THE
WEEPING
ASH

BOOKS BY JOAN AIKEN

The Weeping Ash
The Smile of the Stranger
The Five-Minute Marriage
Last Movement
Voices in an Empty House
Midnight is a Place
A Cluster of Separate Sparks
The Embroidered Sunset
The Crystal Crow
Dark Interval
Beware of the Bouquet
The Fortune Hunters
The Silence of Herondale

JUVENILES

The Shadow Guests
A Touch of Chill and Other Tales
Arabel and Mortimer
Not What You Expected
Go Saddle the Sea
Arabel's Raven
Street: A Play for Children
The Mooncusser's Daughter: A Play for Children
The Green Flash and Other Tales
Winterthing: A Children's Play
The Cuckoo Tree
Died on a Rainy Sunday
Night Fall
Smoke from Cromwell's Time and Other Stories
The Whispering Mountain
A Necklace of Raindrops
Armitage, Armitage Fly Away Home
Nightbirds on Nantucket
Black Hearts in Battersea
The Wolves of Willoughby Chase

JOAN AIKEN

THE
WEEPING
ASH

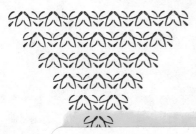

DOUBLEDAY & COMPANY, INC.

Garden City, New York

1980

Library of Congress Cataloging in Publication Data

Aiken, Joan, 1924–
The weeping ash.

I. Title.
PZ4.A289We   1980   [PR6051.I35]   823′.914
ISBN: 0-385-15719-3
Library of Congress Catalog Card Number 79–8431

PROLOGUE

On the night of April 4, 1775, a sad and singular event in the life of Henry Goble, a professional gardener in the employ of the third Earl of Egremont, was to change him overnight from a cheerful, even-spirited fellow, fond of a mug of beer, a game of bowls, and a friendly argument, into a silent, withdrawn, brooding misanthrope.

The chain of events which led to this transformation began by mischance. Goble had, in his kindhearted manner, gone surety for one of his workmates, a lively feckless Italian landscape gardener named Ridotti, who had been brought over to Petworth, where Lord Egremont had his principal residence, to assist in the work of improving the park and gardens of Petworth House.

Ridotti, a spendthrift, carefree Latin, albeit a clever gardener, had been so thoughtless as to incur a huge debt for à la mode clothes and a few gardening books, become bankrupt, and then succumb to an inflammation of the lungs, due to the foggy English winter, which quickly carried him off, so that when his creditors arrived all they could do was seize his handful of possessions in part settlement of the debt and have the unfortunate Henry Goble cast into Petworth jail.

Goble, a steady, middle-aged citizen of Petworth, was at first not too distressed by this incarceration, apart from the affront to his pride. Lord Egremont, at present visiting estates in Northumberland, was expected back within a couple of days and as soon as he returned it was all Lombard Street to a China orange that he would advance the necessary funds to his gardener, for he was a kindly, liberal employer and had a strong sense of justice.

Meanwhile Goble settled down philosophically enough in his dismal accommodation. Apart from himself and a drunken carter, who had been taken up for rowdiness and causing a breach of the peace, the Petworth prison was unoccupied at present, which was just as well.

Goble, munching the penny loaf which was a prisoner's allowance of food for the day, decided that one of the first things he must do when released was to draw Lord Egremont's attention to the dismal state of the town jail. It would be easy enough to mention it while they were pacing out the new pleasure grounds, or in the park, discussing the depth of the ha-ha—all that airy space would present a most forcible contrast to this wretched little pair of rooms, barely six feet high, which, on occasion, might have to accommodate ten or twenty prisoners, male and female, all higgledy-piggledy together. There was no source of heat, no water, no yard, no means of earning money. A leather bag outside the door bore a label, "Pray Remember the Poor Prisoners," but Henry, in previous days, passing by on his lawful occasions, had not, that he could recall, ever seen any food or money placed in it. Indeed earlier that year, in January, three out of a batch of eight had died of hunger and cold after only two or three weeks' incarceration. Shivering, Henry Goble thanked his stars that Ridotti's creditors had turned up in April; even now the dank little stone-walled brick-floored room was wretchedly cold.

Perhaps God sent me here, Goble thought, for he was a religious man in a simple, straightforward way; perhaps He arranged it because He reckoned I could persuade his lordship to make some improvements to the place.

This being resolved to Henry's satisfaction, he relieved himself in a corner, with reluctance (since no receptacle was provided), rolled himself up on a truss of straw, and attempted to forget his situation in sleep.

He had no success. The place was too chill, too dank, too foul. The smell—so different from honest garden muck—nauseated him, the wet atmosphere seemed to penetrate his bones. The carter, lost to the world, snored shatteringly in his corner.

Out of all patience, at last, Goble yelled for the aged keeper.

"Bring half a dozen candles, Mudgeley, you old weasel!"

Candles, at least, would help disperse the stink, and he could warm his hands over them.

"Candles? Where be the money for them to come from?" replied

Mudgeley sourly on the other side of the door. He was aggrieved at being woken from his first sleep.

"My mother will give it you in the morning, you know that."

"Ah—an' she'll think shame to have her son in the lockup," Mudgeley said spitefully.

Goble's parents kept a bakery in a narrow street called Bywimbles, near the church.

"Never you mind what she'll think, you fetch me a light!" said Goble.

"Ar right, ar right," grumbled Mudgeley, and slowly hobbled off to a chest where he kept various perishables, out of the way of the rats. Returning at length, he thrust a bundle of tallow dips through a grille in the door, with the admonition, "Don't 'ee call me again, now—for bawl as much as 'ee will, I shan't pay no heed." And he retired to his own unsavory couch.

Tucking the damp straw under him, Goble set his candles in a ring, fixing them to the bricks by their own wax, and then huddled himself over them, warming his hands on their tiny heat. How long would they last—a couple of hours, three? Daylight at five, that gave him only two hours of dark to endure.

He did his best to distract himself by making plans to sow peas, order a load of gravel for the pleasure gardens, and remind his lordship that the young trees in the park must be fenced or the deer would nibble them.

Then—some white wavering brightness higher than the light from the candles catching his eye—he looked up, to find himself confronted by an undoubted specter.

Henry Goble had never seen a ghost in his life but there could be no possible question about this one. It was translucent, vaporous, gleaming, undulatory; but it had a recognizably human face and two piercing eyes with which it mournfully fixed him.

"Eh! Wh-what do you want?" whispered Goble. The apparition's whole aspect was one of sad, earnest pleading; Goble found that he was not afraid for himself, but nonetheless this spectral visitor filled him with a deep sense of doom and foreboding.

"My name is Wilshire!" announced the specter. "Ned Wilshire—poor, poor Ned Wilshire. Remember that!"

Afterward, in the hundreds of nights that he spent pondering over this scene, Goble could never recall how the tones of the specter's voice had sounded to him—only that they had possessed a singularly penetrating quality, had seemed to strike straight through to his very soul, rather than impingeing on his fleshly ears. Each word the phantom addressed to him remained in his memory, as if recorded on granite, until the day he died. "My name is Ned Wilshire, and I was most inhumanely starved to death in this place! I ask for vengeance. If my heartless brother had paid heed to my necessity, I should be living yet. Remember poor Ned Wilshire—poor Ned Wilshire that died of hunger! I ask that my brother be sought out and that my anguish be visited upon his head. Remember me!"

After the inconsiderate manner of its kind, the specter then vanished, without revealing its brother's name or direction, or even divulging if the latter were yet alive.

Needless to say, poor Goble, after this shocking visitation, remained awake, rigid with cold and horror, for all the remaining hours of that night, while his candles slowly guttered and went out. When at last morning came, old Mudgeley was relieved by Boxall, the day keeper, a distant cousin of Goble's, whose twenty-pound-a-year salary did not render him too proud to chat with the prisoners; of him Goble instantly demanded to know whether a man called Ned Wilshire had ever been shut up in Petworth prison. The name Wilshire was not a local one. Boxall did not recall such a name, but he had held his position only two years; he good-naturedly agreed to look through the records and presently came back to report that there *had* been a Wilshire, who had died three years ago, of the jail fever.

"Fancy that, now! He told ye a true word," Boxall repeated several times wonderingly, as if specters could not, in general, be relied upon, and one that spoke the truth was something quite out of the common way.

"Wilshire?—I wonder where he come from?" muttered Henry

Goble. As yet he felt nothing but a kind of weary impatience—the fatigue of a busy man who has a new and unlooked-for task thrust upon him when he is already put about with work. Somehow he was now faced with the necessity of finding this man's brother and bringing him to a consciousness of his criminal neglect.

"Maybe he come from Wiltshire," suggested Boxall helpfully. "There do be a lot o' folk down that-a-way, I hear tell."

This unconstructive dialogue was now rudely interrupted by the clattering arrival of a coach and four outside the prison.

"Hey there! Open up!" bawled a voice outside.

"*Now* what's to do?" muttered Boxall, stumping off to the entrance. "'Tain't the day for petty sessions, nor that bain't Constable Hoad's voice; onyway, he be away to Byworth."

The coach outside proved to contain a couple of impress officers, on their way through from Godalming to Portsmouth. They had with them a group of captured smugglers, very sheepish, shackled together, but the officers were in a sour humor, having hoped to secure a much larger gang in a midnight pounce at a well-known smugglers' rendezvous called Gunshot Heath on the far side of North Chapel. Evidently word of their intentions had got about beforehand and the haul had fallen far short of their hopes.

"We'll relieve you of your jailbirds, at all events—that'll be a saving for you on victuals," the impress officer said to Boxall.

"Eh, I dunno about that—by rights the magistrates did oughta know, afore ye take 'em," Boxall said doubtfully.

"Damn it, don't argue, man—here's my warrant, and you shall have a receipt for them, all right and tight. Hurry up," he called to his men, "fetch them out!"

With considerable reluctance, Boxall gave in; Goble and the dazed carter were thrust into the coach, chained together, along with the group of smugglers. Goble was hardly less dazed than the carter at this sudden turn in his affairs; he knew about the exactions of the press gang, naturally, but, safe in his lordship's employ, had never expected to be seized himself and was, indeed, approaching the upper age limit of fifty-five, beyond which a man was supposed to be immune. But of course no restrictions attached to prisoners in jails; they were fair game for anybody.

He found voice to say, "Tell my mother," to Boxall, who still stood gaping, at the door of his empty jail; then the driver's whip cracked, the horses broke into a trot, and the coach clattered out of town. Goble was not to see Petworth again for thirteen years. During that period he had abundant time to meditate on the last piteous commission of poor Ned Wilshire.

I

When sixteen-year-old Fanny Herriard became, through the instrumentality of her father the Rev. Theophilus and with his full consent and approval, betrothed to forty-eight-year-old Thomas Paget, the regulating officer of Gosport, she was under no illusion as to the romance of the match. She did not make any attempt to convince herself that Mr. Paget was a heroic or dashing character—despite the fact that he preferred to be called *Captain* Paget; in point of fact, as she knew, a regulating officer was hardly to be distinguished from a civilian—and besides, Papa said that Mr. Paget only carried the rank of lieutenant. Moreover the prospective bridegroom was a widower, with two daughters already older than Fanny herself, and one younger, and until this year he had possessed little more than his pay of one pound a day and additional ten shillings subsistence money. (His previous wife, it was to be inferred, had been able to bring him some money of her own).

Recently, however, Captain Paget had benefited by a stroke of good fortune which, quite unexpectedly, enabled him to contemplate a second marriage, one this time for pleasure rather than for convenience. A distant cousin of his, whom he had never even met, having herself succeeded to an immense—and quite unanticipated—legacy, just as she had contracted an alliance with a wealthy man of rank, had the happy and liberal notion of seeking out the more impoverished members of her family and sharing her good fortune with them. The astonished Thomas, therefore, found himself not only endowed, out of the blue, with a handsome competence, enough to enable him to buy a thriving business, but also possessed for an indefinite period of a larger and much more comfortable house than his own, at a very reasonable rental.

The reason for this additional piece of luck was the devoted attachment of his generous cousin Juliana to her new-wedded husband, a

Dutch nobleman who, up to the time of his marriage, had served as an equerry and intelligence agent in the entourage of the Prince of Wales. However, during the previous year, 1796, Count van Welcker had been delighted to find himself repossessed of some family estates in Demerara, upon the recapture of that region for the British by Laforey and Whyte. In consequence of this, the count was obliged to take leave of absence from the prince's service and make a journey which might be of some years' duration. His bride, unable to contemplate the prospect of such a long separation, had elected to accompany him, and she therefore obligingly offered Thomas Paget her own house in Petworth until the (doubtless far distant) date of her return.

With all these advantages, it could not be said that Captain Paget was particularly handsome or interesting in his person: he was a plain, spare, dry-looking man, with sandy hair, rather thin lips, pale blue eyes, two fingers missing on one hand, discolored teeth, and a curt, short manner of speaking; but still it was to be hoped that having been the recipient of such generosity would release in him hitherto suppressed qualities of kindness and liberality; and in any case several of Fanny's unmarried sisters (she was the youngest of eight) thought, and said, that Fanny had done very well for herself, very well *indeed,* considering that Papa could afford to give his daughters only £200 apiece as dowry. The Rev. Theophilus Herriard was a hard-working Church of England rector, long since widowed, and his daughters might think themselves lucky to catch husbands at all.

Only Fanny, a shy, sensitive girl with a considerable reserve of delicate pride, knew the full measure of her own luck: that she was enabled, by this marriage, to get away from home before her sharp-eyed siblings could discover the intensity of the anguish that she was going through on account of her rejection by Barnaby Ferrars, the squire's happy-go-lucky son.

"Marriage?" he had said, laughing heartily. "You thought we might be *married?* Why, goosey, my father would never allow it! No, no, my dear little sweetheart, we must be like two butterflies, that flutter and dance and kiss in mid-air—so!—and then flit on to other meetings;

you will find some good, kind, worthy fellow who will cosset and spoil you all the days of your life; and I—I shall never forget you, dear little wild rose, and the happy haymaking we passed together, when I am married to some dull lady of fortune who will help repair the inroads that my father's gambling has made on his estates. Gold—gold —I must be sold for gold, my angel—" and he had tickled her chin with a buttercup. For their flirtation—innocent enough, heaven knew —had taken place during a warm and beautiful June, when the whole village—school children, grandparents, squire's sons, and rector's girls —had all helped in the meadows to get in the splendid crop of hay. But then Barnaby's father, Squire Ferrars, had fulfilled his promise to buy his son a commission in the Hussars. Fortunately by the day, some weeks later, when Barnaby came whistling along to inform the Herriard family, assembled for evening tea drinking, of his imminent departure to join his regiment, Fanny, too, had been able to gather the shreds of her pride and dignity around her—it was that little air of self-possession and reserve which, did she but know it, had attracted his notice to her in the first place—and could tell him, with cool decorum masking a breaking heart, that her own betrothal had been arranged; that she would be marrying Captain Paget, a school acquaintance of her father's, in September.

"Why, that's famous! Dear little wild rose, I'm delighted to hear it. Good luck to you both," said Barnaby, not very interested; and after he had informed the Herriards that his regiment was ordered out to India to keep a sharp eye on Tippoo Sahib, he bade them all a carefree good-by and swung happily off into the dusk.

"Barnaby's very pleased with himself," said Harriet.

"You'd think the squire would wish him to marry and get an heir before he goes off abroad," said Maria.

"Maria, such thoughts are unbecoming to you and, in any case, no concern of ours," reproved her father.

"At *one* time I quite thought that Barnaby had an eye to our Fanny," said Kitty with a spiteful sidelong glance at her youngest sister. But Fanny said nothing, merely bent her head lower over her stitching—they were all hemming sheets for her bride linen—and was immensely relieved when the rector said, "Enough chatter, children; it is time for evening prayers."

By September the hot, haymaking weeks were a thing of the past, long forgotten, and it was in weeping gray autumn weather that Captain Paget assisted his youthful bride into the carriage which, after the simple wedding ceremony had been performed by her father, was to take them from Sway, in the New Forest, where Fanny had spent the whole of her life up till now, off to the new home in Sussex.

It was a cold and dismal journey. Rain penetrated the cracks of the ancient hired conveyance, turned the roads to quagmire, and reduced the stubble fields on either side of the turnpike to an uninviting dun color, but nevertheless Fanny, who had never traveled in her life, was prepared to find interest in all that she saw. Although she did not feel it likely that she would ever come to *love* her taciturn bridegroom, she was exceedingly grateful to him for taking her away from her sharp-eyed sisters and a home which had come to be associated with excruciating unhappiness; she fully intended to be friendly, affectionate, and biddable, to do as much as lay in her power to make her marriage a success.

However she soon found that her polite questions and comments about the villages they passed through met with but a brusque reception; the necessities of Captain Paget's rather dismal profession took him traveling about the country for large parts of every week, on horseback or by coach; landscape was of no interest to him, and his only present wish was to reach home and inaugurate the new period of connubial comfort with as little delay as possible; sharply, ignoring Fanny's polite remarks, he ordered the coachman to flog up his brutes of horses and get them to Petworth before the rain turned to a deluge.

Fanny prudently resolved to keep silent; but after a few moments a wish to learn something about the house toward which they were bound made her forget her resolution, and she inquired wistfully:

"Will your cousin Juliana be there to greet us, sir, when we arrive?"

A cousin, such a kindly, well-disposed cousin, would, she thought, be more inclined to be friendly than those three rather daunting unknown figures, her stepdaughters, whose presence their father had not considered necessary at his wedding.

"Juliana? No, no, she is halfway across the Atlantic already, she and that fancy Dutch husband of hers."

Considering the benefactions that Countess van Welcker had heaped upon him, Mr. Paget's tone did not sound particularly cordial, Fanny thought; it is much harder to receive gracefully than to give, and perhaps he was already discovering that to be the recipient of such generosity posed its own problems.

"What is the name of your cousin's house, sir?"

"It is called the Hermitage," he replied shortly, his tone suggesting that he considered this name far too fanciful and would, if it lay within his power, change it to something plainer. He added, "I believe there was once some monastic foundation upon the site; no doubt the name derives from that."

"The Hermitage!" Fanny shivered; to her the name had a chill and dreary sound. She pulled the carriage rug more closely around her shoulders. "And what is the house like, sir?"

"Like? *Like?* Why, it is just a house."

"No, but I mean, is it old or new? Does it lie within the town of Petworth or in the country outside?"

Captain Paget replied briefly that the house was a new one, built within the last twenty years, he understood, and that it lay on the edge of the town, which numbered about three thousand inhabitants.

"It will be very strange to live in a town," murmured Fanny, and added in what she hoped was a cheerful and lively manner, "I greatly look forward to seeing the shops and warehouses and the stalls in the market place."

"I trust your recourse to them will be infrequent. A good housewife contrives all that she may without quitting her own home," was her husband's somewhat discouraging rejoinder.

Fanny had learned already that there were to be four servants in her new home: a cook, a housemaid, a knife- and bootboy, and an outside man who would sleep over the stable and attend to the garden and the horses; she found the prospect of responsibility for ordering such a large establishment an alarming one and said timidly:

"And shall you continue in your profession, sir, now that you have bought the mill?" For she had been told that, with part of his cousin's gift, Captain Paget had been able to acquire a small flour mill at Haslingbourne, a mile outside the town of Petworth, the revenues from which would make a comfortable addition to his income.

"Continue in my profession? Certainly I shall!" he said sharply. "What can have given you the notion that I should not?"

"I did not—I had not meant—" Fanny knew that she must never, at any cost, betray how odious she thought her husband's calling; she faltered out something about regretting that it required him to be so much from home.

Thomas Paget glanced impatiently out of the carriage window— they were slowly descending a steep hill and the driver had been obliged to put on the drag, or the vehicle would have rattled away faster and faster, out of control. Fanny, looking out in the other direction, over a wide prospect of blue-gray, misty weald without a house in sight, battled desperately with the onset of tears. Her throat felt tight and choking; she swallowed and clenched her hands together. For the thousandth time she remembered an afternoon during haymaking— the peak and pinnacle of her flirtation with Barnaby, as it turned out, though at the time she had thought it but a prelude to greater and greater happiness. He had encountered her behind a new-made rick and rained a shower of light, laughing, impudent kisses on her face and neck, until the voices of two other approaching haymakers made them fly guiltily apart. Dizzy with joy, her blood sparkling in her veins like home-brewed cider, she had believed during that moment that a life containing unimaginable radiance and bliss lay stretched ahead of her.

And it had all ended so soon!

Peeping around the corner of the carriage rug at her grizzled bridegroom, Fanny thought, *Could* I ever feel like that about *him?*

Captain Paget had kissed her only once—a brief, formal touch of the lips after the marriage ceremony. He is a cold man, Fanny thought in some relief; well, he is *old*, after all, probably no longer interested in kissing and fondling. Which is just as well, on the whole, for I'm sure I don't want it. At least, not from him.

Bred up in conventual ignorance with her sisters in the rector's household, Fanny had only the vaguest, most rudimentary notion of what husbands and wives did together. Her mother had died shortly after her birth, and the Herriard girls were discouraged by their father from gossiping with servants, who, in that busy, straitened household, were, in any case, too hard worked to have time for telling tales to the young ladies. Upon her engagement her father had held a short, reluctant conversation with her, during which he had informed her that she and her husband would be one flesh—an obscurely repugnant phrase —and that she must bear herself wifely and dutiful to him in all that he might demand of her. Well, she had promised, and would do so, Fanny resolved; gulping, she tried to put away the recollection of Barnaby's firm young lips at the base of her throat; but she did fervently hope that wifely duties would prove not to entail too *much*. Perhaps Mr. Paget, who, after all, had three children already, would just hug and cuddle her, as a father might, as her own had never had time to do; that would be pleasant and comforting, Fanny thought hopefully; and if he did so she might easily come to love him, in a friendly, daughterly way.

He glanced around at her, drumming his fingers on the elbow loop, and she gave him a strained, nervous smile.

"Are those *tears* in your eyes?—Why, pray?" he demanded, his voice sharp with suspicion.

"It—it is a little cold. And I was—just for a moment—missing my home," Fanny stammered.

Her husband subjected her to a curious, raking scrutiny; there seemed to be anger in it, hostility, even jealousy; surely nobody, she thought in horror, could have told him anything about her brief acquaintance, nobody could have mentioned the name of Barnaby Ferrars? Nobody had known—not a soul—not even her sisters. Besides, none of them had ever been left alone to converse with Captain Paget.

She had never been alone with him herself until now. And fortunately her father had not the least notion that she and Barnaby had ever exchanged more than a few words.

No, Captain Paget could know nothing. His next words reassured her.

"It is true, you are hardly more than a child," he said. "When your father suggested that I might marry one of his daughters, I purposely picked you, as the youngest."

"We—we did wonder why—when Kitty is so much prettier—" ventured Fanny.

"Pretty," certainly, was not a term that could be applied to Fanny herself. Her face was a clear oval, with a pointed chin, a straight delicate nose, a pair of dark hazel eyes, and a sensitive mouth. A mole on her left cheekbone had been the subject of many malicious comments by her sister Kitty and was regretted by Fanny herself; she did not realize that it gave her face a pleasing touch of irregularity and that a fashionable lady in London would have placed a beauty spot in just such a position to add piquancy to the classic calm of her countenance. Her looks were not striking, but the eye of the observer, once caught, tended to linger on her; what seemed at first a serene, demure symmetry could break up in a flash to a most vivid awareness—intensity—sympathy of intelligence. Her hair, a shining, silky hazel exactly the same shade as her eyes, was banded smoothly around her small nut-shaped head and knotted on the nape of her neck.

"Tush!" said Captain Paget rather shortly. "What are looks? When a flower is showy, the bees gather around. I wished to secure a bride whose fancies had not been—could not have been—allowed to stray. Your father assured me that this was so in your case.—*Is that the truth?*" he suddenly rapped out.

"Y-yes, sir!" lied Fanny, digging her nails into her palms.

"I am relieved to hear it! Let it continue so, always.—Now, at last, we are approaching Petworth," he went on in a different tone, glancing out at the rain-streaked dusk. "Another ten minutes and we shall be at home, thank heaven. I hope those two idiots, and my sapskulls of servants, will have succeeded in arranging the furniture with some tolerable degree of order and comfort."

"Was the house not furnished, then, sir?" inquired Fanny, immensely relieved at a change of subject.

"Would I be obliged to bring in furniture if it had been?" he demanded. "No—my cousin Juliana—for reasons best known to herself—chose to take all her furnishings and household goods with her to Demerara."

By now they had reached the town of Petworth, of which little was to be seen in the twilight, save a tollhouse and a few timbered cottages. The carriage rattled through narrow, cobbled streets and shortly drew up on the graveled sweep in front of what could only dimly be seen to be a plainly built stone and brick gentleman's residence.

The door instantly flew open as the carriage came to a halt; Fanny's apprehensive gaze beheld what seemed like at least half a dozen persons waiting inside. However several of these were servants, whom Thomas instantly ordered to unpack the baggage; and he hustled Fanny through the door, pushing two young ladies and a child unceremoniously out of the way.

"Martha, Bet, *will* you shift aside? Pray, how do you expect me to get into the house? No, Fanny does *not* wish for a cup of tea—why should she need to maudle her insides and spoil her digestion with such stuff when dinner is only an hour or so away? She will do very well till then. Good God, what a hurrah's nest do I see here—what in the world have you all been *doing* with yourselves?" he went on furiously, looking around the hallway which they had entered. It was a medium-sized room which did, in fact, present a very forlorn appearance, with half-unrolled rugs, boxes in process of unpacking, straw scattered about, and a haphazard air of furniture standing in temporary positions.

"The carts only came with the furniture an hour ago—" began the taller of the young ladies.

"Be silent! Do not trouble my ears with excuses! Why could you not have sent a messenger to hurry them? No, I do not wish to hear any more now, thank you! Well, I will take Fanny up to my room now—I trust *that*, at least, has been set in order?" he said in such a threatening tone that both girls instantly chorused:

"Oh yes, Papa! And there is a fire lit—"

"Very well.—And when we come down I shall expect this disorder to have been cleared away and dinner made ready. See to it!" he snapped, pushing Fanny before him up a narrow but short flight of stairs, around several corners, and at last into a fair-sized bedroom.

Fanny felt quite dazed. She had hardly been given time to take in her stepdaughters—apart from the fact that one was tall and pale, one moderately pretty, and one a mere child—or to make any acknowledgment of their welcome—and she *would* have liked a cup of tea! —Doubtless her husband would feel better after his dinner, she thought, recalling her father's shortness before meals, particularly in Lent.

"Wh-what a pleasant room!" she ventured in a placating manner, glancing around her. The bedroom was scantily furnished as yet, with a chest, a small rug, a bed, and two chairs; a hastily kindled fire burned rather flickeringly in the grate. One charming feature was a large, semicircular bow window which commanded a prospect of dusk-shrouded lawn, rosebushes, and yew hedge. "How delightful this will be in summer—" Fanny was going on, wondering if it would be in order to voice a wish for hot water, when her husband said curtly:

"Take your clothes off."

"What—?"

"Make haste—undo that dress."

"But it was such a short way from the carriage—I am not at all wet—"

"Don't be a fool—do as I say!"

And as she was still slow to follow his meaning, gazing at him with startled eyes, he began himself pulling undone the fastenings of Fanny's striped muslin overdress—breaking a couple of tags in the process—dragged the garment off her shoulders, and tossed it on the floor. "Now your petticoat—don't just stand there staring!"

"But—"

"*Your petticoat, girl!*"

Exasperated by her slowness, he kicked off his own boots and breeches, then flung her on the bed.

What followed was so appalling to Fanny that, though it was to be re-enacted over and over during the weeks and months to come, every grim detail of the first occasion remained stamped on her memory for the rest of her life. The furious intentness of her suddenly red-faced, blind-eyed husband on his own purpose, as he thrust and battered at her, panting, cursing, and muttering to himself, only, it seemed, occasionally noticing her existence enough to snarl, "Open your legs wider, idiot!"—the totally unfamiliar shock of the whole experience, and its suddenness—the complete disparity of her expectations with this aspect of Thomas Paget—all these things in combination worked upon Fanny with almost shattering effect.

Some ten minutes later, when her husband matter-of-factly pulled himself upright and began hunting for his breeches, which had got kicked under the bed, Fanny lay still, limp, gasping, and shocked, horrified not so much by the pain—though that was certainly the worst she had ever felt—as by her own ignorance and fear of what he had done to her, what damage he might have done, tearing and bruising areas of whose very existence she had not previously been aware.

"Well, don't lie there like a gaby," he said irritably. "Get up and put your clothes on! Dinner won't be long. Some of those fools will be along soon, I dare say, with the baggage."

"I'm bleeding—"

"So I should hope—or I'd have had a word to say to your father!"

"There's blood all over the sheets," she said, beginning to sob.

"Well, tell the maids to wash them!—Where's my cravat? Damn it, Frances, can't you be some help? Don't just lie there! I want to go out to the impress rendezvous and see if my placard has brought in any volunteers—For heaven's *sake*," he broke out in exasperation, "I thought I had got myself a wife, not a whining little mawkin. I'll have you show me a cheerfuller face than that when I get back, my girl, or I'll know the reason why!" And, slamming the door to demonstrate his justifiable annoyance, he ran smartly down the stairs, shouting for Jem the bootboy to bring him his officer's greatcoat.

Fanny lay dazedly for a few minutes longer, then, hearing muffled footsteps on the stairs, she huddled among the untidy bedclothes and pulled the sheet over her nakedness.

Thomas Paget was a many times disappointed man. Indeed, by the middle of his life he had fallen into a habit of setting up his expectations so high that it was inevitable he *should* be disappointed; this was possibly the only way in which he found any gratification.

Son of an ineffectual younger son, in a family of decayed aristocracy, he had discovered in his teens that, while his cousins were all due to inherit money or places, the most that he could expect was to be assisted into a naval or military career by wealthier relatives, whether or not such a prospect was congenial to his taste. This was indeed done, a great-uncle bought him a commission in the navy, and Thomas might, with luck or ability, have prospered and risen in his profession; but luck was lacking; in his very second engagement—and that a wholly unimportant one, with a Spanish privateer—he was so unfortunate as to have the finger and thumb of his right hand shot away, thus rendering him ineligible for further active service. Other sailors might, perhaps, have surmounted such a disability; but Thomas Paget was not of this caliber. It is true also that he was not a favorite with his companions or superiors, being of a jealous, exacting, contentious nature, prone to argue the rights of every matter, however trifling, that touched on his own prestige or position; his messmates were thoroughly glad to see the last of him.

Having been on active service for so short a period, he could not hope for a pension, and the sole opening left him, after such an abbreviated naval career, was to become a "yellow admiral" or regulating officer, that is, a shore official of the press gang, which, by government warrant, seized men, whatever their calling, and forcibly enrolled them in the King's service at sea. A very few professions were exempt: fishermen, harvesters—also males under eighteen or over fifty-five; but these exemptions were often conveniently ignored. Every town in the country had its own press gang, varying in size from fifteen to thirty men, and each gang was commanded by an officer with naval rank, known as the regulating captain. Press officers were usually thwarted men, men whose careers, for one reason or another, had gone wrong.

Thomas Paget, in due course, had been lucky enough to marry a girl whose plainness had been offset by the fact that she sincerely loved him and had some money of her own, for she was the daughter of a wealthy undertaker. But Thomas had mismanaged her money, and his wife had disappointed him bitterly, first by giving birth to nothing but female children, and subsequently by a series of miscarriages and still-births. Perhaps simply because he was denied a son, Thomas became obsessed by longing for one; a son, a boy, who might be able to achieve everything that his father had not. And then—even more aggravatingly—his wife, after the fifth or sixth faulty birth, had, not died, but gone melancholy mad, so that she could not be divorced, or even put away without shocking expense, for she was not raving; she had to be kept locked in a room at the top of the house. At first, even then, her husband had not wholly given up hope of a son; even after her incarceration there had been a couple more miscarriages. After the second of these, Thomas *did* give up hope; unfortunately, even then, the first Mrs. Paget survived for another ten years, mumbling and crying and throwing her food about, while downstairs her husband silently raged and the acid of frustration ate into the fabric of his nature.

In the end Mrs. Paget mercifully died, of an obstruction of the bowel; Thomas lost no moment, as soon as the obsequies were over, in negotiating with his school friend, Theophilus Herriard, for the youngest and healthiest of his eight daughters; the rector must be delighted to get one of them satisfactorily off his hands before his own demise—for he was a failing man.

And now at last Thomas's fortunes seemed to have taken a dramatic turn for the better, with his cousin Juliana's astonishing offer of house and fortune. The loan of the house, indeed, proved a particular blessing, for neighbors in their previous locality had been saying—as neighbors always will—that the first Mrs. Paget, poor soul, had not died natural, there was something fishy and havey-cavey about it, a guinea to a groat her unfeeling husband, having failed to get a son out of her and spent all her money, had finally made away with her. By moving to a different neighborhood, therefore—and with a cast-iron excuse for doing so—Thomas had been able to leave all that disagreeable talk behind. He had, in fact, deliberately delayed his marriage until he could take his new bride directly to the new abode. Also—another stroke of luck—there was no press gang at either Petworth or Chichester, although there were gangs at Godalming, Littlehampton, and Shoreham; a gap ran clean across the county of Sussex just at that point, so Thomas, who had previously been regulating officer of Gosport, applied to the Admiralty for a transfer and was graciously granted it. All he had to do now was comb the ungleaned area for a profitable supply of men at a shilling a head, garner the income from his mill at Haslingbourne, and enjoy the comforts of his new marriage. Life had indeed opened out for him.

With a slightly more cheerful aspect than usual, Thomas allowed the bootboy Jem to slide his greatcoat over his shoulders, pulled on his cocked hat, and strode out into the downpour.

Five minutes after her husband had stamped out of earshot, Fanny summoned up the resolution to get off the bed.

Moving stiff-legged, like an old woman, letting out little involuntary whimpers of pain and misery, she stumbled vaguely about, hunting for her scattered clothes. "Dinner won't be long," Thomas had said. She was terrified of displeasing him again by being late for the first meal in his house.

Besides, what would his daughters imagine that she was *doing* up here all this time?

She picked up her muslin dress from the floor, but it was dusty, crumpled, and torn. And her boxes, with the rest of her belongings, had not yet been brought up. She could find no needle or thread in the room, to sew up the torn lacing; also, she badly needed hot water to wash herself. She felt soiled, stiff, cold, dreadfully damaged; the delicate pride, which had carried her through the pain of Barnaby's careless withdrawal and helped her hide her agony from her sisters, seemed now completely shattered; she was conscious of being wholly broken in spirit, fit for nothing except to be a kind of slave. Dimly she contemplated running away—but where could she run to? Not to her father —he would never take her back. And there was nowhere else. . . . But she was really too cowed and weak to entertain serious thoughts of escape.

Outside the door she heard stifled voices.

"Well, I'm sure I'm not going in. Let her manage on her own!"

" 'Tisn't *my* place."

"Blest if I go—"

"Let Tess take in her things and help her—if she wants help. One thing is certain—I'll never call her Mamma. A girl of sixteen!"

"Hush, Martha, she might hear you. Go on, Tess, tell her there isn't much time—that Papa hates to be kept waiting."

"Yes, miss," said a much lower, timid voice.

Two sets of steps went away downstairs, and after a moment Fanny heard a tentative tap on the door.

"Come in!" she called faintly, brushing the tears from her cheeks with a fold of the petticoat she had been clutching. And she huddled the garment around herself as the door opened to admit a small servant girl dragging behind her one of Fanny's two boxes of clothes.

"Please, ma'am, I'm Tess, and I'm to help you," the girl said.

Fanny, in her misery, thought the maid's voice sounded pert and knowing; she was eying Fanny curiously; no doubt she would hurry back to the servants' hall to describe to her companions the plight in which she had discovered the master's new young wife.

"I don't need any help; thank you. You may go," Fanny said, trying to make her voice cool and stop it from shaking. She stared down at the petticoat in her lap, forcing back tears.

"Shan't I open the box, then?" Tess sounded astonished. "Don't you want *nothing* done?"

"Oh, very well—yes—open it.—Can you bring me some hot water?"

"I dunno, ma'am," the girl said doubtfully. "I dunno as the copper's hot enough yet." And she added, "Miss Martha said to tell you, ma'am, that dinner will be served directly the master's back, and 'e—the master—can't abear to be kept waiting."

Fanny made a slight movement of her head, to indicate acknowledgment of this message. She heard faint sounds of activity, as the cords around her box were unloosed and the lid raised; then there came the click of the door closing behind Tess, and Fanny buried her head under the pillow in a renewed agony of tears. But she did not dare lie weeping long, for she imagined that Tess might soon be back with the hot water.

This did not occur, however—presumably the copper had proved recalcitrant—so, after waiting as long as she dared, Fanny was obliged to manage as best she could without. She had some Hungary Water, and some lotion of rosemary that her sister Maria had made for her. At least, as one of the hard-up rector's eight daughters, she was accustomed to managing without the services of a lady's maid—but she did, now, for the first time, regret the inevitable presence of her seven sisters, their ceaseless fire of comment and criticism—"Lord, child, that sash isn't straight, come here and I'll tie it again—stand still, your lace is crooked—your hair wants smoothing, wait while I comb it—"

For once, even Kitty's presence would have been welcome.

The notes of a gong boomed through the house, and Fanny tied the strings of her slippers with shaking hands, did her best to straighten the counterpane over the horrible sheets, then snatched up her reticule and, holding her head high, opened the bedroom door and walked slowly down the stairs, trying to disguise the stiff painfulness of her descent by what she hoped would pass for dignity.

The downstairs hall, she found, had been vigorously tidied since her first entrance. No sign of disorder remained, save a stray curl of woodshaving on the bare boards. Nobody was there, but doors stood open to right and left. Glancing through the left-hand door, Fanny could see a table laid for dinner, but, mercifully, there was no one in the room. She turned to the right and timidly entered what must be the drawing room, or parlor; it was sited under her bedroom upstairs and had the same pretty semicircular bow window, looking out onto darkness, for the curtains were not yet hung. Glancing cautiously about the room, she observed a threadbare rug, a few pieces of sadly shabby furniture, placed in positions of rigid exactitude, and, in attitudes hardly less rigid, three young ladies. No: one of them was a child.

Since the young ladies stared but did not speak, Fanny was obliged to open the conversation. She did this with considerable reluctance, for their looks were far from friendly.

"Good evening," she said, nervously polite. "I—I believe we must introduce ourselves."

Silence, while they directed hostile stares at her embroidered dress of white Spitalfields silk, cut low on the shoulders and gathered into a lace fichu in front. It was quite her prettiest gown, the single new one she had, apart from her wedding dress, and she had been greatly relieved that it lay right at the top of her box, since only its elegance, she felt, could sustain her through this difficult encounter. She had expected Thomas's daughters to be stylishly dressed. But now she felt awkward and overfine, for the two elder young ladies wore plain round gowns of brown and blue mull respectively, while the little girl was in blue and white striped gingham covered with a pinafore.

"I shall have to guess which of you is which," said Fanny a little desperately, as Paget's daughters still did not speak. "You," to the tallest, "must be Elizabeth—and you Martha—and you must be Patience." The words "I am your new mamma" absolutely stuck in her throat, as three pairs of cold gray eyes regarded her.

"It—it is very absurd, is it not?" Fanny persisted, since all three remained obstinately silent. "You—you two are both taller than I, I believe."

The words "And older, too," were silently formed by the lips of Martha, at whom Fanny nervously smiled, but she did not speak out loud; however little Patty cried out, "Of *course* they are—much taller!" directing a scornful glance at the newcomer.

All three girls were, in fact, remarkably stoutly built and well grown for their ages, which were, Fanny knew, nineteen, seventeen, and eight. They resembled their father in being sallow-complexioned and large-boned, with sandy-fair hair and watery blue-gray eyes, pale mouths, and unforthcoming expressions. Only Martha, the middle one, had any pretension to good looks; her cheeks were pinker and her eyelashes darker than those of her elder sister, her mouth, nose, and jaw were a better shape, and her hair, which was a little darker, appeared to curl naturally. Bet, poor girl, really was regrettably plain; no doubt this was one of the reasons why she still remained unmarried at nineteen. Her nose was thick, with a bump in the middle, her mouth shapeless, her lank, sandy locks dangled limply about her neck, save above her brow and ears, where the hair had been twisted into unconvincing curls; and her thick, white, almost lashless eyelids covered eyes so pale in color that it was amazing they could hold such a sharp expression. Little Patty projected her lower lip and wore a scowl of frank antagonism.

The front door slammed.

"There's Pa come back," announced Martha in a tone of relief.

Fanny dreaded seeing Thomas again but felt, nonetheless, that his presence would relieve this uncomfortable encounter. He walked in, gave a glance at Fanny, and said, "You have made the acquaintance of the girls, then, I see; good.—That gown is by far too fine; whatever possessed you to put it on, we are expecting no company. You will be half frozen in the dining room."

"Would you prefer that I change it?" faltered Fanny, and thought she saw a quick exchange of glances between Bet and Martha at this evidence of submission.

"What, now—when dinner's all but on the table? No, no," said Thomas impatiently. "One of the girls can find you a shawl—Bet—fetch something from the lobby for your stepmother."

Bet moved slowly from the room, with lips pressed together and an expression of decided resentment, either at the errand or because she disliked hearing Fanny referred to as her stepmother.

"Make haste!" Thomas called after her, and then he strode into the dining room and shouted angrily through a further door, which apparently led to the kitchen:

"Kate! Tess! Jem, where are you all? Where the devil's dinner?"

Placating voices responded, and Fanny heard a scurry of footsteps and a clink of cutlery. "Come along!" Thomas called to his daughters and Fanny. "If they see us waiting, perhaps they will pay a little more heed to the fact that it is more than eight minutes after the hour."

As they began to sit down at table, and a stout, red-faced woman carried in a tureen of soup, Bet came hurrying back with a mud-gray shawl which she thrust ungraciously at Fanny, who was obliged, there-fore, to eat the meal in considerable discomfort, with the shawl con-tinually slipping from her shoulders.

The meal was not a convivial one. Thomas sometimes addressed a remark to his daughters, or a question as to the disposition of his effects. More often it was some withering reproof. When little Patty dropped her soup spoon he snapped:

"Have not either of you girls succeeded in teaching her proper man-ners *yet?*"

Fanny gathered that little Patty was not often accorded the privi-lege of eating with her papa.

"She does well enough as a general thing," Bet answered shortly. "I dare say she is shy in company."

"She will have to get used to the *company,* as you call it," Thomas remarked, casting an unflattering glance at his new wife. "Let it be your task, Frances, to improve her table manners."

The awkward meal was soon over, ending in a blackberry and apple tart which contained a sour mush of blue-gray fruit and innumerable seeds. After this Kate, the red-faced cook, brought in and set before her master a dish of deviled bones. Thomas said curtly:

"Ah, that looks tastier. You'll have to do better than this tomorrow, Kate, or I'll be advertising for a new cook-maid."

Kate muttered that one could not get used to a new stove all in a flash.

"You have a new mistress, too, don't forget. I shall look to see a great improvement in the next few weeks—or there will be changes made!"

Kate darted a resentful glance at the new mistress in question, and

Fanny felt, with a sinking heart, that her position in this household was being impaired before she had even established it, without her being able to do anything to set herself right.

Thomas addressed himself to his wife and daughters indiscriminately, as he poured himself a small glass of port.

"Run away now—all of you. I have business to attend to and shall retire to my garden room. I may drink tea with you all later. Send the child to bed."

Patty began a protest but was hushed by Bet, who escorted her up the stairs. Martha, with a discontented expression, followed Fanny back to the parlor. There the fire had burned up in the hearth, and its light was reflected eerily, ten times over, in the curved panes of the bow window. Outside, a wind was beginning to rise, which sighed in the boughs of invisible trees, and thumped and whistled in the chimney, as if a live creature were imprisoned there.

Fanny shivered in her thin, pretty dress, pulling the shawl close about her and moving near the fire. With a heavy heart she remembered how cosily, last night, she had bundled into the big sagging bed with Charlotte and Kitty; there had been teasing and laughter and fun; even Kitty, for once, had seemed sorry that her younger sister and willing servitor was going far away.

However at least Martha, on her own, seemed less inclined to be hostile than when supported by the presence of her sisters.

"Pray, Fanny, have you ever been to Winchester?" she demanded. "Or Salisbury? They say there's some monstrous fine shops there."

Fanny was obliged to confess that she had never set foot in those towns, but she soon discovered that Martha's principal wish was to describe her own single visit to Brighton, two years since, under the escort of an aunt, her mother's sister. The splendors of this town, its circulating libraries, pastry shops, Pavilion, the hair styles and toilets of the ladies, and the ogling effrontery of the beaux, occupied her happily for many minutes. Bet, returning during these eulogies, cast up her eyes in exasperation; evidently the glories of Brighton had a wearisome familiarity for her.

"Well, *you* wasn't there, Bet," Martha said defensively. "Aunt Phillips didn't see fit to take you; I was just telling Fanny."

"Has Papa given you leave to call her that?"

"No, but it don't signify; I certainly shall not call her Mamma; Lord! I would not demean myself to address somebody who was younger than me in such a fashion!"

While the two sisters were disputing this, Bet declaring that Martha would have to do as her father bade her, and Martha stoutly affirming that she would not, Fanny seized the opportunity to slip upstairs and fetch the rush basket in which she kept her needlework. She had hemmed a set of handkerchiefs and was embroidering them with Thomas's initials; such a gift, it had been decided by her family, would constitute a suitable offering from bride to groom.

When she returned to the parlor, the girls seemed to have shifted their ground; they were now arguing about the merits of Petworth as a place of residence.

"I say it's none so bad," Bet said shortly. "I saw a pretty-enough-looking haberdasher's shop as we came through—and a tailor—and a deal of shoe shops. And at least, as it's such a small place, perhaps Pa won't object to our walking out on our own; at all events, there's no sailors here."

"Well, I know *Pa* don't like the town," said Martha, "for I heard him say, if it weren't for getting Cousin Juliana's house at such a low rent, there's no town in the kingdom where he wouldn't sooner set up house."

"How strange! I wonder why?" remarked Fanny involuntarily.

Bet said, "Oh, I dare say it's because it is such a muddy, poky little hole, where he's not likely to take many men for his impress."

"No," contradicted her sister, "it's because he don't care above half for Lord Egremont, up at Petworth House."

"La! Why ever not?" demanded Bet.

Martha glanced toward the door and said in a lower tone, "Lord Egremont has only mistresses, not a proper wife! And I believe one of them lived in *this very house,* at one time, before our cousin had it.

She was a French lady, and Lord Egremont built the house for her, and she died of a putrid fever."

"Who told you that?"

"Kate. She heard it from the chimney sweep."

"But anyway," objected Bet, "what's Lord Egremont to Pa? He hardly ever mixes with the gentry, wherever we are. Nobody wants to meet an impress officer."

Both sisters fell into a silence of depression, considering this unpalatable truth. But then Martha said stoutly:

"But still, our cousin Juliana was a friend of Lord Egremont, so perhaps he *will* come to call."

"I dare say Pa won't allow us to see him."

To turn the conversation, Fanny inquired, "Tell me about your cousin Juliana. Did you know her well?"

"La, no! She's gone abroad. We never met her," Bet replied in her flat way. But Martha cried out:

"She was a monstrous pretty girl, though! That's her miniature, over the pianoforte. And she had all manner of adventures in the French Revolution—they were going to cut off her head, but she floated over to England in an air balloon—and she married a Dutch count—and was left a whole heap of money by a rich old nabob uncle in India who was no better than he should be. So that was why she wrote to Pa—"

"The uncle was not in India, Martha—he had come back and died in England."

"Well, what does it matter where he died? Pray don't be so particular!" exclaimed Martha impatiently. "Then Cousin Juliana was given this house by the French lady who died—so she offered it to Pa to live in while she was abroad—"

"Did she share her fortune with any other relations?" inquired Fanny, fascinated by this prodigal generosity which (she was obliged to admit to herself) seemed a characteristic wholly lacking in Juliana Paget's cousin Thomas.

"Yes, I believe she writ to an old lady cousin in Bath—but *she* had already died, falling from a carriage—and two more cousins out in India."

"Pa was rare put about when he learned she'd done *that*," commented Bet sourly.

"Why? Who are the cousins in India?"

"They are twins—by-blows of the old nabob," Martha began, and received a very quelling look from her sister. "Well—why shouldn't I tell it, Bet? She"—with a meaningful glance at Fanny—"she's a married lady now, no harm in her knowing it."

Fanny eased her aching spine against the hard upright back of her Windsor chair and wondered rather dismally what the state of being married had to do with the story of the twins out in India.

" 'Tisn't a proper tale for you to tell," Bet said primly, and pressed her pale lips together.

"Oh, stuff! Anyway, Miss Fox told me, and *she* wasn't married! It was this way, you see, Fanny. The old nabob in India—General Henry Paget, that is, who left his fortune to Cousin Juliana—had a pair of love children by a lady who was half a Portugee and half a heathen Hindoo—"

"*Martha! Will* you mind your tongue! What would Papa say?"

"What could he say? It is no more than the truth, and that is why he was so put out when he heard that Cousin Juliana had writ to the twins as well as to us. They call themselves Paget, though I dare say they've no claim to, since their mother was never married to the nabob, or not that anybody knows—"

"But if he was so rich, *surely* he left his children provided for?" said Fanny, puzzled. "Even if they were not born in wedlock?"

"No, *that* he didn't. It seems, when he came back to England, he had the intention to send the Portugee lady some money, but when he wrote to where he left her, she was gone, nobody knew where. And so then he said, 'Devil fly away with her, she's gone off with somebody else. I wash my hands of her and the twins—' "

"But there might have been a dozen reasons why she was not where he had left her," objected Fanny, distressed at this seeming injustice.

"Oh, ay, well, I dare say he was in the right of it. He *knew* her, after all," replied Martha. "Anyway, after he had left all the money to Cousin Juliana she met with some army officer who had been in north India, and he said he had heard tell that the Portugee lady had died, but he thought he knew the direction where the twins might be found. So Cousin Juliana wrote to them. But 'tis all Zanzibar to a nutmeg that the letter never reached them," said Martha reflectively. "Or we'd have heard by this time. I think it's a sad shame."

Bet, who had been listening with a self-righteously disapproving look, said dryly:

"Oh yes, for sure you'd clap your hands for joy if they was to come walking in the door now!" She broke off her thread with a sharp twist.

"Why—did Cousin Juliana invite them *here?*" Fanny asked in astonishment.

"Ay, that was the one thing that stuck in Pa's craw. 'Use my house, and welcome,' says Cousin Juliana to him, 'for I shan't be needing it myself while I'm off with my dear Count van Welcker in Demerara, and I'd be lief to think there was a happy family living here.'" She rolled up her eyes with a derisive grimace and so missed her sister's expression. Bet's pale, sardonic eye moved around the room and then fixed on Martha with a look so strange, so bleak, that Fanny felt a curious cold shiver move between her shoulder blades.

"'All I ask is,'" continued Martha with histrionic relish, "'all I ask,' says Cousin Juliana, 'is that, if ever Great-uncle Henry's children should come to England, you give them houseroom in the Hermitage, and a kind welcome—'"

Here Bet sniffed to herself, taking little picking stitches in the square of canvas she was embroidering.

"'For, after all,'" finished Martha, "''tis *his* money we're all living on.' Which Pa could not deny."

"They'll never turn up," said Bet with finality, biting off her thread.

"'Tis certain Pa hopes not," said Martha.

"How old are they? The twins?" Fanny imagined a pair of tiny golden-haired children—the only twins she had ever seen were those of flaxen-headed Ned Woodley, the carpenter at Sway—wandering forlornly hand in hand down the gangplank of a huge ship.

"Who's to say? 'Tis four, five years since old Great-uncle Henry Paget died. They'll be in their teens, maybe," Martha said carelessly. "If they did come, it would be somebody else to talk to, at least."

She gave a great yawn, hardly bothering to cover her teeth, which were white and even, much better than those of her sister. Bet's, in keeping with her clumsy nose and undershot jaw, were gappy and yellow as a bad ear of corn.

"Lord," Martha went on, walking restlessly over to kneel on the window seat and look out of the black window, "Lord, it feels as if we had been in Petworth an age already. I declare, I almost wish that Miss Fox had come with us!"

Who was Miss Fox? Fanny inquired, and learned from Martha that this lady had been the Paget girls' governess until the remove to Petworth.

"But then Pa gave her her marching orders. He said he reckoned I was too old for a governess—and Bet is, that's of course!—and he was pleased as Punch to get rid of her. Now he can save her wages and you will teach Patty for nothing. Poor Foxy—how she did weep and wail and take on, when Pa told her she was to go."

Martha gave a sudden chuckle at the recollection, and Fanny thought she noticed another swift, significant look between the sisters.

"How long had Miss Fox been with you?" she inquired—not that she was particularly interested in the ex-governess, but she felt more at ease while there was a trickle of conversation to attend to, while her own thoughts could be kept at bay. Here she was, trapped in this house, with these two dull girls, in whom she did not think it would ever be possible to confide or invest any affection, and their father. . . . But it was best not to think about *him*. Also she could not conceal from herself that there seemed to be strange undercurrents in this family, curious elements of hostility and tension, and not only relating to herself. What did the girls feel toward each other, toward their father? She had come into an unhappy household, Fanny thought.

"Miss Fox?" replied Bet, careless. "Oh dear, she was with us an age —since long before Mamma began to fail in her health—ten, twelve years, I dare say."

"She's old now—thirty at least; on the shelf," agreed Martha. "Though, in any case, who would marry a governess? However, at one time, I believe she quite hoped she'd nabble Pa, when she was in her twenties."

The sisters laughed quietly together.

Fanny said, "She must have been very young, then, when she first became your governess?" deciding that, although Bet appeared to behave with more hostility toward her personally, Martha seemed the more spiteful-natured of the pair.

"It was a fine position for her," Bet said sharply. "She'd only been a nursery governess before that. In those days, Mamma used to teach us."

"But then Mamma began to fail in her wits," explained Martha, and earned an irritable glance from her elder sister.

"Oh dear—I did not know that about your mother," Fanny said faintly.

Bet raised pale eyes from the needle she was threading. "How should you? It was not generally known."

But Martha went on irrepressibly—from a desire, Fanny suspected, to annoy her sister:

"Lord, yes, our mamma was crazy-mad any time these ten years past, and whatever you may say, Bet, it did get about; I am sure that is why none of the beaux in Gosport would offer for us, and why we were glad to move here, for I dare say they all thought we might take after Mamma. Though *I* believed what Dr. Plornish told us; he always did say it was not true madness and that we need not fear we would grow like her, but that, being of delicate health to begin with, too much lying-in had turned her wits."

"Martha! Mind your tongue!"

"Oh, la, Bet, how you do fuss on—our stepmamma is a married lady, a'n't she? Twelve babies in thirteen years," went on Martha significantly, with her eyes all the time fixed on Fanny's face, "and all but three born dead; wouldn't you think that might be enough to turn anybody's wits, *Mrs. Paget?*"

Fanny felt the heat of the fire burn in her cheeks; there was a fierce throbbing in her temples and a dry sourness on her tongue. Her back ached and her feet were frozen with cold. Dizzily, she thrust her work into the rush basket and, standing up, said:

"I am very weary from traveling, I think I had best go upstairs."

She felt that she could not bear to remain in the room with these girls another moment.

Bet said, "Pa won't be pleased if you miss evening prayers."

However the front door slammed at that moment and Mr. Paget, putting his head into the room, remarked:

"It is too late now for tea. I found a great deal of work awaiting me. We had best go to prayers directly."

The servants had already assembled in the dining room for this ceremony. Mr. Paget read the prayers from a book, and afterward, with Jem and Kate, went around the house making sure that all doors were locked and the windows closed and shuttered. Then the family and servants retired to bed, Jem to sleep in a small basement cubbyhole, the maids in one of the attics, Martha in a room that she shared with Patty, while Bet had a small room to herself. Thomas and his bride retired again to the master bedroom which, Fanny was relieved to find, had been set in order during the course of the evening; the bed had been remade with clean sheets, her clothes put away, and a hip bath of hot water brought up.

This stood steaming behind a screen, and Thomas made use of it first.

"Females can't stand water so hot as a man," he said. "No use in heating up *two* baths. Coals and firing cost money, as I trust you will bear in mind."

He spent some time in the bath, splashing and grunting; then it was Fanny's turn. She, though far from eager to go to bed, found no inducement to loiter; the water was no more than lukewarm by now, besides being somewhat thick and scummy from her husband's ablutions. He, already in bed, soon became impatient.

"Do not be dawdling in there all night, Frances! Candles cost money too, remember!"

Fanny would not have minded taking her bath in the dark; outside the window a great orange-colored autumn moon could be seen through the branches of a leafy tree that swayed and swung and danced in the rising wind, casting a series of sliding shadows over the bedroom wall.

"Draw the curtains closer to, Frances," ordered Thomas.

Even so, after she had come to bed and he had blown out the candle, the whole room seemed filled with the sighing and the presence of the tree outside, as if its restless boughs came thrusting right through the wall.

"And *there's* a case of female stupidity for you, if ever I saw one!" grumbled Thomas. "Imagine planting a tree so close to the house—it cannot be more than four or five yards from the wall. Bound to cause damp and cut off the light. I'll have it chopped down first thing tomorrow."

Fanny made a small sound of protest, as he moved and grasped her arm with an ungentle hand; she hardly knew if she appealed against the tree's fate or her own.

"*Now* what is the matter, Frances? Why do you lie on the edge of the bed? Come here."

He rolled over and seized hold of her.

The click of the latch woke Fanny next morning; slowly, reluctantly, she opened her eyes to discover that the fire had been newly kindled and burned cheerfully, the curtains were partly drawn back, and a ewer of hot water stood steaming upon the chest. Beyond the curtain shone a clear blue sky; a brilliant morning had succeeded the stormy night, and from where she lay Fanny could discern the tops of several stately trees, their autumnal color gilded by the early sun. This agreeable prospect, however, did little to disperse her wretchedness, and she lay wondering, almost in despair, how her new life was to be borne.

Why, she demanded of herself for the hundredth time, how could she have been such a fool as to imagine that marriage, any marriage, no matter to whom, would be preferable to enduring the pangs of unrequited love at home, under the sharp scrutiny of her sisters, and being subjected to the sad and troubling spectacle of her father's failing health? Now she had only herself to blame, she was justly served; she could have refused Captain Paget's offer, Papa had told her that he would not constrain her in any way (though she knew he had been greatly relieved when she accepted).

Beside her, Thomas, on his back, arms flung wide, occupying two thirds of the bed, still snored gustily in heavy slumber. As well he might, Fanny thought with a shudder; for half the night his savage, repeated, insatiable onslaughts had hurt, shocked, and bewildered her; he had used her, not like a human being at all, but like some rag doll, a pliable, boneless object, incapable of feeling, or dignity, or response. She had heard the church clock strike two, strike three, strike four . . . She was covered in bruises, and her lips were sore and swollen where, again and again, she had fastened her teeth on them in a struggle not to cry out. Bet, she was only too well aware, slept in a small room next door; and Fanny could not bear the idea that anybody—let alone her eldest stepdaughter—should guess what she was going through, how she was humiliated. Bad enough that it should happen, intolerable that anybody should know about it.

Terrified that Thomas might suddenly wake and make yet more demands on her, she wriggled carefully out of the bed and, with a silence and speed acquired during sixteen years of sharing a small room with two older sisters, she washed in a cupful of hot water (fearful of her husband's anger should she use too much), hastily combed out her hazel-brown hair and put it up in its knot, then pulled on a soft blue wool dress, long-sleeved and high in the neck. It was an old dress, not fashionable, for nobody wore wool any more, but it would cover the worst of her bruises. Then, softly as a ghost, she slipped from the chamber. Her well-justified apprehension at the thought of Thomas's ire when he woke and found that she had given him the slip was quite outweighed by the desperation of her need to be alone, if only for a short while. It was yet early; she had heard the church clock strike seven not long before she got up, and she knew the family breakfast was not served until eight; she would have at least half an hour to herself.

On the ground floor sounds of domestic activity could be heard in other rooms: a brush wielded on a mat, the scrape of a shovel in ash, a knife being sharpened down below in the basement kitchen. Anxious to avoid encounter with any of the servants, Fanny picked up the gray shawl Bet had procured for her the evening before, which had been left on a chair in the hall; thus equipped, she found a glass-paned door leading into the garden, unlocked it, and slipped quietly through and out into the crisp autumn morning, huddling the shawl tightly around her slender arms and shoulders.

The door gave onto a flagged path which skirted the house. The first thing that met Fanny's eye, as she stepped out, was the tree that had so excited Thomas's wrath on the previous night.

It was a graceful young ash, perhaps thirty years old, tall, well shaped, its topmost boughs reaching already as high as the roof of the house. The smooth silver-gray trunk was still no thicker than a ship's mast, but the upper branches were already beginning to spread wide. The fingerlike, pinnate leaves, which in the windy night had swung and sighed and shaken so wildly, now hung calm in the morning light, their color, already nipped by the first frosts, a delicate, radiant pale gold; the branches that had groaned and wailed like the strings of some giant's harp now held their elegant position unmoving against the cool sky. *Yggdrasil,* thought Fanny—for among the Rev. Mr. Herriard's theological library there had also been many books on mythology and Fanny had read them all—Yggdrasil, Odin's ash tree, the sacred stem, the axis that holds earth and sky together; and her heart lifted, in acknowledgment of the tree's peaceful gold-and-silver beauty.

Beyond it lay a drift of mist, beyond that a hillside shouldered up on the far side of a small, deep valley. No houses were to be seen.

Fanny carefully tiptoed the length of the house on the flagged path, then took a diagonal across a dewy lawn to reach the edge of the garden, which, she now saw, occupied an extensive, wedge-shaped terrace of land. Beyond the boundary wall the ground appeared to drop away steeply.

Descending a short, shallow flight of steps, Fanny found herself on a lower level, a long, grassy walk which ran the entire length of the garden on its valley side. The walk was screened from the house by a yew hedge; on its far side a low wall gave onto the valley; beyond this wall the drop was quite steep—from ten to twelve feet—so that the garden seemed bounded by a rampart.

Fanny caught her breath at the beauty of the prospect over the wall: in the bottom of the valley, visible here and there between drifts of mist, a clear brook meandered, its course marked out, from curve to curve, by an occasional oak or clump of osiers; beyond the brook meadows ran up steeply to the top of a small hill crowned with a spinney; and beyond this hill a higher, darker mass of woodland stretched away into the distance. To the north of the ridge the country flattened out into a blue expanse of weald—plowland, pasture, and small patches of copse extending far away to a distant line of blue hills on the horizon, possibly thirty or forty miles off. Perhaps London lies there, thought Fanny, whose notion of distance was very inexact; and she strained her eyes, searching for smoke or the hint of a city on the misty plain. Barnaby had gone to London to be with his regiment until it sailed for India; perhaps he was there still. . . .

Fanny did not know how long she stood absorbed, the morning sun warm on her cheek, drinking in the beauty of this landscape. As long as I can come here, she told herself; as long as I can see this—even if only once a day—I shall be able to bear *anything*.

Having formed even this small plan comforted Fanny a little; she felt as if she had been able to make *some* effort to regulate her new life. Then, recalling to mind that the breakfast hour must be fast approaching, she turned to ascend the steps and retrace her way to the house.

She had, overnight, wholly abandoned any notion that she might ever find it possible to love Thomas Paget. Try as she would, she could discover in him no quality that she could admire, or even like; he might conduct himself with rectitude in his professional sphere, no doubt he did, but at home he was churlish, parsimonious, unloving to his daughters, and apparently so completely lacking in delicacy or sensitivity that he neither knew nor cared if he subjected his wife to severe physical suffering.—He was unlovable, that was all there was to it. —Obey him, though, Fanny must and would; she would take pains to carry out his will in domestic matters and do her best to ensure that day-to-day life in the Hermitage ran smoothly. This she resolved, and hastened toward the garden door so that her lateness for breakfast on the first morning should not be an immediate cause for his displeasure.

Reaching the flagged path, she hurried along it; but the flags were smooth, slippery with dew that was almost frost, and she slid on one of them and would have fallen, had not a hand grasped her arm from behind. A voice exclaimed solicitously:

"Careful, ma'am! They stones be main gliddery, yet!"

"Oh, thank you!" Fanny gasped, recovering her balance with an effort.

Turning, she found herself looking up into the dark blue eyes of a tall young man who had jumped forward to catch her, dropping the lawn scythe he had been carrying; he wore a gardener's hessian apron, and his curly black hair was tied back with a piece of bast; his face and hands were brown as those of a gipsy. Long, and strongly boned, his face looked as if it wore a habitually serious expression, but now it broke into a smile, with a flash of very white teeth, as he released her arm, and she stood up straight, shaking her blue dress to rights.

"Eh, it would never do for the new mistress of the Hermitage to slip and break her ankle, first morning out! That'd be a bad omen for sure, that would!"

"But one which you have luckily averted!" Fanny said, smiling too. "Thank you—no harm is done. I am much obliged to you for your quickness. You must be the gardener; but I am afraid that, as yet, I do not know your name."

"It is Andrew Talgarth, ma'am."

"Did—are you—" Are you one of the servants that my husband brought with him? Fanny wanted to ask, but the phrase, somehow, seemed inapplicable to the tall, black-haired young man who stood so easily beside her holding the scythe which he had picked up again. "Do you belong to Petworth, or did you come here with my husband?" she finally said.

"I was working here as gardener, ma'am, before you came, for Madame Reynard, the French lady, and then for Miss Juliana—but I dunna belong to Petworth. I come from Breconshire, from the Black Mountains; Lord Egremont fetched my father an' me here, a long time since, to work in the Petworth House gardens and park; and then he asked me to help lay out the garden here, for Madame Reynard, when he had this house built for her, sixteen, seventeen year agone."

"So long ago as that?" asked Fanny, surprised. "You hardly look old enough!"

"I'm thirty-two, ma'am, but I've been a gardener's boy ever since I was weaned, as you might say," he answered, smiling. "Born with a trowel in my hand. My da was used to work for a mort of different gentry, all over the country, laying out their pleasure grounds—afore he settled down with Lord Egremont, up at Petworth House yonder."

Talgarth gestured toward the western end of the garden where, Fanny now noticed, beyond a stone barn, a high wall, and a pair of coach houses, there rose the red-tiled roofs of the town. Beyond them, higher still, severely rectangular, the stone portico and slate roof of an impressively large mansion could be seen. It seemed almost as big as a castle.

"Dear me, is that Petworth House? I had no notion that it was so close. Or so large! Does your father still work for Lord Egremont?"

"Nay, he's retired now, ma'am; Lord Egremont builded him a liddle house, up in the dilly woods yonder"—Talgarth gestured across the valley—"where he has his bean plot and his gillyflowers an' his pipe an' 'baccy, an' plays his fiddle; but he still danders over to the big house, now an' now, just to make sure all's well wi' the garden. Lord Egremont, he do set great store by my da's opinion; anything new that's to be done, he likes my da to come and talk it over.—Tending a garden, ma'am, be like to rearing a child, I reckon. You do grow mortal attached. Seems you're bound up, forevermore, to a plot where you've once set your spade in the marl—like as if you been tethered to it with bass bark—and you can't noways forget it."

In demonstration of his point, he pulled a hank of bast from the pocket of his apron and wound a twist of it around two of his fingers.

"I can quite understand that," said Fanny. "You have made a very beautiful place out of this one, indeed."

She looked about it with simple pleasure. On the level area between the house and the long yew hedge there was a formal garden, flower beds intersected by narrow brick paths. Although it was late in the season, the beds, between small clipped box hedges, blazed with color and were beginning, now the sun grew warmer, to give off sweet, aromatic odors. Beyond the formal garden beds the turning leaves of two small sturdy cherry trees growing in the lawn made splashes of red-gold; a shrubbery of lilac bushes and evergreens lay between the house and the stone barn; fruit trees were carefully pleached against a distant high wall; climbing roses grew up the side of the house and against two small summerhouses at either end of the yew-tree walk, their tendrils still smothered with late blossoms. Bees hummed in a lavender hedge, which had been clipped once and was flowering again. Although it was no great estate, the garden, perhaps half an acre, had been carefully planned so as to give the greatest possible variety and to seem larger than it was.

"The kitchen plot an' orchard's over yonder behind the wall," Talgarth said, pointing toward the barn. "There's aplenty late beans yet, do you fancy 'em, ma'am—artichokes—medlars—pears—an' some fine Ribston pippins. 'Tis time they were picked; if the master sees fit, I'll be setting to that today—"

His voice died as a door slammed behind Fanny, and he glanced past her, politely touching his black forelock. "Morning, sir!"

Thomas's voice exclaimed angrily:

"*Frances!* What in the world are you doing out here? I have been seeking you all over the house! Did you not hear the gong? Why do you not come to morning prayers?"

Through his indignant tones the church clock could be heard chiming eight. Fanny had spun guiltily around at the first sound of his voice. She almost slipped again on the greasy flagstone; but this time Talgarth made no move to assist her, and she recovered herself by laying a hand against the house wall.

"I—I am sorry, sir—I was just coming, indeed—"

Thomas looked both incensed and mistrustful; he held his watch in his hand; his mouth was set in a hard line; his suspicious gaze moved from Fanny to the gardener, as if he had detected them plotting against him.

"Truly I had no notion that it was so late," faltered Fanny.

"And yet you can clearly see the church clock from the garden! —Go indoors at once; I will speak with you presently. As for you," Thomas said to the gardener, looking at him with a marked lack of liking, "you are Talgarth, I infer?"

"Yes, sir."

"What you are doing so close to the house at breakfast time I do not know, but since I see you here I may as well tell you now—your first task for the day shall be to cut down that tree there."

He gestured toward the ash.

"Cut it down, Captain Paget, sir?" Talgarth's voice was startled; he looked as if he could hardly believe what he had heard.

"Oh *no!*" Fanny cried out piteously at the same moment, forgetting that she had been told to go indoors. "Oh, pray, sir, do not have it cut! It is so beautiful!"

"Frances! When I wish for your opinion I will invite it; otherwise, I must request you to be silent! Besides, did I not just order you to go inside? Yes—cut it down," Thomas commanded the gardener. "The tree is by far too close to the house; whoever planted it there must have been clean out of his senses. It blocks out the light from the parlor and my bedroom; it is bound to bring damp—insects—probably disease. And its wood will furnish us with a plentiful supply of firewood.—Though why I should trouble myself to give an explanation of my orders, I do not know! You may commence at once; by the time breakfast is over, I wish the tree to be gone."

Talgarth, however, stood his ground.

"Begging your pardon, I'm sure, sir, but I can't do that," he said, wooden-faced.

Thus calmly contradicted, Thomas flew into a cold fury, which Fanny observed with terror. The visible marks of rage were two white spots at either side of his nostrils, a congestion of the eyes, and a quickening of his breath. He said in a gritty voice:

"And what, may I ask, is your justification for this insolence? Do you wish to be dismissed out of hand?"

"No, sir," replied Talgarth calmly. "But Miss Juliana—Lady van Welcker, as she be now—she did say to me that, while she were away, she didn't wish for no big changes to be made in her garden, no trees nor hedges cut down, nor new paths laid, naught o' that nature, for she be main fond of it the way it be now, an' wishes it kept so, in memory o' the lady as left it to her, Madame Reynard. Miss Juliana were *particular* fond o' this ash tree, sir, for Lord Egremont himself gave it to the other lady; I wouldn't hurt it for the world, or go agin her wishes in such a matter.—Anyhows," he added practically, as Thomas, clenching his hands, drew a breath of fury, "I believe it bain't in your power, sir, to go agin Miss Juliana's wish, for she did tell me, afore she left, as how she'd had a lawyer's piece writ out for ye to sign, as named all those things ye could do about the place, an' those ye couldn't."

The silence maintained by Thomas for some moments after Talgarth's words appeared to indicate that this shaft had gone home; evidently such an agreement *had* been signed, which, in the exasperation of the moment, he had overlooked; but Fanny felt fairly certain that, now it was recalled to his mind, the severe rectitude and rigidity of his nature would prevent him from taking any further action to contravene it. This was not likely to sweeten his temper, however, and Fanny now had sufficient discretion to step softly in through the open door without attempting to catch the eye of Talgarth, who still stood, in a perfectly respectful attitude, awaiting his master's further orders.

Without waiting to hear what these might be, Fanny hastened to the dining room where she found the remainder of the household assembled, the servants with expressions of hungry resignation, while

Paget's children appeared startled at this variation from routine, and decidedly impatient. Fanny slipped in to align herself with her stepdaughters, and a moment or two later Thomas strode into the room with a brow as black as thunder.

Without pausing an instant he snatched up the prayer book from the sideboard and began reading rapidly:

" 'Almighty and most merciful Father, who has safely brought us to the beginning of this day . . .' "

Outside the window, Fanny could hear the gardener's footsteps crunching away along a gravel path.

After breakfast, when Fanny had a moment alone with Thomas, who had eaten the meal in ominous silence, she thought it best to apologize again for her lateness and did so speedily, before she had time to lose courage.

Thomas listened without comment and then said:

"Very well; pray do not let it occur again. Frances! I trust that you will remember your position in this household as *my wife*. You are no longer a child, among your sisters, but a woman grown, and must comport yourself as such, with suitable dignity and reserve."

"Yes, sir." She could not bear to look at his face; she kept her eyes, instead, upon the three-fingered hand, holding his cocked hat.

He said, "I do not wish to discover you laughing and talking with menservants—with any such persons. It is wholly unbecoming to your station. You are married to *me* now; please keep this in mind at all times."

Fanny did not feel she was at all likely to forget, but his look was so forbidding that she merely repeated her apology.

"I am going out, now, on impress business, and shall very likely be absent until the late afternoon," Thomas went on. "I have directed Patience to bring her slate and copybooks down to this room where you may give her her lessons until noon. Then I have instructed Kate to wait on you with the housekeeping books and a list of the stores, so that you may be fully conversant with the running of the household. And you had best discuss with her the disposition of the furniture and make certain that the pantry and all the closets have been set in order. This afternoon you may go out into the garden, but pray do not go unescorted—either take one of the maids or, better, have Bet and Martha accompany you."

Rather faintly, Fanny inquired, "May I not go into the town?"

Bending a frowning glance upon her—while he gave her his instructions, Thomas had kept his gaze averted, as if the sight of her was displeasing to him—he said:

"Why should you wish to do *that?* You can have no need to buy any article yet, surely? Your father assured me that he had expended on you sufficient funds to equip you with all the usual bride's gear?"

"Oh yes, sir, he did, of course—" Fanny's voice trembled at the thought of her father, parting with guineas he could ill spare to buy her linen. "I—I merely had a wish to inspect the town, to see the streets.—And your daughters might enjoy it also."

"I prefer that you do not," Thomas said shortly. "If there is some particular necessity, such as thread, or lamp oil, you may send one of the servants to buy it."

Now the sound of his horse's hoofs could be heard outside the front door, and he departed without more ado. Fanny could feel only relief at his going, although these various admonitions and prohibitions had left her decidedly limp, low-spirited, and despondent; by contrast her life at home, free to walk in the fields or the village as she pleased, alone or with her sisters, appeared the height of liberty and independence; here, she was virtually a prisoner.

But perhaps he will change his views after a week or two, Fanny thought hopefully. For one thing, I cannot imagine that Bet and Martha will submit for long to being confined to the house and garden —remembering their conversation on the previous evening. She suspected that Thomas had little notion of his daughters' real natures.

However the two elder were now occupied, diligently and with due propriety, Martha stitching at a large canvas fire screen, while Bet practiced the pianoforte, so Fanny applied herself to the instruction of little Patty. This proved a decidedly unrewarding task; firstly, Patty was a dull and backward child, having poor natural abilities and a somewhat spiteful and disobliging nature; secondly, she seemed filled by a sullen resolve to learn as little as possible, countering any instruction Fanny gave her with an objection which varied only slightly in its form:

"Miss Fox never taught me so!" "Miss Fox never said that!" "That was not the way Miss Fox did it!"

By the end of the morning, out of all patience with the child, Fanny could not avoid wishing Miss Fox at the bottom of the sea. Wearied out, irked, and disheartened, with flushed cheeks and throbbing temples, she leaned against the window sill and looked out at the autumnal tints of the trees, longing to walk in the garden, but, mindful of Thomas's interdiction, not daring to do so unaccompanied. Talgarth was not to be seen; perhaps he was working in the kitchen garden. At least, Fanny thought with a small throb of satisfaction, the ash tree had been saved; from where she stood she could not see it, but the mere thought of its color and grace gave her pleasure.

"Try not to let your pencil squeak like that, Patty," she said, sighing.

"I can't stop it," grumbled Patty, who was copying out scriptural texts with a scowl very reminiscent of her father. Deliberately, as it seemed, she made the pencil squeak even louder on her slate, and Fanny had to master a strong temptation to box her ears.

Kate, the cook-housekeeper, tapped at the door.

"If you please, ma'am, the master said I was to show you over the stores and books at noon, and, please, there's a gipsy come selling lavender bags and clothes pegs, and would you be wishful to buy any?"

Fanny shook her head. Thomas had not yet given her any housekeeping money and, in any case, even if he had, she felt certain that he would never countenance such a frivolous purchase as lavender bags.

"You look fagged to death, ma'am," said Kate, glancing from Fanny to the sulky child. "Should I be making you a cup of tea before you go over the stores? Or a nuncheon, you and the young ladies? It wouldn't take but a few moments."

Fanny was greatly tempted but—remembering the price of tea, over eleven shillings a pound—shook her head. "No, thank you, Kate; but I will take a glass of water."

"You're sure you wouldn't touch a glass of my cowslip wine, ma'am? You look fair wore out, begging your pardon."

Fanny shook her head again but was a little comforted at Kate's unexpected friendliness. And presently, walking about the house, inspecting first the basement kitchen, then the storerooms, pantry, and servants' attics, discussing the disposition of linens, furniture, and food stores, Fanny, to her own surprise, felt a certain uplifting of the spirits. Despite her several grounds for unhappiness—homesickness, the thought of Barnaby far away and forgetting her, sorrow and foreboding for her father, the hateful recollection of last night, and the expectation of tonight and all the nights to come, the repulsive looks of her stepdaughters when she met them about the house, and the recollection of Thomas's evident distrust and censure—despite all these things, when she glanced, from one window or another, at the sunny valley or the golden ash tree, which seemed to stand preening its pale plumage in the fine autumn weather, she could not deny to herself that some influence all around seemed encouraging her to take heart.

It is as if the *place* were speaking to me, Fanny thought illogically; as if the house or garden liked me and wanted to make me welcome.

"Is this house haunted, do you know, Kate?" she asked suddenly.

Kate gasped and let slip a bundle of bed linen she was holding.

"*Haunted,* ma'am? Dear, what a shock you gave me! I should hope not, indeed! They say the house has only been built eighteen year or so —quite modern, it is, not the place for spooks or specters! Though I believe there was an old ancient monastery builded here, hundreds of years ago; but there's no ghosts, ma'am, don't you go filling your head with such notions, or you'll frighten yourself to death!"

Fanny did not try to explain that she rather enjoyed the notion of a friendly spirit, the guardian of the place, keeping watch on behalf of its absent mistress. Perhaps, she thought fancifully, perhaps the house spirit dwells in the ash tree; how lucky it is that Thomas was prevented from cutting the tree down, or some terrible punishment might have been visited on his head. . . .

She smiled and said, "No, I am not in the least frightened, Kate, thank you, only a little tired with being indoors all morning. I think I will find Miss Bet or Miss Martha and see if they would like to take a stroll in the garden."

"Yes, you do that, ma'am. Only wrap up warm, for you look particular pale, all of a sudden."

Martha, now heartily bored by indoor occupations, was pleased enough to leave them and explore the garden with her young stepmother; and little Patty was likewise encouraged to put on a pelisse and come out to bowl her hoop. However she rapidly tired of the hoop and demanded of Jem the bootboy where he had put her kite—she must have her kite! At last, after much search, the kite was forthcoming, it having been accidentally deposited in the barn, which was large enough to serve as both stable and garden shed.

Patty's stepmother and sister soon had cause to wish that the kite never had been found, for its owner was far from expert in the handling of it, and it frequently became entangled in the boughs of various fruit trees; Jem had to be summoned each time to release it. Finally, after much tugging and ill-use, the string broke, and the truant kite soared away up the lane leading to the town.

"Oh, quick, *quick!* Let us go after it!" cried Patty, tugging at her sister's hand. Martha was willing enough to go, but Fanny had scruples.

"Your papa does not wish us to go into the town, Patty. We had better not go up the lane, or he will be displeased."

"But the kite will be lost! Some other child will find it!" whined Patty. "It is not far—I believe I saw it come down just around the bend in the lane."

"We had best send Jem to look for it."

But Jem had gone off to buy saddle soap and boot blacking, and the other servants were all occupied on tasks too important to leave for this trifling quest.

"*I* will take Patty up the lane; there can be no harm in going just as far as the street, after all," proposed Martha, regarding her stepmother with some scorn. "If you are so frightened of Papa's displeasure, Fanny, you had best stay here."

Stung by this taunt—although it was true, and she *was* frightened—Fanny at last said that if Martha and Patty went she had better accompany them; she had better not let them go unescorted; but in any event, none of them must proceed farther than the end of the lane.

As they walked past the gate leading into the walled kitchen garden Fanny glanced through, wondering if Talgarth was at work picking the apples; but he was not visible, either there or in a small glasshouse beside the barn.

"Oh, *there* is my kite!" Patty shouted joyfully, running up the rutted track to where the kite could now be seen, perched in a holly bush.

Next moment she had slipped and fallen on the muddy, uneven ground and was letting out loud uncontrolled shrieks and wails.

"Oh, oh, oh, my knee, my *knee!*"

"Hush, Patty!" said her sister with great impatience. "Do not be making such a coil about nothing. It is nothing of a scrape! You always go on as if you had half killed yourself."

"It hurts, it hurts dreadfully!" sobbed Patty, hoisted to her feet by the unsympathetic Martha. Her face, hands, and knees were mud-covered, and a small bead of blood had started out on her leg. "Look, it is bleeding! Oh, oh, oh!"

"Dear, dear, here's a sad commotion!" observed a cheerful voice over the heads of Martha and Fanny, who were both trying to set Patty to rights and stanch her wounds. They looked up in surprise, not having heard anybody approaching, and saw a gentleman, plainly but neatly clad in a riding jacket with buckskins and top boots, and holding two pointers on a leash. He made them a polite bow, doffing his hat, and with his free hand proffered the missing kite, remarking:

"Perhaps this will help to quench the young lady's tears! I presume the kite is your property, my dear? Allow me to return it to you."

Without a word of thanks, Patty seized the toy, directing a suspicious look at its restorer from swollen, tear-filled eyes.

"Patty! Where are your manners?" reproved Fanny. "Pray let me hear you say thank you to the gentleman." And on her own behalf she added, "We are very much obliged to you, sir."

"Oh, pray don't name it, my dear ma'am," he said easily. "Am I right in supposing that I see in you Mrs. Thomas Paget? Your husband's cousin Juliana is a very delightful and charming friend of mine; I trust that we shall soon be equally good neighbors. Allow me to introduce myself—I am Egremont, you know, from over there—" and he waved a hand in the general direction of Petworth House, which, from here, however, was invisible, concealed by some intervening trees and roofs.

Fanny was very much startled and somewhat at a loss, unable to decide how she ought to deal with such an unforeseen encounter. She could not help being interested in this nobleman, who did not at all seem to live up to his scandalous reputation—except, to be sure, in the ease and unceremonious friendliness of his bearing. He was very fresh-complexioned, though he must be at least in his late forties, with decidedly humorous, twinkling eyes, slightly downturned at the corners, a long, rather hooked nose, and a long-lipped smiling mouth. As Fanny dropped her curtsy, somewhat flustered, and in a halting manner introduced herself and Martha, Lord Egremont went on affably:

"You'll forgive my coming around so soon, when I dare say you are all at sixes and sevens still, probably ready to consign me to the Devil! But we are country folk hereabouts, you know, and don't stand on ceremony. If there is anything you lack at present—a piece of game, for instance, a pine, or a few nectarines—say the word—I shall be happy to let you have any amount of fruit from my succession houses."

"Thank you—you are very kind," replied Fanny nervously, wondering with the deepest apprehension what opinion Thomas would entertain of this call and its lack of formality. She herself could not help liking Lord Egremont—finding herself greatly attracted by this very ease and want of ceremony—but she was very much afraid that it would have exactly the reverse effect upon her husband. Martha, meanwhile, was frankly gaping, all eyes, and Lord Egremont turned to say to her with great kindness:

"You will always find a sufficiency of young company up at Petworth House, my dear—my daughters and their friends, plenty of girls to play piano duets with—boys to lead your ponies or partner you for a dance—impromptu hops, you know, nothing formal! I cannot abide formality, but a small comfortable entertainment with the young folk all enjoying themselves is what I like best in the world; so feel free to step over whenever you like. Another pretty girl is always welcome!"

Martha colored up at this praise but did not take it at all amiss; and Lord Egremont, then turning back to Fanny, inquired with more formal politeness:

"Is your husband—is Captain Paget at home, ma'am? I have not yet had the pleasure of meeting him but should be glad of the favor of his company for a few moments, over a small matter of business."

Fanny was beginning to make his excuses and explain that he was from home, when she was interrupted by the sound of a horse's hoofs and Thomas's own voice from behind her, somewhat louder than usual, raised in tones of very decided displeasure.

"Frances? Do I find you here? With my children? And in what company, may I ask?"

"Ah, is that you, indeed, Paget? Delighted to meet you!" Lord Egremont turned with a cordial smile to greet his new neighbor, who seemed very far from returning the friendly sentiment, as was evidenced by his scowling brow and outthrust lip. "I was just saying to your wife here—"

Since Thomas continued to fix a fulminating stare upon Fanny, she hastily intervened, in case he should come out with some disastrous rebuff or piece of discourtesy.

"This—this is Lord Egremont, sir—very kindly come to inquire if we have all we require. We—we chanced to meet him here, in the lane—"

"Your youngest little miss had suffered a tumble, running after her kite," Lord Egremont explained with his cheerful smile. "But it's all forgot now, eh, Miss Puss? I'll send you a fine big bunch of grapes, and you'll never think twice about those scraped knees. I was saying to your young lady, Paget, that your daughters will be kindly welcome if ever they wish to step over and take potluck with my young people—we seldom have less than ten or a dozen young things there, skipping about."

Fanny dared not look at her husband while this offer was so ingenuously made; she could almost feel the arctic chill issuing from him as he replied with extreme formality:

"That is excessively kind of your Lordship, but I believe they had better remain at home. Too much gratification of a wish for social pleasure may lead to self-indulgence and a reversal of all the principles in which they have been brought up—"

"Well, well, well, we shall see, we shall see," said the earl easily, not very interested or choosing to pay too much heed to this speech. "But what I really wanted to see you about, Paget, was this matter of Talgarth—your gardener, you know; he is such an excellent young fellow that when he came to me and said you had dismissed him I felt sure there must have been some misunderstanding that could all be cleared up in a minute—Talgarth is as sober and steady a young man as I have ever come across in my life, and a first-rate gardener too; indeed I could not have considered letting him go to Madame Reynard if she had not been such a dear friend of mine! So I dare say it was a mistake, eh, and the lad is quite in error when he tells me that you turned him off?"

Fanny caught her breath sharply, but Thomas replied, in a cold, measured voice:

"No, my lord, he was not mistaken. Excellent gardener he may be, I have not the least doubt of it, but I cannot have in my employ somebody who coolly and impudently defies my orders, and that was what he did."

"Oh, come now, Paget my dear fellow, come, come, come!" expostulated Lord Egremont good-naturedly. "Young Andrew told me the whole, and I understood that it was to do with the business of cutting down that young ash tree—capital tree, you know, gave it to Madame Reynard myself, helped with the planting of it eighteen years ago—

perfectly enter into Miss Juliana's wish not to have it felled, can't call that impertinence, only carrying out his mistress' orders, you know! So forget about the whole business, eh, tell the young fellow, he can come back to work, won't you, now?"

"I am afraid, my lord, that is quite out of the question," said Thomas icily. "The *cause* of the dispute may, to you, seem a trifling one—and, indeed, being now aware of Countess van Welcker's predilection for the tree, I have relinquished my plan to fell it—though a more injudicious situation for planting a tree of that size I have never encountered!—but I have the strongest possible reasons for refusing to reinstate the man Talgarth. His manner was insolent—assertive—overweening; such airs in a servant I cannot and will not tolerate."

"Talgarth insolent?" exclaimed his lordship, very much astonished. "Sure, sir, you mistake? It is just not possible! The politest, sweetest young fellow in the whole countryside! You must have misheard something he said! Come now, forget about the whole matter and take him back!"

"I thank your Lordship, I have excellent hearing," replied Thomas, who was now in a silent rage, "and I have not the least intention of taking him back."

"Well, I am very sorry to hear it," said Lord Egremont. "Sorry for *your* sake, since Talgarth kept that garden in tiptop condition, and you will have far to go to find his equal. For my own sake I am glad, since I shall be happy to have him back at Petworth House, and indeed already promised that he should become my head gardener, should my intervention with you prove inauspicious.—*Sure* you won't change your mind, now?"

"That is quite out of the question, my lord," replied Thomas. "In fact, I have already engaged another gardener."

"Well, well, I can see you are a fellow who don't let the grass grow under his feet," remarked Lord Egremont, "but still I confess I am disappointed.—By the bye," he added with apparent irrelevance, "I dare say you will be wishing to lock up the underground passage?"

"Underground passage?" Thomas sounded both suspicious and bewildered.

"Underground way, you know, between your little summer pavilion and Petworth House. Perhaps you will not have discovered it yet? The children have been used to run along it at all hours of the day," said Lord Egremont cheerfully, "they were great friends of Miss Juliana, but I told them they were not to until you were settled in, just in case you did not care for the notion. I am afraid it has been used by the runners, too, from time to time—free traders, you know; I dare say, as an impress official, you, however, may not wish to countenance such activities."

"I most certainly shall *not*," replied Thomas glacially. "I should be greatly obliged if your Lordship would take immediate steps to have the passage closed off."

"Very well, very well! And I will bid you good day," said Lord Egremont, sighing a little. He now appeared resigned to the fact that his new neighbor did not intend to reciprocate his friendly overtures in any way. Indeed it seemed to Fanny that his glance at her contained some commiseration as he bowed and remarked, "Good afternoon, ladies. I trust that you will be very happy during your stay in the Hermitage."

Thomas removed his own hat and bowed stiffly; then stood waiting, holding his horse, until Lord Egremont should have passed out of the lane. But the latter turned to say, on an afterthought:

"By the bye—who is the new gardener that you have hired?"

"His name is Goble—Henry Goble," replied Paget repressively, as much as to say, *What business is that of yours?* "He is a native of Petworth, I understand, but recently returned from long service in the navy."

"Goble? *Goble?* Great heavens, yes—I well remember the poor fellow. Worked for me at one time—excellent gardener—snatched off by the press gang when my back was turned. Now there's a piece of irony for you," remarked Lord Egremont, his customary good humor apparently restored by this item of news. "Pressed off to sea for dear knows how many years—comes back—and goes to work for a regulating officer! Well, you certainly have a capable gardener there—yes, yes

—you can't go wrong with Goble—and I have Talgarth back—so perhaps it is all for the best."

And, chuckling, he called his dogs to heel and walked off up the lane.

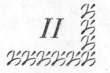

II

The twins had quarreled on the evening of their birthday. Not seriously—their disagreements never went deep; Scylla had raised objections when she found that Carloman had accepted an invitation to spend the evening at the palace with the young Maharajah.

"You know perfectly well what will happen if you go," she complained. "You will stay up there till two or three in the morning—drinking wine and smoking water pipes, and, for all I know, taking opium—"

"Only the prince, my dear; you know I never touch it—"

"And he will lose more and more money to you, so that he will want to go on playing longer and longer to win back his losses—How much does he owe you now?"

"I think it's about twenty thousand rupees," replied her brother cheerfully.

"Yes, and if he ever does pay you, which I dare say he never will, it would very likely be in *shawls*. Of what use would that be?"

"We could hire an elephant and dispose of them to the nearest East India Company factory. Stop scolding, Scylla, my dear! You know it would be foolish to offend Mihal. We shall not have a debauch, I promise you. I am going to read him some of my poems.—Why don't you come up to the palace with me? You could pay a call on poor Mahtab Kour."

"Thank you, dearest Cal, I spend enough time in the purdah quarters as it is! And you can read your poetry to me at home, after all. Does Mihal understand it, may I ask?"

"He likes to think he does. And that puts him in a good humor. So it is really a piece of practical diplomacy to visit him."

"Oh, undoubtedly!" she said, laughing. "Well—*pray* try to come back before midnight! It *is* our birthday tomorrow, after all. And you *did* promise that we should ride to the Great King's tomb—"

"Did I?" He sounded taken aback. "All the way to the Great King's tomb?"

"Which means starting early, as soon as the boys have done their lessons, before it becomes too hot—"

"I must have been mad to promise," grumbled Cal. "It is quite twenty miles away."

"Miss Musson has offered to pack us a nuncheon. And, remember, the hot weather is almost here—if we don't go soon, we shall have to wait until after the rains," pleaded Scylla.

"Oh, very well!" Cal was really fond of his sister and generally prepared to indulge her if it did not mean a great deal of trouble for himself. "I promise that I will come away as early as I can."

"That's my dear brother!"

"Do I look presentable?"

"Correct to a shade! Except for your hair—come here—"

They were of equal height, both medium-sized and slender, so that she, for a girl, seemed tall, and he, for a man, just below average height. While she smoothed back the fine, soft, dark hair, which would fall forward in streaks over his brow, he stood placidly accepting her ministrations, then let her help him into a fresh white linen coat.

"Now you are as fine as fivepence!" she teased. "Dress you up in uniform and you would be the spit image of that dashing young French general Buonaparte—whose picture was in the *Gazette*—except that your face is thinner—"

"Wear uniform? Thank heaven I don't have to," yawned her brother. "That's one advantage of being cast off by our dear father. No obligation to go into some terrible cavalry regiment where they all look and sound like horses—including the horses themselves—" and he adjusted a pith helmet carefully over his interesting profile and walked out onto the veranda, shouting for the syce.

Next moment she heard the sound of his horse's hoofs cantering up the sandy causeway toward the great gate of Ziatur.

Naturally—in spite of his promise—Cal did stay late at the palace. She had known that he would. It was hard to resist Prince Mihal's pleadings. "My dear Padg-ett—it is so deucedly boring here. Just one more game! What difference can the time make to *you?*"

When Scylla woke next morning, to the usual sound of crows bickering on the town ramparts up above, there was dead silence from her brother's part of the bungalow. She could tell, because even the punkah was silent.

Throwing aside festoons of mosquito netting, she pulled on a voluminous cotton wrapper and walked out onto the veranda. There the punkah wallah, whose duty it was to keep moving the long pole with a deep frill of material fastened along its length, was lying fast asleep.

Scylla gave him a prod.

"Wake up, Ram! What time did my brother come home last night?"

"Cal Sahib did not return until the third hour, mem," he answered, hastily beginning to pull on the punkah rope, which was attached to his big toe and ran through a hole in the wall. "The sahib was very weary and gave orders not to be called till noon."

"Oh, he did, did he? The wretch!"

Scylla grimaced to herself as she returned to her own room and splashed her face and arms with water, which was already lukewarm, from the big earthenware jar. Then, sighing with her usual irritation, she struggled into the muslin chemise and petticoats which Miss Musson considered essential for a European young lady to wear among the heathen. If only I could wear a sari or perjamas, how cool and practical it would be, how much less notice it would excite, thought Scylla, as she had so many times before. But Miss Musson was positive that her ward's adoption of native dress would be the first step in a downward progression that would inevitably terminate in slavery, degradation, and death. "It is all very well for me, my dear Priscilla, to wear Pahari trowsers, because I am aged and hideous and nobody takes me for anything but what I am, an eccentric old lady from Boston who chooses to try and teach ways of cleanliness and godliness to the idolaters. But you are so pretty that it would give rise to immediate misapprehension. No, no, you are best as you are."

If only she knew how often I had worn a sari before I came here, thought Scylla crossly, pulling on a blue calico riding dress with a full skirt and gathered high to the neck. The material was already faded almost white along the tops of the gathers from the Indian sun, and showed stains under the armpits in spite of frequent ferocious scrubbings by the dhobi.—At least, however, Miss Musson had relented about Scylla's hair; it would have been senseless folly to attempt in Ziatur the fashionable high-piled style which was still worn by ladies in Calcutta long after it had vanished from Paris and London. Scylla's hair had been shorn when she had had fever at the age of twelve, and it had never grown very long since then; now her soft, silver-pale curls clustered in comfortable disorder above her brow and ears; half a dozen strokes with a brush, and her toilet was complete.

"How—with your coloring so different—you and that brother of yours can be *twins*—" Miss Musson often said at first.

"We are not identical twins, ma'am," Carloman had pointed out. "The non-identical ones are frequently quite different, I understand; and how lucky for me! Who would wish to look like Miss Monkey Face there?"

"Carloman! You should not speak so of your sister!"

But Scylla only laughed. She did not, in fact, resemble a monkey so much as a charming little pug dog; her nose was exceedingly short and straight, with a slight upward tilt to the nostrils; her soft pink mouth was triangular, with dimples at each corner; and a pair of huge guileless gray-blue eyes gazed trustfully out at the world from under level brows which were rather darker than her silvery curls.

"It's those eyes of yours that really gull people," Cal said admiringly. "They make you look such an innocent! Father was the only one who knew you thoroughly, apart from me."

"He knew you too—wretch!"

"I am quite aware of that!"

In fact the nabob, casting a jaundiced eye over his infant progeny, as they kicked and waved their tiny arms in a silk-lined basket in the house at Umballa which he had hired for their mother, recoiled from the spectacle and exclaimed:

"Good God! Caliban and Sycorax! What have I ever done to be saddled with such a pair?"

The nabob was not philoprogenitive and had been far from delighted to have the lazy and lighthearted relationship with his charming Goanese lady complicated by the advent of the twins. Caliban and Sycorax they remained, so far as he was concerned—or Scylla and Charybdis, if he were in a classic humor—until a protesting Portuguese priest insisted on equipping them with a more Christian pair of names, picking the closest that he could find to their heathen designations, as their languid mother showed little interest in the matter. But Cal and Scylla were the names they continued to use for each other, and so, in the end, did most of the people who had to do with them. Cal and Scylla they remained.

Glancing past the curtain into her brother's darkened room, Scylla observed that he still slept, flung out motionless as a corpse under his mosquito nets. No doubt he would continue to sleep for hours. . . .

Well, he would just have to wait for his birthday gift until evening. And as for the Great King's tomb—She tossed an exasperated kiss in his direction and went on her way.

Breakfast was already waiting for her in the veranda on the other side of the house; the sharp-eared servants had heard her moving about her chamber and gauged her progress to a nicety. The day was warm already, and she had little appetite but had learned from experience that the sights and sounds of Ziatur palace had less power to disturb or nauseate her after a sensible meal, so she resolutely forced herself to swallow hot tea, crisp thin flaps of wheat bread fried in butter, and a slice of melon. Miss Musson, who ate like an anchorite, had already sipped a cup of tea and was making her preparations to leave for the hospital.

"Good morning, my dear. A happy birthday to you!" the older woman said. Miss Amanda Musson was not a lady given to effusiveness or sentimental gush. So large a part of her life had been devoted to punishingly hard work in what seemed like an almost hopeless cause that she never permitted herself to expend energy upon lesser objects in her scheme of priorities. She did not therefore kiss her young protégée now but gave her a very affectionate smile as she handed Scylla a tiny package, adding in a dry tone:

"Seventeen! My, what an advanced age!"

"It seems so, certainly, ma'am."

"To think that you have been here five years. Indeed my brother often said that he regarded you quite as his own children—if he had ever had any."

"He was a great deal kinder to us than our own father ever was—*dear* Uncle Winthrop," Scylla said warmly. "I still miss him as if he had died yesterday—and what *you* must feel—"

"Oh well, child, when you reach my age, you at least have the comfort of knowing it won't be long before you are reunited with your dear ones," Miss Musson replied briskly. "But open the package—I must be off."

"Oh, *ma'am*—" Looking inside the little box, Scylla found a small plain silver brooch—not Indian silver, this was heavier and darker in color, with scrollwork surrounding the word "Mizpah." "Your own brooch you are giving me!"

"Psha, child, don't take on! The—the person who gave it me has been dead for thirty years—I am sure *he* would raise no objection at my passing it on to somebody of whom I was fond." Benignly, she watched Scylla fasten the brooch into the collar of her blue dress. When Miss Musson smiled, the pale brown skin that was stretched so tightly over the bony structure of her face broke into countless wrinkles; seeing this phenomenon for the first time at the age of twelve, Scylla had thought it impossible that her face could ever straighten out again without the skin cracking into shreds, it seemed so dry and parchmentlike. Indeed, with her deep-sunk eyes and snowy knot of hair, Miss Musson strongly resembled Time's elder sister. Exactly how old she was the twins had never discovered, though they guessed that she must be well into her seventies. She could remember the Afghan invasion in 1748. She seemed indestructible, impervious to the passing of years. She wore the loose woolen trowsers and black vest of a mountain woman, covered by a burqa, and a huge leather hat, also from the mountains, over which she now draped a voluminous muslin veil. She was an impressive figure as she hopped onto the small pony that the waiting syce held for her and was borne away, riding sidesaddle, toward her hospital; women in the street dropped to their knees and bent their heads to the ground in reverence as she rode by.

Scylla herself followed, ten minutes later. On three mornings a week she helped Miss Musson at the tiny hospital; on the other three she taught reading, writing, geography, English, and French to Amur and Ranji, two of the princes in the palace who were still young enough to reside mainly in the purdah quarters; and she also gave basic lessons in what Miss Musson called common sense and elementary hygiene to any of the Maharajah's ladies who cared to attend.

Pulling on her own hat and veil, Scylla accordingly set out, accompanied by Abdul the gardener. Already, at six in the morning, the narrow, camel-trampled streets of the town below the citadel exuded the heat of a brick-lined oven. Patches of dung and dead dogs were smothered in flies. Stifling odors of mutton fat, spices, rotting vegetables, sweet-scented flowers, and urine issued in almost visible clouds from the open doors and windows of the little flat-roofed houses which were crammed together at all different levels below the palace on its red rock. Picking her way among the dried turds, Scylla called after Abdul to moderate his pace; she wanted to conserve her energy for the last punishingly steep climb, a causeway constructed over ribs of warm, polished rock up to the great gate.

"Wait a minute, Abdul! I wish to look back!"

Immediately below, the congested streets were full of people—women in saris of pink, saffron, turquoise, vermilion, or indigo, carrying children on their hips or baskets on their heads; men driving bullock carts; children scurrying everywhere. Sweetmeat sellers shrieked their wares. Humpbacked Brahman bulls with brilliantly painted horns puffed their way among the crowds, snatching fruit and vegetables from market stalls. Loaded camels slouched and grunted and snarled.

But outside the town—which ended very abruptly, one bowshot from the palace walls—the endless plain stretched far into the distance, a featureless, dun waste of sand, cactus, a few prickly bushes, with only an occasional banyan or mango tree casting its tiny shadow under the huge sun. Southward the plain appeared to continue forever; but, looking northwest, Scylla could just make out, through the heat haze, the distant blue line of the Sangur Hills, which were foothills of the faraway Hindu Kush. Among these foothills lay the ancient tomb which she was curious to visit, four or five hours' ride to the north, in a deep gully full of jungle grass. It was just the kind of place, she had thought, to stimulate Cal's enthusiasm and perhaps inspire one of his poems—but if the wretched boy were not interested, let him sleep all day! She would visit the tomb by herself.

This resolve formed, she moved on to join the impatient Abdul.

The wooden palace gate, between high crenelated red rock towers, was massively reinforced with iron bolts and bars, also with ferocious-looking spikes, a defense against elephants and battering rams; this was the only way into the citadel, which otherwise overhung a semicircular precipice. The town of Ziatur occupied its own little outcrop of hill, a toe that had become separated from the northern foothills and had, in many Muslim wars, served as an outpost and advanced warning station against invasion from the south. Now, with the Sikh states on the point of confederation, nearly all in subsidiary alliance with Britain, the threat of Muslim attack had receded, but never entirely. In this slow-moving land memories were long, the atrocities perpetuated by Jehangir and Aurangzeb seemed no longer ago than yesterday. The hinges of the gate were kept oiled and the spikes sharpened. Besides, what if the British were driven out in their turn?

Today all was peaceful. A magician with an earthenware teapot was demonstrating his magic in the gateway, passing a stick through the spout of the pot so that both ends remained visible; and a fortuneteller with a large cage containing a parrot and a sparrow was urging the passers-by to spend five annas and discover the future.

Resisting these temptations, Scylla passed through. "*Sat Sri Akal* [God is good]," she greeted Saroop Singh, the gatekeeper, whom she knew well. He, replying in kind, greeted her with a flood of local information; some travelers had arrived, Feringi, though not Angrezi or Yagistani; and they were even now with the young Maharajah. No, not with the old one; the latter was not well, not well at all, his despondency of the spirit had come on him once again. He would probably be pleased to see the Mem Periseela, who always cheered him up.

Scylla thanked Abdul for his escort, instructed him to return for her in two hours' time, and walked into the first courtyard, pulling her veil well down over her face as a concession to local mores.

The first courtyard was bare and sandy; in it, a number of soldiers in red tunics and baggy pink trowsers were lolling about on straw mattresses. An elephant was being washed, stamping and trumpeting with pleasure while its mahouts scurried around it with pails of water and long straw brushes. In this court, also, the Maharajah kept his menagerie; chained and collared hunting leopards reclined with bored expressions on rope beds, tigers paced to and fro behind bars.

The next court held the stables, where some of the Maharajah's eight hundred horses were housed. There were carriages as well—a curricle with ivory fittings, a perch phaeton brought from Calcutta, a chaise with gold lamps, and a landaulet. To a Londoner, it would have seemed strange to see these elegant European conveyances gathering dust amid such surroundings, but Scylla had never been to England and passed them without regard, as she did the palanquins with lacquered panels of cedar and silver fittings and gold brocade cushions, the silver elephant howdahs, and the jeweled, velvet-lined saddles, hanging rack on rack in open-fronted sheds.

The next court, paved all over with white marble slabs, had a central fountain and a pair of hoopoes admiring their reflections. Fifty or so of the horses were being led slowly around and around, so that their paces could be inspected by the Maharajah, who reclined near the fountain on a charpoy with a frame of silver and straps of woven elephant hair. He was not paying a great deal of attention to the horses, though; he looked sick, hollow-eyed, and preoccupied. A faint spark of pleasure came into his eyes when he noticed Scylla crossing the court.

"Aha, it is Mademoiselle Periseela, come to batter a little learning into my wayward sons!" He spoke in French, of which he had acquired a fluent command, in days gone by, at the princes' school in Ajmer.

"Good morning, Excellency. How do you find yourself today?"

Scylla curtsied but did not approach him too closely, remembering how he had flinched away when once, absent-mindedly, she had extended a hand to help him out of his chair. Enjoy her company he might, but she was still unclean, untouchable, so far as he was concerned.

"I am not well," he said irritably. "This accursed pain—distracts me from business, from pleasure, even from my horses." He clapped his hands. "Take them away, Umr Singh."

The horses were led clattering through the gate.

"Now sit down a moment, mademoiselle, and tell me something amusing."

A couple of barefoot servants in knee breeches and turbans ran forward to shift the cushions under the Maharajah and set a chair for Scylla—it was made of deer's antlers and was very uncomfortable. She politely declined a bowl of sherbet, but the Maharajah thirstily drank down a silver mug of opium and water, after which he looked a little more cheerful and a tinge of color came into his wax-yellow cheeks. He was a tall, thin man with a grizzled, bushy beard; his long, uncut hair was wound up into a turban stuck about with aigrettes of diamonds, and the knee-length tunic he wore was stiff with gold embroidery and jewels. His hands and feet were tiny, proof of his ancient—and inbred—Rajput descent.

"Amuse me!" he said again hopefully. "How are the wars going now, in Feringistan?"

"I dare say your news is more recent than mine, Excellency," said

Scylla, "for our last Calcutta *Gazette* came three weeks ago and took two months reaching us. There had been a great battle off Cape St. Vincent, and Admiral Nelson blockaded the Spanish in Cádiz."

"Where is Cape St. Vincent?"

"Well—if I had something to draw with—"

A boy servant brought a stick of kajal—lampblack used for painting eyes—and Scylla drew a rough map on the marble flagstone.

"Here is Spain, see—and this is the Mediterranean—the French were here—Admiral Jervis was here, based on a Portuguese river, the Tagus—"

"And where, from there, is Angrezi?"

"Up here." Scylla rapidly sketched in England, adding Ireland off to the left. "The French also tried to invade Ireland, up here, in Bantry Bay, but something went wrong and they sailed home again."

"The French are not good fighters?" he rapped out. "The English are better?"

"I *think* so," answered Scylla cautiously. "But that French General Buonaparte seems to be a very clever soldier. I read that he said he would like to take his armies eastward, like Alexander the Great."

"Aha, Iskander Bey—another great Feringi general. One of my ancestors, without doubt." The Maharajah's eyes flashed, and Scylla was reminded that he came of dedicated fighting stock; ever since the first day of spring in 1699, almost a hundred years ago, the Sikhs had designated themselves a warrior clan and had sworn adherence to the five Ks—Kanga, the comb, for cleanliness, Kara, the steel bracelet, symbolizing contentment, Kesh, unshorn hair, for strength, Kachh, the divided undergarment, for chastity, and Kirpan, the sword, to slay the enemies of righteousness. The word "Singh"—lion—formed part of every Sikh name. The Maharajah's full name, beginning with Mansur-i-Zaman Amirul-Umra Mohinder Singh went on for at least five lines of text, but he preferred to be known as Bhupindra Bahadur —Bhupindra the great fighter—despite the fact that he personally had never been in a battle.

"And do you really think, then, that the French plan to invade our country?"

"They would have a long way to march from the Mediterranean," Scylla replied, laughing.

"So? Where is the Punjab on this map of yours? Where is Kafiristan, and the Khaiber Pass?"

Rather hastily and sketchily she filled in the eastern end of the Mediterranean. "Now, see, here is Istanboul, here is Baghdad. All this is Persia. Up to the north—Turkmenistan and Russia. Here, farther east, Afghanistan."

"Put in Kabul," he ordered, and she placed a dot to the west of the Khaiber Pass. "Now, Peshawur." She put another dot, to the east.

"How many parasangs from Istanboul to Peshawur?"

"I should think it would be about six thousand miles—four miles to a parasang." She calculated. "Perhaps fifteen hundred parasangs."

"It takes a camel caravan forty days to cross from Persia to Herat in Afghanistan, it would take twice as long to reach the Khaiber Pass. We would know, from our spies in Afghanistan, many weeks before the armies were halfway here. They will never attempt it."

"But horsemen could do it in a much shorter time—ten to twelve days," objected Scylla.

"Aha! You should have been a soldier, mademoiselle! Do not forget, though, they have to drag the guns with them—big guns, much heavier than these."

The fountain was embellished, at its four corners, by amazing old brass cannon, whose muzzles consisted of elaborately ornamented lions' heads.

"Also," said the Maharajah, "the road from Baghdad here is impassable in the winter, because of snow and, in summer, because of drought. I do not think they will come."

He sounded disappointed; Scylla could not be sure whether he regretted the lost opportunity for a battle or whether he had hoped that the French might expel the English, who now had virtually undisputed dominion over a large part of southern India.

A servant came up, bowed low, and said, "The Shahzada Mihal Singh asks when you will be ready to receive the Feringi emissaries?"

"Mihal is always troubling me to see somebody," grumbled the Maharajah fretfully. "Now it is these French." He shot a sly glance at Scylla. "You see, mademoiselle, the French are closer than you think!"

He stood up with difficulty, and Scylla, knowing better than to offer assistance, curtsied again and went off toward the women's regions.

When she first entered the purdah quarters of Ziatur palace, with Miss Musson, she had found it unbearably depressing. By now time had acclimatized her, but even so she never passed in without a shiver, remembering that, while she could come and go freely, many of the inhabitants of this place would spend the rest of their lives there and never set foot outside. Cal had once estimated that the palace might easily have a population of four thousand, of whom at least two thirds were women. There was a larger population unseen, for the dead were all buried underneath, and had been for hundreds of years past.

The women's quarters, occupying a natural spur of the hilltop on which the palace perched, were isolated from the rest of the apartments and were labyrinthine in their complexity. Staircases wound and twisted up and down, passages ended abruptly in openings on the cliff, hundreds of empty rooms remained dark and unused, their silk and cedarwood furnishings moldering quietly behind fretted marble screens. There were dwelling chambers on all levels—some of them sixty feet below ground, for the sake of coolness in the raging summer, others opening onto roof gardens two hundred feet up, unguessed at from ground level. Windowless inner rooms and passages were somberly lit by blazing rags soaked in linseed or mustard oil and placed on pronged holders or in cups. Here and there oil lamps with colored glass chimneys were placed on brackets so as to illuminate huge paintings—many of them hideously obscene—on walls and ceilings. Miss Musson, on her first visits, had sternly instructed Scylla to avert her eyes from these, but by now, as with so much else, custom had habituated her to them, and she passed with but a perfunctory glance at the intricately writhing limbs. On other walls, hundreds of portraits of bygone maharajahs hung in disregarded ranks; nobody glanced at their swords, turbans, or dangling mustaches. Along some passages, cows roamed; smells of cooking, incense, and garbage issued from dim, shuttered rooms, or sweeter scents of musk and jasmine. Distant music could always be heard—sitars, flutes, and finger drums. Occasionally, glancing through a doorway, Scylla would see a juggler, storyteller, or group of dancing girls who had been asked in to entertain the bored inmates. The Maharajah was no longer interested in his women—not even the youngest of them, the beautiful, wily Rani Sada, who had been the daughter of his subadar, had been treated as a daughter, as a pet, by the Maharajah when she was a child, allowed to ride with him in his palki when he went out; then, when she was thirteen, he had her sent to school in Amritsar and given an allowance of five thousand rupees a month. And at fifteen she had returned to Ziatur and wasted no time in ousting Mahtab Kour, the true Maharani, from favor, and establishing herself as first lady in the palace. For three years her reign had been supreme; but now it was said that she, too, was neglected, that the Maharajah never bothered to visit her apartments. The boredom of *her* empty days, Scylla thought with a shiver, would be even worse than for the others, because she had been away into the world, been to school, and knew something about the life that went on outside Ziatur. . . .

However, attempting to alleviate Sada's boredom was not Scylla's business, and she now climbed a great many stairs and then turned left into the chamber that had been allocated to her as a schoolroom in which to instruct the young princes Amur and Ranji.

Nobody was occupying it at the moment, and Scylla, walking over to the screened window, looked down through an exotic profusion of dangling vines with scarlet, white, and crimson blossoms to a little courtyard cut into the face of the cliff. Beyond, the great plain stretched away southward and the sun beat down mercilessly. Both princes were in the shaded courtyard, playing a game called bull and cows. Leaning out of the window, Scylla summoned them in a way that would have scandalized Miss Musson: placing two fingers in her mouth, she emitted an ear-piercing whistle. Cal had taught her this trick. Looking up, the boys saw her, laughed, and soon came clattering up the stone stairs. While they did so she had leisure to notice an open exercise book on the table with a drawing of a dragon, quite skillfully executed, and underneath the legend *"Mademoiselle Paget est un bête féroce!"*

Clever little monkey, she thought, studying it; I wonder what will become of him? Perhaps the Maharajah will make him into an ambassador. For Ranji, son of a minor wife, had no hope of succeeding to his father's kingdom; that would go to Mihal Shahzada, the eldest son of Mahtab Kour. Unless, of course, the Rani Sada succeeded in regaining her power over Mihal's father . . . But in either case Ranji would never succeed.

The two princes came bounding into the room, and Scylla said severely:

"You are late, both of you!"

"But *you* were late yourself, mademoiselle," pointed out Amur with perfect truth.

Both boys were slender, dark, and extremely handsome, like graceful wild creatures, deer or gazelle, Scylla frequently thought. They wore uniforms which had been sent up from Calcutta, white doeskin breeches, gold-laced tunics, gold spurs, which scratched the furniture shockingly, and turbans set with clusters of jewels which were a perpetual nuisance, dangling in their eyes and impeding their vision.

"*I* was kept in conversation with your father," Scylla said, "but *you* should have been getting on with your translation in the meantime. And, Ranji, *bête* is feminine—*Mademoiselle Paget est* UNE *bête féroce!* I have a mind to make you write it out fifty times."

"Oh, pray do not, Mademoiselle Periseela! Look, we have got some sweets for you." Ranji's look of pleading, laughing dismay was irresistible, and the sweets in the palace were usually delicious—made from cream, sugar, fruit juices, and nuts—but Scylla said firmly that it was too soon after her breakfast for sweets and that the boys were to translate at least a chapter from English into French before anybody touched so much as a single nut.

After some sighing and expostulation the two princes set to work. Scylla was making them translate *Tom Jones*—which she had discovered among the books of Mr. Winthrop Musson—and fortunately they found it quite amusing, frequently bursting into peals of laughter as they collaborated on a rough rendering. Meanwhile Scylla corrected their English essays and collated a sheaf of geometry exercises to take home to Cal, who, in a rather lackadaisical way, took charge of this side of their education, since Scylla was not mathematically minded.

"There are some Frenchmen come here to see Taba yesterday night," Ranji presently looked up from *Tom Jones* to say. "They are telling my father that he should have a *Francese compo*—a French division—in his army. Maybe so that he can fight the English like Tippoo Sahib!"

"There: you see now how useful it is to be able to speak French," Scylla pointed out in a schoolmistressy voice, but then spoiled the effect by adding, "And will he do so, do you suppose?"

"Mihal would like him to," Amur began, but Ranji interrupted:

"Taba will not let Mihal have any say in the matter."

"But your father is not very well," Scylla said involuntarily—indeed the Maharajah had looked to her like a dying man. "If he should become really ill, then perhaps Mihal might have to take charge of the army."

"What Taba is hoping for is that Kamaran Sahib will return with all the guns that he promised to bring from Feringistan—"

"Yes, double-barrel muskets that will kill at a thousand paces, fuses, brass cannon—they are far better than matchlocks—carbines, pistols, and cuirasses," put in Ranji eagerly.

"Bows and arrows are better for a true Sikh," pronounced Amur firmly, but his brother said:

"There is not much sense in being armed with bows and arrows if your enemy has guns that will kill at a thousand yards."

"But do you suppose that Kamaran Sahib ever will come back?" said Scylla.

She had heard tell of this personage, but neither she nor Cal had ever met him, since he had left Ziatur three years ago, before they began to frequent the palace. The princes, who revered him, said that he was a Yagistani—American, like Miss Musson, who knew him somewhat but rather disapproved of him. For several years he had been in charge of the Maharajah's armed forces. His real name, Scylla understood, was Cameron, Colonel Cameron. Nobody seemed to know about Kamaran Sahib's origins, whether he had previously been an officer in the British, French, or Russian armies. He had traveled, Miss Musson reported, widely; he had sailed around the world; he seemed to have no wife, children, or attachments. He was a very frivolous man, she said severely. Winthrop Musson had been fond of him and thought him a clever, cultivated fellow; the princes revered him as a kind of demigod.

"But of course he will come back," predicted Amur confidently, breaking in on Scylla's train of thought, "for Kamaran Sahib *always* did what he promised; and furthermore Taba had a message last month from Karachi to say he had arrived there with a load of carbines."

At this moment a messenger arrived to ask if the Mem Periseela would visit Mahtab Kour on her way out. Scylla, consulting the watch that hung on a ribbon around her neck, saw that the boys' hour was up. Hastily setting them another assignment, she bade the relieved pair good-by, urged them not to eat too many sweets, and followed her guide along a dark, narrow corridor, up and down innumerable stairways, and across several courtyards, until they came to the queen mother's suite. Once, when halfway across a wide antechamber, feeling rather than observing a presence above her, Scylla paused momentarily and glanced up; a screened, curtained gallery ran transversely over the room she had just entered. Leaning over the fretted balustrade was a girl, richly dressed, hung with ropes of jewels, a girl whose extreme, indeed dazzling beauty did not in the least disguise a look of concentrated malignity on her face. The two pairs of eyes met for a moment; then, with a whisk of curtains, the angry beauty withdrew from view. It was the Rani Sada. But what in the world makes her so angry with *me?* thought Scylla, rather startled, since only an hour before she had been experiencing profound feelings of sympathy for the other girl. Possibly Sada had been expecting somebody else. . . . Just the same, the odd little encounter left a shiver of unease in her bones, a sense of decided disquiet.

Another five minutes brought her to the region of Ziatur palace that was occupied by Mahtab Kour and her attendants. This part was central, and very old; traditionally always used by the reigning queen. Much of it was in very bad repair: flights of crumbling stone steps led downward into unguessable horrors of darkness; there were said to be huge underground cisterns where ancient crocodiles, now grown to vast size, were fed live goats daily by priests (and also performed, if necessary, the duty of crunching up any of the royal ladies who were discovered to be unfaithful to their lord). Great dim halls here contained worn stone statues of incalculable antiquity—Shiva the Creator, Ganesha, the elephant-headed god of wisdom, Kali, Shiva's wife, horrific with a garland of skulls, red protruding tongue, and hand grasping a bloodstained sword; six-armed Bhairava, holding a trident, a sword, more skulls, his face smeared with somebody's offering of food. . . . These were Hindi gods, left over from some previous dynasty, but up here in the north all gods were respected and propitiated. There were Kafir deities too, Imra the Creator and Gish the war god. The citadel had changed hands many times through the centuries and the general feeling of the inmates was that it would be folly to offend any divinity.

Mahtab Kour must once have been very beautiful, but now all animation had left her face. Married to the Maharajah at twelve, she had been brought, in a curtained litter, six weeks' journey from the Deccan, in the south, traveling only at night, never allowed to look between the curtains. Miserably homesick for her own family and place of birth, so far away, she had known from the beginning that there was hardly the slightest chance of her seeing any of her own relatives again, or ever leaving Ziatur; if she had proved infertile she might, perhaps, have been permitted to go on a pilgrimage to a queens' praying at the Golden Temple in Amritsar, the holy town of the Sikhs— but, as it turned out, fortunately for her, she had presented the Maharajah with an heir, Mihal Shahzada, when she was fifteen. After that she had borne a succession of daughters and had soon sunk into disfavor. Now, past the age of thirty, her life was, to all intents, finished; not for years had the Maharajah bothered to come to her apartments, nor did she leave them; she had the soft white transparent pallor of a flower that has grown in darkness, and the slow, sad, languid movements of a creature who no longer cares what happens to her. The first three of her little daughters had long ago been dispatched in closed palanquins to be brides of distant rulers; and it was rumored that the last had been hurled as a newborn infant into the crocodile tank as a punishment to its mother for having given birth to yet another girl child. Mahtab occupied herself, as best she could, with elaborate embroidery, with eating—she had grown immensely fat—and with making pets of slave girls, whose favor waxed and dwindled with erratic unpredictability. Even her son Mihal very seldom came to see her any more. Miss Musson, intensely sorry for her, had attempted to interest her in learning to read, to draw and knit, in acquiring knowledge of other lands, of other cultures; but it was of no use; her spirit had wilted and died inside her. The Rani Sada, a vital, impatient, ambitious girl, coming from a warrior caste, not a decayed, inbred royal family, made no secret of her contempt for the older queen.

"*Sat Sri Akal*—greetings to Your Royal Highness," Scylla hailed Mahtab, in as cheerful a tone as she could muster, walking rapidly into the queen's apartment. And she curtsied, wondering how soon she could get away. "What service can I render you?"

Mahtab Kour opened obliquely. First she offered tea, sherbet, coffee, or almond-curd sweetmeats. These Scylla politely declined.

"Well, I will have a sweetmeat," said Mahtab Kour, and did so. She was like a huge mass of unbaked dough, Scylla thought, lolling back on her pink and scarlet silk cushions, wrapped in brilliant gauzes, strung with jewels on her arms, ankles, neck, ears; a deep red ruby dangled on her forehead—and two profoundly sad eyes, the currants in the loaf, looked out uncomprehendingly and beseechingly from under the ruby.

"My little Persian girl Laili has a trouble in her ears, Mem Periseela. Will you look at them and try if you can heal them?"

"Certainly," Scylla said, knowing with dismal premonition what she would see. Mahtab clapped her hands and the child was brought in— a pretty little black-eyed, olive-skinned creature, probably no more than seven or eight, one of the succession of slave favorites who came and went, treated as pets at first, then, presently, falling from grace, either because the queen found a newer distraction or because they came under the influence of the Rani Sada, who liked to have a spy or two in her rival's retinue, even though that rival had long fallen from power.

"Show the mem your ears, Laili!" ordered Mahtab, and the child, whimpering with pain, allowed Scylla to turn her head from side to side. It was instantly plain what the trouble was: her ears must have been pierced with a dirty implement, probably some old brass pin, and the small wounds had become hideously infected.

"Why did you not tell me about this days ago?" asked Scylla, trying, as always, to keep any hint of impatience and anger from her voice.

"Dr. Nuruddin said the child had a demon in her ears and that if we prayed and made offering to the goddess Durga the demon would infallibly be cast out. I have prayed and offered a kid, but the demon must be a very strong one; it has refused to go."

"Dr. Nuruddin is—" Scylla checked herself.

"Now I thought perhaps you could put your ointment on and drive the devil away," said Mahtab hopefully.

"Ointment will not help in this case, Highness," Scylla said. "The child is badly sick—see how languid are her eyes, how hot her forehead. The devil is *inside* her now, not just in her ears. Will you not allow me to have her carried out, to the Mem Musson's hospital? She needs much medicine and careful nursing."

But this, of course, was quite out of the question. First, Mahtab could not possibly part with the child; and secondly, it was unthinkable that a palace slave girl, even so small a one as Laili, should be allowed out through the streets of the town. Scylla accordingly did what she could—washed off the paste of dung and ground-up owl's feathers which had been applied to Laili's ears (on the theory that, as owls have sharp hearing, their feathers must be good for aural afflictions); then, muttering objurgations against Dr. Nuruddin, she applied some healing balm.

"Poor little thing—I fear she may die, as my little Zindan did when the monkey bit her," Mahtab said with a kind of fretful resignation.

"It is plain the gods do not look kindly on me; all my favorites come to harm. Perhaps it is just as well that my dear son Mihal does not visit me any more—he, too, might incur the gods' displeasure.— Huneefa, Lehna, Lakshmi!" she called. "Take the child away; the sight of her is distressing to me. Carry her far off where I cannot hear her crying."

When this had been done and Scylla was on the point of taking her leave, Mahtab came to the real reason for her summons.

"Mem Periseela—it has been said to me that you are greatly favored with the confidence of the Maharajah—that he listens with respect to the things you tell him."

"Oh, hardly that, Your Majesty," Scylla answered with considerable caution, wondering what was coming next. "Sometimes—when the Maharajah is feeling tired or indisposed—he amuses himself by chatting with me for a few minutes. But I doubt very much if he pays heed to anything I say. He likes to practice his French—that is all."

Behind her, in a sibilant whisper, could be heard the comment of one of the attendants:

"It certainly *must* be her wit that our master admires—if indeed he does. For who could find anything to admire in that pink and white face of a pig, with the nose that turns upward and the mouth like a doorway—it is enough to make you die of laughing just to look at her!"

The whisperer spoke Urdu, not Punjabi; glancing around, Scylla saw that she was Huneefa, the big dark-skinned ayah whom Mahtab had brought with her from the south, many years before. Huneefa was a great friend of Nuruddin, the palace physician (the witch doctor, as Miss Musson indignantly called him) and without doubt would retail to him the fact that his treatment had been disparaged by the Feringi maiden.

Abruptly, Mahtab Kour ordered her women to go into the next room. "No—*all* of you—how do I know which of you is a tattletale, a spy who will carry reports of what I say to the ears of my enemy?"

Scowling with annoyance—particularly Huneefa—they left. Mahtab Kour went on in a low tone:

"That female viper from the Punjab—she who stole my place in my lord's affections—I will not speak her name aloud for fear even the word should poison me—I have heard that, since she, too, lost my lord's favor, she has committed an even more atrocious wickedness and is laying her nets, casting her wiles, in order to entrap my darling son Mihal. Even to speak of such betrayal is like arsenic on the tongue— but I have heard it, and I believe it."

Scylla had heard it too—not in the bazaars but from her brother Cal, who had several times commented laconically that the Rani Sada and Prince Mihal seemed to be becoming as thick as thieves.

"And not surprising when you think about it," he said.

"His own *father's mistress?*" Scylla had indeed been somewhat scandalized.

"Why not? They are much of an age, and she is pretty as a tiger lily. And also she is as shrewd as she can hold together—Rani Sada knows which side her chupattis are buttered on! What do you suppose would happen to her when the Maharajah dies—which, from the look of him, he is bound to do within the next year or so?—Unless Sada had taken care to ingratiate herself with the next ruler, what would you give for her chances? Mihal used to be fond of his mother—quite a mother's boy—and Mahtab Kour would probably part with all her rubies for a chance to stick a dagger between Sada's ribs. But Mihal has an eye for a pretty girl; he's easily beguiled, and Sada knows that; she is taking her precautions in advance."

Now Mahtab Kour went on vehemently. "The very gods would hide their faces for shame at what that creature does—but she is shameless! She is my lord's *wife*—for it is true, indeed, he had the karewa, the betrothal ceremony, performed when she returned from Amritsar, and though that is not so important as the chadar dalna, the marriage, it means that her child by my lord is legitimate—and now she betrays him! With his own son! It is profanation of her vows! It is treason!"

"But," said Scylla, very uneasily, "even if indeed it is so—"

"Without a shadow of a doubt it is so. She brings infamy to the name of my lord's family!"

"Why are you telling me about it?" said Scylla bluntly.

"Because I wish you to bring this news to my lord!"

"The Maharajah? Oh no—impossible! I—I could not transgress on his privacy to tell him a thing like that."

Scylla had a very poor opinion of Prince Mihal. She had hardly met him, except when he called at the bungalow, for it was not considered suitable that an unmarried Feringi lady should consort with the heir; but he and Cal were cronies to a degree that sometimes caused Miss Musson to say, "I wonder if it is wise for your brother to see quite so much of that young man?" And even Scylla, not usually a prey to anxiety or sisterly misgivings, could not feel that Mihal Shahzada was the best of companions, or likely to be a good influence. He gambled insatiably; he was addicted to wine and French brandy, which he had imported at vast expense from Calcutta; he smoked opium and hasheesh; and he could be idly and viciously cruel as the whim took him; Scylla had once arrived in the middle entrance court to find that he and some companions had set a pariah dog on fire and were laughing uproariously and laying bets on the length of its survival, as the shrieking bundle of flame dashed crazily around and around the yard; Scylla's anger on that occasion had been so intense—luckily Miss Musson had been with her and the combined insistence of the two Feringi ladies had finally persuaded one of the soldiers to pick up his curved sword and chop off the animal's head—that ever after that day Mihal Shahzada addressed her mockingly as the "Mem Dog-lover," and she felt quite certain that he had not forgiven her for spoiling his sport.

If he and Sada had indeed become allies—that might account for the malignant look that Sada had given her from the upper gallery. More especially if she thought that Scylla was being employed by Mahtab Kour to pass on information to the Maharajah.

Scylla did not point out the usual fate of talebearers. She said:

"Truly, Your Majesty, I could not tell the Maharajah a thing like that! Besides—do you not suppose he may know it already? Surely nothing is hidden from him?"

"This, assuredly, he does not know. For if he did, his wrath would be terrible. Bring the news to him, sahiba, I beg of you."

Scylla, however, replied firmly that she could not undertake to do so. "I could not bear him such tidings, Majesty. Besides, if His Excellency does talk to me—and sometimes weeks go by when we do not meet—the subjects he wishes to discuss are European wars, and whether the English will permit Ranjit Singh to capture Lahore."

"Men's talk!" said Mahtab impatiently. "But it is known that you talked with him today. Of what did you speak?"

Scylla marveled, as always, at the speed with which gossip traveled in the palace. It seemed to her highly improbable that, considering how difficult it was to keep anything hidden, the Maharajah did not know of his son's intrigue. Perhaps he felt too old and sick to care.

She replied, "We were talking about the battle at Cape St. Vincent, lady."

"Oh!" the queen exclaimed with a grimace of impatience. "If only *I* had his ear!"

"I will tell him, and gladly, lady, that Your Majesty wishes to consult with him—if I should be so lucky as to speak with him again."

Scylla would promise no more, and the rani had to be content with this.

"And Your Majesty will not think again, and allow me to take the little Laili off to the hospital?"

"No—no—certainly not!" snapped Mahtab Kour. "You have my leave to depart, Mem Periseela."

Sighing, Scylla walked back through the great courtyard. Oh, to travel away from here, she thought impatiently, to leave this nest of petty intrigue and spite.

She longed to set out for Europe, to see England, her father's country—London, Ranelagh, the Pantheon, Drury Lane, fashionably dressed ladies, Pall Mall, Sadler's Wells. She had read about these things in the Calcutta *Gazette* and stray copies of the *Gentleman's Magazine*. But three obstacles stood firmly in the way of her wishes. The first was Miss Musson—who had adopted the twins when they were orphaned, friendless, and poor, had given them a home, and treated them with uniform kindness and affection. Now, by helping with part of her work, Scylla was able, she felt, to repay some part of this kindness, and she did not see how she could possibly go off and leave the old woman alone in Ziatur, the only European resident in the town. The second obstacle was that of money. When General Paget, father of the twins, returned to England, with vague promises of presently sending for them, he had left Manuela, their mother, several thousand rupees and the house in Umballa, and had given an undertaking that more money would presently be dispatched from England. But the promised funds had never arrived, their mother had fallen ill from anxiety, the house had had to be sold, and presently Manuela had died. . . . Scylla did not like to remember those days. The last of the money was spent, she and Cal were desperate, almost starving, when Miss Musson and her brother, who at that time were running a small mission hospital in Umballa, had adopted the two children. Winthrop Musson, a gentle, cultivated man, had taken a great liking to the quick-witted pair and had enjoyed teaching them, imparting some of his very considerable fund of learning. Cal and Scylla, starved of knowledge all their lives—for Manuela, a beautiful, languid creature, a born courtesan, had never troubled to see that her children received an education, was interested in nothing but her lover, and when he left sank into melancholy—Cal and Scylla had mopped up all that Winthrop Musson could teach them like thirsty sponges. Musson had encouraged Cal's budding gift for poetry and had been delighted with his progress and talent. When the Mussons moved to Ziatur, because Winthrop suffered from a lung complaint and it was thought better for him to go northward, to be near the hills —naturally the twins went along too. And now, here we are, stuck, Scylla sometimes thought. We may very likely remain here for the rest of our lives! The third obstacle to a removal, of course, was Cal himself, who liked the life in Ziatur very well. Clever, lazy, wholly unambitious, he was perfectly content to read in Winthrop Musson's capacious library, amuse himself with Prince Mihal, go riding with his sister in the cool evening, and pay no attention, not the least in the world, to what happened in Europe, in France, in Spain, in the Mediterranean. To the news of the fall of the Bastille and the Terror in France, he had merely replied:

"How extremely shocking. What rhymes with 'arable,' Scylla?"

"Parable. Have you *no* interest in what goes on outside this place?"

"I am a poet," he pointed out negligently. "A poet's first study is himself."

Miss Musson, Scylla believed, felt some concern over Cal and what would become of him, but Miss Musson felt that her primary duty was to her patients; and furthermore she had a rooted disapproval of interference and believed that people should be left alone to work out their own problems; only in extreme cases (like that of the burning dog) would she take a hand.

When Scylla turned in at the entrance to Miss Musson's house it was early still—barely ten. Going inside, Scylla found, as she had expected, that Cal still slept, in exactly the same position as when she had seen him last, motionless, fathoms deep in oblivion. He had an extraordinary capacity for sleep: ten, twelve, fourteen hours he could pass at a stretch, in a kind of trance, hardly seeming to breathe, impervious to heat, cold, or any amount of noise. When the twins had been younger, when Scylla needed her brother's company for play or comfort, before and during their mother's illness, or in the frightening months after her death, Cal's gift for escaping from his difficulties in sleep had often filled her with a mixture of envy and exasperation. She could not rouse him, she knew; he would mutter some response, roll over, and flop into a new position of utter relaxation.

Now she was older, Scylla guessed that, as well as being his form of escape from the unwanted complications of life, Cal's ability to sleep for such lengthy periods had some connection with his poetic talent; he would surface from these long spells of oblivion crackling with new ideas and solutions to problems in his writing; often, indeed, after having woken up, he would be almost equally inaccessible because he would hurl himself into creation like a mongoose pursuing a cobra into a hole, feverishly anxious to capture all the elusive thoughts and images that had come to him in sleep, to pin them to ground before they could escape.

"Just a moment—pray don't distract me until I have this down—there's a love—" and then hours would go by while he rapidly scribbled down lines and then scratched them out again, his hand moving over the blotted page like a living entity with a mind and purpose of its own.

Adhering to Miss Musson's precept that people had best be left to resolve their own affairs in their own way, Scylla had long ago given up any attempts to wake Cal from sleep or to entice him away from his frenzied bouts of writing.

But this *was* their birthday after all.

She went into his shaded room, and, leaning over the charpoy, said loudly in his ear:

"Cal! Fiend, devil that you are! Brother! Cal! Wake up, it's your birthday!"

No response. She tried again, even louder. He moved a little, then his head flopped into the pillow, with a grunt of relief, as if he had encountered and dealt with some small, tiresome piece of business. She shook him vigorously; he smiled in his sleep and murmured, "Whoa, there, Kali! Gently, mare . . ."

Shrugging, Scylla let go her hold of his shoulders and walked back into the main room of the house, which ran clean through from front to back, so as to receive any breath of wind that blew.

"Missy and Cal Sahib go riding? Mem Musson left word to prepare a picnic. It is ready. I pack it up for Cal Sahib to carry?"

The khitmutgar indicated the birthday feast that Miss Musson had provided. Touched, Scylla regarded a cold chicken, a bottle of wine, a plate of fruit—shaddock, grapes, banana, pomegranate.

"Cal Sahib is fast asleep; I go by myself, Habib-ulla. Pack up the chicken and the fruit, but not the wine; it is too heavy for me; and order the syce to saddle Kali."

"It is not correct—or at *all* wise—for Missy Sahib to go riding on her own," objected the aged Habib-ulla. "And as for taking Kali—what will Cal Sahib say to that, when he wakes and finds out?"

"Cal Sahib can consider himself justly served for lying asleep when he had promised his sister to go riding with her," Scylla retorted. "Tell Ibrahim to put my saddle on Kali and bring her around."

Kali was her brother's most cherished possession—apart from his manuscripts: a thin, high-bred little Kathiawar mare, supple as a shadow, obedient to every touch of the rein, yet full of spirit; she could travel all day at the native lope, between a trot and a canter, yet never tire; she was infinitely faster than Scylla's bay, Tom Jones; she could, it was said, outrun even the Maharajah's hunting leopards. She came from the royal stable; Cal had won her at cards from Mihal.

Since Miss Musson was not at home to disapprove, Scylla rapidly changed into a hill woman's costume of loose black trowsers and vest, with a burqa and wide-brimmed hat. She tied a veil over her hat and walked out to the front of the house where Ibrahim, muttering his opinion of young misses who rode out unescorted, had reluctantly attached the picnic bundle to the back of Kali's saddle.

"Good; tell Cal Sahib, if he wakes and asks for me, that I will return a little after sunset," ordered Scylla, and swung herself into the saddle. Kali, dancing with delight, was eager to be off; Scylla gave the mare a formal tap with her crop and, after one preliminary bound, she settled into the easy, deceptive lope that, while not appearing particularly fast, soon ate up the miles. Kali could cover sixty miles in ten hours, if she was required to, so she made nothing of a mere sixteen.

At the start they passed orchards and melon beds, fields of opium poppy and sugar cane, an occasional fig or banyan tree, or, in the distance, a dark green mango grove. The sound of cicadas rattled around them, loud as a drum; it seemed as if the hot dry earth itself were vibrating. Sometimes a porcupine scuttled across the road, or a wild pig could be heard rooting and grunting in a sugar-cane patch. Then, farther from the town, the cultivated areas dwindled and ceased; nothing grew here but cactus and huge dry-looking thistles; an occasional kite swung high in the pale sky. The distant white hills crept closer, and Scylla could distinguish granite outcrops on their bare crests, and sometimes a scrub of low bushes.

Not long after the hour of noon they reached Scylla's destination: a narrow valley between two low, sandy spurs of rock-studded hill, outcrops from the foothills of the Sangur range. Skirting around a bluff, they came within sight of the ruined temple, which lay midway between the two spurs. The road had been climbing steadily for the last five miles, and the ground here was no longer bare but covered with high, silvery jungle grass, over Scylla's head if she had been on foot, thick and impenetrable as a curtain on either side of the track. Scylla did own to herself a slight qualm as she passed between those living screens—anything, any marauder, might be lurking unseen in that cover—but Kali, she knew, would be lightning-quick to detect the presence of any beast of prey and could almost certainly outrun anything that might give chase to them; besides, it was midday, the hour of sleep, when beasts of prey are not abroad.

The temple itself lay mostly concealed behind a tangle of wild fig and other trees which had grown up in the centuries since it had been abandoned. A hundred-and-fifty-foot-high tower of rose-red stone, slender and still apparently in good repair, appeared above the growth of vegetation; here and there below it a portion of masonry could be seen, a section of marble dome, or a pillar, or a stretch of wall.

Dismounting, Scylla led Kali through what was left of the great gateway. Beyond it, the relics of a wide avenue, colonnaded with red marble pillars on either side, led forward to an entrance that was now choked with vegetation. Beyond the marble pillars there must once have been beautiful gardens; orange trees still grew there, wild and neglected; great screens of climbing rose battled with the wild fig and karela, the jungle creeper which formed a curtain over the cultivated trees. A gleam of water showed where a marble cistern still held some of its contents, half smothered in green slime and water plants.

Tethering Kali to the root of a banyan tree, Scylla decided to take her nuncheon before exploring farther. Sitting on a great block of marble which had fallen from the top of an arch, she opened the bundle Habib-ulla had provided and munched chicken, shaddock, and pomegranate. There was, of course, far too much food—she put most of it back.

"Now we had better find you some water, Light of My Eyes," she said to the mare. "Or Cal will say I have neglected you, and it would be true."

Exploring the overgrown purlieus of the temple, she found another cistern, a much larger one, evidently fed by a spring, for the water at one end of it was clear enough. The place was evidently a sanctuary for wild creatures and birds: a pair of cranes flapped heavily away from the cistern as Kali drank thirstily, cohorts of wild apes gamboled and chattered and chased each other in the tangled branches of the camphor trees, and on a stretch of unbroken pavement a wild peacock pecked and preened and gave out at regular intervals its keening cry.

Scylla, wandering about the empty courts, passing with difficulty through bramble-choked archways, peering through marble lattice-work inlaid with garnets, turquoise, agate, and lapis lazuli, venturing cautiously into great dim halls divided by rows and rows of fantastically carved pillars, inspecting countless statues of gods, known and unknown, portrayed in every conceivable posture—sitting, standing, dancing, grimacing or benign—could not withstand a deep regret that Cal had not accompanied her. I *must* bring him here another time, she resolved. It is exactly the kind of place that would excite his imagination.

Aware that she ought to start for home, Scylla still lingered, reluctant to leave. It occurred to her that she had not yet located the Maharajah's tomb itself; her informant had said this was not in the temple itself, but about a quarter of a mile away, at the foot of the nearby hill.

Untying Kali, she led the mare out of the temple precincts, following a small paved path which crossed the valley, running in between great clumps of bamboo. Stone gods frowned or smiled down from pillars at regular intervals; here and there one had fallen from his place and lay staring upward from the ground.

At the end of the path a flight of steps led downward, under a low stone archway. Here Scylla did pause with some doubt and misgiving. The tomb entrance was set in the side of a hill, just where the ground began to rise. The hillside above was not firm but consisted of shifting, flowing sand, loosened and eroded by years of drought and hot winds.

A two-foot parapet of masonry above the doorway arch had parted the streams of sand sliding down from above, so that they fell on either side of the entrance and had mounted up into high ramparts, while the doorway itself remained clear. But, looking up, Scylla could see that it was only a matter of time before a great dry outcrop of loose earth, not far above the doorway, became detached and slid down, which would almost certainly block the entrance altogether. Might the sound of her footsteps start it sliding? Dare she go in? Anything might set off a landslide: a sudden gust of wind, a wild pig running over the slope, even a kite landing on it.—On the other hand, Scylla felt that she would hardly be able to forgive herself if, after having ridden so far, taken such pains to get here, she lacked the courage to carry out her final intention. She had brought lucifer matches and tapers with her; she could imagine Cal's scornful voice: "You rode all the way to the temple but were *too cowardly to go into the tomb?* I have a faint-heart for a sister! And I had thought you were pluck to the back-bone!"

Gritting her teeth, Scylla flung Kali's bridle rein over a loosely dangling bough on a fig tree at some distance from the doorway, so that, if her mistress were trapped by an avalanche, the mare would in time be able to pull herself free without too much difficulty. Then, having lit her taper, Scylla edged her way forward, slowly and with extreme caution, between the high ramparts of sand on either side of the doorway, and at last under the overhanging arch. Once down the steps and standing on a firm stone floor, she breathed a little more easily, though feeling tension inside her all the while, as her ears strained themselves to catch the least sound of rumbling or sliding up above. Perhaps even her presence in the vault would be enough to start a movement on the hillside up above? But she heard nothing and, when her eyes became accustomed to the dim candlelight, she plucked up courage to go forward. The tomb, she found, consisted of three chambers, one beyond the other, floored, walled, and roofed with marble. But this place, too, it was sadly evident, had been rifled, either by invading armies or local robbers; the plinth, in the last room, under a great fretted canopy of carved stone, where the coffin should have lain, stood empty, and there was no sign of the legendary treasure. Disappointed but also, in some way, relieved, Scylla retraced her steps toward the entrance and was about to extinguish her taper and carefully tiptoe up the stone stairway when, beyond the door, she heard a sound that terrified her: a low, rumbling, muttering growl. For a horrible moment she believed that it was the beginning of the landslide, but the reality was hardly less frightening; Scylla had walked past the Maharajah's menagerie too often not to be familiar with the voice of a tiger. —Why would a tiger be out hunting at this time of day? But the sound came again, followed by the mare's whinny—a shrill, terrified appeal for help. Scylla had no weapon with her, but instinctively, dropping her taper, she snatched up a couple of stones and flew up the steps, without worrying as to whether her haste might start a landslide. If the tiger were to attack Kali—!

Emerging into the daylight, she was obliged to stop and blink for a moment while her eyes grew accustomed to the white glare of day; thus pausing, she heard the tiger's yowling cry again, much closer; this time it was the eerie, ventriloquial, caterwauling whine, seeming to come from all around, with which the hunting tiger panics his prey, often into running straight toward him. And again came Kali's stamp and shriek of alarm. In a moment she will drag herself loose and gallop away—I must get to her first, thought Scylla, and she began to run toward the mare, still clutching her pebbles. Panting, stumbling, she saw a flash of black and yellow—the tiger, emerging from a bamboo cover off to her right. He seemed unbelievably huge—far, far bigger than the cowed, mangy beasts in the menagerie. His great striped head was like some carved, cruel god's face, heavy and powerful. Unexpectedly confronted with *two* objects—the running girl and the stamping, rearing horse—he stood for a moment, swinging his head, trying to decide which to make for; then began loping forward.

The pebbles fell from Scylla's hand. Faced with the massive, formidable actuality of the tiger, she could see that, as ammunition, they were of no more use than grains of rice would have been. She flew to

Kali—just in time, for the foaming, frothing, terrified mare had almost succeeded in dragging herself free—and grabbed at the reins. Mounting was another matter though.

"Steady—steady!" Scylla panted. "Keep *still* a moment, daughter of an idiot! How can I mount while you are dancing around like a dervish?"

She shouted, hoping to startle the tiger into pausing for a moment in its purposeful, stealthy, forward creep. It yowled again—and then, astonishingly, Scylla heard two sharp cracks, one quickly after the other, and a voice shouted:

"Keep still, woman! Hold that accursed horse quiet! We are going to shoot again!"

Dragging down with all her strength on Kali's rein, Scylla turned in utter amazement to see that two men had run out of the bamboo clumps. One was reloading a musket at feverish speed, while the other knelt, aiming at the tiger, who, apparently confused by these new arrivals, had bounded off sideways and now crouched, with lashing tail, unable to decide which prey to attack first. But then Kali whinnied again and he began once more his low-bellied, creeping approach toward the girl and the horse that had been his original objective.

Crack! went the musket again, and the tiger leaped, snarling, into the air, then turned and galloped away in the direction from which Scylla had come, toward the tomb entrance.

"Got him!" shouted the kneeling man exultantly. To Scylla's bewilderment, he spoke this time in English—before, he had addressed her in Punjabi. "After him, quick, Therbah!"

The two men began to race after the escaping tiger.

"He is wounded, lord—he is making for the cave," panted the smaller man. "We can trap him there."

Indeed, the tiger, leaving a trail of blood splashes behind him on the bare ground, was loping toward the tomb doorway. Both men fired again as he disappeared into the dark door hole. Both—Scylla thought —missed; small puffs of sand spurted up on either side of the doorway.

And then a portentous thing happened. Either because of the shouting, or the sound of shots, or the impact of the bullets on the sandy hillside, the portion of hill above the entrance that had been waiting to fall became loosened from its base and, with a strange, soft rushing roar, a huge mass of sand, stone, and grit came pouring over the archway and completely blocked the cave entrance. When the dust cloud had cleared, "God *damn* it, Therbah!" burst out the man who had shouted at Scylla, the taller of the two. "*Look* at that! We've lost him!"

"Alas! We have indeed, lord," the little man agreed lugubriously, approaching the entrance and scratching his head with the hand that did not hold the musket. "The king of tigers has gone to his rest in a king's tomb. It would take two weeks' digging to get him out of there."

"By which time, all his hide would be fit for would be to feed the jackals."

The taller man turned furiously on Scylla, who, having succeeded in calming the panic-stricken Kali, had pulled forward her bedraggled veil and now walked over to thank them, leading the mare.

"Why in the name of Eblis did *you* have to arrive on the scene just at this moment, woman? If it had not been for you and your thrice-accursed mare, the skin of that tiger, which we have been stalking for the past two weeks, would have made a highly acceptable present to take to the Maharajah of Ziatur. Now all we can take him is the information that the tiger is putrefying in his great-grandfather's tomb."

"The Maharajah is a very sick man," Scylla replied composedly. "I do not think he would have been very interested in your tiger. And I do not at all see why you should blame *me* for the tiger's having gone into the cave! There is no reason to suppose that he would not have done so whether I was there or not. However—and be that as it may—I am very grateful to you for saving my life.—Though it is true," she added reflectively, "if you had not been chasing the tiger, I dare say I would never have met him, so saving me was the least you could do."

At the commencement of her speech the taller man had started; he now looked at her very attentively.

"Who are *you*, in the name of all the djinns?" he asked curiously. "You are no Sikh or Dogra woman? What are you doing here? And how do you come to know so much about the Maharajah?"

Scylla had been studying him with equal curiosity. He was unlike anyone she had ever met before. To begin with, he was extremely tall; he would, she thought, easily overtop the Maharajah, who was the tallest person she knew. His beard, eyebrows, and mustaches were a bright gold-red in color, contrasting strangely with his bronzed, weather-beaten complexion. From under the bushy eyebrows looked out the most brilliant blue eyes she had ever seen—vividly, startlingly blue, they seemed lit by an inner light, as sunbeams glance through blue water. His face was long, thin, high-cheekboned, haughty, and hook-nosed like a Shushbaz hawk. And, strangest touch of all, he was dressed from head to foot in Scottish plaid: a jacket and trowsers of black and green checkered material (later she learned that it was the Gordon hunting tartan)—even a turban, made from a length of the same material, topped with an egret's plume, which was held in place by a diamond the size of a mulberry. Both he and his servant—a little man, brown and wrinkled as a nut, dressed in hillman's clothes—were dusty, grimed, and weary-looking, as if they had traveled for days and days in the open country.

"I come from Ziatur—I teach the younger princes in the palace," explained Scylla. "That is how I know about the Maharajah. And, now I come to think of it, I can guess who you must be." She switched to English from the Punjabi they had been speaking. "Are you not Cameron Sahib?"

His rather fierce, probing look broke up into a smile.

"I suppose you have heard about me from those two little monkeys, Amur and Ranji."

"Oh, many people talk about you in the court at Ziatur. The Maharajah has been hoping to see you these weeks past, I believe."

"Just as I feared! And that is why I stopped to try and bag old Whiskers in there"—he nodded toward the cave. "I thought a fine new tiger pelt—and he was a beauty, as big as any I've come across—would help sweeten the news that I have only half the carbines I promised, and only a third of the cuirasses."

"Why is that?" she inquired with interest.

"Why, because I have been used to buy arms in France. But now the

French wish to keep their arms for themselves—or do their own selling."

"Oh!" she exclaimed in sudden enlightenment. "Perhaps that is why —that accounts—"

"Accounts for what?" he asked keenly.

"One of the boys was saying that the French emissaries were trying to persuade the Maharajah to start a *Francese compo* in his army."

"The French? Are there French in Ziatur *now?*"

"Two men. I do not know if they are traders or official emissaries."

"Their names?"

"Ducroze and Valhomir."

He nodded as if the names were familiar to him. "That pair have been flattering and cajoling their way all across Central Asia. I have come across their traces everywhere. First they were at the court of the Shah of Persia, telling him that France will soon rule the whole of Europe; then they were in Kabul making love to the Amir; and now I find them even in Ziatur!—Have they blackened my name to Bhupindra Singh?"

"Oh no, I think he is wearying to see you. But they have made great friends with his son."

"Mihal? He must be a grown man by now. Has he much influence at court?"

Scylla considered, and replied, "I would say, very much—in his own way. And more so, now that the Maharajah is ill and disinclined for activity."

Her own last words reminded her that she was tired—indeed, shaking with fatigue and reaction after the terrifying encounter with the tiger. Although the adventure had lasted only a few minutes, while it was going on the time had seemed to stretch out in a dreamlike, or rather nightmarish, manner, and she felt as if she had lived through several exhausting hours of experience. And she still had a sixteen-mile ride ahead of her.

She said, "I must return to Ziatur, or my friends will begin to worry about me. Are you—"

"You came out here *alone?* Without any escort or companions?" He looked at her in real astonishment.

"After all, I did not expect to meet a tiger in broad daylight," Scylla said, laughing. "If you had not been pursuing him he would have been holed up somewhere, fast asleep—like my brother. If I could have woken him, *he* would have been with me."

"Your brother—and now I have guessed who *you* are." Cameron Sahib studied her again—his keen, piercing blue stare was highly disconcerting. Scylla blushed, aware that she was hot and dusty, her boots and trowsers torn by brambles, her veil dirty and crumpled. She must present a very tatterdemalion appearance. But he went on quite civilly:

"A brother and sister, English, living in the household of Miss Musson, the American missionary lady—but I am not certain if your name is Da Silva or Paget?"

"It is Paget," Scylla said, flushing again.

"Miss Paget! Very good! I am happy to make your acquaintance," he said, and swept her a formal bow.

"Oh, this is so ridiculous!" She could not help laughing, but her curtsy was as graceful as she could make it in her pahari costume. "How can you *possibly* have heard of me? Do you come from Umballa?"

"No, my dear ma'am, I have come from England."

"England? Then—"

"And not only have I heard of you, but I even carry a letter addressed to you. However," he said, with upraised hand checking her astonished exclamation, as he glanced sideways to verify the sun's position, "you were right in what you said before, you should return to Ziatur immediately, or your friends will certainly worry about you. We too may as well proceed there, now that we are disappointed of His Royal Highness in there," and he cast a last regretful glance toward the tomb entrance.

"Have you horses?" asked Scylla, thinking that otherwise it would take them at least five hours to make their way to the city.

"We do, but they are tethered a mile away. Therbah, go and fetch the horses," Colonel Cameron said, and, still addressing the little man, he broke into a flood of unfamiliar dialect, pointing off, first through the bamboo thickets and then in a southeasterly direction. The little man nodded intelligently, touched his forehead in a gesture that was both respectful and dignified, then handed both muskets to his master and disappeared at a rapid trot among the bushes.

"Mount your mare, ma'am," directed Cameron. "She is all of a sweat, it will do her good to walk her for a mile, till she dries off—I will lead her until Therbah meets us with my pair. She is a beauty," he added carelessly, noting Kali's points. "Does she not come from Bhupindra Singh's stable?"

"Yes, my brother won her from Mihal at cards. Sir"—Scylla could restrain her curiosity no longer—"*do*, pray, tell me from whom in England you can possibly have brought me a letter?"

He burst out laughing. "I will tease your curiosity a little longer! The letter is in my saddlebag—you must wait until Therbah brings it.—This is our road, is it not, along the causeway?"

As they left it, Scylla could not help glancing back at the temple with regret. Gilded in the late afternoon light, the soaring red tower and glimpses of marble domes and tracery now appeared strangely magical among the fig and camphor trees; she wished, more than ever, that Cal had been with her to share the adventure.

"So you and your brother have lived in Ziatur for the last four years? For it must be at least that since I left," continued Colonel Cameron, walking easily beside the mare with the two muskets balanced on his right shoulder. "Have you never wished to see any more of the world, may I ask?"

"Oh yes, sir, very greatly." She glanced down—all she could see was the top of his turban and the egret's plume, and the glint of red hair along one strongly marked cheekbone. "But what could we do? We had no money of our own—and Miss Musson, our guardian, wishes to remain in Ziatur. She is growing old—we cannot leave her. And although I confess I long to see England—France—Italy—many countries!—my brother, I believe, would be quite content to pass the rest of his life here in northern India."

"He wishes to remain and help Miss Musson in her charitable activities?" inquired Colonel Cameron. "That is very creditable in a young man of his age."

Scylla was not certain whether in his voice she could detect a certain tinge of irony, but she replied calmly:

"No, that is not precisely the case—though, to be sure, he is very fond of Miss Musson. But he is a poet, and poets, you know, having so many resources within themselves, are not particular as to their place of residence—any situation will satisfy them."

"Is that so, indeed?" responded Colonel Cameron. "I have not had the fortune to be acquainted with many poets.—Do you consider your brother to be a *good* poet?" he added.

"Why, yes, sir, I believe he shows considerable talent," replied Scylla judicially. "Up to the age of fourteen his work displayed no particular genius, but at that age he profited very greatly from the critical advice of our dear friend and guardian, Dr. Winthrop Musson, and I believe that his verses now can compare very favorably with those of Goldsmith or Gray or Cowper. And I myself greatly prefer them to those of Isaac Watts or Matthew Prior."

"Well—I shall look forward to reading them with great interest," said Colonel Cameron. "I perceive that, as well as being a remarkably courageous young lady, you are a well-read one.—But tell me, you speak of yourself and your brother and your guardians—your own mother, I collect, is no longer alive?"

"Our mother died, sir, six years ago. I think," Scylla said matter-of-factly, "it was grief that killed her, after my father went off to England and left us." Then she exclaimed, in a burst of overwhelming curiosity, "Oh, sir, the letter that you bear, is it from *him?* Have you—do you know our father in England?"

Colonel Cameron turned, pausing a moment, to study her with interest and some compassion.

"Were you so attached to your father, then, my child? Did you, too, miss him when he went off to England?"

"No, I was not in the least attached to him," replied Scylla bluntly. "He was never particularly kind to me. And I thought that he treated our mother with a wretched lack of civility and consideration. She came of a good Portuguese family on her father's side. Why did he go off, leaving her with so little money? But of course if he has repented and sent us some money now, I shall try to think more kindly of him."

"Well, he has not done so, because he is dead," replied her companion in an amused tone. "I am relieved to discover that you will not be too stricken at finding yourself doubly an orphan.—However, in fairness to your father it must be said that he left India in some financial straits, having lost a great deal of money by gambling—"

"So it is from *him* that Cal inherits the taste!" exclaimed Cal's sister.

"I understand, too, that a letter he had dispatched to your mother from England failed to find her, so I suppose he concluded that she had found some—" Some other protector, he had been about to say, but altered this to "some other source of revenue."

"Instead of which, I presume the letter arrived after she had died," remarked Scylla rather bitterly. "And by that time, no doubt, my brother and I had gone with the Mussons to northern India. But, sir, pray satisfy my curiosity. What did my father do then? Did he apply to you? Did you meet him in England?"

Colonel Cameron did not reply immediately. He was shading his eyes, looking westward. "Here comes the Therbah with our beasts," he remarked.

The two ponies that came loping toward the causeway, one ridden by Therbah, one led, were short, shaggy, and thickset in build, though with something of distinction in their head and bone structure. Their coats were so long that the hair almost reached the ground and covered their eyes. The dusty gray bestridden by Therbah carried a pair of heavy goatskin saddle bags, and Colonel Cameron, rummaging in one of these, found a packet wrapped in oiled cloth and extracted from it a letter in a somewhat grimy cover, which he handed to Scylla.

"I can see, ma'am, that your curiosity has reached almost unbearable proportions," he remarked, half gallantly, half teasingly, "so I will oblige you to restrain it no longer. Besides, in another fifteen minutes the light will be gone, so you had best read it while you may."

The letter was addressed to "Mr. and Miss Paget, last heard of in Umballa, India, by Courtesy of Col. Robt. Cameron."

Scylla would have torn it open, but the little servant, Therbah, forestalled her. "A moment, missy sahib," he said, and, taking it from her, pulled from his belt a ferocious-looking curved kukri, or Afghan knife, and neatly slit it around the edges, handing it back to her with a polite salaam.

About to read it, Scylla bethought herself of her only half-eaten picnic.

"I have some chicken and fruit here," she said. "While I read this, would you care—?"

"Would we care, ma'am? You see before you two famished men!"

So while she read they demolished the rest of the birthday feast.

> *My Dear Cousins:*
>
> *Having, through no Merit of my own, succeeded recently to your Late Father's Fortune, I am anxious to rectify this Sad Injustice, in so far as lies within my Power. Colonel Cameron has been so obliging as to undertake to seek you out when he returns to India. If this letter does indeed reach you, pray write to me and send me your Direction, so that I may share with you the competence which should, by rights, have been entirely yours. And if you should consider coming to England (which I sincerely hope may be the case, so that I may have the Pleasure of meeting two unknown Cousins) pray consider my house to be your Home for as long as you may wish to remain under its roof. I myself have known the discomfort of arriving unfriended and with but limited Resources in a Foreign Land, and it is my earnest wish to help you avoid such a Disagreeable Experience.*
>
> *Your sincere well-wisher and Cousin*
> *Juliana Paget van Welcker.*

Scylla read this epistle once, and then again, with the utmost astonishment.

"Good heavens! Who is this Juliana? Have you met her, sir? Are you aware of the contents of this letter?"

"Yes, I have met the countess," he replied, negligently flinging a leg over his diminutive mount. "But—forgive me—I think we should now press on, for darkness comes so swiftly here. You may, after all, question me as we ride."

"You are very right.—But who is Juliana? Where did you meet her?" Scylla wanted to know.

"I met her at Almack's Assembly Rooms in London, ma'am."

"Almack's!" breathed Scylla on a sigh of envy. "The very place of all others that I wish to visit! Oh, how lucky you are!"

"To have been at Almack's?" He glanced at her in surprise. "Why, it is the most insipid place in the world—nothing but lemonade and orgeat to drink, dismal, rigid propriety prevailing throughout, and the rooms crowded to the doors by young misses with not an idea in their heads, save that of catching a husband."

"Then why, sir, were *you* there?"

"I consider it necessary to see any place *once*," he briefly replied. "In fact, I was passing through London on my way to Scotland. Lady Jersey introduced me to the Countess van Welcker, as she had done with many others coming from the Indian continent, for the countess was attempting to ascertain the whereabouts of her missing cousins. When I told her that I would, in due course, be traveling east again, she ran into the cardroom, borrowed her husband's tablets, and wrote this letter for me to give you, in the event that I should encounter you."

"But how—"

"I had chanced to mention that I knew the Mussons, who are my compatriots—it seemed that a Dr. Musson had been mentioned to the countess as being one of those who might conceivably know of your whereabouts, since he and his sister had befriended your mother while General Paget still remained in India. Now, is the chain of connection clear?"

"Yes, I believe so," said Scylla after some thought. "But who, precisely, is this Juliana Paget—you say she is a *countess?*"

"At the time when I met her she had recently married a Dutch nobleman—a Count van Welcker who was in the service of the Prince of Wales. Miss Paget was, I understand, the granddaughter of your father's elder brother."

"Our cousin once removed. I see. And she says that our father left her all his fortune? But I thought you said that he was in straitened circumstances through gambling debts? How can he have had any fortune to leave?"

"When General Paget left India his fortunes were at low ebb. But it seems that he had saved the life of an Indian prince who, after a period of time had elapsed, rewarded him with considerable munificence; the money arrived when General Paget was on his deathbed, however, and, to spite his brother, with whom he had quarreled, he left the whole to that brother's son, the father of this Juliana."

"Why should that spite his brother?" asked Scylla, puzzled.

"Because the brother—yet another General Paget—had quite cast off his son, who would not follow in his father's profession and go into the army.—You appear to belong to a combative and contentious family, ma'am," said Colonel Cameron with some amusement. It struck him as noteworthy that this member of it did not choose to repine over the neglectful behavior of her father—who, after all, having come into a fortune, might reasonably have been expected to make *some* provision for his abandoned children. Her interest was all in this newly discovered relation.

"What was she like—my cousin Juliana? What age is she?"

"I should judge, about your age, perhaps nineteen or twenty—very pretty, with a brown complexion, sparkling dark eyes, and dusky curls; very much attached to her husband, who seemed some ten or twelve years older."

"I should dearly like to meet her," was Scylla's reflection.

"Well—now you will be able to, ma'am," remarked Colonel Cameron dryly. "You have but to accept her invitation."

Scylla frowned, thinking this over.

"Alas! It is by no means so simple! I have my brother and Miss Musson to consider. But I will certainly write to my cousin.—Oh!" she exclaimed in an irrepressible burst of pleasure. "It will be so *wonderful* to have a correspondent in England. She can tell me about the fashions—and the Prince—and Mr. Fox—"

Then something struck her. She looked at Colonel Cameron in puzzlement. Dusk was falling rapidly now, and she could distinguish little more than the craggy outline of his profile.

"You said the Mussons were your compatriots, sir?"

"Why yes, I, as they did, hail from America. But from a different region. They are Bostonians—New Englanders; whereas I was born in the Huron Mountains, on the shores of Lake Superior."

"But you must surely be of Scots descent?"

Scylla smiled privately in the dusk, thinking of the tartan turban.

"Oh yes; my grandfather left Scotland as a young man, at the time of the 1715 rising, and founded a town in his name on the Red Cedar River, about a hundred miles to the south of where I was born. And then, many years later, I had a curiosity to visit the land of my ancestors. Which is one of the reasons that took me to Britain."

"Did you find any of your family, sir?"

"Oh!" he exclaimed rather impatiently. "Who's to tell? I found Camerons in plenty, and many a tale of lads who had left in haste when the Stuart rising was put down, but which of the many Donald Camerons might have been my grandfather it was beyond my power to fathom."

She guessed that the visit had been a disappointment to him and asked instead about his childhood. He said:

"Well, I was born with a roving foot, ma'am, and that's the truth of it. Perhaps it was the sight of the Red Indians coming down to our village to trade with the boats that plied along the lake—so proud and free, they stepped, in their grand feathers and leggings; they used to sell their furs and skins, then away, back to the mountains; no petty shopkeeping life for them, or digging the same patch of soil, year in, year out. My father was a doctor and wanted me to follow his calling, but I knew I could never stay in one town all my life. By the age of seventeen I was away. I have worked my passage on schooners and feluccas and dhows; I have been a camel driver in desert caravans; I have fought in other men's battles from Kashmir to Baghdad; and all so that I might catch a sight of some new part of the globe.—And yet there still remains so much to see!"

Scylla did not immediately reply, but her deep sigh suggested how much she envied Colonel Cameron. After a while she exclaimed:

"*Why* may not women travel so? It is unfair!"

"Well, my dear," replied the colonel in a tone of some amusement, "you have only yourselves to blame, you know! If you will all be so pretty and beguiling, is it to be wondered at that, as soon as you poke your charming little noses outside the front door—or the town wall—some brigand will pounce down on you and carry you off to his mountain castle? Why, I have seen a beautiful slave sold for twenty or even thirty thousand rupees—we value your sex too highly, you see, to let you go roaming around by yourselves!"

Ignoring this pleasantry, she persisted, "It is unfair. I wish I could dress up as a boy and travel to all the places you have seen."

"And yet many an English young lady, I dare say, would give the pearls around her neck to see India and the citadel of Ziatur. And here I find you riding unescorted through the jungle—neither an English nor an Indian lady may do *that*.—Which reminds me," Colonel Cameron added, dropping his bantering tone for a serious one, "is the Rani Sada still in the ascendant? Can she still twine the Maharajah around her little finger? The last thing he did before I left was to give her a necklace of pearls the size of cherries."

"No, it is different now," Scylla said, thinking of her interview with Mahtab Kour. "The Maharajah has no favorite at present, I believe—or if he has, it is a very closely guarded secret; and he is ill, very despondent in his spirits; but it is said that Sada has—has become friendly with Mihal Shahzada."

Colonel Cameron let out a long, concerned whistle.

"No, has she indeed! And still has her head on her shoulders? The Maharajah *must* be in a bad skin—or is the real government now in the hands of Mihal?"

"I would say," remarked Scylla after considering his question, "that matters are just about to come to a crisis."

"It is always the way!" he exclaimed rather aggrievedly. "And should be a lesson to me never to return to a place for a second visit. If I do so, it is invariably to find that it has become a regular hornets' nest! But I had promised the Maharajah to come back one day with some carbines, and, fool that I am, I kept my promise."

"Well, *I* certainly have cause to be grateful to you," Scylla remarked, noticing with relief that the lights of Ziatur now sparkled like a tiny diadem far away across the dark plain. "I am deeply grateful to you, sir, for keeping your other promise, to Countess van Welcker. It is my birthday today; thanks to you, I find I have a new cousin as a present."

"And a new friend," said Colonel Cameron chivalrously. "If, as I hope, ma'am, you will allow me that honor?"

III

About four months after the newly married Fanny Paget had arrived at the Hermitage an unprecedented thing happened: Thomas announced that he was going to London for a few days and intended to take his wife with him. From the astonishment of his daughters, it was plain that a trip to London, for Thomas, was hardly more to be expected than a pilgrimage to Mecca; and for her own part, Fanny was dismally aware that her inclusion in the program was by no means to be regarded as a treat or mark of favor; on the contrary. Ever since her unplanned encounter with Lord Egremont, Thomas's attitude toward her had been compounded of total lack of faith in her judgment, suspicion of her motives, and a plain intention not to let her be on her own at any time. She was never out of the company of her stepdaughters unless Thomas was with her. Fanny, homesick and dejected, wondered bemusedly if all men were so. Or if it was her misfortune to have married a man who had a singularly, an inordinately jealous and mistrustful nature. In the circumstances, although naturally she had always wished to visit London, a trip to the capital with Thomas could offer no prospect of enjoyment but was more likely to be a penance, and she would very much have preferred to remain at home, enjoying the unaccustomed tranquillity of her husband's absence.

Another reason for this preference was that she felt particularly unwell nowadays; queasiness, headache, and languor afflicted her all day, but especially in the morning; her back and legs ached, her ankles swelled up, and she found herself only just able to struggle through her household duties. At first she thought, with a certain resignation, that perhaps she had fallen into a consumption and would presently die; then she would be happily reunited with her father, of whom she had dismaying tidings in her sisters' very infrequent letters. But as to her own state, the rector's wife presently enlightened her.

That comfortable lady had come calling a few days after Fanny's arrival at the Hermitage, and since Thomas could think of no rational excuse to forbid Fanny's returning the call—though he did stipulate that she must always be accompanied to the Rectory by one of her stepdaughters—a friendship had grown up between the households. The Rev. Martin Socket was a gentle, unpretentious man, generally to be found absorbed in some scientific experiment, with stains on his fingers and acid holes in his waistcoat; his wife, plump, untidy, and friendly, was the devoted mother of three small boys who spent the principal part of their free time enjoying the delights of Petworth House and all its miscellaneous company; both the rector and his wife were strongly attached to Lord Egremont and could not speak too highly of his lordship, who had indeed sent Mr. Socket (previously the tutor of Egremont's sons) to the University of Oxford and paid for his tuition there, so that he might acquire the necessary qualifications to become rector of Petworth. The fact that, in consequence, it had been necessary for Egremont's youngest boy, Charles, to accompany his tutor to the university, so that his lessons might continue, was regarded by the Sockets as nothing out of the common.

Mrs. Socket instantly diagnosed what was the matter with Fanny.

"Why, child, you are as pale as a whiting," she said one morning when they were sorting clothes for the poor in the Rectory drawing room. And to Bet, who was with them, she added, "My dear, will you be so good as to step into the garden, where I see Nurse hanging out the boys' washing, and ask her to make up one of her brandy possets for your stepmamma."

After Bet had somewhat reluctantly obeyed this order, Mrs. Socket turned to Fanny and inquired:

"My dear, are you increasing?" And as Fanny looked her incomprehension of the query, she added more explicitly, "Do you think you are with child?"

At the girl's expression of shocked, wide-eyed amazement, she went on, smiling, "It is very often the way, you know, with young wives!"

A little more questioning soon proved that this was the case, and also revealed the great depths of Fanny's ignorance on the matter.

"My dear, where can you have been all your life? Did your mother not tell you—?"

"She died, ma'am, when I was born."

"Ah, I see, you poor child.—Well, I will put you in touch directly with an excellent midwife, Mrs. Damer, and ask Dr. Chilgrove to step around and have a talk with you; we shall soon have you in a more comfortable way, I promise you!"

The kindness and concern thus exhibited quite unmanned Fanny, and she broke down in a burst of tears and sobbed out some of her anxieties and troubles. Mrs. Socket listened with a slight crease marring the normal placidity of her brow.

"If only Mr. Paget—did not seem so distrustful of me! He never lets me be alone—never! I must always be with one of the girls—or the housemaid, or Kate—if I so much as step outside the door to throw a handful of bread to the birds he is *so* angry. And—oh, ma'am! If only someone—if perhaps you—could persuade him not to take me to the mill any more—truly I find it so fatiguing that sometimes I think I am likely to die!"

Twice a week, in between his press gang duties, Thomas found time to pay a visit of inspection to his mill at Haslingbourne. There were two approaches to the mill for vehicles, either through the village of Byworth or along a cartway called Grove Lane, but usually, to spare his horses, Thomas went on foot, by a path which wound for about a mile along the bottom of the Shimmings Valley below his house. Moreover, by thus arriving on foot, he could be sure of taking his men unawares; it was his belief that if they were in constant expectation of a surprise visit they would be less given to idleness and loitering.

From the first, Thomas had expected Fanny to accompany him on these visits. And indeed in October and November she had greatly enjoyed the walk, which crossed and recrossed the brook in the winding valley by a number of small footbridges and passed below a picturesque series of hanging woods along the valley sides. But latterly she had felt so ill and tired, and the path was so slippery with ice and mud —for an early and bitterly cold winter had the whole country in its grip—that she had come to dread these excursions. Her hands and feet frozen, she had much ado to keep up with Thomas, who strode on ahead, wrapped in his own uncongenial thoughts, without troubling to see how she managed, apart from an impatient call of "Hurry up, Frances. Make haste! We cannot be dawdling about all day," if she fell too far behind.

The hour or so spent at the mill was always purgatory to Fanny. It was a high-roomed, freezing, drafty place, vibrating always to the roar and grind of the mill machinery; there was nowhere to sit down, and wherever she stood, she inevitably felt herself in the way, some man wheeling a barrowload of sacks would be obliged to call, "Mind yerself, missus!" Also she could not help being aware that her husband's visits were extremely unpopular with the men, who scowled at him behind his back and received his suggestions for more efficient organization with unconcealed hostility and contempt; she had caught their nickname for him, "clung-headed ol' regulator," and felt herself included in their scorn and dislike. By the time the visit was over Fanny was always exhausted and miserably cold, her ankles swollen with standing about; then there was the half hour's walk back along the valley to be faced, with the biting north wind full in their faces, an excessively steep climb up the slippery valley side at the finish, and Thomas in a bad temper because of all the opposition and ill will that he had encountered.

Some of this distress Fanny managed to convey to Mrs. Socket, who said, "Well, my dear, in the general way I would say that it did nothing but good for a girl in your situation to take regular exercise on foot —Lord, when I was expecting Johnnie and Frederick I used to go out riding every day with Mr. Socket and never thought anything of it!— but I can see that you are not quite the thing at present, and I will speak to your husband on the matter."

That she had done so was evidenced by Thomas's extreme annoyance and displeasure. "Who told that busybody to come prying into my affairs? *I* am the proper person to decide what is best for you, and I say that a healthful walk down the valley twice a week is better than dawdling inside the house all day long!" Thomas flatly refused to permit Fanny to discontinue her visits to the mill, nor did he allow the attendance of the midwife, Mrs. Damer—"*I* will engage to procure such a person when it is necessary, which at present it is not!"

However a couple of weeks later, after an exceptionally severe frost, Fanny slipped on a patch of ice when returning home up the steep wooded track, known as the Glebe Path, that led to the back gate of the garden. She fell and bruised herself so severely that for a few days a miscarriage was apprehended; Dr. Chilgrove, who had to be summoned, insisted that she stay in bed for at least a week, and forbade the resumption of walks to the mill for another six weeks, in spite of Thomas's furious expostulations.

"A woman who is always indoors coddling herself will never produce a healthy child. I wish my son to be a strong-limbed and active boy—not a puling milksop!" And he shook his three-fingered fist in the doctor's face.

"Very true," said Chilgrove, "but," he added bluntly, "you are going the best way to ensure that your son is born *dead*, sir, rather than healthy and active. Let your wife take outside exercise, to be sure, but let it be of a more moderate nature, in the garden, where she may walk to and fro and then return indoors when she is tired. Mrs. Paget is young, sir, and on the frail side; she may live to bear you many more children, but only if she is looked after carefully at the present time."

None of which speech pleased Thomas; he strongly disliked being obliged to take orders from someone else and was enraged at the thought that, in spite of his care in picking Fanny, he might have saddled himself with yet another bad bargain, a sickly, unhealthy wife who would not be able to give him the heir he so passionately wanted. However he found himself forced to take notice of the doctor's warning, and the unwonted luxury of a week in bed did Fanny so much good that after the end of that period she was able to get up and resume her household occupations.

Taking exercise, as prescribed by the doctor, with Bet or Martha in the garden, she had occasion to regret the exchange of the pleasant, friendly Talgarth for Goble, the older gardener who had replaced him. Goble was a gloomy, taciturn man who never had anything to say unless asked a direct question; he went silently about his work, digging, potting, and pruning; occasionally he could be heard muttering some biblical quotation, generally of an ominous and condemnatory nature; the look on his face was sour, withdrawn, and forbade any approaches.

One day, however, shortly after her regime of garden exercise had commenced, Fanny was impelled to speak to Goble when she found him at work on the ash tree with a ladder and a bundle of wires and leather thongs.

"Oh, what are you doing, Goble?" she exclaimed in distress and astonishment, for, balanced on the ladder, he was slashing the bark on the upper sides of the boughs, bending them, and tying them pointing downward, binding them tightly to the trunk of the tree, which was also tightly strapped around with leather thongs and hempen cords.

"Master's orders," he grunted shortly, and then, as she persisted, "But why? What are you doing that for?" he explained.

"Master wants 'er made into a weeping tree, so 'er won't cut off so much light from the 'ouse. That's why I'm a-tying of 'er branches and binding up the trunk, so 'er won't grow no 'igher."

And he took a pot of tar and began slapping brushfuls of it over the gashes he had made in the bark, so that the tree's silvery elegance was marred with great black spots.

Fanny was aghast. By now she knew that it was useless—indeed, would do nothing but harm—for her to remonstrate or argue with Thomas. She felt quite certain that, unable to fell the tree, he had thus vented his spite and frustration by crippling it. Every time she passed the bare bole after that, and saw its naked boughs tied down and constricted by those punitive bonds, the ugly splashes of tar on its bark, she felt as if it were her own body that had been so cramped and humiliated.

Thomas himself took considerable satisfaction in the spectacle.

"If I can't cut it down, at least I can *train* it," he was wont to say, rubbing his hands. "Next summer, when the leaves are on, we shall see what a difference that makes!"

Fanny tried to appease her own indignation and make atonement to the tree by planting daffodil bulbs around the tree, but Goble told her gloomily that it was too late in the year and they would never flower.

And Thomas's relatively good mood caused by the coercion of the tree was due to be short-lived, for two events occurred to put an end to it.

The first, in January, was the arrival of a letter.

"Lord, Stepmamma!" cried Martha, running into the parlor one day (she had recently adopted this mode of address, usually spoken with such a satirical drawl that Fanny suspected she used it out of malice, rather than any increase of friendly feelings). "Lord, there's a letter come addressed to our cousin Juliana, and with *such* a foreign-looking cover—I dare swear it's from those twin cousins I told you of, out there in the East Indies!"

"Good gracious!" exclaimed Fanny. "How very unfortunate! They do not know, I suppose, that your cousin was obliged to leave England. I wonder how this letter may be sent on to her? Perhaps Thomas may enclose it in one of his own, next time he has occasion to write to Countess van Welcker."

Fanny herself had not yet achieved her intention of writing to her cousin by marriage; every time she suggested it to Thomas he had replied that it was not necessary, he himself had said everything that was proper; a letter from Fanny would add too much extra weight to the packet of business communications that he was dispatching.

The strange, foreign-looking epistle was placed on the hall table and lay there all day awaiting the return of Thomas and arousing intense speculations in the minds of his daughters. He himself, when he came home, cut short all discussion by immediately opening the cover. He did not read the letter aloud or divulge the purport to his interested family, but since, having perused its short contents, he then flung down the paper and walked upstairs with an exclamation of annoyance, Bet was able to pounce on it and acquaint herself and the others with its contents, which were dated in August of the previous year.

> *"Dear Cousin Juliana* [she read aloud],
> *I cannot tell you with what surprise and delight I received your kind note delivered by Col. Cameron, and what a happiness it was for my Brother and myself to learn that we have a Cousin in England—and such a generously disposed Cousin, too! Had your letter arrived only a few weeks since, I wd not have thought it likely that we wd be able to avail ourselves of your very Welcome Invitation, but now Circumstances render it urgently necessary that we leave Ziatur, the town where we have been living, with our Friend Miss Musson, and we shall, therefore, be extremely happy to accept your Offer of a Home in England under your Roof. Our journey to England must necessarily be taken by a somewhat roundabout & Circuitous Route (due to reasons which I will not go into here, lest this paper should fall into the Wrong Hands). I cannot, therefore, give any very precise indications of when you may expect us, but I wd guess that it may not be for a number of months after you receive my Letter (which I am entrusting to a Mr. Wharton, an American Dental Practitioner who is bound for Surat and assures me that he will see it safe on to a*

*Ship). Sometime then, in the course of next year, dear
Cousin Juliana, my Brother and I will hope for the Delight of making your Acquaintance. In the meantime,
pray accept the grateful and Sincere Thanks of,*

*Your two Cousins,
Scylla and Carloman Paget."*

"Well! Upon my word, that is cool!" exclaimed Bet. "They call
themselves *Paget* when I dare say they have no more right to the name
than Jem bootboy!"

"Wait, there is a postscriptum," pointed out Fanny, picking up the
paper.

*"I fear it will be of no use my putting any Address or Di-
rection to which you might address correspondence, since
we are to set out immediately, and are not able to desig-
nate any places that we might pass through on our journey."*

Needless to say, this letter provided food for endless speculation,
comment, discussion, and wonder among the female occupants of the
Hermitage for many days and weeks after its arrival.

"When our cousins come—" "After our cousins have arrived—" was
a phrase constantly on the lips of Bet and Martha. They very soon
learned not to allude to the subject in the presence of their father,
however, for it threw him into such a black mood that his displeasure
was likely to be visited on the person who raised it. The thought that
two uninvited guests were liable to arrive, that he was powerless to
prevent them or to put them off, having no knowledge of their present
whereabouts, that they were people he had never met, who had no
personal claims on his generosity, and that they might intend to
remain under his roof for an indefinite period, put him into a perfect
passion of indignation. For already he had fallen into the habit of considering the Hermitage as *his* house, regarding it as less and less probable that the real owners would ever wish to return from Demerara and
claim it.

This impending visitation, therefore, was one of the reasons for his decision to take a trip to London.

"I shall visit Throgmorton," he said (Throgmorton was the Countess van Welcker's man of business who had arranged the terms of the contract under which Thomas and his family occupied the house). "I shall visit Throgmorton and discover precisely what my rights and obligations are in the case."

Fanny wondered why Thomas, usually so frugal, did not merely indite a note to the lawyer, instead of going to the expense of a trip to the capital, necessarily lasting two or three days. However in the course of time she learned that he was obliged, in any case, to go to town; his presence being required by the Admiralty in a matter involving alleged bribery of a press gang official. Usually such cases were tried internally, by courts-martial, but in this instance a wealthy Portsmouth saddler, who had given a press officer fifteen pounds to release his best journeyman, was not unnaturally aggrieved when the officer, having accepted the money, then forgot to release the impressed man. The saddler therefore took the matter before the civil courts. Thomas, who had been the senior officer in the case, had been summoned by the defense to appear and give evidence as to character, greatly to his irritation. However this was somewhat appeased by the fact that his coach fare would be paid to London, besides his expenses at a hotel while he was obliged to remain in the city.—Otherwise, Fanny felt certain, he would hardly have considered taking her along as well.

Thomas, in fact, thought it best to travel to London while he might. Buonaparte had recently signed a treaty with Austria and was massing his troops in the north of France—a force known as the "Army of England." Tales were circulating about England as to the construction of huge French rafts two thousand feet square, propelled by giant windmills, each capable of carrying two divisions of men with ammunition. If the French landed, a journey to London might have to be indefinitely postponed. He resolved to set off without delay.

Captain Paget's mode of travel was a subject of great disapproval with Mrs. Socket. Thomas, always unwilling to tire his own horses, had at first considered hiring a hack post chaise but, finding that it would be cheaper to go by the accommodation coach, which ran from Petworth every other day, he resolved on that means of transport, since the Admiralty allowance, sufficient for a post chaise, would not cover Fanny's expenses at the hotel.

"Obliging his poor little wife to ride in that barbarous stagecoach!" said Mrs. Socket to her husband. "It will take them quite five hours, and she will be shaken half to pieces. If she miscarries, he will have only himself to blame. The man is a monster!"

But she had abandoned all attempts at remonstrance with Thomas, suspecting, rightly, that her intervention only rebounded upon Fanny.

Fanny did indeed feel horribly ill in the coach, and had it not been for a fat kindly haberdasher's wife, who was traveling with her three children to visit her sister in Edmonton, she might several times have fainted. That lady, however, carefully propped Fanny among her numerous bundles and administered cowslip cordial and an extremely powerful vinaigrette whenever her young companion appeared noticeably paler or to be on the point of falling off the seat. Thomas knew nothing of these vicissitudes; one look at the three children and he had elected to travel outside, where he had a comfortable conversation with a fellow passenger about the outrageous new taxes levied to pay for the war: taxes on windows, on male servants, on horses, carriages, and Lord knew what next. The lack of her husband's presence was a source of considerable relief to Fanny, who felt too ill to notice the countryside they passed through and was unable to take any nourishment when they stopped to change the horses at Dorking.

Arrived at the small and unpretentious hotel in High Holborn selected by Thomas, she was only too glad to go straight to bed and soon sank into a troubled sleep, vaguely aware of the incessant noise outside in the street, and haunted by dreams of Barnaby, for the pain of his loss had been renewed by this visit to a place where he might possibly still be found—supposing that his regiment had not yet been ordered abroad.

If I should encounter him in the street! was one of the thoughts that beset her feverish slumbers, for she had been too unwell as they drove along to apprehend how very large a city London was, and the extreme unlikelihood of this coincidence. And she tortured herself over wild improbabilities: Barnaby's loudly greeting her in the street, calling out, "Why, there's my dear little briar rose!"—the rage of Thomas at such a piece of familiarity to his wife—the possibility of a duel—seconds, choice of weapons—pistols at dawn on Wimbledon Common.

After such a night, fagged, feverish, queasy, and wretched, Fanny was in no case to get up next morning and go out into the streets. This, in fact, really suited Thomas's purpose quite well. He had only brought her to London because of a vague general dislike and distrust of leaving her to her own devices without his supervision; but he had not come to any practical conclusion as to what he was to do with her all day long while he was obliged to attend the sittings of the court. If Fanny were too ill to get up, very good; she might remain in bed; and Thomas paid the chambermaid a small sum to bring her tea and toast, and went out with great relief, dismissing her from his mind.

For two days Fanny lay in bed, gradually recovering from the journey and listening, with slowly reviving attention, to the busy voices of London in the street outside: the cries of oyster women and hot-pie vendors, the rattle of wheels, clatter of hoofs, the raucous music of street performers. Perhaps, she sometimes thought, Barnaby is walking past outside; perhaps those very footsteps are his!

On the third day, which was a Sunday, she felt sufficiently improved in health to rise from her bed. This was just as well, for the court was not in session, and Thomas would have required her to get up and accompany him to church even if her recovery had been far less advanced. Fanny, weary of the stuffy, poky inn bedroom and the casual ministrations of the chambermaid, was glad enough to wrap up warmly and accompany Thomas along Kingsway and down the Strand to the Church of St. Clement Danes.

It was a crisp winter day and the Sunday streets were relatively clean and quiet; she looked about her with interest, trying to store up impressions to take back to her stepdaughters when she returned—for they, poor things, had been consumed with envy at her luck and had besought her to describe all the ladies' fashions.

This was not a fashionable part of the town, she knew, but still she saw many toilets far superior to those of Mrs. Socket or the ladies who assisted in her parish duties: a walking dress of striped poplin with a quilted petticoat, an exceedingly elegant riding habit of blue velvet with a tight page's jacket, frilled stock, and black hat with a cock's feather; a bonnet shaped like Athene's helmet, a ravishing pair of pink shoes, and a wonderful pink and green embroidered Norwich shawl. These interesting sights compensated for the taciturn demeanor of Thomas, who was annoyed because the court case seemed liable to drag on for at least another two or three days, and he feared that the men at the Petworth press gang rendezvous, without his regulating presence, would be falling into mischief and idle ways. He had hoped to return at least by Monday.

The church service was shorter than those Fanny was used to, and the sermon sounded more like a dramatic recital than a message from heaven—the clergyman waved his hands so, and rolled his eyes, and his voice boomed from low to high and back again—but still, Fanny found comfort in the familiar ritual and prayed earnestly that she might be helped to goodness and acceptance of her lot. She prayed too for her unborn child, that it might make Thomas happy and be a means to bring him closer to his wife.

They had arrived early in the church, which had filled up very considerably after they were settled in a pew. When the service ended they were obliged to remain seated for many minutes, despite Thomas's impatience to be gone, and, even when they were able to rise, their progress along the crowded aisle was very slow. The reason for this became apparent when they emerged, for a light sleety rain had begun to fall, and parishioners were delaying on the church steps to put up umbrellas, summon carriages and sedan chairs, or look in vain for hackney coaches, thus hindering the exit of those behind them.

"This is nothing of a shower!" said Thomas irritably, turning up his collar. "We can be back in High Holborn in ten minutes if we walk briskly, so come, Frances—do not be loitering—" and he was about to take her arm when a jostling movement of the crowd pushed them apart. Fanny, craning about to find him, suddenly received such a shock as nearly made her heart stop beating, for there, not six feet away from her in the crowd—she was sure of it!—was Barnaby! She could not mistake! True, she could see only the back of his head, but it was a neck and ear she had studied so often and so lovingly that she felt not the slightest shadow of doubt. Even then, though, habitual caution, propriety, and timidity prevented her crying his name aloud; but she must, she *must* get a glimpse of his face, and, moving between the foot passengers with a speed and energy of which she would hardly, ten minutes before, have believed herself capable, she worked her way through the crowd in his direction. People were pushing everywhere, cursing, shouting for cabs, summoning their carriages; she thought she heard Thomas's voice indignantly raised behind her: "Frances! Where have you got to? Come here to me directly!" but she paid no heed, only went on. At last she came out of the thickest part the crowd and saw two young men threading their way across the street through the slow-moving traffic. Both wore uniform and surely —surely—one of them was Barnaby. Slipping nervously behind a carriage, darting boldly in front of two horses, Fanny followed them.

I won't speak to him, she was saying to herself. I won't even let him see me—but oh, just to look at his face again, just for one moment— perhaps God meant me to have that indulgence. He *could* not have meant to torment me by just letting me see the back of Barnaby's neck!

The two young men turned to their right, along a side street that led uphill quite steeply. Fanny, blind, deaf to everything but her one objective, followed as fast as she could—but they were striding out at a smart pace, talking and laughing together—she began to be left farther and farther behind; still she followed, in hopes that they would pause somewhere so that she might manage to come up with them. Now that they were away from the main thoroughfare there were fewer people about, so that at least it was easier for her to keep them in sight. And they, walking briskly through the gathering rain, were quite unaware of Fanny hastening behind them in her thin, soft slippers.

Now they had entered a region of narrow, short streets. Shabby, poor-looking people, going about their business, stared in surprise for a moment at the pale, distraught young lady in white muslin who ran by them, and then shrugged and forgot her; London was full of distraught young ladies; she was not their concern. Still Fanny ran on; having come so far, she felt that she *must,* in the end, be rewarded by a sight of the loved face; Heaven would not, surely, be so unkind to her.

But heaven was keeping its own counsel; presently rounding the corner of an even shorter, even shabbier street, Fanny was at first over-joyed to find that the two young men had stopped to speak to a third; also, very fortunately, they were just beyond a whelk and cockle stall, under cover of which she was able to come up close enough to study them without herself being observed. So far, she was lucky. But when she did arrive near enough to see them plainly, then there was pre-paring for her a most bitter disappointment, for the young man she had seen on the church steps was *not* Barnaby—indeed, when she saw him full face on, he was nothing like Barnaby—she did not know how she could ever have been so mistaken! The blow was so severe that Fanny actually staggered, putting her hand to her heart.

"You all right, missus?" said the whelk seller.

"Yes, thank you," said Fanny with absent, mechanical politeness. But in truth she was not all right; when the three strange young men walked away down the street, talking and laughing together, she felt as if the whole side of the universe had been torn away, leaving her naked and cold, exposed to the blast of Heaven's scorn. There was a flight of steps behind her, a church entrance; trembling, she sat down, regardless of her thin muslin cloak, and began to cry in bitter, racking sobs, as if something had broken inside her.

Thomas, meanwhile, was cursing the day he had ever decided to bring Fanny to London. Furiously he walked from side to side of the crowd, calling her name. Then, when the crowd had completely dispersed and she was still not to be seen, he went back inside the church, in case she had taken shelter there. Failing to find her, he at last returned to the hotel; he did not place much dependence on Fanny's sense, but she might have enough presence of mind to remember to ask her way back to High Holborn. Finding that she had not, he became seriously disturbed. Could she have been abducted? It seemed highly improbable that anybody should wish to abscond with Fanny, so pale as she was nowadays, and plain from ill-health, quiet, unassuming, and dressed by no means in the first stare of fashion. But then—could she have run away? Even to the mistrustful mind of Thomas this seemed most unlikely: Fanny was so humble, so docile, tried so hard to do what was expected of her. Why should she have taken such a step as that? The fact remained, however, that she was gone.

At first he thought, Well, she has got herself lost and is wandering about the streets. When she has the sense to ask her way and finally comes back, I shall give her such a scold! But when dusk fell and she *still* had not come back, he became very seriously disquieted and began to wonder if he should report the matter to the constables. However, as yet, his anxiety was overborne by his reluctance to appear in the somewhat ludicrous aspect of a deserted husband; he could imagine, only too well, the knowing looks, the winks, the private comments of his auditors, when he related his tale.

"Your good lady is *twenty-five* years younger, sir? Quite a young girl, then. Young ladies *are* sometimes rather flighty, we all know that. Depend upon it, she'll turn up all right and tight, if you just keep your patience, sir. Increasing, you say? The females *do* get taken with queer notions at such times, as you must be aware. One thing, sir—she being in such a condition—there's no chance of anyone else getting her with child, so you may rest easy there. . . . She'll not come to much harm, depend upon it, sir. . . ."

Perhaps he should return to Mr. Throgmorton, whom he had already consulted in regard to the Paget twins? No, Throgmorton had been totally unhelpful there, why would he be of any more use in this predicament?

Thomas went out and walked angrily about the streets until late at night. Then he hurried back to the hotel, expecting that at least by now Fanny would have returned. But she had not. And so he retired to

bed, perhaps more uncertain, angry, harassed, perplexed, sore, and suspicious than he had ever been before in his life.

Next day he was obliged to go early to court, and in the evening
when he returned, quite late, Fanny still was not there. The chambermaid, puzzled, asked if Mrs. Paget had not slept there the preceding
night, and Thomas was driven to make up a tale of her having been
taken ill and obliged to stay with friends.

The following day saw an end to the court proceedings shortly after
noon, and Thomas walked slowly back to High Holborn in a wretched
state of uncertainty. How could he make plans to return to Petworth,
with Fanny still missing? And yet, if he stayed on in London, it must
be at his own expense.—He was angry, too, about the court case—in
spite of his testimony to the effect that Wilkes, who had been his sub-
ordinate officer in Gosport, had been a man of the utmost virtue and
integrity, the Court had, without hesitation, found him guilty of accepting a bribe. Thomas felt that this reflected upon him. The whole
trip to London had been a complete waste of time, quite apart from
the disastrous loss of Fanny. Throgmorton had told him roundly that
he was absolutely bound by his agreement with Countess van Welcker
to entertain her cousins from India; there was no avoiding *that* im-
position.—He was the most unfortunate man in the world.

Wrapped in such a cloud of gloom and uncertainty, he glanced neither to right nor left, he strode through the inn hallway and up the
narrow crooked stairs to his chamber, still not sure whether to begin
packing, summon the constables, or order a bottle of sherry and try to
drown his problems in drink.

He flung open the bedroom door and came to a sudden halt on the
threshold, almost startled out of his wits. For there sat Fanny on the
one upright chair, pinched, hollow-eyed, and motionless, like some
strangely quiescent and passive little ghost, with her hands in her lap
and her shawl around her shoulders. She raised her eyes to her husband as he came into the room and seemed to draw herself together, as
if nerving herself for his onslaught. But she did not speak.

Thomas was so amazed and, momentarily, relieved to see her that
he did not immediately commence on the tirade which she evidently

expected. He stood staring at her, wholly at a loss for words, while he gradually took in the astounding fact of her safe return; that now it would be possible to arrange for their journey to Petworth, that he need not call in the constables, or write to her father, or ask to see the drowned bodies that had been dragged out of the Thames in the last two days.

However his tirade, when it finally did come, had lost nothing by the delay. Kicking the door to behind him, he drew a deep breath and began in a low biting voice to rid himself of all the fury, frustrations, fears, and suspicions that had ridden him for the last two days. On and on he went; using language normally reserved for the press gang rendezvous, words and phrases such as Fanny's ears had never heard before; he stepped up close in front of her and stood over her with his fists clenched and trembling, as if he would like to shake her to pieces, to pound her into pap.

Where had she been? Where the —— —— —— had she *been* these last two days? Did she think she could play this kind of trick on him and get off scot free? What kind of a fool did she think he was? And again, for the fifth or sixth time, in a voice grown hoarse and thick from raging, where had she been?

Fanny at first made little response to his outburst, seemed hardly to hear it, indeed; her muscles tightened slightly as he shouted at her, she bowed her head, as if under a bitter blizzard, but she did not attempt to answer his questions. Only when his language—for a man who was usually such a model of propriety—became startlingly obscene did she raise great blind shocked eyes to his, and then, after a moment, bend her head forward and press her hands over cheeks and ears. But he furiously dragged her hands down again.

"*Listen* to me, answer me, you bitch! Where were you? Where have you been?"

At that, as if his physical touch had worked some spell to bring her back an immense distance from another, far-removed region, she gave a long sigh and, when he shook her again, said in a very small, soft voice:

"I can't tell you that, Thomas."

"*Can't?* How do you mean, you can't tell me?" he raged. "You —— —— well *will* tell me!—Or I'll—"

Here he came to a stop, temporarily thwarted. For what *could* he do to her? He could not beat her or physically punish her; the frustration of it made his eyes bulge, and straining cords stood out on his neck.

"I'll lock you up!" he blustered. "I'll have you put away in Bedlam —you shall never see any of your family again. *Where were you*, God damn it?"

And again, in that soft voice, barely above a whisper, she answered:

"I can't tell you, Thomas."

She had never called him Thomas before; it had always been *sir*, occasionally Captain Paget, if she had to address him directly; *your father*, if she spoke of him to the girls, *the master*, to the servants. Half consciously his ear noted the fact as his mind observed that, in spite of her pinched, haggard, wan appearance—frail as a wisp, she looked, likely to go off in a faint at any moment—in spite of all this, there seemed something collected about her; he could not quite put his finger on it.

"You certainly *can* tell me, my girl, and you will, too! If you've been up to wrong I can have you committed to prison, you know—and I'd not hesitate, not for a moment."

Idle threat; she seemed hardly to hear it. There she sat, huddled up, like a waif, like a changeling; time seemed to mean nothing to her, she appeared ready to sit like that all night if he wanted to go on scolding her.

And in fact he did go on, for a long time, storming and questioning; she listened absently, as if to the wind. Her eyes, in their great bony sockets, were so sad that Thomas, in sudden superstitious fright, came to a stumbling halt; what the deuce was she *thinking* about, in there? And what was all this going to do to his unborn child?

"When did you come back?" he said more quietly.

She gave her long sigh again.

"I am not certain. An hour—two hours ago."

"Did you have anything to eat during the day?" said Thomas, angry again at the thought of such carelessness, flighty, willful neglect of maternal duty.

She shook her head as if she really had no idea; exasperated, he summoned the chambermaid and ordered wine and soup. These she took obediently and, when he ordered her to do so, went to bed, where she lay silent as some creature inside its cocoon; Thomas, lying beside her, staring into the darkness, could not tell if she slept or no.

Next morning she seemed more like her old self; ate some toast-and-water gruel for breakfast; prepared, with docility, to accompany Thomas in a hackney carriage to St. Martin's-le-Grand and then on the stage to Petworth; at no time did she volunteer anything about her experiences during the time she had been missing, but occasionally made some perfectly practical remark about the contingencies of their journey. "Is not that the Petworth coach over there? I think I recognize the driver." "Thomas, have you given the man something for putting our bags into the trunk?" And on the coach journey, though she became deathly pale, she retained command of herself and was able to make polite rejoinders to the inquiries of a solicitous female fellow passenger. There were no children aboard this time, and Thomas traveled inside; but he did not exchange two remarks with Fanny during the whole course of the journey. He watched her, though, with baffled, thwarted, gnawing, unceasing, engrossed attention; watched her more than he had probably done in the whole course of their married life hitherto. She, as if unaware of this scrutiny, kept her eyes absently fixed on the rainy gray landscape beyond the window glass, but not as if it occupied her thoughts; where these were it would have been impossible to guess.

When they were at home again and Fanny was submitting to the bustle of arrival, still with that same blind-eyed stare and absent docility, Thomas irritably thrust his daughters out of the way, ignoring their questions about London and demands to know how the case had gone. He said to Fanny:

"Get upstairs to bed! And you are not to stir out of your chamber until I give you leave!"

"Is Stepmamma ill?" demanded Martha, and little Patty cried:
"Has she been naughty, that you send her to her chamber?"

But Fanny silently, like a sleepwalker, mounted the stairs, entered her bedroom, and took off her travel-stained garments. Only once did she pause in her mechanical preparations; while she was doing her hair she halted, brush in hand, to give a long, preoccupied, frowning look at the tethered ash tree outside her window; then, sighing, she put on her nightgown and climbed into bed.

IV

For some days after Colonel Cameron's arrival in Ziatur he was not seen by the Paget twins. Cal reported rather discontentedly that Cameron spent a great deal of time with the Maharajah, who, now that his Yagistani friend had returned to entertain him, seemed to have improved greatly in health and spirits. Moreover the promised arms—or at least some of them—had come from Karachi, and the Maharajah was diverting himself by watching his men being equipped with the new weapons and taught new drills by Kamaran Sahib. Meanwhile the French emissaries found themselves in sudden disfavor, never able to obtain an audience, and were kept kicking their heels in antechambers for days together. This state of affairs pleased Mihal Shahzada not at all, and his resentment and ill temper rebounded upon Cal. The latter, although it amused him to bear the prince company in lighthearted diversions—drinking parties, dice games, or quail fights—was not in the least prepared to listen for hours on end to Mihal's discontents or become involved in court intrigues; he therefore found it more convenient to stay away from the palace, and so for some days the household at Miss Musson's bungalow heard little about royal affairs. Cal, usually so easygoing and good-tempered, had been a little ruffled by his sister's borrowing his precious Kali and going off on a whole adventure by herself; and the fact that this was due to his own dereliction of brotherly duty only added the acid of guilt to his vexed feelings. These were not vented in any positive way; he merely became rather withdrawn, but as, at the time, he was in any case deep in the first canto of a long heroic poem about Alexander the Great's invasion of India, which was to conclude with the battle between Alexander and King Porus by the Jhelum River, his withdrawal was hardly noticeable, except to his sharp-eyed, quick-witted sister, who shrugged, laughed, and went about her own affairs, knowing that he would soon come around; Cal never harbored a grievance for long.

The two little princes, Amur and Ranji, had been granted some days of holiday so that they might watch and enjoy the army drilling; Scylla therefore spent a greater part of her time helping Miss Musson at the little hospital.

This was a shabby, inconvenient building, a derelict Jain temple, converted to its present function by a few bamboo partitions. There was a neglected dusty garden in front, where lines of outpatients hopefully squatted, a colonnade of three stone arches, under which lay piles of dirty linen waiting for the dhobi, and a number of charpoys and straw palliasses inside, laid in rows on the stone floor.

The treatments were of the simplest kind: wounds were kept clean (camel bite was one of the most frequently treated afflictions), feverish patients were dosed with quinine, and those suffering from stomach afflictions with rhubarb; balsam and plasters were applied to snakebite to draw out the venom; and Miss Musson had various infusions of honey, vinegar, cinnamon, cloves, gum arabic, and ginger which she used for sore eyes, toothache, and muscular pains. Winthrop Musson had been a doctor, and his sister faithfully followed the principles and practice he had laid down; having worked with him for over forty years, she was perfectly acquainted with all his clinical rules; but also in the course of time she had familiarized herself with a great deal of native lore in regard to herbs and minerals; as she said herself, briskly, "Half my cures are because I give people the confidence to recover, but of the other half, three quarters are because I use the herbs of the country; the jackal that lives on the hills of Mazandaran is best caught by the hounds of Mazandaran." Miss Musson was full of local proverbs, which, like the treatments, she had picked up over the years in her dealings with her patients.

Scylla had been helping Miss Musson with a long and difficult childbirth: a tiny girl, the gardener's daughter, who was in labor with twins. At first the husband had not wished to allow his wife to come near the hospital, but, as Miss Musson cannily pointed out, "Who is better able to help you than the Mem Periseela, and she a twin herself? She will bring you excellent luck"; and though Scylla was not, in fact, very experienced in midwifery, this argument had finally carried the day. Miss Musson, with the help of a shrewd old lady called Jameela, and Scylla as an auxiliary to hold the towels and the implements, had, after a serious struggle, brought the twins safely into the world, and the parents and grandparents were rejoicing while Scylla washed and wrapped the babies, when Colonel Cameron strode unannounced into the hospital.

"So this is where I find you!" he greeted Scylla, and then, perceiving Miss Musson, impressive in her black burqa, made her a low bow.

"Still in the healing line, I see, Miss Amanda, my dear! How many legs have you cut off, I wonder, since I saw you last?"

"Oh, I dare say it may be nine or ten," replied Miss Musson, rapidly washing her hands in a basin of water that Jameela was holding for her, before holding out one of them to the colonel. "How do you do, Rob, my dear boy? I must confess, I am surprised to see you back in Ziatur! I was under the impression that you never returned to a place where you had been before."

He laughed. "Well, one is occasionally obliged to alter one's habits, after all! And I *had* been so injudicious as to give a promise to Bhupindra Bahadur that I would come back and bring him some new toys to play with."

"Well, I think the better of you for it.—Oh, not for bringing him all those cannons, or whatever they are, but for keeping your word to a sick man. He is very happy at your arrival, I understand."

"And you have a new helper since I was here last," said Colonel Cameron, staring with undisguised admiration at Scylla, who, having wrapped both babies in swaddling bands, was now kneeling to hand them to their anxious mother. She looked delightful, her blue dress protected by a voluminous white apron, with its bands wound twice around her tiny waist and her curls tied up in a piece of white muslin, so that her long slender neck and charming blunt profile were displayed to the best advantage. She was laughing at the young mother's astonishment, as she displayed the identical likeness of the babies, her short upper lip crinkled in amusement, revealing brilliantly white teeth.

"Why did I never see her before?" demanded Cameron.

"Oh, she and her brother were two dusty, skinny children when you were here last, in the schoolroom learning their lessons with Winthrop; you would not have come across them."

Scylla's laughter was infectious; the colonel laughed too as he looked at her.

"Pray, what is amusing you, Robert?" tartly inquired Miss Musson.

"The complete unsuitability of your young colleague, my dear Miss Amanda."

"What *can* you mean?" she demanded. "Priscilla is a perfectly good girl in every way—sensible, hard-working, and kindhearted, not to mention quite devoted to that brother of hers. I allow, she is a *little* too independent—" Miss Musson had been slightly shocked by the tiger episode, though, as was her wont, she had forborne to scold Scylla.

"Also a rogue and an adventurer and a *femme fatale,*" Cameron said. "Take her to court in Paris or London, dress her up in style, and she'd have gallants by the score, slicing each other to ribbons, shooting each other full of holes, for the sake of that turned-up nose and that absurd upper lip."

"Fiddle-de-dee!" said Miss Musson.

"There is no fiddle-de-dee about it, I assure you! And you must allow, Miss Amanda, that I know what I am talking about."

Miss Musson gave him a glance full of disapproval. She did indeed know Colonel Cameron's character very well, having, on his previous visit, cured him of a flux—an ailment which notoriously eliminates restraints in those afflicted by it; there was little she had not heard about his rakish, wandering existence, and nothing to earn her commendation.

"In that case," she remarked, "it is just as well that the dear child remains here with me in Ziatur, where she can come to no harm. The local people find nothing at all to admire in her looks, I can tell you; in fact the ladies of the palace call her Monkey Face."

"Poor dear!" said Colonel Cameron, laughing again. "But I am not certain that you are right, Miss Amanda, in believing that she can come to no harm here. To tell the truth, I am concerned for her safety, and yours too. That is why I dropped in to see you. I am uneasy about the state of affairs up at the palace."

Miss Musson smiled at him indulgently, her keen, wrinkled old face creasing like some ancient piece of parchment.

"Rob, Rob, don't waste thought and anxiety on our account, I beg! There is always trouble up at the palace, and nothing ever comes of it. Besides—if there *were* any danger—which I am persuaded there is not —I have many friends here, people I have cured, or whose children I have cured."

He shook his head. "I would place no dependence on them."

"And the Maharajah himself is very favorably disposed; he set much store by Winthrop's opinion and treats me with great kindness in his memory; it was he who endowed this hospital, you know."

"The Maharajah will not live forever. Indeed, my dear Miss Amanda, it would ease my mind amazingly if you would only consider removing to some larger city where there were a few Europeans."

"Stuff and nonsense, my dear boy. Your head is full of fancies because you have been careering about so long in the wilds. If you stay here a few more weeks you will see that there is no occasion for anxiety.—Now run along with you; unless you wish to help me stitch up that poor fellow who was bitten by his camel."

"No, thank you, my dear Miss Amanda; I meet with quite enough of that kind of task when I am careering about in the wilds."

"You can come to dinner this evening if you do not object to one of

Habib-ulla's curries!" she called after him. "And why do you not take this child for a ride later, when the heat has died down—she will have had enough of pills and bandages by then."

He crossed to where Scylla was helping an old woman take a little rice.

"Should you care to come for a ride with me this afternoon, Miss Paget?"

"Why, thank you, Colonel Cameron, that would be delightful!" she replied, the formal politeness of her curtsy offset by her captivating triangular smile.

They were accompanied on their ride by Cal, who, having completed the first canto of his poem, had reverted to his usual sunny frame of mind and was prepared to be friends with everybody in the world.

"And so have you written to your cousin the Countess van Welcker, to thank her and accept her very obliging invitation?" the colonel inquired as they put their horses into a trot past the melon beds and the sugar-cane patches.

Cal replied cheerfully, "Why, no, sir; my sister was all agog to, of course, there's nothing she would like so much as to strike up a correspondence with this unknown Cousin Juliana, but the thing is, there has been nobody leaving the town in the direction of a seaport since you brought us the letter. You know how it is in Ziatur: lacking the luxury of a regular postal service, we must be dependent upon the good offices of merchants or travelers such as yourself. However we are in hopes that a fellow countryman of yours, a traveling dental surgeon, will pay a visit to the town during the next week or so; he generally arrives before the rains; and if no other messenger has turned up in the meantime we can make use of him."

"Wharton? Ay, I have run into the fellow; came across him in Peshawur, on my way here, about to drag a molar out of an old begum who could ill afford to lose it, for she had only two others in her head."

"But in any case," Cal went on carelessly, "it don't greatly signify whether we answer this Cousin Juliana or not, for it's all Peshawur to a pie that we never get to England. We can't leave our guardian alone here, and for my part I've no wish to leave; Ziatur suits me very well."

Cameron caught Scylla's look of resignation and gave her an encouraging smile.

"Tell us about your own travels, Colonel Cameron," she suggested. "I collect that, having dispatched the Maharajah's armaments by sea from wherever you acquired them, you yourself traveled overland to India. Pray tell me, why did you do that? Is it not a much longer journey than the sea voyage? And more dangerous? Did you come through the Holy Land or Turkey? Have you seen Jerusalem and Constantinople and Baghdad?"

"I dispatched the Maharajah's arms by sea because there are too many marauders along the land route," replied Colonel Cameron. "Baluchi brigands from the south—Turkoman robbers from the north —there are plenty of Afghans, too, who would give their dyed beards to get their hands on a consignment of carbines and ammunition. So, for the arms, the sea trip is safer. But I have been around the Cape of Good Hope five times and that is quite enough; four months at sea I consider a dead bore. I find the overland journey more amusing. Besides, I have friends all along the way. And a few enemies, too," he added. Then, guessing quite correctly what Scylla hoped of him, he broke into a lively account of his adventures between Gibraltar, where he had consigned his cargo to the care of a merchant captain, the passage through the Mediterranean to Tyre, and the overland journey to the Khaiber Pass, by which gateway he had finally entered India.

Cal could not help being interested in this narrative, particularly as so many of the places mentioned by the colonel had also been visited by Cal's current hero, Alexander of Macedon. He wanted to know how many towns along the way were still named Alexandria, what traces yet remained of the Greek army that had passed through, and if any inhabitants still bore signs of Greek descent. Scylla, rejoicing to hear this catechism, rode quietly smiling to herself as Colonel Cameron good-naturedly answered all the questions he could.

"One would think, my boy, since you are so interested in campaigning, that you might wish to become a soldier yourself?" he remarked.

"Become a soldier? Good God, no, sir! Are you out of your senses?" Cal exclaimed. "To have had a general for a father is bad enough; thank heaven I was born on the wrong side of the blanket—or more or less so. There need be no question, for me, of following the family tradition, for which I can never be sufficiently thankful! No, no, my dear Colonel, any interest that I have in campaigning is wholly a literary one. I like to *write* about campaigns, not take part in them."

"I wonder?" Cameron pulled his long red mustaches thoughtfully, eying his young companion with some interest. "I wonder what you would do, for instance, if a party of wild Baluchis came galloping over that hill yonder, waving their spears and firing their matchlocks?"

"Do?" said Cal, laughing. "Take my word for it, sir, I should indubitably make off at top speed, *ventre à terre,* as the French say, and head for the town, leaving you and Scylla to bring up the rear."

And he gave a teasing glance at the colonel as he set his mare into a gallop.

At dinner that evening, while eating Habib-ulla's excellent meal of curry, rice, and fruit, Colonel Cameron, whose humor seemed of an eccentric and personal nature, quietly chuckled as he glanced around the table.

"What is amusing you *now,* Rob?" tartly inquired Miss Musson. "I suppose after carousing with amirs and shahs and khans all over Central Asia (none of them any better than they should be, I dare say) you find our appointments too simple?"

"No, not at all, my dear Miss Amanda, I find your appointments eminently suitable, and the meal was delicious. No, I was remembering the last dinner I ate in a Company official's house in Surat—soup, roast fowl, mutton pie, forequarter of lamb, tarts, cheese, butter, bread, and a plum pudding, if you please, all accompanied by copious draughts of Madeira. And this in a temperature hot enough to fry an egg out on the maidan! It is a wonder that all those English do not die of apoplexy. They have no notion of regulating their lives by the custom of the country—except, it is true, that quite a number of them keep zenanas," he added thoughtfully.

Miss Musson, with a disapproving glance in Scylla's direction, was about to turn the conversation when there was a slight bustle outside and Habib-ulla came in with a bow to announce that a servant from the palace had brought a package for the Mem Periseela.

"The palace? Who was it from, Habib-ulla?"

"The Rani Mahtab Kour, sahiba. The servant said it was a gift in requital for a healing Missy Sahib did on the young slave girl, Laili."

Greatly surprised, Scylla undid the fastenings of the package, which was swathed in layers of unbleached muslin. There was no accompanying note—Mahtab Kour, like most of the ladies in the palace, could not write—but inside she found a very beautiful sari, made from the most delicate silk gauze, of a color somewhere between rose and brick red, interwoven with a pattern of black and gold, embroidered all over with a myriad tiny seed pearls, so that it shimmered in the lamplight. The choli, or blouse, that accompanied it was of pure silk, also embroidered with pearls.

"Good gracious!" she said, staring at the shimmering folded material. "All I did was wash the little girl's ears and anoint them with lotion. It is a miracle if *that* was sufficient to heal them."

"Perhaps Mahtab Kour wishes to ask some favor of you, and this is a preliminary move," suggested Colonel Cameron, whose keen eyes did not miss Scylla's look of somewhat frowning uncertainty as she gazed down at the costly gift.

"Very pretty," was Miss Musson's dry comment. "It is too bad that our humdrum existence allows you so few chances to wear such finery, my child. Are you going to try it on?"

Despite the sari's beauty, Scylla was more than a little reluctant to do so. Strongly suspecting, as she did, that it was intended as a bribe to persuade her to act as a talebearer to the Maharajah, she would have preferred not to accept it at all. However there would be no way of returning it which would not be a mortal insult, so she merely resolved never to wear it and said, laughing:

"You know, ma'am, that pink is not my color. The palace ladies would have even more occasion to call me Monkey Face and Daughter of a Pig were I to stroll about all swathed in rose color!"

"You are very right, Scylla my dear!" congratulated Cal. "If you wore that plum-colored robe, it would make you look exactly like one of those sticks of crystallized rhubarb they sell in the bazaars." And he remarked to Colonel Cameron, "You might not believe it, sir, but my sister has a decided sense of style. Take her into high society, and, in spite of her looks, I fancy that she would shine them all down after a week or so, when she had got her bearings."

"Indeed I do believe you," said Cameron, amused. Miss Musson was about to make some moralizing rejoinder when Cal, glancing at the clock, said to the colonel:

"I have an engagement, sir, to go with Prince Mihal to see a very uncommon fortuneteller from beyond Samarkand who has just come to the town. He is a yogi; it is said he lives high in the mountains, at a height of over twelve thousand feet, where no normal person could survive. He is said to have very remarkable powers—would it amuse you to accompany us?"

Cameron had seen a legion of fortunetellers in his time and had no very elevated opinion of them; he would much have preferred to remain comfortably where he was; but, catching a certain pleading look in Scylla's eye, he correctly divined that she thought his company a useful corrective to that of Prince Mihal for her brother and would be glad if he joined Cal on the excursion. He therefore said gallantly:

"If Miss Paget is not going to delight us by trying on the queen's gift—"

"No, no," interrupted Cal. "It wouldn't delight you the least bit, my dear fellow. I tell you, she would look like a stick of rhubarb."

"And I have my accounts to cast up, so we will bid you good night," said Miss Musson firmly.

As soon as the two men had gone Scylla pulled the folds of muslin back over the queen's sari and laid the bundle on a cedar chest in her room.

By the time that Cal, Colonel Cameron, and the prince entered the house where the fortuneteller had taken up residence it was already past midnight. Mihal had insisted on their spending several hours at the palace, drinking Kafir wine and sherbet and watching a series of nautch dancers. The dancers were skillful but Mihal paid little attention to them; he was being exceedingly affable to Colonel Cameron, who wondered, with his inborn caution and skepticism, what this unwonted civility betokened; hitherto Mihal had appeared curt, if not hostile. He was a smoothly handsome young man, a little shorter than Cal, stockily built—indeed, already running to fat, like his mother; at Mahtab Kour's age, he, too, might be mountainous; under the jollity of his manner was a total reserve, and his cold dark eye was deep as a bottomless pool.

The hot weather was fast approaching and at midnight the town was still buzzing with life and activity; families talked and laughed on rooftops, the smell of spices, urine, and mutton fried with onions and cabbage was almost suffocating; drums and conches sounded in the distance, ballad singers and storytellers occupied every street corner.

Prince Mihal had put aside most of his jewels, armlets, serpeches, and the ruby-hilted kirpan that he generally carried; he wore a plain blue muslin turban with steel quoits and a blue tunic which, though made of the very richest material, was not conspicuous.

A skinny old lady stationed in the doorway of the fortuneteller's house let them by with a cursory nod when Cal dropped a couple of pice into her outstretched claw, and they climbed up a narrow, stinking flight of stairs and came into a medium-sized room, very dimly lighted by a series of small lamps with red glass shades. There appeared to be no window; when his eyes were more accustomed to the obscure light, Colonel Cameron perceived that the walls were covered with tapestry upon which embroidered devils were engaged in every possible kind of unpleasant activity. A veiled girl motioned them to sit down against a wall where cushions were piled, and Mihal gave her a handful of rupees.

Now they could see that in the middle of the room there was a large earthenware basin, flat and shallow, apparently filled with red liquid. Cameron wondered cynically whether the liquid was really blood or merely water reddened with betel juice; it was evidently intended to look like blood. On the far side of it, cross-legged, sat a motionless man, clad only in a loincloth; by degrees, becoming accustomed to the dimness, they were able to observe that he was as bald as an egg, also plainly blind; his eyes were overlaid with a white cuticle, like those of a leper. He took no notice whatever of the newcomers but remained sitting, apparently wrapped in thought. The girl who had let them in now began to play softly on a flute.

After five minutes or so Cameron noticed that the water in the basin commenced to undulate a little, like a pool where a crocodile is lurking below the surface. Now the motionless man broke into speech; his lips, however, did not move, and the voice that recited the names of a whole catalog of demons, convoking and summoning them to appear and lend their aid, did not appear to come from his throat but, eerily, from a far corner of the room; Cameron, though, watching closely, perceived that the muscles under his jaw occasionally rippled as the sonorous names rolled out, polysyllabic and ominous. Cal was observing the man with dispassionate, critical attention; he seemed, Cameron thought with some amusement, to be memorizing the scene for use in some future versical work. But Prince Mihal began to appear decidedly uneasy and fidgeted with something under his tunic; Cameron suspected it to be a pistol.

Now the water in the bowl became violently agitated, and suddenly an object bobbed up from below the surface; even Cal drew in his breath sharply, for the round dark bobbing thing was the head of a baby; as it seemed, freshly severed from its body. The lips parted, and it spoke.

"What do you ask of me, O Father from the past?" it asked in a gnatlike high-pitched whine.

"*Sat Sri Akal!*" muttered Mihal, and he began softly reciting passages from the Adigranth, the holy book of the Sikhs.

The seer said:

"These unlettered ones seek to learn of your wisdom, babe from the black deeps. They ask you to look into the stars and see what fate has in store for them."

"Let each one, then, hold in his heart an image of that which he longs for most; and wait, patiently, while I call upon my great masters."

Now ensued a long, muttering silence. The veiled girl left off her flute playing and blew upon the smoldering charcoal in a brazier, tossing on handfuls of incense until the room was filled with pungent coiling clouds of blue smoke. Meanwhile the endless incantation to the demons went on; aid was besought from demons of every denomination: demons from the dry winds of the desert, demons from the snow of the hills, serpent demons from the jungle, and female vampire demons, souls of women who had died in childbed, who walked at night with feet turned backward on their ankles; demons of fire and of plague; demons from the far distant sea.

Colonel Cameron, listening, wondered irreverently what were the images that his companions had summoned up to symbolize their hearts' desire: for Mihal a crown perhaps—riches, power, glory? Was that his wish? And what of Cal da Silva Paget, that gentle, soft-spoken, amused young man who apparently wanted nothing, valued nothing, regretted nothing, esteemed nothing that he did not have already? Was such insouciance really the secret of his nature? Had Cal no hidden longing? As for himself—a man who had long ago buried all his hopes and affections on a windy hillside five hundred miles south of Hazrat Imam—Cameron shrugged and smiled; at present his chief wish was a well-filled hookah, comfortably bubbling; a glass of cognac, a cup of coffee, and perhaps a spoonful of mangosteen or guava jelly. . . . But then, strangely enough, the face of Scylla Paget flitted through his mind. It was a charming face, certainly—with that absurd short nose, that bewitching three-cornered mouth, and those enormous, innocent eyes. . . .

Too young and innocent for you, my boy, Cameron told himself. The only thing for you to do is to steer well clear of her. A girl who sees a European male perhaps twice a year; flirt with her, and you leave her with a broken heart. Marry her . . . But the *last* thing I want is to saddle myself with a wife. No, no, Rob, old fellow, you had best stay away from the Musson bungalow; besides, you are twice her age.

The child's head was speaking again in that eerie ventriloquial squeak.

"O thou descended from Baba Nanak . . . in whose veins the royal blood runs like a river of gold . . . son of a warrior clan . . . Your star is bright, you have far to go before its setting . . . mark well, though, the warning that comes from beyond the blind winds of desolation . . . the tree must be pruned before it will bear fruit . . . the old wood must be cut away, the unruly shoots must be lopped . . . an Akali, a warrior, must also be a martyr in the cause of strength . . . if thy leg be lame, strike it off at the knee!"

Dangerous stuff, thought Cameron rather uneasily; downright seditious, in fact. Mihal was listening with silent intensity; his knuckles gleamed white, gripping the handle of his pistol as he leaned forward to catch the batlike shrilling of the voice, which, Cameron observed, spoke the same hill dialect as the blind seer had used.

"And as for thee, warrior from afar, who bringest weapons for the sons of Nanak, the children of Gobind . . . beware lest the spear thou bearest should turn in thy hand and pierce thine own heart . . . meddle not in the strife of the holy contenders . . . except thou hand his weapon to the true Ruler, it were better to be gone . . . betake thee to thine own place, the river of crimson trees. . . .

"Laughing youth, child of love, beware the lightning flash! Beware the black stroke that smites behind the eyes, bringing vision and forgetfulness!"

The brat in the basin is becoming rather overexcited, Cameron observed to himself lightly, to distract himself from the slight shudder he felt down his spine as the head bobbed and shrilled, seeming now to turn in Cal's direction. Cal, on his cushion, was motionless, rapt, absorbed; the embroidered devils behind him could not have been more silent.

"Watch for the sacrifice by the weeping tree!" squalled the supernatural voice. "And look for my return! You cannot leave me behind; although you may cross water I shall accompany you; I shall be there before you. By the weeping tree you will see me again! I bring you what you ask for, and I take it again; while I am with you, men will hear your voice; when I am gone from you again, your lips will be dumb!"

The voice died away, as it seemed, to an immense distance. And then, as Mihal stood up with an abrupt movement, the bowl of water overturned; he had kicked it to one side and a black pool spread over the floor; next moment his pistol roared and blazed; with a groan the blind seer fell backward, blood flowing back from his mouth to cover his sightless eyes.

Wailing in terror, the veiled girl ran from the room.

"Mother of God!" Shocked out of his usual phlegm, Cameron turned on the prince. "What in the name of Eblis made you do that?"

Mihal was sweating profusely, and very pale, but quite calm; he replaced the pistol in its sheath and said matter-of-factly:

"It is always necessary to stop the mouths of those who prophesy to princes, lest, in their pride, they become dangerous, or boast to the multitude."

Cameron had spent too long in the wilds to hold human life particularly dear; he had seen whole clans wiped out in Afghan blood feuds, or by the headhunters of Kafiristan; and he did not esteem the blind seer to be a particularly valuable citizen. Nonetheless there was something about this cold-blooded statement that struck him with peculiar force. He said, however, half admiringly:

"Well, you surely are a cool customer, Prince.—Does that mean, then, that you *believed* what the fellow told you?"

"Indeed yes," replied Mihal. "And you, too, Kamaran Sahib, you would be wise to believe it! My star shines bright and I have many miles to go before its setting. Serve me, Sahib, and I will reward you. Be my daroga, Kamaran, and I will pay you well. I ask this of you! You shall have twenty-five hundred rupees a month, and many hectares of land."

"What use is land to a man with a roving foot?" Cameron replied composedly. "You are very good, Mihal Shahzada; but I am in the employ of your royal father. A man cannot serve two masters." And then he added, to cut short this difficult dialogue, which, he could not help feeling, should not have taken place at all:

"Had we not better do something about our young friend here? He appears to have been seized with some species of fit."

In point of fact Cal had fallen sideways onto the floor and was lying flat, completely rigid; his eyes were turned upward so that only the whites showed. He looked almost as dead as the soothsayer, save that a trickle of frothy saliva ran from his mouth. Cameron's investigating hand, however, found a slow but steady heartbeat and even slower breathing.

"Merciful gods! Is he poisoned, think you?" muttered Mihal, much more discomposed by this than by his dispatch of the fortuneteller. "Can that girl have thrown poisoned incense on the coals—?"

"No, no, set your mind at rest," replied Cameron soothingly. "He has merely thrown an epileptic fit; I have seen several such seizures before, in men who were greatly stirred or overset by some portent. You need not be too concerned about him." He gave a rather satirical glance at the prince and added, "I am afraid you will have to help me carry him down the stairs, though; he will probably sleep like this for many hours now, and we can hardly leave him here with the dead body; it would certainly be thought that he had done the killing."

Rather sulky at having to perform a service so out of keeping with his royal estate, Mihal complied. The old woman at the doorway was gone.

"Wait here, Colonel, with the boy, and I will have a tonga sent to carry him home," ordered Mihal, and swiftly disappeared into the shadows. Cameron propped Cal's inert body against the doorpost and waited for a few minutes.

Time passed and the promised tonga did not come. It occurred to Cameron that Mihal might equally well send somebody to knife or garrotte him and young Paget, thus eliminating two more inconvenient witnesses to the seer's prophecy.

Thus reflecting, he picked up Cal—who did not weigh so very much, after all—and began walking through the hot, dark streets in the direction of Miss Musson's bungalow, with the unconscious boy dangling over his shoulder.

He chose a rather circuitous route.

Scylla made her way up to the palace early the next morning, for she considered that Amur and Ranji had been indulged long enough and should now return to lessons; accordingly she had sent a message on the previous evening that classes would recommence on the following day.

The first thing she saw, on gaining the inner courtyard, was Kamaran Sahib himself, demonstrating to the Maharajah the correct way of putting on a French-made steel cuirass faced with brass; it was a handsome piece of armor, fastened at the sides with buckled straps, ornamented with a laurel wreath and a Gallic crowing cock in brass inlay, and must have weighed sixteen to twenty pounds. The Maharajah, reclined on his charpoy, today wrapped in a blue, gold-embroidered dressing gown, was greatly taken with the cuirass; so was his youngest son, little Chet Singh, who was sitting on his father's knee, clapping his small fat hands with enthusiasm as the early morning sun fetched sparks out of the steel and brass while Cameron, now buckled into the chestplate, drew himself upright and struck various dramatic military attitudes.

"*Shabash,* Sahib Bahadur!" shouted little Chet.

"That is a very fine piece of armor," said the Maharajah. "Is it not, little prince of my heart? I only wish we had ten thousand of them."

"I will wear it, *I* will wear it!" clamored the little boy. He jumped off his father's knee and ran to clasp Cameron around the leg—he could only just walk, being aged a little over a year. He was the Maharajah's favorite child, born of a young wife, Raj Kour, who had unfortunately contracted puerperal fever and died shortly after his birth. Some rumors in the palace had it that Raj Kour had been poisoned by her displaced rival, the Rani Sada, but Miss Musson contended crossly that it had been a straightforward case of fever—common enough, heaven knew!—and, if anybody had followed her instructions, need not have been fatal.

"*Thou* wear the armor, princeling?" said Cameron, picking up Chet, who immediately began hammering with his tiny fists on the bright steel, shouting, "Bang, bang, bang!" "Thou couldst not even lift it off the ground! Wait till thou art a man grown, my lord—then it will be time enough to shoot off big guns and wear heavy armor."

"Nay, Sahib, I have other plans for this prince," said his father fondly, receiving Chet back as Colonel Cameron began to unbuckle the breastplate. "He is to go to school in England and learn to be a wise administrator, versed in the laws of the Feringi and cunning in their diplomacy. Yes, I have it all planned; he is to go to Eton, where they send their prime ministers to school, when he is of an age to travel."

"*Eton!*" said Cameron, startled—he met Scylla's eyes as she came up to curtsy to the Maharajah and exchanged a smile with her. "Will he be happy there, do you think, Excellency? At an English school? It is so cold in England, and it rains so often!"

"Happy? It is not for a prince to be *happy*," replied the Maharajah severely. "It is for Chet Singh to acquire the white men's cunning and skills, so that he can advise his brother Mihal." The Maharajah's tone confirmed a belief already entertained by Scylla that the father did not hold a particularly high opinion of his eldest son's abilities. "This little one is to become a learned doctor in Belaiti law. It is all decided long since. That letter you carried for me, Kamaran Sahib, to my cousin

Gobind Tegh Bahadur in London, was to make the necessary arrangements; the funds are now transferred, and my cousin will take charge of the boy when he is old enough to leave this place. But previous to that, I hope that the Mem Periseela—to whom I have discourteously not yet said good morning!—will teach him all that a Feringi boy may need to know before he attends a madrisseh—a school such as Eton."

"Good morning to you, Excellency!" replied Scylla, curtsying and dimpling again. "Indeed I doubt if I am equipped to teach the little one *all* that he needs to know; but still, before the sad day comes when he has to go away, I feel sure that you will be able to secure some wise English tutor who can show him how to go on in a school such as Eton."

Just the same, she could not help feeling sorry for little Chet, now happily pulling his father's beard; it seemed a long, cold way to send him into exile, and she had heard that great severities were practiced in English schools. Cal had often congratulated himself that he had escaped such a fate.

"What do you think of the armor that Kamaran Sahib has brought me, mademoiselle?" inquired the Maharajah. "Will not my soldiers shine splendidly in these breastplates? And my friend here assures me that they will keep out a musket bullet at anything over one hundred yards and perhaps even closer."

"It is certainly a very handsome article," agreed Scylla, admiring the cuirass. "Only, I ask myself, will the Maharajah's soldiers, who are used to lighter clothing, be able to stand the weight when fighting, especially in hilly ground, for instance, and under the hot sun of this country?"

The Maharajah looked affronted, but Cameron laughed.

"She has a head on her shoulders, this young lady," he told the Maharajah. "You should employ *her* as your daroga, Excellency!"

"The soldiers will practice wearing the breastplates daily, until they are accustomed," the Maharajah said testily.

Scylla, seeing that she had ruffled the royal sensibilities, was about to take her leave and go on, when the colonel drew her to one side, taking the opportunity of doing so as the Maharajah, first embracing him tenderly, handed over little Chet to an ayah who came salaaming to receive him.

"I hope that you are not too anxious about your brother, Miss Paget," he said in a low voice. "I do not believe that the seizure was a bad one or need give you any particular concern—but of course I would not have encouraged his going to such an affair had I known that he was subject—"

"*Seizure?* What are you talking about, Colonel Cameron?"

Scylla had gone very pale and stared at him with enormous eyes.

A couple of questions by Cameron elicited from her the fact that Cal was still sleeping, and the servants, believing that he was in a state of stupor caused by drink or opium, had not mentioned that he had been carried home unconscious by Colonel Cameron in the small hours.

Cameron rapidly explained the situation.

"I am sure that your guardian will tell you there is no cause for alarm," he ended reassuringly. "I have known highly strung young men like your brother occasionally taken with such spasms—ten to one he'll grow out of the tendency in a few years—"

In spite of his assurances she still looked pale and startled, and murmured to herself, "Oh, I *wish* I could get him away from this place." Then, recalling her whereabouts, she thanked Cameron very warmly and ingenuously. "I collect, sir, that you had considerable trouble escorting him home; we must be exceedingly thankful to you for that! Heaven knows what would have become of him otherwise—it does not bear thinking of—"

She was about to leave him when the Maharajah called to both of them.

"There is a thing that I would like to say to you both—my Yagistani friends," he announced. Wondering what he had in mind—for he looked extremely serious—Scylla did not trouble to correct his error in making her into an honorary Yagistani but listened politely, as did Colonel Cameron.

"There is a charge I should like to lay on you," the Maharajah continued, "for I am aware that you are both people of honor and responsibility—as also is my friend the Sahiba Musson, but she hardly ever comes to see me any more."

"Yes, Excellency? Whatever it is that you wish, you know we will gladly do it, if it is within our power," Cameron said.

"Ah, but it may not be easy. That is why I ask you both together, so that you will be a reminder, one to the other." The Maharajah's river-brown eyes moved from Cameron to Scylla and back. "I ask you—if anything of an untoward nature should happen to me—as the gods in their wisdom know may happen to all mortals at all times—will you both promise to me that you will undertake to convey my little Chet Singh to my cousin in London, or see him conveyed there? Even if he is yet too young for the madrisseh? For although I may be with the gods, I think my heart would be anxious about him, and I shall rest more happily if I know that he is away in that foreign land with my cousin. The palace of Ziatur might not be safe for him if I am no longer here."

"May Your Excellency live forever," Scylla said promptly. "But let us hope that Heaven allows you many more years yet, until your little son is old enough to order his own traveling arrangements—"

Her eyes met those of Cameron; she observed him to be as troubled as she was. Cameron, in fact, could not help uneasily remembering the soothsayer's words of last night and Mihal's look of total composure, surveying the dead body, as he said, "It is necessary to stop the mouths of those who prophesy to kings."

"Nay, but promise!" the Maharajah insisted. "Swear on your Yagistani gods."

So they both promised, and then Scylla hurried away, late again, to her other pair of princes, who were impatiently awaiting her, pulling straws, meanwhile, as to which was to have first dip into an enormous plate of sweetmeats, honey and curd nuggets, globes of sugar spun on a thread, and sugar-coated crystallized fruits, which had been sent to them by their stepmother the Rani Sada. Scylla forbade either of them to touch a single candy until lesson time was over; wondering, meanwhile, with one corner of her mind why Sada should trouble to

send a gift to her stepsons, for whom she entertained the most profound
indifference, concentrating, as she did, all her affections upon her own
child, a fat spoiled little boy of three called Ajit, who was seldom seen
outside of her apartments. But perhaps she, also, was looking ahead
and cultivating possible friends all over the palace. . . .

Scylla was too perturbed about her brother to have much attention
to spare for palace politics today, however. She could not wait to get
away and study Cal for herself—ask him if this was the first such seizure he had suffered, or had there been others? Did Miss Musson
know of this tendency? Did he remember last night's attack, or was the
occasion blanked out in his mind? Now, putting her own impressions
together with facts gleaned from Miss Musson about other such cases,
Scylla could see that everything about her brother's temperament
dovetailed with the likelihood of his having an epileptic tendency—his
dreaminess, moodiness, fits of energy alternated with lethargy, his
strange detachment from the world about him, his tendency for deep,
deep sleep. . . .

Never had two hours gone so slowly.

"Good-by, boys," she said at last, gathering up their geometry exercises to take to Cal. "Don't eat yourselves sick, now. And I will see you
tomorrow at the same time—"

"Au revoir, mademoiselle! Will you not take a bonbon, mademoiselle?"

"Thank you, no! I do not wish to become as plump as Mahtab
Kour," she said outrageously, and left them giggling at such an
improbability.

On her way along one of the palace galleries, Scylla was intercepted
by a servant with a message that the Mahtab Kour wished for her
company, but she excused herself on the grounds that her brother was
sick and that she must hurry home with all possible speed, promising,
however, to call in the following day, and sending a message of extravagant thanks for the beautiful sari.

As on a previous visit she sensed, rather than heard, a presence overhead, and looked up in time to catch a twitch of a curtain in an upstairs gallery; the palace felt even more alive than usual with whispers

and tiptoeings, unseen watchers and listeners. Scylla hurried out into the courtyard with relief, wondering absently why Mahtab Kour's servant—the fat, surly Huneefa—had seemed so astonished to see her? But all other considerations were overborne by her anxiety about Cal as she summoned Abdul from his shady spot by the great gate and made her way homeward through the teeming streets.

Cal, when she reached the bungalow, had just sleepily strolled out onto the veranda and was attacking a large slice of watermelon. His only emotion, when Scylla burst out with solicitous inquiries, seemed to be a mild impatience and disgruntlement.

"Oh, botheration! It was nothing—the merest trifle! Do not be boring on about the confounded business, my dear."

Questioning, however, elicited the fact that he could recall nothing at all of the circumstances of his seizure or how it had come about; could not, indeed, remember anything much about the visit to the fortuneteller.

"There was a skinny blind fellow in a loincloth, calling on Tazreel and Bezroth and a whole lot of other djinns and demons—it was a decidedly tedious occasion, if the truth be told; oh yes, and a girl was playing wearisome stuff on a flute; I think I must have fallen asleep."

"But do you feel in good health now, Cal dear?"

"Lord, yes, never better! In perfectly plump currant. I'll take you riding to the Great King's tomb, if you wish!"

"Do not be absurd! It is by far too hot! But tell me, love—has this ever happened before?"

Intensive questioning elicited the reluctant answer that he had had one or two minor seizures of a similar nature in the last few months—generally when something had occurred to startle or trouble him, or, sometimes, as a result of external physical circumstances, such as dazzling or flickering lights. These brief attacks had passed over as swiftly as they had come, and seemed no more than a momentary spell of oblivion, an "otherwhereness" as he put it.

"But, gracious heavens, Cal! Supposing such an attack were to occur while you were on horseback, miles from the town!"

"I do not think it would," he replied, after considering the matter.

"I feel almost certain that such attacks do not occur while I am mentally or physically occupied. They seem to accompany inertia, not activity. Now pray, Scylla dear, do not plague me about it any more—if *I* do not trouble my head about it, why should *you?* I have a great notion for a section of my poem about the olive—the sacred tree of Athens—and how Alexander brought it, or the legend of it, to India, and it became transformed into the sacred tree of the Hindu scriptures —so, please, leave me in peace, will you, like a sweet girl, and let me work?"

"But if your attacks come as a result of immobility," said his exasperating sister, "should you not be up and about, taking exercise?"

"Which is the more important—my poetry or a few trifling physical symptoms?" he demanded. She was obliged to agree that his poetry was important.

"Oh, by the bye, Ram says that dentist fellow, Wharton, has been seen in the town. Why do not you occupy yourself by writing a letter to our cousin Juliana?"

"You think you can fob me off. Oh, very well, I will leave you in peace!"

Scylla made her way to the hospital, intending to ask Miss Musson's opinion about Cal's state. She found that lady very preoccupied and worried, however, over the case of little Bisesa, the cook's daughter, who acted as maidservant and ayah in the bungalow.

"It came on so suddenly! I cannot decide what ails her. It is not prickly heat—nor mango rash—and although the symptoms, thank heaven, do not seem those of smallpox, the poor girl is in great distress —none of my remedies, at present, seem to help at all. She was perfectly well at breakfast time—then a couple of hours ago her father brought her here in *such* a state—I devoutly hope that it is not some infection that will spread like wildfire."

Scylla went in to see the girl, for whom she had a great affection. Bisesa was only fourteen or so, a slender, pretty creature, slim as a gazelle, with enormous, velvety eyes. Normally her skin was a pale smooth brown, but now it had become thickly covered with tiny angry blisters; the chief areas of infection were her shoulders, arms, and upper torso, hips, thighs, the sides of her neck, even the top of her head under the hair; the irritation from the blisters was so excruciating that Miss Musson had bandaged her hands, in an attempt to prevent the poor girl rubbing her skin or scratching it—but the bandages were of little avail, she lay frantically rasping herself raw with her bandaged fists and weeping with agony, calling on her dead mother to come and cure her.

"I shall have to give her a dose of opium," said Miss Musson, much perturbed, and did so. "Now stay with her, Scylla, talk to her and soothe her until it takes effect; I have sent for her sister Ameera to come and be with her."

Scylla sat with the poor child for several hours, gently preventing her from scratching herself and trying to distract her, talking about her forthcoming wedding and all its ceremonies, singing lullabies, until at last the opium acted and she fell into a troubled sleep. Miss Musson and Scylla covered her with lotions, but these, usually efficacious in cases of prickly heat, seemed slow in having any beneficial result.

When they went home at dusk, leaving Bisesa in the charge of her sister and old Jameela, Scylla unburdened herself to her guardian about Cal's disability. She found, as she had half suspected, that this news came as no surprise to Miss Musson.

"He is of an epileptic constitution; I have apprehended as much for the last year. But do not be putting yourself in a pucker about it, my dear child; there is nothing to alarm you. Think how many great men have been similarly affected—Julius Caesar—St. Paul—indeed quite half the saints, I understand; it seems an affliction particularly disposed to single out those of a saintly disposition, or men of genius. If our boy is *that*," she said, smiling, "we must not repine, should Providence think fit to touch him also with the accompanying weakness—perhaps as a reminder that no man can be expected to be quite perfect!"

"No, ma'am, I see," Scylla agreed, somewhat comforted. "Cal, certainly, is not perfect—I know that! What must we do, then?"

"Why, try not to kick up a great dust about it—as Cal would say— but make sure, unobtrusively, that the dear boy has plenty of wholesome food, enough exercise, and—if possible—a calm, well-ordered life, without unsuitable excitement. Sometimes young men grow out of such disorders, acquired in the teens—the visitation may be an accompaniment of sudden late growth."

"I see, ma'am. Thank you. I will try—I will try to be sensible about it."

While Scylla was inwardly demanding of herself how such a well-ordered life as Miss Musson prescribed could be achieved among the unpredictable oriental ups and downs of their existence in Ziatur, they arrived back at the bungalow.

There Cal, to be sure, seemed innocuously engaged on the veranda, ink on his brow, wreathed about with reams of scribbled paper and the dozen or so quill pens he liked to have by him when inspiration struck; he gave them a vague nod and returned without pause to his writing.

Miss Musson and Scylla repaired to their respective chambers to wash and rest before the evening meal. In her room Scylla noticed with absent surprise that the rose-colored sari, Mahtab Kour's gift, which she had left swathed in its muslin wrappings on top of her wooden chest, seemed to have been unwrapped and untidily tossed onto the floor. Perhaps gray apes had got in, as they were sometimes prone to do, from the loquat trees in the garden, to scamper about and make mischief; but it was odd that nothing else had been disturbed, Scylla thought, glancing around the room. It seemed almost as if someone who had a spite against her, who resented her having been sent the gift, had played this childish prank—but who could have done such a thing? The thought of the Rani Sada did just brush Scylla's mind—but that seemed too improbable; besides, how could she, or any emissary of hers, possibly have had access to the bungalow? No, it must have been apes; if poor Bisesa had not been at the hospital, she would have picked up and refolded the sari, and its owner would never have known about the occurrence. Or no—she must have learned about it, Scylla found, picking up the garment and rather hastily and distastefully rewrapping it (she could not get out of her mind the notion that it was intended as a bribe for informing the Maharajah about Sada's intrigue with Mihal). The accident could hardly have been concealed from her, for the choli was quite badly torn at the neck. Well, what does it matter, I should never have worn it, Scylla thought, bundling it all together inside the muslin; and, going to wash her hands, she resolved to mend the choli as invisibly as possible and give the garment to little Bisesa for her wedding—even torn as it was, with all those seed pearls it must be worth a handsome sum, and the child would have nothing else so fine; besides, she would certainly treasure it, as it came from the palace.

They were just finishing supper—for which Cal had with difficulty been dragged from his writing—when Colonel Cameron was announced. He entered the room pale, dusty, and evidently laboring under very considerable distress. Miss Musson took one look at him and sent Habib-ulla for brandy-pani. When a large dose of this had been administered, "What is it, my friend?" she asked quietly.

"The Maharajah is dead," he said.

"Oh, the poor man!" exclaimed Scylla. "How strangely sudden! Why, he did not look so ill this morning."

"It was not illness." Cameron pushed a hand over his dusty brow. Unobtrusively, Miss Musson refilled his brandy glass. "They will be crying it in the streets any minute now. I came to tell you so—so that you can be deciding what is best for you to do."

"*Not* illness?" Miss Musson queried. "Then—an accident?"

He gave a grim snort. "No more an accident than the rising of the sun—if I am any judge."

"What happened?"

Even Cal was attending now, having come out of his poetic trance to listen, though still with a somewhat disengaged air.

"Why, we were returning from a review of the troops out on the plain—you were right," Cameron said to Scylla, "it will take months of wear before the men become accustomed to those French breastplates—but the Maharajah was pleased with them and thought they looked very fine—he was riding ahead on his elephant, I following behind on another—as he went through the archway of the great gate, a huge stone became detached from the masonry and fell on him, knocking him off his beast."

"It *could* have been an accident, surely?" interjected Miss Musson.

"What followed certainly could *not*," Cameron said harshly. "He was lying on the ground—I had jumped down and was coming to his aid, and the mahout of his elephant was on the other side—when the beast shouldered past us; it knelt on him, carefully and deliberately, on his loins, his chest, his knees—I heard his bones crack, I heard him scream. Oh, dear God, I have seen plenty of deaths in my time, but none more horrible than that—"

"Could the beast have gone *musth?*" demanded Miss Musson, looking very appalled.

"No, ma'am, that elephant was not mad, it was as calm and collected as you or I. It had been trained to that little trick. And I—heaven help me—I should have seen this coming—heaven knows, I had clear warning—perhaps I might have been able to take steps to avert it—"

"My dear man, how could you possibly have done that?" demanded Miss Musson. "You are not Providence itself, to be everywhere at once! There is not the least sense in accusing yourself so. Rather let us be considering what is best to be done next. You were very right to come to me at once—I must be off to the palace directly."

And she called loudly for Abdul.

"Up to the *palace?* My dear ma'am—Miss Amanda—are you run quite mad? Why up there? The palace is the *last* place to be visiting just now—"

"Of *course* I must go to the palace," retorted Miss Musson, equipping herself as she spoke with her large hat, her burqa, and a copy of the Holy Scriptures. "If I do not go there instantly and apply all my powers of argument, that poor silly woman will be persuaded that she ought to commit *sati,* and probably a dozen others along with her!"

And despite all Cameron's arguments she brushed him aside and departed, urging him to remain in the bungalow and take some supper— "for I am sure you have had none"—and keep the twins company.

As she rode off on her pony they could hear the wailing begin, high on the walls of the citadel, accompanied by the sound of drums and conches and the solemn boom of ceremonial cannon.

Cameron sat unnoticingly gulping down the food brought him by Habib-ulla. He looked both sad and angry.

"No doubt Mihal will arrange a huge state funeral now—just the kind of thing he would do, to display his pomp and wealth to all the neighboring princes—after having taken pains to arrange for the fatality—"

"You think he did so?" asked Scylla uneasily. Not, indeed, that she had any doubts on the matter; she thought so herself.

"My dear child, there is no possible question—What is the matter?" he broke off to ask. Scylla had been absently rubbing her hands together for the last few minutes as if they irritated or pained her; now she looked down at them with an exclamation of surprise and annoyance.

"My hands—I was rubbing lotion on that poor little girl in the hospital and it looks as though I must have caught her infection—I do trust Miss Musson has not taken it too—"

Scylla's hands were covered all over with a close, thick sprinkling of little red, angry-looking blisters.

V

For six weeks after her return from London, Fanny Paget was confined to her chamber. Thomas gave it out to the family and neighbors that she had been taken ill in London; the coach journey had been too much for her, she was to see no one, speak to nobody, not even her stepchildren. She herself seemed glad enough to accede to this prohibition.

The girls, wondering, intrigued, mystified, discussed the matter much among themselves—had Fanny somehow disgraced herself in

London? Committed some extravagance? Made eyes at some young fellow? (This was Martha's contribution.) Asked for some piece of finery? (This was little Patty's idea.) None of them came near the truth. Kate, the housekeeper, who took Missus her meals, reported that she picked like a sparrow and looked like a shadow, hardly able to raise her head from the pillow. Indeed Dr. Chilgrove had to be called in and shook his head over her; he could not discover anything constitutionally wrong but said she was in a dangerously low state and prescribed port wine, nourishing broth, and cheerful company. Perhaps one of her sisters, he suggested, might be summoned, to be with her for a few weeks until the birth of her child, now some three or four months distant, and help raise her spirits?

"Tush, sir, she may have plenty of *cheerful company*, as you call it, if she chooses to avail herself of it, in the persons of my daughters," said Thomas, annoyed.

"Yes, my dear sir, I am sure, but—her own family, you know—women at such times—not creatures susceptible to reason—I'll ask her how she feels in the matter—shall I, eh?"

And without bothering to wait for Thomas's permission, he returned to the sickroom and said to Fanny:

"How would it be, ma'am, if we were to fetch along one of your sisters to bear you company and sit with you—would that please you—hey?"

It was amazing how the poor child's eyes brightened.

"Oh yes, Doctor, if you please," whispered the threadlike voice from the bed. "If my sister Lydia—that is, if the others can spare her since poor Papa's death—but they may be glad to find somewhere for her to stay—since they are all obliged to leave the Rectory—"

For the expected news had come that Fanny's father had succumbed to his long illness and the hard winter, and Fanny's sisters must shift out of the house to make room for the new incumbent's family, and go off to live with various harassed and unwelcoming aunts. The Rev. Theophilus must have been happy to know, as he died, that he had managed to leave at least *one* of his daughters safely settled. And now the thought that she might be able to offer a home to Lydia rejoiced Fanny's heart.

"Heaven only knows where we are to put her—she will have to go up in the attic!" exclaimed Thomas furiously when the doctor reappeared with the firm instructions that Lydia was to be sent for. And, when Chilgrove had gone, Thomas walked in to look at his wife with the usual feelings of baffled rage, thirst of unslaked curiosity—in a word, total frustration. For there she lay, weak as a blade of grass, pale as a wraith, wholly at his mercy—and yet in no possible way, by no means of persuasion at his power, could he wring from her any information as to where she had been during those days in London.

Whatever menaces he offered did not, apparently, seem any worse to her than her present state; she was invulnerable to him there. Physically, to be sure, he could still frighten her, and did; she shrank when he came into the room, and still more when he walked up to the bed; he took a certain pleasure in that; but mentally she had somehow escaped him and, whatever he might do, he could not come up with her.

However this notion of Fanny's sister visiting her could soon be scotched; and was.

Thomas's elderly mother, who had removed to the Isle of Wight upon her remarriage, and had continued there after the death of her second husband, living, upon the annuity he had left her, very modestly, in a small cottage, with a companion, was obliged, upon the death of the latter lady, to make some demands upon the doubtful kindness of her elder son. She would probably have avoided doing so if she could; there had been a total breach between them some years after her second marriage, due to Thomas's detestation of his stepfather and half brother; but that was long ago; the old lady was now half blind and nearly senile, with nobody else to call upon; and so, very reluctantly, in her difficulties, she had recourse to Thomas. He, if differently circumstanced, would very likely have found it more convenient to house her in a tiny cottage, looked after indifferently, for a pittance, by some old sloven; but as things were he was glad to make a virtue of necessity and say to Dr. Chilgrove next day, with a clear conscience:

"I am sorry to confound your plans, my dear sir, but it is quite out of my power to accommodate Mrs. Paget's sister at present. I am obliged to take in my old mother to live with me. She is on the Isle of Wight, you know, and I cannot leave her there, with gunboats stationed at all the ports and invasion expected from week to week. And my mother will need an attendant with her in the house; as it is, I am forced to get rid of my good old housekeeper Kate and have a woman come in by the day instead, so that Kate's room will be free for my mother's nurse."

The doctor was obliged to acknowledge the force of this argument and hoped, verbally (although his private expectations were not so sanguine), that the interest of caring for the old lady, and her company, would have a beneficial effect upon Fanny's low spirits.

Thomas was delighted to have a good pretext for getting rid of Kate, who had shown, of late weeks, a somewhat defiant and partisan spirit, tending to side with her mistress over trifling matters. She was, accordingly, given her notice and turned off; a Mrs. Strudwick, a widow who lived in Petworth, was hired to come in daily and take care of the housekeeping; thus, at one stroke, Thomas was rid of a potential troublemaker and also satisfactorily reduced his household expenditure; for a daily woman need not be paid so much as one who lived in. And the arrival of his mother, though tiresome, would, financially, be a positive gain, for he would derive the benefit of her annuity, plus the proceeds from the sale of her cottage.

He assumed that his mother's annuity must perish with her own demise, but in the meantime he would have the administration of it, so it was quite in his interest to preserve her alive for a while; and when she did die, he felt sure that she must have *some* savings, for her second husband had been a well-to-do coachmaker—and there might be a few trinkets, which would come in handy for the girls.

Quite cheered by these reflections, he was in an unusually benign mood and prepared to listen indulgently, for once, to a request from his daughter Martha.

"Papa, will you not let me take lessons upon the harp? You would not in Gosport because it would have meant the use of the carriage to take me quite across the town, but here there is a lady living very close, in East Street, who gives harp lessons—only two shillings an hour—and it is but five minutes' walk from our house, Tess says—please, Papa?—Unless indeed you would *buy* a harp so that we could practice at home—Jem bootboy told me of one he saw advertised in Midhurst, only twenty pounds—"

"*Twenty pounds?* Are you out of your mind, miss?" exploded her father.

But cunning Martha had phrased her request that way around on purpose, knowing that, in comparison with a twenty-pound harp in Midhurst, two-shilling harp lessons just around the corner appeared an economy; and permission for the lessons was duly given, provided that Bet accompany her sister to the lessons and they were escorted to and from the house of the instructress—a Mrs. Dawtry—by Tess or the new housekeeper.

Thomas had in fact of late been feeling a certain dissatisfaction with his daughters. Tiresome though Fanny was—obstinate, secretive, willful—he could not help seeing that, in her gentle manners, her education, all her small graces, elegancies, and friendly, solicitous ways, she was far superior in charm and appeal to his girls, and he had begun dimly to wonder how much chance they had of catching husbands. He had relied upon Fanny's example to instill in them some idea of how to comport themselves, but nothing like that seemed to be happening; and he most certainly did not wish them to be left upon his hands unwed all their lives, eating far too much butter on their bread, constantly wanting new ribbons, and needing a fire in the parlor every night. If lessons on the harp would advance their chances of matrimony—and since the lessons only cost two shillings an hour—lessons would be sanctioned. Bet could doubtless pick up a few hints while watching Martha.

Accordingly the following week saw two major changes in the household at the Hermitage; Bet and Martha went off, two mornings a week, to Mrs. Dawtry's house, whence harp notes could be heard emanating, somewhat discordantly, from an upper window; and the old lady arrived with her attendant from Ryde.

A third event was that Fanny came out of her chamber.

This occurrence might not have passed off with so little remark had not Thomas been greatly preoccupied, at that time, with press gang affairs.

Although merchant-navy seamen and fishermen were, theoretically, exempt from impressment, as were harvesters and "navvies," workers on roads and canals, this exemption was by no means total. Sailors were often taken from privateer ships, even though these were supposed to be protected by their letters of marque, and fishermen were impressed so frequently that, some years before, the entire fishing community of the town of Worthing had banded together and purchased a term of immunity in return for a contribution of five men, who self-sacrificingly volunteered, and a cash payment of forty pounds. At the time, the neighboring village of Brighthelmstone, or Brighton, had expressed great scorn over this pusillanimous and servile behavior; its fishermen had declared that they would never so demean themselves as to "pay off the scurvy gangers." No, the free fishermen of Brighton were not going to submit to that! In consequence, their defiance of the press gang, over the years, had reached such a pass that the inhabitants had now put up a placard declaring that the whole male population of the place considered themselves immune; and this act of what practically amounted to treason was regarded very seriously indeed by the regulating officers of the local press gangs.

Brighton did not properly come within Thomas's province—the town had a gang and regulating officer of its own, Captain Pankhurst, but as his gang, numbering only fourteen men, was by no means large enough to deal with the situation, he had sought help from the neighboring impress officers. A sudden surprise attack on the town was planned, and the regulating officers were obliged to hold many meetings, at much inconvenience to themselves, and loss of local revenue, in order to arrive at a time both suitable to all of them and strategically satisfactory. Times and tides therefore had to be taken into account, and also strict secrecy had to be observed; it was a knotty business altogether and kept Thomas much from home at this time. He greatly begrudged the day required to bring his mother back from

Chichester harbor and settle her into the Hermitage; and, having wasted as little time as possible on the latter process, he was off at dawn the next day to collogue with his brother regulating officers at the town of Shoreham, giving his household a terse intimation that he could not say when he would be back.

The new housekeeper at the Hermitage, Mrs. Strudwick, did not seem an accommodating woman. She was a widow, stiff, upright, with a knot of gray hair, a whaleboned torso, and a glacial eye; which factors had served to recommend her to Thomas.

However when she presently marched into Fanny's chamber with a basin of toast gruel and the rehearsed announcement that she "would not be able to keep on this running up- and downstairs with basins on trays now the old lady was come," she was startled to find her mistress already out of bed, weakly but resolutely tying her petticoat strings.

"Thank you, Mrs. Strudwick; you may leave the gruel. I will drink it up here and be downstairs very soon," young Mrs. Paget said with gentle dignity. Her pregnancy was very visible by now; only a couple more months to go, Mrs. Strudwick judged with expert eye; and she looked drawn and fagged, her wrists as thin as angelica stalks, but quite composed in herself, as she pulled the cambric petticoat about her.

"If you would be so kind as to send Tess to me, in about ten minutes, to help me with my hair, I should be obliged," Fanny added, as the housekeeper stood somewhat taken aback "with the wind taken out of her sails" as she would have expressed it herself, and she found herself replying:

"That's right, ma'am, you shouldn't be lifting your arms overmuch, not while you're expecting," in quite a friendly tone.

"Is my husband's mother quite comfortable?" Fanny inquired.

"As to comfortable, ma'am, I'm sure I can't say; she's a rum 'un and no mistake. You can't get much sense out of her. And as for that one that's supposed to be looking after her—" Mrs. Strudwick cast her eyes to heaven expressively.

Fanny, however, showing no disposition to listen to gossip, said, "Thank you, Mrs. Strudwick. That will be all, then," in so soft but positive a tone that Mrs. Strudwick found herself outside the door before she hardly knew how she had got there. She consoled herself for this oddity, however, by thinking, Well, *she's* in store for a shock when she sees what's come to the house, that's one thing certain.

Fanny, left alone, threw a calico wrapper over her petticoat and walked to the window, holding the bowl of hot toast gruel. There was a semicircular seat inside the bow; she sat there, with one foot curled under her, enjoying the warmth of the morning sun on her aching back, and looked out at the garden. She could hear the birds, bursting with song, and see buds on the trees; a splash of yellow showed where daffodils bloomed in front of Thomas's garden house; and a couple of cherry trees were in tender transition from coral-colored buds to the full fountain of white blossom. Beyond, the green angelic hill soared upward, the blue plain stretched off into the distance.

April will be here in a few days, Fanny thought, her heart lifting; and she remembered how young and untroubled the April of last year had found her. What a gulf of experience stretched between then and now! But daffodils and cherry blossom remained forever the same, and she murmured (for she had read immense quantities of poetry in her father's library and had a fund of it by heart):

> *"Fair daffodils, we weep to see*
> *You haste away so soon;*
> *As yet the early-rising sun*
> *Has not attained his noon. . . ."*

And then, as had so often happened at her childhood home, or in the walks and fields of Sway and the New Forest, notes of music danced, unsummoned, into Fanny's head and supplied an accompaniment for the lines she had just spoken. They sang themselves to her, words and tune knitting indissolubly together into a little spring of refreshment that seemed to come straight from something exterior to herself—the house, perhaps, she fancifully thought; perhaps this strain of music was the method the house found to communicate its feeling of good will. For she still—despite many periods of utter, black unhappiness—had this abiding impression that the house was her friend—it had something to say to her, a message of warmth, of reassurance. We are here for each other; my time, too, is short, but while I am here I will enfold and cherish you, as you cherish and care for me. Something of this nature the house imparted to her, and Fanny, listening, did take comfort.

A tap sounded at the door: Tess, to help with her hair.

"Come in!" Fanny called.

The little maid crept into the room, and Fanny turned in quick concern.

"Why, Tess, what is the matter? You look dreadful."

Tess Goodger, the underservant, was a pale, gaunt little fourteen-year-old who looked hardly more than ten or eleven. Her thin, sharp features were half concealed by her cap; mostly she went about her work in the quiet apathy of timidity and undernourishment. It was plain that something was very wrong, for her drawn cheeks were the color of whey and there were great purple hollows under her eyes; the hands that combed out her mistress' ringlets were shaking uncontrollably.

"It's n-nothing, ma'am; I don't wish to worrit ye."

"But indeed I am worried, Tess; are you sick? You look so weary."

"No, I bean't sick, ma'am; but—b-but—"

Tess burst into tears, and the story came out.

Her household duties began at five, when she had to get up and light the Rumford stove in the kitchen for the servants' breakfast, sweep and scrub the kitchen, heat water for the housekeeper and men-servants to wash, lay the kitchen table, rake out the ashes in all the downstairs fireplaces, and prepare the servants' breakfast of bread and porridge. Kate, the previous housekeeper, had owned a small clock which she had allowed Tess to take to her room every night (if room it could be called; Tess slept in the loft at the top of the house, reached by a ladder) so as to ensure that she woke in time.

"Just having the clock by me bed, ma'am—I set it up on a pair o' bricks—helped me so's I never did overlie. But Kate, she took her clock with her when she was turned off—an' I ast Missus Strudwick but she won't loan me her clock acos she live at home—an' it *is* so hard to know when five o'clock come—I worrit about it all night long. Ten, fifteen times o' night I slips down the stair to look at the grandfather clock in the hall; once or twice I has just set down there, say from 'alf three to five, for I dassn't go back up, 'case I oversleep. I did, once or twice, and Missus Strudwick was *that* angry—"

"But this is ridiculous! Why can you not take the kitchen clock upstairs to bed?"

"There bain't no kitchen clock, ma'am. It got busted in the move, simmingly, an' master said 'twasn't worth getting another, for we can see the church clock do we step out into the garden."

This was true, Fanny knew; there was just a little more justification than usual for Thomas's parsimony.

"Can you not hear the church clock strike during the night, Tess?" she asked gently. "I have heard it myself, many and many a time." She shivered a little.

"No, ma'am. There bain't no window, see, where I sleep; an' to tell truth," Tess said nervously, glancing at her mistress past the strand of hair she was gently combing out, "to tell truth, I'm a bit deef; I believe it was on account of my auntie useter belt me over the ear'ole with a rolling pin if I riled her—"

"I see." That accounted, of course, for the occasions when Thomas, irritated, had shouted at Tess for not obeying him more promptly; doubtless the poor child had not heard his order the first time.

"Well, you must certainly have a clock," Fanny resolved. "Here, now—let me see—"

During her illness Thomas had abandoned his former practice of giving Fanny a small sum of housekeeping money daily; instead this had been handed, first to Kate, latterly to Mrs. Strudwick. She, when applied to, said she had no cash to spare for a clock; master had given her only enough to buy the meat, candles, green baize, and soda that were immediately required. Her expression indicated very fully that the purchase of a clock was the most wasteful, indulgent, frivolous notion that she had ever heard in her entire life.

Then Fanny was visited by a hopeful notion.

"Perhaps the old lady, Thomas's mother, will have a clock. She after all had a whole houseful of furniture; she must have brought some of her belongings with her. In any case it is certainly my duty to wait on her and find how she goes on."

Accordingly, Fanny made her slow and cumbrous way up the flight of stairs that led to the top floor and the two attic bedrooms where Thomas's mother and her attendant had been housed.

This had seemed to Fanny most unsuitable quarters for an invalid; it meant that food, slops, coals, and laundry all had to be carried up and down two flights of stairs, many times daily; and how was the poor old lady ever to be conveyed down, when she recovered from her journey enough to wish to go out of doors and take the air? Thomas, however, did not concern himself with the fatigue of domestics and did not anticipate that his mother would ever need to leave the house; indeed he thought it better that she should not, for exercise could only wear out shoe leather and increase her appetite. At present, in any case, there was no question of such a thing, for yesterday's removal had greatly exhausted the old lady and she lay in her bed, hardly able to move.

Inconvenient the attic may have been, but the view from its window was certainly superior; it faced southeast, down the valley, and commanded a prospect of the long, gradually ascending road that came into the town from Byworth and the newer gentlemen's residences which were building along the valleyside beyond the Angel Inn. Close at hand were some young apple trees, planted by the Countess van Welcker, but their tops were far below the level of the window, and the only tree that gave any promise of every reaching to such a height was the weeping ash, now so severely constrained, which grew directly outside.

The other garden trees, the hedge of young yews, and the oaks and willows in the valley were all gaily tossing their branches in a March wind; only the ash, like a prisoner with arms tied to his sides, remained motionless. To Fanny's impressionable mind the tree appeared to be brooding darkly on its wrongs: hunched, silent, immobile, it seemed to be sending vibrations of ill will toward the house. It was not the first time she had thought this.

However her business was not with trees, and she moved past the window toward the bed with its recumbent figure. Thomas's mother had been housed in the smaller of the two attics, because it was the one that possessed a fireplace (in which a very meager fire now burned); there was exceedingly little space in the room; an armchair, a washstand, a tiny table, and the bed almost completely filled it; the old lady's clothes had apparently to be accommodated in the nurse's chamber. Fanny, glancing about, could see no clock; the appointments here were sparse indeed: a clean cloth on the washstand, a hairbrush, comb, and washing utensils; nothing more.

Nobody had answered her knock, and Thomas had, in fact, warned her that his mother was somewhat hard of hearing, so she walked up to the bed and said in her clear, pretty voice:

"Good morning, ma'am! I hope that you find yourself recovered from your journey? Welcome to the Hermitage!" in a somewhat louder tone than she would normally have employed.

"Eh? Eh, what's that? What did you say?" came in a faint quaver—nervous, weak, mistrustful—from the bunched-up figure on the bed; and the old lady, who had been lying with her face to the wall, slowly turned over to peer at her visitor.

"I am sorry, ma'am, that I was indisposed and not able to greet you yesterday, on your arrival. I have not been very well," Fanny explained apologetically. A pair of pale blue, bewildered eyes surveyed her, and she held out a hand, saying with a friendly smile, "I dare say you may have guessed by now that I am your new daughter-in-law: Thomas's wife, Fanny."

"Eh—what's that? Didn't quite catch. Brandy, do you say?"

"No, ma'am, I am FANNY, your daughter-in-law."

"Daughter-in-law? Where's Emma, then? The girls' mother?"

"She has—has died, ma'am, I fear. I am Thomas's new wife."

"His new wife? Eh, yes, he did say something about her. I disremembered it." The old lady slanted a look at Fanny under her eyelids in which slyness, apprehension, and timidity seemed equally mixed; then, after a moment, she brought from under the covers, and extended, a thin, yellow, blotched claw which was visibly trembling;

Fanny took it in a firm clasp and smiled at Thomas's mother as reassuringly as she could.

"I do hope that you will be happy with us, ma'am; I will try my best to see that you are so, I promise."

Did the old lady hear? It was difficult to be sure. Her faded eyes had a restless, wandering, agitated stare; they hardly dwelt on Fanny but were off around the room, like those of some animal that finds itself in a trap. Indeed the predominating element in her character was fear—fear of the people with whom she had to deal, of her husband, her son, the nurse, her daughter-in-law—she feared all, trusted none. Only one person had not inspired fear in her, and he was dead.

"Thank you, dear, thank you," she murmured vaguely now, apprehending that some response was expected from her. "Seems strange— poor dear Emma—married to Thomas for so long—now all gone and forgotten—Eh, dear me!"

Fanny pulled up the little straight-backed padded nursing chair, which had been bought for her by direction of Dr. Chilgrove, but which she had instructed Tess to take up for the old lady, and sat down on it.

"I hope we shall soon see you out of bed, ma'am, and coming downstairs among us," she said.

"Eh, dear? No, no, Thomas would never allow it, never hear of it," said the old lady, with a fearful glance toward the door.

"Thomas is out all day, ma'am," Fanny said coaxingly. "And I am persuaded that it would be better for you to take the air, now and again—we may procure you a basket chair, you know, and Jem bootboy can push you in it—or at least you could come and sit in the parlor. Will you not do that? Did you not walk out of doors where you lived before, in the Isle of Wight?"

"Eh?—Yes, out all the time—shops, circulating library—haberdashers," replied the old lady when the question had been repeated a couple of times. She showed, now, a gleam of pleasure and intelligence as she made the reply, confirming, had she but known it, all her son's worst fears about her spendthrift habits.

"What should I call you, ma'am?—for Thomas, I am afraid, omitted to tell me your married name—I know it is not Paget."

This question, however, appeared too complicated for the old lady; she frowned, shaking her head so perplexedly that her nightcap almost fell off, and Fanny had to help her retie the strings over her scanty white hair, which was scraped back into a plait.

"Well, I will call you Mother—may I do that? For my own mother died at my birth, so I never had the comfort of one and shall be glad to do so now."

It was plain, however, that most of the comforting would have to be on the other side, but a nod presently indicated that the purport of these words had found its way into the old lady's bewildered mind and she timidly returned Fanny's clasp.

"What can I do for you now?" Fanny inquired. "Shall I read to you —or is there any service I can render you?"

This question, also, took some time to penetrate, but presently, when it did, the old lady intimated that she would be glad to have her back rubbed, for it was paining her severely after the long, unaccustomed ferry and coach journey, or, as she herself put it, "It do fairly give me the jip, dearie."

Fanny who, due to her advanced pregnancy, frequently suffered from pain in her own back, had every sympathy with this request and had been gently massaging her mother-in-law's lower spine for seven or eight minutes, and making such simple conversation as occurred to her, when there was a brisk step on the stair, a clink of crockery, and the door was unceremoniously thrust open.

"Lord! I'm sorry, I'm sure, ma'am—I'd no notion that anybody was in the room," said the newcomer, dumping a tray with a basin of bread and milk on the table, and she went on, addressing the old lady in a loud cheerful voice as if she had been a small child, "There we are, then, missus, all right and tight! Nice breakfast for you! You just set up in bed and eat it as quick as you can. Why, fancy that—has Mrs. Paget here been a-rubbing of you—that was monstrous kind, now, wasn't it? Fancy your demeaning yourself to do such a thing, ma'am!" and she darted a glance at Fanny that was half scornful, half condescending.

Fanny, quietly removing herself from the bedside, said that she would intrude no longer but asked the nurse to let her know if anything lacked in her own quarters or the sickroom. From the somewhat contemptuous smile bestowed on her, she inferred that it had already been made abundantly plain that all orders and supplies must be expected from the master of the house or Mrs. Strudwick, and her own insignificant role had evidently been conveyed to the nurse, who, however, curtsied slightly and said missus was very kind and obliging, but nothing was needed.

"Lord bless you, I dare say the old lady won't be a mite of trouble," she added with a smiling, disdainful glance toward the bed, where the lady in question was already avidly gulping down bread and milk. "Biddable as a lamb, she do seem, compared with some I've had charge of."

"Indeed? You appear young to have had such wide experience," Fanny replied politely. "I am afraid I have not been told your name, Miss—?"

"Baggot, ma'am—Missus Lily Baggot," said the nurse with a simper. "Mercy, yes, I've seen a-many into their coffins, my name is well known in Gosport, I promise you—Cap'n Paget knew what he was about when he hired me to come and take charge of the old lady. I'll take famous care of you, shan't I, Missus What's-your-name," Nurse Baggot went on, removing the empty bowl from her patient so briskly —indeed before the old lady was quite ready to part with it—that a small quantity of milk was spilled on the sheet. "Tt, tt, missus, we shall have to be carefuller than that, shan't we?" she observed, playfully slapping the wrist of her patient, who flinched back in alarm. "No spilling on sheets, ma'am, or master'll be *that* put out! Now then, here's the hot water; I'll just wash your face and get you all redd up for the day."

Fanny, at this hint, was about to withdraw, but from the doorway inquired softly, on an afterthought:

"Nurse, can you tell me my mother-in-law's name? I know it is not Paget, for she was married again after my husband's father died."

"Ay, but master don't care for her other name," the nurse said with a grin. "He gave word as we were to call her Missus Paget here; and it don't make any odds to her, for the old girl's as deaf as a post, you could call her Mrs. Punchinello and *she'd* never know any different— would you, dear?" she added as she vigorously hoisted the old lady up in bed, propped her with a bolster, and removed her nightcap.

Fanny took herself slowly and thoughtfully downstairs. She was not sure that she liked Mrs. Baggot, who had a high color, a mass of tightly curled glossy black hair, sharp dark eyes holding a somewhat predatory expression, a wide mouth that smiled a great deal, displaying two gold teeth, without giving the impression of real good nature, a buxom hourglass figure, and an arm like a leg of mutton. Doubtless the nurse was strong and capable at her job, but Fanny wondered, rather doubtfully, whether she could be trusted to be altogether kind to the old lady. However so long as Thomas's mother was frequently visited by other members of the family and spent a fair proportion of her time downstairs, it should be possible to ensure that her treatment continued all it ought to be.

Now Fanny recalled that one of her original motives in paying the visit had been to discover whether by any chance her mother-in-law possessed a clock she did not immediately need that might be spared for the use of Tess. Having now observed the simplicity of the old lady's appointments, Fanny doubted the utility of this errand but was turning to retrace her steps when she encountered Mrs. Lily Baggot coming down with the empty breakfast bowl.

"Not that it ain't Tess's job to fetch it," remarked the nurse with a kind of cheerful irritability, "but a body can wait half the morning for *her*—and meanwhile there's nowhere to lay so much as a hairpin."

"Do you by any chance know if my mother-in-law has such a thing as a spare timepiece—to save my troubling her again?" Fanny inquired, thinking how strange and grasping the request must sound.

"Lord bless you, no, ma'am! Master stopped off in Chichester yesterday and sold all her trunks full of bits to an auctioneer," said Mrs.

Baggot carelessly, going on down the stairs. "He said there was no space for her to bring more'n a couple of gowns here, and no need, either, for she'd not be stirring out o' doors, there's none as knows her in this town, and she might as well keep her chamber. All he kept back was a few trinkets, as much as'd go into a dressing case, but her household gear was sold off—no sense in keeping a passel of old, worn things as'd only remind her of times gone past, he said." And Mrs. Baggot bustled off with a flounce of her striped poplin skirts.

Fanny returned to her own chamber and took a pair of unworn silk stockings from her drawer. She had been saving them for some special occasion, but it seemed unlikely that such an occasion would ever arrive, and she felt no particular pang at parting from them.

Downstairs, ten minutes later, Fanny was putting on her shabby pelisse when she was startled to hear the nurse say to Mrs. Strudwick:

"Did master come back from Shoreham? I must speak to him."

"Ay, he came back; he's in his garden room. But no one's allowed to disturb him *there*, not nohow."

"Well, he's going to hear from *me*," said the nurse, and swung on her heel.

"Don't blame me if you come back with a flea in your ear!" Mrs. Strudwick called after her.

Aghast, Fanny watched through the drawing-room window as Mrs. Baggot marched down the yew walk and rapped on the door of the garden room. This was a small stone building about fifty yards away from the house, at the northern end of the yew walk. It had been built so as to overlook the valley and commanded a magnificent view from the window on the valley side. Fanny had gathered that the lady for whom the Hermitage had been built, Madame Reynard, had used the little place for a summerhouse and (so rumor suggested) a rendezvous in which to meet her lover, Lord Egremont, who had visited her by means of an underground passage leading from a vault under the building to Petworth House. The passage was there still but Thomas had had its door nailed shut and the trap door to the vault secured with a padlock. He himself used the garden house as a study and workroom. Here he did the mill's accounts and went through a good deal of press gang business also, for the impress rendezvous in the town was merely a dismal little room hired from the Bull Inn. Members of his household were strictly forbidden to enter the garden room at any time (except for Jem bootboy, who was periodically summoned to make up the fire) and Fanny would not have dreamed of setting foot in the place. Indeed she carefully avoided that end of the yew walk unless certain that Thomas was away from home. To see Mrs. Baggot imperiously rap on the door and then open it, plainly without even waiting for a summons, turned Fanny pale with fright. She lingered, petrified, expecting to see the nurse come flying out with scarlet cheeks the very next minute, but, astonishingly, this did not occur, and the door was closed.—Possibly she was discussing with Thomas some medical aspect of his mother's condition.

It occurred to Fanny that now would be an advantageous time for her own errand, while Thomas's attention was otherwise engaged, and she went quietly out by the back door and along a brick-laid path which skirted along the edge of the shrubbery, beyond the view of the garden-house windows. Thomas had been persuaded by Mrs. Socket that there would be nothing improper in Fanny's going unescorted to the Rectory, since a path led there from the Hermitage garden, crossing a disused graveyard, so that it was possible to walk from one house to the other without setting foot in the public street. Unfortunately the door through the wall that led into the graveyard was situated in the corner directly beside the garden house, and Thomas was only too likely, if he saw Fanny setting off in that direction, to demand why she was going and find plenty of reasons to prove that her errand was unnecessary and trivial. On this occasion she really did not know *what* she could tell him if he discovered her. . . . But luckily the blind was drawn over the garden-room window and she was able to slip past unobserved, through the door, and into the graveyard, where she drew a breath of thankfulness.

Any time now spent away from Thomas seemed like a holiday. While he was at home his eye seemed to follow and oppress her wherever she went, whatever she did. He could not, these days, lay claim to her in bed, for it was too close to the birth of her child, but because of this sexual abstinence (enjoined by Dr. Chilgrove) his spirit loomed all the more heavily. In one way Fanny dreaded the baby's birth, because, once that was over, there would be nothing to prevent Thomas from resuming his marital rights.—She really did not know how she was going to bear that, but hoped and prayed that God would send her the necessary strength and endurance.—On the whole, though, she looked forward to the baby. It will give me something of my own, she thought optimistically; one small province in which I am the authority; forgetting, in her inexperience, what terrible importance Thomas attached to this event, this child who was to be the perpetuation of his image. Secretly, Fanny would have preferred that the baby should be a girl; she felt that she could understand a girl better, manage her better; hardly guessing at the disgrace that would await her should she produce a fourth daughter.

When she arrived at the Rectory she was dismayed to see that a harnessed pony and trap waited on the neatly raked gravel sweep by the front door. Evidently Mrs. Socket was just going out, for she appeared in the doorway wearing an old blue velvet riding dress and cloak and a silk and whalebone calash to protect her cap.

"Aha, you are come in a good hour, my dear!" she exclaimed, however, on seeing Fanny. "I am just about to try my new equipage, and you can come with me!"

"New equipage, ma'am?"

"Why, yes, Lord Egremont has given it to me—is he not a love? The kindest man in the world, I do believe. Hearing that the old pony was almost past work, what must he do but give me this beautiful dapple-gray animal and a charming new cabriolet to go with it. Will you not come for a drive in it, my dear?"

"Oh!" Fanny was immensely tempted; the thought of going out for a drive, having a chance to get a glimpse of the countryside, which as yet she hardly knew, on such a charming spring day, was just what she needed to refresh her spirits. But, remembering the certain intensity of Thomas's disapproval, she said forlornly:

"It is exceedingly kind of you, ma'am, but I believe I must not. Thomas does not like me to go abroad in—in my condition. He thinks it immodest."

"What, is that ogreish husband of yours putting his foot down again? Fiddle-de-dee, my dear! A drive is just what you need—your cheeks are by far too pale. In any case, Captain Paget could find nothing to cavil at on this excursion, for I am not going through the streets but merely into Petworth Park. So you may accompany me without the slightest anxiety. Nobody will see you. And furthermore I will wrap you in a shawl so that your condition is not observable.—Pringle, help Mrs. Paget into the carriage."

Thus urged—indeed, almost ordered—Fanny had not the heart to refuse. Comfortably swathed, she settled in beside Mrs. Socket, who, an accomplished driver, took the reins, while Pringle accompanied them, riding beside on the old pony—"Just to open the gates, like," as he put it.

"What he means is that he is not going to let me out of his sight until he is sure of the new pony's manners," Mrs. Socket cheerfully remarked. "But I am very sure that Lord Egremont would not bestow on us any animal that was not guaranteed sweet-tempered and biddable beyond the ordinary—he knows what Martin is like as a driver; Lord Egremont has the very highest regard for my husband, and no intention of letting him break his neck."

Fanny looked about her with lively interest as they drove up the Rectory lane, trotted a few yards northward along the London road, then turned left through a gateway in an immensely high wall and threaded their way among the outbuildings of Petworth House. They passed a farrier's forge, a coachhouse, a couple of cart sheds, and what looked like servants' cottages with neat little vegetable gardens. A man was walking through one of these. He glanced up at the sound of hoofs and, recognizing Fanny, gave her a flashing smile.

"You know Lord Egremont's gardener?" inquired Mrs. Socket, a little surprised, as they went on.

"Why, yes—that is—I have spoken to him; he was to have worked for my husband but—but Thomas found him too independent."

"Of course—I recollect." Without further allusion to this episode, Mrs. Socket went on, "Now here, you see, we pass under the pleasure gardens of Petworth House; this tunnel leads us directly into the park."

Fanny had been somewhat exercised in mind as to whether they might run any risk of encountering the inmates of Petworth House— the very last thing Thomas would wish for her, she knew full well; so she was much relieved to find they had such an inconspicuous means of ingress to the park. They drove under a stone archway and along a tunnel wide and high enough to allow a horse and carriage to pass through; it was about thirty yards long and brought them into a sunken driveway which terminated at a wrought-iron gate. Mrs. Socket had driven rather slowly through the tunnel; now they discovered that Andrew Talgarth had been walking behind them; he quickly made his way past Pringle on the cob and opened the gate for them, touching his cap to Mrs. Socket and giving Fanny another smile. As he closed the gate behind them he said a few words to Pringle, who, coming up beside them, said:

"Begging your pardon, ma'am, but young Talgarth there says best not to go up to the north end of the park today; one of the old stags hasn't shed its antlers yet, and it be in a very twitty, tempersome skin."

"Very well, thank you, Pringle; in fact I had not been intending to go that way," Mrs. Socket said. "I am simply going to drive around the pond."

Beyond the entrance gate a steep grassy slope cut off the view. Mrs. Socket turned her pony's head to the right and they ascended a gradually rising track which circled around a high, grassy knoll. Browsing deer moved across a shallow valley ahead; the animals moved with elegant grace, flicking their tails, black with vertical strips of white; the bodies of the deer varied from dark brown to a light fawn color. Suddenly they all broke into a run, and the whole herd flitted away, moving so lightly over the ground that they seemed more like insects than animals.

"Oh, how pretty they are!" exclaimed Fanny. "Surely they are too timid to be dangerous?"

"As a rule they are not at all dangerous—very timid indeed. But in spring the stags drop their antlers, and I suppose that makes them fidgety—Now you may see Petworth House, over to your left."

They were passing the end of a piece of ornamental water winding away from them in a series of elegant curves between gently rising heights of ground. All this landscaping, Mrs. Socket informed Fanny, had been performed by Capability Brown, about forty years previously. "It cost a fortune! But I believe the park was a very scrubby, poor-looking place before that." At the extremity of the lake, beyond another stretch of park, lay a large, rather plain gray house—a rectangular central block with a slight wing at each end. On top was what Fanny at first took for an extraordinary kind of cupola, until she realized that, in fact, it was the steeple of Petworth church, seen over the roof.

"What—what a lot of windows it has!" was all she could find to say about the house. It seemed to her very plain.

"Twenty-one, my dear, on each floor. Is it not a handsome residence? Lord Egremont is one of the richest men in England, you know; as well as being the kindest. He has upward of a hundred thousand a year!"

Despite this splendor, Fanny preferred the view of the lake, which was delightfully studded with picturesque islets, each planted with ornamental trees, weeping willows, birches, and evergreens. Rushes fringed the edge, and a flock of waterfowl floated over the calm surface, which reflected the house beyond. Then they drove past a grove of chestnuts, and the house was cut off from view.

"Ma'am," said Fanny, who had been screwing her courage to the sticking point for some time past, "I have a favor to ask of you."

"What can I do for you, my dear?" Mrs. Socket turned to give her a very kind smile, which illumined her plain, weather-beaten face. "Anything I can do, you know I shall be very happy."

Quickly, stumblingly, Fanny explained the need for a clock and the difficulty of procuring one. Pulling the rolled-up silk stockings out of her reticule, she offered them, saying:

"I am afraid I cannot give you any money, dear ma'am, but these stockings are quite unworn and made from best Spitalfields silk—I believe they could be sold for a sum which might be sufficient to procure a clock—"

"Oh, you poor child!" exclaimed Mrs. Socket. "Really, it goes beyond all bearing, it makes my blood boil, so it does!" And she muttered something to herself about penny-pinching miserly curmudgeons which Fanny thought it best not to hear.

"Of course I can find you a clock, child—there are clocks ticking in every room at the Rectory, you may choose one of a suitable size when we return. You need not give me your stockings for it!"

"Oh, but indeed, ma'am, I must pay you—it is odds that I shall never have occasion to wear them—"

"Nor I, my dear—with those freezing stone floors at the Rectory I keep to good thick woolsey"—she stuck out a sturdily clad foot—"though it is true I put on a little finery when we dine up at the house. Lord Egremont, by the bye, is very sorry that your husband so resolutely refuses all his invitations!—Now you may see the village of Tillington," and Mrs. Socket pointed with her whip over to the right. "Those hills ahead of us are the South Downs."

Just at this moment Pringle, who had been riding behind them, called out in a voice of alarm:

"Ma'am! Mrs. Socket! Watch out for that beast there!"

One of the darker-colored deer had been moving toward them, half trotting over the smooth ground so gracefully that its pace was deceptive; unlike all the rest of the herd, which fled off at the sight of humans, this one was coming in their direction, holding its antlered head high. It had an oddly lopsided appearance, since one of its antlers had fallen off and one still remained, giving it a rakish look.

Letting out a strange, loud, guttural cry, between a snort and a whinny, the beast lowered its head and charged straight at their dapple-gray pony, who, not unreasonably, bolted, leaving the cart track and dragging the light carriage at breakneck speed across the wide expanse of short grass between the lake and the great house.

"Oh, *mercy!*" gasped poor Mrs. Socket. "Who would *ever* have *imagined*—" She fought to regain control of the panic-stricken gray, who had got the bit between his teeth. "If it had been our old cob now—Mrs. Paget—Fanny—*hold tight onto the rail!* Do not let go, whatever you do!"

"I *am* holding on, ma'am," gasped Fanny between chattering teeth —chattering from the jolting speed of their passage rather than from fear. "Pray do not worry about me!"

"Oh, heavens, whatever will Martin say? He is apt to tell me that I am a shatterbrain—but indeed there seemed no harm—"

Despite her brave protestations, Fanny did now begin to feel some alarm. The panicky gray was making for a ha-ha consisting of a deeply sunk ditch with a high wall beyond it, the latter topped with an iron-spiked fence. Peril suddenly seemed imminent. The hand that was not grasping the rail Fanny pressed against her mouth to stifle a cry of fright.

However, just when it seemed inevitable that they must plunge into the ditch and be thrown out of the carriage or dashed against the wall, two rescuers arrived simultaneously. Pringle came galloping up on his cob and headed the gray sideways. He swung wildly to his left—and there was a man running to catch his bridle and drag him to a halt— Andrew Talgarth, the gardener, who must have seen their predicament from inside the ha-ha fence and raced out to the rescue.

In a moment, all was well. The gray, sweating and trembling, was being gentled and made much of by Pringle, who had jumped from his mount. Andrew Talgarth was asking Mrs. Socket if she had sustained any hurt, and that lady was thanking both men in her lively, unaffected manner.

"Upon my word! That was something like an adventure! I thought we were really in the suds! Who would ever have expected such an occurrence? I thought you said, Talgarth, that the distempered stag was up at the north end of the park?"

"So he was, ma'am, but he must have come a-wandering down, faster than anybody reckoned—"

"However, thanks to your both acting with such promptitude, no harm is done—Are you *positive* that you are not hurt, my dear?"

"Yes, thank you, ma'am," faintly said Fanny, who, now that the danger was over, did begin to feel a little strange. Catastrophe had seemed so terrifyingly close. She felt her heart give a great throb, or was it the unborn child, kicking in her womb?

At this moment three more persons arrived on the scene, hurrying from an open french window in Petworth House. One was Lord Egremont—who had on a most disreputable old hat, which went oddly with his correct morning costume and snowy neckcloth. Another was a plump, friendly-looking woman, perhaps seven or eight years older than Fanny, wearing a very ravishing dress of pink mull embroidered all over with cattails in turkey work and a most becoming cap to match; both of these people looked exceedingly worried and discomposed. A third man followed close behind them.

"My *dear* Mrs. Socket! My very dear ma'am! What a horrifying spectacle! What can I say? Such a shocking misadventure—your very first outing in my gift—I beseech you to tell me that you and your companion are unhurt? If not I shall be obliged to go away and shoot myself without loss of time!"

Mrs. Socket assured him, laughing, that, thanks to their prompt and valiant rescuers, both she and Mrs. Paget were perfectly stout and not overset in the least by their experience.

"Then I shall merely go and pour dust and ashes over my head," he said, taking his hat off and bowing to Fanny. "Dear Mrs. Paget—can you ever forgive me? First for giving Mrs. Socket that wicked animal—"

"It was no fault of Dapple—I will not have him blamed! I should have seen the stag sooner—"

"And," Lord Egremont continued without regarding the rector's wife, "secondly, for having such a dangerous beast as that stag in my park. He shall become venison without delay."

"Psha, my lord, he will probably feel quite the thing again when he has shed his second antler. Leave him alone! I am persuaded that he would be very tough."

"Are you sure that you are neither of you any the worse?" now inquired the lady who had come out with Lord Egremont. "Should you not come into the house for some refreshment? Yes, I am certain that you should. The poor young lady, Egremont, is as white as your neckcloth. Will you not make us known to each other, if you please?"

"I beg your pardon, my dear! This is our charming neighbor, Mrs. Paget, whose husband, Captain Paget, is the impress officer in Petworth—I have mentioned him to you, I know. Mrs. Paget, may I present Mrs. Elizabeth Wyndham."

"How do you do, ma'am," Fanny said faintly. "I beg you not to trouble about me—I shall be perfectly well once I am at home again—"

In fact the park was beginning to swing around her in dizzy circles, and Lord Egremont, observing her sway and turn pale, said brusquely:

"No such thing, ma'am! You must come into the house for a nuncheon. Henriques, help me carry Mrs. Paget in—carefully now!" A couple of menservants brought a chair, and on this Fanny was solicitously carried indoors by Lord Egremont and his friend, who was a dark man, very fashionably dressed.

She was laid on a sopha beside a marble fireplace in which a great pile of logs quietly smoldered. Mrs. Socket and the lady known as Mrs. Wyndham then plied her with smelling salts, but Lord Egremont, brushing them aside, said with decision:

"Take away those damned fumy, vinegary potions, Liz! Here is something that will do Mrs. Paget a great deal more good," and he obliged Fanny to drink the greater part of a glass of dark, sweet nutbrown liquor, which did indubitably have a most fortifying and sustaining effect on her. "One of the last tuns of my father's madeira; he used to say that and turtle soup would have brought King Charles back to life even after his head was cut off.—*Have* we any turtle soup, Liz my dear?" he demanded of the lady called Mrs. Wyndham.

"I will send to ask Conrad Leidenberg," she promptly replied. "It's odds but he has some—he is the most resourceful and well-supplied cook in the world. Now, lie back quietly, my love, and in no time at all you will be quite the thing again. *I* am always queasy when I am increasing, so I feel the greatest sympathy for you—and to be exposed to such an adventure as that—! Do you not think Dr. Chilgrove should be summoned, ma'am?" she asked Mrs. Socket, who, anxious and conscience-stricken, almost as much in need of stimulant as Fanny, was also being plied with madeira by Lord Egremont.

"Did you sustain any bangs or bumps that you can recollect, my dear?" she inquired of Fanny. "On—on that part of your anatomy?"

"I believe not, ma'am." Fanny blushed at having her condition thus alluded to in front of the strange gentleman addressed by Egremont as Henriques. He had remained close at hand and was regarding her with unconcealed interest. She now had time to observe that he was a thick-set, strongly featured man of middle age with curly grizzled hair. To avoid his glance, which made her feel very uncomfortable, she gazed around the room and was greatly impressed by its size and magnificence. The furniture was gilded and scrolled; there were tables with porphyry tops, and ornaments in bronze and marble. The walls were completely paneled in elaborately carved wood (limewood, the rector's wife told her later) and adorned with a profusion of carvings in which birds, fish, beasts, and naked cupids flew and scrambled among wreaths, baskets of flowers, bunches of grapes, cornucopia, and dangling swags. A portrait of King Henry VIII stared down at her from over the hearth and seemed to demand what she was doing there amid all these splendors—little Fanny Herriard from Sway. However, to mitigate its splendor, the room was decidedly untidy—newspapers, pieces of embroidery, and opened books lay scattered about and a great mound of ash had fallen from the hearth onto the stone floor in front.

"I think it best that the doctor be fetched," Lord Egremont pronounced. "Captain Paget would wish it, I dare say."

At the thought of her husband, Fanny almost fainted in good earnest and turned so white again that Mrs. Wyndham hustled the men out of the room.

"Something warm inside you is what you need, my love, and it will be here directly," she told Fanny in a voice that was wonderfully comforting, for it was halfway between a chuckle and a coo. "Now do not be distressing yourself—I think it unlikely that you have done yourself or your baby any harm—and I ought to know—should I not, Mrs. Socket?—for I have had three."

"Good gracious, ma'am, I should never have believed that," Fanny said feebly. In fact Mrs. Wyndham hardly looked over the age of twenty-five and was wonderfully pretty, with a kindly, smiling, open, buxom beauty, like a full-blown pink and white rose that will soon let fall some of its petals but still exudes a lavish summery fragrance. Fanny was greatly charmed by her looks and by her simple friendliness. When the turtle soup came, on a silver tray with rolls and grapes, she sent the footman who brought it away—"For servants are so clumsy and fidgeting"—and insisted on feeding Fanny spoonful by spoonful, until the latter, laughing, declared that she could perfectly well manage by herself and must not trouble her hostess any further (for, from Mrs. Wyndham's air of command and the deference paid her by the servants, it was evident that she was the lady of the house).

Dr. Chilgrove was now announced—evidently a summons to Petworth House was obeyed at speed—and Fanny was transferred to a smaller chamber for privacy of consultation. Before the doctor was admitted and while Mrs. Socket was in another room, consulting with him:

"Now, my love, tell me—are you afraid of your husband?" demanded Liz Wyndham. "I saw you turn as white as your fichu when George spoke of him—and I have heard that he is an exceedingly severe, quarrelsome individual—is that what troubles you? Will he scold you for this scrape?"

"Oh, ma'am—yes! I—I am sorry to seem impolite—when—when you have been so very kind"—Fanny's voice faltered and a couple of tears, mortifyingly, slipped down her cheek—"but, indeed—the thought of what he will say when he hears about this—fills me with *dread!* He will be—he will be quite shockingly angry—"

"Humph! About the accident in the park—or the visit to this house?"

"Both, ma'am, I fear. He sets so much store by my bearing him an heir—since he has daughters, but as yet no son—and—and—"

"And, besides risking the baby's life, he will believe that his innocent little wife has been dragged willy-nilly into a foolish escapade among the most immoral set of loose-living people between here and London," Mrs. Wyndham completed the sentence. "Well—well then, it seems we must contrive that news of your mishap does *not* reach his ears."

Fanny doubted if such concealment would be possible, but when Dr. Chilgrove came in and examined her he was bracingly reassuring about her condition—"Not a penny the worse, my child, I give you my word!" and contributed an item of news that immediately sent Fanny's spirits bounding up, for he went on, "Now we won't trouble to tell your husband about this, my dear, for he'd be up in the boughs directly—I know his fidgety ways—and besides, it would mean sending a messenger posting after him, for he's not at hand; I saw him, with all his scurvy wretches of impress fellows, posting off along the Brighton road as if the Devil himself were at their heels."

"Oh, *what* a fortunate circumstance," breathed Fanny. "He was, I know, planning to go to Brighton quite soon, as soon as the summons should come—"

"I have heard of this Brighton affair," remarked Chilgrove. "All the men of the town standing on their rights not to be impressed, hey? A sticky time the press officers will have of it, if they try to take all those sturdy rogues of Brighthelmstone fishermen—I do not at all envy them the task. Depend upon it, your husband will hardly be home tonight, my dear."

"In that case," said Liz Wyndham, "Mrs. Paget had best remain here, where we can look after her."

Dr. Chilgrove would have endorsed this suggestion, but Fanny was so alarmed at the idea that it was agreed she should merely pass the afternoon at Petworth House and then, when she was sufficiently rested, be transferred to Mrs. Socket's residence. That lady accordingly went home to inform her husband of the mishap, enjoin him to silence about it, and air bedding, heat warming pans, and prepare a room for Fanny; and a servant was dispatched to the Hermitage to inform Mrs. Strudwick that her mistress would be spending the night at the Rectory. This in itself seemed such a wild departure from normality that Fanny was alarmed all over again, but Liz Wyndham told her firmly that she would be far better to pass the night under the roof of a sensible woman of mature years who had children herself and knew how to go on rather than be left to the ineffectual care of a parcel of servants and schoolroom misses. It did then occur to Fanny that she herself had a resident nurse just installed at the Hermitage, but various reservations in her own attitude toward Mrs. Lily Baggot, plus a doubt as to whether Thomas would wish that person's attentions diverted from his mother's needs, disposed her to keep silent on this head.

Liz Wyndham sat down by Fanny and said, "Now I mean to make the most of your visit! I have been so much wishing that I could make your acquaintance, do you know! For the two previous occupants of your house were my dearest friends, and I miss them sadly. I feel that Fate must have intended us to meet."

"Oh, did you know my husband's cousin Juliana? I have so much wanted to know what she was like. She must be the kindest creature!" Filled with curiosity, Fanny forgot to be on her guard and was soon chattering away unrestrainedly.

She could not help being charmed by Liz Wyndham's friendly, caressing ways and ingenuous directness.

"Will your husband be *very* angry if he hears that you have been allowed to meet me?" she inquired straightforwardly. And when Fanny, blushing and distressed, admitted that she could hardly imagine the depth of Thomas's ire and outrage, Liz said, "Well, I am sorry for it, for *your* sake, because that makes him sound such a disagreeable, narrow-minded man, and I pity you deeply at being obliged to live with him. *Is* he very disagreeable?"

"Oh yes—very," sighed Fanny from the bottom of her heart. "You cannot conceive how disagreeable."

"Poor Fanny! Well, you must just conceal this visit from him. Nobody wishes to be involved in deceit, it is so tedious and vulgar, but these mean, ill-judging puritanical characters force it upon us. What concern is it of *his*, pray, if George and I choose to remain unmarried?"

Fanny could not help wondering why they did so, but delicacy prevented her from asking; however Liz continued as if the question had been visible in her face: "Really we prefer it, my dear, because it removes the necessity of entertaining such dismal, prune-faced, quizzy persons as your husband; and there is no lack of the other sort, I promise you! We have more friends than we can contrive to see. We have had Mr. Fox here, times out of number, and Mr. Creevey; the Seftons, and half the Melbourne clan—it is true Creevey complains about the damp sheets and the servants' free-spokenness, but he returns again and again. Prinney, too, used to be a great friend of George's, but these days he is grown too fat and lazy to come over from Brighton."

Fanny could only gaze, wide-eyed, at this recital of great names.

"The truth is," Liz went on reflectively, "that George is not partial to the married state. The thought of it makes him nervous. He was engaged once to the most beautiful girl in England—Lady Maria Waldegrave—oh, a diamond of the first water!—but he cried off. That was nine years ago. I do not think he will marry now. There is something about the stiff decorum and formality of wedlock that does not sit with him. If we were married we would have to spend half our time at Egremont House in Piccadilly and give grand dinners to the *ton* and spend hours worrying about who takes in whom to dine, and whether barons' younger sons walk in before viscounts' elder daughters. Here we see only our friends, comfortably, as we choose.—George has offered to marry me, it is true, but I have said no any number of times; what would be the use *now?* That would not make his sons legitimate, which would be the only practical consideration. And George does not give a rap for that; let his brother William's son get the title, he says. The boys will be sufficiently provided for in a practical way."

Fanny was astonished at this novel view of marriage and lay gazing wonderingly at her hostess.

"But *your* husband," Liz went on. "You say he is anxious for an heir?"

"Oh, indeed yes, ma'am—"

"I wish you will call me Liz, child—everybody does! And may I not call you Fanny?"

Strangely, at this casual invitation to intimacy, Fanny gave an involuntary sob.

"What is the matter, my love?" Liz was greatly concerned and came to pet and comfort her with a rustle of muslins and a waft of delicious fragrance. "Do I tire you? Is my chatter oversetting you? Had you rather be left alone?"

"Oh *no*, ma'am—dear Liz—it is just—I *know* my husband will never, never allow us to be friends—so what is the use of our even learning each other's names?"

Liz Wyndham puckered up her broad, smooth brow.

"Well, as to that—who knows? Perhaps we may contrive to meet somehow. And then, your husband is not a young man, after all. He was married before, was he not?"

"Oh yes. I have three stepdaughters, two of them older than myself."

"Disgusting," said Liz with indignation. "What was he thinking of, to marry a child of your age?" And she immediately answered her own question. "He wanted a young, healthy wife who would provide him with a son.—Strange, is it not, how men will always be wanting what they have not got? Once he has an heir, two to one but he will never look at the boy twice in a day, or care what becomes of him—witness George with his four!"

"Four, ma'am—I thought you said three?"

"Ah, but he had a son and daughter by another lady, you see—my great friend Elise Reynard, who lived in the Hermitage before your husband's cousin. Indeed George built it for her."

"Oh, the French lady who died?"

"That one, yes." Liz fell silent a moment.

Fanny found herself wholly confused by the Earl of Egremont's relationships but resolved not to ask any more questions on what was evidently a sad theme.

"So your husband wishes for a son," Liz resumed presently in her meditative manner. "Well then, for your own sake, dear Fanny, I hope that you succeed in providing him with one."

"Oh, *so* do I!" Fanny shivered at the thought of Thomas's disappointment if the baby proved to be a female. "Disappointment" would hardly be the word for it, she thought.

"Does he abuse you in bed?" Liz said with a sudden, very penetrating look. Fanny gasped and turned white. She had not expected ever to divulge to a living soul the anguish that she went through behind the closed door of her bedroom; to have her painful secret thus calmly brought into the open gave her an almost physical shock.

"I—I cannot—I cannot talk about it. No, not even to you," she said, when she was a little collected.

"Poor child." Liz looked at her compassionately. "You do not think that talking would help?"

Fanny shook her head.

"You see," she managed after a moment or two, "I should begin to pity myself. If I were to talk about it. And that would never do."

Liz stood up and began pacing hastily about on the handsome Exeter carpet. Her round, smiling face was clouded; she turned and looked perplexedly at Fanny.

"Perhaps—if you present him with a boy—he will be better to you. Do you think?"

"Very likely," Fanny said without confidence. "But if I should bear him a girl—"

"If you do bear him a girl—Have you *no* one to turn to? Your father, your family?"

"No. Papa is dead. And my sisters must live with relatives. Poor things, they have no money; they are all unmarried."

"Anybody would think we women were slaves!" Liz burst out. Then she laughed at herself. "Listen to me! I am so lucky—who am I to complain? But, oh, it makes my blood boil—! Well, there is nothing for it, my dear—if matters become too bad at home, you must run away to us! Come to Petworth House. We would look after you charmingly, I promise you."

"Good—good heavens!" Fanny stammered. "But, ma'am—but, Liz, only consider! It is not to be thought of! My husband could sue through the courts for my return—"

"And expose himself to all that scandal and gossip? I am sure that kind of man would die rather than do so."

Fanny did not believe that Liz's estimate of Thomas was at all correct; she thought he would fight, most tenaciously, for anything he considered his right, at whatever cost.

"Oh, I never, never could do such a thing," she sighed. "But thank you for making the offer. It was very kind in you."

"Oh well," Liz said optimistically, "it is odds but he'll die soon, of falling from his horse; or one of those poor fellows that he caused to be impressed will escape from the navy and come home to shoot him through the head. Or some such thing. And then you will be a comfortable and well-established widow, and we shall be able to see each other as often as we wish, and I shall find a charming second husband for you. So do not be too downhearted!"

She smiled at Fanny, who did her best to smile back, and, feeling a little recovered by now, she mustered up spirit to put a timid request.

"Ma'am—dear Liz—Mrs. Socket and I are so much beholden to your brave gardener for running out and catching our horse's bridle—he incurred a great risk of being dashed against the wall—might I, would it be possible just to see him for a moment and thank him? Mrs. Socket's groom I frequently see, but I am not at all likely to encounter the other man again—"

"Andrew Talgarth? Of course you may thank him," agreed Liz Wyndham, rising to pull at a bell rope. "I am very glad you asked it, for I am desirous of doing so myself. He is such an excellent young man! George has the very highest opinion of him—thinks he will become another Repton—and is in the habit of asking his views on all manner of topics, so I dare say it was no surprise to *him* that it was Andrew Talgarth who ran forward and stopped the horse.—Oh, Towson, will you discover where Andrew Talgarth is, if you please, and have him sent here? Mrs. Paget wishes to thank him for her rescue."

"Yes, ma'am. I believe Talgarth is in the library, ma'am. I will have him sent here directly."

Fanny was somewhat amazed to hear that Lord Egremont's gardener was to be found in the library; Liz, however, explained.

"Talgarth is forever reading Tusser, or Lawson, or *The Gardener's Labyrinth,* or some such work, and he has even learned enough Latin from the boys' tutor to study Pliny on the art of gardening; George encourages him to make use of our books. After all, as George says, what is a library for, if not to provide instruction for one's household?"

While Fanny was reflecting that there was no end to Lord Egremont's unexpected qualities, Andrew Talgarth made his appearance. It was plain that his curly black hair had been hastily disciplined with a wet comb; otherwise he looked much as Fanny remembered him from their first meeting in the Hermitage garden: brown-faced, weather-beaten, grave, but with a latent smile in his very blue eyes. He stood in the doorway, neither bashful nor overeager, and said politely:

"You sent for me, ma'am?"

"Mrs. Paget here wished to thank you for saving her life," his mistress said. "And I, too, wish to commend you, Andrew. You are a brave fellow! *I* should not have liked to jump at that horse's bridle as you did—I should have been too afraid of being pulled onto those iron spikes!"

"Ah, Your Ladyship don't carry the weight that I do!" the gardener answered, his serious face breaking up into the smile that Fanny remembered. She stretched out her hand to him, saying softly:

"I am very sorry that you did not continue working for us at the Hermitage, Talgarth; I was greatly distressed at—at what happened. But it was certainly lucky for me that you were in the park today! And I can see that there are better opportunities for you here. I am so deeply obliged to you for your bravery."

"It was nothing, ma'am. I am glad to have been of use," Talgarth replied quietly. He bowed over her hand, touched his forehead, and left the room again, his soft tread making hardly any sound on the carpet.

"Imagine being his wife," sighed Liz, looking after him.

"Oh?—Is he married?"

"No, he is not, and it always amazes me, for I am sure dozens of girls in Petworth are on the catch for him. My own maid, Clara, is fit to break her heart every time he brings me a posy—he never even looks at her! He thinks only of gardens. It would be like being wed to a woodland god! When he hands me a bunch of clove pinks or gillyflowers, I expect them to last forever and never fade."

At this moment a footman came to announce that Mrs. Socket's carriage had returned to take the young lady to the Rectory.

"I hope it is the old cob between the shafts again," said Liz, laughing, "though I feel thankful to that naughty Dapple for giving me the chance to become acquainted with you." She kissed Fanny warmly. "Now, remember that you have a friend, my love, and one in George too—he thinks you are as pretty as a primrose, he said so! George is a great flirt but you may trust him never to go beyond the bounds of what is proper. The man I should perhaps warn you against is James Henriques." Liz lowered her voice, and Fanny remembered the grizzle-haired man whose eyes had dwelt on her so uncomfortably. "He is a rake, a gambler, and a shallow-minded fellow—never trust him. However you are not likely to come across him again.—Good-by, my dear neighbor and friend—I hope that we may meet again before too long. I shall do my best to contrive it!"

"Good-by—and—and I thank you, most sincerely!" said Fanny, whose mind was in a whirl, as the rector's two menservants carefully assisted her out to the carriage.

Liz strode wrathfully back into the Grinling Gibbons paneled room, where Lord Egremont and his friend were talking about old days at Pampellone's school, where they had both been as boys along with Charles James Fox; and reminiscing about the subsequent careers of various wild fellows and jumped-up counter-coxcombs who had also been at the school with them.

"Though why *you* should care for such snobberies, Egremont," said Major Henriques quizzingly, "you who allow your farm hands to play cricket on your lawns and your gardeners to make use of your library —you are a true Radical!"

"Ay, but there is a wide difference, James, between what one chooses to *give* and what one may not wish to have *taken*. This Buonaparte, now—it looks as if he is about to conquer Sardinia, without more than a bleat from the miserable Austrian—It is time someone took a hand to him."

"It is time somebody took a hand to that miserable wretch Paget!" Liz declared. "That poor little creature is kept mewed up, more—

more like a slave in a harem than a British Christian lady. You ought to have her odious husband put in the pillory, George, for people to throw rotten eggs at him!"

"I must admit I don't like the fellow, m'dear," Lord Egremont peaceably replied. "But this is a free country, you must remember, where a man may use his own wife as he thinks best."

"Which is why you never had one, eh, George?" suggested the major. "But *does* her husband use her so ill, ma'am? She looks to me like an engaging little charmer—when she ain't quite so big in pod— I'd have thought any husband would want to ply her with comfits and kickshaws."

"Not that monstrous Paget," said Liz. "I suspect he uses her quite villainously. I have told her that if she can endure it no longer, George, she must seek our protection."

Egremont raised his brows.

"You might find yourself in devilish hot water, m'dear, if she should ever take you at your word. Suppose the incensed husband comes after our blood? Still, we'll jump that rasper when we come to it. Well, James? Have you lazed indoors long enough? Shall we ride out and look at my Southdowns? Rapley tells me this is the best year for lambs since '84; they have lost only three and they are growing fat as butter."

"You are a cunning rascal, Egremont," Liz heard Henriques say as the two men walked out of the french doors. "If I had a dear little bird such as that, nesting just outside my coverts, damme if I wouldn't encourage her to fly off from her keeper, by gad!"

"Stretch your own snares where you choose, James," replied Lord Egremont without heat. "Never trouble your head about *my* preserves."

Fanny, solicitously cared for at the rector's house, was put to bed by her hostess immediately after an early dinner. But it was many, many hours before she went to sleep.

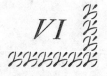

VI

During the night the little maid, Bisesa, died. Scylla was with her at the end. Shortly after the departure of Miss Musson for the palace an urgent message came from the hospital, asking for the sahiba, as the maid's condition had deteriorated alarmingly. Scylla sent Ram up to the citadel with instructions to find the mem if possible and summon her to the hospital but was not surprised when Miss Musson failed to appear. In the grief-stricken chaos at the palace it might not have been possible to locate her, or she might have felt that her duty to Mahtab Kour took precedence.

Scylla herself hurried with old Abdul to the hospital. There she could see at once that Bisesa's fever had reached a critical point: her body was ragingly hot, the whites of her eyes had gone yellow, and every inch of her skin was now covered with the sores that had developed with such mysterious speed. These were now oozing bright yellow matter and were so painful that, even at the height of her delirium, Bisesa constantly attempted to rub or scratch them; her hands were being patiently held down by her sister and sister-in-law sitting on either side of the charpoy. There was practically nothing Scylla could do for the poor girl except dull her pain with opium, which she did. The fever reached its height shortly after midnight, and the girl's slender frame was simply not strong enough to bear it. Just before she died she had a moment's comparative calm, during which she opened her swollen gummy eyes and recognized Scylla, who was bathing her forehead with essence of rosemary.

"Oh, Mem Periseela! Truly I am sorry that I tried on the queen's gift—I knew I should not have done it—and now I am being punished —but indeed I did not think it so very wrong, not a great sin—"

"Of course it was not a sin, my poor child—in any case I am going to give it to you for your wedding robe—so you must make haste and get better!"

"I shall never be better, mem," gasped Bisesa, and on that she died. The women around her bed instantly broke out into heartbroken wailing, but Scylla could only be glad that the unfortunate girl's sufferings were over. While trying to tend Bisesa, she had been too preoccupied to think about the pain of her own hands, but now, while old Jameela and the girl's relatives washed and laid out her body, Scylla went into the small closet where the medicines were kept and found some lotion of honey and gum arabic to rub on her blistered, stinging palms; she wondered, with a kind of exhausted resignation, whether by the next night she, too, would be in Bisesa's condition.

Rousing old Abdul, who dozed in the forecourt, she returned home and found that Colonel Cameron, whom she had left asleep in a basket chair, had woken and was pacing anxiously about the main room of the bungalow.

"You should not have left the house without informing me!" he said harshly. "At any moment now, insurrection and bloodshed may break out—this is hardly the time to be gadding around Ziatur in the small hours."

Scylla raised her brows. She was, however, too weary to trouble about defending herself, though she was not sure by what right he berated her.

"Excuse me—I am very tired—I am going to bed," she answered shortly, trying to move past him in the direction of her room.

"Where have you been?"

"At the hospital, with our maid, who was dying."

Removing the burqa that covered her hair, she lifted her hands. Cameron exclaimed, as he saw them:

"Good God, girl! You cannot go to bed with your hands in such a condition as that! They must be treated! What is the matter with them?"

"I think I must have taken the infection from Bisesa," she said tiredly. "You had better keep away from me."

Sharply he questioned her about the maid's illness: when it had come on, what course it had taken, what clues, if any, Bisesa had let fall as to what might have caused it. "Did she mention anything she had eaten or drunk?"

"No, she gave us no clue at all. Her last words, poor child, were an apology for trying on my new sari. I had intended to give it her any-way—for her wedding," Scylla said, her voice breaking with fatigue and grief.

"*Sari?*" he demanded swiftly. "You don't mean that red affair with the pearls—the one Mahtab Kour sent you?"

"Yes, why?"

"She had tried it on? Where is it?"

She gestured with her head.

Cameron strode into her bedroom and, snatching up a riding whip that lay on a chest, he gingerly poked aside the muslin wrappings and inspected the gauzy rose-colored garment, holding a lamp near it so as to get the sheen of its light over the fabric; then, raising a fold of material on the handle of the riding crop, he very cautiously sniffed at it.

"Mahtab Kour never sent you this," was his verdict. "I'll stake my head it was that scheming snake Sada."

"*Sada?* But why—?"

"It has been dipped in datura poison. You may think yourself fortu-nate, my child, that rose color does not suit your complexion—that you did not put it on," Cameron said grimly.

Lifting the bundle of material, holding it balanced on the riding crop, he carried it into the garden, took out flint and tinderbox, and set fire to it. Then he stood watching it flare up until the last shred of gauze was consumed.

Returning to the house, "Have you any bread dough set to rise?" he asked Scylla.

"*Bread?* I dare say Habib-ulla may have a pan of dough—why, in heaven's name?"

Without bothering to answer, he went off to the kitchen and came back with a big earthenware crock of soft, raw dough, set to rise for the morning.

"Habib-ulla will be *very* angry," Scylla said, half laughing, as Cameron pulled the soft dough apart into two large shapeless lumps.

"Doubtless he would prefer his memsahib to retain the use of her hands," Cameron laconically replied. Having pulled and stretched the two pieces of dough into flat cakes about a foot square, he wrapped each piece around Scylla's inflamed hands, pressing the soft stuff close to the wrist. "Now I need some cloth; yes, table napkins will do," and he bound these over the flaps of dough to hold them in place.

"What is datura?" Scylla inquired as he knotted the second napkin into place.

"Thorn apple. One of nature's deadlier poisons. The sari must have been steeped in a strong infusion; if you had worn it you must have died like your maid. Raw dough is a fair specific against its external use, fortunately."

"Good God," Scylla said slowly. "But why should Sada wish my death?"

Somehow the news came as no particular surprise to her. She had already felt convinced of Sada's hatred.

"Oh, why, *why?* Who asks *why* in Ziatur?" Cameron said impatiently. "She wishes the Angrezi to leave; she believes you—or Miss Musson—might be a threat to her position.—Now you had better try to sleep."

"How am I supposed to undress myself with my hands tied up like plum puddings?" Scylla demanded.

"Unless you wish me or your brother to unrobe you, you will have to sleep in your clothes," he replied coolly.

"I wish no such thing," retorted Scylla, much affronted; adding, "Where *is* Cal, by the bye?"

"Asleep." The impatient, fatigued note in his voice made her study the colonel with some compunction. He looked deathly tired; his cheekbones seemed more prominent than ever, for his eyes were sunk back in their hollows; his dark red hair was in a considerable state of disorder and damp with sweat.

She said apologetically, "Indeed, I am very much obliged to you,

Colonel, for your skill. I do not believe even Miss Musson knew of this remedy. My hands begin to feel better already."

"Keep the dough on all night," was his only answer. "Stay—you should have some brandy now. It will help you sleep."

And, with the impersonal efficiency of someone administering a draught to a sick animal, he assisted her to swallow a sizable dram of cognac, holding the glass carefully to her mouth. Scylla protested and spluttered—she was not accustomed to drink spirits—but he sharply adjured her not to be a ninnyhammer and tipped the liquid down her throat.

"Now—go and lie down on your bed."

She could only obey, observing to herself with some indignation that Colonel Cameron conferred his kindnesses like punishments; but no doubt he considered the Paget twins a dead bore, always having to be rescued from some predicament or other, and a thoroughly inconvenient responsibility; rather dismally Scylla reflected that he had reason to do so. Moreover it was all too plain that the placid course of their existence in Ziatur had come to an abrupt end. Being Miss Musson's old friend, Cameron no doubt considered that he had a duty to see her and her young companions safely out of the place; though whether he could bring Miss Musson to see the necessity of this would be another matter.

Having reached this unsatisfactory conclusion, Scylla succumbed to the effects of the brandy and the day's exhaustion and alarums; she fell into profound and dreamless slumber.

When she woke, many hours later, it was to find the bungalow empty and silent. Venturing to strip the bread dough from her hands, she discovered that the inflammation had gone down; Colonel Cameron's remedy had been remarkably efficacious. If only we could have used it on poor Bisesa! Scylla thought sadly.

Having washed and changed her clothes, Scylla went out to the veranda, where she found Cal, deep, as usual, in his epic poem on Alexander the Great. He nodded as she came out but hardly looked up. Of Habib-ulla, who brought her tea, melon, and chupattis, Scylla demanded:

"Where is the Mem Musson? Is she still at the palace?" and, learning that this was the case, resolved to go immediately in search of the older woman.

"Shall I come too?" inquired Cal, who, having successfully reached the end of a canto and vaguely realizing that they were faced with an untoward situation, was prepared to render assistance, but Scylla said:

"No, thank you, love, for in any case you could not enter the women's apartments. You had best remain here, in case Miss Musson comes back by a different route and we miss one another."

She pulled on a pair of white cotton gloves to protect her tender hands; the effect was bizarre with the burqa and hat.

"Well, don't be too long," Cal said, "or I shall be uneasy about you. There's a devilish queer feeling about the town today."

Scylla had noticed it too. A deathly hush lay in the streets; only the sound of wailing and fumes of incense filled the air.

In the palace the atmosphere was even stranger and more unnerving. Agitated whispers ran through the hush; distant gongs boomed; saucers of incense burned before every god and goddess in their niches along the winding corridors; and marigold petals were scattered everywhere, adding a sickly fragrance to the general miasma. Colored rice crunched under Scylla's slipper soles as she walked the accustomed route to the princes' schoolroom; not that she proposed to give them any lessons on such a day of mourning, but she wished to see them and offer her condolences on the death of their father, to whom they had been very attached.

No condolences were needed. She saw the princes indeed—and the sight was enough to drive the blood from her heart and the breath from her lungs.

Hideously swollen and distorted, with blackened faces and starting eyeballs, the boys lay sprawled together on a divan in their workroom. Ranji had died clutching at his stomach; Amur was doubled backward, his face contorted in a final rictus of agony. The room smelled acid with vomit. Both bodies were stiff and cold; it was plain they had been dead for many hours.

"Oh, God! My God!" Scylla whispered with dry lips. She turned to see Nuruddin, the Maharajah's physician, standing behind her.

"A very sad sight, is it not, Mem Periseela?" he greeted her smoothly. "Those two devoted boys, in grief for their father, both swallowed poison in order to follow him. Was not that a touching and beautiful deed?"

Scylla looked at him stonily. She remembered the tray of sweetmeats that Sada had sent the boys. She thought of the rose-colored sari.

"I do not believe they killed themselves," she said. "I believe they were poisoned."

"I most strongly recommend that you do not go uttering these thoughts aloud in the palace, memsahib," Nuruddin replied. "Indeed, if you are a sensible young lady you will go directly back to your home; now, at once."

"I wish to find Miss Musson," Scylla replied curtly, and walked past him.

"You will find your friend with the Maharani Mahtab Kour. If you value *her* safety," the physician said, "you will advise her also to return home."

Mahtab Kour's part of the palace was even more shrouded in gloom than usual, and suffocatingly stuffy. Scylla paused at one point by a shuttered window and pushed the slats of the shutter aside to inhale a little outside air; but then she wished she had not done so. Outside, in a courtyard of the zenana, a huge pyre was being built; shuddering, she guessed at its purpose. Averting her eyes from it, Scylla hurried on.

She found Mahtab Kour, her portly bulk shrouded in white mourning robes, rocking to and fro, moaning and lamenting. Her women were about her; and all her immense quantities of jewels, robes, boxes of stuffs, cosmetics, carpets, chests of coins, diamond-studded slippers, silk shawls, embroidered bedspreads with jeweled fringes, silk floor cloths, and other personal belongings were being brought before her on trays, so that she could arrange for their distribution among various friends and relatives, who surrounded her with bowed heads, joining loudly in her lamentations.

A new pet slave girl (the little Persian, Laili, had died of her infected ears) huddled dolefully against her mistress, gazing up with large, hypnotized eyes at Mahtab Kour, down whose face tears incessantly streamed, who continually murmured invocations to the gods, at the same time continuing in quite a businesslike way to make arrangements for the disposal of her possessions.

"And this packet of gold dust for my friend the Mem Musson," she directed; a small silk-wrapped package was handed to Miss Musson, whom Scylla now noticed for the first time, sitting swathed in her black burqa among the shadows behind the queen; she held a Bible, marking the place in it with a finger, and looked exceedingly angry, harassed, and weary.

Bowing respectfully to the queen, Scylla slipped around to join her guardian and sat on the floor beside her.

"Those hopeless, silly heathen!" Miss Musson exclaimed in English —Scylla had never seen her so shaken out of her customary calm. "One might as well talk to a herd of *cows*—they take no notice at all. They seem utterly bent on self-destruction."

Scylla could not wonder at it. What real pleasure or purpose did the existence of these poor women hold, that might constrain them to wish to hold onto it? And their future lot, as castoff retainers of a defunct queen, would be dismal indeed; death might well seem preferable to a life of prostitution and ignominy.

"At least, Highness, let me take this little one away with me?" suggested Miss Musson, who apparently, in the course of the night, had most uncharacteristically given up on the major issue. She patted the head of the slave child on Mahtab's lap.

"Take my little Lehna? But then, whom shall I have for a pet and plaything in the next life?" demanded the Maharani in astonished and injured tones.

"My dear Queen, in the next life you will not require cheering and solacing—you will not require *playthings*," the American lady told

her forcefully. Mahtab Kour appeared wholly unconvinced. However
after a long argument she finally agreed that little Lehna, at least,
should be spared from the funeral immolation.

"Quick, take the child away before the wretched woman changes
her mind!" hissed Miss Musson to Scylla. "Go *now;* take her back to
the bungalow; I will come when I can."

"I wish you would come too," Scylla murmured urgently. "Pray do,
dear Miss Musson! There seems no more that you can do here. Colonel
Cameron is exceedingly anxious about your safety. And so am I!"

The older woman shook her head.

"I cannot, child, while there is the least hope of saving any of these
miserable, stupid enslaved women.—I will come only when I am convinced there is nothing more for me to do. But do you take that child
away!"

When the child Lehna realized that she was to be separated from
her mistress she struggled and screamed. Scylla did not care to drag
her bodily; she stood nonplused. Mahtab Kour said in an exhausted
voice:

"Go with the mem, Lehna! She will take good care of you."

"I do not wish to leave Your Highness!" wept the child.

"I am to be burned on a great fire; that is not a fate for such a little
one as you."

"I wish it, I wish it!"

Suddenly Mahtab Kour recaptured some of the royal command that
must have dignified her at a younger age. Her eyes flashed.

"*Go* when I tell you, child!"

Silent and humble, Lehna crept from the room with Scylla.

But as they were crossing a courtyard high among the battlements of
the women's quarters Lehna suddenly dragged her hand away from
Scylla's clasp and, shrieking, "I will join her this way, if not the
other!" she ran to the low parapet and threw herself over it. Appalled,
rushing after, Scylla leaned out and looked down. Twenty feet below,
injured and moaning, the child lay on the cobbles of a lower courtyard, the very one where the pyre was heaped; one of her legs stuck
out at an unnatural angle; plainly it was broken. Gritting her teeth,

Scylla looked about, found a staircase that led to the lower court, and ran down it. But already when she reached the spot where Lehna had fallen some of the queen's women had picked her up and were carrying her away.

"Her Highness says, if the child is so determined to die with her, then she shall have the honor to accompany her on the pyre. Go, leave us, mem."

Silent, sick at heart, Scylla walked away past the huge heap of wood and bamboo and thorn splinters. She saw men pouring great jugs of oil over it, to make it blaze up as rapidly as possible when lit. A platform had been erected in the middle, and a flight of steps was being constructed, leading up to it.

Supervising this work with an expression of calm approval and satisfaction was the Rani Sada Kour. She was wearing, not her usual robes, but a high-waisted European dress of striped jaconet and a Parisian bonnet, over which a veil was draped. She sparkled with diamonds, which were set in her hair, her ears, her nostrils, around her neck, her wrists, her ankles; she looked, Scylla uncharitably thought, like the pictures of chandeliers in the Bombay *Gazette*. The queen appeared slightly startled at the sight of Scylla, her gaze flickered from top to toe, like the tongue of a snake, paused on the white gloves, and then she said smoothly:

"Surely this is no place for you, Feringi lady? I did not look to see you here today."

"No?" Scylla retorted, making no attempt to keep the hostility out of her voice. "Nor I you, royal lady—unless, indeed, you had thought fit to join Mahtab Kour on the funeral pyre. But that, I gather, is not your intention." She let her eyes rest for a moment, ironically, on the young queen's fashionable attire.

Sada's glance darkened. She said, "Beware your insolent tongue, Angrezi, lest I order it to be cut out. My lord Mihal will do all I ask him."

"Allow me to congratulate you on your good fortune," Scylla said coolly. She swept Sada an angry curtsy and walked on, turning to say as an afterthought, "I believe I have you to thank, Rani, for a beautiful sari that was sent me. Unfortunately an accident befell it—I regret to say that it was all burned up."

And I hope you suffer a similar fate, she thought, remembering poor Bisesa's death agonies and the two wretched little princes. She hurried on out of the gate, leaving Sada staring after her, furious and puzzled.

Old Abdul at the main entrance demanded, "Where is the Mem Musson?"

"She would not come home, Abdul. She said she must wait as long as possible. Do you wait here for her. I am not happy about her."

The old man scowled, thrusting out his lower lip. "It is not right for the young mem to go home unescorted."

"Nonsense, Abdul. I know the way backward and shall do very well. I order you to remain here!"

Grumbling to himself, he squatted down again, and Scylla hurried on through the narrow, rutted streets, noticing yet again the town's unnatural hush.

There were signs that the hot weather was coming to an end. The monsoon was near. Heavy, threatening masses of cloud piled up in the sky over the distant hills, then broke and moved off, but always reformed. The air felt humid and oppressive, saturated with heat and moisture, full of small stinging, biting flies. Hastening homeward, Scylla thought, Shall we have to leave, to travel, just as the rains begin? Shall we not stay for the autumn festivals, for the winter?

She loved the winter in Ziatur. Freshened by the monsoon, the air became tingling clear, like iced wine. Smoke from camel-dung fires smelled nutty and pungent in the sharp evenings, the mountains put on coats of snow and glowed at sunset, the sheepherders came down from the hills with their jingling flocks. Suddenly all the winters of the past five years seemed to present themselves as one moment, irretrievably dear, the last of childhood. Where shall we be next year this time? she wondered.

A silence in the street made her pause and glance around her. The few people about, white-swathed women lamenting on doorsteps, peddlers calling their wares, had all, it seemed, been struck mute and were staring in her direction. Glancing sideways, she realized the reason for this. An enormously large, tall man, white-robed, bare-footed, was rushing down a narrow side alley. He seemed mad, or drunk; he was veering from side to side, waving his arms and bobbing his head; his features were distorted in a crazy grimace; he held an enormous curved kukri, or hillman's knife. As when confronted by the tiger, Scylla was held in almost fatalistic calm. He is coming straight for me, she thought; he is running so fast that I cannot possibly escape him. Turning her eyes with an effort from the approaching man to the women seated on their doorsteps, she realized that nobody was going to help her; so far as they were concerned, she was dead already. Perhaps word had been sent out from the palace . . . or perhaps they merely knew, intuitively, that it would be bad luck to help the Feringi or Yagistani. They would watch calmly as she was sliced in half.

Strangely enough, the approaching madman did not decapitate her with his kukri; instead he snatched her up as if she were made of straw and, shouting, "God is great!" rushed off along the street. Scylla, dangling helplessly, head down, over his shoulder, saw the red betel-stained cobblestones flash past and wondered, with detached irony, where Colonel Cameron was at this moment; it seemed so unlike him not to be at hand to rescue her.

After a time it seemed that her captor's footsteps were slowing down; presently, to Scylla's utter astonishment, he came to a standstill and placed her respectfully on her feet. When her head had stopped swimming and she had her eyesight back, she realized that they were in the forecourt of Miss Musson's hospital; also, looking at her companion, now that his face was no longer distorted, she recognized him. He was an Afghan, Sirafraz Ali, who had been in the hospital with a severe brain fever, caused by a camel's kick on his skull; Miss Musson had succeeded in curing him, after a month's care, with infusions of camomile tea and poultices of cold wet sand, but he had remained completely bald thereafter and somewhat unsettled in his wits. However now he appeared rational enough; he was shaking Scylla urgently and saying over and over:

"Missy sahib, tell the mem that she must *not* come to the hospital— ever again! Missy and Cal Sahib and Kamaran Sahib must all leave Ziatur—the danger here is too great. None of the Feringi will live until the rains if they do not leave now. Does the missy sahib understand?"

He shook her again, as if to force the information into her. Looking over his shoulder into the hospital, Scylla saw that all the string bed-steads and bedding rolls had been taken away; the drug closet was open and stripped; nothing of the equipment remained but some handfuls of straw and a broken crock or two.

"Soldiers coming here soon," Sirafraz muttered in Scylla's ear. "Prince Mihal gave the order. Shoot the Feringi ladies, cut their heads off. Understand, missy?" He shook her again, menacingly, then, pick-ing her up once more, resumed his wild dash through the town, up one alley, down another, all the time, by degrees, drawing closer to Miss Musson's bungalow. As he ran he shouted, "Slay the heathen! Crucify the unbelievers! God is great, God is great!"

At last, depositing Scylla gently in a lane that ran down beside the bungalow garden, he laid his finger on his lips, writhed his features into a last frightful grimace, and bounded away.

Scylla walked very thoughtfully into the house, to find Cal, for once not writing, but pacing about on the veranda, looking very anxious.

"Is Miss Musson not back yet?" she asked. He shook his head.

"Not yet. And Cameron has been summoned for an interview with Mihal."

"Perhaps Mihal wants Cameron to command his army, as he did the Maharajah's," Scylla said wearily. "Where are all the servants?"

"I think they have run away. All but Habib-ulla."

"I have just been warned that we must all leave Ziatur or we shall be killed," Scylla remarked.

"Oh, things will blow over, I dare say, once Mihal feels secure of the kingship," Cal said. "He is not a bad fellow, after all. By the bye, do not forget that the dentist fellow, Wharton, is in town, and going on to Surat; have you written a note for him to take? He can see that it is sent to our cousin in England, with the Company's mails."

"If we are to leave in any case, why write a letter? We may go to England ourselves and get there before it."

"Not if our guardian can discover any means of remaining here," said Cal with a grin.

About two hours before dusk Colonel Cameron arrived at the bungalow. When he heard that Miss Musson was still supposedly at the palace he let out such a string of heartfelt curses that Cal gazed at him in admiration.

"I beg your pardon, child," Cameron said then, glancing at Scylla—he looked, she observed, even more exhausted than on the previous night, his hair dusty and dark with sweat, prickles of sweat marking the hollows of temple and cheekbone, the whites of his blue eyes bloodshot. "I beg your pardon, but if that woman's obstinacy is the cause of our all being trapped here and cut to pieces, it will be enough to put a saint in a passion. And I am no saint."

Fortunately, soon after this Miss Musson herself appeared, riding slowly to the front of the house on her black pony. "Where is the syce?" she called, dismounting.

"Don't worry, ma'am, I will see to your pony," Cal said, and led the beast to the stable, while Scylla ran to fetch her guardian a long cool drink.

She did not like to ask how Miss Musson's mission had sped, since it was all too evident, from the older woman's ravaged and angry appearance, that it had gone ill; but Cameron had no such delicate scruples and said with his usual bluntness:

"Well, ma'am? Is it all over? Did they all roast themselves?"

"You may see for yourself," Miss Musson replied briefly, nodding her head toward the citadel, from which, Scylla now saw with a shiver, a thick, sluggish column of black smoke was coiling up into the humid air. "They all accompanied Mahtab; all the wives and most of her women; even that poor wretched child, with her broken leg, was there, allowed, as a mark of special favor, to sit on the queen's lap. And that Jezebel, Sada, watching from a window with *such* a satisfied expression; I would gladly throttle her."

She sipped at her drink, then pushed it away, exclaiming, "Oh, how can I drink after seeing those poor women in agony? It is disgusting!"

"Come now, Miss Amanda," Cameron said abrasively, "you know perfectly well that those women died completely happy, believing that they were carrying out the wishes of the gods and assured of a superior position in the next life. Also, that if the miserable Mahtab Kour had *not* immolated herself it's dollars to doughnuts that her serving maids would have dropped a paving stone on her in her bath. She *could* not have survived for long. So let your grief for her be equally brief, I beg. We have the future to consider. And it does not lie in Ziatur. Your hospital, ma'am, is no more. And we have only a few hours' grace—if that—before soldiers come to chop off our heads. In order to gain a little time, I told Mihal that I had another consignment of guns and ammunition on the way here—so that he might think it worth while leaving me alive long enough to show his men how to use the carbines; but it was not true, and I am not sure he believes me. I am in bad odor because I declined the honor of running his army. The French emissaries have Sada's ear; they have won her favor with a package of Paris fashions. The ways of diplomacy are strange! Who would have thought that an embroidered muslin gown and a bonnet shaped like Athene's helmet would change the course of history? But so it is."

He was talking, Scylla thought, in order to give Miss Musson time to compose herself. She quietly handed the older woman a plate of fruit and said:

"Come, you must eat something, my dear ma'am! Colonel Cameron is very right, we have to make a plan. As he says, the hospital has been pillaged; I am afraid the patients are all gone, and the contents carried off. It is quite plain, I fear, that we must not stay in the city any longer."

Cameron gave Scylla an approving nod, and Cal, coming in from the stable, added his mite:

"All those brutes of servants have run off, and they have taken our horses."

"What?" exclaimed Scylla, shaken out of her attempted calm. "*All* the horses? Not *Kali?*"

"Kali too," replied her brother grimly.

Cameron grunted, as if he had expected this.

"So you see, Miss Amanda, little though you may like it, the time has come to up sticks and go."

Strangely enough, Miss Musson did not seem inclined to argue the point. She had spent all her argumentative powers up at the palace and merely replied, wearily:

"No, I perceive that we must do so. But how is it to be managed? We have no horses, and it is unlikely that we shall be able to buy or hire any. How shall we travel?"

"Spoken like a woman of sense!" exclaimed Cameron approvingly. "Now, if you will all attend, I will tell you the plan. We must not all leave together, or we should assuredly be noticed and stopped. Disguise yourselves as beggars, carry as little as you may, only a few absolutely essential possessions, and some food for the journey. Meet me outside the Kohat gate at dusk, just before they close the gate. Come singly," he repeated. "I will be there and will arrange to have transport waiting. Is that agreed?"

"I fear so," said Miss Musson with a sigh. Cal merely nodded, with an absent expression; his sister guessed, sympathetically, that he was calculating how best to pack up all his poetry, his quills and cakes of ink, and which of his books must be left behind.

Scylla herself said, "There is just one thing, Colonel Cameron."

"Well, what?" Immediately he looked ruffled, ready to flare into exasperation at any opposition to his arrangements.

"Do you not remember our promise to the Maharajah? That if anything happened to him we should undertake to see that little Prince Chet Singh is conveyed safely to England, to his cousin in London?"

"Oh, that."

"Yes, that, Colonel Cameron! I do not forget a promise, even if you do!"

"Hold your fire, my dear." Cameron looked at her kindly and sadly. "I respect a promise, child, as much as you do. But this one we shall be unable to honor—and I must confess that our journey will therefore be relieved of a decided encumbrance. To be carrying a child with us, the way that we must go, would necessarily slow our pace and make us more vulnerable to attack."

"But why may we not take little Chet Singh?"

"Because little Chet Singh, child, was thrown over the battlements, by Sada's orders, early this morning. Already the crows will have picked his bones clean.—Now I must leave you. I have many things to arrange.—Dusk, then, at the Kohat gate. Wear old clothes, but warm ones. Miss Amanda, if you have any medicines in the house, you had best bring a bagful—" and he was gone.

Hastily, discarding the accumulated possessions of a lifetime, Miss Musson and her two wards packed a few necessities. It was, in a way, a relief that they were given so little time for thought or conjecture.

Scylla went to the deserted kitchen, where Habib-ulla remained, alone of all the servants. Giving the old man a month's wages, she told him that he had best forget he ever served the Feringi ladies, who now found themselves obliged to travel away from Ziatur.

"Alas! But how will the mems ever manage without me?" he inquired dolefully. "When do you go?"

"Tomorrow," Scylla replied, mindful that even he, faithful though he had always been, might by now have been perverted by Sada's minions. "Bake us plenty of bread, therefore, tonight, for our journey, Habib-ulla; also, go now to the bazaar and buy a big sack to carry provisions. And take this letter to the Sahib Wharton, who lodges in the Street of Silversmiths. Here is the money for the sack."

When he had hobbled off sadly on this errand, Scylla swiftly collected what food she could, along with such drinking and cooking utensils as would not immediately be missed, and packed them all in a skeepskin pouch. Her own clothes and trinkets were of little value. She left them all.

Cal, working with commendable speed, had wrapped up a parcel of his manuscripts and a few books, in layers of muslin and oiled silk, and now declared himself ready; only Miss Musson, though she had put together a bundle of medicaments, seemed anxious and ill at ease, unready to take her departure. Scylla felt a deep pang for her guardian; leaving this house must, for the older woman, mean abandoning the last home she had shared with her dearly loved brother Winthrop. It was a step forward into a bleak and unpromising future.

"What is it, dear ma'am? Something you are trying to remember? Can I be any assistance?"

"No, my dear child, thank you; no, it is nothing. Do you and Cal start off now, dusk is beginning to thicken; I will follow in a few moments. Colonel Cameron said that we must not all leave together."

Cal, nodding, strode off into the twilight, adjuring his sister to allow five minutes to elapse and then go after him but take a different route to the Kohat gate.

"Ma'am," said Scylla, troubled, "you do *mean* to come with us, do you not? You are not proposing to remain here, or—or do anything dreadful?"

Miss Musson's hawklike face broke into its rare, brilliant smile.

"No, no, child—have no fear of that! I shall be with you as soon as I may. But warn Rob Cameron to be prepared for a little delay—I must wait for an important message, here, before I depart. Now run along with you—veil your face and be as prudent as possible."

With this rather unsatisfactory reply Scylla had to be content. Carrying the bundle of food on her back, she slipped out of the house and along the street, moving from one patch of shadow to another. For once Miss Musson had relaxed her rule about European dress; Scylla wore a hill woman's black headcloth, a voluminous white homespun wool cloak pulled forward over her face and latched at one side so that only her eyes were visible; under the cloak she had a red wool tunic, Pahari trowsers, and goatskin mountain boots. At present they felt stiflingly hot; she was bathed in sweat and found it difficult to hurry. The air was vaporous and steamy; every now and then a distant mutter of thunder came as a reminder that the rains were due to break. A mad time to start a journey, thought Scylla dispassionately as she slipped, like a humble village woman bowed with her burden, between the armed guards who stood on either side of the gate in the town wall. They did not concern themselves with her; bored, chewing pan, they were informing an old fortuneteller with a fat, sleepy python in a basket that he must either come in or stay outside for the night, in which case he would inevitably be devoured by wolves; he was begging them to keep the gate open just one more half hour for his apprentice, who was following behind but had been delayed by a thorn in his foot.

"No more than a half hour, then, old man! Our orders are to shut the gate when the evening star shines clear of that peepul tree."

"But, Your Worships, suppose clouds cover the star? How will you know then what time to shut the gate?"

It was true, Scylla noticed, that, blotting the green twilit sky, huge mushroom-shaped clouds were growing above the distant mountains, black as ink; darkness was coming on apace. She moved inconspicuously away from the gate and along by the side of the great red wall to where a buttress, thrusting out, would screen her from the view of the guards. Beyond the buttress a great peepul tree grew, and under it a mahout was grooming his elephant. It seemed a strange time of day to be doing this, Scylla reflected idly, and then, looking again, she was startled to see that the mahout was Cameron's Therbah servant. He salaamed to her briefly, placing a finger on his lips.

A hand gripped hers; Cal moved quietly from the far side of the tree.

"Is not this famous?" he breathed in Scylla's ear. "I did not above half care to leave Ziatur, but Colonel Cameron knows how to do a thing in style! He is the most complete hand! Where do you suppose he got it? Can he have stolen it from the palace stables?"

There were stone rest shelves around the peepul tree, for travelers to pause a moment and take the weight off their loads; Scylla perched herself on one of these, thinking, An elephant! How masterly! Really, there is no end to Colonel Cameron's resourcefulness.

The town gate was about to close. They could hear drums being beaten, a gong boomed, and the guards bawled out their evening message:

"All ye who are without, make haste if ye wish to enter the town! Oh, townspeople, prepare to be shut in for the night!"

"Miss Musson, where can she be?" gasped Scylla.

"Hush!"

"Ai, aie! My poor apprentice!" wailed the old man with the python. "He has not come yet! How will he know where I am gone? I shall have to remain outside and wait for him."

"Stay outside, then, with the jackals and wild boars, what do we care?" replied the guards, and the gates clanged together. Just before they did so, a stooped figure in a black burqa slipped between them; Scylla breathed out a heartfelt sigh of relief. Hurrying forward, she clasped the arm of the older woman, who murmured:

"Careful, my dear. He is asleep, do not wake him. A cry *now,* and we are lost!"

"Ma'am? What can you mean?"

With utter astonishment Scylla realized that, as well as the pack she carried on her back, Miss Musson was cradling a bundle in the folds of her voluminous black garment—a warm, tiny bundle that moved and breathed.

"*A baby?*"

"Hush! When we are well away from the town I will tell all."

"But—good God, ma'am!—oh well—let me take your pack, then." Scylla led Miss Musson to the elephant, which was now kneeling to accommodate its passengers. They climbed into the howdah, where Cal was already settling himself. A moment later, and they were joined by Cameron. Scylla was astonished to recognize in him the old fortune-teller; she would not have thought it possible that the tall, vigorous Cameron could appear so hunched and stooped.

"But what have you done with the python?" she whispered. "I trust you have not brought it as well?"

"No, child." She could hear the ghost of a laugh in his reply. "The python is rejoicing in unexpected freedom; I left him under a fig tree. —Are you ready, Therbah?"

"Yes, lord."

"Then let us be off."

Silently as a cloud the elephant rose to its feet and drifted away downhill, rapidly leaving the town behind, taking a zigzag route through the orange orchards, the melon beds, and the opium fields.

"Best not to follow any road," Cameron whispered.

"Where are we going?" Cal inquired. "South, to Surat, to ship for England?"

"What is your will, ma'am?" Cameron turned to the silent Miss Musson in her corner. "Is it to be Surat, and a ship?"

"No, I think not," she replied after a moment's considering pause. "When Mihal discovers what has happened there is bound to be a hue and cry, and he will be looking first along the road south, to Surat. We had therefore better go west, to Peshawur and Jellalabad. Rob, do you not agree? Once we are through the Khaiber Pass, Mihal will hardly pursue us. And that is little more than a hundred miles, but Surat is many hundreds, and his vengeance could follow us all the way."

"I am in agreement with you, Miss Amanda—though, I must confess, I am surprised that you plump for the land route!"

"But the baby!" burst out Scylla, who could contain her curiosity no longer. "What baby is that, ma'am? Not little Chet?"

"*Baby?*" Colonel Cameron, who was sitting at the front of the howdah, suddenly screwed around as if a hornet had stung him. "In God's name, ma'am, what act of madness have you committed now?"

"It is the Maharajah's youngest son," placidly replied Miss Musson, glancing down at the anonymous dark bundle she carried. "He was born only this afternoon, to that Khalzai girl who was Bhupindra's last favorite. She, poor wretch, was thrown into the underground crocodile tank, by Sada's orders. But I bribed a servant with a bag of gold dust to bring the babe to me. He has not yet been christened; perhaps we should do so without delay. Do you have any liquor on you, Colonel Cameron?"

"Yes," he replied in a strangled tone. "I am glad to say I have a flask of brandy. I can think of better uses for it but—"

He handed the flask to Cal, who knelt by Miss Musson, dragging the leather stopper out with his teeth.

"Perhaps we should christen this little fellow Chet Singh too, like his poor unfortunate brother," Miss Musson observed, sprinkling a few drops of spirit on the sleeping child's forehead. And she murmured rapidly, "In the name of the Father, the Son, and the Holy Ghost, I baptize thee Amirul-Umra Bhupindra Mohinder Yadu Chet Singh, Prince of Ziatur," before recorking the flask and passing it back to the stupefied colonel. "There," she added in a consoling tone. "Now you and Scylla may feel that, in some part at least, you will be able to keep your promises to that poor old man."

Cameron was speechless, but Scylla said warmly, "*Thank* you, dear Miss Musson."

Almost directly overhead a tremendous, earsplitting clap of thunder, loud as the trump of doom, caused them all to flinch in their seats. A glare of lightning illuminated the cactus-studded plain which they were crossing. The elephant trumpeted nervously and lengthened her smooth, gliding stride.

Huge drops of rain began to fall.

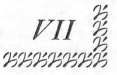

VII

To Fanny's utter amazement, her escapade in Petworth Park went unreported to Thomas and unrebuked by him. The reasons for this were various.

Firstly, Thomas did not return from Brighton for two days, and when he did, he was in a morose temper. The expedition to capture the Brighton fishermen and press them into naval service had been a total failure. The regulating officers, with their combined force of men, had encircled the town and pounced at dawn, expecting to catch all the able-bodied men still in their beds; but somebody had been beforehand with the information and the birds had flown; or rather, put out to sea at low tide, having left their boats moored farther out than usual. Only their womenfolk remained to jeer at the disappointed impress officers, who spent the next twelve hours in angry recriminations among themselves, trying to decide whether it was worth waiting and attempting another pounce.

Thomas, therefore, returning angrily to Petworth, was in no mood to listen to domestic gossip. His daughters, furiously banished from the dinner table for daring to inquire after the success of his expedition, were not inclined to inform their father that Fanny had spent a night away from home, at the Rectory, and they themselves had not heard about the earlier part of the affair, the adventure in the park. Mrs. Socket had merely sent a note to the Hermitage informing the household that Mrs. Paget, finding herself a little unwell, had been recommended by Dr. Chilgrove to rest at the rector's house until the following morning. Thomas was not esteemed by his domestic staff, and none of them was in the least tempted to mention a matter that might lead to trouble for their gentle mistress. Fanny had begun to realize with some surprise that the servants were her friends—in any question involving Thomas's displeasure they would be likely to take her part. And, fortunately, Nurse Lily Baggot, who was disliked by the other servants because she would not take her food with them but expected her meals to be brought upstairs, along with old Mrs. Paget's, never discovered that Fanny had passed a night away from home.

For the next few weeks Thomas was even more lowering and illhumored than usual; he spent much time in his garden room (which the warmer weather now rendered more comfortable) and refused to listen to any but the most urgent domestic requests.

One of these, made by Fanny, was that his mother must be conveyed out into the garden each day for an airing.

"Fiddlestick!" was his first angry retort. "There's not the slightest occasion for it. Besides, she has no outdoor clothes. In any case, she can never be got up and down those stairs."

However when Fanny represented to Thomas Dr. Chilgrove's opinion that the old lady's life would certainly be shortened were she confined all the time to the stuffy little upstairs chamber and deprived of air and exercise, he could not help but remember that it was in his own financial interest to preserve her alive for as long as possible, since her annuity would die with her. He therefore grudgingly and aggrievedly gave permission for her daily airings and began wondering within himself whether Cousin Juliana van Welcker, his landlady, might be persuaded that the house needed an extra room or two on the ground floor. It would be much simpler to wheel out the old lady if she were on ground level. And when she died he could use one of the rooms for an office. Accordingly he wrote off this request to Demerara, though he must resign himself to not receiving a reply for some three months. He was tempted to set about the work in the meantime—for his cousin was sure to agree, since the additional space would do so much to improve the house—but, reflecting that if he began without her agreement *he* would be obliged to pay for the operation, whereas when she knew of the project she might well pay for it with her usual generosity, he decided to wait.

Meanwhile he ordered that his daughters transfer to the attics and his mother, with her attendant, move down to the rooms which the girls had occupied. This edict was received with no pleasure at all by Martha, Bet, and Patty, who suddenly found their space reduced by more than half. Thomas himself had recently installed a bed in the garden house and quite often, these mild spring nights, slept out there. These unanticipated absences from the conjugal bedchamber were times of inexpressibly blessed respite to Fanny, who, attempting to deserve such fortune, bestowed as much attention as possible on Thomas's old mother.

She acknowledged to herself in secret, however, that it was hard to like the old lady. Although when she had settled in she became less confused and more conversible, she still proved, on closer acquaintance, to be a dismaying mixture of stupidity, malice, and rather primitive cunning. She disliked her son, but feared him more, and was all propitiation in his presence, repeating over and over her unbounded gratitude for being brought to reside at the Hermitage. In his absence, however, she did not scruple to revile him for his parsimony, unkindness, and selfishness. She did this only with Fanny, though, having rapidly discovered that Nurse Baggot was in Thomas's confidence and that any complaints disclosed to *her* would be passed on straightway to *him* and subsequently punished by deprivation of comforts or other penalties. Poor Fanny, however, was obliged to listen to many grievances.

"And the way he treated his poor brother, dearie—my second husband's son Edward, you know—was shocking as can be. Ah, poor dear Edward! Such a sweet-tempered, easygoing boy as he was! But Thomas was always unkind to him—jealous, as you may imagine, because Edward's father was more partial to his own boy—and Edward such a bright, lovable little fellow—whereas Thomas always showed that surly, selfish temper from his earliest years. I was obliged to protect little Edward—or Thomas would be forever abusing him, for he was five years older, and stronger—taking his toys and breaking them, or snatching his food, or cuffing and pinching him—so the end of it was that my second husband said Thomas must be sent away to school. And it's my belief he never forgave his brother for that."

Though she could no longer make any attempt to like or esteem Thomas, Fanny did begin to feel some stirrings of compassion for his childhood. She could see how this usage might have helped to sour still further a nature already arrogant, self-centered, and touchy.

"Thomas could never bear his stepfather's authority," the old lady disclosed. "And my second husband, though he could be liberal on occasion, would never brook insolence or sulkiness; oh, I have been frightened, many and many a time, dearie, by the shocking scenes. 'You keep out of this, Maria,' Mr. Wilshire (that was my second husband's name) would say to me, and then, to punish Thomas for some unkindness to little Edward, he would be obliged to beat him till the blood ran down."

"But, ma'am! Did you never remonstrate with him? Was he always perfectly fair to Thomas?"

"Remonstrate? Oh no, dearie. I would shut myself in my bedroom on such occasions. Mr. Wilshire knew best; what he did was right.—

Besides, he was a very quick-tempered man—he would brook no interference. In that way he resembled my first husband—Mr. Paget,
Thomas's father, had a very severe nature. I dare say it is true of most
men. They will have their own way, whether right or wrong, and we
females have to defer to them."

Sighing, Fanny thought of her own father, who, a scholarly, un-
worldly man, though much preoccupied with his pastoral duties, had
always been the epitome of gentle impartiality and kindness to his
daughters; Lord Egremont, too, she felt certain, would be perfectly
fair-minded and benevolent in all his dealings; however there was no
purpose to be achieved in arguing with the old lady, who had plainly
been too frightened of both her husbands to think well of the male sex
or behave with justice or equity to her two sons.

"What became of your younger son, ma'am?" she inquired. Thomas
had never spoken to her of his brother.

To her dismay, the old lady began to weep.

"Oh, pray do not, ma'am!" Fanny exclaimed. "Indeed, I am sorry
to have distressed you."

It was a wet April afternoon; both older girls were out, Bet accompanying Martha to her harp lesson; little Patty, who had fortunately
taken a liking to Mrs. Strudwick, was downstairs in the kitchen learning how to make a gingerbread man; Fanny and the old lady were sitting in the big bow window of the parlor, Fanny alternately stitching a
robe for the coming baby or gazing out at the rain-swept garden and
green valley beyond. Nurse Baggot was off in the town on her own
purposes.

Gently, Fanny leaned forward and wiped the old lady's tears away.

"Look, ma'am, see that patch of sun moving up the far side of the
valley. In five minutes we can go out. Do not be troubling your mind
with sad thoughts."

"No, I will tell you about it, dearie—for it will give you some notion
of Thomas's jealous, niggardly ways." Fanny sighed. "I had a little
money, you see, left me by Mr. Paget, my first husband, on his death.
So this, of course, passed into the hands of my second husband, who

bought an orchard with it; the income from the sales of fruit was to be divided fairly between my two sons, after the death of Mr. Wilshire."

"That seems a fair scheme," said Fanny cautiously.

"Of course it was fair, dearie; Mr. Wilshire would never make any arrangement that was unfair. But my son Edward—ah, I am afraid he was a sad shatterbrain, the very sweetness of his nature led him into scrapes, since he would be always helping out his friends, who, knowing his liberality of spirit, applied to him for money. And he was forever spending money, also, on inventions which he believed would presently make his fortune. He had an idea for a machine to cut grass by a system of whirling blades. Thomas, of course, thought nothing of such a notion, and indeed, I fear it would never have worked—"

Fanny glanced out of the window at old Henry Goble, the gardener, who, with a sack over his head to protect him from the rain, was scything the lush April grass that grew on the bank leading down to the yew-tree walk. A machine to cut grass! What a strange, fantastic idea.

"So what happened then, ma'am?"

"Edward, you see, wished the orchard to be sold so that he could realize his part of the legacy and make use of the money for his schemes. But, for that, Thomas's agreement had to be obtained, and Thomas was at sea then, in the navy, you know, and perhaps Edward's letters did not reach him, or perhaps he had no time for such business; at any rate, he did not reply, and I fear my poor Edward meanwhile fell into debt and had recourse to moneylenders; he did apply to *me*, but I could do little for him, I had not much. . . . And then I believe he took to gaming and betting—hoping to retrieve matters, you know—and found himself in bad company—and—and I am afraid he was sent to jail—and took the jail fever—and that was the end of him!"

"Hush, hush, ma'am—do not be weeping any more—you will tire yourself out!"

Patting, consoling the old lady, Fanny thought: What a sad, unsurprising tale. No doubt the poor young man had done nothing particularly bad; if he could have been rescued from his unfortunate predicament and helped, he might have given up his youthful wildness, might have become a decent, hard-working citizen—might have been a comfort to his mother in her old age; would probably not, like his half brother, have accorded her grudging houseroom and repulsive looks. Very likely, though, it was her unwise indulgence in Edward's childhood that had caused him to turn out feckless and improvident. . . .

"See, ma'am," she said, rising, "here comes the sun. I will send for Jem to bring your basket chair, so that we may take a turn out of doors."

Going out onto the flagged path by the house, "Goble!" she called. "Will you send Jem to me, please."

The gardener straightened himself from his task, presenting his usual unforthcoming aspect; impatient, it seemed, at being withdrawn from his own thoughts; grave, somber, verging on hostility.

"Eh? What's your will wi' the boy, missus?" he demanded. "I sent him over to Shimmings Farm for a load o' peasticks."

"Oh—" Fanny was rather dashed. "I wished him to push my mother-in-law in her wheel chair for half an hour, now the sun has come out. Dr. Chilgrove has forbidden me to do it any more."

"Where's yon wumman as calls herself a *nurse?*" he demanded in a grumbling tone.

"It is her time off."

Goble's face expressed what he thought of both Nurse Baggot and her lavish free time.

"Reckon I'll hafta leave off this-yer work and shove her along myself, then," he muttered ungraciously.

"Would you, Goble? I should be very much obliged to you."

Fanny had decided that the only way to meet Goble's surliness was to behave to him, always, with a grave, formal politeness; she saw no sign, as yet, that this was in any way winning his friendship, but at least he was no more uncivil to her than to any other members of the household; perhaps a little less.

"I'll be fetching her chair," he said in a grumbling manner, and limped off.

While Mrs. Strudwick and Tess were helping the old lady into various borrowed shawls and pelisses, Fanny, slipping on a pair of pattens, strolled over the lawn to the yew walk and, leaning on the wall that overlooked the valley, gazed out across the green and blowy prospect. Down at the bottom the brook shone, reflecting the changeable sky; on Fanny's back and shoulders the sun felt deliciously warm. How Thomas can wish to exclude the sun! she thought. He had lately complained that its beams, shining into the garden house, dazzled his eyes and distracted him from his accounts; he had caused venetian blinds to be installed in all the garden-room windows.

Voices coming from the public right of way below the boundary wall caught her attention, and, glancing down, she saw one of the liveried footmen from Petworth House carefully escorting a plump lady in a pale pink dress, whom he shaded from the sun with a parasol. Because of the parasol, Fanny could not at first see the lady's face, but a sudden premonition was making her step back from the lookout wall when the lady, becoming aware of Fanny's presence, looked up and laughingly waved to her, then gestured to the footman to proceed farther along the path.

"So there you are, my love! I have discovered a means of reaching you in spite of your incarceration! Is not this famous! I declare, you are exactly like Fair Rosamund, shut up at Godstow by the wicked Queen Eleanor. Now I have found out your hiding place, I intend to take no more rambles in the park but walk this way every day, exercising Pug," exclaimed Liz Wyndham, glancing down at the diminutive dog she had on a leash.

Her round face broke into its irresistible dimpling smile. "I hardly dared hope that I might see you! I told Egremont that I was not satisfied the brook in the bottom of the valley was being kept properly dredged—our coal is all fetched up it by boat, you know—and some other commodities that I will not mention! Now I shall report to him that the brook requires a *great* deal of attention and that I must come to inspect it with the most meticulous regularity. Do you not approve?—How are you keeping, my sweet friend? You look pale and hagged—did you receive the basket of peaches and nectarines that was sent to you *from the Rectory?* Come now—could you not contrive to

lower a basket on a rope so that I could pass you up *Horrid Mysteries,*
The Orphan of the Rhine, The Necromancer of the Black Forest,
and *The Castle of Wolfenbach?* I am sure reading those delicious romances would do you more good than all Chilgrove's potions and
nostrums. He, however, assures me that you go on just as you ought
—in spite of *you know what*—and that your baby will be born within
a few weeks. Do you really feel tolerably stout, my sweet creature?"

Fanny could not help laughing, though she glanced in terror toward
Thomas's garden house at the far end of the walk. Mrs. Wyndham's
conspiratorial looks and glances were very funny, but what if Thomas
should appear? In a low voice, but with heartfelt sincerity, she assured
her friend that she went on very well, that the nectarines had been
most gratefully received, and that, since they were sure to be discovered and would lead to serious trouble, Mrs. Wyndham must not on
any account think of lending her books.

"Oh—! Such stuff! You promised to call me Liz, remember? Why
do you keep looking at the gazebo? Is the ogre within?" With a ro-
guish look she shook her fist at the garden house but lowered her voice.
"Then I will be more circumspect. Are you truly in good health? I
rejoice to hear it. Now I will not embarrass you any further! Adios!
But, I warn you, I shall somehow contrive to see you again. Come,
Pug!"

Blowing kisses to her friend, Liz Wyndham moved on along the
path. Fanny thought that she seemed like an emanation of spring itself: a cluster of pink apple blossom, a cloud drifting in the sunlight.
—She had departed only just in time. The door of Thomas's garden
room opened, and he strode out, glancing suspiciously at Fanny.

"To whom were you talking just now?"

Fanny, naturally a truthful person, had resolved that, whatever the
circumstances, she would never tell a lie to Thomas, for if she once
began to do so, she could imagine that her life would become in no
time a terrifying tissue of falsehoods and mendacity. The silent sup-
pression of fact that she already practiced made her feel quite sufficiently guilty as it was. In the present situation she would have been

hard put to it for a reply, but fortunately at this moment two children ran by along the path below, searching for a lost ball. Thomas concluded that she had spoken to them and withdrew again, saying sharply:

"I do not choose that my wife shall hang over the wall like a servant girl, talking to all and sundry who pass by. You will oblige me by withdrawing to some other part of the garden."

"I was just waiting for your mother," Fanny replied mildly. Indeed Goble now appeared at the end of the walk, pushing the old lady in her chair.

Thomas scowled. "Do not be keeping Goble from his duties for more than twenty minutes."

He went back into the garden house and slammed the door.

They had taken no more than half a dozen turns along the yew-tree walk when Bet and Martha returned from the harp lesson. Fanny could not help wondering, sometimes, about these harp lessons, in what lay their great attraction. The girls today were giggling and red-cheeked, full of some mysterious excitement, hardly likely to be called forth by a series of scales and arpeggios. Both girls had lately blossomed out in new ribbons for their gowns and new strings for their bonnets; these, they asserted, had been bought with money given them by Thomas's mother. The two girls passed by now, ignoring Fanny and the old lady; they were laughing and whispering together. Fanny caught a few words.

"Even if he plagued me to death I would not tell him for the world —they are both amazingly saucy—I shall not pay them the compliment of seeming to give them any attention—they cannot put *me* out of countenance, I promise you!"

They passed into the house. Fanny looked after them in some perplexity. If they were not getting into some scrape! But she felt the delicacy and difficulty of her situation. Being younger than they were, she did not like to seem to pry or dictate her own notions of propriety —particularly since, considering her own clandestine acquaintance with Liz Wyndham, she felt that she herself stood on very debatable ground.

"Have you had enow of trundling to and fro, Mrs. Paget, ma'am?" Goble was inquiring of the old lady, who, hunched down in her chair, had let out a querulous murmur to the effect that the sun had gone behind a cloud, she believed the damp air was giving her a rheum, her feet were unconscionably cold, and no one cared if she died of the influenza.

"Eh? What did you say?" she demanded, peering up at Goble irritably.

"Do you wish to go indoors, Missus Paget?" impatiently repeated Goble in a voice that had, when he was a boatswain, summoned men from all over the ship.

"You do not have to shout! I am not deaf!" peevishly replied the old lady. "Yes, I *do* wish to go indoors, and have done any time this last ten minutes. What's the pleasure in going up and down, up and down a grass path, pray? Why can't we go into the town? And my name is not *Paget,* I'll have you know! It is Wilshire, and pray remember it."

Without a word, Goble turned and directed the course of her chair toward the garden door. Fanny followed, reflecting how swiftly an April day could pass from brilliant sunshine to cold, dark threat; the air had become icy, a great bank of black cloud had crept up, and there was promise of another heavy shower before dusk. She hoped that Liz Wyndham would contrive to return home safely without a drenching. . . .

As she stepped indoors, heavy drops of rain began to patter on the flagged path.

About to slip off her pattens, Fanny paused and put her hand to her side with an involuntary startled gasp of indrawn breath. For a moment a sudden transfixing stab of pain held her motionless; she clenched her teeth and gripped her hands together. Then, as the pain slowly withdrew, she went carefully on into the house and pulled the bell cord for Tess.

"Tess? Is Jem come back yet? No? Then will you please go to Dr. Chilgrove's house and ask him to come here as soon as he conveniently can. First tell Mrs. Strudwick that I have sent you on this errand. Say to Dr. Chilgrove that I think my pains have begun."

And, turning on her heel, Fanny toiled wearily up the stairs to her own chamber, where she began walking to and fro at a slow but steady pace.

Fanny's labor lasted for more than thirty-six hours. Afterward she was to look back on the time with a kind of wondering disbelief, as a species of nightmare that could not possibly have happened or, if it had, must have happened to some other person, not herself. It seemed impossible that she could have survived such an experience, and indeed, at many times, both during and after the birth, her life was despaired of. Her main recollections were twofold: firstly, of walking to and fro, to and fro, exhorted to do so by Dr. Chilgrove, until the pain in her back became so consuming that she felt as if it were likely to split her in two; then of lying on her bed, speechless, bewildered with agony, unable to do anything, even cry out, nothing but mutely demand of whoever came within her range of vision *why* this was happening to her and when this undeserved torture would be over. Dimly she was aware that little Tess, the maid, called in at some point to help rub Fanny's back, had burst out blubbering.

"Oh, jeemany, Doctor, I can't a-bear the look in her eyen!—Bain't there *some* way ye can put her to rights? Poor lady—and she the deediest, kindliest mistress a body could have—niver taffety or grummut—oh, *do* summat for her, Doctor, do!"

"I am doing all I can, my girl," grunted Dr. Chilgrove. "Do you fetch Mrs. Strudwick and tell her to bring more hot water and a strong, hot cup of her camomile tea. And send that nurse, Bagshaw, Baggot, whatever the woman calls herself—where the devil is *she?*"

There were long, confused intervals when pain was the only reality: pain vaguely apprehended by Fanny on two levels, a deep, continuous basic gripping drilling torment that grew steadily more and more severe until she could see it would finally rise to a pitch when it became wholly intolerable; and a sharp, intermittent pang whose sudden assaults, when they came, were so ferocious that they depleted her ability to endure the more continuous agony.

"I am sorry—Oh! I am sorry!" she gasped when one of these acute spasms shook her out of control and she felt the sweat pour down her cheeks.

"Don't you be sorry, ma'am, you got naught to be *sorry* for—" That was Mrs. Strudwick's voice. She felt as if she were in a hammock of friendly hands and voices, but they could do nothing for her, she was merely conscious of their well-meaning impotence.

Sometimes she was aware of dissident notes in the concerned chorus. A frightened twittering at the door—that must be her stepdaughters; she tried to call out, to tell them that there was nothing to be frightened of, but her voice would not carry so far, would hardly come out of her throat. And in any case, she thought confusedly, perhaps there *is* something to be frightened of—did not their own mother die in childbirth? I cannot recollect. Or was it mine? She—Thomas's first wife—went through this so many times, they very likely know more about it than I do—what did Martha say that first evening, twelve babies in thirteen years? Oh, dear God, think of going through this *twelve times* . . . and an overmastering onrush of pain deprived her momentarily of sight or hearing as she battled in a thorny twilit region of anguish and delirium. Out of this she came at some point to hear Dr. Chilgrove's voice, sharp with anger and disgust:

"Get out of this room, woman, you stink of geneva! God knows by what authority you term yourself a *nurse,* but I do not scruple to say that you are wholly unfit for your office. I would as soon employ a milkwoman or a stone picker—" And then Mrs. Baggot's tones, loud, hectoring, and abusive: "I dare say I have as much right in here as you, sir! I am employed by Captain Paget, not by *you,* I'd have you know—"

"Oh, send her away, pray send her away," Fanny murmured faintly to whoever was within earshot. "Her voice is so loud—if the truth be known, I do not like her above half—and if I am going to die I had as lief die among friends—" and she was off again, hardly heeding Dr. Chilgrove's robust exhortations.

"Psha, ma'am, let's have no more of this talk of *dying*—why, we shall have you in plump currant in no time, I promise you—now, pray take a little of this cognac—"

More angry voices: that of Thomas, this time. "What the deuce is all this pucker about? A young, healthy girl, not yet eighteen— Frances, *Frances,* let us have no more of such mawkish, sickly, swooning affectation! Pull yourself together, I beg! Good God, Chilgrove, my first wife went through this twelve times, I am not a man to be told my business when it comes to childbirth, I assure you! Get the infant *out* of her, that is all I ask."

"That is all I am trying to do, Captain Paget—" Dr. Chilgrove's voice, ragged with fatigue and irritation. "Your first wife, sir, must have been a lady of remarkable stamina if she indeed experienced such a labor as this twelve times; though, as I apprehend that she finally succumbed, perhaps her strength was less than you gave her credit for. The present Mrs. Paget is young and small in frame—the infant I am attempting to deliver is a remarkably large, fine one, even though slightly premature—"

"Boy or girl?" Thomas's voice, quick, eager.

"That, sir, the Almighty, in the fullness of time, will disclose—now, if you please, Captain Paget, there are enough persons in this room as it is—Mrs. Strudwick, pray hand me that hot plaister, I wish to apply it to the poor lady's extremities, which are becoming dangerously chilled—"

Fanny wished that the plaister could have been applied to her back, where the pain was rapidly becoming so terrible that she feared it might rip her apart like a pea pod.

"Pray, Dr. Chilgrove, if I die, see that my green morocco slippers go to my sister Maria, they are but hardly worn and her feet are the same size as mine—"

"Come, come, Mrs. Paget, be of good heart, ma'am. Never mind the slippers now! Hark, the cocks are crowing. Let that brave sound raise up your spirits!"

"Have you e'er tried snuff, Doctor?" she heard Mrs. Strudwick's tired voice inquiring diffidently. "Time my daughter was took so dannel bad with her fourth, a haitch o' snuff were what pulled it out of her, handsome as a herring—"

"Well, well, Mrs. Strudwick, the old country remedies are sometimes worth trying—let us see what snuff can do." In an undertone, not meant for Fanny to hear, she caught a few words: "Last resort, I fear —strength is ebbing rapidly—"

Indeed, Fanny did begin to feel a strange, dreamlike slipping away of all her faculties; very agreeable, she thought vaguely, if this be death, I am not in the least afraid of it; besides I shall see dear Mamma and Papa in heaven, he promised it, and Barnaby also perhaps—

A gust of sharp, stinging, burning powder up her nose made her gasp, gasp again, and inflate her lungs in a series of shattering sneezes: they were followed and overborne by a pain compared with which all those that had gone before seemed mere twinges, irritations.

"Mercy!" she screamed, and on the word her child was born.

"Bravo, ma'am! Mrs. Strudwick—make haste, hand me those—"

"Oh, ma'am! Thank God, thank God!"

"Well done, missus, that's the dandy—"

Now I can lie back, Fanny thought, now I need never stand up again. Limp, flat as an ell of soaking-wet gauze, she sank back on her pillows. She felt boneless, drained, evanescent.

"Quick, Tess—the smelling salts, girl—she be going—"

"No, I am not," said Fanny faintly. "The child—I wish to know— is it a boy or a girl?"

"Oh, ma'am, the most beautiful boy! Blue eyes, and fair as an angel!"

"A fine little fellow, Mrs. Paget, one to be proud of—eight pounds, if he's an ounce, or I never pulled a fish out of Benbow Pond! Now sup this cordial and let you lie back and rest, you have done your part—"

"He should be called Mercy," whispered Fanny. "Let me see him, let me hold him if you please—"

"One moment, my dear ma'am, while Mrs. Strudwick sets him to rights. Then you shall have him."

But by the time her son was ready for her Fanny had fainted dead away, and her next sight of him was not to be for some ten days, during which period she nearly died from loss of blood, and Dr. Chilgrove, a sporting man, predicted her chances of recovery as one in fifty. Thomas, privately, felt it would be no bad thing if she *were* to die. He had his son, which was really all that mattered. And another wife, one with less of Fanny's silent obstinacy, reserve, and something he could only define to himself as undeclared rebellion, would be a considerable improvement, and not at all hard to find.

Meanwhile a wet nurse, Jemima King, was found for the baby, who was christened, not Mercy, a wholly unsuitable name for a boy, but Thomas, after his father.

It was six weeks after the birth of the second Thomas before Fanny was permitted by Dr. Chilgrove to leave her chamber. In the course of that period, several things of considerable importance occurred.

The first took place during an interview between Thomas and Dr. Chilgrove in which the latter bluntly told Captain Paget that another pregnancy and birth such as that before at least two years had passed would in all probability kill Fanny.

"A speedy recovery of tone to her system cannot be hoped; we must watch for hectic symptoms and hope that her whole constitution has not been dangerously undermined; in short, my dear sir, I shall hold you morally responsible for her death if, before at least fifteen months shall have elapsed, Mrs. Paget is again found to be with child. She has given you a fine boy, in whom you can take just pride; you must be satisfied with that for the present."

Thomas, of course, was *not* satisfied; far from it. He had already begun considering that two strings to the bow were better than one—

for heaven knew, and he, personally, was only too well aware, to what ailments and accidents young children were constantly subject. He fell into a fury at this piece of unwarrantable interference in his domestic affairs. "Outrageous!" "Insupportable!" were some of the adjectives he applied to Dr. Chilgrove. But the latter calmly and firmly held his ground, only agreeing to re-examine Fanny and reconsider the matter at the end of six months; and Thomas, possibly recollecting that there were some questions regarding the death of the first Mrs. Paget that he would not wish to be reopened, finally contented himself with a great deal of angry bluster and with being exceedingly short, curt, and irascible during his visits to the chamber of Fanny, whom he roundly abused for not making more push to pluck up her energies, get back on her feet, and resume her household duties. Indeed Thomas was startled and annoyed to discover how much less comfortably the household ran when her quiet presence was lacking to give it order and direction.

The second notable event was the sudden disappearance of Martha, who, in the classic manner, was found to have vanished one Sunday morning when it came time for church, leaving no trace but a note pinned to her sister's pillow which cryptically said, "Dear Bet, gone with C, you may guess where. Wish me happy!"

Given time to think and recollect herself, Bet would certainly have concealed this note from her father, since its purport indicated some considerable degree of knowledge and complicity in herself. But her own indignation and astonishment at her sister's departure almost equaled that of Thomas, who, indeed, after one tremendous explosion of rage, began to consider that he was now quit of the troublesome keep and care of a daughter whom he had never particularly regarded and would not miss—and, furthermore, without the expense of having to find her a dowry.

"She shall never set foot in my house again!" he declared. "That is for certain! She may come begging and praying, in tatters, sick, or starving, she will find no pity here."

Blubbering and contradicting herself, Bet swore that she knew nothing, nothing at all of what had been going on; well, only just that sometimes Martha had loitered on the way home from harp lessons to talk to a young fellow who was sometimes to be seen down in the Shimmings Valley overseeing the work of dredging out the brook; he was a very well-set-up handsome superior young man who, from his bearing, might be rather a militiaman or excise officer than a mere civilian—

"Then what the devil was he doing ordering the dredging of the brook?" thundered Thomas. "And what the devil were *you* about to let her walk down that way and talk to him? Depend upon it, he was merely some steward or foreman of Egremont, who, I dare say, will give the pair of them a cottage on his estate to live in—as if my name were not disgraced enough in this town already!"

Whoever the young man was, he did not reappear, nor did Martha; Thomas was far too touchy and jealous of his reputation to make any inquiries after them. He did, however, place a crippling interdiction on Bet, who was forbidden to leave the grounds, bawled at, and deprived of all treats, until, as she tearfully complained to Fanny, life was not worth living, and she had as lief hang herself from the weeping ash tree.

Fanny could not help secretly feeling it quite a blessing that Martha's elopement had taken place during the second week after the baby was born, while her own life was still in danger and she therefore could be expected to play little part in the family disputes and recriminations that followed. She imagined that Martha's selection of this time was no accident; while attention was concentrated on the mistress' sickroom and the household at sixes and sevens would be a very favorable opportunity to escape from it.

The third change Fanny was not to discover until, after six weeks, by Dr. Chilgrove's permission, she was finally able to leave her chamber for an hour or two and venture down into the parlor window seat, which in the morning, at this time of year, was flooded with warm sun. By now May was running out. It was close, unusually warm weather for the time of year. The daffodils around the knobbed roots of the weeping ash were fast withering, and foxgloves were growing up to take their place. The baby, little Thomas, lay out of doors at Dr.

Chilgrove's recommendation, swaddled in flannel bands in his bassinet, under the shade of the ash tree. Fanny looked out at him wistfully— but he was in the care of his nurse Jemima King, who sat by him; she, his mother, had been allowed to handle him for little more than a moment or two, once a day; she hardly felt that he belonged to her. But when I am better . . . she thought. In the meantime, since she was not yet permitted out of doors, she asked Tess if the old lady, Mrs. Paget, would not like to come and sit in the parlor for a little while and talk to her.

"For I have not laid eyes on her since before the baby was born."

"I'll see, ma'am. She haven't hardly stirred from her chamber since you was laid up," Tess told her.

While waiting for the old lady, Fanny looked out at her son again. The fettered, crippled branches of the ash tree, bound with leather straps so that they pointed downward to the earth instead of upward to the sky, had, as if in frantic reaction against this abnormal confinement, sprouted thickly with green featherlike leaves, so that the tree now formed a natural umbrella of dense foliage; it was only just possible to see the baby's basket crib and the white cap of the nurse-girl sitting beyond him on a stool with her head nodding low; tired, poor soul, thought Fanny, who had heard the baby cry many times in the night. Although large and strong in spite of his premature birth, he was of a colicky disposition; but this, Dr. Chilgrove said, was not at all uncommon, and he pooh-poohed Thomas's anxieties about it. "The child cries in the nighttime, but he sleeps soundly by day; he is doing very well, sir, you need be under no apprehensions." Now, however, Fanny suddenly heard the baby give a loud, indignant scream, and then she heard Jemima King's sharp exclamation: "*Do* not be doing so, Miss Patty! Fie for shame! Bad, bad girl! I shall tell your mamma what you did!" There was also the sound of a slap, and little Patty emerged from among the dangling feathery branches, red-faced and resentful.

With an effort, Fanny raised the window sash a little higher and leaned out.

"What has happened, Jemima?" she called.

"Oh, ma'am! I didn't see you there." Rather confused, red-cheeked like Patty, Jemima came across the grass to the window and curtsied. "That wicked little hussy crept up to the baby while I—while I was not looking—and poked him with a twig. You have to watch her all the time, she is as naughty and sly as a barrel of weasels! Why, she might have put his eye out!"

"Come here, Patty," Fanny quietly said.

Patty came, scowling and dragging her feet.

"Tell me, why did you do so? Did you not know that it was wrong? The baby is only little, and feels pain very easily."

"She is forever trying to come at him and tease him," Jemima put in.

"I wanted him to open his eyes," Patty said in a grumbling tone.

"Her nose is out of joint, ma'am, that's the truth of it," Jemima said. "She can't abear not to come first. But girls must take second place to boys, she knows that."

This was such an evident truth that there was no gainsaying it. Still, Fanny, though it was hard to be fond of her youngest stepdaughter, who stole sugar and cakes, then put the blame on Tess, told untruths at every turn, constantly broke or mislaid household articles which she used for her own purposes, left disorder behind her everywhere, and was rude and disagreeable to her stepmother, could not help being a little sorry for the child. No one in the household could tolerate her, except, occasionally, Mrs. Strudwick, and of late she must have felt lonely and neglected, for since the baby's birth Fanny had been too weak to resume the morning lessons. She resolved, now, to begin again at once; at least, in those, Patty had been showing a little improvement.

"I am sure that Bet and Martha did not use *you* so when you were a baby," Fanny suggested hopefully.

"Yes, they did! They never left off plaguing me!"

"Well, if I find you tormenting Master Tom again, straight to your pa you go," Jemima threatened.

"Now run along, Patty, down to Mrs. Strudwick, and tell her I said you were to learn how to make a posset," Fanny said swiftly, and when

Patty had departed, thrusting out her lower lip, Fanny told Jemima, "Never mind informing Captain Paget this time, Jemima; he takes the child so to task that I fear it only makes her dislike the baby more."

"Very well, missus; but, to my mind, she'll never mend her ways without a good birching," Jemima, a plain-faced country girl, said roundly. She had two children of her own at home and had just lost the third, so she felt she spoke with authority. Fanny sighed.

"Thank you, Jemima. That will do."

Tess came into the parlor, supporting the old lady, who hobbled at a slow pace. Fanny was startled and dismayed at the change that had come over Thomas's mother in the past six weeks.

"Mercy on us, ma'am! Are you not well?"

"What is that, dearie?" mumbled the old lady, looking around her vaguely as Tess assisted her to sit down in a rocking chair and wrapped her knees in a shawl. She seemed to have aged five years; her face was puffy, her eyes dim, her thin hair unkempt and greasy-looking; her bodice was only half laced, a dirty dimity petticoat showed under her crumpled muslin gown, her gray stockings hung in wrinkles.

She looked as if no one had helped her to dress; or, indeed, washed her, brushed her hair, or assisted her with her toilet for many days.

"This was how I found her, ma'am," Tess said apologetically. "Mrs. Baggot had gone out on an errand—and I'm a bit behind with my work—"

"Well, never mind, Tess; thank you. I will speak to Mrs. Baggot when she returns," Fanny said, though with sinking spirits, for Mrs. Baggot these days treated her with hardly veiled insolence.

It was soon apparent to Fanny that the old lady, besides being physically neglected, seemed to be greatly deteriorated and confused in her wits; indeed Fanny began to suspect that she had perhaps been dulled by repeated doses of opiates. Her replies to questions were rambling and incoherent, she appeared interested in nothing, and, unless addressed, tended to fall into a doze with her chin dropped on her chest and a drool of spittle sliding from the corner of her mouth. When Fanny sent for Jem and the basket chair so that the old lady might have an airing in the garden, she was shocked to learn that Thomas, considering these promenades no longer necessary, had ordered the chair to be sold.

"Is Mrs. Baggot come back from her shopping yet?" demanded Fanny.

"No, ma'am, I believe not."

Fanny found the old lady's condition so dismaying that, in spite of Thomas's total interdiction on visits to the garden house, she resolved to go and speak to him about it without delay.

She wrapped a shawl around her and walked out onto the flagged path. As she did so, Will the postboy came whistling down the lane and into the garden.

"Morning, Missus Paget! That's good to see you about again! Here's a letter as'll cost ye a deal of money, for it's all the way from furrin parts!"

Receiving the letter from him, Fanny saw with amazement that it was addressed to herself in a completely unfamiliar handwriting.

"Thank you, Will; go in to Mrs. Strudwick and she will give you the money," she told him, having none about her, and she broke the seal with hasty fingers.

> *Demerara, January 1798.*
> *Dear Cousin Fanny (for so I shall call you without ceremony):*
> *I write to extend a Welcome to you and hope that you will be very happy in the Hermitage. I am delighted to hear that you and my Cousin Thomas (whom I have never met) have married, and I am sure you will prove a kind Mother for his orphaned daughters. It pleases me to know that a young and growing Family resides in my house while I am in the West Indies. I trust that you may soon have Children of your own, playmates, perhaps, when they all meet, for my twins, little Charley and Gussie. Speaking of twins, it has Occurred to me that, since I requested you and my Cousin Thomas to be kind enough to receive our other Cousins Priscilla and Carloman Paget into your Household, should they travel*

to England from the East Indies, you may hardly have house-room enough to Accommodate them besides your own brood. I therefore gladly authorize my Cousin Thomas to build an Extension on to the house (if he thinks fit) and have instructed my Bankers, Messrs Coutts in Leadenhall, to issue funds to cover the cost of the work. I am certain, dear Cousin Fanny, that you will treat our young kinsfolk kindly when they arrive; poor Children, I fear that, up to now in their lives, they have received little but neglect and hard usage, abandoned by their father (my great-uncle Henry) and thrown on the mercy of strangers after the death of their mother. Of their precise age I am not certain.

My husband joins me in extending warm greetings to You and Cousin Thomas:

Juliana van Welcker.

Fanny read this letter slowly, pacing along by the shrubbery, and her first reaction was, What a very great difference there must be between this unknown Juliana and her cousin Thomas. How I wish she were in England, Fanny thought, forgetting that, in such a case, Thomas and his family would be obliged to quit the Hermitage and resign themselves to greatly inferior quarters elsewhere.

During the last months Fanny had not given much consideration to the two unknown cousins presumably making their way from India; the possibility of their arrival had been overlaid by other events, indeed almost forgotten. And yet, for all anybody knew to the contrary, they might appear at any moment. Now, reflecting on the practical aspects of this prospect, she thought: Poor children, this is *not* a happy household for them to be received into, I wish they might find some kinder harborage, though for my part I shall be glad to welcome them. But I fear that Thomas will be surly, and Bet sullen, and little Patty spiteful. . . . It is too bad indeed that their first experience of England should be among such a disagreeable family.

Having arrived at which depressing conclusion, she took a deep breath, squared her shoulders, and tapped firmly upon the garden-house door.

After a considerable pause Thomas's voice called out sharply:

"Who is that?"

"It is I, Fanny. I wish to speak to you."

"*Frances?*" His voice sounded both astonished and wrathful. "What in the world are *you* doing out here? Chilgrove has not given permission for you to leave the house yet."

Still the door remained closed.

"It is a very warm day," Fanny said. "And I have an urgent matter to discuss with you."

Another longish pause ensued, and then the door was flung open. Thomas stood in the doorway with a decidedly forbidding aspect. He said:

"I am very displeased, indeed, that you should have come out here, entirely counter to the doctor's instructions! Pray return to the house directly! Whatever you have to say can surely wait until dinnertime."

His eye then fell on the letter in her hand. "What is that letter?"

"It is from our cousin Juliana van Welcker. But that is not—"

Thomas's brows flew together. He said, "How *dare* you open it without permission?" almost snatching it from her hand.

"But it was addressed to me!"

"To *you?*" He was astonished. "Why should she do so? What can Juliana be about, writing letters to *you?*"

"It is merely a very kind, civil letter of welcome," Fanny explained. "Oh, and she authorizes you to add an extension onto the house if you see fit."

"Hah!" His expression lightened a trifle. "Very well—*I* will reply to my cousin Juliana about this matter. There was no occasion at all, however, for you to be coming out here on such a trifling matter. Now, pray return indoors at once."

"But that was not what I came about," Fanny persisted. "I am very distressed about your mother, Thomas! She does not look at all as she should. I am afraid that Nurse Baggot has been neglecting her shockingly."

To Fanny's astonishment, Thomas's face became suffused with rage. He glared at her as if she had bitten him.

"Is *that* all? How dare you lay such accusations? Nurse Baggot, I may inform you, is somewhat better qualified than *you* to pronounce on my mother's state. Indeed, she is here now, with me, discussing it."

He moved a little to one side revealing the figure of Nurse Baggot behind him in the shadows of the room, arms akimbo.

Though very taken aback, Fanny held her ground.

"Why does the old lady look so dirty and uncared-for? Her hair has not been done, her clothes need mending—and I am persuaded, too, that she is suffering from the effects of opiates—she seems so drowsy and confused in her mind."

"Of course she has opiates!" Nurse Baggot came and stood by Thomas. She smiled scornfully at Fanny. "Ma'am, you had best not be interfering in what you know nothing about and what does not concern you."

"It does concern me." Fanny's voice trembled a little; the combined hostile regard of her husband and the nurse had begun to make her feel a little sick; how long had they been in there together, so quietly? What could they have been talking about all that time?

She went on as steadily as she could. "It concerns me to see her looking so neglected. It is not right."

"My dear Frances," Thomas said sharply, "as Nurse Baggot has said, it is no concern of yours, but since you are so inquisitive I may as well inform you that my mother is beginning to fail in her wits and requires frequent doses of laudanum, otherwise she becomes impossibly quarrelsome and abusive, even violent; for which reason, because she is so difficult and intractable, Mrs. Baggot finds it best to wash her and perform her toilet but once a day, instead of twice. Now, are you satisfied?"

"Does Dr. Chilgrove know about this?"

A white patch appeared around Thomas's mouth.

"Certainly he does—do you dare to doubt my word?"

His look was so menacing that, almost unconsciously, Fanny took a step backward from the doorway and supported herself against the elbow-high stone wall that overlooked the valley.

"No, of course not, Thomas—but she seems quiet enough now—"

"Naturally she is. I have just told you why. She is under necessary opiates. Now, pray leave us!"

At this moment it became apparent to both of them that their conversation was audible, in some degree, to a couple of persons walking below on the valley path. Fanny turned pale. For the pair in question were Mrs. Wyndham, looking more ravishing than ever in a diaphanous dress of gauzy pink and gray mull, and the gentleman who had witnessed the carriage accident, Major Henriques. Observing Thomas, the quick-witted Liz Wyndham inclined her head (adorned with a delicious chip-straw hat) giving no more than a tiny half-smile; but Major Henriques doffed his elegant hat and swept Fanny a polite bow.

"Your servant, ma'am! Servant, sir!"

"I am not aware of having the honor of your acquaintance, sir," said Thomas glacially, and, to Fanny, in a terrible voice, "Frances— withdraw!"

Fanny could only obey, and returned on trembling legs to the house.

When Thomas came in, which he did much later, he sent for Fanny and said at once, "Frances, I wish to know how you came to be acquainted with those people."

"I met them while with Mrs. Socket, sir."

"Very well. Then there are to be no more visits to the Rectory. If I had any *idea*—But it is to be expected, if one must live in a town like Petworth, where those who ought to be models to the lower orders display nothing but outrageous vice and infamy!"

Fanny inferred that he was speaking of Lord Egremont.

He said, "Go to your chamber. I will attend you there presently."

Dry-mouthed with fright, Fanny obeyed him; but she had to wait for several hours before he appeared. She wondered if he intended to beat her; he had threatened to once or twice previously, but her pregnancy had deterred him. Surely he would hardly dare do so now, while she was still under the care of Dr. Chilgrove?

At length he came. To Fanny's dismay, Nurse Baggot followed him, holding a bundle of material over her arm. She shut the door behind her.

"Remove your garments, Frances," Thomas said.

She looked from one to the other of them in terror. The scene was all too reminiscent of her first arrival in the house—but *surely* Thomas could not intend anything of the sort that had happened then—not in the presence of that woman?—and while she was still so weak? Dr. Chilgrove had told her most categorically that she must not become pregnant again—

Her thoughts tumbled one over another in horrified confusion.

"Make haste and do what I bid you! Strip off your garments," Thomas ordered again curtly, and, as Fanny clasped her hands in mute protest, he turned to the nurse. "Lily—get her clothes off her back!"

Mrs. Baggot darted a rather disagreeable glance at Thomas but proceeded briskly enough to undo the fastenings of Fanny's gown and petticoat.

Thomas said coldly, "Since I have for some time, Frances, been aware that I am unable to trust you out of my sight, I have devised this corset for you. I had not purposed obliging you to wear it for another sennight, until you were out of the doctor's care, but finding you so froward and disobedient, there is nothing for it but to bring it into use at once."

Dumb, astounded with horror, Fanny found herself being fastened into a stiff calico corselet which was laced with extreme tightness up the back and tied in a knot, by Mrs. Baggot's strong fingers, between her shoulder blades, where she could not possibly reach it herself. A thick strap of canvas webbing was drawn between her thighs, pulled up behind her back, and fastened under a leather belt, to which it was locked by some kind of clasp that she could not see, as it was in the middle of her back.

"There!" said Thomas. "You may wear your gowns and petticoats over the top of that. Mrs. Baggot will lace you up each morning—I shall undo you when I come to bed at night.—In this way I need be under no anxieties regarding your behavior. Your friend Dr. Chilgrove has forbidden another pregnancy for fifteen months; this garment, I trust, will ensure that his veto is not contravened. Your fine acquaintance up at Petworth House may go on in whatever licentious way they choose—the women—I will not call them *ladies*—cohabiting with grooms, stableboys, or any males they chance to encounter—I do not choose that *my wife* shall behave with a like freedom."

Fanny gazed at him, totally speechless.

He turned to leave the room, Mrs. Baggot following. The latter had remained silent throughout the scene but now darted one cold, triumphant look at Fanny, who could only gasp, as Thomas opened the door:

"Sir! How can you! It is inhuman! How, in this garment, may I contrive to—" Obey the calls of nature, she wished to say, but delicacy and shame prevented her. Thomas, however, turning in the doorway, replied coolly, understanding her:

"You should have thought of that before your provocation obliged me to take such a step. You will have to rise betimes in the morning. I trust this may teach you, Frances, that I am not to be defied. When I am convinced that you have fully learned this lesson—when you are able to assure me of your humble and dutiful intention to be a loyal and faithful wife—then I may permit you to leave off this remedial garment, which, in the meantime, I trust will be a constant reminder to you of your past faults."

The door clicked to behind him, and Fanny sank trembling onto the bed. The canvas web cut into her legs; the belt and tight laces nearly choked her. Dr. Chilgrove will never allow this, was her first stunned reaction, but her second was that the doctor, kindly and well intentioned though he was, really had no means of preventing it. Thomas had a perfect right to tie up his wife in a strait jacket, did he so wish; many husbands subdued their wives by even harsher means. Indeed it was not the harshness, which by now she was long accustomed to, but the humiliation that now caused tears of anguish to roll down her cheeks.

It was a considerable time before she could summon up the resolution to walk with stiff and clumsy steps downstairs. The canvas webbing cut painfully into her thighs at every step, the calico corselet pressed so severely on her still enlarged and tender breasts that she was obliged to hold herself ramrod upright as she moved along. Indeed, though she did not realize it, the penitential garment gave her a new sedate and touching dignity.

Since it now wanted but a very few minutes to dinnertime, Fanny walked slowly into the parlor to wait for the gong; although very doubtful whether her distress and the fearfully constricting stays would allow her to swallow any food, she did not wish to give Thomas the satisfaction of seeing her completely subdued or crushed. Aware of a rebarbative atmosphere in the parlor, where Thomas was reading the daily paper, while little Patty teased the cat, and Bet darned a pair of stockings, Fanny quietly took her seat in a rocking chair.

Thomas suddenly flung down his paper with an inarticulate exclamation of disgust.

"Tcha! It passes all bounds!"

"What does, Papa?" demanded little Patty, who had lately been promoted to eat dinner with the rest of the family, since none of the servants was prepared to carry her food up two flights of stairs.

Addressing himself to nobody in particular, Thomas went on:

"That *Mr. Pitt*—that the first minister of England—a man whom I have been used to esteem as a model of superior sense—should become involved in a *duel*—it is beyond comprehension!"

"A duel, Pa? Whom did he fight?" Even Bet, who rarely occupied herself with public affairs, was interested in this.

"Where did the affair take place?" Fanny softly inquired.

"Upon Wimbledon Common! Upon my word, I do not know what outrage we shall be hearing of next! Pitt was obliged to fight some rogue of an Irishman named Tierney, who had the insolence to challenge him in the very House of Commons itself! And, furthermore, there has been an abominable uprising in Ireland—close on thirty thousand armed ruffians are laying waste the country around Wexford. If the French should land in Britain now, we should, I dare say, be quite at their mercy!" He glared at his womenfolk as if all this were their fault. "The army hardly numbers more than thirty thousand men all told, and most of them must have been sent to Ireland to put down the revolt."

Although these were distressful tidings, Fanny could not help being relieved that Thomas had something other than her own shortcomings to occupy his mind.

"Do you truly think that the French will invade us, Papa?" Bet inquired presently, over the boiled chicken, the roasted bullock's heart, and the mutton-and-apple pie. "Mrs. Dawtry says a French scientist named Monsieur Monge has constructed an armored raft two thousand feet long, capable of carrying a whole army across the sea! It is propelled by windmills and guarded by hundreds of cannon. Boney and all his men could be here by next week!"

She looked as if she quite relished the prospect.

"Fiddle-de-dee, girl," said Thomas disagreeably. "Such notions are nothing but moonshine. Why, a raft of such dimensions would weigh upward of fifty thousand tons. Pray, how could it be constructed? Where is there a forest large enough to supply timber for such a vessel?—Still, it is by no means impossible that the French *may* land," he added gloomily enough.

"La!" exclaimed Bet, her eyes sparkling at the thought. "Imagine the Frogs marching into Petworth in their shakos? I should die laughing—would not you, Stepmamma?"

Fanny shook her head without reply. Thomas cast a sour look at her and requested Bet to keep her mouth shut if she had nothing to offer but stupidities; but it was evident that he, too, was occupied by unpleasant apprehensions as to the likelihood of a French invasion.

That Thomas was not the only person to entertain such forebodings was evidenced by a note that arrived after dinner, brought by one of the Petworth House footmen.

Thomas digested its contents in silence:

> *Lord Egremont presents his compliments to Captain Paget, and requests the pleasure of his company at a Meeting to discuss the formation of a Petworth Volunteer Corps which Ld. Egremont proposes to finance. Ld. Egremont ventures to hope that Capt. Paget will do him the Honor of captaining the troop, and requests his suggestions as to uniform, equipment, service pay, types of*

> *belts, cartouche boxes, firelocks, haversacks, canteens,*
> *pistols, swords, etc. The time suggested for the Meeting*
> *is Wednesday, May 30, at noon, if convenient to Capt.*
> *Paget.*

"Humph," remarked Thomas, not wholly displeased, after reading this missive from the third earl. "Well—at least that shows some sense! I don't like the man—can't stand his Whig affectations and his rakehell friends—but he certainly displays a proper feeling and respect —very proper—in applying to me during such an emergency.—Mind, I have my hands full as it is, with my impress duties—he might remember that—but still, I dare say I *am* the best-qualified person to take over the command of such a troop."—And it will show those local tow-row rogues a thing or two, he added inwardly, for Thomas received very little respect in the town, partly because of his unpopular calling, partly owing to his miserly ways.

"What does Lord Egremont write to you about, Pa?" demanded Bet, agog with curiosity. Thomas explained, his pride and gratification at the invitation growing, as he reread it. " 'A nuncheon will be provided,' it says—as if I cared for that. Still, I dare say other gentlemen may have rid in from some distance. Ha! here is a postscriptum.

> *"Lady Mountague of Cowdray is convening a meeting of*
> *local ladies in Petworth House at the same time, regard-*
> *ing measures to be taken in the event of an Invasion—*
> *such as establishment of field hospitals, evacuation of*
> *women and children from the battle area, etc. etc. The*
> *attendance of your wife and grown daughters is respect-*
> *fully solicited for this purpose."*

Thomas knitted his brow very doubtfully over this last, but Bet was already exclaiming, "What, *we* are bidden to Petworth House also? Oh, famous—is it not, Stepmamma? We shall see all the nobs—Lady Mountague! Just fancy! I dare say the Duchess of Richmond may be there also, it is not far to Goodwood House."

"Quiet, miss!" said her father. "I have not yet said that you may go."

"But for *such* a purpose, Pa? It would be patriotic. Do you not wish to go, Stepmamma?"

Fanny said quietly that she was not sure of feeling strong enough. Constricted in what, by now, felt like a suit of chain mail, she really did not see how she could enjoy or play any active part in such a function. It was therefore to her intense astonishment that Thomas, after long meditation, said finally:

"Well, I think you had best go, Frances. I know Lady Mountague to be a very excellent and distinguished personage—of the *highest* respectability—she might, should she take a liking to you, prove a most useful patron and neighbor. She lives at Cowdray Park, only seven or eight miles off; her acquaintance could do you nothing but good.— Yes; you had better go. Bet must accompany you."

And as Bet, amazed and delighted at this unlooked-for indulgence, began clapping her hands for joy, Thomas added in his most quelling manner:

"Mind, no dressing up too fine for this affair, now. It is not a party, nor an assembly. Neatness and propriety will be all that is required."

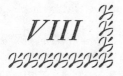

VIII

The first few hours after the escape from Ziatur were passed in somewhat unprofitable recriminations between Colonel Cameron and Miss Musson.

"Stealing that baby, ma'am, was probably the most arrant piece of folly you have committed in your entire existence. Indeed I do not scruple to assert that it was downright suicidal! Before, we might have had some tolerable hope of leaving the country without pursuit and the threat of vengeance; *now* there is virtually none. How *came* you to be so muttonheaded?"

"My dear Rob"—Miss Musson glanced placidly at the exasperated colonel as if he were a sixteen-year-old schoolboy—"you are not about to teach me my Christian duty, I hope? Where there was an opportunity to save life, I must seize it—particularly in the case of this little innocent." She looked fondly at the dark downy head of the sleeping baby. "I might say that it was an equal piece of foolhardiness on *your* part to steal an elephant from the royal stable—"

"Not *this* one," Cameron replied grimly.

"How in the world *did* you manage to purloin the beast, sir, without its mahout?" Cal put in at this point. "As a rule these fellows stick to their beasts as if they were their children."

The stolen elephant was being guided, with his customary efficiency and calm, by Cameron's Therbah servant. He glanced around now, from his position on her head, to remark:

"We stop, I think, tomorrow to buy goat, yes, sahib?"

"I was able to purloin the elephant because its mahout was dead," Cameron answered Cal shortly, ignoring the Therbah's suggestion. "*He* had been strangled by Mihal's personal order."

"But why?" demanded Scylla, astonished. "Mihal is a monster, we all know that—but why should he require to have a mahout strangled?"

"Because this is the beast—her name is Parvati—that killed his father."

"Good heavens!" exclaimed Miss Musson in affright. "Then, is the animal safe? Will it not run amok with us?"

"Have no fear, ma'am; that death was no accident. The elephant was made drunk on palm toddy, I imagine."

"Oh, I see," said Scylla. "And that was why the mahout must be killed."

"Just so. To prevent any possibility of his confession. This beast was regarded by all the stablemen as unlucky; it would probably have been slaughtered too, if I had not appeared with a large bribe; so very likely its absence would not have been considered important, my dear Miss Amanda, but for your little essay in child-snatching."

Ignoring this shaft, Miss Musson imperturbably replied, "Your Therbah is right, Rob; we must stop somewhere tomorrow and purchase a milch goat."

"A milch goat!" The colonel flung up his hands to heaven. "And I suppose we must also purchase swaddling bands—gowns—gripe water —doubtless shawls and a rush basket—our course will be as noticeable as if we were traveling in a royal progress! Your having saddled us with this little encumbrance materially changes our prospects, ma'am. We must on no account now think of attempting the Khaiber Pass. It would be sheer madness to leave the country by such an obvious route. Mihal's assassins will follow us farther than that, I can assure you."

"What route *must* we take, then?" calmly inquired Miss Musson. "I am sure that you will know what is best to be done, my dear Rob."

He pondered. "We had best travel into Kafiristan by river. That is our most likely means of slipping away unobserved. Not the Kabul River—that is too close—but farther north, the Kunar. We must go through the Lowacal Pass north of Arnawai, then over the Weran, and then turn south, down through Kafiristan, toward Jellalabad."

"There! You see! I knew that you would have a capital plan for us," Miss Musson said.

"It is *not* a capital plan, ma'am!" he said wrathfully. "From Peshawur to Jellalabad is barely ninety miles. What would have taken us not more than three or four days on mule- or camelback now becomes a journey of more than three times the length, and through dangerous country—we must travel at least seventy miles to the north, then west through mountainous regions, then south again. I had proposed to dispose of the elephant in Peshawur and purchase camels there, but now I am doubtful if we dare do that. I think we had best avoid all large towns entirely until we are well out of India."

"I am sure you are very right, my dear Rob."

Scylla could not help quietly laughing; Miss Musson, having decided on a course of action that meant abandoning all her previous occupations, her whole way of life, and confiding herself to the colonel's care, had done so in her usual thoroughgoing manner; she appeared serenely certain of his ability to undertake this charge.

"You will have to climb some exceedingly high mountains!" he said irascibly.

"Oh, that will be like old times when I was a child in New England," Miss Musson replied with unimpaired calm.

"No, it will not be, not in the least! These mountains, my dear Miss Amanda, are not the Berkshires! The Weran Pass is fifteen thousand feet up."

"I am sure we shall manage very well."

At this moment the baby woke and began to cry; a thin, mewing, threadlike sound that caused Parvati, the elephant, to snort and spread out her large ears inquisitively.

"Have no fear, royal lady," the Therbah muttered to her in Pushtu. "It is only the memsahib's little piece of foolishness."

Miss Musson produced from among her black draperies a large gourd full of milk and capably fed the baby, who went back to sleep again.

As the sun rose, shining on their backs and right shoulders, it became plain that already they were entering more hilly country. Beyond them, to the north and west, great serrated ranges of the Hindu Kush sliced the sky, their snowy peaks flashing crimson and gold with the first rays. The party were crossing, at present, a wide, cultivated vale intersected with many streams and small rivers. Some of these Parvati waded; others she swam, while her riders maintained a vigilant lookout for crocodiles. "Plenty of the brutes in the Indus," said Cameron, "and all these little tributaries flow into it, only fifty miles off; crocodiles can travel great distances when water is low, as it has been this summer."

"What a fortunate thing it is, Rob, that you are so familiar with this country," Miss Musson said comfortably.

"It will be by far the best course, ma'am, to leave that infant of yours at some monastery along the way," Colonel Cameron remarked brusquely when the baby had to be given its noontide drink of milk. "How are we to procure milk for it all the way across Afghanistan—a most mountainous, rugged, and inhospitable region—"

"Why not take a goat with us, as the Therbah suggested?"

"—whereas in a monastery—I can think of several excellent and suitable ones—he would be reared to a harmless life of useful piety and fruitful activity. *Why* you should be so resolved on dragging him all the way to *England*—"

"So that he can go to Eton. It was his late father's wish."

"And what will be the outcome of that?" demanded the irate colonel. "When he is grown he will return to Ziatur—foment civil war if it is not already raging—probably get himself killed—and all to what purpose?"

"You know as well as I, Colonel Cameron, that if only more Western-educated rulers could be introduced into Indian states there might be some chance of inculcating a system of democracy and equality such as we have in America. As it is: look at the condition of this wretched land—Tippoo Sahib intriguing with the French in the south —the Maratha princes all at odds—three hundred and sixty-two independent, warring states in the Punjab alone—civil war and chaos everywhere."

"And you believe that dragging one puling infant all the way to England—"

"How remarkably fast this elephant moves," tranquilly put in Scylla at this point—she felt the argument would never be resolved and had much better be shelved. "What a very fortunate choice of yours she was, dear Colonel Cameron. At what pace would you imagine her to be proceeding?"

Cameron's mouth twitched in a reluctant grin under his red-gold mustaches.

"I should think she may be capable of achieving so much as fifteen or even twenty miles an hour, Miss Paget—certainly faster than a man can run—so long as we are on level ground, that is. But very soon, unfortunately, we shall not be."

By now they had left the wide vale and were crossing a series of narrow tributary valleys on their way northward. The orchards, pomegranate and orange trees, and the banyans were giving way to deodar and rhododendron forest, through which Parvati crunched and crashed her way, displacing great drifts of aromatic scent, wonderfully refreshing to the travelers accustomed to the dry and fetid odors of their enclosed town.

The sun, after its early morning promise, had retreated behind a bank of cloud, but the full rains had not yet begun; the air was moist, a little cooler here among the foothills, and thunder rolled occasionally in the distance. Miss Musson had prudently equipped herself with an ancient rusty-black umbrella, but as yet there was no occasion for its use.

That night they camped in a belt of rhododendron forest at the head of a narrow valley by a deep rapid brook that came bounding down a rocky stairway from the hills above in clouds of spray. There was enough thick grass growing by the water, and young tree shoots around about, to satisfy the elephant's hunger without beginning on the fodder they had brought for her. After browsing she enjoyably drank and sprayed herself with water from the brook. The Therbah lit a small fire and cooked millet porridge and chupattis for the party, but Miss Musson had come to the end of the milk in her gourd and declared that she must go down to a village which they had glimpsed through the trees some half a mile down the valley and purchase either more milk or a goat.

This was a fresh cause of friction with the colonel.

"Oh, confound it, Amanda! Cannot the infant eat porridge like the rest of us?"

"No, it can*not!*" testily replied Miss Musson.

"I dare say strangers come hardly once in two years to such a little foothill corner as we are in. The news will be all over the province in a flash."

"By which time we shall be on our way. Come, come, Rob; you know we cannot let the baby starve."

"Then you had best let me go—or the Therbah," he replied hastily. "A Feringi lady they will be *sure* to remember."

"Nonsense, Rob—you are quite as conspicuous yourself, with those red mustaches of yours—whereas I, if I speak Pahari dialect, might be any old hill woman from another region."

There was some truth in this and reluctantly, at last, Cameron let her go. But she was a very long time in returning, and he became extremely anxious about her, his anxiety bordering on exasperation. "If she is not up to some piece of folly!" he muttered.

His fears seemed justified when at length she returned with a train of interested observers following: country people who all wanted to stare and wonder at the strangers.

At last the visitors were politely shooed away, the baby was fed— "*What* a little angel!" remarked Miss Musson in a self-congratulatory way; "I only wish he *were* an angel," bitterly replied Colonel Cameron —and the party were left to settle down to sleep, which they did underneath the elephant, who provided them with shelter from a light rain that had commenced to fall—she being shackled by the leg to a couple of trees. However she showed in any case no disposition to move and lived up to the character for docility and good nature that she had so far established.

Dawn came late in their deep valley but they were up long before the sun, breakfasted hastily, and started off while the crows and the bluejays were still waking the forest with their morning screams. From down here the higher mountains were hidden, but the track lay steeply uphill, through dense green forest, and presently, in a dip between two acute hillsides, they could see distant peaks, indigo blue.

Parvati was making slow work of the climb.

"We shall have to dispose of her today," Cameron said. "She will be no use to us in these hills."

However she had not yet outlasted her usefulness to the party. There were several more valleys to cross which were bisected by the shallow, shingly, fast-running rivers of the region. These Parvati gallantly forded, struggling sometimes in the deeper channels, slipping on the loose scrambling stones, and trumpeting with anxiety, while the Therbah gentled her and encouraged her with words of praise.

At about the sixth of these rivers—which was, in fact, a confluence of two tributary mountain streams that came together in a flat-bottomed, steep-sided valley to make a quarter-mile stretch of shallow, turbid water studded with sandbanks—Parvati had hardly entered the current when her riders were startled by the sound of rifle shots from downstream.

"Oh, heavens—look!" exclaimed Scylla.

Parvati trumpeted excitedly, and at the same moment Miss Musson exclaimed, "Good gracious, what *can* be the matter with my umbrella?" staring at it in amazement. She had been left with hardly more than the handle—the upper portion had been torn away.

Narrowing his eyes against the light from downstream, Colonel Cameron stared for no longer than five seconds before pronouncing:

"I recognize the uniform of Milhal's bodyguard. The wretches must have been hard on our trail all this time. Therbah—make the elephant go faster. Paget—is your weapon loaded?"

"Yes, sir."

"Then take aim and fire. Aim for the leader—the fellow on the black horse."

Staring downstream, Scylla perceived a small troop of men. Her vision was by no means so keen as that of Colonel Cameron who, she had discovered, had eyes like a hawk; she could just detect the movement of their horses, the white flash of their turbans, and the puffs of smoke as, having reloaded, they fired again. All their shots this time fell short or wide; she could see the splashes kicked up by their bullets on the water and the furrows carved on a shallow sandbank which Parvati was just approaching.

Cameron discharged his own musket, and one of the pursuers toppled off his horse.

"Ha!" grunted the colonel. *"That's* made 'em ponder; and now they've got to reload again; they *still* have no notion of staggering fire, in spite of all I have taught them. Hurry up your beast, Therbah! Once we gain that bluff on the far shore we shall have the upper hand of them."

The Therbah, however, was troubled. "Parvati not moving well, sahib."

"Why, what is the matter? Can she have been hit? She did not cry out."

The elephant did cry out now, though: a long, strange shrill trumpeting shriek of fright and dismay.

"Oh, what can it be?" exclaimed Scylla, and then, in horror, "Why, look, Colonel Cameron—she is sinking into the sand!"

"The devil! So she is! Poor beast—no wonder she was not able to go any faster. A quicksand, by God! Therbah! Can you not urge her out of it? Discharge your pistol behind her ear—that may help to startle her forward. If not—I fear we must prepare to abandon her forthwith. Miss Musson—Miss Paget—make ready to jump for it!"

"Into the *quicksand?*" exclaimed Miss Musson. "My *dear* Rob!"

"Devil take it, ma'am, what else is there to do? Where an elephant may sink, a human may, with luck, venture safely—that is, if he looks sharp about it and don't dawdle—leap as far forward as you may, into the sand, then run fast, for your life, into the deeper water where you may swim."

The Therbah discharged his pistol behind Parvati's ear, but to no avail. Indeed the wretched beast's floundering start of terror at the sound only served to sink her deeper into the quicksand.

"*Jump!*" roared Cameron, and his fellow travelers launched themselves out of the howdah while he, hastily reloading, fired two more shots at the pursuing troop. Another man fell, and a horse staggered. A hail of fire came back in return, but the elephant was now interposed as a barrier between pursuers and fugitives; many of the shots, in any case, fell wide or short.

Scylla, leaping into shallow water, felt the horrible suck of treacherous sand beneath her feet; she struggled hastily forward until she was waist deep in water and could swim, then turned to see how her companions were faring. Cal, with a pack on his back, was assisting Miss Musson into deep water and had taken the baby from her; the Therbah, holding his musket above his head with one hand, swimming strongly in a deep narrow channel, had the elephant's lead rope in his teeth and was endeavoring to drag and persuade her forward.

"It is useless, Therbah!" Cameron called from the howdah. "One of those villains' shots has taken her in the neck; one way or another, I fear she is done for, poor beast. Here—be ready to catch these—"

He was hurling out of the howdah the rest of the scanty bundles that constituted their luggage. Fortunately the sandbank that had proved so treacherous to them was rather beyond the middle of the river, and many of the articles that he flung out reached the far bank or fell into shallows where they might be rescued.

"Rob! Do not be lingering there but come quickly!" called Miss Musson in agitation.

"Don't put yourself in a pucker, ma'am! Here I come," replied Cameron, and, holding his weapon muzzle down, he sprang into the water from the slowly subsiding elephant, who was still trumpeting in despair and terror. In a few rapid strokes he had caught up with the rest of the party.

"Now—quick, before they have time to reload—make a dash for the shelter of those rocks and so up the bluff. Each for himself—who has the baby? Ah—very well. *Run!*"

Scylla, in shallow water, dared not look behind her. One thing, she thought, there has been no time to worry about crocodiles. She gained the reedy bank, scrambled up it, turned to assist Miss Musson, who was close behind, and half led, half dragged the older woman up to the ridge of red rocks that outlined the shore to their left. In the shelter of this they sank down gasping. As they did so a prolonged, mournful bellow from the doomed elephant ended abruptly. Either she had been hit again or she had finally sunk under water. Stealing a glance above the rock, Scylla perceived that the surface of the river was empty: the poor beast had been completely submerged.

"Keep *down*, Miss Paget!" furiously roared the voice of Colonel Cameron. A shot smacked the sandy ground not twelve feet from Scylla.

The colonel was lying on his stomach nearby, reloading his weapon. "Aha!" he muttered. "Now their flank is thoroughly exposed," and he fired through a crack between the rocks. *"Paget!* Why the *devil* are you not firing?"

"Well done, sir!" shouted Cal, ignoring this. "You got the fellow on the black." Next moment he discharged his own weapon.

"That's given the villains something to think about, anyway," grunted Cameron, lowering his musket to study the attackers through the crevice. "Yes; just as I thought; they haven't the pluck to attempt that river without their leader."

The horsemen were conferring together at the spot where Parvati had entered the water; they were looking up and down the banks irresolutely. Evidently the elephant's fate had discouraged them. Cameron fired again and succeeded in picking another rider off his horse. Without more ado the rest of the troop turned and made off in the direction from which they had come.

"Dismal curs!" remarked Cameron. "If I were Mihal I'd behead the lot of them—as he probably will! Didn't even stop to hinder us from collecting our baggage. They might at least have waited until dark."

As it was—after allowing a prudent interval to elapse—the survivors of the quicksand were able to go down to the water's edge and retrieve their scattered belongings—wet, certainly, but intact.

"All the flour is sodden!" lamented Miss Musson.

"Let that be a lesson to you, ma'am! Wrap up your supplies better in future. All the weapons, you will observe, are heavily greased, and the ammunition is encased in so many layers of oiled leather and silk that Neptune himself couldn't get at it."

"Don't brag, Rob," said Miss Musson sharply. "You, after all, are *used* to these sorts of alarums—it is your profession—but *we* are not accustomed to scampering off into the wild at short notice and being shot at."

"Miss Musson is very kind," here coldly put in Scylla, "but the fault regarding the flour was mine. *I* had charge of the stores and shall undertake next time—if there *is* a next time—to wrap the flour in as many layers of oiled silk as you please to direct, Colonel Cameron."

All of a sudden she felt exceedingly angry with the colonel—if she had been asked why, she could hardly have said. Partly it was because he had shouted at her so loudly and rudely to put her head down when she was still shaking with fright and effort. Partly because he had seemed so callous regarding the fate of their poor elephant. And partly just because she was cold and wet and exhausted and could not imagine what they were to do now.

As if to aggravate her indignation, Colonel Cameron now addressed Cal.

"Paget, why in heaven were you not quicker off the mark with your covering fire? By thunder! I wouldn't have *you* in a troop of mine, not if you couldn't get down and begin firing faster than that!"

"Sir," very composedly replied Cal, "I was holding the baby; which I had taken from Miss Musson while we went through the water."

"Holding the baby! —— —— the baby! Why couldn't you set it down, man?"

"Enough of this!" interposed Miss Musson. "We are all very much obliged to you, Colonel Cameron, but the main requirement at the moment—I fancy—is to put some distance between ourselves and the scene of this unfortunate occurrence. And then we had best light a fire and dry our possessions."

"You are in the right of it, ma'am," rather curtly replied the colonel.

Ruffled, wet, and not best pleased with one another, the party retired up the hillside into the gathering dusk. Still shaken by the recent adventure, they were inclined to straggle, but Cameron, visibly impatient, waited until they all came up with him and then harangued them.

"Listen to me if you please!" he said. "Heaven knows, I had no particular wish to become involved in this business; but since I *am* involved and, owing to my experience, am the most capable to take charge of the expedition, I must request that you all follow my directions and, particularly at moments of crisis, give me instant obedience. You, Paget! Did you hear me, sir?"

"What was that you said, Colonel?" absently replied Cal, whose thoughts evidently had been miles away—he had probably been, his sister suspected, composing an elegy on the drowning of the elephant. "Oh yes, instant obedience in times of crisis—certainly."

"And don't straggle!" snapped the colonel, regarding them with exasperation. "In country like this we *must* all keep together. Soon we shall be entering a region of Kafiristan where head-hunting is a regular practice. It is a sport for them, like polo: successful hunters, on returning to their villages, are showered with wheat. I must request you not to behave in a manner which will put your companions at risk by obliging them to halt and turn back in search for you. Do you understand?"

"Of course we understand, Rob," replied Miss Musson calmly. "We none of us wish to lose our heads. You have experience, you are the leader; the children perfectly comprehend this. No one questions your authority."

"Very well," Cameron said. "Now: a further point. We are making for the pass of Lowacal, which is, I conjecture, some forty or fifty miles from here. We shall try to procure mules, but I doubt if we shall succeed; and part, indeed most, of the journey will in any case have to be done on foot—and it must be done *fast;* the rains are upon us, but as soon as the rains reach these lower valleys the rivers begin to flood and may become impassable; furthermore, higher up, the rains become snows, and Lowacal itself may be blocked unless we reach it with all possible speed. Therefore we must make haste. No dallying to pick bouquets or gaze at romantic vistas—is that understood?" he demanded, gazing sternly at Scylla.

She nodded, biting her lip; then, as he still held her eyes, replied in a cool detached manner, "Certainly it is, Colonel Cameron; you have made it abundantly clear."

"Very well!" He added, "It is becoming dark, and we have put a fair distance between ourselves and the river; I think we may venture to stop here for the night."

Their path was climbing beside a cliff face, and, at one point where it curved around, a rough cave had been dug in the mountainside, evidently used as a shelter by other travelers before them; one or two heaps of pebbles were crowned by withered marigolds, probably in propitiation of some mountain god.

Thankfully they set down their loads, the men gathered brushwood for a fire, Scylla fetched water from a spring to make lentil soup, Miss

Musson fed the baby, and Cal returned in triumph from a wood-gathering excursion with a pouch full of walnuts.

They were all tired out and lay down as soon as they had eaten, wrapped in their half-dried cloaks, the women at the rear of the shallow cave, the men in front. A misty moon threw pine shadows on the rock wall; some beast howled in the distance.

"Are there wolves in these mountains, Rob?" Miss Musson sleepily inquired, and he answered briefly:

"Wolves, tigers, bears, leopards—hyenas, jackals, apes—"

"Oh well, I dare say they will not greatly trouble us," she murmured. Next moment Scylla heard her softly singing an Urdu lullaby to the child: "'*Roti, makan, chini, chota baba nini* [Bread, butter, sugar, little baby sleep].'" And she went on, even more softly, into one that her own mother must have sung to her: "'By-low, baby, my wee baby, By-low, baby, Mother's little lamb.'"

Outside, an owl hooted among the pines; Scylla felt waves of sleep drifting over her.

In the cave entrance Cal said to the colonel, "How long do you think it will take us to reach the Lowacal Pass, sir?"

"We shall try to procure a guide in a mountain village. Then, with luck, perhaps three weeks."

"Three *weeks?* To go fifty miles?"

Cameron merely grunted, "You will see," and, burrowing his head into his sheepskin jacket, composed himself for sleep.

They did see. They soon began to understand how, in that country, it was sometimes a matter for self-congratulation if they achieved half a mile in an hour. They managed to obtain a guide in a hill village, where Miss Musson also purchased a goat. But mules were not to be had. The goat, Ammomma, sometimes seemed of more use than the guide; she had an infallible instinct for picking her way along a treacherous track that was half washed out by rain. The guide, Hazarah, a sad-looking little man with slightly mad, wandering eyes, appeared to be an outcast in the village where they hired him, and to Scylla he seemed the last person likely to be able to conduct the party through these confusing, precipitous hills to a far-distant mountain pass. But Cameron professed himself satisfied. "The man is a Kafir; he comes from Weran; he has trodden that trail many times."

The trail itself was a nightmare. Sometimes it led over slopes of shale, which threatened at each step to slip down and set the whole hillside sliding into an avalanche; sometimes they must cross gorges, over crazy cantilever bridges of tree trunks; sometimes the bridge was but a single trunk with branches left on, or a trunk split in half. Sometimes, traversing the sides of a precipitous gorge, they found that the path became no more than a rickety platform of pine branches woven together and jammed into cracks in the rock, extending from the cliff face hundreds of feet up, over white water roaring among boulders, or wicked-looking black mountain lakes which the sun never reached, so deep were they sunk among their slimy cliffs; sometimes the party must clamber up nearly vertical slopes where the path was but a series of toe holds and a single slip would have meant a fall of half a mile; sometimes they were slogging knee deep through snow, high above the tree line in a windy valley, or exposed to frightful gusts, traversing some immense rocky shoulder; at other times, having gone down, down, down, exhaustingly, till the backs of their legs felt ready to split with agony and their toes threatened to push through the tips of their boots, they must cross rushing mountain torrents where already crusts of ice were beginning to form along the bank.

Scylla could not imagine how Miss Musson, at her advanced age, managed to bear up. She herself was often so weary, her heart pumping furiously, a metallic taste like blood in her mouth, that she longed for nothing but to throw herself down by the track and be left there to die; only pride kept her going. But the older woman plodded on, indomitable, and always appeared serene, cheerful, even able to take an interest in what lay about them. When Scylla was staggering on, her whole attention engaged in counting her steps on the muddy, sliding stones under her feet—"Five hundred and two, five hundred and three —" Miss Musson would lightly touch her arm.

"Do see, my dear, the bear in the cherry tree!"

"A bear, ma'am?" Scylla would gaze foggily up to where her guardian pointed. "Will he attack us?"

"Not he! Much too engaged with his own affairs!"

And indeed the black bear—"moon bear," Hazarah called him—was busily occupied, perched in the branches, pulling them toward him and munching the wild cherries, then bending the stripped boughs into a platform on which he reclined, reaching out for more distant clusters and dragging off the fruit with his claws; he hardly spared a glance for the procession winding slowly past his tree.

Or, as they balanced precariously along some hideously slippery sloping track, barely eighteen inches wide, that snaked its way across a vertical wall of rock, while Scylla tried to remember Cameron's various exhortations on equilibrium, she would hear Miss Musson's quiet voice ahead:

"Do, my dear, pray observe this eagle hovering so close to us; a lammergeier, I believe my dear brother would have termed it; only see, what an immense creature! I believe it must be at least nine feet across the wings!"

And, casting a cautious, sideways glance at the great golden-headed bird floating so serenely beside them without a single flip of its pinions, Scylla could not help a faint lifting of the heart.

There was no sympathy, during these hardships, to be had from Cameron: at the end of an exhausting day's march he expected each member of the party to do a fair share of work in fetching wood and water and making camp; the women were shown no favor, not even Miss Musson, though he accepted with stern resignation the fact that most of the older lady's evening duties lay toward the baby; Scylla sometimes relieved her of those tasks but Miss Musson seemed to have a natural gift for child care and could feed, reswathe, and dandle the little creature with such calm, swift, and gentle movements that it hardly roused from its daylong slumbers.

"You are the best baby in the world," she could sometimes be heard murmuring to it, and even Cameron was obliged to acknowledge that, as babies went, it gave remarkably little trouble.

Scylla was more concerned for Cal; slender and small-framed like herself, he had never been of an athletic turn, although a good horseman; and since she had learned that his moods, silences, tendency to long, heavy slumber, and moments of strange blank inaccessibility were caused by an epileptic disposition, she had been in a state of constant subdued concern about him, which was greatly increased by their present situation of danger and hardship. Suppose, for instance, he should take an epileptic spasm while crossing one of these vertiginous pine-tree bridges? But when she privately confided these fears to Miss Musson, on a rainy morning as they waited for the men to jam back into place one such tree-trunk bridge that had slipped from its precarious anchorage, the older woman was reassuring.

"Do not be troubling your head about it too much, my dear; I believe that, so long as our boy's attention is fully engaged, he does not run the risk of taking a fit; I have observed this with other epileptics, even those much more severely afflicted than Cal; it is when their minds are vacant, or lulled by music or regular movement, such as that of a fan, for example, that a seizure is likely to occur. In general I believe that all this outdoor activity is doing your brother nothing but good."

This statement, Scylla was bound to agree, certainly accorded with Cal's own remark that his attacks seemed to follow inertia, not activity. Nevertheless, his sister continued to worry about him, for she knew that he very much disliked heights, as she did herself; with all the sympathy of one twin for another, she could sometimes *feel* his distress as they inched their way along some narrow dizzy path, with wet rock on one side and giddy vacancy on the other. But then, suddenly, the telepathic sensation of strain would lift and, glancing aside, she would notice the red-gold flash of a maple tree in the mist far below, or the cloudy white ribbons of half a dozen waterfalls winding their zigzag way in silence down the opposite cliff, half a mile distant; and, thankfully, she would realize that the exhilaration of such a sight had power to turn his mind away from his own ordeal.

Once, though, they came to a bridge of a different kind. They had been creeping along the lip of a deep gorge all day and in midafternoon arrived at a point where a sheer vertical wall lay ahead of them; the path appeared to come to an abrupt stop.

"It must go on somewhere," Miss Musson remarked with her usual placid certainty.

But even Hazarah appeared momentarily perplexed; apparently a recent rockfall had caused the blockage in front of them; he scratched his head.

Then the Therbah, uncharacteristically taciturn, pointed in silence to a tree that stood near the path, a great twisted mountain oak. Peering through the misty rain that was falling, the travelers could just perceive what seemed to be a rope which snaked down from its branches—down and out, across to the opposite side of the gorge; the human eye could hardly follow its threadlike progress, but it seemed to terminate in a similar oak tree low down on the farther bank.

Cameron asked some question of the Therbah in his own language; he replied with a single word. Then, setting down the conical basket in which he carried his load, he climbed with rapid agility into the oak tree, up to the fork where the rope was attached.

"You don't mean to say that we have to go down *that?*" Scylla demanded in tones of incredulous horror.

Cameron remarked coolly, "Can you suggest any other means of crossing the gorge, Miss Paget?"

Of course she could not. Below the slope on which the tree grew, as she was aware, a vertical cliff fell three hundred feet to the river beneath. And ahead of them the way was blocked—

"To go back?" she suggested uncertainly.

"All the length of the gorge? Are you mad? Think how long it has taken us. Besides—" Silently he pointed back and down, to a lower, far-distant section of the track they had followed. Dimly, faintly, Scylla perceived the flash of metal, white dots of turbans, the movement of six, eight, ten, twelve little objects as they rounded a corner.

"Who is that?" she breathed in horror. And then: "After us?"

He shrugged. "Perhaps. Perhaps not. In the mountains, one does not wait to see."

Now the Therbah descended the oak again and reported on the condition of the rope, which he had tested by hanging from it; the rope itself, made from twisted, plaited canes, appeared to be in good condition, but the fastening to the tree itself needed reinforcement.

"But how shall we manage? Surely we do not hang by our arms from that rope?" Scylla murmured, appalled, to Miss Musson, as the four men began slashing among the undergrowth to procure suitable lengths of sapling. "And what about the baby? The goat?"

"There should be a species of hanging chair—I remember Winthrop telling me about such a means of crossing rivers, from a high bank to a low, but I have never seen it myself," Miss Musson replied composedly. "There should be two ropes, I believe, one to pull the chair back, but I suppose the second one has perished. They will have to construct it, and the chair also, which is likely to take them some time; while they do that, we might as well prepare a meal. Do you kindle a fire, my dear."

And in the most matter-of-fact way she laid little Chet Singh down between two massive tree roots and walked off to a nearby spring to fill her water pot.

Scylla did not mention the glimpse of armed men on the distant road; since Cameron had not seen fit to do so she assumed he did not wish to raise alarm in the party before it was necessary.

A dish of barley porridge and some chupattis had been prepared before the fastening was mended and the second rope constructed. Meanwhile the Therbah, whose eyesight was even keener than that of Cameron, declared that he could see the missing chair on the far bank. Having gulped down his meal at speed, he proceeded, without the least apparent disquiet, to climb the tree again, make fast one end of the new rope, tie the other end around his waist, and shake out the rest of its length so that it hung free. Then, holding onto the original rope with his hands, he hooked his knees over it also and launched off, with a cheerful shout, into space.

Scylla gasped in sheer disbelief, watching his small, muscular figure shoot downward and dwindle almost to the size of a fly as the curve of the rope took him out over the water.

Would the rope hold? Unconsciously, they had all suspended their breath. Miss Musson peered shortsightedly and let out a little sigh of anxiety.

"You require hard hands to perform that trick," Cameron remarked to her in a dry, quiet tone. "If any one of *us* had tried it, our palms would have been cut to ribbons."

Miss Musson smiled at him, as if grateful for the relief of his prosaic comment.

"Look! He has got there!" exclaimed Cal.

Far away, on the lower bank, the Therbah's tiny figure waved a triumphant arm. Then he busied himself with something on the bank and waved again.

"He has found the chair," observed Cameron. "That has saved us hours of work; which is as well."

His glance just brushed that of Scylla and moved on past her; she turned to follow where he was looking, but a mist had crept up the side of the gorge; she could see nothing.

Presently a third signal from the Therbah indicated that they were to pull in on the secondary rope. Cameron, climbing the tree, did so, and in due course up came a thick, wishbone-shaped piece of wood, carved from a tree root. Between the two arms of the wishbone, which pointed downward, a kind of leather saddle hung suspended. This was not in good condition; more time had to be spent repairing it with pieces of leather cut from the end of a goatskin tent which Cameron had purchased for the women. At last it was declared ready.

"Good," said Cameron. "One of the ladies had better go first. Miss Paget."

Scylla drew in a sharp breath but said nothing as she met the cold stare in his unrelenting blue eye. Attempting to still the violent tremor which, quite independently of her control, had started up in her arms and legs, she clenched her teeth together, pressed her clammy palms against her thighs, and replied in, she hoped, as dispassionate a tone as Cameron's:

"Very well. Shall I take the baby?"

"No; Miss Musson has a better hand with him," Cameron replied baldly. "You had best take charge of the stores and the medicines."

Sick with fright, thankful at least that her thick mountain garments concealed what she felt must be the visible thudding of her heart in her breast, Scylla scrambled up into the oak tree, assisted from above by Cameron and from below by her brother; she would have liked to avoid Cal's eyes but could not help meeting them, and the tortured comprehension in them did nothing to allay her own terror—rather augmented it. She wriggled herself uncomfortably into the insecure, frail-seeming perch and passively allowed Cameron to tie the bundles of food and medicines onto her back and into her lap; this he did with brisk efficiency and as little emotion as if he were loading up a pack mule.

"Good. Now, raise your hands above your head and grasp the arms of the fork. Are you balanced? Off you go," he said, and without a pause dispatched her into the gulf by means of a strong push in the small of her back.

Scylla shut her eyes and felt freezing wet air shoot past her cheeks; her hands, frantically gripping the wooden arms of the wishbone, became numb at once; she could feel nothing but the rain dashing in her face, hear nothing but the whine of the wind and a strange humming noise that rose to a shriek as her ramshackle sling chair shot down the wet cable.

I *must* open my eyes, she thought. I have to know what is ahead of me, I have to be ready, but her eyes refused to open, a fierce ache of cold burned her temples; fighting with her mutinous eyelids, she traveled on, down and down; the descent seemed unending; at last a warning shout ahead roused her from this almost trancelike state of fright and, by themselves, her eyes opened to see the wooded riverbank approaching her at a hurtling pace, a terrifying pace—"Watch out, missy sahib!" shouted the Therbah once more, dancing up and down in agitation on the bank, and some words that she did not catch, ending in "Jump, must jump!" She grasped his meaning, realized that if she did not eject herself from the sling in time she ran the risk of having her brains dashed out among the branches of the mooring tree and, as the sloping bank shot by under her she gulped, let go, and launched herself sideways, landing with bent knees, rolling over and over along the wet ground.

"Oh, very well done, missy sahib—very good done!" yelled the Therbah exuberantly in her ear as he ran to pick her up. "No bone broke, not even medicine bottle—might have been crossing river every day of life!"

Filled with pride at her survival, though still shaking violently, Scylla staggered to her feet, waved, and shouted. But the distance was too far for sound to carry.

"They see you come safe, no worry," said the Therbah, busily resetting the wishbone seat so that it could be hauled back across the river. "Miss Musson Sahib now come too also probable."

However a pause now ensued of some considerable duration. Scylla's fear rose again. What about that party on the lower road? Where were they now? A bend in the gorge cut off the view from here; she could only conjecture. Or had something gone wrong with the sling? Were she and the Therbah to be marooned on this side of the river, with the rest of the party unable to reach them? Could Miss Musson have balked at the crossing? The Therbah, frowning, puzzled, stared across and up, shading his eyes with his hand, muttering:

"Master tie Memsahib in seat I think yes perhaps? Very dangerous tie in seat. Get ready quickly catch I believe yes understand *very* quick, missy?"

He directed Scylla where to position herself so as to grasp and slow down the speeding sling the instant it came within reach; it was not hard to see that this would be a very tricky proceeding, rather like trying to halt a galloping horse that was about to come shooting down out of the sky.

"Can it be because of the baby?" Scylla wondered, perplexed. But Miss Musson had adopted the mountain women's practice of carrying the baby in a sling on her back, where he was perfectly secure; it seemed unlikely that this would raise any additional problem.

When the seat at last came down, however, at its previous breakneck pace, they saw between the wooden arms, not Miss Musson's white head, but Cal's dark one; and he seemed to be lolling unconscious in the leather cradle, his hands were not grasping the arms of the fork.

"God in heaven! My brother must have fainted!" exclaimed Scylla, horrified. "No wonder they must delay—"

"Quick, missy—be ready—catch legs, push back—NOW!"

Working together like herdsmen to stop an escaping beast, Scylla and the muscular little Therbah simultaneously gripped the sling seat and Cal's inert body, struggling to bring him to a halt before he smashed into the tree. They were dragged, scrambling, along the ground with him, and all came to rest together in a tangle of boughs just short of the trunk.

"Well done, missy," the Therbah said again. "Break no leg I think very lucky. Cal Sahib got sick—not good time get sick."

Scylla could only agree, but as they worked to unfasten Cal, who had been strapped into the seat with massive knots and twists of plaited cable, presumably by Cameron, she could feel within herself exactly what must have precipitated an epileptic attack in him just then: it had been the dizzying, horrifying spectacle of his twin sister, almost part of himself, shooting down at such nightmare speed into the gulf. What a mercy that the attack had occurred before he had taken his place in the sling, and not on the way down, in which case his hands would have loosened their hold and he been plunged to destruction.

Colonel Cameron must have been very angry about it, thought Scylla uncharitably. Heaven knows how they hoisted him up into the tree.

The empty seat was sent back and Miss Musson came next with the baby; by now Scylla and the Therbah had achieved some degree of experience in how much to give way, how much to resist a body approaching them at full speed; in comparison with Scylla's arrival, that of Miss Musson and the baby was almost decorous.

"Well!" exclaimed the older lady, extracting herself neatly from the seat. "*That* was certainly a novel and diverting experience, and reminds me of the games that we used to play in the big old maple tree when I was a child! But how is poor Cal—did you manage to bring him safely to land?"

"Yes, ma'am, but I fear he may be unconscious now for some time," Scylla said worriedly. "I believe the seizure has turned into one of those deep slumbers that he falls into. It was a most unfortunate moment for it to occur—"

"Unfortunate, but not in the least surprising—the poor lad turned positively green when he saw you diving through the air like a falcon."

"Was Colonel Cameron very displeased?"

"Displeased? No, why should he be? He perfectly understands Cal's disability."

Scylla reflected that Cameron often seemed disposed to be more lenient with Cal than he was with herself. Not that he ever permitted Cal any reduction in his share of work and hardship—nor, indeed, that Cal expected it; but the colonel allowed himself more of an easy, relaxed manner with her brother—a smile now and then, an occasional joke; whereas to Scylla, lately, his manner had been curt to the point of dislike.

Her somewhat unprofitable train of thought was interrupted by the need to receive the guide, Hazarah, who now came down across the gorge, a reluctant co-passenger with the terrified goat; and after him, lastly, came Cameron himself.

He was bleeding, they noticed, from a scrape wound on his brow.

"What is that, Rob?" demanded Miss Musson.

"Some fellows came up and shot at me just as I was starting off; I think we had best cut the rope," he said negligently, and did so. "How is the boy?"

"He will do well enough," Miss Musson said. "But his seizure has changed to a sleep and I am strongly of the opinion that he should not be roused from it; the sleep is nature's way of compensating for the violent convulsion that he has undergone. I am afraid, Rob, that you must resign yourself to make camp here for the next twelve hours."

"I had apprehended as much," he said shortly. "We had better retire out of range from the opposite bank; not that there is much chance of hitting a mark with all this foliage in the way. Therbah! Help me carry Cal Sahib to a safer stopping place."

"How will travelers manage who wish to cross the gorge in future?" Scylla wondered as she and Miss Musson went to and fro, carrying stores up the riverbank.

"They will choose some other route," Cameron, overhearing her reflection, commented dryly. "I had thought that must have been obvious, Miss Paget."

She blushed, feeling foolish, and walked away from him without reply. But she heard Miss Musson demand:

"Rob! The men who shot at you? Were they mountain brigands?"

"No, Miss Amanda, I think they were soldiers from Ziatur; I am afraid Mihal has not given up the search for us yet. He has a longer arm than you credited him with."

Cameron visibly chafed at the delay, but the rest of the party were grateful for the hours of rest enforced on them by Cal's seizure. The women availed themselves of the opportunity to mend worn footwear and patch torn garments; Miss Musson cleaned and dressed Cameron's graze; Cameron engaged in a long discussion with Hazarah as to the best routes ahead once the party had crossed the Lowacal Pass into Kafiristan. The result of this discussion was a certain cautious optimism.

"Hazarah thinks that, if we can cross by Lowacal and then surmount the Weran Pass, which is the watershed between the Kokcha and Kunar rivers, there may by that time have been sufficient rain so that we may travel by raft down to Jellalabad; which, I need hardly say, would be a considerable easement in our mode of travel."

"By raft? Oh yes! What a delightful prospect!" exclaimed Miss Musson. "I shall look on that as quite a holiday, indeed!"

"But before that, ma'am, I must warn you, lie some extremely arduous stretches of trail."

"Arduous?" put in Scylla, though she had not been directly addressed. She raised her brows. "More arduous than those we have hitherto traversed, Colonel Cameron?"

He glanced at her briefly. "In comparison with what lies ahead, Miss Paget, our journey up to now will seem like a mere Sunday school picnic."

"Tell me, Rob," said Miss Musson while Scylla was digesting this, "who now reigns in Afghanistan? Is the country in a settled condition since the death of the Amir Thaimur?"

"No, ma'am, far from it," he replied bluntly. "Crossing Afghanistan must be regarded as merely the lesser of two evils. Better than being assassinated by Mihal's agents in Surat, no doubt; but I fear that lawlessness and civil strife are prevalent all over the country since the death of Thaimur—he left behind, as you may be aware, twenty-three sons—"

"Twenty-three? Dear me!"

"Twenty-three sons, none of whom had been positively nominated by him as his heir and successor."

"You were in the employ of Thaimur, were you not?" said Miss Musson.

"I was, ma'am; for three years before his death I had charge of his army. I will say that those wild Pathans make fine soldiers! Devils when roused, given to relentless blood feuds, yet they have a great sense of honor and discipline."

"So why did you leave Afghanistan?" inquired Scylla, interested despite herself.

Cameron continued, addressing himself to Miss Musson. "When Thaimur died, his son, Zaman Shah, briefly gained control of the throne, adopting Peshawur as his capital. He asked me to continue in his employ as commander of the army but I—did not see eye to eye with Zaman. He was extravagant, wild, cruel—almost a maniac, indeed! His ambition was to invade India, drive out the British and French. He occupied Lahore, as you know. But then the canny British, taking him in the rear, set up an alliance with the Persians, who began nibbling at Zaman's western frontiers. And then a year later his brother Mahmud, who is Prince of Herat, started gathering forces against him. Mahmud was my friend, so I transferred my allegiance to him when the father died."

"So why are you not in Afghanistan still?"

"Because Mahmud is a prisoner in Kandahar. A third brother, Shuja'-ul-Mulk, has since then seized power and installed himself on the throne."

"I collect," thoughtfully remarked Miss Musson, "that you are not in favor with brother Shuja' either?"

"No, Miss Amanda. That is why I left Kabul and traveled to England."

"May it not be somewhat dangerous for you to pass through Afghanistan?"

"Why no," he said indifferently. "I did it on the way to Ziatur—in disguise, naturally. And who knows? Perhaps by now Mahmud has succeeded in releasing himself; Fatah Khan, the son of his father's chief minister, was working to help him, when I last heard. Or, very likely, some one out of the other twenty brothers has had a snatch at the throne. Do not be putting yourself in a pucker over the dangers in Afghanistan, Miss Amanda; we shall have plenty of more immediate perils to contend with!"

Scylla stood up, leaving the other two, and walked up the slope to where Cal lay asleep, rolled in his traveling cloak, with his head pillowed on a clump of moss. He looked peculiarly young, innocent, and defenseless. None of the men had been able to shave since the expedition began, but, whereas this had merely added another inch to Cameron's luxuriant red-gold beard, not materially altering his appearance, Cal, previously clean-shaven, now had a soft dark fringe of fuzz over his upper lip and chin, which made him look even more youthful than before. A loose lock of soft black hair had fallen forward over his face; kneeling by him, Scylla gently smoothed it back out of his eyes. He did not even stir when she touched him. He slept very deeply, drawing long, slow breaths that could hardly be heard.

Looking up, after a moment or two, Scylla was astonished to find that Cameron stood beside her. He had moved as silently as some creature of the forest. He stooped and laid a finger on Cal's wrist to feel the pulse.

"He will do well enough.—It is a strange affliction, this epilepsy—very inconvenient—*devilish* inconvenient in a situation such as ours," he remarked abruptly, and then added, "For twins, you are singularly unlike!"

"I am sorry, sir"—she could not keep a note of anger out of her voice—"I greatly regret that my brother's disability causes you such *inconvenience.*"

"Oh, confound it!" He turned on his heel and strode away again. As he crossed the clearing she heard him mutter the word "Women!" in his beard.

Scylla knelt on by her brother. Despite the welcome rest and the comfortable presence of Miss Musson, softly singing, "'*Roti, makan, chini, chota,*'" across the clearing, she felt desolate, weary, lonely, and very low-spirited.

IX

The meeting at Petworth House was quite frightening to Fanny, after such a long period of seclusion and virtual confinement at the Hermitage. To be going into company—to walk through the streets of the town with Thomas and Bet, just like any normal family—was in itself an extraordinary novelty. She had hardly set foot in the streets of Petworth during her nine months' residence there. For the occasion Thomas had even thought of taking out the carriage; parsimony had warred in his breast with the wish to make a creditable appearance among the other gentry who would be arriving at Petworth House; but parsimony had won. It was only a five-minute walk, after all! Every minute of this, though, was of fresh interest to Fanny: the handsome town hall in the central square, built only five years previously by Lord Egremont—with a great black and white broadsheet stuck up on its door, terrifyingly depicting hideous brutish Frenchmen raping and devouring English women and children while houses flamed in the background; then there were the shops—drapers, mercers, shoe shops; there were the farmers in their leather breeches and leggings, round hats and neckerchiefs; the butchers' stalls adorned with burning candles; so many impressions poured in upon her that by the time they reached the great front gates of Petworth House, Fanny was already quite dazzled.

"Make haste, Frances!" Thomas said irritably. "Do not be staring about so! It will not do for *us* to be late, as Lord Egremont has invited me to take command of the troop."

Fanny, however, could not go any more rapidly; even at a moderate pace, buckled into her corselet, she could hardly breathe, and the linen webbing cut cruelly into her thighs; she said softly:

"I can go no faster than this, Thomas. But see the church clock; it still wants five minutes to noon."

The gravel sweep before the house was a confusion of barouches, landaus, curricles, and phaetons; ladies and gentlemen were laughingly greeting one another as they descended from their equipages and stood about enjoying the warmth of the sun.

"What's this, James, is it true what I hear, that you have contributed ten thousand pounds to Pitt's defense fund—and you a Whig? Fie!"

"Well, if some wretched Lancashire calico merchant can subscribe ten thousand, it behooves us poor farmers to put our hands in our pockets—"

"Dearest Lady Susan, *how* do you go on, over there, south of the Downs? Are you not afraid to open your windows in the morning, in case you see the French walking up the garden?"

"Why, no, my love, for I have only to look southward to see a perfect forest of masts in the roadsteads off Portsmouth Harbor. I feel well protected!"

"But they say that Rouen and Cambrai are packed with French troops, waiting to embark."

"I am persuaded that Admiral Duncan would never let them cross the Channel."

"What about that ill-starred landing of Popham's at Ostend, though? A most shockingly botched and ill-conducted business! Fourteen hundred men obliged to surrender to the Frogs!"

"The force was simply not strong enough—it should have been at least double that number—"

"Just let them try landing on British soil, that's all—the very sheep will fly at them—"

"I quite agree with you, sir. This new semaphore telegraph will have the whole nation mustered within a space of hours. What a magnificent invention—news flashed from all the ports to the roof of Westminster Abbey, faster than a bird can fly!"

"For my part, I do not believe Buonaparte means to invade us at all. I have heard rumors that French engineers at Alexandria have been collecting information regarding the routes to Suez and the navigation of the Red Sea. I am of the opinion that Boney means to strike eastward, to India; after all, he is in league with Tippoo Sahib—"

"Well, if he does so, it will be a cursed shame, after all our preparations—"

Shy and silent amid all this cheerful babel, Fanny and Bet stood in the shadow of Thomas, who, also somewhat quelled by the sight of so many well-dressed, loud-voiced, confident people, stood looking about him with a kind of nervous hostility. His clothes suddenly appeared countrified, his broadcloth shabby, his neckcloth skimpy, and he himself small, pale, and ill assured.

Bet was avidly taking in the ladies' toilettes. Up to this moment she had considered Fanny and herself very creditably dressed. Regardless of Thomas's admonitions, they had put on their best walking gowns—Fanny's gray and white striped poplin, somewhat old-fashioned, but it suited her, with its frill at the neck and a tilted hat over a lace cap; Bet had her spotted India calico, a Norwich shawl over her shoulders with the long dangling ends crossed in front and a pink sash tied over them. The shawl was too hot for such a warm day but it was by far the finest thing she had, and she had been determined to wear it. Now she saw that she and Fanny looked like a pair of dowds among these ladies, who were all dressed in the most exiguously scanty garments, low-necked muslin gathered in front with gauzy fichus, no hats to be seen, but only bonnets, some of them shaped like Athene's helmet (for in spite of the war, Paris fashions still floated across the Channel), worn over bewitchingly pretty mobcaps with ribbons at the back and rosettes on top. And such lovely slippers! Morocco leather, and satin in every color of red, blue, and green. Surreptitiously Bet shuffled her own feet under the skirt of her gown.

Fortunately at this moment Lord Egremont himself appeared unceremoniously at the entrance to the house, thrusting aside the butler and a couple of footmen. As usual he was impeccably dressed except for a somewhat battered hat resting comfortably on the back of his head.

"Why!" he exclaimed good-naturedly. "Do I find my whole assembly taking place in the garden, and I not present at it? Come in, come in! I would recommend that we hold our discussions out of doors—but that I have a deal of maps spread out on the library table—which would all fly away in the breeze—and Liz has I do not know how many cakes and strawberry syllabubs and cold fowls prepared for the ladies. For that matter, I dare say even the gentlemen will not refuse a cooling glass. But come in, come in! Faith, it's as hot out here as the Earl of Hell's kitchen!"

At these hospitable words there began to be a general move toward the door of the house. Lord Egremont stood by the entrance, greeting his friends without ceremony.

"Ha! Milsom, is that you? It is good of you to come such a long way on such a hot day. Lady Mountague, Liz will be happy to see you! She has been depending on your advice. Now you may have a snug coze together. Captain Holland, how d'ye do? How does that leg go on? Famous, famous. Mrs. Johnstone, pray step in, out of the glare; ay, ay, Liz will soon find you a cool seat and a glass of sherbet or shrub. Lady Susan—Mrs. Whitaker—Miss Louisa Whitaker—what news of your husband, ma'am? He has left St. Vincent's fleet and is sailing to the

Mediterranean with Nelson? Well, well, now that poor fellow has recovered from his wound and returned to action, I dare say we shall soon hear of some lively work! Tickle Boney on his underbelly, that is what *I* say, then he will have less inclination to come bothering us here in Sussex. Not but what we shall be rare and ready to give him a warm welcome if he does come!"

Then, setting eyes on Thomas, who with his female encumbrances was still hesitating at the edge of the group, Lord Egremont walked forward to him very cordially, saying:

"Why, here you are, Paget! I am delighted to see you. And Mrs. Paget too, and Miss! I believe I am to congratulate you, Mrs. Paget, on a recent happy event. Ay, ay, Liz will be wishful to hear how you go on. But"—hastily recollecting himself—"Paget, let me make you known to Milsom here, and Captain Holland, and Sir Archibald King—Captain Paget is to command our troop, Milsom, d'ye know—but come along, come this way into the library—now, Paget, what do you say as to uniform—helmets with feathers, do you think, or hair cockades? Or bearskins? And if we have a scarlet jacket—as I believe we should—need the lapels be of the same color?"

So talking, he thrust Thomas ahead of him into the library, while the butler, with more decorum, ushered the ladies, of whom there were fewer in number, to a large cool dining room with handsome paintings all around the walls and a table spread with a variety of cold meats, cakes, syllabubs, and beautiful pyramids of fruit. Many of the guests immediately clustered around the table. Fanny, who was both hot and nervous, sank down onto an exceedingly uncomfortable little straight-backed Venetian chair. Here she would have remained, despite the impatient looks Bet was giving her, had she not been sought out by Liz Wyndham, who came floating up to them, her laces and gauzes quivering with suppressed laughter, her eyes sparkling.

"Why, my dear—my very dear Mrs. Paget! And Miss Paget! Miss Paget, pray let me make you known to Miss Sefton, I dare swear you two girls will have a great deal to say to one another—" and having thus rapidly disposed of Bet, she turned back to Fanny and whispered to her, bubbling over with laughter:

"Is not this famous? I was bound to see my dear friend *somehow!* And I knew how it would be—I told Egremont! 'Depend upon it,' I said, 'Paget will *never* be able to resist *such* a bait! Being appointed commander of the town troop—even *his* surly contumacious nature must have some weak spot by which its defenses can be breached.' And, you see, I was right!—But how do you go on, my dearest creature? Are you in plump currant again? You are dreadfully thin! Quick, let me feed you. No, do not rise. Remain there—you look weary—I will bring you some strawberries—or would you prefer a wing of chicken?"

And, despite Fanny's protests, she fetched with her own hands a quantity of good things and placed them near at hand on a French giltwood table. "Is not this pretty? George brought it back from Paris in 1772—along with Mademoiselle Duthé, his first mistress! Now I have shocked you—I keep forgetting. I am so delighted to see you! But tell me, how is your baby? Chilgrove says he is very big, and beautiful as an angel. Do you love him very much? Or," sinking her voice to a whisper, "does he too much resemble his papa?"

Fanny could not help laughing at Liz's nonsense and being greatly cheered by her warmth and affection. She wished that it had not been necessary to meet in the midst of such a public gathering, for she had two troubles that she longed to divulge to this lighthearted yet practical and unshockable creature. One was the corselet. She would have wished to know Liz's opinion, to hear her comments about this indignity. Just to disclose her own horror, her humiliation, to an understanding friend would be an incalculable relief. But *that* she could certainly not mention in such surroundings as these. And the other distress was, in a way, even worse, because it revealed Fanny to herself as a heartless, unnatural monster; this one she thought she *must* confess, even at the risk of being overheard.

"Truly, Liz, you did not—did you?—*really* persuade Lord Egremont to appoint Thomas as head of the troop—just so that he could be persuaded to come here to Petworth House?" she breathed in horror.

"Truly I *did!*" Liz said, laughing. "Egremont was not at all certain that he would make a good commander, but I overbore all his objections! 'It will get the man away from his house more,' I said, 'so that poor persecuted little angel can have a bit of respite from him.' And— who knows?—if he is inveigled into meeting a few more people of *ton*, perhaps he will learn a little how to go on, and that a man ought not to treat a wife as a mastiff treats a bone, to be growled over in the back of his kennel."

This image was so apt that Fanny could not repress a shudder.

"But now you have provided a son and heir, is he not at least delighted with that? And are *you* not delighted?"

"Oh, Liz!" Fanny said wretchedly. "I cannot love the baby as I ought! He is big and beautiful, it is true, but I find I—I do not like babies! Indeed I find I can hardly love him at all. To me he seems just a big, damp bundle, smelling of milk—I cannot feel that he has ever been part of me. Am I not dreadfully wicked?"

Tears trembling on the tips of her lashes, she looked piteously up at Liz, who replied roundly:

"No, my dearest creature, you are not in the least wicked. How could *anybody,* situate as you are, love anything that derived from that man? I dare say in your case I should have been tempted to strangle the little monster."

"Liz, Liz, hush, how can you! But you *love* your children."

"Ah, true," said Liz, and a most characteristic expression came over her face—tender, teasing, fond, resigned, dispassionate, reflective, indulgent, mischievous—as she added, "But then, I have the good fortune to love George."

"Then—then you do not think me heartless, unnatural?"

"*No,* my poor child, I think your heart is full of good and faithful feelings, and it but requires the right occasion—perhaps the right person—to bring them out. Meanwhile—do not utterly despair of coming to love your brat," Liz added cheerfully. "You may find he improves as he grows. Myself, I must confess I loved mine better as they began to walk and talk and behave like civilized beings.—Now I fear that, for the moment, I had better leave you and perform a few of my duties as a hostess, or all my acquaintances will become jealous of you.

—Do not be afraid, though," smiling at Fanny's look of alarm, "I will not allow you to remain alone in this throng, or undefended. Come with me and I am going to introduce you to one who, I hope, will prove a kind friend to you as she has to me."

And, with something more of formality in her manner than she had hitherto shown, Liz took Fanny's hand and, leading her across the room to where an elderly lady was seated in a velvet armchair, said:

"Ma'am, allow me to make known to you my friend Mrs. Fanny Paget, whose husband, Captain Paget, has been chosen by George to lead our troop of volunteers. Mrs. Paget is a dear neighbor of mine whom I see much less than I would wish to," and to Fanny she said, "Fanny, this is Lady Mountague, who resides at Cowdray and knows, I believe, every soul in the countryside, so it is very shocking that she does not yet know *you!*" and smiling, blowing a kiss to Fanny, she floated off to replenish the plates of a hungry-looking trio of ladies in the corner of the room.

"Come and sit by me, my dear," said Lady Mountague, patting a velvet seat beside her. She was a kind-looking, gentle-faced person, very pale, dressed in black, with a quantity of soft gray curls, rather haphazardly arranged under a widow's cap. "I have been looking at you across the room for the last ten minutes and admiring your beautiful carriage! I only wish their governesses could have instilled such deportment into *my* daughters when they were your age. But—forgive me—you are a married lady, though you hardly look old enough for it. Now I am going to be very inquisitive and find out all about you."

Lady Mountague was as good as her word. In five minutes she had elicited all the Herriard family history and discovered a second cousin of her own who was related to Fanny's mother's eldest sister's husband. After that she went on with the same eager interest to a review of the Paget family ramifications. "Paget, Paget, was there not a branch of them at Romsey? *General* Paget of course I know all about, and his brother the other general, Sir Henry (no better than he should be, that one, I may say!), but your husband was from the Romsey branch, I understand? Did not his mother remarry on his father's death and have another son by her second husband?"

"Yes, ma'am, but he is dead. I believe he perished in rather sad circumstances."

"Ah yes—that was it. I believe I heard that there was something rather discreditable about his end—or that your husband did not do his part as a brother, was that it?"

This was news to Fanny, though not surprising, but she said simply:

"I know nothing about it, ma'am."

"Very properly said, child; my indiscreet old tongue tends to run away with me. But now tell me about the wealthy cousins who let you have the house—and are there not some more cousins out in India, children of that old rip, General Sir Henry?"

"Yes, indeed, ma'am, and they may be coming to live with us," responded Fanny, eager to get away from the subject of Thomas's past wrongdoings. She and Lady Mountague enjoyably discussed the possible ages and dispositions of Carloman and Sarah, as Lady Mountague believed the twins to be called. She had heard they were in their late teens, whereas Fanny tended to think of them as children.

"I wonder if they will really come? It is such a long way to India! And if Buonaparte is really in the Red Sea—they must come all the way around the Cape of Good Hope—"

"Well, they are young; when you are young, travel is a pleasure, not a fatigue. My husband was a great traveler, even to a late age. Unfortunately he fell into the river Rhine and was drowned," Lady Mountague disclosed matter-of-factly. "So, having no house and no husband, I must e'en occupy myself nowadays with my neighbors," she went on, turning her deep-set gray eyes on Fanny and smiling with a sudden unexpected radiance. "I live in a small house in Cowdray Park, where I go on very comfortably, and I hope that you will come to visit me there as soon as possible, Mrs. Paget. Will your husband allow you to visit me?"

"Oh yes, ma'am, I am sure he will," murmured Fanny, remembering Thomas's homily to the effect that Lady Mountague "might prove a most useful patron and neighbor."

During the next two hours the more energetic of the lady guests, or those who had a talent for organization, tore up old sheets and rolled them into bandages, as a long-term precaution against the possible siege and bloody defense of Petworth. A plan was prepared whereby, if the French army were to be seen advancing over the Downs, all the families who resided in outlying farms should be informed by courier and transported to the comparative security of Petworth House.

Fanny was introduced by Lady Mountague to numerous other guests—Mrs. Holland, Mrs. Milsom, Lady Sefton, Lady Susan Coates; presently she was able to sit down comfortably beside kind Mrs. Socket and help to make a list of provisions to be stored in the church.

Lady Mountague presently declared herself tired and called for her carriage, bidding a kind farewell to Fanny and declaring that she should soon give herself the pleasure of inviting her young neighbor to come and spend the day. Fanny likewise would gladly have gone home but could hardly do so without Thomas, who was still closeted with most of the other males in the library. She looked for Bet, but the latter had found a handful of congenial younger people, visitors and relatives of the house; they were playing games together and she was not at all anxious to leave.

"Oh, gracious me, Stepmamma, why in the world should you wish to go home?" she demanded impatiently. "We are all just about to take part in an archery contest!"

Indeed the younger members of the party had all strayed out through the french windows onto the grass.

"Where is Mrs. Wyndham?" Fanny inquired, thinking that she might ask Liz if it would be in order to send a message to Thomas in the library. Perhaps he would give permission for her to walk quietly home by herself.

"Mrs. Wyndham went into the garden to order targets to be set up," somebody said. "She went up toward the Grecian Pavilion."

Wearily, Fanny walked out to look for Liz. The cooler atmosphere outside, and a chance to be by herself, refreshed her; she turned to her right, following the direction indicated, and strolled toward the end of the house, where there was an informal pleasure garden with clumps of rhododendron and lilacs, and larger trees. Liz was nowhere to be seen.

"Why—as I live and breathe—it is George's lovely neighbor—the bewitching Mrs. Paget! What a surpassing piece of good fortune that I should have become fatigued by all those wiseacres in the library and escaped for some fresh air! Dearest Mrs. Paget, you look precisely like some delicious wood nymph—a dryad, slipped out from the trunk of one of the trees to take a turn among the narcissus and the lilies—which *you* so much excel in beauty!"

Fanny spun around, startled out of her wits by this address. Confronting her, having come strolling around a big clump of pink rhododendron, was that Major Henriques whom she had seen on two previous occasions, once at Petworth House, once walking with Liz Wyndham. "A shallow-minded fellow—never trust him," she remembered Liz had said of him. Indeed Fanny herself had felt an instinctive dislike and distrust of him—there was something disconcertingly cynical, far too knowing, in the expression on his swarthy face; his eyes, as they studied her, seemed full of a rather unpleasant amusement, as if he had caught her out in some discreditable activity.

"How—how do you do, sir," she stammered. "I—I was looking for Mrs. Wyndham."

"Of *course* you were," he agreed, the laughter in his voice wholly belying his words. "You were out among the trees looking for our dear hostess, and not at all hoping that some woodland god would come galloping down the glade for a little charming sylvan dalliance! But will not *I* serve instead? Truly I am only too anxious to serve you, Mrs. Paget—in any way I may—and have been, I promise you, ever since I first set eyes on your enchanting countenance!"

"Pray, sir, *pray* do not be talking so," said Fanny, greatly disconcerted. "Indeed I am not used to it and do not like it—it—it is most improper! I—I would remind you that—that I am a married woman —you should *not* be addressing me thus!"

Indignantly she pulled away the hand that he had taken and had been about to raise to his lips.

"Now come, come, what's all this to-do about?" he said teasingly. "A married woman? Of *course* you are! That is why I did not expect such missish airs from you! For heaven's sake, my sweetest creature—

my angel—where is the harm in my taking your hand, in my telling you that the charms of your person have stirred up such a fire in my heart that I cannot rest until I have expressed it thus—"

So saying, he attempted to repossess himself of her hand, but Fanny, with an inarticulate exclamation of distress, broke away from him and turned back toward the house. She could not run—she could not even walk fast, her corselet was too miserably constricting and uncomfortable; the reminder of this indignity, and the thought that Thomas, did he know of her present situation, would consider it just the sort of scrape to be expected of her—had even *anticipated* it—made her all the more desperate. She was half sobbing as Henriques came up with her in two strides and barred her escape.

"Nay, my charmer, you do not evade me as easily as that!"

"Sir, pray, *pray* leave me—*indeed* I wished to find Mrs. Wyndham —somebody said she had gone this way—"

"Find Mrs. Wyndham!" he mocked her. "Why, you sweet simpleton, can you not be aware that dear Liz invited you to the house for *my* sake, because I told her that I so longed to get a glimpse of you at closer quarters? Liz and I, you must know, are *very* good friends!"

Really stunned at this, appalled at such a revelation of duplicity, she stood stock-still, staring at him, while the blood drained from her face.

"I—I do *not* believe it!" she stammered naïvely. *Could* lively, laughing Liz have betrayed her in such a way—have so misread her character? "It *cannot* be the truth."

"Psha, my dear, you are almost too much of an innocent to walk this earth! Come, come, you bewitching little Puritan, give me a kiss— *do*—what is all this coil about?"

And he was again attempting to slide his arm about her waist. Fanny gave a slight scream—tried to struggle, pulling away from Henriques—and found herself suddenly face to face with a young man in a gardener's apron who was walking quickly down the path, carrying in his arms a bundle of bows, arrows, and targets.

"What is the trouble, ma'am? Can I help you?" exclaimed this individual.

Major Henriques let out a heartfelt oath under his breath.

"It is nothing," he said hastily. "The lady thought she saw a snake —but she was mistaken! See, ma'am—there is nothing to be frightened of, nothing at all!" he added with an irritable laugh, and he said to the gardener, "These delicate fine ladies are wont to think they see bogeys in every bush!"

"Yes, sir," said the young man stolidly. He did not move away but addressed Fanny. "May I help you back to the house, ma'am?"

"Oh, thank you, Talgarth—indeed I am perfectly well—or shall be in a moment—I came out to look for Mrs. Wyndham—"

"She is just coming down from the Grecian Pavilion, ma'am; there, you may see her dress among the trees."

And indeed next moment Liz appeared coming down the hill, also carrying bows and arrows. She called:

"Set the targets up outside the drawing-room windows, Talgarth—" and then, her eyes falling on the white-cheeked Fanny and the scowling Henriques, she exclaimed:

"Why, what is the matter, my angel? Are you not well?"

"No—that is—I came to find you—to tell you that I must return home—"

Fanny could not bear to meet the eyes of Liz Wyndham. The thought of the latter's duplicity—surely the startled concern in her voice *must* be pure histrionics—the situation was not to be borne! Pulling herself together with a strong effort, Fanny said in a low voice:

"I should be so much obliged, ma'am, if you could send a servant to ask my husband if he is ready to return home, and—and if he is not, inform him that I find myself rather tired and under the necessity of taking my leave."

"I will tell him myself," said Liz. Handing her burden to the gardener, she tucked her arm through Fanny's and led her solicitously indoors. Major Henriques had already removed himself from the scene; Talgarth, after another concerned glance at Fanny, carried off the archery equipment.

"What is the matter, my dear friend?" Liz asked quietly as they walked along at a slow pace. "Was that man making himself objectionable?"

"You knew—you knew that he would," Fanny burst out. Then they passed in through the french windows and she could say no more, for there were several people about. Quietly detaching her arm from that of Liz, she moved to a chair and sat on it, feeling sick and giddy. Liz stood staring at her for a moment with a doubtful, troubled expression, then said simply:

"I will deliver your message," and went off to the library.

After a few moments she returned, looking even graver, and reported:

"I am afraid that Captain Paget is not ready to leave yet. When I said that I would have you sent home in one of our carriages he gave his permission." She suppressed Thomas's angry rider, *"What, making a damned nuisance of herself again, is she?"* and ordered a servant to see that a conveyance was brought around. Fanny thanked her and apologized for the trouble she was giving.

"Not the least trouble, my dear child. But I wish I knew what was in your mind—why do you look at me so strangely?" she added in a low voice.

Fanny could not reply. There were too many people within earshot —she shook her head miserably. How, in any case, could she explain that she felt betrayed, outraged? Liz might not even understand what she meant. Next moment the servant returned to announce that the carriage waited. Fanny, observing that Bet was outside on the grass, laughing and excited among the archery contestants, murmured her thanks again and took her leave, saying that she would not attempt to drag off her stepdaughter, who could return later with Thomas. The last impression she carried away with her was the quick, warm pressure of Liz's hand on hers and the words whispered in her ear:

"I shall not rest until I get to the bottom of this. Doubtless it was some mischief of that toad, Henriques!"

Fanny was immensely glad of the short carriage ride to quiet her unhappy and troubled spirits. The open carriage—the calm pace of the horses along the cobbled street—the cool air blowing against her smarting eyes and throbbing brow—all these things were helping to calm and soothe her mind. While they crossed the town square and passed the town hall she looked about her, trying to distract her thoughts with outside matters. A sizable crowd was gathered in front of one of the larger alehouses, the Half Moon, laughing, talking, and jostling. She wondered what occupied them.

Suddenly, as the carriage drew near to the group, Fanny heard a terrible, a truly ear-piercing scream, which came from its center. The crowd broke apart as a young man burst out from its midst and ran wildly across the open space. Next moment all the bystanders were after him. Fanny gazed at him aghast as he raced toward the carriage; he was white-faced, thin, wild-eyed, bare to the waist. His dash for escape was hopeless; somebody thrust out a foot and tripped him; a moment later two burly fellows in leather jackets had seized him. Fanny saw with horror that these were members of her husband's impress gang—a tough, callous pair called Noakes and Tanner, who had elected to follow Thomas to Petworth from Gosport.

Meanwhile the carriage driver had been obliged to draw his horses to a halt, since the crowd had blocked the road. "Make way, make way there!" he called authoritatively, and the people, recognizing him and Lord Egremont's equipage, began to move aside, touching their hats and forelocks. The press-gangers gathered around their prisoner once more; Fanny saw a man scoop a dipperful of something out of a heavy leather bucket and pour the contents over the captive's arm; then a second time; she saw steam rising from the ladle; and twice more came that appalling scream.

"*Oh!* What in mercy's name are they doing to that poor man?" she demanded of the footman who stood behind her.

" 'Tis the press gang, ma'am," he replied flatly.

"I know that." Fanny could not avoid a dreadful feeling of guilt for her own connection with the gang, through Thomas; she felt it must show in her face. "But what were they *doing* to him?" she repeated.

"Likely he'll have been shamming epileptic, ma'am. If you're a 'leptic, see, you may claim freedom from impress. So the gangers, what they do is hold a fellow's arm in a flame, or, like now, pour on boiling tallow. If he do truly suffer from fits, 'tis reckoned as how that'll bring one of 'em on; if not, then he's a healthy man, and fit for naval service."

And indeed at this moment Fanny heard the stentorian voice of Noakes roaring out what was evidently a ritual sentence:

"He'll do, alow and aloft! Throw him in the cart!" And the wretched prisoner was dragged, trembling and crying, to a tumbril that stood outside the Half Moon Inn.

As the carriage passed by the cart, Fanny saw that the man knelt beseechingly, extending his manacled hands, while the half dozen other captives looked at him with vague dislike and apathy; she heard him cry: "If I am taken, who will look after my poor mother?"

"They doesn't take loonies and 'leptics and suchlike for sailors, ye see, ma'am," the footman continued instructively as the carriage rolled on, "'case they tumbles down out o' the rigging or sets fire to the ship; so chaps'll get up to all manner of tricks, acting crazy, feigning sickness, scraping their skin sore with copper coins, rubbing their legs with cow itch or sting nettles to bring on scabs, burning theirselves with oil of vitriol even, and making out 'tis the pox; why, I even heard of a man chopping off his own thumb and finger with an ax, so's to 'scape the press."

"I see," Fanny said faintly. She thought of Thomas's missing thumb and finger—for a wild moment wondered if he could possibly have mutilated himself in such a manner; but then remembered that he had in fact been to sea, that the injury had been received in a naval engagement; no wonder he and his men had little sympathy with those who pretended disabilities in order to avoid serving their country.— She must try to think of it in a proper spirit. Of course there had to be a navy—ships, sailors—in order to defend the country from Buonaparte, men must be taken to serve at sea; nevertheless, all she could really think of was that man's face of desperation; his terrible cry still rang in her ears.

The distance from Petworth House to the Hermitage was a very short one, and in three more minutes the conveyance had drawn up at her front door.

Little Patty, hearing the sound of wheels, came flying out in curiosity.

"La! Stepmamma, why do you come home in a coach? And where are Bet and Papa?"

Patty had gone into a sulk for three days on learning that she was not to make one of the party to Petworth House. Her feelings of ill-use were very strong, and now, as Fanny explained why she had returned before the others, they broke out once more.

"It is too bad! Why could not I go? I dare say there were other children my age. *I* should have liked to see the pretty ladies' dresses and the nice things to eat! Why should Bet be allowed to play with bows and arrows when I am not?"

The afternoon had become thunderously close and hot; having changed her dress, Fanny walked outdoors again. Longing for a breeze, she made her way down to the yew-tree walk, closely accompanied by Patty with demands for more details about the party at Petworth House and information regarding the possible visit to Cowdray. Fanny supplied these as best she could, but in a somewhat disjointed manner; her thoughts were distressfully occupied by the encounter with Major Henriques. Was it conceivable that Liz could have arranged the visit to Petworth House to promote the schemes of such a man? Could the relationship of Liz herself with Henriques be such as he had hinted? What, after all, did she really know about Liz Wyndham, save that she lived with a man to whom she was not married and had borne him three children? Very likely she would think of the affair merely as a harmless flirtation, nothing but a frolic. But then, previously, she had expressed what sounded like contempt for Henriques, said that he was a rake—that did not sound like close friendship, surely? Or could these derogatory comments have been made in order to disguise her own interest in him? Or out of pique because he had slighted her?

How *can* I think such hateful and disgusting things about someone who has befriended me? thought Fanny, and pressed her palms against her burning cheeks. But if she turned her mind from Liz Wyndham, it was only to remember Major Henriques and his mocking smile, or to hear again the horrible scream of the man in the square as they poured the boiling tallow onto his arm. How can Thomas permit such practices? she thought. Surely there must be other ways in which to discover whether a man has epilepsy or not?

Fanny glanced over the wall into the meadows below. A storm was

brewing: the high-piled purplish clouds, reflecting the light of the setting sun, threw a strange glow into the valley, making the grass shine
emerald green, the young-leaved hedges flow like shining ribbons;
birds were singing with wild fervor, as if to try and avert the bad
weather. Another kind of whistling caught her ear—a sweet human
tune, lilting and irresistible, one that she had never heard before, yet
its gaiety reminded her of the tunes that she invented for her own
pleasure.

Patty tugged at her hand.

"Come, Stepmamma! Why are you standing and staring so, down
into the valley? Papa does not like you to do so!" And then, standing
on tiptoe herself so as to see over the wall, "Who is that man walking
down by the brook? Why do you look after him?"

"He is one of Lord Egremont's gardeners," Fanny said absently.

"Oh, a *gardener*." Patty's tone dismissed the whole tribe. Nevertheless she added, "Where is he going?"

"I dare say to visit his father, who lives in a little house in the
woods, up on the other side of the valley."

"How do you know? You have never been there? I believe that is
just a story! Who told you?" Patty demanded suspiciously.

Fanny thought how strange it was that she had never been into
those woods, which looked so close.

"See, there is Tess coming from the house; I believe she wants me.
Let us go back."

Tess hurried toward them, looking anxious.

"Mrs. Strudwick sent me for ye, ma'am; owd Missus Paget tumbled
herself out o' bed, and Mrs. Baggot is out, and we fear the poor owd
lady may be poorly; we've put her back in bed but she's unaccountable
mazed, and Mrs. Strudwick wondered should we send for the doctor;
she give her head a proper dunt on the corner of the chest."

"Oh, good God!" exclaimed Fanny. "How very unfortunate that
Nurse Baggot should be out when such a thing occurs."

Tess looked as if she felt this to be nothing surprising. Indeed Nurse
Baggot spent less and less time with her patient.

"Are you quite well, Tess?" Fanny asked, noticing that the little maid, walking a respectful pace behind her mistress, appeared rather more distressed and troubled than the news about the old lady seemed to warrant. Tears swam in her eyes, and her cheeks, under their freckles, were even paler than normally.

"Oh, ma'am!" The child gulped. "'Tis my cousin Tom Rapley, ma'am—he've been taken up by the press gang—the butcher's boy just told me when he brought the beef—and how is my aunt Rapley ever going to manage now, for she be a widow woman, and bedridden these five years! Couldn't ye say a word to Master, ma'am, and tell him how 'tis? Maybe he'd let poor Tom go, if he knew all?"

She gazed at Fanny pleadingly but without real hope; and Fanny gazed as hopelessly back.

"My word carries no weight with the master, my poor child; I will try my best, but I am afraid I already know what the answer will be."

Tess nodded, suppressing a sob; she had expected as much.

"But tell me where your aunt Rapley lives," said Fanny.

"In Bywimbles, ma'am, next and nigh to the church."

"I will write a note to Mrs. Socket about her," Fanny said. "I am sure she will see that your aunt is looked after—that somebody comes in to do for her and run errands."

"Thank you, ma'am," said Tess, sniffing. She still looked very stricken. Fanny wondered with pity if she had a more than cousinly attachment to the boy who had been taken; the sound of his scream came again, unbidden, into her mind.

"Perhaps your aunt might find somebody to lodge with her and help her in the house instead of paying rent," Fanny suggested.

"Yes, ma'am," Tess agreed dully. "I dare say that's what she better do."

Arrived in the old lady's room, Fanny could see immediately that her mother-in-law was in a fair way to be really ill. She was feverish, wild-eyed, continually threw herself about in the bed, and muttered unintelligibly; her lips were dry and caked and her head was very hot.

"It's as much as I can do to keep her in the bed, ma'am," said Mrs. Strudwick, "and me with dinner to prepare and all; what Master will say I do not know—and as for that *hussy* that calls herself a nurse—"

"Pray send Jem for Dr. Chilgrove directly, Mrs. Strudwick," Fanny ordered her. "I will sit with Mrs. Paget until Nurse Baggot returns, so you may go back to your work."

Mrs. Strudwick departed in haste.

Left alone with the old lady, Fanny attempted to soothe her by stroking her temples and bathing them and her wrists with rosemary water. By degrees this had a beneficial effect, and presently Mrs. Paget ceased her restless frantic movements from side to side of the bed and lay still, staring at Fanny with wide, unrecognizing eyes.

"He died in jail!" she suddenly exclaimed. "I was not there!"

"I know," Fanny said in a tone of sympathy, "and I am very sorry for it."

"I do not know where his grave is, even. Thomas would never speak of it. I could not put flowers on my own boy's grave. Thomas is wicked —a heartless, unnatural brother."

"Try not to think about it," Fanny said gently.

The old lady gave her a cunning look.

"You won't tell him I said so? You won't do that, dearie? He is angry as it is. I fooled him finely."

"I am sure you did not, ma'am."

"He thought I had more money," the old woman said in sly triumph. Her eyes slid secretively past Fanny. "He will be angry, though, when he learns the whole. We must conceal it while we can. *That one* might tell him, though—you can't trust her." She seized Fanny's wrist in a clawlike grip and whispered harshly, "Hand in glove! Hand in glove!"

"Hush, hush, ma'am. You are overexciting yourself."

Ten minutes later Dr. Chilgrove arrived. He immediately diagnosed the old lady's disorder as a putrid fever similar to some other cases which he had been treating in the town. He shook his head over her prospects but said that with careful nursing she might come through.

"Only tell me what she needs," said Fanny.

Dr. Chilgrove looked at her doubtfully.

"You are only just out of your own bed, ma'am. I fear it will be too much for you, my dear."

"What I cannot do, Nurse Baggot will, I am sure," Fanny said with a confidence she did not wholly feel. Dr. Chilgrove appeared to feel even less confidence in this aid but administered some drops to the old lady, wrote out a regimen, and promised to send a further supply of medicine by his boy. He was taking his leave when voices outside announced the return of Thomas and Bet.

Fanny could tell at once from the raised tones that Thomas was in one of his towering rages. He was shouting orders to Jem bootboy to do something or other—"And do it *directly!* I wish to see it gone in five minutes—make haste about it!" Then came the sound of his quick, angry feet on the stairs, and the next moment he was in the old lady's room.

"What is this I hear—" he began furiously, but Dr. Chilgrove, without ceremony, hustled him out of the sickroom.

"Hush, sir! This is no place for loud voices."

Fanny was glad to remain with the patient and so avoid the first overflow of Thomas's displeasure; and indeed, by the time Dr. Chilgrove had talked with him and reasoned with him, it was evident that he had been brought to see the necessity for the doctor's visit, and his anger had somewhat diminished; also Jem had apparently carried out the orders given him, whatever they were, to his master's satisfaction.

In due course Nurse Baggot reappeared from her afternoon's outing —"visiting her cousin at Heath End," was her only explanation. She had evidently bought a new bonnet, ornamented lavishly with poppies, her color was high, and her breath redolent of gin and peppermint. She listened without comment, but with a scornful expression, to Fanny's account of the doctor's directions; Fanny left her with a sinking of the heart and went to change her dress for dinner. She expected, and duly received, a trouncing at this meal from Thomas, first for having returned home by herself from Petworth House, secondly for having, on her own initiative, called in the doctor for her mother-in-law;

but to her agreeable surprise these offenses were passed over more lightly than she had anticipated; most of Thomas's rage appeared to be directed against some person or persons unknown who had written up several defamatory statements about him, in paint, on the Hermitage gate at the end of the driveway leading into Angel Street; Thomas did not divulge what these remarks had been (Jem had already cleaned them off) but Fanny gathered that they had been scurrilous to a degree.

Recalling the scene in the square, Fanny shivered, thinking how many people in the town—people who had lost sons, brothers, fathers, husbands to the press gang—must have cause to hate her husband.

However presently Thomas reverted to happier topics and grew more cheerful. It seemed that the meeting of the local gentry had been highly successful; a scheme for the local troop had been drawn up, and a long list of volunteers was already in hand; agreement had been reached as to the uniform, accouterments, and weapons; Thomas and another gentleman were to travel to London very soon, possibly next week, in order to make the necessary purchases.

Fanny's heart bounded; several days without Thomas! But then she wondered if perhaps he would expect her to accompany him, as on the previous ill-starred occasion. She dared not broach the question for fear of exposing her hopes; and she suspected, from several angry and undecided glances given her by Thomas, that he himself had not made up his mind on the matter.

Late in the evening Fanny returned to the old lady's chamber. The patient was whimpering and moaning restlessly, with most of her covers thrown aside. Since it was a close, thundery night, with a storm muttering outside, Fanny removed most of the blankets and replaced them with a light quilt. Meanwhile Nurse Baggot slumbered peacefully in a wicker armchair, letting out an occasional snore. Fanny had to shake her arm quite sharply several times before she could be roused out of her heavy sleep.

"I will sit with Mrs. Paget now," Fanny said when she was awake. "Do you go and lie down on your bed."

Nurse Baggot threw her a glance of suspicion and malice compounded, with very little gratitude in it.

"What does Master say?" she demanded.

"I have told him that I am going to sit with his mother," Fanny quietly replied.

When Nurse Baggot had gone, she sat down by the bedside and took hold of the clutching clawlike hand that was restlessly searching, searching, among the crumpled sheets.

"Where is it, where is it?" murmured the old lady. "Where can it be?"

"Never mind it, ma'am," Fanny murmured. "Try to sleep!"

"My poor boy! When he was a little lad I used to sing him lullabies. But Thomas would be so spiteful to his poor little brother. Often he has slammed the bedroom door on purpose to wake the baby just as he had gone off to sleep."

Like father, like daughter, thought Fanny, disagreeably struck by this resemblance to little Patty.

"Then, when he was older, little Edward was so loving to me. He used to sing to me so sweetly. Ah, if only I could hear it now!"

A tear trickled down the thin, withered cheek that had the bright flush of fever like a scarlet penny below the eye.

"I will sing to you if you wish, ma'am," said Fanny softly.

"I would sooner *he* sang," said the old lady in a fretful tone.

"He is not here, though, ma'am."

"Oh, very well, sing, then; my ears are teased to death by all that rumbling," the old lady grumbled.

Indeed, the thunder was loudly audible overhead, even to a deaf ear, and the drawn curtains could not exclude the continuous flicker of lightning.

Very softly, Fanny sang to the old lady, as many ballads, hymns, and lullabies as she could remember, many of them to tunes of her own invention. And when these had run out she recalled the lilting, insidious tune she had heard whistled that afternoon by young Talgarth as he went his carefree way down the valley path, and she hummed that, and then set it to some words that she remembered from a poem by the Earl of Surrey:

> *"And in green waves, when the salt flood*
> *Doth rise by rage of wind,*
> *A thousand fancies in that mood*
> *Assail my restless mind.*
> *Alas! Now drencheth my sweet foe*
> *That with the spoil of my poor heart did go*
> *And left me; but alas! why did he so?"*

X

Some twelve weeks had elapsed since Cal's unfortunate seizure on the brink of the gorge. During that period of time he had not, mercifully, been subject to another severe attack of his malady, but the party of travelers had undergone many other trials and vicissitudes. Hazarah, the guide, from neglecting to follow the precautions advised by Colonel Cameron, had been afflicted with snow blindness; he moaned in agony all day long and was of practically no use to them in his prime capacity, since he could see virtually nothing and must have every feature of the landscape described to him before he could suggest which way to go. Miss Musson made him tea-leaf poultices until Colonel Cameron forbade this use of their precious scanty supplies, saying that it was the man's own stupid fault and he must suffer the consequences.

For a period of many weeks, now, they had been above the snow line; the blond grass hillsides which had succeeded the forests had in their turn been succeeded by unbroken white: sometimes a slippery crust on which the travelers must proceed with the utmost caution for fear of falling and sliding hundreds of feet; sometimes, in the passes and ravines, the snow formed a soft layer, knee deep or thigh deep, through which they were obliged to flounder at a painfully slow rate of progress.

And what Colonel Cameron gloomily apprehended had come to pass: owing to their tardiness, the full severity of winter came down while they were between the passes of Lowacal and Weran, so that they were obliged to pass six weeks of somewhat acrimonious inactivity in a mountain village, before being able to continue their journey. Miss Musson, to be sure, occupied her time in advising the hill people on their ailments, and by learning how to spin goat hair on the locally made spindles; while Cal succeeded in completing his epic poem on Alexander's invasion of India. Owing to a complete lack of writing paper, he was obliged to inscribe his verses between the lines of the few books he had carried with him, cultivating a microscopic script for the purpose. The accomplishment of this task filled him with great satisfaction, and he was now meditating his next work, undecided as to whether it should be a heroic drama on the life of Timur Leng (or Tamburlaine), a narrative saga about Genghis Khan, or a romantic elegy on the fate of the Children of Israel, some of whom, by Colonel Cameron's account—those deported from their homeland by Nebuchadnezzar—had subsequently drifted eastward and come to rest in Kafiristan, as evidenced by the frequent use of the proper name Israel among the natives of that region. Thus absorbed in literary planning, Cal was perfectly contented.

It was far otherwise, however, with Scylla and Colonel Cameron, both of whom, for different reasons, chafed exceedingly at their enforced inaction and were impatient to be on their way.

During this time they were all, also, in some degree affected by the great height to which they had ascended; intermittently they all endured blinding headaches, nausea, shortness of breath, and palpitations. Little Chet Singh, the baby, suffered even more severely than the adults, for besides the trouble from the altitude he also fell victim to a colicky disorder caused, probably, by the poor quality of the provender consumed by Ammomma the goat, who supplied his milk. Consequently the baby, who had been so well behaved on the first stages of the journey, now cried despairingly for hours at a stretch; provoking Colonel Cameron, every now and then, to such exasperation that he was wont, more or less seriously, to urge putting the child out for adoption by some village woman.

"How *dare* you make such suggestions!" Scylla exclaimed on one such occasion. Her eyes bright, her voice unsteady with emotion, she confronted him in the narrow, snow-packed street of a tiny hill town where they had paused to buy such scanty provisions as were available. Little stone houses rose on either side of them, built squatly into the mountainside, their flat roofs held down by large rocks; a couple of hill women, clad in striped blankets, adorned with large brass earrings, paused to gaze in wonder at the recriminations of these strange, fair-haired foreigners. But Scylla went on without regarding their curious looks:

"It is just *like* a man to make such a suggestion—merely because the poor child is sick and in pain. He does not cry expressly to annoy you! What can you know about such matters? I dare say you have never looked after a child in your life!"

"There you are wrong, Miss Paget," replied the colonel coolly. "And show some ignorance and some folly. However that is not to the point. I made the suggestion for the child's own welfare. I dare say, left with one of these hill women, he would soon become acclimatized and thrive well enough. But I am aware that my opinion on this subject is of no consequence. Miss Musson is quite resolved on taking him to England. I only hope that her obstinacy does not imperil all our lives. —Excuse me."

And, turning on his heel, he walked away. Scylla remained fuming for a moment; then, recalling that she was supposed to be buying grain for porridge, she turned to the women who had been watching the argument.

Their wondering stares recalled her to a sense of her own undignified appearance: wrapped, likewise, in a striped blanket, to keep out the bitter cold, her torn boots stuffed with straw, a long, dirty, knitted muffler twined around her neck, and an equally dirty goatskin cap crammed on her head. Miss Musson fortunately had a pair of scissors among her medical supplies, with which she obligingly kept Scylla's locks trimmed short, since washing was generally out of the question. As a result of the constant trimming and the sun that beat

down, day after day, her hair had curled up tightly and bleached almost silver; in contrast, her skin was tanned, and her nose peeling
from sunburn. She felt dirty, disheveled, and miserable from various
itches and sores; whereas the colonel always appeared healthy and untroubled, in good physical trim. He had bought a poshteen, a sheepskin jacket, in one of the villages, walked bareheaded and barehanded
through the fiercest cold, and seemed less affected than the rest of
them by the altitude. It was really unfair!

Returning to the main street with her purchases, she encountered
Cal, carrying half a sheep. He, in the course of twelve weeks, had been
transformed into a decidedly piratical-looking figure, with a curly
black beard (also kept trimmed by Miss Musson) and a skin tanned
almost as dark as the hillmen themselves. He excited far less attention
than Cameron and Scylla.

"Only see what I have managed to obtain!" he greeted her gaily.
"We shall be able to have roast mutton tonight!"

As they hurried to join the rest of the party, Scylla thought for the
hundredth time how blessed she was in her brother; invariably sweet-
tempered, never complaining, ready with a joke when the rest of the
travelers had become despondent from the rigors of the journey, always interested in his surroundings; if it had not been for his epileptic
affliction, he would have been the perfect traveling companion. Sometimes, as they walked, he would be withdrawn for several hours, and
Scylla knew that at these times it was a severe deprivation for him not
to be able to sit down and commit to paper the verses that were forming in his mind; but even at such times he never showed any sign of
bad temper or chagrin; what a contrast to Colonel Cameron, who became daily more curt and acerbic!

However on this occasion the colonel appeared better humored than
usual, made no reference to his exchange of words with Scylla about
little Chet, and informed them of his discovery that from here it was
probably only a week's journey to the point where the Kunar River
would be navigable by raft as soon as the spring thaw had produced a
sufficient body of water.

"Or so this fellow says—" indicating a wrinkled toothless ancient
with a straggling white beard and a large goiter on his neck. All the

hill people suffered from goiter to a greater or less degree; Miss Musson said this was due to a lack of salt in their diet. Salt was an exceedingly precious commodity up here, more valued than money, which, indeed, was of little use in many villages.

Miss Musson appeared from the doorway of a nearby house. Tanned, deep-eyed, hawk-nosed, white-haired, she, more than the rest of the party, looked as if she belonged in the mountains; although very different from the snub-nosed Mongol-featured hill people, she was regarded by them with immediate, instinctive respect. A tall staff which she used to assist her limping progress (having strained a knee joint while crossing a glacier) added to her prophetic appearance. She had been conferring with a local medicine woman about little Chet's ailment and held a handful of wizened roots which somewhat resembled parsnips.

"The hakima thinks that he may well have commenced teething; if so, these will help relieve the soreness and counteract the overacidity. Poor babe! It is rather hard that he should have painful gums as well as the mountain colic. Here, my lamb—"

She broke off a piece of root and offered it to the baby, who immediately thrust it into his mouth and mumbled it avidly.

"Really, Miss Amanda!" exclaimed the colonel in a tone of exasperation. "How do you know that insanitary-looking root will not poison the wretched child?—Not but what its untimely death would relieve us of a decided encumbrance," he added bitterly. Scylla gave him what she hoped was a withering glare.

"No, no, I recall having come across this root before, or something very similar," Miss Musson tranquilly replied, passing the baby to Scylla, who settled him in a sling on her back. "The Huron Indians make use of a similar remedy as I recollect; it is wonderful how many identical medicaments are used in widely differing areas of the world. —I am ready to set off, my dear Rob, shall we proceed?"

Their spirits were all raised, soon, by indications that this arduous portion of their journey was nearly over. The snowy slopes gradually gave way to dry mountainsides the color of bleached bone, often riven by deep, red-cliffed gorges; occasionally, on a sunny day, they would see the glitter and sparkle as a frozen waterfall began to melt on a cliff face.

Ten days later, in a little town called Kotka, they were overjoyed to reach, at last, the river that was to help them on their journey. Up here the Kunar was still a rocky mountain torrent, and they must follow down its banks for some fifty miles before it became navigable, but in Kotka, for the first time, they were able to procure mules, and so would be able to accomplish the next stage at a greatly increased rate and in comparative comfort. Here, too, without regret, they parted from Hazarah, and were also happily able to wash themselves in the stream and purchase a few items of clothing. They also felt it possible to dispense with the goat, for the greater frequency of villages made it possible to purchase milk as it was required.

"What shall we do when we run out of money?" Scylla said to Miss Musson privately. At the time of their flight they had brought with them all that they had in the way of cash, but it was quite plain that their funds would not last them all the way to the Mediterranean.

"I have discussed the matter with Colonel Cameron," Miss Musson replied placidly. "He informed me that there is a nobleman named Mir Murad Beg, residing in Kafiristan not far from the route which we shall take, who owes Rob a considerable sum. This was in payment for helping Mir Murad to plan and conduct a military campaign against a feuding neighbor who had invaded his territories. Rob plans, therefore, to visit this man and collect the debt, which, he says, should be quite sufficient to pay our expenses as far as Baghdad; there I may make contact with the American consul and arrange for funds to be sent by my brother Henry."

This plan did not recommend itself to Scylla. "We must depend on the generosity of Colonel Cameron as far as Baghdad?"

"Since we are already dependent on him for his company and protection, what difference does it make if he helps us with money—a commodity which both he and I regard as of very little consequence?"

Although this made perfectly practical sense—indeed, Scylla herself had never attached particular importance to money, or the lack of it—

she found herself strongly averse to the prospect of being altogether dependent on the colonel. She resented the thought of needing to apply to Cameron should she wish to purchase a head shawl or a new pair of shoes.—Miss Musson, it was true, sometimes received payment from people for her medical services, but the payment was generally in kind, a small lump of salt, a bowl of curds, a gluey handful of dried mulberries. And, more often than not, her patients were so needy that even these offerings were declined if it could be done without offense. "Rather pray for our safety on the journey," was her formula.—Well, there seemed no help for it; they must accept the colonel's bounty. Cal, when his opinion was canvassed, exclaimed:

"Oh, fiddlestick! What do I care? Or what does Cameron care? He's a great gun—a regular out-and-outer. Do not be a muttonhead, Scylla! We can pay him back when we get to England all right and tight—I dare say our great cousins will advance the money till we are in the way of earning some for ourselves. So in the meantime it would be foolish to regard it; and I don't, in the least."

"How can we be sure that we shall be able to earn money in England?" despondently replied his sister, dropping a pebble in the river— they were sitting on a wall in a riverside village called Aq Qara, waiting while Cameron bargained for and organized the construction of a raft.

"My poetry is going to make me famous. It will earn us a great deal of money," Cal forecast with total confidence. "I shall take a house in the best part of London; *you* may buy a perch phaeton (or whatever is in the fashion when we get there), mix with all the *ton*, go to Almack's, rig yourself up in the first stare of the mode, and, I dare say, even meet the Prince of Wales."

Scylla smiled faintly at Cal's cheerful predictions. At bottom, she, too, believed in his talent, and that he would have a great success; very likely all his expectations would come to pass; then why was she not more excited at the prospect? Two or three months ago the greatest ambition in her life had been to reach London, to get a glimpse of the world of cultivated, fashionable society. Then why did this interesting future no longer please as once it would have?

Absently, she looked across the tumbling water to the gray shingle banks, fringed with ice, on the other side of the river. Beyond the shingle, supported on struts, rose the flat-topped Kafir houses, tier on tier. A street bazaar, by the river, was roofed with branches. Single willows and apricot orchards beyond the houses were covered with golden buds. Above the orchards rose the white peaks of Laghman Konarha. A kingfisher darted over the water with a flash of blue. Children were throwing flat stones at a post in the stream. Women, dressed in red and blue, bustled past them carrying triangular baskets of firewood. Flocks of sheep jostled and bleated in the street, being driven to spring pasturage on the lower slopes. Cuckoos were calling. A great brown and white lammergeier floated serenely overhead, hundreds of feet up. The sun, at last, felt warm.

"I wonder how long it will take us to reach London from here?" she pondered.

"Perhaps a month to Kabul," Cal thought. "Then from Kabul to Herat is twenty-five days by camel caravan, Rob says; or ten days on horseback. Then on to Yezd, another thirty-five days by camel."

"Which cost more, camels or horses?" prudently inquired his sister.

"Camels cost more to buy, of course, woolly crown, because they are bigger! But it costs more to join a horse caravan, because they travel faster.—Then from Yezd to Baghdad is another thirty-five days—and then from Baghdad to the sea is no great matter, perhaps four hundred miles. That may be done in a few days by coach, I believe."

Scylla reckoned on her fingers. "So from Kabul to the Mediterranean might be done in perhaps a hundred and ten days."

"After that, I suppose it may take another two months to sail from the eastern end of the Mediterranean to a British port. This is the end of February—we might be in London by mid-September. How strange it will be to see you rigged up in fashionable gear!" he added, regarding his sister, who, at that moment, was wearing a black pleated wool dress that she had bought in the town, over a pair of blue baggy trowsers, or perjamas, fastened tight around the ankle; she had curly-toed shoes, a black wool vest, a wide-sleeved jacket, and a black headcloth. On these items of apparel she had spent most of her dwindling funds, and now wished she had not.

"Even now you look as fine as fivepence!" Cal teased her. He himself had purchased a peaked fur cap, a black sheepskin coat, wide white trowsers, and short black boots, for the clothes he had worn during the mountain journey, like Scylla's, had practically fallen to pieces. "Rob says," he went on, "that fair-haired women from the Kirghiz fetch immensely high prices as slaves here in Kafiristan—as much as twenty thousand rupees. If we could only sell *you* to some rich nobleman, we should have plenty of money for the journey."

"Thank you! And I am to settle down in his tent while you travel to England?"

"Oh, you could very likely run away and join us."

"That sounds like one of your romantic sagas," she said, jumping down from the wall. "Hark! I hear Miss Musson calling us."

The negotiations for the raft were complete. A number of massaks, or inflated skins, had been purchased, and they were now being roped together and reinforced with brushwood.

"Will it really support five people and a baby?" inquired Miss Musson, surveying it doubtfully as it bobbed by the riverbank.

"Certainly it will, ma'am!—I hope you are a capable boatman, my boy," Cameron said, turning to Cal. "If not, you will have to learn."

"Cal and I can both row," Scylla coolly said. "Do you remember, Cal, how we used to go in a boat on some lake near Umballa, when Mamma was still alive?"

"This will not be quite the same as rowing in a pleasure boat, Miss Paget," Cameron dryly informed her. "The paddles are about three times the size and weight. And a great deal of the time we shall be negotiating rapids."

"What a fortunate thing it is, Rob, that you were born on the shores of Lake Superior," Miss Musson said comfortably. "You will be able to show us all how to go on."

Scylla could not help wondering if her guardian intended this remark as gentle mockery of the colonel's somewhat magisterial manner, but, if so, he took no notice, merely addressed himself to the stowing and fastening of the stores. The raft was a strong but fairly light structure, some ten or twelve feet square, with a kind of gunwale around it.

Before embarking, to fortify themselves for the journey, they had a meal at an eating house in the center of the town. Compared with many skimpy meals in the mountains, this seemed like a feast: chicken cooked with wild onions and apricots, rice, and the acid wine of Kafiristan, served on trays, around which the travelers sat cross-legged on the ground. The unwonted comfort and luxury had the effect of relaxing the constraint which, of late, had affected several members of the party.

"What religion is practiced in Kafiristan?" inquired Miss Musson of the colonel, as she neatly bit the meat from a chicken bone.

"Well, ma'am, since the Kafirs have been repeatedly invaded by the Muslims, a large number of them now subscribe to the Mohammedan faith. But the original Kafir religion still obtains in the mountains, where the people worship Moni the Prophet, Imra, the forefather, Gesh, the earth god, and his wife the producer of all things—this pair seem equivalent to the Hindu Shiva and his consort Parvati. Kafirs also reverence sun, moon, fire, and water. They have holy men, called pirs, who live in caves like hermits. And when the Kafir people die, it is customary not to bury them but to leave the body on some mountain peak for the birds to devour."

"How very heartless!" exclaimed Scylla. "If I had a loved one—a husband, parent, or child—who died, I should think it *horrible* to abandon them in such a way. It seems quite shockingly callous. Do you not agree, Colonel Cameron?"

He looked at her, she thought, rather strangely. After a moment or two however, he replied:

"If one lives in a country, ma'am, it is better to adhere to its customs, whatever one's private feelings. It would be impossible to contravene local mores without giving terrible offense. One must subdue one's own inclinations.—And, when all's said and done, what difference does it make, once the soul is fled, what happens to the earthly envelope?"

She was silenced; taken aback at something different in his tone, which, as a rule, was characterized by curtness and dryness, particularly when addressing her. Rather lamely, after a moment, she replied: "I—I dare say you are right."

After the meal the party embarked cheerfully amid shouted good wishes from bystanders who stood on the riverbank, and housewives out enjoying the sun on their flat, wide-eaved roofs. "May you be healthy!" they shouted. "May you never tire! May you remain harmonious, one with another!"

Replying to these good wishes, Miss Musson bowed with dignity as the three men, wielding poles and paddles, untied the raft and urged it on its way.

For several days nothing occurred to trouble them. By day they drifted downstream, sometimes swiftly on rapids through gorges of dark red rock, sometimes at an easier pace through wide, curved valleys where the fields were beginning to show green sprouts of barley and maize, where poplars grew by the water's edge and apple and walnut groves were covered with rosy buds.

At night they erected their skin tents and slept on the bank, unmolested by wild animals.

Cal occupied himself during this time with fishing, at which he soon showed considerable skill, and making notes for his poem on Genghis Khan. He had been unable to find any paper in Aq Qara but had discovered an old book, in one of the teahouses, which he had been able to purchase. That it was in Russian made no difference to him; he wrote in the margins and between the lines. "I dare say I shall be able to procure paper in Jellalabad," he said. Meanwhile he provided them with trout, and Cameron, when he was awake, shot a sufficient quantity of duck and waterfowl to vary the fish diet. The latter, however, passed a great deal of time alseep, unless the increased speed of the raft alerted him to the fact that they were approaching rapids, when he awoke, by instinct apparently, and seized a pole or a paddle.

"He is worn out, poor man," Miss Musson said softly one day as he lay sprawled at length, slumbering deeply, in the mild sunshine. "I fear that it was a great anxiety for him, getting us through those mountains. See how thin he has become."

Scylla realized that this was true. Looking at the defenseless sleeping face, she saw the hollows under the jutting cheekbones, new lines of worry around the closed eyes, a hint of gray in the lion-colored hair. Even asleep, his lips were set together in a determined line, tucked in deeply at the corners, as if to conceal emotion and give nothing away.

"Well, he will soon be rid of us now. He can dispatch us on some caravan bound for Baghdad and heave a sigh of relief."

"Not so," Miss Musson contradicted her. "He intends to escort us at least as far as Baghdad and, if he considers it necessary, all the way to the Mediterranean."

"Indeed?" With a lift of her brows Scylla inquired, "Does he not think us capable of traveling without his aid?"

"Do not be foolish, child," Miss Musson returned equably. "The way is beset with dangers—Baluchi brigands, Turkoman robbers who haunt the passes and at times capture the caravanserais. And there are dishonest local officials who would exact extortionate taxes from unwary travelers—but Rob has been that way many times and knows the hazards. So do not be decrying his usefulness and generosity."

"Look, look!" exclaimed Cal in a thrilled whisper, his fingers digging into Scylla's arm. "A huge wild goose! Should I waken Rob so that he can shoot it?"

Neck outstretched, the bird was flapping slowly across the valley of bean and clover fields.

"Do not waken the poor man—shoot it yourself," Scylla whispered back. "Make haste—or it will be gone."

"I'd miss—and the shot would wake him—then it would be too late and he would be angry."

"Oh—!" Suddenly impatient, she snatched up Cal's gun, which lay beside her, aimed, as she had so often seen the men do, and fired. As she had instinctively taken aim ahead of the bird's flight, the shot was exactly on target, and the goose dropped heavily into the river ahead of them.

"Very good shot, Missy Paget!" exclaimed the Therbah with an approving nod.

Cal gaped, Miss Musson exclaimed, "Gracious me!" and Colonel Cameron awoke to the sight of Scylla, pink-cheeked with triumph, dropping Cal's gun beside him on the raft.

"*Miss Paget!*" Although he had been asleep the instant before, his voice was like the crack of the shot itself. "Did you fire that gun?"

"Of course she did, Colonel!" Cal cried joyfully. "And look what she has bagged us!"

At this moment the raft overtook the floating body of the goose and Cal succeeded in hooking it out of the water with his pole. "See what a markswoman my sister proves to be!" he said, holding up the massive bird. "We should have had her shooting for the pot any time these past three months!"

Cameron darted such a look at Scylla that she found it hard not to flinch. "You might have blown somebody's head off!" he said harshly. Scylla bit her lip. Cal looked mutinous, Miss Musson appeared pensive. There was a terrible silence. Then, suddenly, the colonel burst out laughing.

"I ought to wring your neck or box your ears, Miss Paget, but I will be magnanimous and admit that it was a very fair shot—or a very lucky one! But no more impulsive firing of this kind, I beg; I have not brought us all the way over the mountains only to have somebody killed by mischance on the last leg of the journey."

"I am sorry," Scylla murmured, catching Miss Musson's eye, which was fixed on her.

"Truly, sir, I think my sister is a natural shot," Cal said eagerly. "Will you not instruct her how to handle a gun, as you did me? I think she would prove a far more rewarding pupil!"

"Is that your wish?" Cameron demanded of Scylla. She nodded, bright-eyed. "Very well! It is a bargain." He stretched out his hand, clasped hers for an instant, then let it go. "But I shall prove a very hard taskmaster, I warn you."

"Goose quills!" said Cal, lovingly stroking the great bird. "Now I can make myself some proper pens at last."

Another day and a half brought them into regions well known to Cameron.

"These are the lands of Mir Murad Beg," he said. "I have skirmished over them often enough to recognize the contours of the hillsides."

It was a mountainous area, with dry jagged peaks, and watchtowers built of dried mud perched on the steep hillsides. Soon enough, in a riverside village, a couple of white-trowsered, turbaned men greeted Cameron, bowing deeply and addressing him as "Arb Shah."

"That was my name in these parts," he explained to his companions. "They took me for an Arab, since I said that I came from the Western lands."

"Our lord the Bai will indeed be happy to learn that you have returned to his territories," one of the men said in Pushtu. "We will send him word that you are journeying toward his castle, and without doubt he will dispatch envoys to greet you," and both men bowed respectfully again.

Despite the warmth and evident welcome of the greeting, Cameron seemed oddly constrained and ill at ease, talked little after they had reembarked, but sat in frowning silence, his unfocused gaze resting on each peak in turn as they drifted slowly along the rocky windings of a valley where black and white humped cattle grazed near the water and shaggy sheep roamed on the higher slopes.

Scylla wondered if this return to a place where he had been before was distressing to him in some way; he certainly seemed to derive no pleasure from it.

"What is he like, this Mir Murad Beg?" she ventured to inquire.

Cameron turned to her, his brow lightening.

"The Bai? He is a great autocrat, Miss Paget—a feudal baron, rather after the style of the old Normans. He lives in a fortified castle

—has complete power over his vassals—is of mixed Kafir and Tatar descent. But his rule is fair enough—he cares for his people and is an excellent overlord, after his fashion. He is a handsome old boy, too—I think you will like him. His wives seem devoted to him."

"How many wives?" Miss Musson wanted to know.

"Four, when I knew him last—but also some unofficial relationships." Cameron began to laugh. "I can remember once, when he came back from a trip to Kalat, all his wives beating him with their slippers, upon his admission that he had been unfaithful to them while in the city. And they laid on, too! But he only laughed. He told me that he chose his first wife for style and high birth, the second for beauty, the third as a handmaid, and the fourth as a pet."

"I am sorry for the third!" was Scylla's comment. But Cameron had relapsed into silence again and was once more gazing into the distance.

Toward noon they saw a number of riders on horseback galloping over the hillsides.

"Is it a hunt?" speculated Miss Musson. "Or would these be your friends coming to greet us, Rob?"

Cameron scrutinized the riders for a while with his keen eyes before replying.

"No, it is neither of those things. It is a betrothal chase."

"A betrothal chase? What in the world is that?"

"Do you see that girl riding ahead? The figure in red, on the beautiful black horse, riding with her bow slung?"

"I cannot see the bow, but I see the one you mean, ahead of the rest."

"All those young men behind her are her suitors; she must be some rich man's daughter—or very handsome—to have such a number after her. If she can ride around the mountain and return to her village still with her bow, she may choose the suitor she likes best. But if one of the hunters can catch her and take the bow from her—then he keeps the girl too!"

"Suppose two of them catch her?" Cal suggested.

"Then they fight it out with short swords called katars."

"I hope her father has equipped her with a good horse," remarked Scylla.

Soon they were able to see that the girl had, in fact, been splendidly equipped; she must be a considerable heiress, it was plain. Her shaggy, wiry black stallion came thundering down to the river and splashed across at a fording place where the water was only knee deep. The girl herself was equally handsome—straight-featured and haughty, fair-haired; she wore red breeches and tunic, a leather belt, and a high fur cap with a heron plume on it. Scylla could not help envying her wild freedom as she gave the travelers a swift, incurious glance before setting her steed at the opposite bank, scrambling up, then making off at a gallop around the curve of the hillside, her bent bow held easily in one hand as she grasped the reins with the other.

"Oh, I do *wish* that she will manage to get home with her bow," Scylla could not help exclaiming.

"We shall never know," the colonel observed rather dampingly in a tone of indifference.

But he was wrong. When, later on that afternoon, the travelers disembarked at a riverside village in order to purchase milk for the baby, and eggs, vegetables, and preserved apricots for themselves, they were given a chance to see the end of the race.

In a whirling cloud of dust the main party of the suitors came pelting down the mountain and into the village, laughing, joking, and shooting their guns into the air. Although they were the losers, it was plain that they took their defeat philosophically and in sporting spirit. After their arrival perhaps half an hour elapsed, during which the entire population of the place had time to assemble excitedly at the end of the dusty street, in the shade of a big walnut tree, looking up the mountain slope in the direction from which the party of disappointed wooers had returned. It was plain that many jokes were flying about and expectation had reached a high pitch. At last a shout went up as two riders were seen in the distance coming slowly down the hill. Musicians struck up a tremendous rowdy din, blowing on horn trumpets and beating huge kettledrums. Children danced exuberantly around the walnut tree. As the riders drew nearer it could be seen that the girl no longer carried her bow; the heron plume on her fur cap had been broken short; her clothes were dusty and bedraggled and her expression somewhat abashed; however her suitor made up for her downcast looks by his air of joy and triumph. Girls ran out to fling wreaths of flowers over the pair; more and more blank cartridges were fired off. The girl rode soberly to join her parents, while the lucky suitor suddenly let out a tremendous yell of triumph and urged his tired horse into a gallop once more, performing a wild figure eight over the open fields outside the village, waving the girl's bow above his head.

"He is a handsome fellow," Miss Musson observed comfortably when he re-entered the village. "I dare say she will do very well with him."

And indeed when the bridegroom trotted up to pay his respects to the girl's parents, it became plain that he was perhaps, after all, the girl's own choice, for the looks they exchanged were very frank and comradely. He was a big bronzed fellow with dark red hair and beard. The girl's family greeted him in a friendly manner, and small horn cups of fermented liquor began to be passed about; the strangers, as a matter of course, were offered some of the beverage.

"Kumiss," Cameron murmured in Scylla's ear. "Made from fermented milk. You must drink a little for politeness, but do not take much; it is very strong."

"I assure you I am not in the least tempted to take much," she whispered back, pulling a wry face after tasting it.

Now a great cake of pulverized mulberries was brought out, and a bonfire kindled outside the village, on which two sheep were set to roast; it was plain that the scene was set for a night of celebration, and Miss Musson suggested prudently that this might be a time for the strangers to withdraw.

"Not without giving offense," Cameron warned her.

But at this moment there came an interruption. Dusk had begun to fall while they watched the bridegroom's exultant ride, and in the twilight another party of riders had entered the village almost unobserved amid the general festivity. Now, however, two men in long woolen cloaks and fur caps came up to Cameron and greeted him with polite formality, informing him that they came from the Bai Mir Murad Beg and would be glad to escort him and his party to the latter's castello.

"The Bai is awaiting you impatiently, Arb Shah; he longs to embrace his friend again."

"We shall be honored to accept your escort and will accompany you without delay," Cameron replied promptly. They were speaking in the Kafir language, but Scylla, who had picked up a word here and there, managed to grasp the purport of this exchange.

"Oh, may we not stay and watch the festivities?" she said, rather disappointed.

"Better not, my dear; I dare say they may become somewhat rowdy," Miss Musson murmured. "And the village people will quite understand our reason for leaving; the Bai is their overlord, it seems. Rob will not wish to offend him by delay in accepting his hospitality."

So, somewhat regretfully on the part of Cal and Scylla, and leaving their raft in the care of the bride's father, who proved to be the village khan, or headman, they mounted the shaggy Kazak ponies provided by their host, crossed the river at a ford, and set out up the opposite mountainside at a steady trot.

For Scylla the ride seemed to go on interminably. She became desperately tired; she had been sleeping poorly of late, perhaps due to their sedentary mode of travel; she would lie awake in the skin tent listening to Miss Musson's peaceful breathing, sometimes wriggling her head outside to look at the great piercing stars of Asia; she found herself, these days, increasingly troubled by doubts and unanswered questions: What would she and Cal do when they reached England? What would Miss Musson do, would she accompany them to their cousins' house, or would she wish to return to her brother in Boston? And—even more of an unknown factor—what were Cameron's plans? Did he propose to return to Ziatur? To Kafiristan? Or would he set off to explore some as yet unvisited region of the earth?

This affliction of the spirits, she acknowledged to herself, had become even worse as a result of watching the village wedding. To see the triumphant wooer and his bride toasting each other out of horn mugs had awakened in Scylla a wild contrariety of feelings: firstly an exhilarated kind of envious happiness, so that she felt she would have liked to remain there, join their party, talk to them, become, if it were possible, their friend, sister, and confidante; secondly, under this lighter mood, a darker one, a depression so deep that she felt she wanted to find some dark corner, crawl into it, and lie down there and die.

Her pony stumbled, and she clutched at the reins, realizing that she had been half alseep.

"Hold up, son of Shaitan!"

"Miss Paget tired," remarked the Therbah, who had changed places with Cameron in the procession, and he kindly took the reins from her and led her pony for the rest of the way.

It was too dark, when they arrived, to gain much impression of the Bai's fortress from outside—save that it seemed to be perched extremely high up, since they had been climbing steadily all the way; they passed through a gateway into a walled courtyard. Here they thankfully slid from their steeds, which were led away.

The party of travelers was then divided, the females being politely escorted to a chamber lit by flickering rushlights where a couple of servant women invited them to take off their clothes and enjoy a bath. A large earthenware tub of warm water stood steaming before a fire of yak's dung, and the prospect of a real wash in hot water was so enticing that they had no hesitation in complying. They rubbed each other's backs to alleviate the stiffness brought on by riding, while the slave women admiringly tended little Chet.

By Ziatur palace standards the amenities of the castle were primitive enough, it seemed—their room had sheepskins for carpets, and a few stools and cushions formed the only furniture—but in comparison with their recent lodgings it was unbelievably comfortable. The women—who had braided hair hanging to their waists and wore loose trowsers and wool vests—brought similar clothing, but of rather finer quality, for their guests.

Scylla's costume was particularly handsome—dark brown raw silk trowsers, a velvet vest embroidered with tiny chips of turquoise over a loose silk shirt, and a pair of gold-studded sandals. The women clucked disapprovingly over the shortness of her curls but brushed them out until they crowned her head like a nimbus.

"You look exactly like a cherub, my dear," said Miss Musson, laughing, as she slipped on her own fine wool vest embroidered with silver thread, and, over all, the chadar which she preferred because, she said, it was easier to watch people through the eyeholes without giving offense.

One of the women then beckoned them to follow her. None of the servants spoke Urdu or Punjabi, and their language seemed to be a mix of Kafir and some hill dialect; Scylla could make nothing of it, and even Miss Musson was driven to communicate by smiles and gestures.

"I wonder if they have purdah quarters in this castle?" the latter murmured as they followed their guide. "I believe Rob said they do not; that the women move freely among the men."

So it proved; for when they had followed down a drafty, dusty stone passage and a flight of worn stone steps they emerged into what was evidently the main hall of the castle, where there were a great many people, seated or moving about, both men and women.

The walls were of rough, undressed stone, but the stone floor was covered with numerous rugs, and dung fires burned in braziers, giving a smoky light. On a carpeted dais at one end they could see both Cameron and Cal, handsomely dressed, seated cross-legged on either side of a man whom Scylla guessed to be the Bai Mir Murad, and thither the two ladies were led, picking their way between the people squatting all over the floor, amid a murmur of interest and admiration.

Noticing this, the Bai looked up and saw them. His eyes lit up, and, addressing some remark to Cameron, he rose to his feet and stepped down from the dais to greet them. Scylla had time to notice that Cameron looked exceedingly startled by whatever had been said to him; next, that Mir Murad was quite a short man, only a head taller than herself, with piercing deep-set Tatar eyes under hooded lids, and a thin, hooked nose above luxuriant gray beard and mustaches—he looked like a fierce little old eagle, she thought—when he reached her and took her hand. Scylla was about to make him a curtsy, as she had been accustomed to do in the presence of the Maharajah, when he startled her nearly out of her wits by throwing his arms around her and giving her a vigorous hug. A roar of laughter went up from the assembled guests or members of the household. Scylla's reactions were somewhat confused—her main impressions were an overpowering smell of garlic and snuff and the sensation of his bristly mustaches against her cheek—when she heard Cal's indignant shout and the sudden clash of steel.

Instinctively and rather indignantly recoiling from the Bai's embrace, she saw that Cal had started to his feet and sprung forward. His way had instantly been barred by two stalwarts in conical caps, who had crossed their short swords in his path; but now Cameron had also jumped up, had addressed one short, imperious command to Cal which stopped the latter where he stood, and was now addressing himself to the Bai in a hasty, urgent, but respectful undertone. As Cameron talked, Mir Murad's aquiline features displayed a series of rapid changes of expression: astonishment, rage, quickly reined in—chagrin, incredulity—and finally a kind of rueful resigned disappointment, a rather touchingly childish regret.

Cameron took six paces forward to Scylla, and said rapidly in her ear:

"It was a misunderstanding—a most *unfortunate* misunderstanding, which I deeply regret. The Bai had—had apprehended that you were a—a slave, a gift brought here as a token of my esteem."

The Bai laid his hand on Cameron's shoulder and made some brief remark. Cameron interpreted.

"He asks your pardon for what has occurred.—And for heaven's *sake*, Miss Paget," Cameron went on rapidly, "don't get into a missish flutter, don't make a big issue of it; *don't* take offense, I beg! Or a most awkward situation might be precipitated—we should all be in the suds." And, to the irate-looking Cal, he added urgently, "Devil take it, boy, *sit down!* Do not be making a cake of yourself or you are liable to have us all cut in pieces. Murad's attendants act first and ask questions later."

Reluctantly, Cal sat down, and Scylla called to him as gaily as she could:

"Nothing to worry about, love! It was just a foolish mistake."

Laughing, she swept a curtsy to the Bai and said to him in Punjabi:

"Your Excellency, nobody could regret the misunderstanding more than I!—And I am indeed greatly honored that you could even *think* that I might—might have had the happiness to become a member of your household. Alas! My destiny must be far otherwise. I am obliged to journey to Ingrezi to rejoin my father's family there."

The Bai listened intently, his eyes narrowed. As Scylla had hoped, he evidently spoke enough Punjabi to understand what she had said, though Cameron made a brief translation into the Kafir language, which caused him to nod thoughtfully. The mixture of arrogant displeasure and childish disappointment left his face and he suddenly smiled—a smile that made Scylla begin to understand why his wives were so attached to him, for it had great and unexpected charm. The hooded eyes twinkled, the stern mouth relaxed, the curved nose came down, and he surprised Scylla by turning to her and exclaiming in careful English:

"What-a-pity! What-a-pity!"

She smiled back at him and, obedient to a warning gesture from Cameron, stepped away to join Miss Musson, who was with a group of ladies seated beside the dais. These greeted the two strangers with smiles and soft hand clapping; they were evidently the wives of the Bai and their attendants.

"What an unlucky misapprehension!" Miss Musson whispered. "But never mind, my dear; it certainly was not your fault. I dare say Rob has brought slaves to Mir Murad before! It was too bad that we had not some handsome gift to bring with us; I know Rob brought a couple of ibex horns, but I dare say the Bai is used to his visitors bringing him gold dust and Persian greyhounds and lion skins. Never mind! Perhaps we can cure him of a quinsy or some such thing. Meanwhile this looks like a very excellent repast."

The feast that followed, served on trays, was indeed sumptuous compared with their recent diet: kebabs and pillaos, sweet, spiced, and salty, fresh cheese curds, and fat, snow-preserved wild mutton dressed with onions and walnuts. These things were eaten from huge copper trays, with horn spoons, and after it they drank ferociously acid wine of Chitral from tiny horn cups.

After the feast the ladies withdrew, and Scylla and Miss Musson thought it prudent to accompany them.

Cal crossed the floor to speak to Scylla when he saw her stand up.

"Are you sleeping with Miss Musson?" he demanded, and when she nodded, warned her, "Bar your door! I don't trust that old potentate!"

"Oh, Cal, do not be foolish. I am sure he is the soul of honor! And I dare say Cameron has told him that I am a highborn English noblewoman on my way to contract a matrimonial alliance with the Duke of Cumberland. I am sure you need feel no apprehension.—In any case I very much doubt if it is possible to bar doors in this castle."

"I am going to give you my pistol," he said, and, as she demurred, "No, no, I shall not rest easy unless you have it. Hide it in your sleeve."

"I am *sure* you need not be uneasy," she said, but he slipped it under her jacket and she was obliged to take it.

"If you have occasion to use it—do not forget that it throws to the left!—I hope we need not remain here long," Cal muttered. "I do not like this place. However in one way it is just as well we came, for Mir Murad has a cousin in Jellalabad, and he has heard that there are spies from Ziatur there, looking out for four Angrezi and a baby— Mihal has sent his assassins there before us, and all our long, roundabout journey would have been to no avail; if we had gone there, we must have been discovered and murdered."

"What must we do, then?" she said, dismayed. "Can we avoid Jellalabad?"

"Oh yes; Rob thinks it possible to make our way overland to Kabul from here. It will take longer than if we followed the caravan route, but it can be done. And Mihal's bravos will hardly travel as far as Kabul.—By the bye, I have discovered something about Rob that will surprise you—when he was here before, he had a wife and child!"

"*What?*"

"Thought that would startle you! One of the first things the old Bai said to him—'Alas, Arb Shah, I fear this place must bring back sorrowful memories of your wife and child.' It seems that ten years or so ago Rob was married to a Kafir princess—some niece or cousin of Mir Murad."

"Good God," Scylla murmured. This news was to her far more startling than the tidings of Prince Mihal's murderous plans. "I wonder what happened to her?"

"Something sad. So far as I could make out from what the old fellow was saying, she and the child came to an untimely end while Cameron was away leading the Bai's army in a local war."

"Poor man! Oh, poor man! No wonder he has been looking so haggard lately. And I said—oh, what a stupid, unfeeling *shrew* I have been."

"Oh, I wouldn't put yourself in a pucker. I've a notion he don't pay much regard to what you say to him.—Mind what *I* said, now, Scylla! Keep a sharp lookout. I believe the Bai still has his eye on you. From the look of him, I would say he is an old tartar, a real rakehell."

"Cal! Hush!"

But it was true, Scylla noticed, as she kissed her brother good night and turned to leave, that the Bai was still observing her; she caught a sudden piercing flash from his deep, hooded eye.

That, and a memory of the wild girl with her slung bow and her heron plume, were the last images that floated through her consciousness before she fell asleep.

XI

Thomas's mother died the night she had been taken ill. Fanny was sitting with her at the time of her death, but the old lady had sunk into a stupor several hours before and did not regain consciousness; the precise moment of her passing was marked only by the cessation of her soft, shallow breathing. Fanny folded the thin freckled hands together and then knelt and silently prayed, commending the troubled spirit to its maker.

Outside, a few birds were just beginning, cautiously, to try their morning notes. It was very early, before five o'clock; the sun was not yet visible over the eastern hillside. After the heavy rain that had fallen during the night, the valley was filled with mist.

Fanny debated with herself as to whether she ought to call Nurse Baggot. There did not seem to be much purpose now, since all was over, in disturbing the woman's repose; she had been up until midnight and might as well be allowed to have her sleep out. Reluctant, however, to stay in the close, fetid sickroom, longing for purer air, Fanny softly opened the door and slipped downstairs; throwing her old pelisse over her shoulders, she made her way to the back door, undid the chain, making as little noise as possible, and stood on the step, drawing in lungfuls of the damp, cool freshness, which seemed loaded with garden scents—she could detect the fragrance of clove pinks, wallflowers, early roses, narcissus, and the cascading fruit blossom in the orchard. After such delicious refreshment, to turn back into the dark, shuttered house seemed out of the question. Fanny was shod in house slippers and dared not seek her pattens for fear of rousing somebody; the rain-soaked lawn was therefore debarred to her. She turned, instead, up the graveled lane which, being on a slope, remained sufficiently dry, and walked slowly past the orchard, gazing up at the opulent garlands of white-covered boughs tracing their fantastic designs against the gray-blue sky. She knew, remorsefully, that she ought to regret the old lady's passing, but in all honesty she could not; she had tried to love Mrs. Paget, but there had been little lovable in that querulous, selfish, sly, self-pitying character. It occurred to Fanny, moreover, with a lightening of the spirit, that there was now no occasion for Nurse Baggot to remain in the house; which would run very much more easily without her rather disagreeable presence.

But I won't think of her now, resolved Fanny; the morning is too fine for that; and having walked as far as the gate at the top of the lane, she stood gazing longingly out into the silent street, wondering if she dared take a turn around the town. Not a soul was stirring and it seemed wholly improbable that anybody would see her or that such an escapade would come to the ears of Thomas.

Intrepidly, Fanny ventured out, almost tiptoeing over the damp cobblestones. She felt as if the silent town belonged to her alone; as if she, rather than the people obliviously sleeping inside them, owned the tiled, thatched, and timbered houses and the little patches of bright garden before them stuffed with primroses, wallflowers, and forget-me-nots. Only in the market square were there signs of human activity; a pair of smocked carters drowsily unloaded a wagon stacked with turnips, greens, wooden milk churns, and dairy produce.

Up past the church Fanny went, along the narrow street called By-wimbles, and now she remembered that she must write a note to Mrs. Socket, commending to her care Mrs. Rapley, the bedridden mother of Tess's cousin Tom, who had been seized by the press gang. She wondered which of the little rickety houses was occupied by Mrs. Rapley; they formed a huddled row between the church and Petworth House, jammed close together against its great enfolding wall, as if for warmth and protection.

Fanny entered the church, which was quiet, dark, and still held some of the warmth of the night; here she knelt again and, after praying for the repose of Thomas's mother, said another prayer for Thomas himself, and asked guidance in her own difficulties, particularly in her relationship with her husband. "Let me seek to do what is right," she prayed humbly, "that is all I ask."

Soothed and strengthened by this brief interlude, she walked out, along the rosemary-bordered graveyard path, and back toward the street. By the lych gate she was surprised to see a woman who might be in her mid-thirties, but so thin and worn that she looked older; she was dressed plainly, like a servant, in brown bombazeen gown, white handkerchief, wool stockings, and trodden shoes; but, strangely enough, she wore a fine lady's hat, or what had been one once; now it was sadly crushed and worn, its feathers draggled; under its frayed brim her face looked pale and wild. She gave Fanny a nervous, calculating glance, as if assessing her alms-giving capacity.

"Can I be of any help to you?" gently inquired Fanny, since the woman continued to stand in her path. "I am afraid I have no money on me, but—"

"No, no, it's not money I require, it's not money. I *have* a very little money, I have sufficient, I am in no anxiety about *that*," returned the woman, in such a quick low mutter that it took a moment for Fanny to understand her. Strangely enough her voice was not that of a servant; it had a certain refinement. "No—no—what I need is a lodging, nothing too fine, just a room, a quiet room, and it must be cheap, very cheap; I have been wandering about the town all night because I did not know where to apply, whom to ask; can you perhaps tell me of a house where I might find such a room? A lodging with a single lady would be best; I do not wish to be in the company of men, no, no, God forbid!"

Fanny wondered what had happened in the poor creature's life to give her such a distaste for men; then, recalling the horrible occurrence of the day before, she had a sudden inspiration.

"In the little house close by the church there is a Mrs. Rapley who is bedridden, and her son has just been—has just gone for a sailor; I think she might be very glad to have a quiet, respectable lodger; if it was somebody who would do a few errands for her, I dare say she would not ask too much rent."

"Close by the church? I should like that. Yes, that would suit me excellently," replied the thin woman, always in that soft, slightly distracted mutter.

"But you had best wait awhile before disturbing her," said Fanny. "It is full early yet. And you—you have references, I suppose—as to respectability, you know?"

"Oh yes, I can furnish references." The woman gave a soft, odd coughing laugh. "References, ay, ay, plenty, plenty of references. I have friends in the town!"

"Then if I were you I should wait a little—"

"Wait a little—yes, I will wait. I will take a stroll out into the fields, until people are stirring—the fields are pleasant at this time of year, are they not, with the ladies-smocks and bluebells, the primroses and cowslips and kingcups by the brook? Yes, yes, the fields are pleasant enough in *summer!*" And, swinging awkwardly on her heel, she walked away. Fanny stood gazing after her, wondering if she had done right in directing this poor crazed wanderer to Mrs. Rapley.

But I will mention it to Tess, she thought. I will give Tess leave, by and by, to slip up and see if the woman is lodging with her aunt; if she does not seem satisfactory, I will tell Mr. Socket. He will know what to do for her.

The church clock now striking six reminded Fanny that she had better not linger, or the servants would be stirring, and astonished to see her. Rapidly, therefore, she walked along East Street to where the Hermitage lane ran down past its orchards.

Re-entering the gate, she was startled and appalled to discover an inscription in six-foot-high letters splashed in white paint across its wooden slats: SCOUNDRELLY MURDERER! they proclaimed raggedly; the paint from the final *R* had run down and made a white pool on the gravel below. *Could* I have missed noticing *that* on my way out? Fanny wondered, aghast, and then realized that the paint, in fact, was still wet, the white still trickling down; somebody might have come and painted the message while she, Fanny, was walking around the town or in the church. Thomas will be almost mad with rage, she thought, and then remembered that there had been a similar incident on the previous evening; he had sent Jem to wipe away the offending inscription. Well, she must do the same; perhaps, with luck, Thomas need not come to hear that the unpleasantness had been repeated. Jem should be at his work by now, cleaning the knives and boots, fetching water from the well. Or Goble might be in the garden. *Who* could have done it? A relative, perhaps, of the impressed Tom Rapley had furiously splashed up the word before setting off to his morning's work?—But just to have had a kinsman taken up by the press gang hardly seemed sufficient cause for such venom?

At the foot of the lane, Fanny was relieved to see the bent figure of Goble in his sacking apron and leather leggings, carrying a bale of straw to the strawberry bed.

"Goble!" she called softly. "Here a moment, if you please!"

"Ma'am?"

"Goble, some wicked person has written shocking words on the gate —will you wash them off, please, before Captain Paget goes that way?"

"Words, ma'am?" He looked as puzzled as if she had addressed him in a foreign language.

"Unkind—untruthful things." Fanny could not bring herself to repeat the inscription. "Pray wash it off as soon as possible, Goble." She was going on toward the house but, on reflection, turned to add, "Oh, Goble, I am sorry to inform you that old Mrs. Paget was taken ill and died last night. I know that you—were fond of her." She was not truly certain if this had been the case, but at least there seemed to have been some kind of a bond between the old lady and Goble, who had been prepared to push her about the garden in her wheel chair and exchange disconnected, rambling remarks with her. Fanny went on, "When you have cleaned the gate, would you be good enough to pick some bunches of flowers that I may put in her chamber."

Goble looked at her vacantly. Sometimes, of late, Fanny had wondered if he were beginning to fail in his wits, his manner was so strange, wandering, abrupt.

"Died?" he repeated. "Eh—died? Who died then?"

"The old lady—my—Captain Paget's mother. Old Mrs. Paget. Whom you were used to push about the garden in her basket chair."

A spark of understanding came into his eyes. "Oh! Ah! The owd 'un. But *her* weren't Missus Paget. Missus Wilshire, *her* were."

"Yes, I am sorry, you are in the right of it," Fanny said gently. "We had fallen into the habit of calling her Paget, because my husband preferred it. Will you pick some flowers for her, please, Goble?"

And she went into the house.

But, behind her, she could hear Goble muttering to himself, over and over, "Her weren't no Paget. *Wilshire,* her were."

The funeral arrangements for old Mrs. Paget took a week and necessitated the deferment of Thomas's trip to London to purchase accouterments for the Petworth troop. This put him in a bad mood, as did the discovery, communicated by her lawyers in the Isle of Wight, that the old lady's fortune had been totally sunk in her annuity and there was no more to come; Thomas discovered to his great chagrin that he was out of pocket over the whole affair and would have to pay the funeral expenses himself.

The black temper thus engendered should have been a warning to Fanny not to raise other dangerous topics, but she was so anxious to have the matter settled before his departure for London that she risked his displeasure.

"Thomas," she said to him timidly as he was shaving on the morning of his departure. "Now that your mother is—is no longer with us, should we not dispense with the services of Mrs. Baggot?" He swung around, razor in hand, and stared at her with so intent a gaze that she became even more nervous, but persevered. "After all, there is very little for her to do now—indeed I hardly know how she occupies herself all day long—and—and her wage must constitute a considerable part of the household expenses, which I know you are always concerned to reduce—"

She faltered to a stop under the ferocity of his expression. He said venomously:

"Just because *you* have taken that poor woman in dislike is no reason wholly to overlook the interests of the rest of the household. But that is always your habit! Selfish, sullen—never thinking of others' convenience, but only of your own! You know full well why I do not permit you to accompany me to London. Because I cannot trust you out of my sight, after what happened last time.—Are you prepared to tell me *now* what you did with yourself during that period when you were gone?" he suddenly demanded, grasping Fanny's arm so tightly that the bruises and nail marks remained on her skin for days afterward. *"Are you?"*

"No, Thomas, I cannot do that," she said quietly, clenching her knuckles to prevent herself from crying out with pain.

"Tell me, curse you!"

"I cannot," she repeated.

"Then damn your eyes for a sly, secretive bitch!—And you expect me to dismiss Mrs. Baggot—why, *she* is the only one in this household that I can trust! Who is to advise Mrs. Strudwick? Who is to take little Patty for walks, pray, if Mrs. Baggot leaves? Who is to instruct Bet in sick-nursing? Who is to rub my back, which, of late, has been giving me such shocking pain that, without her ministrations, I sometimes do not know how I am to endure to the day's end?"

Fanny's mouth fell open under the injustice of this tirade. She did not like to say that never, to her knowledge, had Mrs. Baggot been seen walking with little Patty or instructing Bet; she murmured:

"I did not know, husband, that your back pained you; *I* could rub it for you, I am sure, if you would tell me where it troubles you—your mother used to like me to rub her back—"

"*You?* Of what use are *you?*" he said savagely. "All you are good for—" and he added such a string of obscenities that she stood in stunned silence with her face the color of chalk, so frozen that she could not even put her hands over her ears. "Mrs. Baggot remains in the household!" he concluded. "So let me hear no more on this matter!"

However the arrival, soon after breakfast, of the one-legged Captain Holland, who was to accompany Thomas on his mission, raised the latter's spirits again, and he bade farewell to his family with a briskness that was his closest approach to geniality, and urged his daughters not to be idling during his absence but to work hard at their tasks, and perhaps he might bring them a ribbon apiece from London. "But only if you are good, mind," he added.

Fanny, seizing advantage of this milder-seeming mood and the public occasion, displayed a note which had just arrived by messenger, and, as her husband turned to bid her a cold good-by, said to him:

"Thomas, here is an invitation just come to hand from Lady Mountague, asking me to spend the day with her at Cowdray Park next Friday. Will it—will it be proper to accept?"

Thomas's expression betrayed his conflicting emotions. On the one hand, he did not wish to lose this promising and eligible connection.

On the other, he wanted to deprive Fanny of any possible pleasure. After a moment's struggle, he replied shortly:

"Very well. You have my permission to accept. You must take the girls with you, Patty and Bet. It will be of value to them to study the usages of good society, to see how things go on in an aristocratic establishment."

He climbed into Captain Holland's chaise, which was to carry both men to London. His daughters waved their handkerchiefs, the driver cracked his whip, and they were gone; Fanny stepped back into the house with a wonderful lightening of her spirits and sat down to write an acceptance of Lady Mountague's invitation.

The next few days passed in unusual and delightful good humor and calm; the absence of Thomas and the peevish melancholy spirit of old Mrs. Paget rendered the household so much more agreeable that there seemed a benign spell over the Hermitage. It soon became plain that Mrs. Baggot had been instructed by Thomas to keep a sharp watch over his wife, and for the first two days of his absence Fanny was half humiliated, half entertained by the pertinacity with which Mrs. Baggot followed her about wherever she went. By degrees, however, this surveillance slackened; it was evident that the nurse had received extra pay in advance for these services and that some of this had been laid out in spirits; on the third day she was not to be seen, and a strong odor of gin and peppermint was exuded from her chamber. Happy in the termination of this disagreeable espionage, Fanny now spent as much as possible of her time working in the garden, where her assistance was accepted by Goble with a sort of morose resignation. Even, very occasionally, her suggestions were followed, though never without modification, argument, and the lapse of a certain amount of time.—"Do you not think, Goble, that a border of heartsease and forget-me-nots would look pretty around the wellhead, inside the brick path?" "Dannel it, missus, why do 'ee allus be ettling to clutter up the place wi' such clung-headed notions? Who needs posy flowers about a wellhead?"

"But it would be something pleasant for you and Jem to look at,

Goble, as you draw the water?" At such a nonsensical suggestion he only snorted derisively and added, as if that clinched the matter, " 'Sides, I can't shift they heartsease afore we gets a haitch o' rain; soil be unaccountable dry." Yet, a few days later, the pansies and forget-me-nots would be planted around the well, just as she had envisaged them. She soon learned not to be too quick and obtrusive in her thanks, or she would elicit some sour, sarcastic snort and muttered comment about "Okkerd grummut fanteagled notions"; it was better to let a number of days elapse and then casually remark, "The pansies are looking well after the rain, Goble." "That's as may be, missus." A sniff. "Don't some mouldiwarp dig 'em all up, they'll maybe do."

The garden was a pleasant place, these days, with Goble muttering biblical texts to himself among his rosebushes in the formal beds, little Patty bouncing her ball against the stable wall, Bet with her needle-work under an apple tree, and Jem tunelessly whistling as he scythed the grass; no Thomas in the garden house to reprove Fanny if she paused from her labors to stroll the length of the yew-tree walk and lean over the wall, gazing at the valley's green bowl, where a cuckoo called all day long.

On Friday there came a check to all this amiability. Little Patty appeared at breakfast with a thick red rash covering her face which, on further inspection, proved to extend all over the rest of her body. She was irritable, querulous, and lachrymose; bursting into a passion of screams and tears when Dr. Chilgrove, on being summoned, diagnosed a sharp case of nettle rash and recommended that she be kept in bed on a low diet.

"But I wish to go in the carriage!" she kept bawling. "Papa said that I might! It is not fair! It is too bad! I wish to see Lady Mountague's house!"

"Do not be such a little goosecap!" exclaimed her sister. "You cannot think that Lady Mountague would wish to see you like *that!*"

"No, my dear, I fear you must wait for another time," Fanny assured her. "Dr. Chilgrove says you are not well enough to go on an outing at present. You would not enjoy it. You must remain in bed."

Fanny, indeed, was greatly exercised as to whether Thomas, on his return, would not feel that she had committed a dereliction of domestic duty if she deserted Patty to keep her engagement to Lady Mountague. Ought she to stay at home with the child? But as Thomas had particularly desired her to pay the visit, duty seemed to pull in two directions. And she was reinforced in her decision to go by Dr. Chilgrove, who said bluntly:

"The child is in no danger, ma'am. Bless me! What's a touch of nettle rash? You go off and enjoy yourself—Lord knows, you get out little enough. Besides, haven't you a whole parcel of women in the house— Susan Strudwick and little Tess and the baby's nursegirl and that other female, what's-her-name?—If they can't look after one spoiled brat among them, you had best turn them all out of doors and hire some others!"

So the departure of Fanny and Bet on their day's pleasuring was rendered uncomfortable and discordant by the shrieks of little Patty, held forcibly in her chamber by Tess and Mrs. Strudwick.

"You are the greatest beasts in nature and I will *never* forgive you," she yelled from the window, running to hang out in her night shift.

"If she can bawl like that there's not much amiss with her," remarked Dr. Chilgrove callously, hopping up onto his cob.

Despite this adverse beginning, the day was full of unexpected pleasures.

The drive to Cowdray Park was a delight. They took the road to Midhurst, which ran along the side of a gently sloping rise of land all the way, giving a view southward over the wide valley of the river Rother to the curving grassy Downs some five miles distant.

"Jem says the smugglers come along that river," said Bet, pointing to the gleam of distant water.

"Ah, they do that," said Jem, who was driving.

Fanny was quite astonished.

"But surely they do not continue smuggling, when the French may land at any moment?"

"Bless you, ma'am, a free trader bain't a-going to leave off trading and lose a fair profit just acos the government say we are at war wi' the Frenchies," Jem told her pityingly. "In any case, 'tis the moonlighters as brings word most often as to what the Froggies are up to over there. Why, who do you think the Sea Fencibles are, as Prime Minister Pitt praises uphill and down dale? They're none but the Gentlemen, given a new name! When they flits back from Rouen or Lille with a dallop o' tea and a keg or two of eau de vie, they brings back a whole passel o' news about the disposition of the French forces. —See, mum, now we be a-passing through Cowdray Park."

Owing to the country's state of war, some of the green and rolling slopes of Cowdray Park had been plowed and sown with a crop of wheat which in that hot summer was already well grown and shimmering under the cloudless sky; but presently they came to a shady stretch of oak and beechwood, massive trees, under which grazed fallow deer, strolling gracefully in and out of the shadows.

"Oh, Stepmamma, are they not pretty!" exclaimed Bet, but Fanny sighed, remembering the deer in Petworth Park that had been the instrument of her first meeting with Liz Wyndham.

Now, emerging from the wood, they beheld a sad spectacle: a great stone mansion, almost a castle, some distance to their left, which had been completely gutted by fire; only a central portion, some casements and chimneys, and a few blackened pillars of stonework still remained. Fanny was very much struck; and Bet broke out in exclamations, protesting that the ruins of Cowdray Castle exactly resembled the scene of a novel that Martha had once borrowed from Mrs. Dawtry, the harp teacher.

Jem, obviously well informed as to Lady Mountague's place of residence since the destruction of Cowdray Castle, now turned the carriage down a cart track that led into a copse to the left of the road, and soon they pulled up in front of a small thatched house.

"Is *this* it?" exclaimed Bet, quite laughably dismayed. "You cannot mean to tell me that Lady Mountague resides *here?*"

But Jem had already jumped down to open the carriage door, and a curtsying maid was waiting to lead them into the house.

Lady Mountague's establishment was certainly quite other than Fanny had foreseen, and she could not help suspecting that it would shockingly disappoint Thomas's expectations of an aristocratic household where, unlike Petworth House, matters were managed with propriety and respectability. Propriety there was, but on such a small scale! It charmed Fanny but greatly disconcerted Bet. Lady Mountague, with her cook and footman, lived in a cottage not half the size of the Hermitage, and they were ushered into a tiny room, half filled, it seemed, with plants and birdcages. Since several large windows had been introduced into the south wall, the sunlight was dazzling, and it took several minutes before their eyes were accustomed and they could discern the occupants of the room. These were Lady Mountague, exactly as she had been at Petworth House, smiling, composed, and dignified in a wing armchair and—to Fanny's extreme astonishment—her stepdaughter Martha and a strange young man.

"My dear Mrs. Paget!" said Lady Mountague as Fanny curtsied to her. "I am so delighted you can spare the time to come and visit an old recluse such as myself. As a reward for your goodness I have prepared this little surprise for you—I hope it is a pleasant one!" she added, laughing. "One never quite knows what will be the result when close relatives meet."

But it was plain that all the participants were happy with the present reunion. Fanny had always found it easiest to get on with her middle stepdaughter—though recently, to be sure, Bet's nature had improved as a result of not having to compete with her prettier sister.

Martha now ran to Fanny and gave her an exuberant kiss.

"Stepmamma! Now I can make my husband known to you! Oh, I am so happy that Lady Mountague has been kind enough to arrange this meeting. This is Charley! Is he not a fine fellow! A real nonpareil! Aha, Bet! You little thought, last time you saw me, that on our next meeting I would be able to take precedence of you! I am an old married woman now—Mrs. Penfold, if you please!—and may go ahead of you up the stairs!"

"Only there are no stairs to be climbed at present," said Lady Mountague, smiling. "Martha, my dear, why do you not take your sister and your husband to feed my peacocks—you will find a basket of stale crusts there on the sill."

So, after Fanny had greeted her new stepson-in-law—he seemed, indeed, a pleasant, well-set-up young man, who behaved to her with the greatest civility and respect, but had a lurking smile in his eyes which seemed to suggest that when not on best behavior he could enjoy a joke with the best—the three young people walked out through a french window, leaving Fanny alone with Lady Mountague.

"Ma'am, I am so *very* much obliged to you for this!" exclaimed Fanny as soon as her stepdaughters were out of earshot. "My husband had strictly forbidden any inquiries to be set on foot regarding Martha —he will not hear her name mentioned, indeed!—but I have been exceedingly anxious about her. I am so delighted to discover that she has reached such a comfortable and safe harbor. How did it come about?"

"Oh, Charley Penfold is quite a favorite of mine," said the old lady, smiling. "He was the son of my husband's steward but worked hard at his books—my husband had him sent to the Midhurst Grammar School and destined him for the church. But then he turned out a little wild, we discovered that he was engaged in running contraband goods with the local free traders, so it became plain that a clerical career was not for him. A couple of months ago Charley came to me in a very proper spirit, informed me that he had quite amended his ways and become a captain in the local Sea Fencibles. He told me, too, that he had married, and asked if he could rent one of my cottages on the Cowdray estate. I was glad to allow this, and even more so when I found that he had married Captain Paget's daughter. Indeed he is very anxious to be reconciled with his wife's family if it can be arranged."

Fanny thought that Thomas's objections might not be insuperable once he learned that the young man enjoyed Lady Mountague's favor; however she could not engage to answer for her husband, and said as much. Then she inquired cautiously:

"Can the young man support a wife, ma'am?" remembering what Jem had said of the Sea Fencibles, that they were, in fact, merely the smugglers promoted to a more respectable-sounding name.

"I can see that you will make an excellent mother-in-law, my dear! Yes, Charley does any amount of work for me on my estate, in between his Fencible activities—and most capably, too; so I pay him the wage of a junior steward, and they have the nicest little cottage, down by the Easebourne gate. At first I was not too inclined to take to your stepdaughter, I thought her a flighty young minx, if the truth be known; but marriage has improved her out of all recognition, and it has worked wonders for Charley too; they seem to deal together admirably and are becoming quite steady and sensible."

During this speech Fanny had been greatly startled to see a mouse run across the floor, climb the bulbous legs of a Jacobean table, and begin busily nibbling some grain that had fallen from one of the birdcages on the table top. Lady Mountague paid no heed to it, did not even move aside her gray brocade skirts.

"Ma'am! Is not that a mouse?"

"Yes," replied the old lady calmly. "They come in after the birds' grain. That is why I keep my plates of kickshaws on vases."

Fanny had indeed wondered why two or three plates containing tarts and wafers were balanced somewhat precariously on the tops of long-necked jugs and candlesticks.

"The mice are very clever," said Lady Mountague, with an affectionate smile at the one which was nibbling crumbs two inches from her sleeve, "but I am one too many for them there! Now, shall we go out and join the young people? I thought we would take our nuncheon in the grape arbor.—I say *young people,* but you are as young as any of them, my dear," she added, taking Fanny's arm as she moved somewhat limpingly to the garden entrance. "How does your baby go on? When shall I come to see him? And the other little girl? Have you not a third stepdaughter?"

Discussing Fanny's household, she passed along a grassy path which led down to the river Rother. This was a sizable stream, wide and deep enough to take a coal or timber barge; Fanny could understand how the smugglers made use of it. Indeed Lady Mountague informed her, with a certain pride, that most of the houses in the town of Midhurst, which could be seen from where they stood, had long underground passages leading from their cellars to the riverbank, for the easier transport of contraband.

"But do you countenance smuggling, ma'am?" inquired the startled Fanny, following Lady Mountague over a footbridge.

"Bless you, yes! I doubt if the tea you are about to drink has paid duty. Foolish laws lead to inevitable infractions."

Beyond the river lay the formal gardens of the ruined Cowdray Castle, where Martha, Bet, and Charley were feeding three peacocks and a couple of swans which had floated to the riverbank. A velvety lawn led to a grape arbor, where a table and chairs had been set, and to this cool and tranquil haven Charley and a footman brought baskets containing a light repast—cakes, fruit, and wine. A syllabub was made on the spot by leading up a brindled cow from a neighboring field and milking her (Charley did this) into a dish of white wine; Fanny thought she had never tasted anything half so delicious.

While Lady Mountague was giving some instructions to her gardener, after the repast, and the two girls were exchanging all the sisterly gossip that, apparently, they had been missing for the last two months, Charley addressed Fanny in a low voice.

"I didn't know whether to trouble you with this, ma'am, or not," he said. "I talked it over with Marthie, and she thought maybe 'twasn't needful; *she* says she don't care if she never sets eyes on her pa again—and she don't care what becomes of him. But I'm one that likes all things shipshape; if I'd thought there was any chance of the old gentleman giving his consent to the match, I'd have asked him, fair and square. But Marthie said he'd *never* give his permission in a year of Wednesdays—and I've heard the same about him from others, in Petworth—so there was nothing for it but to elope."

Fanny, somewhat startled to hear Thomas referred to as "the old gentleman," could only agree with Martha that he would never have given his permission but said that for her part she was delighted to discover that Martha had found such a kind husband. However she feared that she could not promise to procure a paternal forgiveness.

"No, no, I'm not making up to ye for that, ma'am, don't take me up wrong," said Charley quickly. "If Cap'n Paget'll forgive Marthie, very good; if not, *I'll* not weep millstones. We do very well as we are. That wasn't what I was asking ye; no, I was wishful to warn ye. I've many

Petworth friends, and it has come to my ears as how there's some in Petworth wishes ill to the cap'n, an' I believe he should be put on his guard."

"Somebody that wishes him ill? Who can it be? Have you any notion?"

"There's more than one, ma'am, so the tale goes. One's a woman— but she's a poor, crazed being, I doubt *she'd* do him much harm. But she might stir up those as would. I told Marthie about her and she said directly, 'Oh, that sounds like our old governess that Pa turned off; Miss Fox, her name were!' "

"Miss Fox—good God!" said Fanny, aghast. "Why, I believe I have even met her—I myself suggested . . ."

She fell silent, remembering her meeting with the strange woman on the morning after Mrs. Paget's death. "But surely that poor deranged woman cannot harm my husband?" she said presently.

"There's another, ma'am, so I understand. As to who it be, I know not, but that there Miss Fox has been heard a-mumbling and a-muttering threats. 'Now I've got me an ally,' says she, 'I'll *surely* have my revenge on him, and he'll live to rue the day he slighted Maria Fox. Now I've got an ally I have power over him.' "

"Good heavens. How very shocking! Whom can she have been referring to?"

"That's all I can tell ye, ma'am," said Charley Penfold soberly.

And, apparently feeling better now that he had disburdened his conscience of this weight, he turned to pick up the nuncheon baskets and carry them back to Lady Mountague's sylvan cottage.

Martha was very urgent that her sister and stepmother should visit *her* cottage and see how nicely it was appointed. "It is all so neat and snug! It is the best little house in the world! And there is even a bed for you, Bet, should Papa ever allow you to visit us."

Fanny, however, decided that this visit of inspection must wait for a subsequent occasion. She had two motives for this decision; firstly, she could see that Bet was falling back into her old habit of envying her sister's superior good fortune. The novelty of the meeting had at first allayed those bad feelings, but now the familiar sour, jealous expression was visible in her face, the grudging ill-natured note in her voice; Fanny feared that the sight of the cottage might prove the last straw and wreck the better relationship that at first had seemed to be springing up. Also, for herself, Charley's warning had stirred in her a vague but profound uneasiness; she could not wait to be back at home again and make certain that all was well with her household.

Without further ado she said to Lady Mountague, "Ma'am, this day spent with you has been the happiest for me since—since I left my father's house. But Martha's husband has told me something that has made me anxious to return home and make sure all is well there. Also I am persuaded that we have tired you long enough! But I thank you more than I can express for all your kindness."

"My dear, I have enjoyed it quite as much. Come, give me a kiss! And let me see you again soon—I trust your husband will permit?"

"Of course, ma'am!"

"Then I shall come and take my nuncheon with you, as informally as you please, one of these fine days."

Fanny made such undertakings as she could, kissed Martha good-by, shook hands very cordially with Charley Penfold, and climbed after Bet into the waiting carriage.

Bet was somewhat markedly taciturn during the drive home; she huddled her shawl discontentedly around her shoulders. The evening had turned cool and cloudy; a dark gray thunderous bank in the western sky promised a storm later; and a light rain was beginning to fall.

The streets of Petworth were empty as they drove through the town. Fearing the storm, doubtless, the townspeople had retired early; the place seemed unnaturally quiet. But, strangely enough, as they passed down the Hermitage lane the sound of voices could be heard ahead— quite a number of voices, it seemed.

"How curious!" exclaimed Bet, listening. "One would think there was a crowd of people assembled in our garden! Do you suppose that Papa can have returned home already? Can they be assembling the troop—or some such thing?"

"We shall soon see," said Fanny, who found herself unaccountably trembling.

When they rounded the curve of the lane and came in sight of the house, they could see that, indeed, quite a large group of people had assembled in the garden—all the members of the household, Tess, Jemima, Mrs. Baggot, Goble—besides a number of other persons whom she did not know. They were all crowded around the well.

Tess came flying over the grass as soon as the carriage appeared.

"Oh, ma'am! We was about to send a messenger for you! Oh, the most dreadful thing—!"

Mrs. Strudwick followed her, arriving just as Fanny stepped out of the carriage.

"Ma'am, thank God you are come—though I hardly know how to tell ye—"

Behind Mrs. Strudwick came Jemima, the nursegirl, her face all streaked with tears.

"I only left him for two minutes!" she sobbed. "As God's my witness, 'twas not longer than that!"

"What has happened, Mrs. Strudwick?"

Fanny spoke as quietly as she could, but with a knifelike feeling in her heart.

"'Tis Master Thomas, ma'am! Oh, ma'am, he've tumbled down the well!"

XII

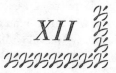

After spending three days in the castle of the Bai Mir Murad Beg, Scylla became decidedly restless and impatient. She longed to resume their journey and said as much to Cal, in one of the rare chances she found to catch a word alone with him.

The male guests were being lavishly entertained—hunting parties in pursuit of musk deer and a beast called rero, hawking parties, shooting matches—and, at night, much feasting, from which the females judged it prudent to absent themselves.

"It is very fine for *you*," Scylla said to her brother. "But all that is thought suitable for us is endless gossip with the Bai's ladies and being taught how to weave blankets and ferment goat's milk."

"*I* wouldn't object," said Cal. "All this target practice is a dead bore! I haven't had a moment to work on my poem since we arrived here. I would be happy to sit at home with the Bai's wives—one of them is uncommonly pretty."

Scylla glanced at him a trifle anxiously. There had been a note of sincerity in his voice; and it had not escaped her notice that during the last feast his gaze had been frequently attracted to the Bai's youngest wife, a beautiful kittenish laughing creature called Sripana, hardly more than fourteen, the pet of the whole establishment. Once or twice Cal had achieved a short conversation with her, mostly conducted in dumb show, since she spoke only a Kafir dialect; Scylla had been rather horrified to see him teaching her the game of cat's cradle, which she learned with much laughter and teasing. Theoretically the ladies of the castle were not debarred from converse with men, but Scylla had caught a look of what she thought was decided disapproval on the Bai's countenance as he observed this interchange. She said now:

"I *wish* Colonel Cameron could collect his debt from the Bai so that we might be off. I have had enough of washing wool and pounding up barley for porridge!"

The ladies of the household lived, indeed, an extremely active and hard-working life. Although the Bai was a rich man and a landowner, a noble and local administrator, there was no idling in his establishment, which was like that of a wealthy farmer. Hens in the great courtyard were tended and their eggs collected; sheep and goat wool was sheared or carefully collected from the low-growing shrubs on the mountainsides, washed, carded, spun, and woven; the Bai's wives, it was true, did not engage in the rougher work, but they spent their days in spinning, weaving, embroidery, and the more complicated forms of cookery, shaking milk into cheese, cream into butter, pounding dried mulberries, apricots, and honey into tremendously sweet confections. Two or three days of participating in this life was interesting enough, and Miss Musson, enjoying the spell of leisure, occupied herself by learning about the dyes the Kafirs used for the brilliant colors in their rugs and tunics; but Scylla, after the adventures of the journey and living on an equality with her male companions, found such an exclusively female existence heartily tedious.

"You must see that Cameron cannot just turn up here and ask for his money!" Cal objected. "I am sure that wouldn't be etiquette. The matter has to be treated with proper formality. I dare say in two or three days' time he will come around to it."

"*I* don't think the Bai intends to pay him," said Scylla. "I don't like the look in his eye."

Here she did the Bai an injustice. Mir Murad was a highly honorable man who would not have dreamed of defaulting on a debt, but at present he was rather short of cash, having recently been obliged to find a dowry for the daughter of his middle wife. He therefore cunningly suggested to Cameron that the latter should accompany him on a raid against a neighboring and rival chieftain whom he suspected of having purloined some of his cattle.

"From that rogue's stolen goods, Arb Shah, you may collect half your debt, and I can provide the other half; thus, honor will be satisfied."

Cameron demurred; his party had no time to waste in raiding; the Angrezi ladies were anxious to resume their journey and press on toward their far-distant destination.

The Bai was greatly disappointed. "The Yagistani chieftain has lost his delight in battle?" he remarked with a slight touch of scorn in his voice. "I had hoped to ride into a fight again with my old comrade at my side."

Cameron was not to be drawn. "We are older now, Mir Murad, and I have women under my care; suppose I should be killed in battle. How would they ever win through to Europe?"

The Bai looked sideways at Cameron under his bushy gray brows.

"If you, their protector, were killed, I would offer them honorable asylum here to the end of their days; or," he added reluctantly, "an escort as far as Baghdad if they wished it."

Cameron considered him with care. He could see plainly that the

Bai was still suffering from some slight disappointment over the misapprehension regarding Scylla; it was most unfortunate that he had taken her for a beautiful slave from the Kirghiz obligingly brought for him as a present by his friend Arb Shah; apparently he had always wanted a Kirghiz woman for his collection and now found it difficult to put the mistake out of his mind. Several times he had said to Cameron wistfully, "You are *sure*, Arb Shah, that she is an Angrezi and that young boy's sister? They seem so different!" eying Scylla in a manner that made Cameron a trifle fidgety; Mir Murad was the soul of honor, he knew, within his own code, but within that code many things were possible; if Scylla had but known it, Cameron was as eager as she to quit the Bai's hospitable precincts. Moreover he, as well as Scylla, had observed that Cal was dangerously prepossessed by Mir Murad's youngest wife; to be sure, it was only a fit of calf love, the boy meant no harm in the world, was perhaps hardly aware of his own state, but his eyes followed Sripana continually, he seized every chance to approach her, and this had not escaped the keen attention of her husband. The whole situation, in fact, was fraught with awkward possibilities, and Cameron was blaming himself for having brought the party to the castle in the first place.

Now the Bai, still thinking yearningly of exotic additions to his female entourage, had another and even better idea for raising the rest of the money owing to Cameron.

"I have heard," he observed, "that the chief wife of the Amir in Kandahar, Shuja'-ul-Mulk, greatly desires an heir. I have it on good authority that on the first day of the Afghan New Year the Shahzada, together with all the ladies of the harem, set forth on a pilgrimage to the great shrine at Hazrat Imam, with an escort of fifty sowars and a great treasure in gold and rubies, to pray for an heir. And God He knows they need one! Since the Amir Thaimur died, leaving none of his twenty-three sons designated as his successor, there has been nothing but civil war among the princes and the cities of this land.—*I* stay in my castle, on my own hills, I take no part in it.—But for your sake, Arb Shah, my old friend and comrade, I will ride out, as in the bygone days, and raid that queen's procession. What are fifty sowars to such as you and me and my brave sons? We can dispatch them in one morning. And then you may take your pick of the queen's treasure. And we could ransom her," he went on, his eyes brightening, "for three thousand gold tillals, I dare say!"

"What!" said Cameron, scandalized. "Raid a procession of pilgrims on their way to a holy shrine? And *queens,* into the bargain? No, no, Mir Murad Beg, I am a fighting man, but I do not engage in battle with pilgrims or women—nor do I recall your doing so, in the bygone days! Furthermore the lady is the wife of your own Amir!"

"Persian dogs!" The Bai spat disgustedly. "What are the Persians to us? We Kafirs are from Scythia. It would be no more than shearing a flock of sheep, Arb Shah. At this very time, probably, they are traveling through the Kundera Pass; we could fall on them like a thunderbolt."

But Cameron said it was not to be thought of.

At this negative reception of his good idea, the Bai became very silent and morose.

"I beg you, my dear friend," said Cameron, "forget the debt! What is such a trifle between brothers? I will come back to you when I have escorted the Angrezi ladies to Baghdad—or maybe Damascus or Acre —when I can be certain they are assured of a passage on a boat to their own lands—then I will return to your castle and we shall have great feasting and hunting and maybe, if God wills it, a battle or two against your enemies, and much talk about the happy days of long ago. And then, if Providence has smiled upon you, you may let me have such few monies as are still owing."

"But it is *now* that you need the money," said Mir Murad, glumly pulling on his gray mustaches. Then he brightened again. "After all, it is the New Year! I will send out messengers to inform my people that they must pay their spring taxes before the wild rose trees are in flower. I will dispatch my killadar immediately."

Cameron was greatly relieved. He could see that the Bai considered this a poor-spirited way of raising money, in comparison with a foray against enemies, but it seemed a satisfactory compromise. Even Miss Musson's delicate conscience need not scruple to make use of money received as proceeds from a tax (she would certainly have been appalled had she heard the Bai's plans to abduct the Amir's ladies and hold them up for ransom); and Mir Murad was, by the standards of his country, an excellent overlord, who protected his people from bandits and did not tax them unduly.

Eased in his mind, therefore, Cameron accepted an invitation from two of the Bai's sons to go out after a mountain leopard which had recently been troubling their father's flocks. He hoped very much that, by the end of the day, sufficient rents and taxes would have been collected to remit the larger part of the debt and satisfy the Bai's sensitive conscience; then they could take their departure on the morrow, or perhaps the day following, without loss of face to anybody concerned.

Scylla and Miss Musson, meanwhile, had been making the acquaintance of an old lady named Khalzada who, by virtue of her years and wisdom, had acquired a very important status in the Bai's household. She came from north of the Kirghiz—possibly, Miss Musson thought, from Samarkand or Tashkent; she had been a slave belonging to the Bai's grandfather, had won a position of respect owing to her knowledge of herbs, oracles, and omens, graduated from slave to wife, and had managed to survive into a gnarled and revered old age.

Except in high summer, Khalzada remained mostly in her own chamber, reached by a narrow flight of stone stairs. Here they found her, seated in state on layers and layers of differently colored felts and supported by a bolster. Khalzada spoke neither Urdu nor Punjabi, but Habiba, the Bai's second wife, who came from Kabul and had respectfully led them into the old lady's presence, remained to act as an interpreter.

The room was fustily warm: a dung fire burned in a brazier, and a couple of girls stood behind Khalzada wielding dyed yaks' tails to keep off the flies. The guests were offered tea in small copper pots and a dish of maing, made from curds and butter, also pinches of snuff and wizened little black objects, which, Miss Musson murmured to Scylla, were probably dried snow mushrooms. Miss Musson valiantly accepted both the snuff and the mushrooms; Scylla politely declined them, which at once brought the old lady's sharp scrutiny on her, and Khalzada asked some question.

"She says," translated Habiba, "does the Angrezi lady refuse snuff because she is bearing a child?"

"No, no," said Scylla. "Tell her that I am not yet a married lady."

"Not married, and yet you travel abroad with two men? This is very singular!"

"One of them is my brother, sahiba," replied Scylla. "And this lady" —she laid her hand on that of Miss Musson—"is my adopted mother."

"The younger man is your brother? The other, Arb Shah, I know from many years already."

Evidently the old lady had been observing the visitors from some point of vantage.

"The young man—what is his name?"

"Cal Bahadur," said Miss Musson.

"There is something very strange about him—I think he is afflicted by a djinn."

"What makes you think that, sahiba?" asked Scylla, startled.

"I have seen others thus afflicted. There is a look about the eyes, the skin, the hands, the whole bearing—do not his eyes, on occasion, go red? Does he not cry out in a strange tongue?"

"Yes, this has been known to happen, certainly, sahiba—or something like it," agreed Miss Musson. It was true that after one of his epileptic spasms Cal's eyes were often very bloodshot.

"I knew it. He has a djinn," repeated the old lady, nodding. "Is it a bad one or a good one?"

"Oh, a good one," asserted Miss Musson. "It inspires him to write wonderful charms on paper."

"I thought so," said Khalzada. "My grandson the Bai is not easy in his mind about that young man, because he gazes too often at the lady

Sripana, but I told Mir Murad that it would be wrong, even dangerous, to harm somebody who is possessed of such a powerful spirit."

"Yes, *indeed* it would," exclaimed Miss Musson, startled and
anxious.

"Also," pursued the old lady, "I do not think any harm will come to
our household from the young man. I have looked into the salt bowl
and I see no danger from him.—And yet I *do* feel danger—I feel trouble. It seems to come from among your party. Give me your hand,
Angrezi lady."

Miss Musson stretched out her hand; Khalzada scrutinized it intently.

"No, there is no harm there; only great wisdom and goodness." She
peered closer, seemed about to speak, checked herself, and looked
sharply into Miss Musson's eyes. The American lady sustained her
regard calmly but sighed a little, as if, Scylla thought, the two women
had exchanged some unspoken message, as if Khalzada had told her
something she knew already, something, indeed, that she had been told
a wearisome number of times.

"Imra, Moni, and Gish watch over you. We shall be friends and
shall exchange many secrets," Khalzada said to Miss Musson. "Now,
child," to Scylla, "give me *your* hand."

Over Scylla's palm she pored for many minutes as if perplexed,
screwing up her eyes, muttering to herself. "These lines are so faint, I
can make nothing of them.—Bring me the salt bowl, girl," she said to
one of the slaves, who fetched a flattish black curved pottery dish with
a handle at each end and a very small handful of rather dirty salt in
the bottom.

"Stir that with your finger," said Khalzada. Scylla accordingly
stirred it, then the old lady carefully shook the dish and inspected the
pattern thus formed. "It is very singular," she murmured to herself. "I
see much trouble here—a dead man, a dead child—"

"Oh no!" Scylla was horrified, her thoughts flying to little Chet,
happily playing at this moment with a teething toy made from
markhor tusk which had been presented to him by another of the Bai's
wives.

"Do not interrupt, Angrezi! I see trouble for my grandson, too—grief—he is hurt, and suffers. I think you do not mean to hurt him, lady, but still the thing happens, and by your agency."

Rather uneasily, Scylla wondered if this hurt referred to the Bai's undisguised wish to add her to his zenana; she tried to withdraw her hand, but the old lady still clutched it in her muscular claw, peering at the salt in the black dish. "I think you had best not stay too long in my grandson's fortress, Angrezi girl; I think it may be you who bring trouble among us."

"I am sorry for that, sahiba," Scylla said simply.

"Now, here is a strange thing!" Khalzada shook the dish, peered again. "I shake it away, but still it re-forms! I see a great tree, a great twisted tree—it is not like a tree of our country. It is a sacred tree but far away, far in the north; it is a tree of great anger and power; there is a man woven in among its coils, like a beast in the embrace of a snake. You have a dark, troubled road ahead of you, Angrezi girl! Hai mai! I cannot read it all, and it is giving me a headache!" She peered up into Scylla's face and said, "Yet I can see no harm *there*. It is a fate laid on you by the gods. Truly, you are young and delicate to travel such a dark distance. Wait, and I will give you two things that will be of use to you.—Or no, come with me."

Raising herself with surprising agility, she hobbled, still keeping hold of Scylla's fingers, into a windowless inner closet, where she rummaged under dusty gauze hangings to open a massive wooden chest. Inside it, Scylla was amazed to see a shimmer of blazing color: the chest was packed to the lid with silky glowing materials in brilliant scarlets, blues, greens, jeweled and tinseled and tasseled; in startling contrast to the old lady's well-worn, thick dun-colored apparel. Khalzada probed down, but with a careful and gentle hand, among this unexpected gorgeousness and pulled out two things. "Habiba!" she screeched, and Habiba, who had lingered in the other room, not certain if the old lady wished her to follow, came hurrying in with a propitiating smile.

"Explain to the Angrezi girl what these two gifts are for, Habiba!" And the old lady broke into a rapid string of directions.

"This," said Habiba, putting it on Scylla's finger, "is a gold ring, looped with camel's hair. My grandmother-in-law wishes you to have it, so that you will not injure her grandson, whom she loves; it is the signet ring of the tribe that she came from, far to the north; for she was once a queen in the great plains where the Kafir Niham River runs into the Kunduz; this ring can render any action right or wrong, can give or take away, make or unmake laws—"

"But," protested Scylla, "indeed, I am deeply grateful to the sahiba for this honor, but I intend no harm to her grandson, not the least in the world—why should the lady give her precious ring to me?"

To this the old lady snapped out some impatient retort which Habiba interpreted.

"She says do not interrupt, and that you *are* to have the ring; you must wear it always unless—until you can give it to a man whom you know that you can love until you die."

The ring was tarnished and heavy, wound with coarse black hairs, but it still sat loosely on Scylla's middle finger; seeing which, Habiba pulled a handful of black sheep's wool from a yak-hide sack and wound the circlet thickly with the wool until it became a better fit.

Meanwhile Khalzada had rummaged in the chest again and came up with something that looked like a wizened thorn twig which had been dyed or dipped in red juice, and a little muslin bag of red powder. This she handed to Scylla, with a brief muttered injunction to Habiba—evidently directions as to the use of these articles—and then hobbled away back to Miss Musson in the outer room.

"What are they for?" inquired Scylla, eying the twig mistrustfully—it had an ominous resemblance to implements of witchcraft which she had sometimes seen employed back in Ziatur.

Carefully Habiba explained how the twig and the powder were to be used. "It is because our honored grandmother feels a kindness to you, lady. She wishes you to leave this place in peace, cherishing no resentment against us, and to reach the end of your journey in safety."

"Please tell the respected lady that I thank her with all my heart," said Scylla. "Assure her that I wish no ill to any in this castle, particularly to her grandson—and in token of my good intentions I give her—"

What offering would be suitable and appropriate, impressive enough to assure the old lady of her friendly feelings? Regretfully, but feeling that it was the only possible gift, Scylla slipped over her head the ribbon that supported her watch. The watch was an old silver one that had once belonged to her mother; it was prettily engraved with flowers on the back, and Miss Musson's brother had had her own name, Scylla, inscribed on the case. It had never kept very good time, however, and since their adventure in the quicksand had stopped, once and for all. Since then it had undergone so many other mishaps, immersion in rivers, being knocked against trees, scraped on rock faces even glazed completely with ice in blizzards, that Scylla had not the least expectation of its ever telling the time again.—She was sorry to part with it nonetheless.

"Give Khalzada this charm," she said, handing the watch on its draggled ribbon to Habiba.

She had expected Khalzada to express a fair degree of gratification upon receipt of this handsome and interesting gift, but, rather to her chagrin, the old woman merely looked cursorily inside the case, which Habiba snapped open for her, then nodded, as if she had expected something of the sort, and continued a dialogue with Miss Musson which the two of them seemed to be conducting in a kind of sign language.

Feeling slightly rebuffed, Scylla curtsied and, as Khalzada took no further notice of her, quitted the room and went down the dusty stairs again, to where she had left little Chet in the care of Sripana and the Bai's third wife, who had several small children of her own. The two women greeted her kindly with the usual beaming smiles. They could not get over their admiration of her silvery, curling hair, and every time she entered a room some of the ladies would come up to stroke and smooth it with cries of wonder.

Scylla, however, was in no mood for female gossip. Feeling sad, confused, and apprehensive after the strange interview with Khalzada, she picked up the baby and, shaking her head politely at the welcoming, cushion-patting gestures of the Bai's ladies, strolled out into the castle courtyard to give Chet a little fresh air. She longed to get away from the castle, to be out on the mountainside; but, while Cal and Cameron could go galloping off over the wild-rose- and juniper-studded hillsides at liberty with the Bai's sons, she and Miss Musson had been given firmly to understand that females stayed within the castle walls, unless some suitably escorted wool-gathering or herb-picking party should be arranged. Any female who strayed outside was rounded up and gently led back again.

Today, however, there was plenty of action in the castle courtyard to entertain her. The Bai, it seemed, had not gone on the leopard hunt with his guests but had remained at home to receive tribute. Formally dressed in a leopardskin mantle and a two-foot-high leopardskin cap, he was seated on a throne of carved rock covered with a sheepskin. A procession filed past him in a ceremony which had evidently been going on for most of the day. Villagers approached one at a time, gave their names to the killadar, or steward, who stood at the Bai's right side, and presented their rent offerings, which were received with lengthy debate and consideration. The payments offered were of every possible kind: skins full of butter, rangy goats, skinny fowls, carefully tied bundles of firewood or sacks of charcoal, sometimes a shaggy pony, fat sheeps' tails which had been preserved in snow, packets of dried pepper, asafetida, very occasionally a few copper coins called zerubs, and one or two small lumps of turquoise. All these things were estimated by the killadar and his naib, or assistant; their value was calculated on a kind of abacus with brown clay beads strung on wires, a mark was made on a sheepskin tally, and the tenants were informed whether the toll paid had been sufficient or whether there remained still more to pay.

Toward the end of the procession came a bearded, fur-capped man whose face was vaguely familiar; cudgeling her brains, Scylla was trying to remember where she had seen him before when, following him with hands tied behind her, and pulled along by two of the Bai's warriors, she was horrified to recognize the handsome scornful girl who had galloped her shaggy black horse across the river, who had worn her heron plume so proudly. She was the village bride—now dusty, disheveled, and tear-stained; and the angry bearded man was her father, who addressed the Bai in a long, vehement harangue. The Bai appeared to listen to this dispassionately, then shook his head and made a dismissive, denying gesture with his right hand.

Scylla noticed that Cameron's Therbah servant had come quietly to stand by her; proof that the hunters must be on their way home, for the Therbah never stirred very far from his master's side, though he manifested a certain fondness and respect for Scylla.

"What are they saying, Therbah?" she whispered to him. "Can you understand what is happening?"

The bride's father now fell on his knees. He looked stricken to the heart. The girl still stood behind him held by her guards; she appeared to be almost in a state of trance, moving like a sleepwalker, hardly aware of her surroundings.

The Therbah explained.

"Bai, he say: no give permission for marriage. No bride price paid. Wife cost two horse, five cow, forty sheep, three hundred guest feast for seven day. Bai get half."

"And it wasn't paid him? But surely"—Scylla was puzzled—"surely it is the husband's duty to pay the bride price? Where is he?"

She looked around for the handsome young man who had ridden that triumphant figure eight, firing his gun at the sky.

"Bai angry. Husband was not a man of this region. Husband say, no duty pay Mir Murad bride price. And Mir Murad, he say, no bride price, no marriage."

The Bai now made another dismissive gesture, and the bearded father was hustled out of the courtyard, while his daughter was led toward the castle. To the last, the father still shouted, protested, and pleaded, as he was expelled from the gate; but the daughter seemed indifferent, almost calm; until suddenly, at the castle door, a kind of scuffle took place, in the course of which one of her guards dragged from her grasp a short straight knife which was tossed to the killadar's assistant amid head shakings, shrugs, and looks of disapproval from the Bai's retinue. At the loss of her knife, the girl's mask of indifference broke up; she let out a desperate cry and began to struggle frantically with her captors, who, however, easily overpowered her and dragged her inside.

Horrified by this scene, Scylla was wondering whether it would be of any avail to remonstrate or appeal to the Bai—when, perhaps fortunately, the gates opened again to admit the returned hunting party.

One of the Bai's sons proudly carried over his pommel the dangling body of a five-foot snow leopard, its beautiful silvery gray fur splashed with black rosettes, its jaws parted in the grinning rictus of death. Observing this, Mir Murad immediately clapped his hands, dismissing the last group of taxpaying vassals, and hurried to greet his sons and his guests, exclaiming over the dimensions of their prize and calling for kumiss in which to celebrate their triumph.

Cal, seeing his sister, crossed the court and came to speak to her— they had hardly been able to exchange more than a couple of words all day—and Cameron followed after a few moments.

Scylla at once began agitatedly pouring out to them the story of what had happened to the bride and asked Cameron if he could not intervene.

"It is so dreadful! Poor girl, what had *she* done? It was not her fault! What will become of her, Colonel Cameron?"

"I fear, Miss Paget," he said reluctantly, "that in such cases—if the girl marries a man from another region, or if the father fails to pay his feudal lord the proper bride price—both of which faults seem to have been committed here—the usual penalty is for the girl herself to become the Bai's property."

"Oh *no!* But what about her husband? What will *he* do?"

The two men exchanged a grim look.

"Now we know whose head it was," Cal muttered.

"What do you mean?" Scylla demanded.

"No need to have said that, you young sapskull!" Cameron said in a sharp undertone.

But Scylla, given a clue by the direction of their glances, had hurried to the gate. Outside, on a flattish area before the hillside fell away, the Bai's warriors were accustomed to exercise their ponies daily in a kind of wild, disorganized polo game with no rules and any number of players, using a sheep's head or blown-up yak's bladder as a ball. Today, however, the object they were knocking about the stony ground was a human head; under the dust and filth Scylla had some difficulty in recognizing the features of the young bridegroom.

For a moment, leaning against the stone gatepost, she turned sick and faint.

Numbly, she allowed Cal to lead her toward the castle. He would have taken little Chet from her, but she hugged the baby tightly, murmuring:

"No—no, let me hold him. Besides—they would all laugh—those men—if they saw you carrying a ch—carrying a child." Her teeth began to chatter. She felt suddenly chilled to the bone.

"No, I don't think they'd laugh at me too much," Cal said with a certain satisfaction in his tone, which his sister noticed, even in her state of distress.

"What do you mean, Cal? Why not?"

"Because it was my spear that killed the leopard!"

She stared at him in amazement, thinking how much younger than herself he sometimes seemed, despite his gifts of intellect and poetic creativity—or perhaps because of them. Overflowing pride in his exploit could still occupy his mind at such a hideous moment.—To be sure, it was a very astonishing feat for Cal to have killed the leopard— usually he was wholly uninterested in deeds of sportsmanship, especially if they involved killing something.

"Do you think Sripana will come to hear about it?" he went on eagerly; and then she understood. Poor boy, he thought of himself as a knight-errant, performing feats of valor to impress his lady love.

"I am sure she will. The Bai will probably give her the skin to make herself a cloak—he is so devoted to her, he is always giving her presents." Cal's face fell a little at this. Scylla went on, "Cal—if *you* killed the leopard, you will be in good standing with the Bai—he must be grateful to you! Do you not think you could ask him to allow that poor girl at least to return to her father's household? I—I cannot *bear* to think of her being kept a prisoner here. *Do!* Pray try!"

Cal's face fell even more. He said doubtfully, "I am not sure if Rob would think that wise. He says that what he has done is quite within his rights as chieftain of the district.—And *nothing* is going to bring back that girl's husband, after all." He added uncomfortably, "Perhaps she may prefer it here to her father's household. I dare say the Bai is not such a bad old fellow. Or one of his sons may have her. She may settle down here tolerably well."

Scylla flashed him a glance of indignation, almost hatred.

"How *can* you talk so? It is all very well for *you.*" Then, seeing his hurt look, she recollected herself and muttered, "Oh, I am sorry! But pray, Cal, *do* ask Colonel Cameron if nothing can be done. I cannot bear it—that girl's look haunts me."

"Oh—very well," he said. "I will ask Rob. But do not *you* be doing anything foolish, now, Scylla! Mind! You have seen what happens when the Bai is crossed."

He left her to return to the courtyard, and Scylla went on up to the room she shared with Miss Musson, feeling sick at heart. Mechanically she set about the task of washing and feeding little Chet; not until this was completed did her mind revert to the strange scene with Khalzada. Now the old woman's words—"I see trouble for my grandson the Bai—he is hurt and suffers"—came back to her more forcefully. Vindictively, she thought, I wish I *could* hurt him. Why should he be permitted to abduct that poor girl and kill her husband?

When Miss Musson reappeared, Scylla poured out the whole story. The older woman, too, was troubled but, like Cal, thought there was probably nothing to be done. "You must remember, my dear, that this is the custom of the country. The girl herself must have been aware of the risk when she plighted herself to an outlander. And, in her present circumstances, doubtless she has more resignation than you give her credit for."

Scylla doubted this. She remembered the desperate scream—the struggle over the knife at the castle door.

"Oh, I wish we could leave this hateful place," she muttered.

"Well, very likely now the Bai has received his taxes, he can pay Rob what is owing, and we may take our departure," Miss Musson said, but that only exacerbated Scylla's distress.

"*We* brought on that wretched girl's tragedy! It was to collect money for *our* needs that the Bai summoned his vassals. It is blood money!"

"Come, come, child!" said Miss Musson almost sternly. "There is no purpose in working yourself into high fidgets over the matter. Firstly, there is nothing to be done, and, secondly, the marriage would have been discovered sooner or later in any case.—Now I do not want you worrying Colonel Cameron about this, pray! He has enough to concern him as it is, in getting us away from here without disturbing the Bai's touchy notions of honor. And this castle has unhappy memories for him too, do not forget. So show a cheerful face at supper, if you please!"

These were strong words from Miss Musson, who hardly ever found it necessary to reprove her wards, and Scylla took them to heart. They recalled to her mind, too, the story of Cameron's tragedy, which she had been pondering, on and off, ever since Cal told it to her on the first evening. It was so strange—to think that he had been married here, that, ten years ago, he had lived with a wife and child in this very place. And they had somehow perished tragically. Would this be likely to make him sympathetic to that poor girl's troubles? No; Scylla was inclined to think that it might make him less so; she could imagine him callously saying, "Why should her problems touch me? How are they worse than any other?" Before this afternoon Scylla had been feeling deeply for the colonel, wondering if every corner of the castle, every crag of the mountain, did not carry painful memories for him; she fancied that she detected in his face a careworn, grief-stricken expression which made her heart go out to him; but, now, that sympathy was quite quenched; she thought, Among these savage companions, he has reverted to a savage himself. He is probably as ruthless and unfeeling as the Bai himself.

Armed by these feelings of hostility, she washed and robed herself for the evening meal, which was to be yet another feast in celebration of the successful hunt and the equally successful tax levy. The Bai's ladies were dressing themselves up in all their finery: long pleated skirts of shimmering, tissue-like material, and richly embroidered sleeveless jackets embroidered with tiny rubies and turquoises, thick with gold and silver thread; Miss Musson and Scylla were lent similar garments. Then, to Scylla's horror, the captured bride was brought in, her clothes were removed, she, too, was washed, anointed, and carefully robed in a pleated silk skirt, full-sleeved tunic, and embroidered green velvet vest. To all this she submitted limply, apathetically; she seemed to be in a kind of stupor. The women were not unkind to her; they patted her gently, as they were used to do with Scylla and Miss Musson; carefully dressed her long, beautiful black hair in two great plaits, which they wound into a kind of chignon, leaving loose curling locks to hang in front and frame her face, the expression on which was rigid, the calm of despair. She stared straight ahead of her, ignoring her surroundings.

"What can they have done with her?" murmured Scylla, appalled.

Miss Musson put some questions to Habiba, who was carefully draping long chains of gold and amber around the girl's neck. As she did so the girl raised her eyes and looked, briefly and incuriously, at Miss Musson and Scylla; then she dropped her head again, over the gaudy chains dangling on her breast. A horn mug of liquid was brought for her; with passive obedience she received and began to sip it.

"Her name is Dizane," Miss Musson returned to say. "And she is sixteen years old."

"But why is she so quiet and stupefied?"

"I believe it is that drink they have been giving her; it is charas, wine made from hemp seeds. It induces that kind of dreamy stupor. Poor girl, it is very hard," Miss Musson said, sounding riven with sympathy, despite her own advice to Scylla. She added, however, "I dare say it is for the best. The opiates will dull her grief and help her to forget what she has undergone."

Scylla was not so certain. When the women attending Dizane were not close by, she noticed the girl glance swiftly around her, then pour the contents of the horn beaker among the thick sheepskin rugs on which she sat; this done, she resumed her limp, stupid attitude, allowing her head to fall forward and her hands to lie loosely in her lap.

A moment came when all the women, dissatisfied with some item in Dizane's costume, had hurried off in a chattering group to ransack yet another treasure chest of silk and velvet garments. Miss Musson had taken her way downstairs. Scylla, with her bundle of belongings open, was kneeling by little Chet, wrapping and pinning him more securely in his woollen nightrobe, for as soon as the sun went down the air turned bitterly cold. Suddenly she became aware that Dizane had moved, had sprung up and crossed the room in two lithe, silent strides and was now kneeling by her, pouring out a stream of imploring words. Her words were incomprehensible, but their meaning was clear. She fixed her great urgent black eyes on Scylla's face and made a gesture with her hand—the gesture of one who drives a knife into his own heart—then clasped her hands together again, repeating the gesture and the words that evidently meant, "I beg you, I beg you!"

Next, turning to Scylla's bundle, not ungently but at frantic speed, she rummaged in it, searching, feverishly searching—turned in disappointment, made her gesture again—"For God's sake, by all that you hold sacred—if you have one—give me a knife!" Full of anguish and pity, Scylla began to shake her head, opening her hands helplessly to show she had no weapon. At this Dizane frowned as if in perplexity, perhaps disbelief that any person of sense should lack this piece of vital equipment; then suddenly her eyes flashed and fixed: half wrapped in a woolen hood she had glimpsed the stock of the pistol that Cal had lent Scylla. Silent, swift as a panther, Dizane swooped on it and dragged it out. With one imploring look at Scylla—"You must permit this—you *must!*—my need for it is greater than yours!"—she concealed it under her jacket. Kneeling, she pressed Scylla's hand to her forehead, then quickly kissed Scylla; two seconds later she was back in her place, seated, with shoulders drooping and head bowed among the discarded finery. In another moment the women of the castle had returned with a great gold-embroidered black shawl which they wrapped around Dizane with exclamations of self-approval; then they gently raised her up and led her away.

The subsequent feast was a nightmare to Scylla. Almost mechanically she ate what she could of lamb flavored with garlic and coriander, heavily spiced smoked mutton, and dishes made from rice, raisins, and pistachios, curd sweetmeats and cakes of pulverized mulberries, drank tea and, later, tiny cups of coffee. She looked in vain for Dizane among the ladies; the girl did not seem to be there. Perhaps the weapon had already been discovered? Perhaps she had been thrown into some dungeon? Or perhaps she was feigning sleep or sickness, so that she might avoid the feast; or had really succumbed to the drugged wine.

Over and over again Scylla asked herself what she ought to have done, ought to do now. Tell Miss Musson? Tell Cameron? Have him warn the Bai? She did not even know if the pistol was loaded; though she assumed that it was. She remembered Cal's half-laughing caution: "Remember it throws to the left." Suppose that Dizane, instead of using it on herself, which had plainly been her first intention—suppose she decided instead to revenge herself on the author of all her misfortunes and shoot the Bai? Numb with horror, Scylla could see Khalzada's prophecy fulfilling itself on the same day that it was uttered. And, if the Bai were killed, what would become of Cameron and his party? Their lives would not be worth a pinch of snuff. It would be only too plain where Dizane had obtained her weapon.

Besides, did the Bai deserve to die? He had only been asserting his feudal rights.

Oh, what a fool I have been! Scylla groaned inwardly, clenching her hands together in her lap as she sat cross-legged among the Bai's ladies. Beads of sweat rolled down her forehead and her nose; it was stiflingly hot in the hall, among the press of bodies and the burning braziers; with a detached part of her mind she noticed the coiling smoke from the fires, the incessant din from kettledrums, horns, and brass wind instruments, the dancing boys performing in front of the Bai; the discomfort from the ever present fleas in the woolen floor coverings, stirred to leaping, biting activity by the warmth. Scylla felt ill with anxiety and unwonted indecision. I *cannot* betray Dizane, she thought. There in the village, at that betrothal ceremony, I felt as if she were my sister; I feel it still.

The main part of the repast was already over. The men had finished eating and were drinking more and more kumiss and Kafir and Chitral wine; they were laughing and singing and shouting. Miss Musson, sitting not far away, caught Scylla's eye and nodded, indicating that she thought it best to retire. Scylla half rose, then felt a numbing pain in her head; it seemed to sound in her ears like a gong. The pain passed, instantaneously, but in the same instant she realized that the sound she had heard was Cal's voice, raised in an extraordinary cry, which sounded like a distillation of all the woe and dread in the world. She saw Cal beside Cameron, standing up with his arms extended waveringly; then he crashed to the ground as if he had been struck by a thunderbolt. The men closest around him gasped and rose to their feet in horror.

"Oh *dear!* The poor boy!" Miss Musson exclaimed with a prosaic normality that seemed fantastically out of keeping with the impact of this occurrence. "I did wonder if all this emotional excitement might not occasion one of his epileptic attacks! When I heard that he had killed the snow leopard, I suspected that it might overset him—an event like that, mingled triumph and guilt—for I know that he *abhors* killing—is just the kind of thing to throw him off balance. And in his present state too," she added, glancing toward Sripana, who looked frightened to death at this mysterious affliction in the Angrezi youth— as were a great many others. The Bai himself had sprung up in horror, evidently suspecting poison or some terrible disease—until Cameron reassured him, quickly murmuring a few words in a low tone. Then all the men gathered around Cal—Scylla could hear them saying to each other:

"It is a djinn! He is possessed of a djinn!"

"Heat some yak's butter in a pan and hold it under his nose," said the Bai authoritatively. "That is a sure way to drive out a djinn."

The butter was heated, while several of the Bai's sons grasped Cal's legs and arms, gripping them tightly, calling on the djinn to swear by the slipper of Moni the prophet that he would depart and never return.

"Wrap him up in a goatskin!" somebody suggested.

A crowd of interested spectators pressed close around, and Miss Musson exclaimed:

"This is very bad! The boy will never come to himself in such conditions." And she called over the heads of the crowd, "Rob, cannot you ask Mir Murad to have Cal carried to your chamber, or at least somewhere cool and quiet?"

"In a moment," Cameron called back soothingly. "They must be allowed to try their own remedies first."

To the stench of burning yak's butter was now added that of singeing cloth, as charms were inscribed on bits of cotton cloth and then burned close to Cal's face. Scylla began to feel worse and worse. To a violent nausea was added a sensation as if a band of hot wire had been drawn tightly across her temples. Detachedly, with the lucid part of her mind that seemed able to stand aside and observe these symptoms, she wondered if she had been poisoned by something in the feast. Or— a likelier explanation—was her condition somehow connected with Cal's seizure? They shared, occasionally, a telepathic sympathy; when one of them endured mental or physical pain, the other was liable to experience equivalent sensations; but which way around had it worked this time? she wondered. Had her intense anxiety, sensed by Cal, brought on his paroxysm—or were his sufferings now contributing to hers?

"Ma'am," she muttered to Miss Musson. "There is something urgent I must tell you—step aside here a moment. That girl—" she did not say the name Dizane aloud, because so many people pressed around them.

"Why, child! You are as white as paper! Here, quick, Colonel Cameron—she is fainting—"

Indeed, Scylla found that she could stand no longer. The light seemed darkened to her, black specks swirled in front of her eyes. She made a dizzy grab for Miss Musson's arm, her legs gave way, and she would have fallen but felt herself caught and supported by several pairs of arms.

"The pistol—pray tell him that she has it. Indeed I could not refuse her." Had she managed to say the words aloud? Her voice sounded hoarse and strange. Numbness and blackness closed in on her. Vaguely she felt herself being carried; then nothing more.

When she recovered—after an interval of not very long duration—it was to a fresher, cooler atmosphere and the sound of Miss Musson's voice.

"Her eyelids are fluttering—there! I believe she is better. Drink this, child—" and a beaker of something warm was held to her lips.

"Not milk!" she muttered. "Not milk, pray!" Her nostrils still held a memory of the rank smell of burning butter.

"No, no, this is herb tea. What a pair you and Cal are, to be sure—a fine couple to escort through the wilds!" Miss Musson scolded affectionately. "Drink the tea while it is hot. Here have Rob and I been, scurrying from one to the other of you, not knowing which to tend first!"

"*Indeed* I am sorry, ma'am!" Scylla struggled up on to her elbow and took the horn beaker. "How—how is Cal? Is he better?"

She looked around her, trying to discover where she was. Evidently she and her brother had been carried to some chamber close to the banqueting hall. She could see Cal, propped against a pile of bolsters. Colonel Cameron was superintending the Therbah, who was bathing his temples with aromatic spirits.

"Is he better, ma'am?" Scylla repeated anxiously. Something else was troubling her—something at the back of her mind—what was it? She would remember in a moment.

"He will do famously by and by." Miss Musson's tone was reassuring. "You know his way. He takes time to come out of these convulsions—and this was a very severe one."

Cameron walked over to look down at Scylla.

"How do you go on, now, Miss Paget? You and your brother have given us a fine fright! Indeed Mir Murad thought at first you had been poisoned—I had my work cut out to dissuade him from cutting off the cook's head."

His tone was friendly enough but Scylla thought she could detect a note of impatience in it.

"Truly I beg your pardon, sir—I hope I will not disgrace you so again."

"Oh, young ladies are entitled to a few fainting fits," he said lightly. "Or so I understand."

"No, but I was very worried—there was something I had to tell you urgently—indeed, I was quite sick with anxiety—" What had it been? She searched her mind.

"Do not distress yourself. I dare say it can wait until you are better."

"No, no. It was important. It was to do with that girl—"

"I expect, Rob, she means the village bride," Miss Musson suggested in a low tone. "Scylla was horribly distressed about the affair, I know."

"*Oh!*" Now he sounded really exasperated. "Yes, I am aware of the fact—Cal mentioned it—but what can I do? I am not a miracle worker, I cannot bring that wretched young man back to life."

"No, no, it was not that! I remember now!" Scylla rose up to a sitting position. "It is worse—much worse! She has my pistol—" and, as Cameron looked at her with evident disbelief, no doubt under the impression that her wits were still astray, she explained, "The pistol that Cal gave me."

"*What?*" He was still staring at her, with an expression of mingled rage and incredulity, when there came a patter of footsteps, and a soft voice inquired:

"Is it permitted to enter? I come from the lady Khalzada. She wishes to know if the afflicted persons are recovering."

It was Habiba.

"Not a word about the weapon!" Cameron said urgently, and quitted the room at speed, leaving Miss Musson to reassure the Bai's wife and express regret for the anxieties and suspicions that had been engendered by the sudden disturbing afflictions of her two young companions. But Habiba waved her apologies aside.

"It was a djinn. Who can prevent their comings and goings? Doubtless it was to warn of some coming disaster—some war or pestilence. Tomorrow the Bai will send offerings to the Holy Pir at Chaghlar—perhaps he may be able to do something to avert the trouble. Meanwhile the lady Khalzada wishes to know if you require any medicines or charms. If so her skills are at your service—though she is sure that your own arts are equal to any that she can offer—"

She broke off, turning pale. For at this moment a tremendous shrieking broke out somewhere in the castle; also a commotion of running feet, shouts, and, outside in the courtyard, the whinnying of horses.

"*Hai!* What can it be?" exclaimed Habiba. "Imra send that the disaster foretold has not already come to pass—"

She turned to leave the room and encountered Cameron returning.

"The Bai is hurt, Lady," he informed her briefly. "His hurt is not serious, I am glad to say. However you had best go to him."

With a cry of dismay Habiba hurried off, while Cameron strode across the room and stared down at Scylla. There was such fury in his face that, despite remaining traces of vertigo, she struggled to her feet to face him.

"You little *idiot,*" he said between his teeth. "How came you to do such a lunatic thing? I know you to be reckless and headstrong—but I would have thought even *you* might foresee the consequences of such a piece of frantic folly—"

"Rob, Rob!" warned Miss Musson.

"Hush, Miss Amanda!—Have you *no* thought for others at all?" he demanded of Scylla. "To furnish that distraught female with a weapon—and such a weapon! Have you run completely mad? What did you expect her to do with it?"

"It was not *like* that!" Scylla confronted him as best she could, though her face was quivering, her knees shook, and she felt weak and sick at the force of his rage.

"Rob, you *must* not!" muttered Miss Musson. "The child is ill yet—scarcely able to stand."

"She is well enough to hear what I have to say! Thanks to you, Miss Paget, we are all in desperate danger."

"What happened?" whispered Scylla.

"Since the banquet had been disrupted by your brother's very regrettable seizure, the Bai went to visit that girl, who was shut up in a room somewhere."

Guilty as she felt, Scylla could not withstand a prick of resentment at Cameron's dry reference to her brother; poor Cal could not help his affliction, after all. But, eager to learn what had happened, she remained silent.

"She produced a pistol—the pistol that *I* gave Cal—and fired at the Bai. Luckily, even at close range, her aim was not accurate—" Scylla, with slightly hysterical amusement, recalled the pistol's failing—how fortunate that she had not been able to warn Dizane of *that*. "The Bai was wounded, but only in the arm," Cameron went on. "He has lost a deal of blood, but it is not serious. He and his sons have gone in pursuit of the girl."

"What? She escaped?" Despite her disgrace, Scylla could not withhold a leap of the heart.

"While he was still faint from the wound—before he could call for help—she had somehow succeeded in making her way to the stables and abstracting one of the Bai's best horses; apparently, on account of the banquet and the evening's various excitements, no proper guard was kept."

"She has got away? Oh, I am so *glad!*"

"You little *fool!* How far can she get, with the Bai's warriors in pursuit?" Cameron looked at Scylla almost with loathing. "You have no more sense than a baby—than little Chet! They will be *certain* to catch her—they will bring her back—they will question her—they will discover that you gave her the gun—what do you think will happen *then?"*

Miss Musson asked in a troubled voice, "What had we best do, Rob?"

"The only thing we can. Leave now, before the Bai returns." He added impatiently, as they stared at him in astonishment, "Well, do you think I *like* it? Sneaking away like a thief from my old friend's house? Of course I do not! But the alternative is being slowly disemboweled, or seeing you all cut in pieces, or both—I have no choice. Therbah, pack up our possessions—and be quick about it!"

"Yes, lord."

"But the money he owes you—you will have to leave without it?"

He laughed harshly.

"I can hardly ask Mir Murad for money when one of my companions has just supplied a weapon to his would-be murderer! We must manage without."

"But Cal—he is unconscious. How shall we manage?"

"I have thought about that. We shall take camels from the stable— we can say that we are going to help search for the girl."

"*Camels!* But they are costly—two or three would be worth the whole sum of the debt."

"You do not think I would steal Mir Murad's camels?" Cameron said sharply. "I shall arrange to have them sent back. That is the only honorable thing to do."

Scylla could not help being glad that she was not a man. Their code of honor seemed to add almost impossible complications to a situation that was bad enough already.

"Cal will have to travel in one of the saddlebags; they are fairly capacious," Cameron went on. "Now, for your lives, make haste! Bring what you can, say not a word to anybody, meet me in the courtyard in ten minutes—not a moment longer." He added callously, "We can only hope that wretched girl had sufficient start on them so that it will take the pursuit some time to come up with her."

Remembering Dizane's intrepid horsemanship when pursued by her wooers, Scylla could hardly doubt it. She still hoped with fervor that the girl would escape—though a more rational assessment of the case warned that this was scarcely possible. Dizane must be well known in the region—it would be no use taking shelter with her father—who could protect her?

The Therbah reappeared to say that he had packed the men's gear. He and Cameron picked up Cal and carried him out.

"Are you strong enough to return to our room, child?" Miss Musson asked anxiously.

"Yes, yes—" In truth, Scylla felt dreadfully weak, as if she were recovering from a long illness, and was appalled at the prospect of being called upon to bestride a camel, but she saw that there was no help for it. The whole situation was her responsibility, and the least she could do was give as little trouble as possible. Trembling, she hurried after Miss Musson back to their original chamber, where little Chet slept placidly and her bundle of belongings lay open, as when Dizane had snatched up the gun. What an eternity ago that seemed! Hastily she tied up her things, took off the finery that had been lent her for the feast, and put on her own clothes.

"I am ready," she said to Miss Musson, who, holding the baby, was glancing around for any mislaid articles.

"Good. Let us go."

It was fortunate that the castle was in such a state of ferment. Women were rushing to and fro exchanging questions and exclamations on the Bai's narrow escape; incense was being burned and prayers said before statues of Moni and Imra; out in the courtyard more men were saddling up to go after the Bai. In all this tumult it was not difficult to slip through unremarked; and as soon as they entered the courtyard Cameron came quickly and quietly up to Miss Musson, laid a hand on her arm, and jerked his head in the direction of a shadowed corner where there was a kind of postern gate, seldom opened.

Scylla saw that near it two camels, already saddled, were kneeling on the ground. On either side of the wooden, padded saddles dangled saddlebags, attached to the frame. They were quite large, and in one of them, on the bigger camel, Cal had already been placed in a huddled position, curled over, with his head on his knees. He was still deeply asleep or unconscious.

"Get in there," Cameron said curtly to Scylla, gesturing to the left-hand bag on the smaller camel. The right-hand one was piled with the men's baggage. Half relieved, half ashamed that she was not expected to ride the camel, she climbed into the saddlebag, which was made of plaited osiers.

"It is lucky that we are none of us very heavy," Miss Musson said softly. Each camel would be carrying three persons—several hundred pounds' weight. The Therbah quickly loaded the women's bundles in along with the men's, then hopped onto the smaller camel's saddle.

"Harh, harh!" he said, jerking on the headrope, which was attached to a chain around the camel's muzzle.

Cameron had already mounted the larger camel, having helped Miss Musson, with the baby, into his vacant saddlebag. Both beasts rose to their feet, swaying backward and forward, grunting and snarling.

"Where are we going?" Miss Musson softly asked Cameron as they passed through the postern gate.

"To take refuge with the Holy Pir at Chaghlar."

It was a long and miserable journey. At first Scylla worried about the possibility of their encountering the Bai and his retinue of warriors—either still in pursuit of Dizane or returning with her as captive, which would be worse, or returning in frustration without her, which might be worst of all. However this did not happen; presumably Cameron, when he chose their route, had done so with reference to the direction in which the man hunt had set off.

The night was bitterly cold and windy. Clouds scurried over the sky, concealing a moon which gleamed fitfully, giving enough light to show that they were crossing a stony upland plateau with high bare peaks all around. Indeed, they might have been traveling across the moon itself. The camels loped along at a brisk pace, despite their heavy load. How many hours they traveled Scylla could not judge; it seemed endless; she soon became almost numb in her cramped position; her feet lost all sensation; her hands, from gripping the wicker sides of the receptacle, became almost equally stiff.

The motion of the camels—a sideways sway and lurch—was particularly uncomfortable when riding in the saddlebag. By degrees her back began to ache from bracing herself against the forward jerk—then her whole body ached—then it was torture merely to keep in an upright position. She felt guilty when she thought that Miss Musson had the additional burden of little Chet; but the older woman had firmly refused to let Scylla take him, saying simply:

"You are not well enough, child."

It was true that Scylla felt very unwell; before they reached their destination, indeed, she felt ready to die, and thought that death would be infinitely preferable to this cold, this misery, this agonizing motion.

Toward the end of the trip Scylla was overcome by a kind of stupor in which, as if it were happening to another person, she felt cold, pain, wretchedness, and nausea. Only vaguely and dimly, when they arrived, was she aware of the fact that the camel had sunk down onto its knees and hocks; then that she was being half lifted, half dragged out of the basket. The exquisite relief of being able to stretch out her limbs was followed, in a moment, by excruciating cramps, but even these could not keep her awake for long; she drifted into a state of unawareness that was half swoon, half sleep.

When Scylla next woke, it took her a long time to make any sense of her surroundings. She still felt utterly weak; a hand or foot, even a finger, when she tried to lift it, seemed heavy as stone; but the racking cramps and the dreadful sickness were gone.—Where could she be? The light was so dim that at first she began to wonder if she were back in the Bai's castle; in a dungeon, perhaps; but the air was fresh and cool, with a scent of water and rock, as if she were lying out on the mountainside; there was no hint, here, of the all-pervading stench: moldy straw, burning dung, rancid butter, and old sheepskins, that had been such a notable feature of the Bai's residence.

Were they out on the mountain? With extreme difficulty Scylla at last raised herself on one elbow and looked about her.

"Aha; you are feeling better at last; that is capital!" came Miss Musson's tranquil voice. "Would you care for a little tea, my dear? Keep still, and I will fetch you some."

"Thank you, ma'am . . ." Feebly, Scylla sank back; she seemed to be lying on a great mound of feathers, piled deep; they were covered by a camel-hair blanket, but she could feel, here and there, the points of the feathers pricking through the rough weave. Another hairy blanket was thrown over her. Looking upward with sharpened vision, she could now see, high above her, a brownish-gray vault, irregularly shaped. When she turned her eyes sideways she gasped, for the rock wall nearest her was smothered by brilliant paintings in reds and greens and blues: they depicted gods and devils, smiling goddesses, men being chopped up and mutilated in various ways, men praying, worshiping, and dancing; dragons, serpents, and great birds; and yet more gods, beast-headed, bird-headed, six-armed, smiling, contemplative, or cross-legged.

"Where in the world are we, ma'am?" asked Scylla when Miss Musson reappeared with the tea in a small copper pot.

"We are in the cave of the Holy Pir at Chaghlar."

"Oh yes, I remember now. This is a cave, then?"

"An enormous cave, containing I know not how many chambers. It goes far back into the mountain; for aught I know, right to the other side," said Miss Musson, cheerfully drinking some tea herself. "So— which is an excellent feature of the situation—we may remain here as long as Rob thinks it necessary, without feeling ourselves any encumbrance on our excellent host the Pir."

"Have you met him, ma'am?"

"Yes indeed; a most delightful man. How I wish my dear brother Winthrop could have met him too!"

"Shall I see him?"

"Most certainly you shall; when you feel well enough.—He is at his prayers just now. In fact he is at his prayers for most of the time. And I dare say the world would go on a great deal better if everybody followed his example," Miss Musson added roundly.

"What about Cal, ma'am? Is he better?" The tea had roused Scylla. Now she recalled her two sources of trouble: Cal's alarming indisposition and the fact that Cameron was furiously angry with her.

"Yes, my dear, Cal is coming on as well as can be expected." The older lady's voice here held a shade of reserve; anxiously Scylla scanned her guardian's wrinkled, hawklike features for some clue as to her doubt.

"Has he woken, ma'am? Is he sensible?"

"Oh yes. Perfectly sensible. Indeed he and Rob have gone out to gather a handful of wild sage and rosemary (Rob shot a mountain goat this morning, and I prefer the flavor of goat *mitigated*)."

"But you are troubled about Cal, Miss Musson?"

"Yes, my child, a little. He will recover in time, I don't doubt. But I am afraid his feelings for that charming but empty-headed little

Sripana had gone deeper than, in the circumstances, was at all wise. He is very miserable."

"Oh, *poor* Cal." Cal's sister felt a deep throb of sympathy—exacerbated by a slight jealous pang. This was the first time her brother had felt at all strongly about any woman—and what a hopeless situation!

"It is a mercy that we left the Bai's castle when we did," was the outcome of Scylla's reflections. "Or he might have done something really foolish—tried to elope with her, involved her in something that was bound to be discovered—"

Miss Musson agreed. "Yes—for Cal's sake, we left none too soon. Though I do not think that she in the least reciprocated Cal's feelings —which was just as well. He would not have wanted to leave her with a broken heart."

"No . . . poor Cal. So he was really in love with a mirage."

"As most people are when they are in love." Miss Musson's features remained calmly thoughtful, but there was a smile in her voice.

"Is he very downhearted?"

"Very. Rob reports that he has been constantly calling out in his sleep—even walking. Rob has encountered him once or twice, wandering in a trancelike state, quite unaware of his surroundings."

"Oh, poor Cal! He did that for months after our mother died. It is fortunate that we are here, and not in the Bai's castle! His sleep-walking there might have been disastrous!"

"He will be glad to have your company again, my dear," Miss Musson said. "And Rob is good for him—Rob is an excellently bracing influence upon anybody finding himself inclined to fall into a melancholy through unrequited love!"

I dare say, thought Scylla bitterly, and she asked:

"Ma'am, is the colonel still *very* angry with me?"

"Well, I am afraid he *is,* my child, there is no denying it. And, though I have done my possible to reason with him, I can see that, in a way, he cannot be blamed for his feelings. He seems to have set considerable store on his relations with the Bai—which must now be greatly impaired, if not wrecked for good. The Kafir rules of conduct are such that, even if the Bai were aware that Rob himself had no hand in supplying that girl with her pistol, because a member of his party had done the deed he must necessarily be involved in the resulting feud. And of course he has old ties which bind him to this countryside, so the severance of them must be painful to him."

"Yes, I see," said Scylla mournfully. "Did you know about his wife and child, ma'am?"

"Not before we came here, no. But since our arrival we have talked about it. We have had ample leisure—" The smile was back in Miss Musson's voice again.

"How long have we been here, then?"

"Nearly three days now. You have slept the clock around twice—helped by a draught containing, I think, opium, which the Holy Pir advised when you woke up the first time."

Scylla could remember nothing of that. She asked with difficulty:

"Can you *tell* me about Colonel Cameron's wife, ma'am? I—I feel very bad because once—many weeks ago—I said something—something unkind to him regarding little Chet, which, if I had known he once had a child of his own, I would not for the world—I—I am so anxious to avoid making such a mistake again, giving him needless pain."

Miss Musson looked at her thoughtfully and said, "Well, my dear, it is a short, sad tale. When Rob was here before, as commandant of the Bai's troop of picked horsemen—this was before he took service with the Amir Thaimur—I understand that Rob had won some notable battle for the Bai, against an encroaching neighbor chieftain, and the Bai offered him a large monetary reward. But Rob said—like the prince in the fairy tale, you know—that he would rather have the hand of his daughter in marriage. Except that she was not the Bai's daughter but some cousin or niece, daughter of one of the Bai's male kin, who was taking refuge in his castle at the time, because her own father had been killed and his lands ravaged. So the Bai gave his consent, and they were married."

"What was her name?" asked Scylla, after a pause.

"Jindan. And presently she had a little daughter; I do not know what the child was called. . . . Well, then Rob, it seems, collected Jindan's scattered liegemen and followers; aided by some of the Bai's warriors, they recaptured her father's castle and she returned there; but while Rob was off with his troop fighting a final battle with the almost defeated enemy Jindan's own uncle arrived at the castle—not the Bai, another uncle. She, thinking no harm, welcomed him in; but he, on the pretext that she had married an outlander, had her and the child cut up, limb by limb, in the presence of her women; their bones were scattered over the mountainside; and then he took her castle and lands for himself."

Scylla felt deathly cold; she wished she had not asked for the story. But after a while she said hoarsely:

"What did Cameron do when he found out?"

"He fought yet another battle, against the uncle; killed him and razed the castle to the ground. He felt there was a curse on the place; no one should live there. The lands he gave or sold to Mir Murad Beg; I believe that was the origin of the Bai's debt which was not yet fully paid."

"I see . . ."

"Poor Rob. It was a terrible thing to happen. And yet," Miss Musson went on thoughtfully, "I cannot help feeling that his union with Jindan must have presented him with innumerable difficulties as the years went by. Although they are not precisely *savages,* the Kafir ways are so different from what we regard as civilized; even Rob, accustomed as he is to the wilds, might in time have had cause to find fault; for he is *not* a patient man; or he might have wished to return to America, felt a longing for his own country, and then what could he have done? He must have taken Jindan with him, for he would never dare leave her and her territories unguarded; and I do not think a Kafir woman would transplant well; she must have been miserably homesick on the shores of Lake Superior! No, all things taken into consideration, I believe matters are best as they are."

Scylla reflected, without irony, that Miss Musson almost always came to this conclusion.

"How can I put matters right with Colonel Cameron?" she inquired humbly after a while.

"I think you had better simply ask his pardon, my child. Do *not* try to enter into any explanations or give an account of why you acted as you did; that is always *fatal*. *I* can understand very well why you let poor Dizane have the pistol—indeed I do not undertake to swear that I might not have acted likewise—but there is no arguing with a man over such an issue! Repentance is the only answer, if we are all to be comfortable together again."

"Is there any news of—is it known what happened at the Bai's castle after we left?"

"No, child. Not a soul has come this way since we arrived."

Then at least the Bai must have recovered, Scylla thought, remembering Habiba saying that the Bai would send offerings to the Holy Pir to avert the wrath of the gods. Presumably this had not been thought needful.

"How long must we remain here?" she asked.

"Well," said Miss Musson, "of course in the first place we have been waiting until Cal was quite recovered from his seizure and you from your fainting fit—"

"What a cursed *nuisance* he must find us," burst out Scylla.

"Don't swear, child," said Miss Musson equably. "In any case we would not have proceeded any farther until Rob was assured that all danger of pursuit had died down."

"And then how will we go on?"

"Oh, pilgrim caravans pass by here, on their way to and from the great shrine at Hazrat Imam, north of us; many people consider the Holy Pir of Chaghlar quite as important a point of pilgrimage. The season for pilgrims has hardly begun yet; but it is odds that, sooner or later, we shall be able to attach ourselves to some party traveling to Kabul."

"I see. How simple it sounds."

Despite her two-day rest, Scylla felt tired to her bones at the thought of the many months' travel ahead, the great distances to be covered, over the mountains to Kabul, across the desert to Baghdad and on again to the Mediterranean. She said wearily, "I wonder Colonel

Cameron does not simply entrust us to some caravan and then return to put matters right with the Bai."

"No, he would not do that."

"Ma'am," said Scylla after a considerable pause, voicing a worry that had visited her, on and off, since her awakening. "Do you think that I, too, share Cal's affliction? Was my fainting fit a seizure like his?"

"No, it was not, child," Miss Musson replied instantly and with certainty. "I wondered if you had been suspecting that! And indeed such a fear would not be surprising. But you showed none of the true epileptic symptoms. I think, indeed, what happened was that your terrible state of anxiety communicated itself to Cal—for there is no doubt that a strong sympathetic telepathy runs between you—do you not remember that occasion when he, playing truant in Umballa, got himself shut up in a palanquin and you nearly went mad with distress?—and I can remember many other such occurrences—so your state of agitation brought on his seizure, poor boy—and no wonder, for he was already in a fair degree of ferment over Sripana—and that, in its turn, rebounded on *you*."

"Yes, I see. Thank you, ma'am. I am sure you are right." Scylla sighed. "What a tedious pair we are." But she was immensely relieved at this confirmation of what she had vaguely thought herself.

"Not tedious." Miss Musson smiled slightly. "Now I believe you should drink a little goat broth and go to sleep again."

"But—little Chet—you must have such a deal to do, ma'am—"

"Psha. The Therbah is looking after little Chet, very capably. He is the best baby in the world—no trouble to anybody.—Ah, here comes Cal with your broth. I am sure that you will wish to have a comfortable coze together, so I will leave you for the moment."

Scylla, now accustomed to the dim light in the cave, perceived immediately that her brother was looking thin and pale. His faunlike pointed face was even more pointed than usual, for it had great hollows below the cheekbones; and his wide-set eyes under the soft black-winged eyebrows were tired and sad. His look of strain broke up, however, into an affectionate smile when he saw his sister recovered, and he squatted down by her and offered a steaming bowl, saying:

"Drink this disgusting beverage! I have done my possible by scattering wild herbs into it, but it still tastes to me like essence of old rope, if not something *much* worse."

Obediently Scylla gulped it down, and agreed with his verdict.

"How *are* you, dearest Cal?" she asked, searching his face with anxiety.

He took one of her hands and clasped it in both of his.

"Oh, I shall come about!" The lightness of the tone could not disguise the real depth of his feelings. He added after a moment, "No, it is very bad. To tell you the truth, I feel as if I were being stretched on the rack all the time! I have written poetry about love so often, and so glibly, but, sister, you have no idea; *I* had no idea; no idea whatsoever! It is a terrible force; a *fever*. It really burns. And to know that I shall never see her again; ever—ever—*ever*—Oh, it is *not* to be borne!" he cried in anguish, and hid his face in his hands.

"I know," said Scylla softly. "It is very bad. Poor Manny—" which had been her childhood name for him. She knelt up on the pile of feathers and put her arms around him. After a moment he turned his head speechlessly and rubbed his cheek against her hand.

When Scylla woke from her second sleep she was pronounced well enough to be introduced to her host, the Holy Pir; her awakening, fortunately, happening to coincide with one of his short daily periods of intermission from prayer.

Miss Musson escorted Scylla to the rock chamber generally occupied by the Pir; and on the way to it she was able to see for the first time the true extent and vastness of the cave system where they were quartered.

A whole mountainside, it seemed, was pitted by great natural vaults, which, in the course of many centuries, had been enlarged, added to, joined by passages, and made into dwelling places by countless generations of humans. Air holes and entrances at every level allowed light to penetrate to a greater or lesser degree. As Miss Musson had said, the passages delved far back into the mountain, but the chambers nearest the surface were the ones that had evidently been in most frequent use. At one time, it was plain, a huge multitude of people must have inhabited the place; it had been a whole city inside a mountain. Now the sole remaining inmates in this great hilly honeycomb were the Holy Pir and his disciple, who kept their quarters high up on the brow of the hillside. To reach this part the visitors must climb hundreds of worn rock steps, mostly inside the cave, but some of them winding among crags or crossing uncomfortably precipitous rock faces. At last they reached a small, chilly cavern, illuminated by three great round holes in the cliff, which, facing north, allowed in plenty of light and freezing air but no distracting sun. Here the Pir stood all day inside a kind of semicircular barrier, or desk, carved from the rock. With one hand he tinkled a tiny golden bell, with the other he swiftly flicked a set of ancient carved ivory beads along a string; and meanwhile he chanted continuous invocations, reciting the ritualistic words of prayer with incredible speed, acquired, no doubt, by long usage and familiarity. Cal was already in the room, sitting cross-legged on the floor; he seemed thoughtful, soothed and calmed by the devout atmosphere and the peaceful murmuring of the holy recluse. Little Chet sat on Cal's lap, silently chewing the teething toy that the Bai's wives had given him, his round black eyes intently following the to-and-fro movement of the golden bell. Miss Musson sank matter-of-factly to the floor and Scylla followed suit, thankful to rest after the quite arduous climb.

About ten minutes later the Pir's chantings came to a stop. He brought his eyes back from the invisible distances they had been contemplating and laid down his bell. Picking up a censer full of incense that had been standing on his desk, he rotated it on its chain until blue coils of aromatic smoke drifted about the room and out of the window holes. Then, setting down the censer, he raised his string of beads and beckoned Cal to come to him. Cal rose obediently, holding the baby in the crook of his arm, and went forward to the desk; the Pir swung his rosary so that the beads touched Cal's forehead, while murmuring what was evidently a blessing; then he did the same to little Chet. Finally he beckoned to Miss Musson and Scylla, who approached and were blessed in their turn.

When this ceremony had been completed, the Pir's face broke into a smile. He was a very impressive-looking man; quite six feet tall, Scylla thought; his skin weathered almost to the color of old oak by exposure to mountain air. He wore a dark red wool robe, tied around the waist by a hair-rope girdle, and had on his head a pirpank, or conical hat, made of black wool. His face, Scylla thought, curiously resembled some old prints Miss Musson's brother Winthrop had had in his study, depicting those other Indians, the North American Comanches or braves. He had a long hooked nose and high, deeply undercut cheek-bones; his aspect was proud and calm. When he smiled, Scylla noticed his large fine white teeth. She wondered how old he was; his face seemed hairless as from extreme age, but a long black braid hung down his back, under his cap. She suspected him to be far older than he seemed.

"Good evening, ladies," said the Pir, startling Scylla nearly out of her wits. "How do you do, Miss Musson; I am happy that you have brought your young companion to visit me." His smile became wider as he observed Scylla's look of astonishment. "You are surprised, miss, that I speak your language."

Scylla blushed, feeling that she had been detected in discourtesy, and stammered an apology.

"His Holiness has traveled to many lands and speaks many languages," Miss Musson explained suavely; the glint in her eye suggested to Scylla that she had deliberately withheld this piece of information in order to entertain herself by observing her young friend's surprise.

"How do you do, sir—Your Holiness." Scylla curtsied politely. "It is very kind of you to—to allow us to visit your retreat."

"I am very happy to be visited."

The Pir's eye rested on little Chet. "Especially by young persons and children." He studied the baby gravely for a few minutes and then remarked:

"Would you have any objection, Miss Musson, if I performed a simple test on the baby?"

Even Miss Musson appeared slightly puzzled at this. "A *test,* Your Holiness? No, I see no reason to object, but—what kind of a test?"

The Pir walked to a cavity in the rock wall and delved about in it. Glancing around his sanctum, Scylla noticed that it was furnished with all kinds of sacred odds and ends, on rock shelves and in corners —brass goblets, full of moldering grain, highly colored cakes, copper jugs of oil, sacred images, cloth paintings attached to the walls, bells, antelope horns, gongs, scrolls, lamps, and little pots of yak butter.

Presently the Pir withdrew his head and shoulders from the closet and lifted out a flat basket containing an odd mixture of articles— three or four horn cups, a couple of what looked liked aged, brittle loincloths, three or four rosaries, half a dozen small ivory images, a couple of scrolls, two snuffboxes.

"This should really be done after much prescribed ritual and several weeks of prayer," he observed, carrying the basket across the room and setting it down in front of the baby. "But as I am not quite certain how long I am to have the pleasure of your company on my mountain, it is perhaps best to conduct the test without so many preliminaries; it is quite valid in all circumstances."

He watched intently as little Chet, delighted at the sight of so many new, interesting, and unfamiliar objects all set within his reach, studied the contents of the basket absorbedly.

Scylla had been on the point of asking what the test was intended to prove but, seeing from the Pir's expression how much importance he evidently ascribed to its outcome, she closed her lips again and, like the other three, concentrated her attention on the baby.

Presently, with a crow of pleasure, little Chet reached out a hand to finger one of the rosaries. Then he grasped the handle of a cup and thumped it gently up and down. Then he found a bell which gave out a sweet tinkle when he shook it, so he waved it lustily, laughing with joy.

The Holy Pir sighed and gently undid the small brown fingers from the bell handle. "No, my friend," he said, patting Chet's head while he picked up the basket, "you are a good boy and a clever boy, but you are not the boy I am looking for," and he carried the basket across the room and restored it to its place in the rock cleft.

"May one ask," inquired Miss Musson when he returned and sat down cross-legged, "what would have been the result if Chet *had* been the boy you were seeking, Your Holiness?"

"He would have been my successor as keeper of this shrine," the Pir explained. "As you may know, the shrine has had a guardian for many hundreds—perhaps thousands—of years. When one guardian dies, his spirit is rehoused in another body and returns, in course of time, to its place."

"How can it be proved that it is the right spirit?" inquired Cal, greatly interested.

"Why, as you just saw! A child who is claimed to be the new Holy Pir will be able to select, without hesitation, all the articles that have belonged to his predecessors."

"I see; how uncommonly neat! But I do detect a difficulty here, sir," Cal pointed out. "After all, you aren't dead yet! So how could your spirit be rehoused in little Chet here?"

The Pir sighed again. "I am afraid you may be right, my son. It is so seldom that a baby as young as that visits my mountain that I thought, perhaps, by some happy dispensation, it might have been vouchsafed that my successor had arrived *before* I had died, so that I myself would be permitted to train him."

"But that would mean sharing one soul between two bodies," objected Cal.

"Such a situation *might* be covered by various sections of the holy writings," the Pir assured him. "I am not certain that it *has* happened, but it would not be impossible. However it was not to be!"

"I must acknowledge, I am greatly relieved at that!" divulged Miss Musson. "I do not doubt that Colonel Cameron would be delighted to be rid of our charge in such a respectable way as discovering that he was the reborn guardian of a mountain shrine in Central Asia, but as *I* have undertaken to see that little Chet receives the education of an English gentleman at Eton, it must have been a decided setback to *my* plans for him."

The Holy Pir laughed kindly.

"Do not perturb yourself, ma'am! I will not deprive you of your charge. And now"—he glanced at the light in the sky—"I must return to my devotions, but I look forward to conversing with all or any of you again next time I am at leisure."

He returned to his desk, picked up the bell and the rosary, elevated his gaze to the northern sky, and recommenced his chanting as if he had never stopped.

Somewhat awed by this remarkable duality and detachment, Scylla followed Miss Musson on tiptoe from the cave. Outside, above a fairly narrow ledge overhanging the precipice, she noticed an altar, liberally smeared with yak butter and loaded with offerings: goats' heads, green disks of flat buckwheat bread, silver beads and amulets, markhor horns. It was evident that some pilgrims ventured no farther than this, perhaps fearing to disturb the Holy Pir at his devotions.

Cal did not follow his companions.

"He will come by and by," said Miss Musson tranquilly. "I hope that he is learning resignation from that holy man."

They retraced their way down the winding rock steps and when they had reached the foot Miss Musson said:

"If you are feeling truly recovered, my dear, would you care to accompany me in a search for camel fodder? Rob does not dare allow the camels to graze outside because, of course, if the Bai does send any pursuers this way, they would be instantly recognized. And it seems too hard that all the labor of finding forage for them should devolve on the men."

"Of course I will help you," Scylla said instantly. "I shall be glad to see what lies outside the cave."

The view from the Pir's window in the cliff face had shown a series of gradually declining foothills, rippling away northward into a great flat desert plain, of apparently almost limitless extent. But when they left the cave by an eastward entrance, Scylla realized that they must be at the northern tip of the chain of mountains which, she knew, curled through the center of Kafiristan. Great peaks, some of them still snow-covered, surrounded the upland plateau which lay behind the Pir's mountain. Here grew wild sage and wild rose, huge thistles, pale spear grass, leaves of wild hollyhock and uncurling tendrils of wild rhubarb. It did not take the two women very long to gather a large bundle of grass apiece, but, Miss Musson said, "Camels eat a deal of fodder; we had better take in at least a dozen bundles each." Scylla had no objection; it was pleasant, here on the mountainside, going to and fro, and on the slopes sheltered from the keen and constant wind the sun was very hot.

"Pray tell me, child, if you see anybody approaching," Miss Musson said. "My eyes are not as good as yours." And presently, far off across the plateau, Scylla was able to inform her guardian that she could see the tall, rangy figure of Cameron and the shorter, rounder one of the Therbah, carrying some large beast slung between them. As they came closer, this was revealed to be a large, shaggy deerlike animal.

"Cameron Sahib shoot a foo!" called the Therbah joyfully.

Cameron, less enthusiastic, apparently, about the acquisition of the foo, approached the females with a forbidding expression.

"I *did* ask you, ma'am, not to venture far from the cave," he remarked irritably as soon as he was within speaking range. "Supposing the Bai's warriors should ride this way? They could see you for a great distance in this open place."

Scylla was tempted to retort, "In that case, was it not rather foolhardy of you, Colonel Cameron, to go hunting so far from the cave?" but, with an effort, she held her peace.

"I am sorry; I did not think of that," admitted Miss Musson. She did not seem too perturbed, however, and added placidly, "Well, it is fortunate that Scylla and I have collected a great deal of fodder. Now nobody need go out for two days at least, as I see our stewpot has been handsomely provided for; and, by the end of that time, perhaps you may be satisfied that danger of pursuit is over."

"How can I be?" he replied gloomily, and was turning to climb up to the cave mouth (a large cleft in the mountainside, approached by a kind of rock stair) when Scylla walked up to him.

"Colonel Cameron," she said resolutely. "I am very sorry indeed for the inconvenience and trouble that my—my action at the Bai's castle has brought upon you. Heaven knows that we have immeasurable cause to be grateful to you. You must have been tempted to abandon such awkward charges as we have proved many times over, and yet you have borne with us and rescued us from the predicaments in which we have involved you, again and again. I can only apologize and hope that you may be able to forgive me."

She had prepared this speech with some care and spoke it slowly, with a thudding heart. Concluding, she looked up into his face and held out her hand. But his face, she saw with dismay, was set like granite, and he replied dryly, without taking the extended hand:

"Let us proceed into the cave, if you please, before we discuss your behavior at the Bai's castle, Miss Paget."

Deeply mortified at this rebuff, she spun around on her heel and climbed up into the cave entrance, biting her lip to keep herself from tears. When they were inside and she was certain of her voice, she said:

"I have not the least intention of *discussing* my behavior at the Bai's castle, Colonel Cameron," and walked hastily away through the heaps of camel fodder toward the chamber where Miss Musson had arranged her sickbed.

Miss Musson followed her, while the two men, assisted by Cal, who had come down from the upper cave at that moment, set about carrying the fodder into some more remote area where the camels were quartered.

"The camels must be housed deep inside the mountain, poor things," Miss Musson explained in her matter-of-fact way, following Scylla with little Chet balanced on her hip, "for, of course, if a troop of the Bai's riders arrived, and they had any camels with them, they would all call to each other; camels are very communicative beasts, it seems."

"I see," replied Scylla mechanically, taking little Chet from her guardian. His friendly warmth was consoling; she sat down on the pile of feathers and gave him a hug. Noticing her inattentive tone, Miss Musson said kindly:

"Now, my dear child, pray do not be distressing yourself about Rob! He is stiff-necked, as most men are—*especially* those of Scots descent —he will come around by and by. You have done your part by apologizing—you did very well—all you need do now is keep out of his way as much as possible until we recommence our journey, so as to avoid occasions for dispute."

Scylla received this discouraging news without comment.

At the end of two more days' cave life Scylla was heartily weary of in-carceration and longed to be on the move again. Even the Bai's castle would have been preferable! Following Miss Musson's advice, she had hardly seen Cameron—except for brief intervals at mealtimes—but she heard from Cal that he still thought it best not to move on.

During this period the two women mended their clothes and those of the men; the Therbah assiduously groomed the camels and made a new carrying frame for little Chet; Cal spent as much time as he was permitted in theological discussions with the Holy Pir, a good many hours in writing, and the rest of his time holding long conversations with Scylla.

Sooner or later these always came around to the subject of Sripana and his feelings about her; certain that the more he was allowed to discuss his hopeless passion, the sooner he would begin to recover from it, Scylla indulged him in this, though she was beginning to find these dialogues inexpressibly painful.

How Colonel Cameron passed his leisure Scylla did not know, nor did she inquire. But at the end of three days his caution received its justification, for a troop of armed men in the service of Mir Murad Beg came climbing up the slopes of the Pir's mountain.

Fortunately there were no external traces to betray the presence of the fugitives. The incessant wind (the Therbah said it was called "the wind that blows for a hundred and twenty days") removed all foot-prints from the rocky, dusty terrain, and all camel droppings had been thriftily scooped up to be used for fuel. The indignant camels them-selves had had their muzzles tied up to prevent them from roaring, snarling, or shrieking and had been led by the Therbah to the deepest cave he could find that would accommodate them, as soon as the first tiny puff of dust, denoting a troop of horse, had been sighted on the horizon.

The humans, likewise, took refuge far inside the mountain, where they were obliged to remain without light or fire, because the smell of smoke, drifting through the tunnels, might betray their presence. Even little Chet was somewhat dismayed by the cold and the blank darkness; he whimpered dolefully at first but was appeased by Scylla's holding him tightly and singing all the lullabies she could think of, in a voice hardly above a whisper, until he finally fell asleep.

This disagreeable period of imprisonment seemed to last for an eternity. Cameron had asked the Holy Pir's disciple, Buyantu, a small, stocky, taciturn monk with a very Mongolian cast of countenance, to let them know when the searchers departed; but hours elapsed before his shuffling tread was heard coming along the rocky passages, and the glimmer of his taper gradually illuminated their tomblike place of refuge.

Buyantu explained to the Therbah (the only one who understood his dialect) that the Bai's men had been obliged to remain for several hours—it had seemed like days to the captives—because the Holy Pir was engaged in one of his periods of prayer and could not be interrupted. Meanwhile Buyantu had blocked all their questions with the answer, "I know nothing; I know nothing."

The leaders of the troop—two of the Bai's sons—were finally admitted to the Holy Pir's presence.

"Bless the old boy, he was quite equal to them," said Cal cheerfully, telling his sister about the interview later. "Apparently they said to him, 'Have you seen some European thieves and murderers here?' or something like that, and he answered, 'I have seen nothing but God.' He wasn't telling any lie. That's all he does see. And of course they were obliged to accept his word, because he is the Holy Pir."

"Did he learn what had happened to Dizane?" asked Scylla anxiously.

"Yes, they told him the whole story—how the Bai had been

wounded and insulted and deprived of his rightful property—meaning Dizane."

"Where is she?"

"She is dead."

Scylla had expected as much, but still the news came as a kind of numbing grief: she remembered so clearly how the girl had knelt to her, how she had snatched up the gun, the urgency of her speech, the touch of her hand—now all that proud energy was gone, finished.

"What happened?"

"They were following her on horseback, coming closer, and she slowed up a little and turned around to shout back at them, 'You will never catch me, never!' and then she jumped her horse over a cliff."

"Oh, I am glad!" Scylla said fervently. "—Does Cameron know?"

"Yes, he was there when the Holy Pir was telling us about it."

"Did he say anything?"

"No; he asked about the Bai."

"Was the Bai badly hurt?"

"No; he is better now."

"That is fortunate. . . . So now we can continue on our journey?"

"When a pilgrim caravan passes by."

This did not occur for another ten days, during which the party had time to grow exceedingly weary of cave life and a diet composed mainly of mountain goat.

However on the fifth day the Pir, learning by chance from Cal that they were very short of funds, suddenly announced that he would escort them to a spot where they might supply themselves with enough wealth to provide them with provisions and equipment for the rest of their journey.

"How very singular!" exclaimed Scylla when Cal told her this. "Wealth to be picked up in the wilderness? What is this place?"

"A ruined temple, it seems, destroyed by King Ogotai when he came down from the north."

"Ogotai?"

"He was a son or nephew of Genghis Khan," replied the well-informed Cal.

"If there are treasures," said Scylla, thinking of the Great King's tomb at Ziatur, "why have thieves not made off with them long ago?"

"They believe the temple is watched over by a powerful djinn."

It took them half a day's journey to reach the temple of Koh-i-Ruwan; this was partly because of the Pir, who, owing his stationary life, could not move very quickly. He rode on a white ass; the rest of the party walked, and the outing took on something of the cheerful aspect of a picnic excursion, because the Pir was delighted as a boy to have a chance of a day out from his cave and continual orisons.

"I shall have to pray for twenty-one days without stopping at all to make up for this," he confided to Miss Musson. "But yet it will have been worth it! I know that the world we see about us is merely an illusion, an insubstantial show, a shred of vapor, no more important than a dream—but still, it has a very agreeable appearance!"

Miss Musson admired the white ass, a handsome beast, and he told her that he had once ridden it all the way to Mecca. "I have been to all the holy places of Asia.—But there is nothing in Mecca," he said sadly. "It is just a place, like any other. For true sanctity one must look inward."

Scylla discovered with amazement that the Pir had also been to Jerusalem, to Constantinople, and even to Rome, which was where he had learned his excellent English.

"But all this running to and fro in the world is as nothing! Travel, even to the greatest seats of learning and sanctity, weighs nothing in the balance—no, not so much as a grain of sand—against remaining in one spot, withdrawing from temptation, abstaining from all actions, even virtuous ones, and loosening one's ties with everything temporal and corporeal."

Miss Musson sighed.

"I dare say you are in the right of it, Your Holiness. Indeed, as I grow older, the appeal of such a life grows very great. But, after all, *some*body has to make the laws and teach the children and look after the sick and feed the pigs!"

"I see no occasion for it. If men had not already committed a great many follies and wickednesses, such activities would not be necessary," loftily replied the Pir.

Scylla could hardly feel that was a valid argument.

"You mean, because everybody would be meditating in their own little cell? But—if they were—I do not precisely see, Your Holiness, how the human race would continue at all. Surely it would very soon die out altogether because—because there would not be any families to ensure its continuation."

The Holy Pir smiled. "Aha, my child! I see that you, like your brother, suffer from the intellectual curiosity and the disputatious nature which is just as much an enemy to holy abstraction and meditation as—as any other form of worldly activity. Mind! I do not deny that it is very enjoyable to encounter it from time to time," he confessed, as if he found it necessary to apologize for his interest in their ideas.

"I hope our disputations will not disturb your meditations, sir," put in Cal, who was walking on the other side of the white ass.

"No, my son. I am thankful to say that I am too far along the True Way for that. When you are gone from here, it will be no more than as if two birds, flying past, threw their shadows for an instant upon my wall and then vanished forever."

Scylla felt chilled by this image, but the Holy Pir went on, surprisingly, "Now your excellent guardian, Miss Musson here, is different; she has the contemplative habit; if she were to remain with me in the wilderness, I feel very sure that I could soon set *her* feet upon the Way."

Miss Musson remained silent for so long after this remark that, amazed and a little apprehensive, Scylla began to wonder if she intended to take the anchorite up on his unexpected offer. At last, however, sighing, she said:

"The prospect of a tranquil old age learning contemplation in this comfortable wilderness, Your Holiness, is indeed not one to be lightly rejected. But, alas, one is sometimes obliged to decline the greater good in favor of the lesser. I have lines to follow—knots to untie, promises to keep."

Scylla felt herself strangely moved by this, but also a little shocked.

"*Dearest* Miss Musson!" she exclaimed. "If you would truly prefer to remain here—*pray* do not be feeling that any commitment to *us* must take you farther than you wish to go! I do not"—she gulped—"I do not pretend that we should not *miss* you! But we are not children! I am sure that we could manage very well. Cal and I could—could deliver little Chet to the provost of Eton—"

"Certainly we could," agreed Cal, but Miss Musson said calmly:

"No, my dear children; I am very sure that you could manage to admiration without me—but I promised my eldest brother Henry that before it was too late I would return to keep him company. He is—is blind, you know—"

She sighed again and once more fell silent.

Colonel Cameron had been walking a little ahead of the rest and taking no part in their talk. This was not to be wondered at, since the route must have awakened sad memories for him. They had been skirting the mountainside, just above the tree line. Down below them a dark, thickly forested ravine fell away abruptly—so deep, so dark, so densely crammed with trees that it resembled a black crack in the landscape.

"Sun never shine down there," said the Therbah sadly.

And, on the opposite side, on a crag above the trees, they had seen a ruin which, Miss Musson murmured to Scylla, had been the fortress belonging to Cameron's lost princess. By unspoken agreement they all increased their pace past this tragic spot and felt relief when it was out of sight.

Gradually the deep ravine became shallower and formed a series of cup-shaped hollows in the mountainside, linked by tumbling waterfalls; rounding a spur of the mountain, they presently saw that they were on a level with the topmost of these hollows which formed a great natural amphitheater, magnificently situated at the head of the valley. In the center of this great space were more ruins—pillars, round arches, fragments of wall—and the Holy Pir, loosening his rein, said:

"That is the temple of Koh-i-Ruwan, where there was once a thriving community."

"How long ago was this?" inquired Miss Musson.

Scylla had expected the Pir to answer forty or fifty years, but he reflected and said, "It must be some six hundred years now since the priests were all slaughtered. I was a priest there once myself, in a previous incarnation, but that was long before; in the time of the great king Alexander, who visited the temple once, on his way to his northern city of Cyropolis."

Scylla was somewhat startled at the Holy Pir's claim to clear memories of earlier incarnations, but Cal and Miss Musson took them calmly enough and evinced no doubt of his ability to recall events of previous lives.

"So that is how Your Holiness happens to know where the treasure is hidden?" Cal said. "You were there when it was stowed away perhaps? You do not think it might have been removed in the meantime?"

"I think it very unlikely. In those days there was much gold to be found in the streams and rivers of this region. All that men needed to do was lay fleecy sheepskins, weighted down by stones, upon the river bed and leave them there—for about twenty days, as I recall. Then the fleece would be dried in the hot sun and shaken carefully over a white cloth, and many grains of gold would be found. Also there were ruby mines, farther north, in the sandy foothills, deep tunnels like those made by wild beasts, burrowed into the soft rock. Many great rubies were discovered. . . . I recall the king Alexander took a basketful with him, as large as red grapes. There was a great deal of treasure in the temple," said the Holy Pir simply. "I do not think it will all be gone."

On closer approach to the ruined temple, Scylla could well understand why it was believed to be haunted. The situation of the building was awe-inspiring, poised on its natural shelf, overhanging the valley. And the only approach to it was along a single track, part of which, for a stretch of about thirty yards, traversed a narrow man-made shelf across a cliff face, a sheer drop of some four hundred feet into the ravine below. At the far side of this the path ran between the massive, pillarlike legs of an immense equestrian statue. This, like the temple, was shattered: only the legs remained upright, supporting a portion of the horse's body. When the party had passed under it they all paused to exclaim at it. The legs, some fifteen feet high, were carved from black, flinty porphyry with veins of dark red and green.

"It was all cut from one rock," the Pir told them. "I can just remember when it was made—that was in my sixty-ninth incarnation."

"Where is the rider?" Cal asked, looking about.

The head and neck of the horse, carved with wonderful fidelity and skill, were to be seen on the blond grass nearby. The head seemed gazing across the valley. And a portion of the tail and hindquarters lay not far off. But of the rider there was no sign.

"There is a local tale about this horse," said the Pir. "Our friend there"—nodding at Cameron—"will have heard it. Like all such tales, it is part superstition, part fact; every auditor must ravel out the truth, as best he can, for himself."

"Pray tell us the tale, sir," said Cal, and Scylla echoed his request.

"Pray do, Your Holiness."

"Very well," said the Pir, with an indulgent smile, and went on. "This horse is called the Asp-i-Dheha. Once it had wings and could fly. Its master, a giant, lived many thousands of miles to the north, beyond the Hiung-nu mountain range. Every night he flew southward, through wind and storm and blizzard, thousands of miles, to visit the beautiful queen of this region. But she died at last, and one night her lover arrived to find that she had been buried in a tomb on this mountain. The giant was so distraught with sorrow that he cut off his horse's wings and buried himself beside the queen, deep under the mountain. The horse remained on this spot, year after year, grieving for its master, until at length it turned to stone. But even now it still speaks, and sometimes cries aloud, imploring its master to come back to it; you can see how the head looks to the north, where it believes its master to have gone."

"Poor horse," said Scylla softly, and Cal said:

"Does it really speak, Your Holiness?"

The Pir tapped a piece of flint against one of the massive legs and it gave off a clear ringing note, like bell metal.

"When the wind blows between these four legs, it is like a great stringed instrument; one may hear the sound from many miles away. That is why thieves are afraid to visit and rob the temple. But come, now, let me see . . ."

Leaving his ass to stray where it liked, the Holy Pir walked across a wide paved area which must once, presumably, have been the main entrance court of the temple. Climbing a zigzag ramp to a higher level, he made for what looked as if it had been a small shrine, set against the back wall of the amphitheater. This had a double row of columns on each side, some of them still upright, others prone among the pale grass and thistles. At the rear of the shrine stood a weathered block, apparently an altar, and, going to one side of this, the Pir tapped with his piece of flint here and there upon the paved floor, until his ear caught the sound that he was expecting. He called Cal to him and said:

"My son, push this paving slab sideways, depressing the left-hand edge and raising the right; after some centuries, it may be a trifle stiff."

This proved an understatement; and in the end it took the combined strength of Cal, Cameron, and the Therbah to force the slab to swivel. But at length it did so, apparently rotating on a stone axle, and a cavity was revealed below, about the size of a clothes chest. It seemed to be full of birds' bones.

Scylla was too polite to voice her disappointment, but Cal said disgustedly:

"Are you sure this is the right cache, Your Holiness? I see nothing but a lot of drumsticks!"

"Vision without knowledge is little better than blindness," replied the Pir calmly. "Break one of those shank bones, my child, and tell me what you see then?"

The aged, brittle bone snapped like a dry twig in Cal's grasp, and he let out a shout of astonishment.

"It's all filled with gold! Why, those old priests did a better job, even, than Wharton, the traveling dentist!"

The Pir smiled benignly. "Take what you need, my friends. But leave some for other needy travelers."

"Oh yes, indeed, sir; we shan't need a fiftieth of what's here."

"Under the bones, as I recall, there should be a black basalt box. It is full of rubies."

The box was there, carved—probably to deter intending thieves—in the form of a cobra with raised head and hood. The head lifted off, and Cal, cautiously tipping the casket, released a flow of little red nodules, some of them cut, polished, and sparkling vermilion, others still in their rough state. "Take what you need," said the Pir again.

After some discussion among the males, they took a dozen bones and a handful of rubies.

"Wait one moment," said the Pir then, as they were about to recover the hoard. "Give me the box."

Cal passed it to him and he delved carefully among its contents.

"There is one particular stone that I remember," he murmured. "I should like to see it again." For a few minutes it appeared that he was going to be disappointed, then he exclaimed in satisfaction:

"Ah, here it is!"

He pulled out a remarkably large, square ruby, cut and polished to a lustrous perfection. It must have weighed at least two hundred carats and was carved in the shape of a tiny altar. There were letters and characters deeply incised on all four sides.

"What a gem!" breathed Cal. "But surely, sir, that is too good for us. We have taken only a few of the smaller ones, to provide for our journey—"

The Pir smiled at him, and he fell silent, abashed. "No, my son," the Pir agreed kindly. "This is not a stone for needy travelers to barter in exchange for camel hire or millet porridge. This is a stone for one friend to give to another, and"—he stretched out his hand—"as former abbot of this monastery, I choose to give it to my friend Miss Musson. I give it in token of our friendships in former lives and our continuing friendship."

Cal and Scylla politely concealed gasps of amazement, but Miss Musson took the magnificent ruby composedly.

"Thank you, Your Holiness," she replied. "Whenever I look at it— which will be many, many times every day—I shall remember your kindness and this remarkable place. I am not, as you are, able to recal our previous acquaintance, but your statement comes as no surprise to me. I feel in my heart that you may be right."

"Perhaps they were lovers in a previous incarnation!" hopefully whispered Scylla to Cal, who replied loftily, "Psha! Perhaps our guardian was a man in a previous life. Sex may change from one incarnation to another; the Pir told me so."

The object of their excursion having been achieved, when the revolving slab had been carefully replaced over the treasure Miss Musson declared that she, for one, was ready to eat a nuncheon. This she had foresightedly packed in the saddlebags of the ass. Accordingly the party sat on fallen pillars and consumed cold roast goat, excepting the Holy Pir, who would eat nothing but a handful of pulse.

On the journey home, nobody was inclined for conversation. So much unwonted exposure to other people, their chatter and questions, had, it was plain, tired the Holy Pir more than he cared to admit; he rode silently, in meditation, with his head bowed. Miss Musson, too, seemed full of thought. Cameron had been moodily silent all day, and remained so; the Therbah seldom spoke unless it was needful; and Cal, his sister saw, had been much moved and impressed by the atmosphere of the ruined temple and the legend of the stone horse, the Asp-i-Dheha—as indeed she had herself; she suspected that his creative demon had seized him and would not leave him again until the legend had been transformed into poetry.

They were all tired out by the time, close on sunset, that they reached the Holy Pir's mountain. Buyantu was waiting to stable the ass and led it away, with grunts of disapproval and censorious glances at the travelers for having kept his holy master out so long. The Pir retired wearily to his cave, Cal retreated hastily to a distant cell-like cranny which he had adopted for work and reflection, the Therbah hurried off to tend the camels. Cameron was left with Scylla in the open entrance cavern, which Buyantu kept piled high with firewood and stores of grain, salt, dried snow mushrooms, and strings of edible herbs.

Cameron gave Scylla an irresolute glance, moved, as if to walk off to the cave that he used as his sleeping quarters, then turned back again.

"Miss Paget—" he began abruptly. "I have been thinking about what happened at the Bai's castle—"

Scylla was exceedingly tired. The day's expedition had been a long one, in hot mountain sun and biting wind. She had found the sight of the burned fortress across the valley inexpressibly saddening, and the legend of the giant's horse had done nothing to pick up her spirits. She interrupted hurriedly:

"Pray do not allude to that, Colonel Cameron. I am sure there were faults on both sides—no useful purpose would be achieved in discussing it. Indeed, it might well be disastrous."

"But I—"

"Excuse me, if you please. It is bad enough to realize that, if we had only known *then* about the Holy Pir's treasure and his obliging nature, we need never have visited your friend the Bai—about whom I would prefer to hear no more."

"Very well," he replied haughtily but with evident deep mortification, and Scylla made all speed off to her own cave before he could find some other means of reintroducing the topic. The last thing she wanted just then was another quarrel with Colonel Cameron!— Indeed even this passage between them, brief though it was, had power to sink her into such dejection that she cast herself on her feather couch and, to her own shame, indulged in a shower of tears. Little Chet, roused from a daylong nap in a box of sweet-smelling grass, gazed at her wonderingly until she wrapped her arms around him and buried her face in his hay-scented draperies.—She did not know what had overset her, she told herself. Her irritation of the spirits could be nothing but fatigue and stupidity! But she was glad that Miss Musson was not there at that moment to catechize her. Miss Musson had lately taken to long periods of meditation, sitting cross-legged in a high, airy cavern that faced north; sometimes she spent the whole night there.

The evening meal, when the travelers met again, was a very silent one. Nobody had much appetite for the broth which Miss Musson had made earlier, and which the Therbah now heated up. Cal, it was worryingly plain to his sister, had succumbed to such a severe bout of creative fever that he was hardly aware of anything passing about him. His hands shook, his eyes were glazed and bloodshot, he constantly made notes on dried leaves and scraps of parchment. Scylla could only hope that this preoccupation did not bring on another of his seizures. She must be glad of anything that distracted his attention from his lost love, but this theme, perhaps, was rather too close to his own grief to be a true distraction.—After swallowing a few mouthfuls of broth, he made his excuses and returned to his study-cave. Scylla, shortly following his example, bade good night to her guardian and Cameron, giving as pretext that she was weary and wished to sleep. In reality her mind was far too active for slumber, and she sat restlessly with her chin on her fists, or paced to and fro, watching the northern stars while they glitteringly wheeled across the window cranny of her cave. She would have liked to talk to Cal—but he would be busy writing, or asleep. It was unfair! *He* poured out his heart to her, whenever he chose.

At last, restless beyond endurance, she wrapped a black shawl around her and started out in the direction of Cal's eyrie. The way to it led past the communal chamber where they had the fire (when Cameron judged it safe to light one). To Scylla's considerable surprise, a dim glow of light still emanated from this chamber, and she heard the voice of her guardian, whom she had thought to be long retired, in sleep or meditation.

"No, no, my dear Rob! You are all consideration, as always—kindness itself! But my mind is made up on this head. As I told His Holiness—I have other reasons, other commitments. One cannot always do as one chooses."

Cameron's voice came with unwonted diffidence—in a tone he had never used to Scylla.

"Miss Amanda—you may not immediately approve of what I am about to suggest now—but I must ask you not to come to any hasty conclusion until you have heard me out."

A murmur from Miss Musson appeared to accede to this request; he went on: "That girl—that child *must* be a constant anxiety to you—to both of us—until she is delivered to her friends in England. With her appearance—her very considerable degree of charm—and her hasty, headstrong, *willful* disposition—occurrences such as the recent one must, I fear, be all too frequent between here and the Levant. Indeed, I do not scruple to say that, if we manage to get her safe as far as the shores of the Mediterranean, it will be nothing short of a miracle. Hitherto we have been traveling in the wilds—but we shall be passing through towns, Kabul, Girishk, Herat—"

"Oh, come now, my dear Rob—"

"I am not joking, Miss Amanda. I saw the looks that Mir Murad was giving her. If we had not left the Bai's castle when we did—"

"In that case, you have been rather unfairly hard on her," dryly remarked Miss Musson.

"*Hard* on her! If the wretched girl had any notion how I have worried about her—what a desperate anxiety I have been in as to her welfare—"

Here Scylla, listening in a kind of paralysis, almost interrupted to beg the colonel icily not to concern himself about her to such a degree, but he then took her breath away by continuing:

"Ma'am, I have thought it all over very carefully—many, *many* times—and I can only urge you to allow me to bed her now—*here!*—because it is almost impossible that she should escape capture and seduction somewhere along the way and—and by this means we may ensure that at least the child she bears will be white—of European blood—and that she will be somewhat prepared for what she—will understand a little better what constitutes provocative behavior—will know how to go on, in short! Also, I myself would then be in a—in a better-defined position with regard to her!"

There was a considerable pause here, while Scylla gazed ahead of her motionless, trembling, in the darkness; then Miss Musson spoke again.

"I consider that you rate the risks much too highly, Rob. I see no need for the somewhat drastic remedy you propose. Besides—only consider the consequences—suppose the poor girl were to fall in love with you?"

"Well," he said very slowly, "then I suppose I could marry her!"

The dryness of his voice matched that of Miss Musson's. She said quickly:

"No, no—that would be frantic folly! You are far too disparate—in age, in nature, habit—everything! No, no, you have windmills in your brain, my dear Rob! No such desperate remedy is called for. We must trust in Providence. She is a good child—and, in time, will be a sensible one; if she is overtaken by some such misfortune as you suggest, she will know how to bear it with philosophy."

"Oh—you have been imbibing too many of the Pir's doctrines!" he exclaimed in an exasperated tone. "Take no action! Do nothing! Raise no finger to avert disaster! Well, I have made my offer, and, since it is rejected, I will take myself off to bed."

"Good night, Rob. Believe me, I am obliged to you for your practical consideration!" Scylla could hear the smile in Miss Musson's voice. "I dare say you may be glad enough that I did not take you at your word and put it to the test!"

Scylla waited no longer. Silent as night itself, she turned and fled back at top speed to the chamber she had just quitted. Once there, safe from discovery, she allowed her outrage to boil over.

Striding to and fro, folding and unfolding her arms, clenching her fists, she silently fulminated against him. The presumption! The callous, arrogant self-satisfaction!

"I suppose I could marry her!" "Could you, indeed, my dearest Colonel!" she muttered between her teeth. "How very self-sacrificingly kind! What an obliging thought! And you could even overcome your repugnance so much as to bed me, so that my child might be Anglo-Saxon. Very considerate indeed! Shows such a distinguishing regard, to be sure! How exceedingly thoughtful of you it was to save me from the Bai's horrid embraces—at the cost of a slight misunderstanding or two! You need not have troubled yourself, I assure you! I had *rather* be embraced by the Bai!"

And then, giving up all pretenses, even to herself, she sank down on her rumpled couch in a despairing agony of tears. Oh, it's not true, it's not true! I love him, I love him! It's burning my heart out! And all I am to him is a hideous anxiety, an encumbrance that he had better take to bed so—so that I shall know how to go on when some amir carries me off!

Love is a fever, Cal had said. I feel as if I were being stretched on a rack. Sister, you have no idea! But I have, my dear Cal, his sister had silently assured him. I know what you mean only too well.—In fact it was his description of his plight that had sharpened her perceptions of her own. When had it begun? She could not say. How could it end? There was no hope of Cameron returning her feelings—no hope whatsoever. "You are too disparate in everything," Miss Musson had said, and she had spoken nothing but the truth. He would never entertain such a notion. He thought of her as an irksome responsibility. He had loved once and would not be caught twice in that agonizing snare—and who could blame him? He was a rover, besides—would probably never settle again anywhere. His end would be like that of his wife and child—bare bones scattered on some mountainside.

Writhing in misery, shame, and anguish, Scylla thought that she would never find forgetfulness in sleep. But, astonishingly, in the end she did. The day's exhaustion suddenly took effect, and she sank into merciful blankness and lay totally inert, heavy as a sheepskin pegged out in the waters of a mountain brook.

For what period of time she had slept she could not tell; but suddenly she was roused, she could not say how, by the presence of somebody beside her. Sound there was none—but she had a perception of warmth, breathing, awareness—then a hand grasped hers in silence: two arms went around her, two lips met hers. Confused, languid, and dizzy after this abrupt awakening out of her brief and heavy slumber, she was inclined to think it a dream; she had had such dreams before. But this seems *real,* she thought bewilderedly. These arms, these lips; the prickling of a beard. Could I have imagined that? Or the strength, the weight of this body accommodating itself to hers, the desperate urgency of the stroking, caressing touches, the demanding kisses, the wilder and wilder excitement? *Could* I have imagined this? He has come, she thought, in spite of what my guardian said, he has come—not because he thought it right or prudent but because he wanted to! He has longed for this, he wanted it just as much as I did—oh, my dearest, dearest Rob! But no wonder he is so silent—and so will I be too—she thinks it unnecessary—*folly*—better if she does not know, for the present, at least. Oh, but something as marvelous as this cannot be folly! Her whole body was vibrating like—like the great horse on the mountainside, the Asp-i-Dheha—and when he drove into her, with a great gasping shudder of joy and triumph, it was all she could do not to cry out too, in triumph and wonder. So it was of *this* that you wanted to warn me! But you need not have been so concerned for me. It could not have been like this with anybody else. I shall be safe, now, forever; defended by knowledge, protected by love.

He murmured something, yearning and tender, nuzzling his head in her neck. "Hush, love!" she whispered, but he murmured it again, and this time she heard.

"Sripana!"

Suddenly stone-cold with terror, Scylla raised herself on her elbow. Night had paled, infinitesimally; dawn was not here yet, but it was on the way; dimly, now, she was able to see.

And what she saw was her brother Cal.

XIII

"Down the *well?*" Fanny repeated half incredulously. She could only breathe with difficulty; it was hard to speak. "My baby is *down the well?* How *could* he be?"

"Oh, ma'am! That's what we none of us know!"

But Fanny had not waited to hear what Mrs. Strudwick had to say.

With a kind of awed respect—not unmixed with gloating curiosity— the crowd parted to let her through as she hurried across the grass to the wellhead.

Her little flower border had been much trampled by many feet. She knelt trembling in the mud, regardless of her best sprig muslin, and looked over into the narrow brick shaft, which seemed to go darkly down forever. A faint, a very faint cry came up from far below.

"Is he badly hurt?" she whispered. "How can he be reached? How did it happen?"

How, indeed, could it have happened? Little Thomas was unable to crawl yet. Suppose he had fallen from his cradle, twenty yards away under the weeping ash, it was wholly impossible that he should have managed to make his way as far as this, let alone clamber over the low stone wall. And why had the lid been open? The servants had strict orders to keep it closed at all times, save when drawing water.

The cry came again.

"He's not in the water—he is not drowned?"

"No, 'ee bain't in the water, missus," a grizzled man said—vaguely, Fanny recognized him; he was Daintrey, one of the bricklayers working on Thomas's addition to the house. "Lucky for 'ee the water in the owd quill be turble low, 'count o' this drought we been having; that saved the nipper from drowning, reckon. 'E be stuck, like, on a spong o' rock what juts out down thurr; 'countable okkerd it do be getting the bucket past it now an' agen. 'E be just about resting on it, thanks be."

"Hope 'e don't slither offen it," somebody gloomily said.

"Suppose we gets a haitch o' rain, an' the water come down in a lavant," somebody else suggested. "It'll rise up an' drown the dawlin'."

"But can he not be rescued?" Fanny frantically said. "Why does nobody go down after him?"

She looked desperately around at the ring of faces. "Jem? Goble? Can you not—?"

But Goble seemed to have been overwhelmed by a fit of prayer. He was kneeling on his leather apron in the mud and chanting, " 'They shall go down to the bars of the pit, when our rest together is in the dust.' "

This last seemed to be in reference to Jem, who now brought a candle and held it over the edge of the well, endeavoring to show Fanny where the problem lay.

"Ye see, missus, 'tis wide enow up atop here, but lower down the owd quill do become larmentable narrer. 'Tis on'y just wide enow to take the bucket, see? I'd goo down on a rope, and gladly, arter the nipper, but I be too broad in the beam."

Jem, indeed, was a big, broad-shouldered boy, but even so—"Are you *sure*, Jem?" Fanny asked.

"Sartin sure, missus. Daintrey an' them, they h'isted me down thurr afore, but I stuck fast; cardenly they drug me up agen."

"But then what is to be done?"

"Could send for a looksman and borrow his bilbo? Hook out the liddle 'un," somebody suggested.

Surely, Fanny thought, there must be a more suitable implement than a shepherd's crook nearer to hand.

"'Appen us might use a weed hook—or a ditch hook—or a Cannerbury hoe?"

Jem ran off to the shed and came back with a Canterbury hoe, which was lowered on the end of a rope.

"Pray take care!" Fanny cried beseechingly.

The rain now came on harder.

"Let me fetch ye a cloak, ma'am," said Mrs. Strudwick solicitously, and did so, draping it around the shoulders of Fanny, who hardly noticed the attention.

"Can you not reach him?" she demanded as the third attempt with the Canterbury hoe proved unavailing.

"'Tisn't that, missus; but the hoe do slip off 'thout gripping, simmingly, an' we dassn't furrage about, 'fear of tipping the liddle feller off'n the rock. 'Tis a hem setout!"

"Oh, dear God! What can be done?"

"'E be still lively enow, anyways," someone said hearteningly. "Hark at 'im grizzle!"

Indeed the baby's cries, because of the rain, or possibly because he had been scraped by the hoe, now became louder.

"Soon it will be dark. What shall we do then?" Bet said with what seemed like a kind of gloomy relish.

Fanny had an inspiration.

"Jem! Pray run up to Petworth House and ask for Lord Egremont!"

"Ah—I'll fet'n anon, missus! That be a 'countable good notion!" said Jem, and ran off.

"I am sure *he* will know what to do," Fanny said hopefully to Bet.

For though the ring of men around the well seemed kindly enough disposed toward her, she could not feel that their intelligence was of a high order. Moreover they appeared rather inclined to regard the emergency as an interesting event on its own merits, a kind of entertainment to be relished for its drama, rather than a challenge requiring any solution by *them*.

Some, indeed, muttered that it was the will of 'Im up there, and it was best to let such matters alone.

"Ah, I allus did say this was a proper unked owd spot! They do say as 'ow the owd monks still haunts around, from the monastery as used to be here in Queen Mary's time."

"Arr! My owd 'ooman, she saw a black Token down this-a-way on Andring Eve. An' it beckoned to her, but she ran t'other way."

"'Tis larmentable ellynge, here, come bat-flit time. Ye can hear the owd aps tree a-groaning an' the house do give a skreek or a skreel, now an' now; *I* wouldn't live in 'er, not nohow, not for a whole trug o' gold guineas."

To turn the talk from this depressing and unprofitable vein, Fanny asked:

"Can nobody tell me how the baby contrived to fall into the well?"

Heads were shaken. Nobody knew. The bricklayers all asseverated that they had taken pains to make sure the well cover was always closed. Goble, interrupted in his orisons, agreed.

"Ah, she were shut, right enow, time I done watering my greens and brockyloes."

Jemima swore, again and again, that she had only left the baby for a moment, to run indoors and get an umbrella to put over him, as it was coming on to fret with rain. But why hadn't she taken the baby in with her, as it was raining? Fanny asked. "Oh, it didn't look to be coming on muchly, ma'am. If you ask *me*," Jemima said with a darkling glance around her, "'twas liddle Miss Patty as done it! You know how she is—forever tormenting and teasing Master Tom, don't I watch her like a hawk."

"What?" exclaimed Fanny. "You think that Patty—oh no, impossible!"

Privately, it was true, Fanny did believe her youngest stepdaughter capable of *conceiving* such an act—especially when suffering from such a severe disappointment as she had that day—but it was doubtful whether Patty would be physically capable of it. Thomas was a large, heavy baby; his inertia and slowness in learning to roll over had made him unusually stout for his age.

"I don't believe Patty could carry him so far. And you say that you were gone only a couple of minutes," Fanny pointed out.

" 'Count it might ha' been a *liddle* longer—time Missus Strudwick ast me to hurry an' help her in wi' the wash afore it got wet," Jemima said in a defensive tone.

"You were a-drinking a cup of morgan tea in my kitchen!" Mrs. Strudwick contradicted.

"Where is Patty now, by the bye?" Fanny asked, perceiving that it was going to be almost impossible to sift a true tale from these accounts.

"I locked her in her room," Jemima said self-righteously. "She was a-willocking around, an' getting underfoot, so I took an' shut her in."

Fanny let pass without comment the fact that Patty was supposed to be confined to her chamber in any case. Fortunately at this moment Jem appeared at a run and panted out the information that Lord Egremont was following fast behind.

" 'E'll be here drackly, missus; 'e be a-going to the town cage, fustways."

"The *jail?* But why?" Fanny demanded, greatly puzzled.

"Ah!" said Jem, proud of himself. "I ax to see owd Lordy, missus, like ye said, an' I tells him how 'countable narrer 'tis, down thurr. 'Then we'll be needing a 'countable skinny feller to goo down arter the babby,' says Lordy, 'an' the place to find un's in the jail, where the prisoners gits only the vittles they needs an' nothing extry. Tell your missus I'll be down wi' the skinniest poacher or pickpocket they have in the place.' "

And indeed, hardly more than three minutes later, Lord Egremont himself came down the lane, cheerful and good-natured-looking as always, with his hat tipped onto the back of his head, accompanied by the tallest, thinnest, palest man that Fanny had ever laid eyes on, clad in the prison garb of dark-colored waistcoat and breeches and coarse shirt with different-colored sleeves.

"Massypanme," muttered Jem. "I niver did see one nigher a skellington, not in all my borns! If *he* can't do it, no one in the world can!"

Lord Egremont walked rapidly up to Fanny, exclaiming, "Why, my poor child, this is a wretched affair! I was never so shocked in my life as when your garden lad told me what had happened—"

"Oh, my lord, I am sensible of my forwardness in applying to you, but indeed I knew not where else to turn—I am so unspeakably grateful—" she stammered.

"Come, come, no tears now! I dare say we shall find that it is no great matter after all," he added reassuringly. "These good fellows are apt to fall into a despondency at the least setback, you know!"

Two of the Petworth House footmen had followed Lord Egremont, bearing bundles of the rush flares known as fried straws, and they now lit these so as to allow Lord Egremont sufficient light to inspect the situation in the well.

"Hm, yes—I see how it is," he remarked. "Indeed I had no idea that well was built so narrow! I fancy the soil must have subsided, pushing the walls inward. But now, let us consider. What we need here, I fancy, is a pair of fire tongs. Have you such a thing in the house, ma'am—a pair with a decent long handle?"

"Why, yes, I fancy so, sir," said Fanny, and sent Tess running for the long-handled pair from the parlor. Meanwhile Egremont had the prisoner, whose name, it appeared, was Tom Callow, brought up to inspect the well. He peered down it somewhat wanly and nodded without speaking as Lord Egremont gave him his instructions.

Tess came back with the tongs.

"Capital; capital. Now, these must be tied to your wrists, Tom, my man—it would not do if you were to let them drop on the baby, ha! ha!—and the other ropes around your ankles—so—"

"Ah, say one thing for owd Lordy, 'e do allus know 'is mind to a marvel," someone murmured admiringly.

"The man is to go down *head foremost?*" Fanny demanded in horror as Callow was lowered over the lip of the well.

"Certainly he must," Egremont assured her. "Even he, you see, skinny though he is, would not, the right way up, be able to dangle low enough down to reach your little one. What we need is somebody with the girth of a child—but then a child's reach and strength would not be sufficient. However I am in hopes that Callow may succeed with those tongs—if not, we must find a longer implement."

A long-drawn-out, silent, tense period of time ensued. With what seemed intolerable slowness the silent Callow was gingerly lowered, several men holding onto each of the two ropes that were attached to his ankles. Fanny clenched her hands, thinking, first, of the dreadfulness of being hung upside down in a well, and second—a thought which she tried to banish—of how desperate the case must be if Callow could *not* reach the baby.

"I hope that poor fellow may be pardoned for whatever crime he has committed," she murmured in a low voice to Lord Egremont. "It is very brave of him to attempt the rescue."

"Pardoned? No, my child, that would not be right," Lord Egremont said kindly but briskly. "What he has done, he has done. However, as chief magistrate and lord lieutenant, I can see to it that his sentence is as light as possible. He stole a loaf, you know, from a bakery; bakers have to live as well as other people. But you can take Callow a basket of fruit in jail, if you wish to show your gratitude—the prisoners get meat, potatoes, bread, and buttermilk for their daily diet—I dare say they acquire a craving for greenstuff."

Callow, down the well, here let out a muffled guttural sound which the men holding the rope interpreted as a signal of qualified cheer.

"'E kicked twice, that means let down another couple o' feet," said Daintrey.

"No, 'e kicked once, to signify lug 'er up a bit," objected another man.

Daintrey overruled this man, and more rope was let out.

"Liz sent her love to you, by the bye," said Lord Egremont, kindly attempting to distract Fanny at this agitating moment. "She would have accompanied me, only she is laid up—has been, indeed, these ten days—with a putrid sore throat, and cannot leave her chamber. She would have asked you to visit her but feared to communicate the infection—Aha!"

Another, more promising signal from Callow had induced the men to begin cautiously hauling up on the ropes. Egremont went swiftly to the wellside.

"Handsomely now, my lads!—Not too fast, or you may jerk his hold —remember he grasps the child but with a pair of fire tongs—it would be easy to let go—and then all your work is for naught! Handsomely— imagine that you have the biggest carp in Burton Furnace Pond at the end of your line! Half a guinea to each of you if you bring him safe to land!"

Sweating and silent, the men continued to pull. At last Callow's feet appeared above the coping, and all who could reach him laid hold of his body. He was dragged backward over the edge, gasping, dark red in the face with effort and the effect of being upside down for so long, his temples bulging, his eyes bloodshot—but he still grimly grasped the handles of the tongs, and now, with triumph, drew into sight the damp swaddled bundle, wriggling and crying, that was little Thomas, horribly dirty and muddy but indubitably safe and alive. Fanny rushed forward and received the shrieking child in her arms, while Lord Egremont was exclaiming, "Well done! Capitally done, my good fellow!" and the other men were thumping Callow on the back and congratulating him as they untied his ropes. He stood smiling sheepishly, and Fanny, having ascertained that the child seemed unhurt, save for some bruises and scratches, handed Thomas over to Jemima and went forward to clasp Callow's hands and to thank him, over and over.

"And you too, Lord Egremont—oh, I shall remember this to my dying day! I cannot express—"

"Phoo, phoo, my dear," he said, laughing good-naturedly. "Brats will always be getting into these scrapes, as I know full well! There was never a day when mine were not up a tree or locked in a stable or being fished out of some pond—and still it is so, indeed! Is the little fellow unhurt, ma'am?"

"Yes, I think so—but it is *very* strange," Fanny said, frowning, puzzling over the contradictions of the affair. "He appears unhurt because he was so tightly swaddled around with cradle cloths—and that was how Callow was able to drag him up, I imagine—but that means he *could* not have fallen from his cradle. He must have been taken up and carried by somebody."

There was a silent pause while Lord Egremont considered this anomaly. Most of the group, the excitement now being over, had begun to trickle away. Jem silently returned the ropes and tools to the shed. Goble had disappeared on his own concerns. Bet, Jemima, and Mrs. Strudwick carried little Thomas back to the house to wash him and tend him. Tess, at a word from Fanny, ran off to summon Dr. Chilgrove. The Petworth House servants escorted the unfortunate Callow away, presumably back to his place of incarceration. But Lord Egremont still stood scratching his head, his eyes on the heavy well cover which had been lowered back into place.

"Are you aware of any who might wish your husband ill, ma'am?" he asked abruptly, at length.

"Well," faltered Fanny, "you must know, my lord, that his profession carries with it a certain unpopularity—"

"Yes; but hardly to *this* degree!"

Fanny then recollected what had occurred earlier that afternoon, on the pleasant visit to Lady Mountague, which had been quite driven from her mind by the accident.

"Curiously enough," she said doubtfully, "I was warned—this very day, indeed—that Thomas has an enemy in the town—two enemies. One is—was—I believe—his children's former governess where they lived before—a Miss Fox—but this is only hearsay."

From Lord Egremont's expression it was plain that he hardly considered an ex-governess capable of throwing a baby down a well.

"Some old maid at her last prayers! No, no, I do not believe a Miss Fox would do such a thing. Who was the other person, then, ma'am?"

"My informant did not know," Fanny told him.

"Captain Paget is still in London, I understand?"

"Yes, sir—thank God! I must beg that you will not—will not refine too much upon this occurrence, sir, when talking to him. He will be so

—so very angry—" Fanny's voice trembled as she thought of Thomas's probable reaction. His heir, his treasure, thus at risk! Whoever had done the deed certainly knew how to gauge Thomas's vulnerable spot to a nicety.

"Well—I will reflect on the matter," Lord Egremont said at length. "And will talk to your husband on his return. Do not put yourself in a taking, my dear—I will not agitate him unduly! I know he tends to be a trifle sidy, as we say in these parts. But now—do not you be standing any longer in the rain, or you will be laid up like my Liz."

Fanny felt that she ought to ask him in and offer him a glass of wine, but he walked off unceremoniously, giving her a friendly smile and nod.

"Oh, pray give dear Liz my love—my *best* love!" she called impulsively after him. He waved his hat in reply and disappeared around the bend in the lane.

Fanny moved slowly toward the house. By now dusk was beginning to shroud the valley; a rare, rainy evening, for that splendid summer, was setting in, wet and windy. Shivering, huddling her cloak around her, Fanny recalled some of the remarks about the Hermitage that she had heard earlier.

"I allus did say this was a proper unked spot. . . ." "*I* wouldn't live in 'er, not for a whole trug o' gold guineas." Absurd, she had thought at the time; idle talk of villagers who enjoyed scaring themselves with follies. The Hermitage had always felt like a warm and welcoming house to her; she loved it, despite the adversities of her situation, and she felt that it had responded. But now, suddenly, passing the wind-tossed branches of the weeping ash, entering through the garden door, she sensed a different atmosphere—not, exactly, that the house was hostile, but that it was uneasy, mournful, *waiting for something to happen.* I am being fanciful, Fanny thought wearily, pushing back the damp hair from her forehead. I have had a fright and am thinking foolish nonsense, childish fancies; I will put on a warm gown and tidy myself to receive Dr. Chilgrove, and then I will feel better.

It was at that moment that Fanny heard, for the first time, the house give its shriek. She had wondered, earlier, what the man meant when he said, "Ye can hear the house give a skreek"; now, with her own ears, she heard it: an indescribably sad, eerie, keening wail. *Was* it the house, or the ash tree outside moaning in the wind? The sound was repeated twice, then no more. I *must* stop imagining things, Fanny repeated to herself, and went on toward her chamber.

Thomas returned to Petworth next day. As it chanced, he and Captain Holland stopped first at Petworth House, to report to Lord Egremont on the success of their trip and deposit a quantity of equipment in the tennis court, which had been adapted into a drill hall. Thomas, therefore, heard from Lord Egremont the story of his son's rescue from the well, and Fanny was spared the task of breaking the news to him. He arrived home in a predictably black mood, ready to castigate all the females of the household for not keeping better watch over the baby. Even Mrs. Baggot came in for her share of commination, but she retorted sharply that minding the baby was no part of her duty and so Captain Paget might please to remember. Fanny, overhearing the last part of the dialogue as she came downstairs with the doctor who had called in to inquire how the baby went on, was moved to hope that Thomas might consider what a very inessential part Mrs. Baggot played in the household and revise his decision to keep her on; but the nurse walked off composedly enough, only her high color betraying her vexation, and Thomas, with equally high color, came to put stringent questions to the doctor regarding his son's welfare.

Dr. Chilgrove was reassuring. No: thanks to the thickness of his wrappings, the baby seemed to have sustained remarkably little harm. One of his fists slightly scraped—a bruise or two—and a bit of grit in his eye, which the doctor had removed on the previous evening: these were all his injuries. No concussion, no fractures, and, so far as could be ascertained, no psychological damage.

"Are you *sure*, Doctor?" said Thomas menacingly. "If it should prove otherwise in time to come—when it might be too late to call in more expert advice—"

"Tush, my dear fellow! I will take my affidavit that the child hardly knew he was out of his crib! Infants of that age, you must know, are amazingly impervious to such mishaps; and your great boy is as robust as any I have seen—thanks to the excellent care and principles employed in his rearing," he added with a bow toward Fanny, who interpreted this, correctly, as an attempt to shield her from Thomas's displeasure.

"That may be," Thomas snapped nonetheless. "But if *you*"—to Fanny—"had taken him with you on the visit to Lady Mountague, instead of considering only your own selfish enjoyment, the accident would have been averted."

"No—no—my dear Captain Paget," said the doctor hastily, "I could not have sanctioned such an excursion—in fact I *did* not, did I, ma'am? Such a long carriage ride—on a warm day—folly, folly! Infants should be kept quiet, not jauntered about the countryside in carriages." So saying, the doctor made his escape, before becoming further embroiled in domestic dissension.

"I am going to get to the bottom of this business—if I have to call in the Bow Street runners!" declared Thomas ominously, and he summoned all the members of his household into the dining room for an interrogation which soon had most of the females in hysterical tears. However none of his stormings or threats of dismissal could elicit any information regarding the baby's accident.

"Mayhap some piker or mumper or didicai come in and done it," suggested one of the workmen hopefully.

"Fiddlestick, man! Why should one of the gipsies have a grudge against me?" said Thomas impatiently.

"More like 'tis the liddle maid your own darter as done it," grunted Daintrey. This brought a chorus of agreement. "Arr! Dunnamany times I seen 'er a-tormenting the babby, time the nursegirl warn't there to frap 'er knuckles."

"What? You *dare* to suggest that my own child could do such a thing?"

Thomas's wrath was terrible, but it could not modify the popular verdict, and at last, dismissing the servants and workmen to their duties, he turned on Fanny.

"What is this, Frances? You allow my own child to be accused to my face, without speaking a word in her defense?"

As always, his fury made Fanny feel physically sick, but she clenched her hands, digging her nails into her palms, and replied with as much calm as she could muster:

"It is true, Thomas, that Patty has a very jealous, teasing disposition where the baby is concerned, and I have a number of times been obliged to reprimand her quite sharply for disturbing him; but in the present instance I think the accusation is unmerited; I do not believe she is to blame."

"Oh, *indeed?* You are graciously pleased to believe that she is not to blame? And on what is this opinion based, may I ask?" Thomas inquired savagely.

"Come upstairs," Fanny replied, "and we will try a simple test."

"If I find that the child *is* responsible," muttered Thomas, following, "I will thrash her until she—If she is responsible, God help her— and God help *you*, for allowing such a situation to develop!"

The baby was in his crib today, with Jemima keeping vigilant watch over him. Patty, whose nettle rash was still present, though abating, kept her bed in the adjoining room, listlessly snipping up lengths of colored silk with scissors which she had purloined from Fanny's work-bag. Fanny, anticipating this moment, had purposely refrained from questioning the child about little Thomas's accident and had forbidden Jemima to do so; now she called her stepdaughter:

"Patty, come here to your papa and me a moment; we wish to see how strong you are."

"Why?" demanded Patty suspiciously at once. However she could not resist a chance to demonstrate her capabilities, and soon came running through the door in her nightgown with a conceited smirk on her face. "What do you wish me to do?" she asked.

"Your papa," said Fanny, forestalling Thomas, who was about to speak, "does not believe that you are strong enough to lift little Thomas out of his cot. Whereas I am sure that you can."

"Of course I can!" said Patty proudly, and she ran to the cot and endeavored to hoist out the baby. However, owing to the height of the cot and the very considerable weight of little Thomas, this, in fact, proved quite beyond her power; she could not even raise him off the pillow. After several minutes she had to admit defeat, and Thomas obliged her to desist, saying shortly:

"That will do, child; do not upset the baby any further. Go back to bed. And, Patty," he added grimly, "if ever I hear of you touching or tormenting little Thomas, I shall give you such a beating—with my belt!—that you will not be able to sit down for a week after. Do you understand?" Crestfallen and frightened, she ran back to her bed and hid under the covers.

Thomas said coldly to Fanny, "That was well thought of, Frances, and should suffice to give the lie to any calumniators who make such a suggestion in future. But it still leaves us with the question of who committed the crime. I can see I shall have to call in the constables."

Here Bet, who had inquisitively followed upstairs, blurted out:

"But, Lord, Papa, don't you think it very likely that it was Miss Fox who did it? She was such a whining, sneaking, prying miserable creature—it is just the kind of thing she *would* do, I dare say!"

"*Miss Fox?*" Thomas's high color left him completely; he went perfectly white. "Are you clean out of your wits, girl? What should Miss Fox have to do with the matter?—Whom do you mean, in any case? What Miss Fox?"

"Why, you know who I mean, Papa, Miss Fox who used to be our governess. She has come to lodge in the town—we heard so yesterday when we was at Lady Mountague's—did we not, Stepmamma?" Bet artlessly divulged, without, however, mentioning that it was her own sister's husband who had mentioned the matter. "So do you not think, Papa, that it is likely—"

But, with an inarticulate exclamation, Thomas had turned and plunged out of the room, leaving the females to stare at each other.

Thomas was seen no more at home that day. The weather continued gray and rainy, the garden uninviting, and Goble so strange and distracted in his manner that Fanny was almost afraid to go near him. Walking out to ask him if there were enough strawberries for dinner, she heard him mutter:

"Leave a babby under the owd asp tree, can ye wonder if the asp maid abuses 'im? Arr, I shouldn' wonder if 'twas *she* throwed 'im down, powerful aggy, she be, an' can you blame 'er, so tied up and throttled as she be? Better to 'a' left 'im in the apple terre, apple treeses 'ont bear no grudges."

Shivering under his wild wondering eye, Fanny retreated to the house again. Who could he imagine the *asp maid* to be? The spirit of the tree?

Later in the day, risking Thomas's displeasure, Fanny went on two errands into the town. The first took her to the jail.

The Petworth Bridewell was a decent-sized stone building with a notice carved on a slab over the portal informing the passer-by that it had been erected on that spot in 1788 at the expense of the third Earl of Egremont to a design made by J. Wyatt Esquire.

Old Boxall, the jailer—who resembled some ancient Nibelung hobbling out of his crevice in a rock—would have been pleased to show Fanny over the entire building.

"It be a main fine jail, ma'am—ye'll never see a better. Owd Lordy had 'er builded, acos the jail we had afore was so tarnal damp, a-many prisoners died o' the jail fever, 'thout ever coming to trial." Fanny shuddered. "But it bain't so now, missus! They gets a dry cell apiece, two pun' o' bread a day, decent thick cloes, an' looked over by a surgeon does they so much as complain o' the rheumatiz."

Nevertheless, Fanny had no wish to see over the place. She left her basket of provisions for Callow and promised to bring more every day that he was there. Boxall, however, was loath to see her go; it was not often that gentry-ladies visited his domain.

"It be a rare different place now, missus, from when your owd gardener Goble did see a Token 'ere. But that were in the owd jail, see, afore Lordy 'ad 'er pulled down."

"*Goble?* Was he here? In the jail?" said Fanny, startled. In spite of the recent strangeness in his manner, Goble seemed such a respectable character that it was hard to imagine his going to jail.

"For debt, it wurr. 'E tuk on another man's debt; the more fule 'e," said Boxall with some scorn. "An' then the press gang got 'im an' 'e wurr obleeged to go to sea. But while 'e wurr in the jail 'e did see a Token."

"A Token? You mean—a phantom?"

"A Token," Boxall agreed, nodding his aged head up and down. "It wrung its pore hands something crool, an' huffed an' hollered till owd Goble was all of a vlother; 'e couldn' get no sleep 'count of its hollerings and carryings on. 'Remember pore Ned Wilshire,' the Token said, 'what died in this jail. Remember me!'" This was Boxall's most notable story, polished by much telling and retelling during the last twenty-three years, and he invested the specter's words with great dramatic emphasis, fixing his pale ancient eyes on those of Fanny.

He had never had such a gratifying reaction from an auditor.

"*Wilshire?*" she whispered, pale with astonishment, gazing at him wide-eyed. "You say there was a prisoner called Ned Wilshire who died in this jail?"

"Not in *this* one, missus," Boxall repeated patiently. "'Twas in the owd jail, what Lordy 'ad pulled down."

"When was this?"

"Over a score of years agone. When I was a young man in me forties."

"Then if Wilshire died here," pursued Fanny, "where would he be buried?"

"Likely 'e'd be down i' the new graveyard near to Hampers Green way; they doesn't want jailbirds stodding up the Bartons' graveyard nigh to your place. Rackon that's whurr 'e'll be."

Nodding her thanks, Fanny left the disappointed Boxall, who was just on the point of telling his Token story all over again. She walked on, her empty basket over her arm, doing sums in her head.

Thomas had been five years older than his half brother Edward Wilshire—Thomas was now forty-eight, so his brother would have been forty-three—he had died "over a score of years agone"—so he would have been twenty-one or twenty-two—yes, it was feasible that the Ned Wilshire who had died in Petworth jail had been Thomas's unhappy half brother. Then *that* was why—yes, it came back to her now that, on her first evening at the Hermitage, Bet had said her father had some objection to living in Petworth. No wonder, if his brother had died here in disgrace! Knowing Thomas, he must have been anxious lest his connection with the prisoner should ever come out; though there seemed little reason why it should, since the names were different.

Occupied in these reflections, Fanny walked at a quick pace through the great gates of Petworth House and, without giving herself time to become nervous or change her mind, rang the bell at the main door which, as usual, stood open. A manservant asked her business, and she announced firmly that she wished to inquire after the health of Mrs. Wyndham, and see her, if it were possible.

"Sure, ma'am, she be in the library, an' I reckon she'll be main glad to see ye," said the friendly if unpolished footman, and led Fanny off to the left, adding, "'Tis Missus' fust day out of her chamber; she've been in the sheets three weeks, nigh, larmentable ornery she've bin, ever sin' the big randy."

"So I heard yesterday, and I am very sorry for it," said Fanny.

A voice from the library called, "Is that Mrs. Paget?" and Fanny came around a screen to see Liz reclining on a sopha, her face alight with expectation.

"Oh, my dear friend, I have been so wearying to see you! But Chilgrove said my complaint might be contagious, and my conscience would not allow me to send out a call for your company, or even to tell how I was, lest you come and take the infection. But I am so *very* glad you have come! Especially since George told me about the dreadful accident to your baby! What a fright you have been in! Is he really quite unhurt?"

Fanny was touched that Liz should inquire after the baby when she herself was plainly still far from well. She looked very pale, waxen, and was a great deal thinner than when last seen; in spite of being carefully arranged, her curling gold-brown hair had lost its luster and her eyes their sparkle. Fanny's conscience smote her that she had been harboring censorious and unkind thoughts of her friend; at the sight of Liz her suspicions melted totally away. She hastened to make light of little Thomas's misadventure and inquire how Liz really did.

"For indeed you look sadly pulled down."

"Oh, it was a shocking bore, but I am better now," sighed Liz. "And it made an excuse to bundle all our guests out of the house, including that viper Henriques, who I could see was rendering himself disagreeable to you. I am truly sorry for that; the man is a pest, and quite without principle, but the trouble is, there is no getting rid of him. He was a friend of George's in the wild days, when George belonged to the Four-in-Hand Club and the Prince of Wales's set, and now, when he wishes to stay here, George is too good-natured to say no. Thank heaven he was afraid of taking the infection, and departed to find some other accommodating hosts.—But tell me how you go on, my dear friend? And how is that curmudgeonly husband of yours?"

Somehow, without having the least intention of doing so, Fanny found herself relating the story of her visit to the jail and Boxall's astounding revelation.

"Is it not strange, Liz? My poor brother-in-law dying in that jail, and *Goble* having seen his ghost there. Do you believe in ghosts, Liz?"

"I have never seen one myself," Liz admitted. "But I remember hearing George speak of this occurrence—indeed at one time it was a well-known tale, all over the town. George used to think very highly of Goble, you know—he was employed as a gardener here before he was impressed—and George would have taken him on again when he came back from his naval service; but Goble would not; he said he was disgraced. But how could he have imagined the specter? Very likely he had never known Wilshire, who was not a native of the town. It *must* have been a real specter!"

"Goble is so strange now," Fanny confessed. "I am half afraid of him. He was muttering something today about the *ash maid*—saying, I think, that it was she who had flung little Thomas into the well."

"The ash maid? He has been reading Theocritus!" said Liz, laughing. "If it were young Talgarth, now, I would not be surprised. Were not the ash maids hollow dryads who came out of trees to lure travelers to destruction?—But do you not think, Fanny," she went on in a more serious tone, "is it not possible that it was *Goble* who put your baby in the well? As a kind of revenge on Thomas, perhaps, for the death of Ned Wilshire?"

"But why *now?* And how could he possibly know that Thomas was

Ned Wilshire's brother?" Fanny began. Then, however, she recollected that Goble had been used to push old Mrs. Wilshire about the garden in her wheel chair. He might have discovered from the old lady—yes, he might—

"Good heavens!" she burst out. "Liz! What had I best do?"

"Well, it is only conjecture," Liz said quickly. "Best do nothing, is my advice. Your husband is such a hothead, you know! Wait and watch. Do not leave the baby unattended."

"No, *indeed* I will not."

Greatly preoccupied with this idea, Fanny shortly afterward took her leave, saying that she had tired Liz for long enough. Lord Egremont came in as she was going, greeted her in friendly fashion, asked after the baby, and offered to send her home in the carriage. She was laughingly declining this offer when Liz contradicted her.

"Yes, George—Fanny would like to be driven down to the new graveyard. She wishes to lay some flowers on her mother-in-law's grave."

"Oh, but I have none with me—" Fanny began; but Lord Egremont had already given the order, and at the same time dispatched a footman for some blooms from the glasshouses. Two beautiful bouquets of roses and lilies were brought before Fanny had time to utter more than a few words of protest, and Lord Egremont handed her into the carriage.

The graveyard lay a quarter of a mile outside the town by the Billingshurst road upon a grassy eastward slope. There were very few graves in it, as yet, and the planted trees were still young, hardly more than saplings; the place was kept, still, mainly for persons coming from outside the town who had not family plots in the Bartons graveyard near the church.

Fanny, having laid one of her bouquets on the newly turfed resting place of Thomas's mother, which as yet lacked a headstone, turned to scrutinize the rest of the stones, of which there were fewer than a score. Ned Wilshire's must be one of the oldest here, she thought, if he died more than twenty years ago.

Her search was not difficult. A stone in a corner by the hedge that seemed somewhat older than the rest caught her attention, and, crossing to it, she read the brief inscription: "Edwrd. Wilshire Esq. A Stranger to this Town. 'Many that sleep in the dust of the earth shall awake.' Went to his rest 1773."

Seventeen seventy-three. Thomas would have been twenty-three, and his brother eighteen or thereabouts.

Poor young man, Fanny thought. No doubt he was foolish and dissipated, but so were many young men of his years; he might, with increased age, have mended his ways. It did not occur to Fanny at this moment that she herself was only seventeen; so many cares sat on her shoulders that she felt, often, older than the Sphinx. She laid her flowers on the grave and was returning to the carriage when an oddity struck her; among the graves of strangers, many neglected, with grass long and shaggy or nettles growing on them, that of Ned Wilshire was kept clipped and neat. She turned back to verify the fact: yes, the grass was carefully scythed, even the stone looked as if it had been cleaned. Could it be possible that Thomas had paid this attention to his brother's grave? Or hired someone to do it? Puzzling over this, she had walked a few steps away when a movement caught her eye: somebody who had been kneeling beside a distant grave stood up; she was a little confused to recognize the young gardener, Andrew Talgarth. Still, her errand to the graveyard was a perfectly proper one. She went forward to greet him. He had, she saw, been placing a very beautiful bunch of wild flowers—honeysuckle, campion, cowslips, herb Robert, traveler's-joy—on the grave of Jennifer Talgarth, dearly beloved wife of Robert Talgarth and mother of Andrew, born in Llandovery 1740, died in Petworth 1790.

"My mam always liked the wild flowers best," explained Andrew, giving Fanny his slow, wide smile. "So in summertime I try to bring her over a new posy every two–three days; my da comes over on Sundays but he's not so young as he used to be and he finds it a fair step from his house in the dillywoods. Lord Egremont'd send the carriage for him, but that he won't allow."

"Lord Egremont sent the carriage for me," said Fanny, smiling too. "And the flowers! There is no end to his kindness."

It occurred to her that if Andrew Talgarth were of an inquisitive nature he would immediately notice the identical bouquets on the new grave of Mrs. Wilshire and the old grave of poor Edward; it would be simple for him to make the connection and form his own conclusion; but she was certainly not going to stoop to any deceptions about it; she liked him much too well for that. Indeed she went on:

"I have only just discovered that my husband's brother, who died long ago, is also buried in this graveyard. I was quite surprised to find his grave so well tended."

Talgarth's brilliant dark blue eyes turned to follow the direction of her glance; he said:

"Ah, that grave's been well tended ever since old Goble came back from the sea."

"Goble? It is he who keeps it neat? Why should—"

"Because he saw the ghost!" Andrew said, smiling. "It had a rare, sobering effect on old Goble, that phantom did, by all accounts! And I'm not saying I mightn't be the same. If *I* saw a spook, likely *I'd* take care to keep its resting place tidy."

"Good heavens," said Fanny faintly.

Now recalling that all this time she was keeping Lord Egremont's carriage waiting at the gate, she moved on, then, turning back, said impulsively to Andrew Talgarth:

"I was not able to thank you as I ought for the assistance you rendered me that day in Petworth House gardens when I was being persecuted by that odious, odious man! I can hardly express to you how *deeply* grateful to you I was—how *immensely* relieved to see you come along that path—"

His face broke into its flashing smile again. "Ah, it was nothing, ma'am! I didn't like to see you so affrighted; I'd have been glad to throw the chap into a holly bush.—Though I dare say it was punishment enow for him to have me turn up when I did—the poor besotted fool!" He glanced aside, seemed to murmur something—could it have been "Who's to blame him?"—then, turning full to Fanny once more, said seriously, "Any way I can help you, ma'am, at any time, I shall be very happy. You can always call on Andrew Talgarth. I hope you know that?" The blue eyes met hers again, he gave a little bow, rather dignified, then turned and strode away up the slope toward a gate that led out onto the North Chapel road.

Feeling strangely peaceful, Fanny rode home in Lord Egremont's carriage.

This mood of calm lasted through that day and the next and helped her to bear with fortitude the miserable atmosphere in the house, compounded of the servants' nervous hostility under Thomas's threats, his air of black vindictiveness against the whole world, Patty's sulks, and Bet's uneasy excitement and envy of her sister's married state. Only little Thomas, the subject of all this upheaval, seemed unchanged; he slept a great deal of the time; roused to take nourishment; then slept again.

Thomas, to Fanny's infinite relief, now passed several nights in his garden house. Since Fanny had no wish for the distasteful presence of Mrs. Baggot in her bedchamber, she did not summon the nurse, but, as she had done while Thomas was in London, requested Tess at night and morning to help her put on and remove her corselet (rightly guessing that Thomas would instantly notice if she left off the repellent garment). She had been a little exercised in mind as to how to explain it to Tess, but in the end simply said that it had been recommended as an aid to posture, leaving Tess to draw her own conclusions.

Tess accepted this, merely remarking, "Geemany, ma'am, I dunno why *you* need sich a contraption, seeing as you allus holds yourself upright as an ellet-rod. If it had been Miss Bet, now!"

On the third morning after Thomas's accident, Tess appeared in a state of hardly suppressed excitement which burst out as she began the lacing up.

"Oh, ma'am, sich doings! That poor lady as you sent to lodge with my auntie Rapley—Missus Fox—"

"Yes? What of her?" Fanny asked with an instinctive tremor and sinking of the heart.

"She've been found, missus! Drownded! In the pool, down to Haslingbourne mill!"

"*What?* Oh, how dreadful! Who found her?"

"My cousin by marriage Charley Heather. He work down to Haslingbourne as a miller's man, an' when he went to open the sluice gate he see a bit of a feather, yaller, an', thinks he, *That* be no water bird, and he looks furder, an' sees the poor lady a-floating drownded among the mare's tails an' tussocks."

"Oh, my God!" Fanny felt so sick and unstrung that she had to sit down on her bed.

"Hold up, ma'am! I shouldn't ha' told ye so sudden. I'll get ye a cup of water."

"Thank you, Tess. Just leave me a moment and I—I will soon be better."

"D'you think 'twas she, ma'am, as tried to drown poor little Mas'r Thomas, an' then got sad-like, an' dreesome, a-thinking of what she'd done, an' throwed herself in the mill pool?"

"I do not know, Tess," Fanny said faintly. "Perhaps so."

But to herself she added, Perhaps that is what we were meant to think.

True or not, this, at any rate, was the explanation popularly held in the town for Miss Fox's untimely end. A crowner's quest was held in the new town hall—much to the disgust of Thomas, who bitterly deplored and resented the unfortunate publicity of the whole affair; and it was decided that she must have made the attack on little Thomas while in an unbalanced state of mind, and had then drowned herself in a fit of remorse. Many people in the town came forward to say that they had seen the strange lady walking about wringing her hands or distressfully muttering to herself, "hackering an' stammering like she were only half baptized," as the town constable put it; so this seemed a reasonable explanation for both occurrences. Goble was not present at the inquest; he was laid up in the loft over the shed where he slept with one of the putrid fevers so prevalent in the town that summer;

and Mrs. Strudwick reported that he was feverish and rambling and talked no sense at all. Fanny would have visited him, but Thomas furiously forbade this, exclaiming:

"Are you mad, Frances? Do you wish to bring the contagion back to the whole family?"

Two days after Miss Fox's quiet funeral rites—she, also, was buried in the graveyard on the Billingshurst road, and a surprisingly large number of curious bystanders attended the ceremony, but the Paget family stayed away—Tess came to Fanny with a folded paper.

"The constables did come an' take all Miss Fox's things from my auntie's, ma'am—not that the poor lady had much—but they missed this, simmingly. I fund it under the mattress, time I ran up to give the room a turnout. An' I saw the name Paget on it, so I brung it to ye. 'Tis in some foreign language, though, I reckon; I couldn't read no more than the name."

The short note was, in fact, written in French. *"Si quelqu'un me trouvera morte, je veux . . ."*

> *If I should be found dead, I wish it to be known that the man responsible for my sad end is Thomas Paget, my evil genius, who used me heartlessly and despitefully, made many promises that he did not intend to keep, unkindly threw me off, and at the last, deprived me of my poor life, as he had done previously to his wife Emma.*
>
> *Maria Fox.*

The scrap of paper swam under Fanny's eyes.

"Thank you, Tess," she said at length with difficulty. "I shall have —I shall have to think what is best to be done with this. You did right to bring it to me."

Show it to Liz? was her first thought. To Lord Egremont? To Lady Mountague?

But, under such a direct accusation, Thomas must surely have the right to defend himself? He must have the right to see it first?

Papa would certainly say so.

Fanny walked swiftly out into the garden and across to Thomas's sanctum. He was there, she knew; she had seen him cross the grass after breakfast, although it was his usual day to visit the mill.

The weather was close, cloudy, and uneasy; a fidgety wind sighed in the branches of the ash tree and carried the chimney smoke over the garden in sudden blue gusts.

Fanny tapped at Thomas's door and walked firmly into the bare little room, controlling, as best she could, her inner dread.

He was there alone, sitting moodily hunched over a small wood fire. The garden room, with four outside walls and facing north, was damp and cold at all times except in the full sun.

"*Now* what is it, Frances?" he said harshly, turning to fix Fanny with an unwelcoming stare. She noticed that his eyes were bloodshot.

"Thomas . . . I think you ought to see this. It was found in Miss Fox's room."

He read the paper, puzzling slowly through the French. He had learned the language, Fanny knew, during his spell in the navy, enough to understand conversation and, she imagined, the contents of this note. As indeed it proved. Reaching the end, he gave a grunt of rage, screwed up the paper, and, before Fanny could stop him, hurled it into the fire.

"Oh!" she exclaimed. "I did not mean—Do you think you ought to have done that?"

"Yes, I should! And why not, pray?" He turned on Fanny furiously. "When that madwoman was accusing me of—*Why not?* Do you mean to suggest that I—that your husband—?"

Flinching before the look in his eyes, she murmured something about the coroner's inquest.

Thomas took her hand in a punishing grip.

"Listen to me, Frances. You are to forget that you ever saw that mad, lying note. Do you understand me? If I ever hear you speak of it again—if I ever hear that any word about it has got out—I shall know who carried the report. I shall know that *you* are mad—to give credit to such tales about your husband. Do you understand me? You will suffer for it."

He gripped her arm even tighter, until a cold sweat pearled her brow and she gave a stifled cry.

"I must do what I think is right, Thomas," she said breathlessly.

"If you mention that note," he told her, "I shall say that your wits are turned. That it was *you* who threw little Thomas down the well. I shall have you committed to Bedlam. Now go!"

Fanny stumbled out, so paralyzed by the hate and fury in his voice that the futility of his threat was no comfort to her. True, he could not accuse her of throwing her own baby down the well—she had been in Cowdray Park at the time—but she did not doubt that he would think of something just as bad. And would have no hesitation in doing it.

XIV

The town of Kabul was a handsome, prosperous, and friendly place with a great palace—built long ago by the Emperor Thaimur—on a hilltop looking north to the mountains of the Hindu Kush. The city, lying to the west of a spacious plain, ensconced in the angle between two mountain ridges, was built mainly of baked clay— golden, flat-roofed houses, tier upon tier, leading up the hillside. Among the bazaars and caravanserais there were many beautiful fountains and painted arcades. Huge red-flowering trees gave shade at street corners, walnuts and plane trees adorned the public gardens. Despite the uneasy political situation since the death of Thaimur with at least twenty of his sons struggling to obtain mastery of the country, the atmosphere in Kabul was one of luxury, comfort, and frivolity. Dancing girls performed in public places to the music of lyre and tambourine. Innumerable stalls sold wine, food, and every kind of delicacy, particularly the candied fruits for which the town was famous—preserved mulberries and rhubarb, made into a delicious conserve with lime and grape juice, candied apples, pears, peaches, quinces, licorice, and watermelon. Raspberries were preserved in ice with rose water; ice, brought down in great blocks from the mountains during the winter and kept buried in pits wrapped with straw, lay within the purchasing power of any poor citizen, even in the hottest summer.

The females had to take all these delights on trust, however (except the candied fruits, of which Cal brought them supplies every evening). Cameron was warned by a friend of his, a camel dealer in the Kashmir serai, that even here emissaries of Prince Mihal were on the lookout for a party of Kitabi, or Christians, carrying a baby with them. Also, as a known adherent of the imprisoned Mahmud, brother of the Shah Shuja', Cameron would be liable to arrest if he were recognized. He therefore thought it best to appear in the streets as little as possible, and then in careful disguise as an Arab horse dealer. He had accordingly hired a house for his party, where they must remain withdrawn from the public eye until a suitable westward-traveling caravan had been found, to which they could attach themselves.

The house consisted of two rooms, one for eating and one for sleeping. The main room had in it a sandali—a stone table built over a hole in the ground, in which a fire burned all winter long. Around this an Afghan family would sit cross-legged through the winter months—very often the legs of old persons and females were quite numb by the spring, Cameron told Miss Musson, who commented tartly that the Afghanis must be a set of idle good-for-nothings.

Miss Musson was very silent these days. Unless directly addressed, she seldom spoke. Very few of her dry shrewd comments, her brisk, pithy, ironic, yet good-natured observations were to be heard by her fellow travelers; ever since leaving the Holy Pir's mountain she seemed to have fallen into an abstraction. Because of this very uncharacteristic preoccupation and inattentiveness, she had apparently failed to remark the almost equally uncommunicative mood of her younger companions. It was, of course, not uncommon for Cal, when inspired with a poem, to be quiet and dreamy and rapt; his present behavior merely followed the usual pattern as he sat immobile, staring into space, or feverishly covered the stone table with sheets of scribbled manuscript. His long epic about the great stone horse, the Asp-i-Dheha, was well under way, and he raised no particular objections to Cameron's interdictions on the exploration of Kabul, only taking the air at dusk, disguised as an ash-smeared faqir, or a seller of shawls from Kashmir.

But for Cal's sister to be so quiet, so somber and reserved, for such a long period was far from customary, and Cameron occasionally gave her a thoughtful, troubled glance, when he could do so unobserved by herself or other members of the party. She did not appear to be ill or afflicted in any physical way that he could discover; merely sunk in a strange lethargy and lowness of spirit so profound that sometimes she had to be addressed three or four times before she heard what was said to her. She had odd flashes of anger too, though never at Miss Musson; but with the other two she frequently lost her patience in a way that was quite out of character. "Scylla's sulky as a bear these days, I can't imagine what's got into her," Cal confided to the colonel. "As a rule, you know, she's the best company in the world, never out of sorts. What can ail her, do you suppose? I ask her, but she just turns me off, or snaps at me. Can she have formed an attachment for one of those warriors back at the Bai's castle?"

"Young ladies can be very chancy creatures," Cameron answered cautiously, "though certainly your sister has up to now shown less signs of temperament than many members of her sex. I dare say she will come about if we leave her in peace."

Accordingly Scylla was left mainly to her own reflections, and these were far from happy. She would sit for hours together, sometimes, with a stricken expression in her eyes, staring out of the small window, over the descending flat roofs of Kabul, to the faraway snow-covered peaks; and her face appeared almost as frozen and immobile as the distant mountains.

On the night when the glimmer of false dawn had shown her that it was Cal, not the colonel, who had come to her bed, she had been so appalled that her first instinct had been flight, and silence. With desperate, trembling speed, she had removed herself and her few belongings from the cave. Cal was sunk in a profound, swoonlike slumber; he had rolled off the bag of feathers onto the sandy floor of the cave, so she was able to carry the bed away with her. She withdrew herself and little Chet, who slept like a dormouse in his box of hay, to another chamber, and settled down as best she might to pass the rest of the night in a state not far removed from despair. At first her main concern had been for Cal. That he had been sleepwalking she was well aware; but suppose he had woken sufficiently to realize what he had done? His sister could only pray that was not so. Meanwhile she was left with the terrifying realization that his attachment to Sripana must have gone a great deal further than anybody had suspected; the thought of the danger they must all have been in had the Bai discovered this turned her sick with horror, also the thought of Cameron's reactions had he learned about it. Her own fault paled in comparison.

Why did I not know—not guess—that it was Cal? she asked herself over and over. Why had the mental sympathy failed, that had so often united them in thought, in feeling? And each time she came back to the conclusion that for once Cal, obsessed with his own hopeless passion, and she with hers, had been deaf to each other's thought patterns, absolved from reality—or perhaps, she thought, shivering, aware in a deeper, more basic way of the other's inextinguishable need.

Besides her distress about Cal, she was left with the full understanding of her own hopeless, comfortless case; she loved Cameron, bitterly and deeply; just *how* deeply she was now made well aware; and that there was no likelihood of his reciprocating her feeling she also perfectly well understood. His cool reply to Miss Musson had made that quite clear, when she had said:

"Suppose the poor girl were to fall in love with you?"

"Well then"—and a pause—"I suppose I could marry her."

Every tone and nuance of that exchange, Scylla thought, would be stamped in her memory until the hour of her death. I might just as *well* be carried off by some amir and spend the rest of my life in his harem, she thought despairingly; I cannot imagine any other prospect that would be less wretched.

On the following day, however, her misery was mitigated by one degree. Cal slept long and late, as he often did after his epileptic seizures or during intensive, inspired spells of writing. When he finally woke and joined the others, although his sister scanned his face with close, anxious, passionate attention, she could see absolutely no sign of consciousness or guilt; he behaved to her in precisely his normal good-humored casual brotherly fashion; it was plain that the episode must have seemed to him like some fantastic, feverish dream, born out of the longing for his lost love. Thank God, Scylla thought with heartfelt sincerity, oh, thank God for that; he has been spared the guilt and horror that must otherwise haunt him all his life. And with this knowledge, her own agony of spirit was somewhat relieved. Now she had only herself to contend with. Eased in this way, she was now at liberty to reflect that she was still faced with a physical hazard. Girls in her situation—seduced girls—with a wry mouth she remembered another of the colonel's statements to Miss Musson—such girls became pregnant, such embraces were the means by which children were engendered. She knew all about this, theoretically, from her work at Miss Musson's hospital. Well—that was no matter either; with a kind of ironic inner shrug she recalled the bizarre interview with old Khalzada and Habiba in the Bai's castle. Perhaps Khalzada had intended to safeguard her against the Bai! At all events, if she did prove to be with child, she had the means to cope with the situation. Thank God again! Had Colonel Cameron known *that,* she thought with a wry chuckle, he might not have felt it needful to make his self-sacrificing proposal to Miss Musson.

It had been a huge relief to Scylla, who found the continued inactivity in the Holy Pir's cave hard to bear, that three days after these events a southward-traveling pilgrims' caravan passed by the mountain. It was in fact that same queens' procession of which the Bai had spoken to Cameron, suggesting they capture the royal ladies and hold them up to ransom. An elderly princess, the mother of one of the queens, had unfortunately died of exhaustion on the return journey from the shrine of Hazrat Imam, and the caravan had traveled around by way of the Holy Pir's mountain in order to ask if her body might be left in that sacred spot. Permission was given, and the funerary ceremonies occupied two days; after that it was a simple matter for Cameron to request that he and his companions might join the caravan. Since the mountains were known to be full of raiders, the escort of three extra men was welcomed, and the ladies were allowed to ride in the palanquin of the deceased princess. Scylla would have far preferred to ride and see the country they were passing through; but Cameron assured her that, in their present company, this was quite out of the question and she must just make the best of it. She was obliged to obey, but the long hours of traveling in stuffy semi-darkness did not improve her spirits. Miss Musson talked very little during the journey; her mind seemed far away; and Scylla found the week spent on the road to Kabul by far the most miserable part of the trip so far.

During the journey they had hardly a sight of their male companions, who, at night, slept with the armed escort of fifty sowars. Cameron had put it about that his ladies were a pair of nuns from Debuje in the Himalayas, on a pilgrimage to various Middle Eastern shrines, including Mecca, and this was incuriously accepted.

At first Scylla was relieved when, reaching Kabul, they parted from the caravan, which was continuing southward to the royal town of Kandahar. But the inactivity in the little house was even harder to bear than imprisonment in the palanquin. Consequently she was overjoyed, as Cameron had hoped, when, returning one evening, he announced that he had secured them places in a westbound caravan departing in two days' time.

"It will travel south, taking the longer route, along the Helmand River, so as to skirt the Koh-i-Baba range, and the Koh Siah, but we are lucky, since it is a horse caravan; it should take us no more than ten or twelve days to reach Herat. Unfortunately it goes no farther in our direction; but very likely we may pick up some other caravan there."

"What will it cost?" inquired Miss Musson.

"Six sequins apiece, and we must provide our own food, naturally."

Through his bazaar acquaintance, Cameron had disposed of some of the party's gold, and he now went out to procure supplies for the journey and arrange for the dispatch of their camels back to Mir Murad Beg.

Coming out of her own preoccupation somewhat at this news, Scylla noticed that Cameron seemed unusually downcast and taciturn—even more than commonly; later she learned from Cal that he had had a discouraging report of his friend and previous employer, the ex-Amir Mahmud.

"He is being kept imprisoned by his brother the Shah Shuja'; for a time he was in his own town of Herat, but Shuja' has now moved him to Kandahar, and rumor has it that he is ill, as a result of his imprisonment; I believe Rob is afraid that he may die if he is not soon released."

This news aroused in Scylla more compassionate and kindly feelings toward the Colonel than she had entertained of late.

"Poor Colonel Cameron; no wonder he looks so worried." A thought struck her. "Now that he has arranged for us to join this caravan, I wonder that he does not leave us? He must be anxious to try and rescue his friend; he is probably wishing us all at Jericho."

"Just what I said to Rob myself," Cal agreed. "And I believe that, if the caravan had gone right through to Baghdad, he might have considered leaving us to make our own way; but since it does not, he thinks it his duty to accompany us."

If Scylla had been a man she could have exclaimed, "*Damn* Colonel Cameron and what he thinks is his duty!" As it was, she gave a shrug and remarked, "Well, he must do as he thinks best; *we* certainly cannot influence his decision; one might as well order the Holy Pir's stone horse to break into a gallop.—How does your poem go, by the bye?"

"It is nearly done—I will read it to you presently—may I? And I am happy it is nearly finished, for I have had a capital new idea—I find this life of travel and movement quite famous in that way—ideas seem to bubble up all along the road, and I feel that I am writing better and better every day. Even losing Sripana"—his voice shook a little —"even that seems to have opened a door in me—opened my mind in a new direction."

Scylla was silent for some minutes; then, rousing herself, she said affectionately:

"Dear Cal! I am very glad for you. What is the idea for the new poem?"

"It concerns a tree—a great tree. For some odd reason—I do not know how it comes about—perhaps because we traveled through so many of those dark, wooded, vine-grown valleys coming down to Kabul—but ever since we left the Bai's castle, night after night, I have been dreaming about a tree, a great twisted tree."

Scylla stared at him, profoundly struck.

"Why, Cal, how strange! So have I!"

"Do you remember when we were children, we would very frequently be dreaming the same dream? You often used to remind me of what we had dreamed when we were eating breakfast, and Mamma used to scold us and say it must be nonsense."

"So I did," Scylla said slowly. "I had forgotten that. I expect—" She stopped, then said, "Very likely all the adventures we have been through together lately have brought us back into that old childhood connection which we had when our whole world was each other. But tell me about your tree. What is it like?"

"It is an ash; Odin's tree, you know, the lightning tree."

"Yggdrasil! I remember Uncle Winthrop telling us that its roots passed through the center of the world."

"The Greeks, as well as the Norsemen, worshiped ash trees," said the well-read Cal. "Hesiod quotes a myth of man being made from an ash bough. Zeus was nourished by an ash nymph, one of the Meliae, and the goddess Nemesis is sometimes represented as an ash tree."

"Nemesis: Fate . . ." Scylla shivered, remembering Khalzada's words over the salt bowl: "I see a great tree, a great twisted tree—it is a sacred tree, but far away, far in the north—a tree of great anger and power—"

The coincidence was very strange. Had the tree passed from her mind into that of her brother? Should she tell him about Khalzada's prophecy? But it made her profoundly uneasy; there was something shadowy and menacing about it; and she decided to wait until some later time when she was in better spirits. Cal, in any case, had moved on to other matters and was telling her of the Emperor Babur's tomb, which he had visited, and another, quite unexpected one—

"Just fancy, Scylla, the inscription was in English and it said, 'Here lyes the body of Joseph Hicks, the son of Thomas Hicks and Eldith, who departed this lyfe the eleventh of October 1666.' Was not that a strange thing to find in Kabul?"

"He certainly died far from home," said Scylla, and shivered as if a goose had walked over her grave.

The caravan to Herat set off several hours before dawn, and this was to remain the pattern of travel throughout the journey. Taking advantage of the cooler hours of darkness, the long string of loaded horses and mules would make as good speed as they could between 4 A.M. and noon, then rest through the hottest hours of day, then move on again between evening and midnight. Scylla and Miss Musson, heavily veiled, still in the role of holy nuns from the Himalayas, which had served so well on the previous leg of the journey, rode on mules; Cal and Cameron and the Therbah had small shaggy but powerful horses from the northern plains. The journey was uneventful. They spent several days skirting the mountain slopes forming the central massif of Afghanistan: stony hillsides covered with shrubs, wild pistachios, rhubarb, and gooseberries. Occasionally in the distance they would see a group of wild pastoral nomads with flocks of sheep or goats, and black tents, but no marauders came to attack them. The rough stony track was marked along its way with mud towers. Here and there they must climb over a mountain pass or ford a pebbly river, but these mountains were tame and unimpressive compared with the ones they had left behind. The main problem here was lack of water; as spring advanced and the weather became hotter and hotter, the rivers shrank to mere trickles, and often a day would pass without their finding any water that was fit to drink. For this reason, Cameron told them, the route became impassable during the very hot weather.

On the twelfth day they arrived in Herat.

"Why do we have to go so far north?" Scylla demanded impatiently of Cameron. "Does not Persia lie to the west of us? Why may we not strike directly westward to Isfahan?" and he replied simply, "Because there is no road, my child. The land to the west of here is one of the worst deserts in the world, the Dasht-i-Lut. No one has crossed it and survived."

"Oh," she said, quite quenched.

Herat (the Greek Aria, Cal informed his sister) was a thriving town that lay in a beautiful fertile valley, making a pleasant change from the bleak land they had passed through. The town was surrounded by a high mud wall with great towers at frequent intervals (built by Tamburlaine) and, as additional defense, a wide moat, fed by the Hari River. Herat, an important posting stage on the east–west route, had more than twenty serais where silk, wool, and manufactured articles were sold. The skyline was bulbous with the domes and minarets of mosques. In this busy place Cameron was able, without too much difficulty, to arrange for the party to join another caravan, a camel cafila this time, which was due to set out for Baghdad in four days.

Now he will surely leave us and go back to help his friend Prince Mahmud, Scylla thought.

But to her amazement—and, she thought, that of Cal and Miss Musson also—he did not. It seemed there was another friend of his, an exiled adherent of Mahmud, who now lived in Baghdad, and Cameron had decided to make contact with this man and enlist his help. He was a wealthy merchant and could probably do more, if he was willing, than many devoted but humble followers in Herat. Therefore they were to have Cameron's company as far as Baghdad.—Scylla found herself almost sorry that it was so. Since he was bound to part from them sooner or later, she could not help longing, in a kind of feverish impatience, for the parting to be over.

Cameron, however, set about calmly and capably equipping them for this longer desert journey. The distance from Herat to Baghdad, traversing the whole country of Persia, would be about sixteen hundred miles, or eighty days' journey on camelback. The road was not difficult, however, as, for most of the way, it ran across open, level plains; it could even be undertaken by wheeled vehicles during the cooler months, but both Scylla and Miss Musson were emphatic in their preference for riding.

"It will have to be camels, you understand?" Cameron warned them. "It is too hot for horses now; only camels can survive the long dry stretches."

"Then camels let it be," said Miss Musson.

Accordingly Cameron bought seven (he said it was cheaper to buy than hire, and then resell in Baghdad); five riding camels and two for baggage. They were expensive, moreover, since there was a shortage: sixty rupees apiece for the riding beasts and forty for the baggage carriers.

At the last moment Cameron's Therbah suddenly announced that he was not coming with the party; he intended to go and visit his own village to the north of Herat. Briefly, with the minimum of ceremony, he mounted the camel that had been bought for him, took his leave, and departed. Everyone was sorry to see him go, for he was such a friendly, cheerful little man; nothing ever seemed to put him out. Scylla wondered how Cameron would ever manage without him; but there seemed to be a very good understanding between the two men, and it was evident that they planned to meet again when Cameron returned to Herat.

As on the previous portion of the journey, they set out before dawn. The saddles were different from those of the Bai's camels; these consisted of a framework of four upright poles, lashed together by crosspieces, supported on a kind of mattress stuffed with camel hair. The rider sat on the mattress and, when the sun was at its hottest, could stretch a blanket over his head, its corners tied to each of the poles, and so ride along shaded by a traveling tent. In the morning the caravan would set out at a trot, which was not so bad and seemed a fairly fast rate of progress; but as soon as the sun rose the file would slow down to a walk and maintain this pace throughout the day, in order not to overtire the camels. The distance they were covering was too great to allow of carrying much fodder for the beasts, which must therefore graze along the way. These halts were exasperating to Scylla. What a dawdling method of progress this seemed! And the walking gait of a camel was torture to the rider; at the end of the first two or three days she and Miss Musson were so stiff when they dismounted that they could hardly stagger a yard until they had rubbed each other's aching backs and thighs.

There were occasional trees along the route—palms, tamarisks, and a mimosa-like tree with yellow blossoms—but for the most part the land was bare desert. The route was marked along its way by conical pyramids constructed by Shah Abbas to guide travelers. At each stage they found caravanserais built of sun-dried clay bricks, generally in the form of walled courtyards with stalls or cells around them, the walls often twenty feet high, the cells entered by arched doorways. These had been erected for the use of voyagers by various wealthy and pious persons—but they differed considerably: some were ruinous, little more than crumbling shells, while others were in a fairly good state of upkeep. Sometimes there would be a well, and palm trees giving shade, in the center of the courtyard. But often, if the day's march had been slow, the whole caravan would be obliged to pass the night in the bare desert, with the camels crouched around the outside of the camp in a ring and the humans inside. The men would strike their daggers on bits of flint to kindle fires of camel's-thorn. Sometimes Cameron or Cal managed to shoot a gazelle or a desert hare, from which the women could make soup; otherwise the party subsisted on pulse and dried fruit.

The caravanserais offered more privacy at night, with their little cell-like chambers, but these were often verminous, with hundreds of fleas hopping among the dried thorns and reeds left by previous travelers. On the whole Scylla preferred to sleep in the open, though it was alarming, sometimes, to lie shivering in the chill of the desert night under blazing stars and hear the cough of a leopard near at hand among the rocks or concealing sand dunes; at the sound the camels would all begin to roar and gurgle, half rising to their feet; the drivers would curse them and fire a few shots to discourage the leopard; nights in the open tended to be restless and wakeful. And all the way Scylla dreamed, almost every night, about a great tree; and, when she asked him, she learned that Cal did too.

Cal found the desert journey frustrating because, although in Herat he had equipped himself with various notebooks and a slab of Chinese ink which he could moisten as required, there was hardly any opportunity for writing. Consequently his poem remained mostly pent up in-

side his head and he was in a continual ferment lest he forget any particularly choice line.

"Listen, Scylla!" he would call, urging his camel alongside hers.
"Which of these do you prefer:

> *"Nine days of fire, nine piercing nights of hoar*
> *The pierced god hung upon the weeping tree*
> *Whose taproots plumb the still unfathomed core*
> *Of black Ginnunga's chasm, where the three*
> *Dread shadows spin the skeins of destiny—*

"Do you think it should be *pierced* god? Or the *impaled* god hung
upon the weeping tree?"

"You have piercing nights—just before—perhaps it should be impaled, so as not to repeat the word?"

"But the repetition is intentional, Scylla, deuce take it! The question
is, which word sounds better before god, pierced or impaled?"

Scylla gave it as her opinion that pierced sounded better. "I don't
care for the impaled god, Cal. Pray who is he, your pierced god?
Odin?"

"Of course!" he said impatiently. "Odin hung himself upon Yggdrasil for nine days to learn wisdom. Now listen to this:

> *"Nine days he knew that anguish; through his heart*
> *Gungnir the sacred shaft, which only he*
> *Might wield, held with its deadly dart*
> *Odin transfixed above the whispering sea,*
> *Mimir's dark waters, flowing to eternity.*

"What do you think of that, Scylla?"

"Your last line has twelve syllables; all the rest have ten."

"Of *course* it has, thickskull! It is a Spenserian stanza."

Scylla pondered. "If it is a Spenserian stanza, should it not have
nine lines? I believe you have ten."

"Confound you, Scylla," Cal said, laughing. "You are right!"

"What happens next?" Scylla wanted to know.

"Odin prays to the tree for wisdom, and then he creates man and woman out of two branches. Listen:

> *"At which the tree obeys, yields up its store*
> *Of wisdom. Now the god, released, renewed,*
> *Pacing with Loki on the ocean shore,*
> *Perceives two blocks of timber, roughly hewed.*
> *'Ask, be thou man!' The log of ash, imbued*
> *With soul and sense, breathes, weeps, and kneels in praise;*
> *'Embla, be woman!' Elmwood, rough and crude,*
> *Trembles, and is transformed to woman's grace.*
> *The twain are given Midgard as their dwelling place.*

"Oh, huzza, look—there's a hare—I wonder if I can drop him with one shot before he takes fright?—Why don't *you* try for him, Scylla?"

But, since quitting the Bai's castle, Scylla had quite lost interest in shooting. She watched in wonder as Cal, forgetting all about poetry for the time being, went off in happy pursuit of the hare. Sometimes she felt that, although she had been in close contact with him ever since they were born, there were parts of her brother that were a total mystery to her;—witness his total unawareness of what had happened in the Pir's cave; she knew him no more than the desert creature he was chasing; both were equally changeable, quicksilver, elusive. Where *did* he get these strange flashes of illumination?

"Your brother is writing a poem about an ash tree, I understand?"

She had not observed that Cameron, on his rangy gray camel, had fallen back alongside from his place ahead.

Surprised at this inquiry—on the whole Cameron showed minimal interest in Cal's writing—she replied coolly:

"That is so, Colonel. He has had an idea for a poem about Yggdrasil, Odin's ash. Why it should come to him here, in the desert, who knows?"

"Strange; very strange," Cameron muttered.

She put up her brows. "Why so, Colonel Cameron?"

"Well—" he began, checked, and then impulsively, sounding younger, less sure of himself than she had ever heard him, "Och, I dare say you will think it all moonshine and havers, but when I was a child my mother had the second sight, she had forward-looking dreams—she was a Highlander, from Shieldaig—" He paused, then went on, "Well, it happened that on one of the first occasions when I was with your brother I heard a prophecy concerning him. It was connected with a tree."

"A *tree?*"

In her astonishment, Scylla twitched her camel's headrope and the subsequent struggle with the indignant beast made her voice come out unwontedly high and breathless; Cameron, evidently taking her reaction for scornful disbelief, shrugged and said in a cooler, more disengaged manner:

"Well, I do not expect you to believe that. Why should you? No doubt you think I am inventing old wives' tales in order to impress you. It is not so, but no matter."

"Why should I believe that you wish to impress me? You show no such wish in the normal way! I was only surprised because—but that is of no consequence. What was the prophecy that you heard concerning my brother, Colonel Cameron, and where did you hear it? I am very curious, indeed!"

He told her the story of his visit to the seer in Ziatur. "Of course the man was probably paid to warn me off and to say what he did to Prince Mihal. But his remarks to Cal seemed to have no connection with the rest of his mumbo-jumbo; they appeared to be spontaneous."

"A weeping tree; it is really very strange," mused Scylla. "What can it possibly mean?"

That evening, seated under a scrawny tamarisk tree in the courtyard of the serai, Cal said:

"Have you ever heard of Shambala, Rob?"

"The kingdom of Shambala? As a legend, yes. Not as a real place."

"It was of the legend that I was thinking."

"Shambala?" Miss Musson stirred out of her silence and leaned forward; the firelight made triangular hollows of her deep eye sockets. "Is not that a kind of Eden legend?"

"It is the kingdom in the center of the world—somewhere up there—" Cal waved a hand northward, toward the river Oxus and the mountains of Bokhara. "The Holy Pir told me a little about it. It is the place from which all the holy truths and great sacred mysteries emanate. The god Dyans-Pita—the Zeus of the Greeks, or Jupiter—he came from there. Other names for it are Urgyan, Udyala—"

"You wanted to know if ash trees grow in Shambala?" Scylla guessed correctly. "Because it seems the same as the Scandinavian myth—Midgard? Why did you not ask the Holy Pir?"

"I wish I had. But at that time I had not begun having these dreams—"

He stopped because Scylla had let out a sudden low cry. Shifting her position, she had put her hand down on a flat rock and received two sharp jabs, one in the palm, one on the wrist. At her exclamation, Cameron sprang up and gave a kick to the camel-thorn fire. It flared, showing a small snake flicking itself into a crack in the rock.

"Horned viper, damn it! Of all the cursed luck! Where did he get you?"

"On my hand—"

"Here, quick—show me—"

While Cal went after the viper and battered it to death with a stone —"Look for its mate, too," the colonel warned, "you generally find them in pairs"—Cameron hastily but carefully inspected Scylla's hand, holding it close to the light of the fire; and then he sucked hard at the two puncture wounds, repeatedly spitting into the hissing embers. After he had done this half a dozen times Miss Musson said:

"That should suffice, Rob. The venom penetrates very fast. But you must have extracted what is near the surface. Now you had better incise the wounds while I prepare some of my snakebite specific."

"I was going to," said Cameron. Without more ado he pulled out his knife, held its blade a moment in the flames, then, saying to Scylla, "Shut your eyes if you don't want to see," quickly slashed the two small wounds crossways. "I wish I had some whiskey on me," he muttered, "there is nothing like it for washing snakebite. Brandy must serve." He splashed on a quantity from his silver flask. Scylla sucked in her breath at the sudden sting of the spirit.

"Brave girl." Matter-of-factly he knocked the cork back into the neck of the flask.

"Shall I die?" she asked calmly.

"No, my poor child. You would have if it had been a cobra. But you may *wish* that you were dead; I am afraid that you will be very sick for some days."

"Here—drink this—it helps to combat the poison—"

Miss Musson had heated water in a metal pot and infused into it one of her herbal powders. Scylla obediently swallowed down the bitter stuff.

"I dare say it will be nothing, after all," she said hopefully as they settled down for the night.

Her optimism was unfounded. During the night her arm swelled to three times its normal dimensions and became so painful that the least touch felt as if red-hot nails were being hammered into her skin. Nevertheless she made light of it next morning and said that she was perfectly able to travel, if somebody would kindly help her onto her camel.

That day, and many subsequent ones, became like a hellish dream for Scylla. She knew that it would be highly dangerous—out of the question, indeed—for Cameron's party to drop out of the caravan. They had not food for more than the time it would take to cross to Yezd, which was the first town of any magnitude along the way. Moreover if they remained alone at one of the caravanserais they would be in danger of attack from Turkoman brigands or wandering savage tribes from Baluchistan. It was essential to keep up with the rest of the cafila. But the effort required to get on her camel and stay on it throughout the interminable days of travel was something that made any other pains or difficulties in her life seem mere trifles in comparison. Her head swam, she was deathly sick, often half delirious, and her whole body felt hot as fire; she longed all the time for drink but any food tasted repugnant to her. Hour after hour she struggled against an insane urge to throw herself off the saddle onto the desert sand; the camel's gait, consisting of sway—jerk—pause, and then, on the other side, sway—jerk—pause, became an excruciating torture, a recurrent jolting pain on her already pain-racked body so hard to bear that it was all she could do not to groan aloud each time her mount shifted its weight from one pair of legs to the other. At the end of the day, all she could do was roll from the saddle when her camel knelt down, and then lie where she had fallen, with the blood pounding in her head like cannon fire. Her companions tended her kindly and tenderly; she was aware in the evening rest periods of how one or another of them was always with her, coaxing her to drink, washing and cleaning her horribly swollen and inflamed arm.

"Will it have to come off?" she once asked Cameron with difficulty. "Has gangrene set in?" Her tongue felt enormous, like a flap of Arab bread. "No, matters have not come to that yet," he replied coolly.

Toward the end of the journey Scylla became aware of nothing but pain. Night and day were blurred together in her consciousness; she hardly discriminated between the days of travel and the nights of delirium. She could not speak enough to ask questions; occasionally she struggled to mutter, "Sorry—trouble—sorry!" but was washed away on waves of fever before there was time to hear the reply. She dreamed, endlessly: of mountains, rivers, the girl Dizane galloping away on her wiry black horse, turning a mocking face to call, "Catch me if you can!"; of the Rani Sada offering a dish of fruits and sweetmeats which on closer examination proved to be a mass of writhing snakes; of Prince Mihal with a glittering spear about to stab Cal to the heart; of the Bai, shouting angrily, "Where is my wife, where is she? You have hidden her!"; of the Holy Pir, seated on a stone horse, with Miss Musson on the pillion behind him, riding sidesaddle, her unseeing eyes staring past Scylla, who cried helplessly, "Come back, come back!" And, over and above and in among these tangled images, again and again, she felt rather than saw the great twisted tree, which grew up through them, towered over them, dropped its leaves, and cast its shadow upon them.

The later stages of her sickness impinged on her in disconnected images: a huge dim room with smoke, from incense perhaps, drifting sluggishly in blue wreaths and coils; a white-bearded turbaned man, touching her arm, she thought with a feather, though she felt the stabbing pain of a knife; the coolness of ice, laid on her tongue; and then the numbing but healthful bitterness of some opiate which plunged her fathoms deep in oblivion; then, some long time after that, the taste of coffee, suddenly and wonderfully recognizable and stimulating after what seemed weeks of leaden-tongued, fur-mouthed fever, when even fruit had been a slimy horror to the palate. "I am getting better! I must be!" she was able to whisper, and heard Miss Musson's voice, tired but cheerful: "Yes, child! You are indeed!" She could feel now the delicious comfort of down-filled cushions instead of the lumpy, swaying saddle; but was soon swept again into darkness.

Her next sensation was one of motion; but a very different motion, this, from camel travel; it was a brisk, regular, yet soporific rocking: *"Roti, makan, chini, Chota baba nini,"* she murmured, remembering Miss Musson's Urdu lullaby, and heard Cameron laugh somewhere nearby.

"Come, that is capital. She will be better even before the sea breezes have a chance to revive her," somebody said.

Sea breezes?

And then, not suddenly, but in a slow pleasant languor, true consciousness began to come back. By degrees she found herself reclined on a straw-filled couch, covered by a cotton coverlet, in a small clay-walled room full of sunset light. Miss Musson was washing little Chet in one corner by a stone basin of water; the shrill, clear keening of some unfamiliar bird came through the unglazed window.

"I was dreaming about a tree," Scylla murmured.

Miss Musson gave an exclamation and, laying the baby down upon a wadded quilt, crossed the room with hasty steps to peer at Scylla.

"My dear child! *There* you are at last!"

"Yes, ma'am. Here I am." Scylla smiled faintly.

"One moment, and I will bring you some lime juice."

The juice, wonderfully cold and tart, in a large earthenware mug, was like nectar; Scylla thought she had never tasted anything better. While she drank it, Miss Musson propped her on a pile of cushions against the wall.

"Do you wish to lie down again?" she asked when the mug was empty.

"No, let me stay up a little, ma'am. I fear I have given you all a deal of trouble."

"We were worried about you, child; but you did not choose to be bitten."

"It was wretchedly careless." Looking now at her guardian with compunction, Scylla saw that Miss Musson's hair was decidedly whiter and scantier; her keen brown face thinner and more lined; there were unfamiliar furrows between the brows, around the eyes, chiseled deeply from mouth to nostril.

"I shall get better *very* quickly from now on," Scylla resolved. "How long have I been ill, ma'am?"

"Why," Miss Musson was beginning, "to tell truth, I have rather lost count of time—" when there were voices and steps outside— evidently running up stone stairs—and Cal burst into the room.

"Ma'am! Miss Musson! Only imagine! There is an American ship in the bay!"

"*What?*" demanded Miss Musson, but her exclamation was drowned by Cal's shout of joy at the sight of his sister sitting up.

"*Scylla!* By all that's famous! Sitting up and drinking lime juice like a Christian!"

"Like a Muslim, you should say!" Scylla found that words still came slowly to her tongue. Then something extraordinary struck her. What had Cal said before?

"Are we in Baghdad?" she asked. "Where is this place?"

Cal was squatting down by her couch, scanning her eagerly, and exclaiming, "Your eyes are clear, your look is sensible—you are really better!"

Then her question penetrated, and he answered:

"Baghdad? No, indeed, we left there two weeks ago! Do you not remember the carriage ride? Rob would hire the most amazing coach you ever saw; I swear the Shah of Persia himself must have had it built. Springs like pigs' tails—"

Cameron's quick step was heard, and he strode into the room.

"I thought it best to come to you directly, Miss Amanda. It is true, there is an American merchantman anchored out there—the *Lucy Allerton*, from New Bedford—"

"New Bedford!" Miss Musson echoed faintly. Her hands were trembling. "Where is it? Which one? Point her out to me!"

"Right in the middle—there." Unceremoniously, Cameron laid an arm around her shoulders and led her to the window; with the other hand he pointed.

"No; it is no use; I cannot see it," said Miss Musson after a moment. "But is she *really* sailing to New Bedford?"

"Yes, ma'am; in two days' time."

"Two days? Oh, but how can I possibly—"

"Cal!" said Scylla urgently. "What lies outside the window? Where are we?"

"Come—I will show you." He glanced around, snatched up a woven shawl that lay over the foot of the couch, and wrapped it around her. "Up, now!"

Half carrying, half leading, he took her to the window, where Cameron and Miss Musson were engaged in eager argument. Cameron turned with an exclamation of approval at the sight of Scylla on her feet and said to Miss Musson:

"There, you see, ma'am! Now the fever has left her, she will be herself again directly. A sea voyage will be all she needs to complete the cure—"

"A sea voyage?"

Scylla looked out of the window and gasped, almost with disbelief. Below her, flat white roofs interspersed with palm heads and brilliantly flowered creepers fell away steeply. Beyond the roofs, more palms, green and feathery. And beyond those a dazzling background of blue that was almost green, green that was almost blue, stretching to the horizon—

"Is that the *sea?*" she whispered, and Cameron laughed indulgently.

"Poor little land babe! Have you never beheld it before?"

"How could I?" Unaccountably, Scylla felt a rush of weakness and the pricking of tears behind her eyelids. The shock was too great. She had longed, above everything, for the end of their interminable journey, but now the end was here, she was not ready for it. And Cameron had accepted her recovery so matter-of-factly; had not even congratulated her.

"Help me back to bed," she whispered to Cal. "I must lie down again."

"That's the dandy; you will have to take things carefully for a day or two—"

Cal disposed her against her pillows and gave her little Chet to hold.

"I have been such a burden to you all," she muttered.

"Well, yes, we did wonder if you were going to die," Cal said cheerfully. "But Rob brought you to an old fellow in Baghdad who gave you a great dose of hasheesh or some such stuff; and after that you began to mend. And in a way your illness speeded us on our journey, for in some places folk believed you had the plague, so they were not disposed to be too particular at the customs posts."

"Miss Amanda, there is *plenty* of money left," Cameron was saying earnestly, by the window. "Enough to pay all your passages—rig you out in the first stare of the mode—"

"I cannot decide so quickly. I must take time to think."

For once, Miss Musson appeared to have lost her power of forming rapid resolutions.

Scylla murmured to Cal, "But what is the plan? Are we to go to New Bedford? Is not that in America? I thought Miss Musson was to come to England with us?"

Cameron said rather impatiently to Miss Musson, "Ma'am, I informed the captain that I would give him your decision tonight. He must know directly. He has half a dozen applications for places on his ship; since the Mediterranean has been cleared, everybody wishes to take passage."

"What has happened?" Scylla asked Cal.

"It seems there has been a great sea battle off Egypt; Rear Admiral Nelson defeated the French at Aboukir Bay."

"But then—oh, I *do* not understand!"

All these rapid developments were too much for Scylla; two large tears of weakness rolled down her cheeks. She bowed her head over little Chet.

Cameron, looking at her, said calmly:

"That child should rest again. Come, Cal; we are out of place in this chamber.—Miss Amanda, I will await your decision on the terrace."

When they had gone, Scylla, already ashamed of her weakness, said, "Ma'am, pray tell me, where are we?"

"We are in the port of Acre, child. Rob thinks we should not remain here too long, however, for he has heard that the French are marching this way and plan to besiege it—Oh, it is so *hard* to know what to do for the best!"

"And is there really a ship going to America?"

"Yes, to New Bedford; which means that in a little over four months I could be with my brother Henry in Boston. And your voyage to England would be equally easy to arrange, Rob says; you and Cal have only to take passage on some coastal vessel to Alexandria, where there are gracious knows how many French ships that were captured by Admiral Nelson in this battle at the mouth of the Nile; when they have been made seaworthy again, some of them will be dispatched to British ports."

"I see; how very simple it all is."

And how very relieved Miss Musson and the colonel are to get rid of us, Scylla thought, well aware that the pain she felt at this brisk disposal of her affairs was quite unreasonable; but feeling it nonetheless. Now Miss Musson could set sail to her brother, and Cameron could return to help his friend Mahmud in Afghanistan, and neither of them need waste any more concern on the Paget twins.

"Of *course* you must sail on that ship to New Bedford, ma'am," she said steadily, trying to keep all these feelings out of her voice. "It—it is a chance not to be missed. It—it seems like the finger of Providence."

"Well—perhaps it does." The older woman walked about restlessly, then came to sit on a stool by the bedside. Absently she picked up little Chet and pressed his smooth cheek against her own. Her deepset gray eyes looked past Scylla into the distance. She said:

"I do not like to leave you in such a weak state, my dear child. Do you really think you can manage?"

"Certainly I do," Scylla lied stoutly. "Cal will help me—you know how good he is—" A terrifying world of emptiness and desolation opened ahead of her. She gulped and went on. "I dare say there will be English ladies traveling on some of these ships; I might offer my services to one as a companion or nursemaid. And when we reach London we will take little Chet to the Maharajah's cousin—"

She spoke almost with irony, but Miss Musson's tone of reply was absently approving.

"That's my good child. I knew you would be able to go on just as you should. I must tell you that I have a reason for wishing to reach America as soon as may be; if you feel confident that you and Cal can contrive to make your way—" Sighing, Miss Musson stood up, then stooped and kissed Scylla's forehead, returning little Chet to her arms. "Be brave, child; take up each duty as it comes to you; here is the first. . . ." And, with rather a hasty step, she left the room and could be heard, somewhere not far off, saying to Cameron:

"Rob, I have decided; tell Captain Coffin that I should like a berth on his ship."

Scylla noted the approving tone of his lower-pitched reply but could not catch the words; she had turned her head sideways on the cushion and was struggling with a great sob that threatened to overwhelm her. She dared not let it out, lest Miss Musson return; convulsively she hugged little Chet instead.

Two days later she stood on the white-walled terrace of their hired house, watching through a blur of tears while the brown topsail of the *Lucy Allerton* dwindled and disappeared over the horizon. Cameron had forbidden her to come down to the harborside, saying that she was not strong enough yet.

Feeling as if all of childhood had been withdrawn from her reach, Scylla shook herself and turned to amuse little Chet with some pottery animals that Cal had brought him. After an hour or so Cal himself returned to report that Cameron had found berths for them on a Lebanese coaster which would be setting sail next day for Alexandria with a cargo of timber.

"Admiral Nelson wants all the timber in the Middle East, it seems, to mend his ships. It will be rather famous to see half the British navy there! You will be well enough to sail, will you not?"

"Oh yes, I dare say," replied Scylla listlessly. "And I am sure Colonel Cameron will be happy to see us disposed of."

"He has had a capital notion," said Cal. "It seems he is acquainted with a certain Captain Capel, whose ship is reported to be at Alexandria now; she is a sloop, a fast vessel used for carrying dispatches; Rob has given me a letter of introduction to Captain Capel—whose life he once saved, or some such thing—"

"So that we might travel to England on his sloop?"

"No, no, sapskull!" Cal exclaimed impatiently. "They would not take passengers in a sloop! Or only very important ones. But Rob feels certain that Captain Capel would carry a letter for us, to apprize Cousin What's-her-name Paget that we shall be with her in the space of a few months. And so I have formed a famous plan. I have not been idle while you lay raving in your fever; I have made fair copies of all my poems, and I intend to entrust them to this Captain Capel—Rob says he is a very good-natured, obliging fellow—and ask him, when he reaches London, to have them delivered to John Murray's, the publishers—they are those fellows with whom Uncle Winthrop used to correspond, if you recall, they issue a monthly magazine and many volumes of poetry; so, with luck, by the time we ourselves reach England, they will already have my work in process of publication, and I shall be in a fair way to becoming famous."

"Gracious," said Scylla weakly. A hundred possibilities for the disappointment of Cal's expectations occurred to her; she had not the strength to voice one of them. When Cal went on eagerly, "Do you not think that an excellent scheme?" She replied, "Yes; I dare say it will answer very well," in such a lackluster manner that Cal, studying her closely, exclaimed:

"I see how it is! You are blue-deviled with having little Chet on your hands for so long. I will take him off to look at the ships. Come, baby!" And he slung the willing Chet over his shoulder and walked off whistling down the steps. Scylla gazed after him with envy. He seemed to have quite forgotten his unappeasable love for Sripana; or, in some way, dispersed it into his poetry. She wished she had a similar outlet.

Half an hour later, hearing a step ascending the stone stairs, she looked over the parapet, expecting to see Cal returning, but found that it was Colonel Cameron, who climbed slowly up, looking hot and discontented (the month was now August, the weather exceedingly torrid) and dropped down in a basket chair, after glancing about.

"Where is your brother?"

"He has taken the baby to see the ships."

"Oh." After a moment he grunted, "Very obliging of him." Then there was a protracted silence. Scylla felt too weak and sad to attempt engaging Cameron's interest with any remarks. She reflected that it was probably the first time she had been alone with him for many weeks—perhaps since that abortive scene in the Holy Pir's cave. And when, she wondered, would she ever be alone with him again? Perhaps never.

"Are you in truth well enough to set sail tomorrow?" he asked abruptly.

She tried for a light tone. "Oh, mercy, yes! What is a sea voyage, after all, compared with camel travel? We shall have nothing to do but loll about on deck and enjoy ourselves." She went on, gathering resolution, "Colonel Cameron, I have long been intending to say this— I fear that I have been nothing but a nuisance and a burden to you from first to last . . . indeed, the very first time that we met you had to save my life—"

Momentarily, a half-smile twitched his red mustaches at the recollection.

"Very true! And little did I know then—" he murmured musingly, but did not complete the sentence.

Scylla continued with difficulty. "I would not wish you to think, sir, that I and my brother are insensible of how great a debt we owe you. I am very sorry indeed that, owing to my stupid carelessness, you have been obliged to travel so far out of your way—"

He interrupted, with a note of impatience and anger in his voice. "My *way*? My way? What is my way? I do not have one. My life— compared with any of yours—is unplanned as that of a desert nomad. Miss Musson travels off to look after her brother—and whatever other duty, other purpose, she has in mind. Your brother applies himself to his poems—whether they are good or not I cannot judge, I know nothing of such matters, but he seems very dedicated to the business, I dare say he will make a name for himself. And you, indubitably—for you have the same driving energy—will achieve your ambition of going to London, meeting the great men of the day, mixing with high society—"

He sounded so bitter that she felt obliged to defend herself. "I can see that you think poorly of such an aim, Colonel. But what is a female to do? *We* cannot command armies or go to the rescue of princes —we can take no hand in the direction of public affairs. All we may do is go where we can hear such matters discussed. While you are rescuing your friend the Amir Mahmud, I, perhaps, shall be sitting in some London drawing room, listening to gossip about Buonaparte.—Is it true that he is about to march for India, to overthrow the British there?"

"So I have heard it said. It is also said that a French force has landed in Ireland and is about to invade England."

Cameron looked at her irresolutely and added, "I did not tell Miss Musson this rumor, in case it might have inclined her to postpone her journey to America. But I am wondering if I do right in encouraging you and your brother to sail to England just now. There might be more safety for you in remaining here."

She tried to laugh. "Oh, good heavens, Colonel Cameron, what a poor-spirited pair you must think us. Pray what should we do here? How should we earn our living? We cannot continue to live on your bounty, after all."

"How will you earn your living over there?"

Pretending a confidence she did not feel, she said, "Oh, in a dozen different ways, I dare say. I can offer my services to the East India Company as an instructress in Urdu and Punjabi. Besides, Cal is going to make our fortune with his poems. And furthermore, we have our cousin Juliana, whose letter you brought me, who seems so benevolently disposed toward us."

"It is now over a year since she wrote that letter. Many things may have happened in the meantime. I would place no dependence on her bounty."

"Well, at all events, she may give us introductions—find us openings by means of which we may be enabled to support ourselves."

"So that you may contract a rich marriage, you would say?" he said sharply. "You plan to marry some wealthy nobleman and thus contrive to support your brother?"

"I meant no such thing!" she retorted angrily. "And you take an unwarrantable liberty in supposing it, Colonel Cameron!"

He replied, irrelevantly and, as it seemed, reluctantly, "Your brother may go and sample the cultural and intellectual life of London if he chooses. I think it would be by far the best thing, Miss Paget, if you remained here and married me. You would be nothing but a lamb among lions there; *he* will not take much harm, I dare say, but you would fall prey to the first raptor that comes your way."

"Colonel Cameron, I am greatly obliged for your charitable impulse, but please understand that such a piece of self-sacrifice is not required of you. Fortunately! I dare say you mean very kindly, but I would wish you to understand that my brother and I will go on perfectly well without your finding it necessary to enter into what must be a most repugnant alliance to you."

A flush of red appeared on his cheekbones.

"It would not be repugnant. You mistake! If my sometimes hasty temper has ever given you the impression—"

"It *would* be repugnant to *me!*" declared Scylla impetuously. "I must always consider myself under a heavy obligation to you, Colonel Cameron, for having come so far out of your way—having done so much, but—but—but"—she was stammering with indignation and the difficulty of expressing herself with proper dignity—"but I am *not* prepared to be united with somebody whose only motive is a k-kind of reluctant philanthropic—philanthropy! You need not marry me to save me from abduction by amirs, Colonel Cameron, or from any *other* kind of alliance either—I can manage my own affairs very well, I thank you! In fact—if you were the last man on earth I would not marry you for such a reason—"

Her voice trembled dangerously.

"Say no more, ma'am!" He was pale with mortification. "I only regret having embarrassed you with an offer that—that you find so wholly repugnant. I assure you, however, that it was made with the best of intentions."

Scylla could not speak; her throat had closed up.

He said, "Since nothing but embarrassment can attend upon any future meetings between us, I will arrange to take my departure from here without delay, for I have various arrangements to make with my friends in Baghdad."

"Pray feel free to take your departure whenever you wish, Colonel," she achieved. "I am sure that you must have been impatient to set out for many days past."

"I will bid you good-by, then.—I have already portioned out our financial resources between your brother, Miss Musson, and myself," he added as an afterthought. "I think you will find the funds adequate to get you to England. The rent of the house is paid up to the end of the week."

"We—we are obliged for your generosity, Colonel. When—when we reach England we shall be wishful to repay you. Can you give me some direction—"

"Oh," he said hastily, "in care of Baba Mustapha at the Street of the Sandal Makers in Baghdad will always find me sooner or later. But no repayment is necessary, I assure you. The funds were intended for us all and have been so shared out.—Farewell, Miss Paget."

Slowly, she put her hand into the one he extended. Her arm, which had been so swollen with the inflammation, was now thin, weak, and blue-veined; the camel-hair ring Khalzada had given her continually slipped down her finger in spite of its woolen wrappings. She thought he was looking at the ring, but his eyes were on the two little crisscross wounds, still sore and angry-looking, that he had made with the point of his knife on her wrist and hand.

"I trust that the scars will not remain for too long a period," he said shortly, gave her hand a brief, firm pressure, turned on his heel, and strode into the house. A moment later she heard a door slam inside; then there was silence.

Thank heaven *that* is over, Scylla said to herself.

In token of her relief, she leaned against the terrace wall, laid her head on her arms, and cried as if her heart were broken.

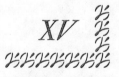

XV

Captain Capel of the sloop *Mutine* was a friendly little man, round and brown as a nut; he readily agreed to carry a letter from the Paget twins to England, and also the parcel of Cal's poems addressed to John Murray's, the publishers in Albemarle Street, London.

"Bless you, that will not be the least trouble in the world," he said.

Cal asked, with diffident politeness, glancing over the busy decks of the *Mutine,* which was within an hour of putting to sea, whether Captain Capel could suggest any ship in the port of Alexandria on which the brother and sister might take passage to England.

"That I can, my boy! I know for a fact that Captain Phillimore, of the *Tintagel,* is desperate for hands; she was a French ship of the line, the *Timoléon,* you know, captured two weeks ago at Aboukir; ran aground on a sandbank, ha-ha! and her cowardly rogues of Frogs all jumped overboard and left her; now she is being patched up to return and form one of the Channel fleet off the Downs. But Phillimore is sadly short of men, he has only a prize crew added to what he can scrape together of riffraff from the port of Alexandria; I am sure he will be happy to give your sister a berth if you, sir, would be prepared to enlist as one of his junior officers for the voyage and work your passage."

Cal was rather startled. "I know nothing of seamanship, sir! I fear Captain Phillimore would find me more of an encumbrance than a help."

"Oh, psha, my boy! Anybody can see that you are a fine, well-set-up young fellow, accustomed to a life in the open air, used to encountering difficulties and perils—as indeed my friend Cameron says in this letter; he gives an excellent account of you. You will soon learn to distinguish the bow from the stern, ha-ha! Ability to handle men is the important thing—if you have *that,* you will be welcome, even if you have no more notion of navigation in you than this sea chest. Wait but two minutes—I'll scribble a note to Phillimore."

"This is very good in you, sir."

Scylla glanced at her brother in slight surprise as Captain Capel, without more ado, sat down on the sea chest and dashed off a note on a tablet. It was true, she thought wonderingly, that Cal, whom she had been used to regard as a dreamy, rather inactive creature, fonder of playing pachisi with Prince Mihal than engaging in any outdoor pursuit, now presented a very different impression to the casual eye. Sunbrowned, wiry, and self-possessed, he stood coolly on the deck, looking about him; his quick, dark glance, under the soft, winged brows, took in all the movements of the men who were busily engaged in making the sloop ready for sail. His brows were drawn together in a frown of concentration as he watched the sailors; he was evidently doing his best, already, to make some sense of their activities.

"There!" said Captain Capel, handing Cal the folded paper. "And

I wish you godspeed! Now I must bid you farewell—your servant, ma'am! You will excuse me, but I have a hundred and one things to attend to before we set sail."

And he bustled away over his cluttered deck but turned to call a warning:

"Mind now! Captain Phillimore is a queer, cross-grained fellow—disappointed many times over promotion, you know! It soured him a trifle—soured him; ay, he's something of a tartar. But now that he has the promotion—he was first lieutenant of the *Leander,* you know, before the battle at Aboukir—now he has his captaincy, perhaps he will be in better skin. For your sakes, I hope so. *Mr. Smiley!* Handsomely with those tubs, if you please."

The *Tintagel* was a very different ship from the trim little *Mutine,* as they discovered when they had succeeded in locating it amid the tangle of shipping in the port of Alexandria. And Captain Phillimore was a very different person from the smiling, round-faced little Captain Capel. Indeed, at first sight of Captain Phillimore, Scylla's heart sank; she had half a mind to urge Cal not to approach him; surely in all this huge port, crammed with craft, there must be some other vessel proposing to set sail for England in the near future? But then, she thought, we might have to wait here for a week, ten days, two weeks, kicking our heels; in her present miserable state of mind, the prospect of such inaction was not to be borne; so she stood quietly by the rail while Cal, having presented his note to the midshipman of the watch, was conducted to the captain on the quarter-deck.

Captain Phillimore was much older than Scylla had expected after learning that he had only just received his promotion from first lieutenant. No wonder he had been soured and disappointed! He must be in his mid-fifties at least. He was a large, stout man with a face that was red, weather-beaten, pock-marked, and almost perfectly spherical; a fringe of reddish beard adorned it, like the tuft of a coconut, a bulbous, somewhat flattened nose occupied a great deal of the center, to make up, it seemed, for the fact that his eyes, set remarkably far apart, were ususually small and slitted. The general effect of this countenance was far from prepossessing.

She saw the little slit eyes slew around in her direction and felt an unaccountable surge of self-consciousness. Hitherto it had not troubled her that she had been unable, partly through lassitude and weakness, partly from the shortness of the time available, to purchase European garments suitable for a young lady about to set sail for England. She still wore a pleated dress and tunic procured in Afghanistan, over embroidered perjamas and curly-toed leather slippers. She noticed Captain Phillimore's eye resting disapprovingly on her sunburned skin and the hair which, during her sickness, Miss Musson had been obliged to cut close to her scalp; now, starting to grow again, it covered her head in short silvery curls like the fleece of a lamb; she had done her best to conceal its immodest shortness by draping a Kashmir shawl over her head, but she was carrying little Chet, who, in his eagerness to see everything around him, was wriggling from side to side, and the shawl had become dislodged and slipped to her shoulders.

Little Chet himself came in for an equally condemning glance; indeed Captain Phillimore seemed to regard him with a kind of incredulous loathing. Since Cal had nodded to Scylla to approach, she moved across the deck and did her best to curtsy politely without loosening her grip of the baby.

Phillimore was saying, "Damned if I ever thought I'd be reduced to carrying a half-caste *blackamoor* brat between my decks—however, what can't be cured must be endured!"

"The baby is no half-caste, sir," Cal said politely. "He is the son of the Maharajah Bhupindra Mansur-i-Zaman Amirul-Umra Mohinder Singh, of Ziatur, and we are taking him to the Maharajah's cousin Prince Gobind Tegh Bahadur, in London, so that when the little prince is old enough he may be sent to Eton."

"Hm; I see," remarked Captain Phillimore, his tone conveying that he did not believe a word of it. "Eton! Ha! Lucky if they take him in there! And you two are *brother and sister*," he went on, in a tone of equal disbelief, glancing from the black-headed Cal to his sister's silvery nimbus.

"Twins, sir," said Cal rather stiffly. "We have our papers of identification—"

"Oh, papers, papers," exclaimed Phillimore harshly—he had an extraordinary voice, both fruity and croaking, as if it had acquired a crust on it through countless years of brandy-bibbing. "Such papers may be purchased in any bazaar, I dare say. Still, Capel was right—I'm damnably shorthanded. If you travel on my ship, sir, you must be prepared to work for your passage."

"I shall be glad to do anything that is required of me, sir—"

"Very well! Very well! It will be work, mind you, not just standing about with your hands in your pockets giving orders. I'll ship you as junior lieutenant, fifth, under Gough, there—he'll take you to your quarters and show you how to go on, and I'll have your papers drawn up by and by."

"And my sister, sir?"

"Your *sister*." Again Phillimore gave the word that disbelieving emphasis. "Understand me now, young man, this is a decent ship! The hands may keep their sluts below decks; such animals must have their doxies on board (besides, women are needed for passing up powder from the magazine) but I require my *officers* to conduct their amours ashore, there is to be no indulging your lusts while shipping under my command, is that *quite clear?*"

"Sir," began Cal, stiff with outrage, but Scylla hastily interrupted him.

"Since Captain Phillimore evidently finds it difficult to believe that we are brother and sister," she said, trying to make her voice as tart and cold as iced lime juice, "it will be best, and will also further the interests of propriety, if I and my charge travel on some other vessel—which I myself would greatly prefer! I do not choose to have my credentials in doubt."

Captain Phillimore's rusty gray brows shot up at the sound of Scylla's voice; and he became a trifle more conciliating.

"Now, now, my dear—there's no occasion to fly up into the boughs!

In point of fact I am already carrying a lady back to England—Mrs. Whiteforest, widow of Captain Whiteforest, who was killed on the *Majestic;* Mrs. Whiteforest has no maid, the black hussy ran off with an Egyptian; so if you, miss, ain't averse to sharing a cabin with the lady and performing a few services for her—she's somewhat down-pin at present, you see, having just lost her husband—"

"Certainly, I shall be very glad to take care of Mrs. Whiteforest," Scylla said calmly, having intercepted Cal's anxious look; she smiled at him, gave a cool, dismissing glance at Captain Phillimore, and added, "Perhaps, sir, you would be good enough to allow Lieutenant Gough to direct me to this lady's cabin so that I may introduce myself to her? And I dare say you will permit my brother to have our baggage brought on board by and by?"

From the start, it was plain to Scylla that their passage on the *Tintagel* could offer no pleasure; the disposition of Captain Phillimore was a guarantee of that. And there was no friendship or distraction to be found, either, in Mrs. Whiteforest; the poor lady, already thin, pale, and weak with grief, was also a martyr to seasickness and during the seven-week passage hardly ventured on deck more than twice. She kept her bunk, and Scylla must look after her hand and foot. Wryly, Scylla consoled herself with the thought that at least she was too much occupied to have time for bewailing her own misfortunes.

She was, however, exceedingly unhappy.

Cal's grief, when he learned that Cameron had gone off without bidding him good-by, had been intense but short-lived. He had questioned Scylla about the final interchange.

"You say he offered *marriage* to you? And you refused him? Well, that was levelheaded enough, you could hardly be expected to share his kind of a roving existence, and he must have had the sense to see *that;* I dare say he only offered because he felt responsible for you; he must have been greatly relieved when you said no. But what I fail to understand is why he felt it needful to sheer off so fast. There need have been no awkwardness; we have all been cheek by jowl forever, after all! It is too bad! I had a hundred things to say to him before he left. And it's odds but we'll never see him again." To this Scylla had dismally agreed.

"I dare say you would not have suited," Cal went on, pondering. (This had been aboard the coastal schooner sailing to Alexandria.) "You never seemed to have much to say to one another. But still, I am half sorry you did not accept him! There would have been something to be said for having Cameron as a brother-in-law. He is a capital kind of fellow—a rare hand in a tight place. You will be lucky if you find anyone like him in London." Scylla said nothing to this. "However I dare say it is all for the best," Cal decided in the end.

Once aboard the *Tintagel,* there was no time for such conversations. Cal, instructed in his duties by Gough and Howard, the two lieutenants immediately senior to him, seemed to be kept busy every minute. The *Tintagel,* a full ship of war, was still severely undermanned.

Moreover she was, apparently, in very bad condition. So Scylla learned from Mr. Fishbourne, the purser, a small friendly man who came to Mrs. Whiteforest's cabin to inquire if the ladies had all they needed. Mr. Fishbourne had been a barber in civil life, before being impressed into the navy, and he still kept all the garrulity of his former trade.

"Oh, a shocking state the ship was in!" he said earnestly to Scylla. "And still is, ma'am, if you'll believe me. Those bloodthirsty rebels of Frenchies may be all very fine when it comes to chopping off people's heads with their guillotine, miss, but keeping a ship in decent trim, that's quite another matter. Her bottom boards was all rotted, miss, no one had so much as scraped off a barnacle in years, and as for stores! There wasn't enough to keep a crew of mice in cheese crumbs. The only thing in plentiful supply was grog, for the Frogs won't so much as pull a sheet without they have their oh-de-vee, as they call it; that's the only thing Captain Phillimore found to approve, he being quite a one for the grog himself. But he's changing all the rest, toot sweet, as the Frenchies say."

Scylla could see that Phillimore was a fierce disciplinarian; men in his crew were frequently flogged; they were ducked from the yardarm, half a dozen times over, until they were gasping and half drowned; hung up by their wrists in the shrouds with weights attached to their feet; obliged, for slowness in obeying an order, to drink gallons of salt water; for other faults, deprived of food, drink, or tobacco; and their tongues were scraped with hoop-iron if he overheard them swearing, though he could be foul-mouthed enough himself on occasion.

Sometimes Scylla wondered if Phillimore's addiction to punishment was due to the fact that he himself for so many years must have felt unreasonably deprived of the power to mete it out; now he was making up for lost time.

She herself, mindful of Captain Capel's advice, kept well out of Phillimore's way. Although she disliked being confined to the cabin and longed to be up on deck, she curtailed the period she allowed herself in the fresh air with little Chet to an hour a day, taken at a time when the captain was at his dinner. This restriction she found easier to bear because, when she did go up on deck, there was such a likelihood of being obliged to witness some distressing punishment and hear the cries of the victims as they were beaten or ducked by the bosun's men.

"It's a damnable shame," Cal muttered, meeting her once by chance on the quarter-deck. "Half those poor fellows haven't committed the faults they are accused of; but what can one do? If you take their part against the captain, it is mutiny and you can be hanged for it. The captain is like God aboard the ship."

"For heaven's sake, then, do not do anything foolish, Cal," his sister warned him urgently. "It is only for a short period, after all."

"Just the same, it makes one's blood boil!"

Setting aside his feelings about the captain, Cal seemed to have fallen into the ship's routine easily enough and to be absorbing information about his duties with commendable speed; he was on friendly terms with the other lieutenants, Gough, Howard, MacBride, Forsyth, and Goodwillie; the sailors seemed to accept him, and the midshipmen, mostly boys between fourteen and eighteen, showed a tendency to hero-worship when it came out that Cal had traveled overland from India through Kafiristan, Afghanistan, Persia, and Turkey, had

climbed mountains, shot a leopard, and resided with foreign poten-
tates. Scylla, too, came in for some admiring and friendly smiles from
the younger officers, but, remembering Captain Phillimore's admonitions and evident low opinion of her, she thought it best to be extremely circumspect in her dealings with them, going and coming to
her cabin (which had been that of the first lieutenant, allocated to
Mrs. Whiteforest) by the shortest possible route, and keeping strictly to
the small patch of deck assigned to her use when taking the air. If
Captain Phillimore chanced to come out, even though she had not
taken her allotted hour, she went below immediately.

As one week followed another, however, in spite of these evasive tac-
tics, she began to be forced to the disagreeable conclusion that Captain
Phillimore was taking an undue interest in her; a great deal too much
for her peace of mind. She felt his eye on her frequently. From time
to time he would intercept her, as she hurried for the companionway,
and ask some question, always in a loud hectoring voice, and with a
tinge of malice in it.

"Your brother—*Miss Paget*—alleges that you have traveled through
the pass of Lowacal and down the valley of the Kunar River in
Kafiristan. Eh? Is that true? How did you find the natives in those
parts? Were they friendly?"

The sarcasm and disbelief in his tone were patent, but Scylla did her
best, always, to answer simply and naturally.

"The natives differed from one region to another, sir, as might be
expected. Some were hostile; but most of them we found friendly
enough."

"Some of them perhaps a little *too* friendly and oncoming, hmn?"
Phillimore suggested with a significant leer at little Chet. "*One* of
them, perhaps, left you with that little token of his friendship?"

"I haven't the least idea what you mean, sir," Scylla said coldly.
"And now, if you please, I must go below; Mrs. Whiteforest will be
needing me."

Slowly the captain stepped aside to let her pass; he had evidently
curtailed his dinner hour in order to come up on deck while she was
still there; his face was flushed and his breath redolent of brandy.

As the voyage proceeded it seemed to Scylla that the captain's potations became deeper; often, after his dinner, he clambered up the companion like some gross fly and walked with a lurching and unsteady step; his loud hiccups and belches could be heard all over the quarter-deck; yet he was never completely inebriated. He seemed to have a remarkably strong head, and however far gone in liquor he appeared, the smallest emergency found him at once perfectly clearheaded and capable of dealing with it.

Off the coast of Spain the *Tintagel* encountered a French privateer. Scylla and the baby were instantly ordered below, not just to their cabin but down to the orlop deck. "Captain's orders, I am afraid, ma'am," said Howard, the first lieutenant, delivering them; "he says he cannot allow females to be anywhere near the operational decks while an engagement with the enemy is in progress." Mrs. Whiteforest protested faintly; the orlop deck was a horrible place, below water level, pitch-dark and infested with rats. But protest was of no avail. Groping their way, the females went below and sat among casks and water barrels, hearing the water rush past terrifyingly close outside, and the thunder of guns overhead. Little Chet set up a frightened wail; Scylla tried to hush him by singing all the Pushtu songs she remembered.

Fortunately the engagement was of short duration. The French ship was in no way equal to tackling a man-of-war and would have fled if possible, but the *Tintagel* could outsail her and had far superior gun power; within a couple of hours the enemy ship had surrendered after being grappled and boarded. The French captain and his officers were taken prisoner, and Howard, the first lieutenant, was dispatched to take command of the captured ship. Some time after, Captain Phillimore recollected that his female passengers were still confined below decks and sent word that they might come up again.

This time it was a midshipman who brought the message; a skinny lad named Owens to whom Scylla had endeared herself by lancing a gumboil that was plaguing him and which he dared not show to the surgeon, who considered such trifling afflictions beneath his notice.

"Mr. Howard's gone to take command of the Frenchman, ma'am,

so we're all to have a step up," Owens told Scylla happily. "I'll be junior lieutenant, now, and your brother's number four. O' course it's only acting promotion; it won't be confirmed till we get to Portsmouth."

"Well, I am happy to hear it for your sake," said Scylla, thankfully assisting Mrs. Whiteforest to clamber up the steep ladder into daylight.

"Cap'n Phillimore ain't half making indentures, ma'am," confided Owens. "He's as happy as a grig. He's thinking of prize money, I dare say! I say, miss, your brother is a prime gun! He was first over the side in the boarding party, and I saw him knock over a big hulking brute of a Frenchman with the butt of his pistol! He's a right top-holer."

Returning to their cabin—which seemed unbelievably light and airy after the horrors of the orlop—Scylla could not help being amazed at how readily Cal had taken to naval life. She longed for a quiet hour to ask him his feelings about it all. Did he not wish for some time—or solitude—in which to write his poetry? She knew that he shared a cabin with Gough, who was extremely talkative. When could he even find the peace and quiet to think? And what of his epileptic attacks? Had they ceased to trouble him? She remembered that he said he was less prone to an attack during action than when at rest; perhaps the almost non-stop action in his present existence was proving beneficial. It was very strange—and frustrating—after so many years of constant unfettered communication to be so close to Cal, to see him often, active on deck, giving orders, talking to his companions, and yet be prevented from exchanging anything but the barest commonplaces.

Sounds of singing and festivity about the ship now made Mrs. Whiteforest very anxious.

"Best bolt the door, my dear," she said to Scylla. "I know what it is like at sea when a prize has been taken!—And the crew on this ship are still a scratch lot, something new and raw, I am afraid they may become out of hand; Captain Phillimore, though such a stern disciplinarian, is, regrettably, so fond of his bottle himself that he will think little of it if they become drunk and unruly. Bolt the door, and let us keep as quiet as may be."

"Yes, ma'am." Although agreeing with Mrs. Whiteforest that this was the only course to pursue, Scylla was extremely hungry, for the ladies had missed their main meal, and it was a relief when, after an hour or so, a polite tap announced the arrival of Bagby, the captain's servant, who brought them their meals. Bagby, like Fishbourne, was an inveterate gossip, and now he brought disturbing news.

"I'm afraid your brother's fell foul of the capting, miss," he said, handing Scylla the tray of boiled beef, sour cabbage, and biscuit which was their almost unvarying diet.

"Oh no, Bagby, how?" Her heart lurched with fright; her hands shook so much that she was obliged to set the tray hastily on the deck.

"Well, miss, I wasn't there for the beginning of the altercation, but it took place while they was all a-celebrating the prize at dinner in the capting's cabing. I come through the door to hand around the port wine, which the capting likes particular when there's something to celebrate, and I saw your brother was a-standing up, white as holystone, I give you my word, miss. 'Captain Phillimore, that is an unwarrantable aspersion on my sister, sir,' he says, 'an' I must ask if you will be good enough to retract it.' An' at that old Philbottle looks him up and down, in that sarcastic way he has, an, 'No, my young shaver, I *don't* retract it,' he says. 'I dare say you think you are a fine fellow after to-day's work, but let me tell you, one engagement does not make a sailor, an' you still have a many things to learn about the navy. And one of them is that, what the capting says goes! An' furthermore,' says he, 'you have just been guilty of insolence to your capting. You are lucky that I am lenient enough to consider it insolence, Mr. Paget, and not mutiny. You will report to the officer of the watch, Mr. Paget, every hour, until further orders.'"

"Good God!" exclaimed Scylla. "You mean my brother must get up at every hour through the night, even when it is not his watch? How monstrous! That man is a brute!"

"Yes, miss. He is that," said Bagby sympathetically, and he went out, shutting the door.

Scylla paced up and down the limited deck space. Now she had no appetite for her meal. Mrs. Whiteforest, perhaps fortunately, had fallen asleep. Scylla's thoughts were turbulent. Her face burned with anger and shame. She could imagine the kind of thing Captain

Phillimore might have said about her, under the influence of drink and excitement. And she could imagine Cal's disgust and indignation at hearing his sister so traduced—in front of the other officers, too!

The night passed slowly. Scylla, unable to sleep, imagined Cal being obliged to rouse up every hour and report himself to the officer of the watch. What a mean, filthy trick!

When she went up on deck next day for her hour's fresh air, she looked around for Cal but could not see him. Perhaps he was snatching a little sleep—or perhaps Captain Phillimore had devised some new penalty for him.

The captain came up while she was there although she had, as usual, chosen his dinner hour for her airing. His face was even redder than usual as, with a truculent gait, he crossed to intercept her as she started for the companionway.

"Good day to you, *Miss Paget*. I am sorry to have to inform you that your—*brother*—is just now subject to ship's discipline. Young gentlemen who come to sea thinking that they know all there is to know must sometimes be obliged to learn that they do not!"

Scylla met his malicious grin with what she hoped was a look of stony impassivity.

"Would you mind letting me by, Captain Phillimore? I wish to go below."

If he had wished her to display temper, argue, or plead her brother's case, he was going to be disappointed. He tried another shaft.

"Young ladies and their *brothers* who travel about the world together cannot always expect to be treated like royalty."

To this Scylla made no reply at all, merely stood waiting in silence with compressed lips, until at last he reluctantly moved aside from the companion ladder enough to allow her down it. She was aware of cautiously sympathetic glances from a couple of other officers within earshot, MacBride and Forsyth; but their pity only made her feel angrier. If only Cal were not so completely at the mercy of this pig of a man, what satisfaction she would take in answering him as he deserved!

That evening, late, after Mrs. Whiteforest and the baby were both asleep, Scylla received a message. It was brought by a little mouse of a boy, Gasgoyne, the youngest midshipman, who was barely twelve years old. He was a tiny trembling creature, terrified of Captain Phillimore, who seemed to take pleasure in tormenting him; knowing that Gasgoyne was nervous of going aloft, he sent him up into the rigging twenty times a day "to harden him off" as he put it. Now Gasgoyne timorously tapped on the door and whispered:

"Please, miss, Captain Phillimore's compliments, and he says to tell you Lieutenant Paget is in the captain's cabin, answering questions as to his conduct regarding the captain, and he asks if you will p-present yourself, miss, for he wishes to have c-confirmation of something or other." Toward the end of this statement it began to seem plain to Scylla that either the little boy had forgotten precisely what he was supposed to say or he was suffering from an extreme attack of nerves; he sounded exceedingly stammering and terrified.

Scylla herself was greatly startled by this message. Completely ignorant as to how ships' affairs were conducted, she thought it a strange time to conduct an inquiry and could not imagine what value *her* presence might have there; she was inclined to refuse, suspecting another of the captain's cruel jokes. On the other hand, if Cal was there, if Cal needed her—

If the captain were likely to deal out a further horrible piece of unjustified punishment—

"I don't think I had better go, Gasgoyne," she said in a low voice.

"Please, miss! For God's sake! The captain'll have me over a gun barrel if you don't!" he snuffled. "I'm bruises from me head to me heel as it is—look!" He held out his skinny little hands, which were, indeed, covered with black weals and cuts. "And you should just see me back —He said he'd slit my tongue if I didn't fetch you directly!"

"Slit your tongue? He couldn't do *that!"*

"Miss, he *meant* it! And he could!"

"Oh—very well." With a helpless sigh of anger and despair, she flung a shawl around her shoulders and followed Gasgoyne along corridors and companionways to the door of the captain's great cabin.

Scylla had never set foot in it, though she knew where it was. Gasgoyne tapped on the door, then stood aside to let her through.

Despite the final outcome, which was inevitable from the start, Scylla would always be glad to think that she had fought as hard as she was able and had managed to do quite a bit of damage before Captain Phillimore finally overpowered her. She kicked, she scratched, she bit his thumb till her teeth met bone, she nearly dragged off his ears, she tore at his hair and beard. The fight was conducted in a panting, stifled silence, because she was too proud to scream for help and reveal how stupidly, how gullibly she had walked into his trap. So *this* was what Cameron really feared for me, she thought at one black moment; how ironic that it should happen, not when or where he expected it, but on the very sea passage that he had taken such care to arrange for us.

Phillimore was drunk, of course, but not so drunk as to be totally inarticulate. "I don't doubt that this is what you are in the habit of doing with *your brother,* Miss Paget," he panted at one point. "Well, now you are going to have the privilege of doing it with an English gentleman." For reply, Scylla sank her teeth in his arm and he dealt her a ringing blow which would, she thought, almost certainly result in a black eye next day.

At last he rolled off her, almost insensible from drink and physical effort. She dragged herself to her feet and stood looking around the room, which was in a considerable state of disorder. Chairs had been overturned, the handsome mahogany table had a great scratch across it; several glasses had been broken, and Scylla's arm had been cut quite deeply by a shard from one of them; there was blood all over the floor.

He had locked the door and put the key in his breeches pocket. From there she retrieved it, let herself out, and left the door swinging. Let anyone who passed think what they would; at this moment she did not care. Feeling sick with rage and disgust, she made her way staggeringly back to her own cabin, flung herself on her bunk, and lay staring wide-eyed into the darkness.

In a way it was fortunate that, on the next day, the *Tintagel* entered the Bay of Biscay. From dawn the turbulence began. Mrs. Whiteforest was too desperately ill even to look up from her pillow; as the ship pitched and rolled, and toilet articles skidded about the floor, Scylla congratulated herself that she had a good reason for not going to take the air as usual, and a plausible means of accounting for her black eye. She could say that she had fallen against the bunk or the cabin door.

In spite of these dismal satisfactions, it was a long, wretched day. The sky outside the port was dark, the ship's motion was horrible, and she had her hands full with Mrs. Whiteforest and little Chet, who was not ill, but very frightened of the strange way in which everything around him was going up and down or sliding to and fro.

Presently, too, it occurred to Scylla that there was something strange and unusual about the atmosphere of the ship. Outside her door she could hear considerable commotion—running feet, excited voices, questions, shouts. Perhaps another French boat had been sighted? Perhaps the *Tintagel* was on fire, sinking? The thought of having to descend to the orlop deck in these circumstances was frightful; in trepidation Scylla wanted for an order to do so. With a sinking heart she opened the door at the sound of a knock.

But the person outside was Cal.

He stared at her in silence for a moment or two, taking in the bruises, the contused cheek, the rough bandage that she had put on her own arm, the black circles under her eyes.

He held something small in his hand.

"I found this," he said. "I picked it up."

It was her camel-hair ring.

After a moment she muttered, "Don't mind it, please, Cal, pray don't mind it; it's of no consequence, I swear!"

Next instant they were in each other's arms, trying to console each other, weeping, murmuring childhood words of endearment.

"We can't talk here," said Cal at last. "Come to my cabin."

"But—Gough—"

"He and the others are having a meeting in the wardroom. Come."

Gathering up little Chet, Scylla brought him along too; Mrs. White-forest had finally accepted a dose of laudanum and was in a merciful sleep.

Once in Gough's cabin they turned to face one another again. "Listen to me," Cal said urgently. He looked pale and grim but composed now. "Captain Phillimore has disappeared."

"*What?* But he—"

He laid a finger on her lips.

"Never mind that! Just listen to this, Scylla. *He has disappeared.* The whole ship has been searched for him. He is not to be found any-where. So—it can only be concluded that he must have fallen over-board. Everybody knows that he was in his cups last night—at least three sheets in the wind. He had drunk a huge quantity of brandy—all the officers saw him. He must have gone on deck for a breath of air to relieve his head. It blew very hard as we were entering the bay. He could have slipped and gone over the side without anybody noticing. That is what must have happened."

She could not speak. She stared at Cal, huge-eyed.

"There will be an inquiry when we reach port," Cal went on. "So long as it cannot be said that anybody had a particular reason to wish the captain ill, Forsyth and MacBride think that it will be accepted that he fell by accident; it seems half the fleet can attest that he was a heavy drinker. But *if* it could be suggested that anybody had a grudge against him—then that person would be in deadly danger. Do you see?"

She did see. She muttered, "He was such a hideous beast—there must be twenty—thirty—fifty people aboard the ship who are glad he has gone." Suddenly the gross, hateful image of the man rose in her mind; she clutched Cal's arm. "Are you *sure* he is gone? Not—not sleeping off his debauch in some corner?" She imagined Phillimore thrusting his way along the corridor, bawling for her brother. Alive, and in the flesh, he did not frighten her; absent, possibly in hiding, he had much more power to terrify.

Cal met her eyes straight. "No, he is gone. You can be sure of that."

He put his hands gently on either side of her face, cupping her cheeks.

"Scylla—I hate to ask it of you, but it is desperately important that you behave as if *nothing had happened*. Can you do that?"

She nodded, gulping back the tears that his gentleness had brought to her throat.

His face worked, momentarily, as he looked at her; the black winged brows nearly met over his nose. He muttered, "That *monster*! He deserved far worse—" Then, urgently, "Scylla! Are you all right? Are you—did he—?"

Taking a long, gasping breath, she shook herself as if to throw off the horrible image and said firmly:

"I am going to forget him. There is nothing the matter with me. Don't distress yourself—*pray*! I shall soon come about. And—and I shall take care to remember your warning." Trying for a normal tone, she added, "What will happen to the ship, now, with the captain missing and the first lieutenant on board the captured French boat?"

"Forsyth has signaled for Howard to come back and take command here. I dare say Howard will send Forsyth over to the Frenchman in his place. Forsyth is really a capital fellow—equal to *anything*." There was an intensity of meaning in his eye as he added the last words. Scylla longed to put the question that was in her mind: "How did you *know* what happened? And who else knew?" but she knew that she must not. She drew another long, shaky breath and said:

"I had best return to my cabin. We should not—should not seem to be speaking too particularly."

"No, you are very right." He opened the door and glanced out. "The coast is clear—you may go now. There will be no harm in your keeping your cabin while we are in the bay—any female might! Be of good heart, love—"

His lips brushed her cheek, then as she turned to retrace her steps toward her cabin he walked swiftly in the other direction.

Contrary winds kept them in the Bay of Biscay for six days, and during that time the *Tintagel* rolled so wildly that her deck seemed to be perpetually at a forty-five-degree angle. Sea water splashed through their port, the wind howled in the rigging, and it was wretchedly cold; Scylla began to realize that her wardrobe was not adequate for northern latitudes.

Off Ushant they encountered and captured another French privateer, and during the action Cal was wounded in the thigh.

Scylla let out a gasp of horror when she saw him next, his leg a mass of bloodstained bandages; but he told her cheerfully that it was no great matter.

"In fact it is all to the good, for I have the surgeon's orders to keep my cabin for a day or two and can begin to set down a poem about the Romans and the Gauls that has begun to fidget me."

As always, Scylla wondered at his power of detaching himself from a past trouble and engaging his mind in new schemes. It was a faculty in which she was totally lacking, and in spite of the wild weather and the constant necessity for attending to little Chet and Mrs. Whiteforest, she had spent a hideous week. Try as she would, she could not drive out the idea that Captain Phillimore was still alive, somewhere concealed about the ship, and likely to make violent entry into her cabin one dark night. Sleep was hateful because she dreamed about him constantly and would wake with dry mouth, clenched hands, and thudding heart, certain that she must have screamed aloud; but fortunately her screams were silent, internal ones, and not audible to her two companions.

At last, rounding Ushant, they came into the English Channel and, suddenly, halcyon weather. Scylla was able to go up on deck once more, and, since her black eye was now fading and her bruises nearly healed, she found it possible to meet the friendly eyes of the officers with a calm demeanor and a steady presence. She told herself that it did not matter which of them knew what had happened to her; the important thing was to maintain her dignity as if nothing had occurred at all.—But she would be careful never again in her life to let a man come closer than arm's length. Meanwhile the *Tintagel* was certainly a far pleasanter place without Captain Phillimore's aggressive presence and malicious innuendoes; she could remain on deck for hours now with little Chet, watching the coast, as the Lizard, Start Point, and Portland Bill slid past, identified for her by whoever chanced to be on the quarter-deck at the time.

"See, ma'am; it's so dry ye can see the stubble fields atop the cliffs!"

The visible coast line of England, so long wished for, dreamed about, and imagined, could not fail to excite her; she began wondering about her Paget cousins, what they were like, what kind of a place they lived in.

Cal hobbled up on deck and joined her in time to see the Needles Lighthouse with its white cliffs behind.

"It is a cursed bore," he said. "Howard thinks that the officers will not be able to quit the ship until the inquiry has been held. But the sooner you are off the scene, the better it will be! I have been asking Gough—he is a native of Portsmouth and he says it is no more than a few hours' journey by chaise to Petworth. I believe you should take little Chet and travel to our cousins directly."

She was troubled. "And leave *you?* But suppose—"

"Suppose nothing. Do not put yourself in a pelter! I will join you as soon as I may, and then we will post up to London, leave little Chet with his uncle, and enjoy ourselves seeing the sights. Very likely our cousin Juliana has a house in town as well as the one in Petworth—after all, Rob said that he met her at Almack's."

"So he did." Scylla felt a faint comfort at the recollection; it seemed to create a link between Cameron and these unknown relatives. "But what about your leg, Cal? Does it pain you very much? I do not see how you will be able to enjoy London if you can hardly walk."

"Oh, fudge. It is only a trifle. Would you believe it, that fool of a sawbones wanted to take it off—only, I believe, because he has invented his own patent circular saw for cutting through smashed thigh-bones! But I told him I was not having any such thing."

"I should think not, indeed!"

She shuddered at the thought.

XVI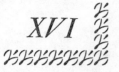

After an early and bumper harvest had been gathered in, there was plenty of time, during the weeks of August and September, for rumors about the French invasion to proliferate.

Thomas and his troop of volunteers drilled continually; other troops were formed in smaller villages. All male persons of an age between fifteen and sixty-three in each village were enumerated. Plans to lay waste the country should the French land were finalized; by every sweet-smelling golden haystack, by every barn packed to its eaves with grain, lay sticks and kindling ready piled to burn up the winter stores before the French could lay hands on them.

During all this national excitement it was not surprising that small personal affairs, such as the untimely death of poor mad Miss Fox and the mysterious accident to the Paget baby, should quickly sink from the public memory and be forgotten. Thomas was fortunate in that respect, Fanny sometimes thought, sadly and wryly; at a time when the whole country stood on guard, who would stop to ponder about the drowning of a poor half-witted spinster? Or wonder how a baby came to fall down a well? The weather, too, favored Thomas and his various projects; in week after week of dry hot sunshine his additional wing to the house was quickly completed and the workmen paid off.

For some weeks the newly completed rooms stood empty and unfurnished.

"Very likely we shall never need them," Fanny remarked one day in early October as Thomas was about to mount his horse and depart for a meeting of the local captains of Fencibles and volunteer groups at Midhurst. "After all, we have heard no more from your cousins in

India; perhaps, with the state of the war so uncertain, they have decided not to come to this country at present."

Thomas remarked, "I need a better room to work in; as soon as the cold weather begins, I shall move my papers from the garden room into one of these."

Let the warm weather continue a long time yet! was Fanny's first thought.

Outside the Angel Hotel in Midhurst, after Thomas's meeting, he encountered the bizarre but impressive figure of Lady Mountague, wearing an amazing gauze tulle confection on top of her old-fashioned high-piled coiffure, a fabulously expensive Norwich shawl, with loose threads dangling from it, over gingham skirts kilted up like those of a farmer's wife to reveal a pair of stout country boots.

"Hey-dey, Captain Paget!" she greeted him briskly. "When are you going to invite me to your house to drink a dish of tay and see how that pretty little wife of yours goes on?"

Thomas fell over himself with expressions of welcoming hospitality. Had not liked to take the liberty—so very kind and condescending of Lady Mountague—his poor house always open to her—

"Well, my friend, since we can hardly expect the fine weather to last much longer—and since the French may land any day, in which case I dare say you will be busy enough—shall we say tomorrow?"

Thomas assured Lady Mountague that her ladyship would be immeasurably welcome at whatsoever hour she chose to present herself at the Hermitage.

"Very well, my friend! At half past ten or thereabouts you may expect me, for I am an early riser. But you are to tell your wife, mind, that she is not to put herself at all out of her way to prepare a nuncheon for me—whatever she may chance to have in the house will do for me capitally—a slice of bread and cheese, some apples—anything of that kind."

Thomas again expended himself in assurances that, without taking any especial pains, not the least in the world, his family would yet contrive to make her ladyship feel as comfortable as if she were in her own home; he then returned to Petworth at a gallop, resolving to inform Fanny that she must instantly bespeak a turkey from the poulterer, a saddle of mutton from the butcher, and order Mrs. Strudwick to prepare a plumb pudding, a blamange, an apricot pie, some cheesecakes, and as many creams and jellies as she could contrive in the time.

Not finding Fanny indoors, he looked for her in the garden and discovered her, to his great displeasure, standing in the yew-tree walk, looking over the wall into the Shimmings Valley. He said angrily:

"How many times have I told you, Frances, not to be wasting your time in this dawdling manner, gazing over the garden wall into the fields?"

Fanny replied composedly, "I was observing the great quantity of blackberries on the hedges running down to the brook. I have already picked all the fruits off our own hedges and those in our Glebe Path down as far as the stile." Thomas now observed for the first time that she wore an enveloping apron, carried a crooked stick, and had over her arm a basket piled with black, shining berries. "If you do not object, husband, I will send Tess and Bet down into the valley to gather some of those berries; Mrs. Strudwick and I are busy making bramble and apple jelly in order to use up the windfall apples which would otherwise go to waste."

Often, these days, Fanny felt herself to be living a strange kind of double life. With part of herself—the everyday part—she regulated her household, maintained as equable a relationship as possible with Thomas, and presented a calm face to the world; the other half, watching, as it were, from a distance, lived in a continual state of apprehension, if not downright terror, endeavoring to suppress the suspicion, the dread, that grew in her from day to day. What *was* this man, her husband, who seemed, in general, so wholly preoccupied with trifling economies, with social anxieties, with small, niggling points of behavior? Did these irritating, trivial shortcomings really constitute a whole person? Did they preclude—or conceal—larger, more horrifying faults—*wickednesses?*

Because a man was snobbish or penny-pinching, did that render him incapable of murder? Or false witness against his wife?

"Oh—ahem! Well, it would certainly be a great folly not to take advantage of such a plentiful blackberry crop—"

As Fanny had guessed, the notion of something for nothing was particularly attractive to Thomas. "But before the girls go fruit-picking, Frances, I wish the house thoroughly cleaned and redd up—" and Thomas informed Fanny of Lady Mountague's forthcoming visit and his orders to Mrs. Strudwick. "Now I must be about my business, for I have a great deal to attend to."

Fanny was about to return indoors when she was appalled to observe the jaunty figure of Major Henriques, very sprucely attired in a riding jacket that was a little too nipped in at the waist and padded as to the shoulders, astride of one of Lord Egremont's hunters, which was picking its way carefully along the dry, slippery valley-side path.

"Holloa there, my charmer!" called Henriques, looking up and giving Fanny a detestably ogling smile. "Were you waiting there for me? I'll wager you were! What a fortunate circumstance that I chanced to come this way! I wonder what can have prompted me to do so? Shall I climb up the wall like Romeo?"

With a look of freezing scorn, Fanny instantly turned her back and withdrew to the house. She was infinitely dismayed to discover that Henriques had returned to the town and could only be thankful that Thomas had left before the major rode by. Her spirits were not raised by noticing the figure of Mrs. Baggot, most unsuitably clad in a muslin wrapper and what looked more like a boudoir cap than anything a respectable person would wear out of doors, strolling along the yew-tree walk, yawningly collecting a bundle of rosemary sprigs to make the lotion with which she frequently anointed her glossy ringlets. If she should chance to see Major Henriques, or to have heard his voice, Fanny was dismally certain that the news would soon get back to the ears of Thomas.

Meanwhile there was plenty to do indoors. Without wholly countermanding Thomas's orders, Fanny contrived to arrange for hospitality on a slightly less disproportionate scale to welcome Lady Mountague on the following day and made sure that the house was in a reasonably respectable degree of order. Then she enrolled Tess, little Patty, even the reluctant Bet, in the immediate business of making preserve. The whole house was redolent with the hot scent of the boiling fruit, and everybody's fingers were stained purple with blackberry juice. For once the atmosphere in the Hermitage was one of cheerful, almost festive bustle.

Fanny's careful planning for the morrow, though, was quite overset by Lady Mountague herself, who arrived that same day, shortly after two. Fanny, espying the phaeton through the kitchen window, gasped, flung off her apron, rubbed unavailingly at her blue-stained fingers, and then ran out to welcome her ladyship.

"The very minute I returned home after seeing your husband," announced Lady Mountague, "I recollected that tomorrow was the day assigned for planning my next week's harvest supper with my steward."

Planting her stick firmly in the gravel, she allowed Fanny to help her carefully down from the carriage, then gave the latter a hearty kiss. "So—since your husband had made such a point that an impromptu visit would not derange you in the least—I e'en tucked up my skirts and posted over directly."

"Ma'am, you know that you are wholly welcome whenever you choose to come," said Fanny. She laughed, displaying her blackened fingers. "You will not object to take us as you find us—we have been putting up blackberry preserves."

"Making bramble jelly!" exclaimed her ladyship. "The one occupation I prefer above all others! Lead me to your kitchen—I will engage to stir the cauldron without allowing the syrup to burn—or peel apples —or perform whatever task you choose to assign me!"

She was as good as her word, and even the scandalized Mrs. Strudwick was soon persuaded to accept her presence with equanimity. "Ah, her ladyship's true gentry," she confided to Fanny in the pantry. "They can go anywhere."

It was to such a scene that Thomas presently returned. Lady Mountague, wrapped in one of Mrs. Strudwick's aprons, and with a towel spread over her gingham, was skimming purple froth from the top of the boiling jelly with a wooden spoon and depositing it in a small pot, while the rest of the household cut up more fruit and chopped a new loaf of sugar into small lumps.

"Fanny, I believe this panful is ready to pour into the jars; it sets like curd cheese as I skim it off," said her ladyship. "Mercy—here is your husband—I dare say hungry for his dinner. But you must know, my dear man, that jam making takes precedence over all other household activities; you must be prepared to forfeit your dinner today and make do with a slice of cold mutton or some cheese; we are too busy to attend to your needs."

Thomas nearly dropped dead of shock. The freezing glare he directed at Fanny would have annihilated her had not Lady Mountague been there to support her. As it was—all his exhortations proving insufficient to move Lady Mountague from the kitchen to the parlor, or to make her wait while a turkey or at least some roast mutton was prepared for her dinner—his glowering, baleful presence in the kitchen soon became so discomposing to his children and servants that Fanny diplomatically suggested they should all adjourn to the garden to eat bread and jelly, cheese and fruit, in the hot October sun under the golden leaves of the cherry trees.

"Besides, you have not seen little Thomas yet; also I want to ask your advice, dear ma'am, about a hundred and one things in my flower garden."

The displeasure of Thomas, at learning that his son and heir had not yet been displayed to Lady Mountague, was very evident; but Fanny explained that he had been sleeping so peacefully, under the watchful eye of Jemima, that it had seemed a pity to wake him. Now, however, having been fed, he was brought out to lie on a blanket and kick his legs among the rest of the party.

Lady Mountague leveled her lorgnette at him.

"Hmn! A remarkably large infant, certainly." Thomas appeared gratified. "I must aver," Lady Mountague continued, "that I have never brought myself to regard infants in the dribbling, crawling stage of their development with any degree of *pleasure*—but still, yours appears a fine, stout child. How old did you say he was?" When told the child's age, she remarked, "Good gracious, should he not be showing a few more signs of progress by now? You say he has not yet even attempted to *roll over?* Dear me!"

Fanny here swiftly put in that Dr. Chilgrove appeared quite satisfied with the baby's rate of development, but the damage had been done; Thomas's brow was as black as thunder. Observing this, Lady Mountague calmly remarked, turning the subject:

"Is it not capital news that has come to London regarding Nelson's victory over the French at Aboukir Bay! If our land forces were but as well ordered as our navy, we should have nothing to fear."

Since Thomas appeared hardly better pleased by this speech, Lady Mountague then proceeded to ignore him and told Fanny that she had received word of some remarkable poems by a new and unknown author which were shortly to be published in the capital. "My correspondent—my cousin Chevenix-Beauchamp—tells me they are works of powerful genius, that nothing has been seen to equal them since Dryden! My cousin has promised to let me have a copy as soon as they are off the press."

Much addicted to poetry herself, Fanny eagerly inquired the name of the author, but of this Lady Mountague's correspondent had failed to inform her; she knew, however, that the publisher was John Murray, and that one of the poems consisted of a long, heroic saga recounting the exploits of Alexander the Great. Here Thomas's lips silently formed the word "Stuff!" but, like his daughter Patty, he was too much in awe of her ladyship to let the sound come out.

Then, taking pity on Thomas, Lady Mountague remarked to him:

"Captain Paget, that is a very pretty little species of pavilion at the end of your grass walk—" indicating his garden room. "I trust you will indulge the curiosity of an interfering old woman and take me to see the interior? I am persuaded that it must command a very fine prospect out over the valley."

All smiles again, "Yes, indeed, ma'am, it does!" Thomas declared. "Can you walk so far as that? Allow me to take your arm!"

"Thank you, thank you, my friend—but I am not quite a cripple yet, I'll have you know!" However, as she really was quite lame, Lady Mountague permitted Thomas to assist her across the grass and along the yew-tree walk.

Fanny wondered if this was a tactful ploy to get Thomas to herself in order to mention his other daughter and her desire for reconciliation to him. She did not immediately accompany the party to the yew walk, but remained behind to pick up her recumbent son from the blanket where he lay peacefully dribbling milk and gazing at the golden leaves overhead. "Poor boy!" she said to him softly. "Poor fat backward boy! I fear you are as great a zany as your mamma!" The baby smiled at her agreeably, and she felt a surge of affection for him —just at that moment he began to seem like a real person, and not merely an extension of Thomas.

Then, to her alarm, Fanny heard raised angry voices coming from the direction of the garden house. "Quick, Jemima, take the baby," she hastily said. "You had best carry him indoors now; the sun is losing its heat," and she hurried across the garden and along the yew walk to the little building.

Here she could hardly credit the scene that met her eyes.

By the door of the gazebo were grouped Lady Mountague, Bet and Patty (who were saucer-eyed and openmouthed), and Mrs. Baggot, in a considerable state of déshabille. Thomas, who seemed almost beside himself with rage, was leaning over the valley wall, directing a tirade of shouted insults, curses, and obscenities at somebody down below.

"Who is it? What has happened?" Fanny demanded in fright, and little Patty exclaimed, "Oh, Mamma, there was a *man* in Papa's garden house, and he was doing something dreadful to Mrs. Baggot—"

"Silence, miss!" said Lady Mountague sharply. "This is no affair of yours. Be off, you and your sister!"

Red-faced, Patty and Bet obeyed, the latter, however, having first directed one look at Fanny and one glance toward the nurse which spoke volumes.

"Now, sir," continued Lady Mountague to Thomas in the same tone of brisk authority, "stop that ranting and bawling, I beg! Pray remember that there are ladies present! You might more sensibly occupy yourself by directing some servants to pick up that unfortunate man—who appears to have broken his leg. Tell them to carry him to Petworth House. It is Major Henriques, who frequently visits Egremont."

Thus sharply pulled up, Thomas started uncertainly back toward the house, took a step or two, then turned to direct a look of concentrated malignity toward Mrs. Baggot and to hiss at her:

"*Doxy!* Fussock! Get out of my house—I never wish to see you again."

"*Well!*" that lady resentfully observed, pushing back a tangled raven ringlet. "There's a nice thing! And me with a month's wages owing!"

"I will see that the money is brought to your chamber," said Fanny swiftly. "Now, pray do as my husband says."

Mrs. Baggot began to walk away, casting indignant glances toward Thomas, who was shouting for Jem. She bawled after him,

"I had rather lay with him than with *you,* I can tell you that!" adding a remark of such lewdity that Fanny could hardly believe her ears and was thankful that Patty and Bet had left the scene.

A loud series of groans now coming from below the wall, Fanny allowed herself one cautious glance over it and perceived Major Henriques prone below the garden-room window, which stood open. A broken ivy branch dangling down the wall gave some clue as to the cause of his mishap. He must have climbed up into the garden room—there he must have encountered Mrs. Baggot—by design or by accident? Had it been an assignation? The nurse had known that Thomas was going to be out on business that day, was not expected to return—

"My dear," said Lady Mountague calmly, "if you do not object to take my arm, I should like to stroll once up and down this delightful walk, and then I believe I had best be on my way; you must be fatigued from making all those preserves; and I fancy that I have discomposed your household enough for one day!" she added with a droll sideways look. "Child, I am an outspoken, intrusive old woman, and I am now about to give you some advice which you may take or reject as you choose.—I collect that your husband is in a passion because his mistress has been discovered in double-dealing."

Fanny gasped slightly at hearing the situation, which she had been endeavoring to disguise to herself for so long, thus flatly brought out into the light of day; but there was something astringently bracing about it too, like the slap of a cold, salt wave.

"Yes, ma'am, I am afraid that is the case."

"Well, child, you are perfectly in the right to pay off that harpy; the *last* thing one wants is such a trollop about the house—a real bird of ill omen! But, having done that, I advise you to say no more about the matter! A wise wife turns a blind eye to such follies.—If *I* had not done so," said Lady Mountague cheerfully, "I should be lying drowned in the Rhine now, along with my husband—instead of whichever barque of frailty he had with him at the time—and I had far rather be here, lecturing you!"

"Indeed, ma'am, I am very grateful for your advice, and I will try not to refine too much upon this incident," Fanny sighed. Then she burst out, "Sometimes I fear Thomas *hates* me—and after this, I am afraid that matters will be even worse."

"*Hates* you?—Why should he do that, pray? You run his household to admiration—you have given him an heir—"

"Oh, Lady Mountague—do you really think the baby is backward in his progress? Do you think—do you think he might be *abnormal?* I am so afraid that Thomas will say—" She checked herself, then added, trembling, "He will be sure to blame *me.*"

"Blame my runaway tongue, rather," said her ladyship. "I am only sorry that I put such a notion into his head. And I dare say it is all moonshine, you know—infants vary prodigiously from one to another."

Fanny longed to confide in this redoubtable adviser the story of Miss Fox and the letter—but she could not, no, she *could* not reveal suspicions that sounded so wild, so lurid, so bizarre. Lady Mountague would take her for a nervous simpleton, someone whose head had been turned, probably by the perusal of too many Gothick romances.

"What we must hope," said Lady Mountague briskly, turning toward the house, "is, either that the French soon invade these shores, which would keep your husband occupied and out of mischief—or that he will very shortly find for himself a charming new mistress who will put him back in a good temper.—Hey-dey," she added, leveling her lorgnette, "you are expecting more company? Whom have we here?"

A dusty hired post chaise had pulled up by the side of the house. Out of it now descended a slender young lady attired with ravishing simplicity in a muslin traveling dress of slate blue adorned with ruffles and ribbons of white and darker blue. An absurdly pretty little matching hat was tilted forward at a provocative angle on her fair curly head—in spite of which protection it could not be denied that her complexion was decidedly tanned. Huge trusting gray eyes, a small upturned nose, and a soft, arched mouth made the visitor, Fanny thought, quite the prettiest girl she had ever seen in the whole of her life. Despite this enchanting appearance, the stranger appeared remarkably hesitant, not to say diffident; approaching them over the grass, she glanced from the younger lady to the older and then, fixing her eyes again on those of Fanny, she inquired with cautious politeness:

"Forgive me, ma'am, for this unheralded intrusion—but—but—but are you my cousin Juliana Paget? I do hope that you are! I am your cousin from India—I am Scylla Paget."

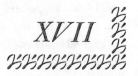

XVII

The first view that Thomas had of his cousin Scylla Paget was late in the evening. After the disagreeable encounter with Mrs. Baggot and Henriques, he had not returned to bid farewell to Lady Mountague—let the old beldame go back without that civility and make the best of it, he thought furiously—if she had not ridden over unannounced and unexpected in that rude and inconsiderate way, none of this trouble need have happened. He had gone off to inspect his mill, where, as so frequently on these visits of surveillance, he found matters all astray.

Dark had fallen, therefore, before Thomas returned to the Hermitage. He had, contrary to custom, stopped in Byworth at the Black Horse Inn to eat a piece of pie and drink a glass of small beer; thus fortified, he planned to wait until his womenfolk were in bed before entering the house, so that he need not meet them until next day.

However, greatly to his dismay, he saw, as Jem ran out to take his horse, that there were lights burning still in the house.

Beset by dismal forebodings, he flung open the front door and strode in. But, seeing lights and hearing perfectly cheerful voices coming from the parlor, he walked into that room and stopped short in amazement.

He heard Fanny's soft "Here is Thomas, at last!" but his eyes were all for the girl who rose from her chair by the blazing hearth and walked to greet him, smiling up into his face with unaffected friendliness.

"Good evening, Cousin Thomas! I have to ask your forgiveness for this unannounced intrusion—the more humbly so as I gather that I am the second uninvited guest to descend upon your house today! I am Scylla Paget, you know—but just arrived in this country from India—"

"Good God, ma'am—Miss Scylla"—for once Thomas was startled out of his usual cold unconcern—"we were under the apprehension that you were about twelve years old—not a beautiful young lady—"

Laughter rippled among the females in the room—Bet, who should have been in bed by now, was there too. Thomas saw with disapprobation the glances of undisguised warm admiration that Fanny bestowed upon Scylla and the friendly smiles exchanged between the pair. Obviously they were already upon terms of great cordiality, and this Thomas mistrusted; he never cared for alliances among other members of his household. However his cousin Scylla seemed so spontaneously amiable, so naturally prepared to like her new relations, that he did his best to unbend; and, indeed, surprised Fanny by the liveliness of his questions and the apparent eagerness of his welcome.

"And where is your brother?" he presently inquired, rather hoping that the latter might have been drowned at sea, but Scylla explained that Cal was obliged to remain at Portsmouth to give evidence at a naval inquiry.

"He will come to pay his respects here as soon as he can; and, if he may, to pass a week or two of convalescence under your roof, for he is suffering from a troublesome wound in his leg. Then we plan to take a trip to London—perhaps we may persuade our cousins to accompany us? And, when his leg is fully recovered, I believe Cal wishes to return to sea; he has found the life of a sailor much to his taste—which, I must acknowledge, amazes *me,* for he was used to be the laziest creature imaginable!"

Thomas was greatly relieved to hear this program, since he did not in the least wish to have his cousin Cal quartered on him. His cousin Scylla, however, was quite another matter.

"I hope you will make this house your home, cousin, for as long as you feel inclined. I am sure we shall be much diverted by the tale of your adventures in foreign parts."

"Oh, for that, you had best wait until Cal is here. He makes a far better hand at descriptions. I paused only to purchase a couple of dresses, in order that I might pass myself off with some credit among your acquaintance, and not cause you to blush for your beggarly connection from overseas."

"No one would do so, indeed," remarked Thomas, studying her simple yet elegant evening gown of pale yellow crape.

"Well, it might have been otherwise," divulged Scylla. "For I traveled all the way from Baghdad in the dress of an Afghani hill woman, and would be wearing it yet, had not my brother come in for a share of some prize money due from two French merchant vessels that we captured on our way from the Mediterranean.—But I fear that I am keeping you all from your beds—also I believe I can hear my baby crying; poor angel, he cannot yet accustom himself to the English diet; and I am, indeed, somewhat fatigued myself; so, if you will pardon me, I will seek my couch."

She left the room with a friendly smiling nod all around, so swiftly that she did not observe Thomas's stunned expression at her penultimate sentence.

"Baby?" articulated Thomas in accents of such shock and revulsion that Fanny was hard put to it not to smile, as she thriftily removed a half-burned log from the fire and checked to see that the shutters were all fastened. Blowing out the candles, she said calmly:

"Why, yes, it seems that our cousins have performed a service for the Maharajah of the state where they resided, in bringing to England the ruler's youngest child, who is destined to receive his education at Eton College and become a lawyer. A dear little fellow, but rather too young for Eton as yet!"

She picked up a candlestick and moved to the door.

"And what is to become of him in the meantime?" inquired Thomas suspiciously, following his wife up the stairs. "I trust we are not expected to house him *here?*"

"No, no; Cousin Scylla plans to take him to London, to his uncle."

"I am glad to hear *that.*"

Fanny was a little unnerved to find Thomas entering their bedroom, which he had not done for some time. Quietly she dismissed Tess, who had been waiting to help undo her corselet, and allowed Thomas to do so instead; he performed the task automatically, as if he had not observed that there had been any interim, and Fanny, likewise, accordingly did her best to behave as if nothing unusual were occurring, and to control the slight shrinking she felt as his hands touched her shoulders and waist. To cover this awkwardness she continued to talk of Cousin Scylla, of how Scylla's brother had served as a junior officer aboard the captured French warship, but that his real interest lay in writing poetry.

"Poetry!" growled Thomas, pulling on his nightshirt. "Good God, what sort of a frippery fellow can he be? I hope he does not remain in this house above a week or so."

Fanny did not voice her ardent disagreement with this hope, or her interest in the prospect of meeting Scylla's brother. She was trying to remember something else that had been said about poetry that day—what could it have been? No, she could not recall; too much had happened. Thank God, that horrible woman was gone at last; thank God, she had flown away—like a bird of ill omen—before this bright new migrant had alighted among them.

"Er—Frances—" said Thomas, rolling into the middle of the bed and wrapping the covers around his shoulders. He was not looking in Fanny's direction. "Frances—that unfortunate scene earlier today—that malicious, lying slut—I trust she is gone, by the bye?"

"Yes, husband."

"Of course there was not a word of truth in her accusations—they were merely spiteful attempts to—"

"Of course."

Fanny expected that he would make some comment on their new cousin's bewitching prettiness and charm. He was silent on this head but said thoughtfully:

"I wonder what their fortune consists of; I believe that my cousin Juliana made some provision for them, Throgmorton said as much; very unnecessarily generous of her! Very likely they had already inherited property on their mother's side. Our cousin seems perfectly ladylike and well bred; she has evidently not been brought up in vulgar or indigent circumstances."

"No indeed!"

Fanny quietly slipped into bed, maintaining a position as near the edge of the mattress as she could contrive to, without actually rolling off. She waited in nervous expectation for Thomas to turn toward her; the first six-month period of connubial interdiction set by Dr. Chilgrove had terminated without remark from Thomas; but she could hardly expect, now that Mrs. Baggot was gone, that he would continue to forbear from claiming his marital rights.

However on this occasion he went straight to sleep.

Scylla, at the other end of the house, did not find sleep so easy to achieve. Little Chet whimpered unhappily in his dreams, and she was tempted to take him into her own bed but reflected that all too soon, now, he must be separated from her entirely; harsh though it seemed, she must begin loosening the tie, accustoming both of them to the severance. My life is nothing but partings, she thought miserably. Next, Cal would be gone from her as well. And by what—by whom—would he be replaced?

She began to speculate about her cousins. It had been a considerable shock to learn that Cousin Juliana, after making all these benevolent provisions, had departed incontinently to the coast of South America; Scylla could not avoid a feeling of decided letdown and disappointment.—Though it was true that Fanny had been as warmly welcoming as any friendless stranger could wish. Fanny was a darling, and it would be the easiest thing in the world to live with her on terms of sisterly affection; but what of her stepdaughters? What of her husband? It must be admitted that they were by no means so prepossessing; Patty a pert, spiteful-looking little minx, Bet uncouth, nervously self-assertive, and, Scylla thought, imbued with feelings of jealousy toward her pretty stepmother; and Thomas? Scylla had to acknowledge to herself that she had taken her cousin Thomas in strong dislike during the first five minutes of meeting him. Since he was her host, it devolved upon Scylla to be friendly and civil to him, and she had taken some pains to be so. But there was something about him—a sourness, a lack of openness, an indication of angry, bitter feelings very close below the surface, that dismayed Scylla greatly. Worse—but here she hoped that she deceived herself—it seemed to her that she detected in his eye an expression that had become horribly familiar in that of Captain Phillimore—a look of concupiscence mixed with dislike, greed and lechery mixed with calculation; the aspect of a man who sees within his reach a fruit that is both tempting and disgusting, delicious but degrading. Surely I must be mistaken? Scylla thought, moving restlessly in her cold, narrow bed. I must have imagined that calculating, acquisitive look. Or is it that all men, like Captain Phillimore—she shuddered at the memory—inevitably assume that travel defiles a woman; that, having crossed Asia and ridden on a camel, I have thereby forfeited all right to respect and may be regarded as unchaste, any man's natural prey? Were the signs of her two experiences, both unsought, but so different—were they, then, as *visible* in her face and bearing as the look in Thomas's eye had seemed to suggest?

I am degraded, she thought miserably; fatally sullied, and he knows it. If I try to enter London society, will the same thing happen? Shall I encounter the same attitude? Oh, if only Cal were here!

She was troubled, too, about Cal; not as to the result of the inquiry, for Gough and the other officers had seemed fairly sanguine concerning that: Phillimore's intemperance being so well known in the fleet that it had been considered only a matter of time before some fatal accident befell him. But Cal's leg was not healing as it should; although he made light of it, she could see that it pained him greatly and was still much inflamed.

Suppose—suppose—

For the twentieth time she composed herself for sleep; but the wind moaning in the trees outside disturbed her, and she heard a strange, keening wail—could it be a wild beast? But surely there were no wild beasts in England? She was reminded of the whine of a leopard in the desert sand hills; heavens, how happy I was then, sleeping in some flea-ridden caravanserai with Miss Musson close at hand, Cal and Cameron nearby; why do we never recognize our good fortune when we have it within our grasp?

It was many hours before Scylla slept.

By the time Scylla made her appearance next morning, heavy-eyed and apologetic, all Fanny's household duties had been done, and there was plenty of time to devote to the guest. Bet, grumbling, had departed to her harp lesson, and little Patty, grumbling even more, had been set to sew a row on her sampler. Jemima was given charge of little Chet, who, greatly interested at his first sight of another baby, tottered across the room (which he had recently learned to do on shipboard) and inquisitively touched the stranger's hands and feet. But Thomas merely lay gaping at this unwonted encounter, without making any attempt to respond.

Fanny sighed despondently and said, "I fear Thomas is sadly backward. How old is your little prince?"

"Oh, he is upward of a year now; quite six months older than your baby; so do not put yourself in a taking, cousin! Babies vary hugely, as I know, having seen so many in my guardian's hospital."

"I am only afraid that my husband may be vexed by the great contrast between them. But come, cousin—if you are sure you have had sufficient breakfast? I am longing to show you all about while the weather is fine."

Scylla was eager to be shown and, in Fanny's company, everything charmed her. The late roses, the scarlet crabapples, the dull gold of the oak trees in the valley, the sky-colored glimpses of the brook down below—"It is all just the way I imagined England to be!" she exclaimed enthusiastically. Then, turning toward the house:

"Good God! What is that tree?"

She had not noticed it before, since they had come out by the back door.

"Oh, that is an ash tree, a weeping ash; Thomas had it tied like that because he was not allowed to cut it down, which he wished to do; he said it blocked out the light." Fanny had a sudden vivid recollection of Andrew Talgarth, a look of resolution in his blue eyes, saying, "Miss Juliana were particular fond of this ash tree, sir; I wouldn't hurt it for the world."

"I hate to see it fettered and cramped in that fashion," Fanny went on, "but Thomas insisted. Are you fatigued, cousin? You look pale. Do you wish to return to the house? Or would you like to stroll in the town?"

Scylla declared that she was not in the least tired, walking exercise was what she had longed for above all things while on board the *Tintagel;* so they strolled up the lane, talking without intermission.

"I feel as if I had known you forever!" Fanny exclaimed once, laughing, breaking off in the middle of a sentence.

"Perhaps we have conversed in our dreams," Scylla said, laughing too.

But under the laughter she still felt vibrations of the shock she had received when she first saw the weeping ash tree: bowed, bent, fettered, casting its golden slender leaves on the ground, it resembled some haggard petitioner standing close to the house, half pleading, half threatening, like a beggar, ignored by everybody because he is so humble, because he is always there. What in the world would Cal say when he saw it? What in the world did it portend?

She felt inclined to tell Fanny about Cal's poem—about the prophecies—but not just yet. Besides, there was so much else to tell Fanny!

Walking into the park, they encountered Liz Wyndham and Lord Egremont, who were standing by the ha-ha, deep in conversation with Andrew Talgarth.

"Good morning!" called Liz. "How glad I am to see you here, my dear Fanny! You can instantly come to my support! I wish to throw an ornamental bridge over the lake, and both Talgarth and George are horridly opposed to the scheme."

"What Capability Brown saw no need to do, when he landscaped the park for my father forty-five years ago, *I* see no occasion for now! But pray make us known to your friend, ma'am!"

Fanny therefore introduced Thomas's cousin, and Scylla entered cheerfully into the controversy over the bridge.

"George is about to dispatch Talgarth on a tour of all Capability Brown's greatest works," Liz told Fanny. "He is to go to Longleat, to Stowe, Blenheim, Hampton Court, Croome, Milton Abbas—we shall miss him shockingly while he is gone, but I am in hopes that when he returns after seeing Milton Abbas he will agree to build me an orna-mental village over there in the middle distance!—There is a *charm-ing* bridge at Blenheim," she told Andrew. "Mind you study it—it is exactly the kind I should wish to see across that water."

"Directly Lord Egremont agrees, I shall be happy to build you half a dozen bridges, ma'am," Talgarth said, smiling.

"Oh, you wretch! That is as good as saying, never! But, Fanny, bring your cousin into the house for a nuncheon. We have the best peaches you ever tasted. (And you need not be afraid of meeting that hateful Henriques)," she added in an undertone, drawing Fanny behind Egremont and Scylla, who were walking toward the french windows, "for Chilgrove set his broken leg and he has taken himself back to London in a closed carriage. I collect that he was discovered in some discreditable escapade, and I am heartily glad to see the back of him.—Fanny, your cousin is *enchanting*. Are you not happy to have her with you? I can see that George is head over ears in love already!"

Indeed, Scylla and Lord Egremont were conversing like old friends; Fanny, listening with half an ear, was amazed at her cousin's grasp of international affairs. How, traveling across Asia from a small state in northern India, had she acquired so much knowledge? They had, too, it seemed, an acquaintance in common, a Colonel Cameron who had encountered Lord Egremont in White's Club in London. Now they were talking about poetry.

"William Blake? Oh, he is one of my brother's greatest heroes! Is he truly a friend of yours, Lord Egremont? And visits you here? I am afraid you will have my brother haunting your house forever, in hopes of meeting him!"

"Your brother is a poet also? Madam here will be happy to hear that—she collects poets like peacocks," Egremont said, as a peacock strolled mewling across the terrace, and Liz threw it out some cake crumbs. "Has your brother published his verses, Miss Paget? Under what name does he write?"

"He has not yet had any of his work printed—mainly through lack of opportunity to show it to a publisher. But he lately sent some poems to the firm of John Murray in London. I think he intended using a nom de plume—in case, you know, our English friends disliked having a verse-writing connection. But what it was I do not know."

"John Murray? I frequently step into his offices when I am in town; I shall hope to see the work in manuscript. I am to go to London in a few days' time; I shall make a point of inquiring about it.—There is talk, you know, of Mr. Pitt's instituting a tax on income—a most unprecedented step. If there is to be a debate in Parliament, I should wish to hear it."

"A tax on *income?*" said Fanny, instantly thinking how outraged Thomas would be at such a notion. Imagine his being obliged to reveal the amount of his income to some revenue official, for tax purposes!

"So it is said. The war against France, ma'am, you know, is proving a severe expense. And now the Tsar is asking for three hundred thousand pounds to equip a Russian force and send it into Holland."

"Well, it is very shocking," said Liz. "Why should we be obliged to pay those Russians? But listen, George, here is Miss Paget desirous of traveling to London in order to deposit her princely Indian babe with his friends—why should she not ride with us on Monday and spend a few days at Egremont House?"

Thus easily was Scylla's journey to London arranged; and though she was sorry not to make her first visit to the capital in Cal's company, she could not but see that there were decided advantages to the scheme. Slight though her acquaintance was with Thomas, it became plain to her after only a day that the sight of little Chet was extremely repugnant to him, whether this was because due to the Indian baby's manifest superiority over little Thomas in walking, moving, playing with objects, and attempting to talk; or whether he secretly believed the baby to be Scylla's own, and felt Chet's presence to be a scandal on his house (which Scylla half suspected was the case); at all events, every time Thomas's eye rested on Chet, Scylla felt most profoundly uneasy. Understanding, also, from Fanny, that their generous cousin Juliana had made a financial provision for her and Cal, she wished to call on Throgmorton, the London lawyer in charge of the funds, and obtain access to them; she and Cal could not live on his prize money forever. And, finally, a note from Cal arriving on the second day of her sojourn in Petworth informed her that he would not be able to travel from Portsmouth for another week or ten days; the result of the inquiry had been satisfactory, but his leg was proving a little troublesome. This last news naturally threw Scylla into a fret, but it clinched her decision to accompany the Egremonts to London. If Cal's leg were paining him, he would not be able to travel to town immediately; it would be best that she should do so and return before he arrived in Petworth.

Thomas, surprisingly, was not at all pleased by this plan, and grumbled to Fanny.

"Why must she go off so soon? Is our house not good enough for her? I dare say she will find London so much to her taste that she never returns here, and we shall be left with her precious brother on our hands!"

Contrary to his expectations, however, Scylla spent no more than a few days in the capital and traveled back with the Egremonts when they returned.

She came back from her visit to the metropolis bright-eyed and bubbling with news. November 29 had been appointed a day of national rejoicing for Admiral Lord Nelson's victory over the French at Aboukir; the rebellion in Ireland was finally quelled; she had met William Lamb, alleged by some to be the natural son of Lord Egremont and Lady Melbourne: "The most delightful young man, Fanny, and indeed I see a likeness!"; she had deposited little Chet with his father's cousin—"The most reverend-looking old man, Fanny, in a long white beard and a blue turban; he is a kind of ambassador and presides over a Sikh college in London; it was such a pleasure to speak Punjabi again. He greeted little Chet with tears of affection, and I am sure will use him with the most tender consideration!"; Mr. Fox and Mr. Sheridan had come to call at Egremont House and were so entertaining that Scylla only wished she could recall half the witty things they had said; she had learned, to her amazement, from Mr. Throgmorton that wealthy Cousin Juliana had endowed her and Cal each with an extremely handsome competence— "So we need not be the least encumbrance on you, dearest Fanny!"; and, most wonderful, most delightful of all, her brother Cal, unknown to himself, was already an amazing, an instant success! His poems, in a volume entitled *The Weeping Ash,* were eagerly being passed from hand to hand and demanded at the circulating libraries; seven thousand copies at half a guinea had been disposed of to the booksellers and a new edition was already in preparation; Mr. Murray assured her that Cal must by this time have earned at least two thousand pounds. "Think of it, Fanny, *two thousand pounds!*"—and was eagerly requesting more works.

In consideration of these joyful tidings, Scylla had taken time out, as well, to rig herself up in the first stare of the mode; she had also purchased tonnish garments for Fanny and Bet which Fanny, though she could not help admiring them, feared that Thomas would think outrageously décolleté and diaphanous, not at all suitable for well-bred females to wear. As well as clothes, she had also bought a parcel of improper reading matter—*Evelina, Cecilia,* and *Camilla,* by Miss Burney, and *The Castle of Otranto,* by Horace Walpole.

"It is so enjoyable to be able to spend money, Fanny; you cannot imagine how poor we were as we traveled through Kafiristan."

She had brought back with her, as well, two copies of Cal's poems, handsomely bound in green leather, embossed with gold.

"The Weeping Ash!" exclaimed Fanny, gazing at the spine. "But, Scylla, how singular! When we have a weeping ash tree here—in our garden. It seems like a premonition! What in the world should impel

him to write a poem on such a subject?" She turned to the title poem and read a verse of it wonderingly.

> *"Wise tree," he prayed, "bestow on me some part*
> *Of your immortal self; breathe out that lore*
> *Founded in ice and fire, show me the art*
> *To make a world where no world was before.*
> *O wind-rocked tree, whose topmost boughs explore*
> *Outermost realms of sky, no lightning's flash*
> *Can ever blast your limbs, nor thunder's roar*
> *Scatter your foliage, nor tempest gash*
> *Your bark, divine Yggdrasil, Odin's sacred ash!"*

"Why, Scylla, it is beautiful! It is by far more beautiful than Crabbe or Cowper!"

She turned eagerly through the pages of the book and said, "May I borrow this? Oh, it is a shame to read it before he has seen it himself! But I shall feel that I know your brother even before he arrives."

"Of course you may have it; indeed I brought it for you and Thomas, and have already inscribed your names in it."

Thomas, predictably, was not in the least grateful for the gift, nor impressed by the poetry, which he apostrophized as "Sad stuff!" leafing contemptuously through the pages. "Poetry! I do not know why grown men will be writing such fustian rubbish! 'Odin, transfixed above the whispering sea'—pah!" Nor was he at all struck by the coincidence of the ash tree. "Why must you be making a mountain out of a molehill, Frances? Ash trees are to be found in all regions of the world. I beg you will not be continually dinning my cousin's name into my ears—I am sick of it before he has even come to the house. I dare say he is a puny, posturing, paltry fellow."

Learning, through Fanny, of Cal's epileptic disposition had engendered in Thomas an extra prejudice against his cousin; in Thomas's experience epilepsy was a hysterical, puppyish affection, nearly always pretense, a mere simulation of illness, a subterfuge adopted by those poltroons who were too cowardly to serve in the navy.

"But Cousin Cal *has* served in the navy," said Fanny unwisely.

"And I dare say this *epilepsy* will serve as an excuse to get out of it again, now Cousin Juliana has given him this fine fortune!" snarled Thomas, and went off about his press gang duties.

Scylla said to Fanny, later that morning:

"Dearest Fanny, will you indulge me? I have a great curiosity to walk in English woodland. May we enter those woods that I see on the far side of your valley? For when poor Cal comes with his lame leg, I fear that our excursions may be restricted.—Also Goble tells me that we may shortly expect snow." (Strangely enough, a great friendship had struck up between the recovered Goble and Scylla; she treated him with an unceremonious friendliness which had punctured the defenses of his surly and eccentric nature.) "He says that all the bright berries we see on your hedges portend an early and severe winter, and if there is snow we may not be able to walk in your woods. So will you give me the pleasure of your company *now?*"

She was astonished to discover that Fanny had never even walked down to the bridge over the brook, let alone up the other side of the valley and into the woods.

"I dare say it must seem very poor-spirited to you, accustomed as you are to rambling Himalayan mountains," Fanny said, sighing. "But Thomas will not allow me to go out unescorted, and Bet is no walker."

Indeed Bet, though jealous of the growing affection between Fanny and Scylla, said grumpily, when she was told of the projected excursion, that she had better things to do than tramp through muddy woods; she was about to alter the trimming of the dress that Cousin Scylla had brought her.

Fanny and Scylla therefore set out unimpeded, picking their way with laughter down the steep grassy slope, past the rector's packed haybarn halfway down, crossing the bridge at the bottom where the brook was already bordered with pale scallops of ice.

"Oh, this is better!" exclaimed Scylla, drawing in deep lungfuls of tingling-cold, frosty air. "I do not know why it is, Fanny, I love you as if I had known you all my life, your house is charming, but there is something in its atmosphere that I find oppressive.—Do you have a ghost?" she added, laughing.

"I am not certain," Fanny said more seriously. "I think it is possible. I have seen nothing myself, but I have felt—something. And the builders' men—simple, superstitious fellows, of course—talked of seeing the ghost of a little child. But Thomas says it is all nonsense."

Scylla shivered.

"The ghost of a child? You make me glad that I removed little Chet to London.—Besides," she added candidly, "I have a notion that Cousin Thomas thought that he was mine—though I assure you, Fanny, that he was not!"

Since Thomas had indeed voiced his speculations to Fanny on this theme, her protestations lacked force. "No matter!" Scylla said, laughing at her in friendly mockery. "I collect that Thomas thinks I have been ruined by my wild life—and in some ways, Fanny, I am afraid that he is right!"

"Oh, what nonsense!" retorted Fanny with unexpected spirit. "It is not what happens to you, but what you *are,* that is important; and anybody can see, Scylla, how good and sweet you are. Why, Liz Wyndham is forever singing your praises—"

"Liz Wyndham—another lost soul. In any case, I do not deserve them," said Scylla, troubled. "If I were to tell you, Fanny—"

They had reached the top of the hill, and stood a moment to get their breath and to look back over the valley at the little cluster of roofs climbing the hill, topped by the majestic oblong of Petworth House and the church steeple above it.

Then they took their way down a short slope and up a steep, beech-bordered path into the woods beyond. "These are called the dilly-woods," Fanny said. "But what were you about to tell me, Scylla?"

Somehow—though without having in the least intended to lay the burden of her confidences on Fanny—Scylla found herself doing so, in part at least, and discovered that Fanny appeared not in the least burdened by them but, on the contrary, sincerely happy to have a friend place such trust in her; and Fanny, in her turn, was soon revealing facts about her marriage to Thomas which she had hitherto felt it impossible should ever be exposed to another person, even to Liz Wyndham.

"—So you see, dear Scylla, how it is that I feel *strongly* that it does not greatly matter what happens to a person—in the way of outside events, I mean—even things that may seem very shaming or degrading or dreadful—so long as that person preserves a kind of core—of self-respect, of integrity—oh, I express myself so *badly*," Fanny exclaimed with impatience. "My father would have said it better, if he were still alive."

Scylla looked at her in amazement. *"Better?*—And you seem such a quiet, gentle, unassuming little creature, who have spent all your short life in small, sequestered places!"

"I do not believe it makes much difference *where* a thing happens," Fanny remarked. "One may be a martyr for one's faith as well at home as in the Spanish Inquisition."

"Yes," objected Scylla, "but Captain Phillimore did not violate my faith; there was no virtue on my side in fighting him off."

"Captain Phillimore's motives are no concern of yours. *Listen,* Scylla," Fanny said, standing still in the middle of the path to accentuate the importance of what she had to say, "you *must* learn to think of what he did to you, however hideous it was, as nothing but a—a kind of natural disaster, as if you had been caught in an earthquake. So long as your spirit did not consent, it need not affect you. We women are so frail. Our position in the world is so weak. The law says that I must obey my husband in all things. As soon as I marry, all my possessions are his; I have no right to anything of my own. Not even a room! But one stronghold we *do* have—one private place—and that is inside ourselves. Listen, I am going to tell you a very queer thing that happened to me ten months ago. It was when I had gone to London with Thomas.—You must know that before I was married to Thomas I loved—thought I was in love with—a young man called Barnaby Ferrars"—she lingered gently on the name—"but I had no portion, so he did not want to marry me. When we were in London—I—I thought I saw him in the street, and I could not resist following to see if it was indeed Barnaby." Her voice trembled a little. Scylla glanced at her in total sympathy. "I had become separated from Thomas in a crowd," Fanny went on, "and then, when I came up with the man, I found that it was *not* Barnaby; was nothing like him indeed. I think the shock of disappointment caused me to faint."

"In a London street? All alone? Good God, what might not have happened to you!"

Scylla had been somewhat startled by her sight of London. Here, at the hub of the world, in Europe's most sophisticated capital, she had seen streets and passageways as dark, dirty, evil, and full of menace as any in Kabul, Herat, Umballa, or the other Eastern towns she had visited.

"Well, that is the strange thing. For when I returned to my senses—and it felt, Scylla, as if I had been away from my body not for hours but for days, even *weeks*—I found myself not lying down but leaning against a wall, by the river, in a street called the Strand. My return to consciousness was not sudden, but a slow and growing awareness of my situation. I felt that I had been walking arm in arm with somebody—or very close—I had been talking with some dear companion—"

"A *companion?* Who?"

"That is the strangest part! I do not know! Have you never woken from a dream, Scylla, certain that you have been in the company of the person you love best, in the world or out of it?"

"Yes—but—"

"And yet you are not positively certain of the identity of that companion?"

Now it was Scylla's turn to stop short and look intently at her companion. "No," she said at length, and there was a wry resignation in her tone. "No, when *I* awake from those dreams I am never in any doubt as to the identity of my companion! But go on, Fanny. This is the queerest story I ever heard!"

"Well, that is all there is to it! I woke, I knew I had been with *somebody*, but he was no longer there. The parting had not been a sudden or a painful one; more as if we both had small duties to perform and had gone our separate ways, knowing that it would not be long before we met again. And—and so I went on walking, alone by the river, and saw the sun rise—"

Now, all of a sudden, recalling that instant, an almost ungovernable emotion did seem to take hold of Fanny; she turned aside for a moment, leaning against a beech tree, and hid her face in her hands. Scylla, immeasurably moved, laid a hand on her shoulder.

"Dearest Fanny—do not tell me if it distresses you—"

"No; no; there is nothing more. It was just the recollection of that feeling—" She took a breath and went on. "I saw a priest enter a little church in the Strand. I followed him in. He was saying his early service. Afterward I went up and spoke to him—told him the story of what had happened to me and asked what I should do. Must I tell Thomas? I asked him. I knew Thomas would not believe such a tale. He would be so angry. The priest—he was a very old man—reflected about it and said that in his opinion I had no duty to tell Thomas about it. I asked if I might remain in his church for an hour or so—I did not feel equal to facing Thomas yet, I still had that strange feeling of *otherness*—and the priest, Father Duarte, said yes, I might stay there, he would go to his house nearby and bring me a little packet of food." Fanny smiled faintly. "But he never did return, poor old man; after we were back in Petworth I read one day in *The Times* that he had died, been found dead in the street; perhaps on that same day. So —after a while—I went back to Thomas."

"And you never told him what had happened?" Scylla's tone was awe-struck.

"I never told him. He was very angry," Fanny said detachedly.

"So I should imagine! And you never had this experience again—or any clear idea as to who the companion could have been?—Do you believe that it was a real person?"

"I do not know."

Both of them now walked in silence. The woods were beautiful, the trees nearly all bare by this time, silvered boughs and lichened, moss-covered trunks, the ground thickly carpeted in yellow and rust-colored leaves.

"To think this was all so close, and I never came here before," Fanny murmured.

Across the valley they heard the church clock strike two.

"Good heavens, have we been out so long?"

Glancing at Fanny, Scylla was struck by her pallor. "I have kept you out too long—I have overtired you," she said remorsefully. "I forgot that you are not in the habit of walking all day long, as I have been used to. Should we sit down for a while on a fallen tree?—Or no, look, I have a better notion—is not that a little house, along there, at the end of that ride? Let us ask if we can rest there, until you are feeling more the thing—I can see that you are quite done up."

Remorsefully, she took Fanny's arm and assisted her to walk slowly toward the cottage. This had evidently been built to provide a picturesque focal point in the prospect across the valley from Petworth House; set in a clearing among the trees, it was provided with a row of counterfeit battlements and a tiny tower; the cottage itself looked to be no more than two rooms, but a thread of blue smoke issued comfortingly from the chimney, and the strip of garden, besides carefully tended vegetables, contained late roses, asters, and a fig tree dropping its great pale hand-shaped leaves across the forest path. Scylla had a sudden sharp recollection of her first encounter with Cameron, and the wild gardens of the ruined tomb, where fig branches had writhed among the cracked marble colonnades.

"What a bizarre little place!" she said, knocking on the door. "It is like a gingerbread cottage in a fairy tale; I half expect an old witch to pop her head out."

"I believe I know who lives here," Fanny was beginning when the door opened.

"Good day! I have walked my cousin too far and tired her out," Scylla said directly to the old man who stood in the doorway. "May we ask the favor of a seat by your fire for half an hour?"

"Indeed you may." Standing aside, the old man gestured them to come in. He was unusually tall, but thin as a cobweb; despite this frail appearance he moved briskly and had, Scylla noticed, an impressive shock of snow-white hair and two of the bluest eyes she ever recollected seeing. Cameron's eyes were as bright, but a greener, sea-blue color; the old man's were dark, hyacinth blue. Where had she seen such eyes recently?

They had come into a little kitchen, stone-flagged, neat as a ship's quarter-deck. On either side of the hearth stood a Windsor chair, black and polished with age; but the old man carefully wiped each with a cloth before inviting his visitors to sit down.

"I believe you must be Mr. Talgarth," said Fanny quietly. "I know your son; I have seen him several times with Lord Egremont. I am Mrs. Paget, you know, and live in the house across the valley."

Of course! Scylla thought. Lord Egremont's gardener had those brilliant dark blue eyes. She observed with interest that the name Paget aroused some reaction in the old man; it seemed as if a shutter had clicked open; the gaze he turned on Fanny was very intent.

"I have heard my son speak of you," he said.

His voice was clear and deep-toned; no hint of a rustic accent in it, but an unfamiliar cadence; Fanny recollected that he came from Wales. She said, smiling:

"Almost every time I have met your son, he has rescued me from some predicament; once, indeed, he saved my life!"

"He was very happy to do it," said the old man simply.

"This is my cousin Miss Paget, who has just come from India."

"You will be finding it rather cold here, I am thinking," said old Mr. Talgarth. "Perhaps you would take a drop of my mead?"

He served the mead, which was very sweet and potent, in tiny, thimble-sized glasses; while he was fetching them from the other room Scylla, glancing inquisitively through the open doorway, saw a bed covered with a great woven coverlet, and two shelves of books. Reminded of the Holy Pir, she said:

"You live here like a hermit, Mr. Talgarth!"

"Ah, you see, I have a right to, now," he said seriously. "I have done my little bit of work in the world and I need no more from it. My son comes by, when he can, to tell me the news; but he is away just now; Lord Egremont has sent him to look at gardens."

"Not a very good time, surely, just when winter is beginning?"

Old Mr. Talgarth's smile was like a sudden brilliant ray from the setting sun. He said:

"My son is very obstinate, indeed! All summer he would not go because there was something that needed doing." And he began to talk about his son's work at Petworth House.

After a while Fanny said to Scylla, "We had best be on our way; it will take us a good hour to walk home."

"Are you certain that you feel strong enough?"

"Yes indeed; Mr. Talgarth's mead has quite set me up. We are so grateful to you," Fanny said to him. "Will you please remember me to your son when he comes back from his travels?"

"I will do that."

"May we come again if we get lost in the wood?" Scylla asked as they left the house, and Mr. Talgarth answered:

"You may come whenever you wish. Even if you are not lost!"

As they walked off down the path he stood on his doorstep looking after them.

On the way home they talked little; both were preoccupied; but there was no sense of awkwardness. Neither of them felt the need for speech, they were in harmony without it. Once or twice Scylla endeavored to slow their pace, thinking that Fanny must be tired; but she noticed that each time it was Fanny who soon began walking faster again.

"I am hoping that we can get back before Thomas returns," she explained as they crossed the bridge over the brook.

"He cannot forbid you to walk in the woods!"

"No; but while I am out my household tasks go neglected."

"Nonsense! You are the most punctilious housekeeper possible."

Fanny did not mention what she suspected would be Thomas's main cause of objection to his wife and his cousin taking a long ramble together: the intimacy engendered, the confidences that might be exchanged.

When they passed through the iron gate into the garden they saw that a carriage stood drawn up by the front door.

"Oh, can it be Cal?" exclaimed Scylla joyfully. "I do hope so! I so long for you to meet him!"

Hastening inside, they came on a curiously constrained tableau in the front hall: Patty, silent, excited, staring; Bet all elbows and angles, agape with curiosity; Thomas, evidently just returned, for he still wore his greatcoat; his whole aspect radiated dislike and hostility. If he had been a porcupine, Scylla thought, his prickles could not have been more evident. Cal, similarly garbed in a many-caped greatcoat, leaned as if wearied out against the stair banister.

"Cal!" cried his sister rapturously, and in the same breath Fanny exclaimed:

"Oh, it *is* our other cousin! Thomas, why do you not invite him to sit down?"

"Pray, love, have a care!" Trying for a light note, Cal eyed his sister warily as she rushed forward to embrace him. "You see I am not quite secure in my balance yet."

Puzzled, suddenly afraid, she hesitated, and then, a new nervous stiffness in his movement giving her a clue, she glanced downward and saw that he was supported on a crutch and had a wooden leg.

XVIII

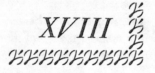

Country people said of that winter, 1798 to 1799, that it was the worst in living memory; nothing like it had been known for fifty years. The bitter cold that began early in December kept most of Europe ice-bound and immobilized until the end of March; even into April the frosts continued. Snow and more snow fell; the water froze in the wells, animals died of hunger, roads were blocked by snowdrifts. An envoy from Mr. Pitt took three months to reach Berlin. Austria declared war on France, but at first this made little difference; nobody could wage war in such weather.

In England the expectation of an invasion from France was greatly diminished, and consequently Thomas had much less to occupy him. Meanwhile the Sussex roads were in so bad a state that for many weeks Petworth was virtually cut off. Tidings of the new tax on all incomes over £60 per annum, passed in December, did come through, and made Thomas quite as angry as Fanny had expected; how *could* Mr. Pitt, a good Tory, do such a thing?

Thomas had a great deal to aggravate him at present. With a

recently amputated leg, his cousin Paget was in no case to go off again to sea directly; indeed for several weeks Cal was obliged to keep his bed, the journey from Portsmouth having inflamed the stump and brought on a fever. Thomas had not even the satisfaction of being able to say that his young cousin was a mawkin or a mollycoddle, for Cal bore his pain with commendable fortitude and left his bed as soon as he possibly could.

Not surprisingly, an instant antipathy had sprung up between the two men. Cal represented, to Thomas, everything that he most disliked: the glamor of having traveled in distant places, of having taken part in battles on land and sea and acquitted himself creditably, so that he could not be put down as a namby-pamby or a coxcomb; then there was his poetry writing, which was disgusting enough in itself, and ten times more exasperating because the fellow had actually made two thousand pounds out of it and had, according to Lord Egremont, half London talking about him.

It was vinegar and gall to Thomas that Egremont had evidently acquired a high opinion of Cal, invited him to come and use the library at Petworth House, and meet flibbertigibbet guests, poets, painters, and other such riffraff. Not that Thomas was courting opportunities to meet such tedious society—but it was infernally irritating that his cousin should, apparently, be idolized by them, and he not even invited! "I know you are too busy," Egremont sometimes said—a lame excuse if ever there was one. Also, naturally, the females at the Hermitage wasted half their time fluttering around the invalid, offering to read to him, sing to him, and God knows what; if the housekeeping did not get disgracefully neglected, it was only because Thomas, deprived of his normal outdoor outlets, had so much more time to pace about indoors, looking into everything. And that wretched sawbones, Chilgrove, was forever underfoot, telling Cal not to exercise his leg too much at first, not to try horseback exercise, not to be in a hurry.

Meanwhile Thomas had interrogated Chilgrove, pretty sharply, several times, about the baby: could he detect any definite signs of backwardness, of slowness in development? The fool had hummed and hawed, said it was much too early to make a definite pronouncement, infants differed greatly in their rate of progress. But what about the tumble down the well? Dr. Chilgrove did not think that could have had any adverse effect. At the back of Thomas's mind was another question that he could not ask: what about that period of time in London, as to which Fanny was still resolutely silent—what influence might *that* not have had on the unborn child? Sometimes, these days, Thomas could hardly bear the sight of his wife or her child. And it made him sick to see the way that fellow looked at her, with undisguised admiration and tender liking. Cal had discovered that Fanny could sing, could make up tunes for songs, and the pair of them spent whole evenings, sometimes, matching words to music, Fanny finding tunes for Cal's poems—faugh, what an occupation for a pair of adults! It made it no better that Fanny always took care to have a piece of mending or needlework in hand, so that it could not be said she was neglecting her duties.

Learning also that Fanny could play the harp, had learned to play while still in her father's house, the Pagets had the extravagant impertinence to send off to a shop in Chichester and order one, which, during a brief period of thaw, was delivered by carrier's cart. And then there was no end to the twangling and jangling, even Bet sometimes taking a hand. "You never told me that you could play the harp!" said Thomas resentfully to Fanny, and she replied, "I was afraid that if I mentioned it you might interpret it as a request for one; and I knew that you could not afford that, for you told Bet so." Fanny always had some piece of self-justification for everything!

Another cause of irritation to Thomas was the fact that his real liking for and interest in his cousin Scylla—now *there* was a fine girl, if you like, spirited, lively, pretty, yet always showing a proper deference to Thomas's opinion—his relations with Scylla were constantly being hampered and obstructed by the strong tie between her and her brother. Any remark in the nature of a setdown to *him* always had an immediately quelling effect on *her*. It was a most infernal situation! And the worst of it was that, if Cal's leg did not recover sufficiently to allow him to go back to sea, he and Scylla talked of removing to London and setting up house together there—a scatterbrained project which Thomas could not at all approve.

There was no real resemblance between Cal and Thomas's deceased half brother Ned—how could there be, indeed?—yet sometimes Thomas found himself possessed by the crazy notion that Cal was an embodiment of long-forgotten Ned, come back to plague him.

"I am afraid this is all a dismal bore for you," Scylla said to Cal one day in the stable. She had come out to find him taking refuge here, visiting Goble, with whom he spent hours talking about the navy and life at sea. Goble, at the moment, was next door in the harness room, making a careful adjustment to the base of Cal's wooden leg in order to change the angle where it met the stump, so that he could walk more comfortably.

"Oh, it might be worse!" Cal's tone was flippant, but his dark eyes were serious. "Fanny is the one I feel for. How can she bear him? And she such a rare creature—"

"*Pray* take care, Cal!" his sister said urgently. "If Thomas had the *least* excuse to suspect—"

"Don't fret your head, love. He shall have no cause. He hates me simply because I am younger and luckier."

"*Luckier!* When you have lost your leg—and he only his finger—"

"That is one of the reasons why he hates me. He had to take his own off. Fate took care of me."

"You mean he *amputated his own finger and thumb?* But why?— How can you be sure?"

"Why? Men do. So as to have a pretext for leaving the navy. How can I be sure? I feel it in my bones."

Thinking it over, Scylla felt sure too. Another cause for Thomas to hate his cousin, who had been honorably wounded, who had sufficient justification to leave the service, yet intended to go back if he could.

"At least Phillimore was not a hypocrite," she said thoughtfully.

"Compared with our cousin, he was a paragon of honesty and uprightness!"

"Cal, tell me—what *did* happen to Phillimore?"

"Gough, MacBride, and I picked him up and threw him overboard. It was not at all difficult—we took him completely by surprise."

"Whose idea was it?"

"Mine. But they were quite in agreement. Phillimore made no secret of what he had done. And none of us felt a single qualm afterward." He added in a matter-of-fact tone, "It is a pity we are not in the Bay of Biscay *now!*"

"Cal! You cannot simply dispose of anybody you happen to dislike!"

"Why not? I only dislike bad people.—Now run along back indoors, or Thomas will think we are conspiring against him. Besides, I want to try to write, and I can't do that in the house."

"Oh, very well."

Still feeling the reverberations of shock—this was a new Cal indeed —she jumped down from the stall partition where she had been sitting. At that moment Goble returned with Cal's wooden leg, saying:

"'Ere, now, Mus Cal, you try 'er on an' see how she do feel."

"Ah, that is a great deal better, thank you, Goble; I shall be dancing a cotillion in no time."

He tried a few steps with his crutch out in the snow, slipped, went white with pain, but recovered himself and laughed.

That evening Fanny shyly revealed that, while she had been helping Mrs. Strudwick chop fruit and suet and prepare the Christmas puddings, a tune had come into her head for Cal's *Weeping Ash* poem. "It came all of itself!" She played it to them on the harp.

"Again!" said Cal. "Fanny, it is exquisite! It suits the words to a nicety—haunting, mysterious, yet swiftly moving. Scylla, can you sing it?"

"Play it over again, Fanny!"

Scylla had a clear, light soprano which had been carefully trained by Mr. Winthrop Musson. She sang:

> *"All-Father! Odin! who did sacrifice*
> *One eye to drink at Mimir's mystic spring,*
> *The lore obtained at such a cruel price*
> *Wrought havoc far beyond imagining!"*

"Bravo, Scylla! Try it a trifle faster!"

Scylla sang again, this time Fanny softly joining in, while Bet looked on enviously, wishing she had the courage to take part.

> *"Ash upon elm our fathers rasped, to bring*
> *Fire leaping from the wood. Those fires now rage*
> *Unquenched in every breast, and, ravening,*
> *Devour the world, and will from age to age*
> *The furious fires of love, that nothing can assuage!"*

Thomas, who had been checking his clerk's accounts in the dining room, came in angrily, intending to say, "Can you contrive to make less commotion, pray?" But, on seeing that it was Scylla who was the singer, he lingered, eying her with reluctant admiration.

"That is my poem about your weeping ash tree, Cousin Thomas," said Cal when the verse was sung.

"I am sure I do not know why you are all making such a to-do about this weeping ash!"

"Do you not think it strange, Cousin Thomas, that Cal and I should have dreamed about it before ever we saw it?"

"Dreams! Fiddlestick!" Thomas did not utter aloud his opinion that the twins had invented their dream in order to impress Fanny, but his feelings were plain from his expression.

"You do not believe, Cousin Thomas, that dreams are a portent of things to come?"

"If I did, I wish I might dream that my mill would make a handsome profit," said Thomas sourly. "It is high time, Bet, that you were abed."

With which strong hint he returned to his accounts.

Christmas passed quietly. Fanny was too careful of Thomas's touchy mood to provide more in the way of festivities than an excellent dinner of beef sirloin, plumb pudding, and mince pies, but the Paget twins produced gifts for everybody, small fairings bought by Scylla at the Petworth shops, and books.—In consequence of which, Thomas was obliged to confiscate and burn Fanny's gift from Cal, a volume of poems by a Scotsman, Robert Burns, which he considered grossly indelicate and unsuitable for a female's eyes.

"I am truly sorry for that," Cal apologized to Fanny several days later when—Thomas having ridden out on press gang business—they were able to converse in comfort without his watchful jealous eye marking every nuance of expression. As the snow had temporarily melted, and only a thick white hoarfrost covered the grass, they were attempting a cautious promenade in the yew-tree walk, Cal in a great-coat, balancing on his crutch, Fanny in a thick shawl and pattens.

"Pray do not regard it, cousin! I think, whatever you had given me, it would have been the same." Fanny then looked conscience-stricken and added quickly, "But I am very sorry, because the poems were so delightful. I loved especially the one describing the flowery banks of bonnie Doon—it made me think of this valley in summer. I wish you could see it then!"

"I hope that I may be able to, sometime. But it is beautiful now: see how the movement of the sun creates shadows of frost, which are out-stripped by the shadows of light."

Fanny turned to look at the gray-green slopes and the ghostly dark-ness of the leafless woods beyond.

Cal was watching her profile; he said suddenly:

"There is another poem by a Scot that reminds me of you, Fanny: I read it last week, up in Lord Egremont's library. It is by a writer with an uncouth name—James Hogg!—but it has the very feel of you about it: a poem about a girl called Kilmeny—do you know it?"

Shy at having his attention thus focused on her, Fanny said she did not, and asked what the poem was about.

"Well! Kilmeny goes out and falls asleep in the wood and vanishes quite away. And then, after a long, long time, when all hope for her has been given up, she comes home again: 'Late, late in the evening, Kilmeny came home.' And she is strangely changed.

> 'As still was her look, and as still was her e'e,
> As the mist that sleeps on a waveless sea.
> For Kilmeny had been, she knew not where,
> And Kilmeny had seen what she could not declare.'"

"And where *had* she been?" Fanny's attention was engaged, she looked wonderingly at Cal. Had Scylla—could she have?—divulged Fanny's confidence, told him about her visit to London? But there was no consciousness in the look he gave her, only a kind of tender gravity.

"She had been to a land of thought—a land of love and light—oh, you will have to read it!—it is a long and beautiful poem. I will borrow it from Liz Wyndham.

> 'But to sing the sights Kilmeny saw,
> So far surpassing nature's law,
> The singer's voice would sink away,
> And the string of his harp would cease to play.'

"You have that very look, sometimes, Fanny—of a person who has *been away*, and come back with reluctance, and still retains memories and secrets from another world."

"Perhaps you have been there too, cousin? A poet must visit many different worlds."

"Perhaps I have! I think some unseen bond unites us—do you feel it too?"

"Oh, pray do not—" she exclaimed in a kind of terror, turning to look up at him, huddling the shawl about her as if for protection against him.

"I love you, Fanny. I think you must know that. Do not be alarmed!" he said, smiling faintly at her stricken look. "I am not about to importune you in any way—I do not wish the wrath of Thomas to descend upon you! I have a notion that wrath is visited on you too often as it is, and most undeservedly. I would be the last person in the world to wish to add to that burden. But when I am back at sea I shall miss you sorely—" She made an involuntary sound of protest at that thought, but he continued, "I cannot stay here forever after all. Firstly it would drive Thomas into a frenzy. Secondly I might —who knows?—give way to temptation, be overcome by the longing to make love to you. So I am going, the very minute I can manage this wooden pin."

"But must you go to sea?"

"It is a good life, Fanny. My friend Howard is hoping to get command of a sloop, and if he does so he has promised me a berth as senior lieutenant. I shall have no time to think of you; or not too much."

With his finger he gently outlined the curve of her lip.

"But can you go—like *that?* Will—will they take you?"

"In time of war—yes, I think I have a good chance. Fanny: I have not asked—I dared not—what—if ever you think of me?"

She looked up at him slowly. The lip that he had touched was quivering; she drew a long breath.

"I should not have asked." His tone was full of remorse. "Forgive me! Consider the question unasked. You are cold; we should return to the house."

He took her arm; they moved up the slope in the direction of the weeping ash.

"I have planted a mass of snowdrops under it," Fanny said shakily. "I wonder if you will be here long enough to see them come up."

"Not if I can help it," Cal said.

Scylla came out to them through the garden door. She was holding a paper.

"Cal! There you are." Her expression, studying them, suggested she felt her interruption had come not a moment too soon. "Only think! I have had a letter from our guardian."

"From Miss Musson? Famous! Did she reach Boston in safety?"

"Oh, I am so glad for you!" Fanny exclaimed. "I know how anxious you have been about her. I will leave you to read it together."

She hurried away to fetch little Thomas from his crib and try to persuade him to take a few reluctant steps. Thomas was now so furious at the baby's lack of progress that Fanny feared he might begin to punish the child for what he called "infernally stupid laziness." Thomas had commenced to study other children, when he encountered them, and was beginning to understand just how far behind the normal state of development his own son had fallen; he was in a state of constant, simmering rage about it, unsure where to lay the blame; consequently Fanny spent hours with the baby each day, endeavoring to stimulate him into *some* activity or response.

Cal saw that there were tears in Scylla's eyes.

"What is it, love? She does not send bad news?"

"Oh, Cal, she has gone blind! That was why—that must have been why—she was often so silent toward the end of our journey. Do you not remember?"

"Of course I do," he said. "I thought it was because she wished to remain and become a female anchorite along with the Holy Pir. Did she find her brother?"

"Yes—but he is dying—well, read the letter."

He took the several sheets, crossed and recrossed. The letter had been started by Miss Musson, but her writing became more and more disjointed and shaky and the final sheet was in a different hand.

"*Poor* Miss Musson," said Scylla in a choked voice. "She, of all people! So independent, so active—"

"Hush, I am reading." But Cal, sitting by her in the window seat, slipped his arm around her waist. When he had finished he looked up, remained silent for a moment, and then said, "Famous! Selling that great ruby, using the proceeds to found a Friends' Home for poor old people—herself as warden, and her brother, while he is still alive— what could be more suited to her talents and disposition? Do not be a goosecap, Scylla! Shed a tear or two for me, if you like, but do not waste sorrow on our guardian. She will always arrange her life in the best possible manner for herself and everybody about her." He looked down at the letter again. "What is this postscript she mentions: 'I wrote the postscript first, in case my sight failed before I came to the end.' Where is this postscript? I do not see it."

With a certain hesitation Scylla produced a scrap of paper.

"It is about Cameron," she said in a low voice.

"Cameron? What—?" He read it.

> *Priscilla, my child: this for you.*
> *At various points along our journey I talked with Rob about you. I hope you may understand by this time that he loves you very sincerely. He has, I know, lived a some-what roving and disreputable life and, I don't doubt, entered into various short-lived and discreditable relationships.*

"Humph!" Cal broke off. "Cannot you just hear our guardian sniff there!" He laughed. "Poor Rob!"

> *But now I believe that his affections are sincerely en-gaged; he has spoken of you many times, with such un-derstanding and devotion that I believe, if you accept him, you will have ensured for yourself a truly suitable and lasting partnership.*

Cal broke off again. "But, Scylla—I thought you said—"

"Go on!" Her voice was strangled. She clenched her hands together.

> *He asked whether I considered it proper for him to offer marriage to you; in fact he had suggested this sev-eral times in a very diffident manner, due to the disparity of age and his wandering way of life. At first, indeed, I could not agree to such a union; and indeed he did not feel himself a suitable partner for you. He looks upon*

you and Cal as such rarefied beings—far above him! Also he felt it unfair to your youth and inexperience that he should attempt to engage your affections before you had a chance to see the world and encounter other applicants.

"Other applicants!" Scylla broke in bitterly. "He should have seen Captain Phillimore! He should see—but go on."

As he put it: "The lass ought to have a chance to go to Almack's, since that appears to be the crown of her ambition. If I snapped her up before she had done that, I fear she might always hold it against me." Upon our parting at Acre, however, being by that time quite convinced of the sincerity of his feelings, I urged that he should make you an offer before you, too, embarked. I strongly hope that he did so, my dear child, and that you accepted him; nothing could make me happier. If he did not summon up the courage, I take the opportunity to tell you now of the depth, true strength, and disinterested attachment of his feeling for you; it may hinder you from contracting in England any shallow or fleeting connections which you might later come to regret.

Yr affc. Guardian,
Amanda Musson.

"Shallow or fleeting connections!" Scylla gave a kind of wretched laugh.

"But you said that he *did* make you an offer?" Cal looked at her in perplexity.

"So he did! And I did not believe he meant it! I sent him away!" She hid her face in her hands. "I sent him away—in the curtest—most repulsive—manner; and why in the world should he ever come back?"

"Well, you could write to him," Cal said reasonably. "To that address he gave you in Baghdad."

"Write? I could never do such a thing! Are you mad?"

"Women!" said Cal in exasperation. "Why were they ever made? Oh, Lord, here comes Bet back from her harp lesson. I'm off to the stable!"

He snatched up his crutch and limped away, leaving his sister to the depressing company of Bet and her own thoughts.

Bitter weather during the following week kept the household mostly within doors. Cal chafed miserably at the enforced inactivity. Whether it was the proximity of Fanny or the atmosphere of the Hermitage, he did not know, but neither in the house nor anywhere near it could he manage to write poetry; his muse remained implacably silent. Indoors, he found it particularly hard to concentrate; the winter wind, which blew so constantly, raised an eerie banshee-like wail somewhere in the house, hideously distracting, for he found himself listening tensely, waiting for it to happen; while wherever he was, in house, barn, or stable, he found himself strangely, exasperatingly beset by the notion that, if he looked up from his writing, he would see a small child, little Chet perhaps, squatting in the doorway, or crouching at his feet, or about to scramble toward him across the floor.

Scylla, too, during this period was unusually quiet and gloomy. Several times, indeed, she was so short with Thomas, upon his attempting to engage her in conversation, that she materially contributed to *his* bad temper.

Thomas was in a particularly sullen and intractable humor; Patty was peevish because the new cousins took little notice of her, finding her a detestable child; and Bet was in a sulk because Thomas had refused to allow her to attend a Twelfth Night party at Petworth House, where she had hoped to wear the gown Scylla had given her.

With tempers in the Hermitage mostly at such an inflammable point, it was to be expected that sooner or later there would be an explosion. This finally occurred one afternoon in mid-January when Cal, driven indoors by cold and frustration, had come into the parlor to find Fanny and Scylla vainly endeavoring to interest little Thomas in the notion of crawling across the hearthrug, by dangling in front of him a charming coral and bells that Scylla had brought him from London. He would merely gaze at it vaguely, extend a languid fist, then lose interest and, as it seemed, withdraw into himself again.

"*I* was able to crawl at that age, was I not?" demanded Patty. "Was I not, Stepmamma?"

"I did not know you at that age," said Fanny patiently. "Come, baby!"

"How different he is from little Chet," Cal murmured involuntarily to his sister, remembering the Indian baby's lively brown smiling countenance and his alert movements; little Thomas was pale, vacant, and seemed half asleep all the time.

"How different from Fanny," Scylla murmured in reply. "He is like a changeling."

"That is it—No, he is like one of those children who have had their spirits stolen away by the trolls. I have it—the child in my poem!" And, his mind on nothing but pursuing his idea to its source, Cal picked up a sheaf of papers which he had been irritably rereading, in the hope of pushing himself to a new point of inspiration, and read aloud:

> "*For he has dwelt within the enchanted mound*
> *By Urdar spring, where time is naught but dream.*
> *What tidings can he bring? No human sound*
> *Disturbs the silence there, no wandering gleam*
> *Pierces the dark, nor fins divide that stream.*
> *No single element in that domain*
> *Has here its image; that immortal scheme*
> *Contains creations his untutored brain*
> *May neither grasp nor guess, remember nor explain.*"

"Hush, Cal! You will distress Fanny."

"No, but do listen! Does not this exactly describe little Thomas:

> "*Poor child! The birds will sing for him in vain.*
> *For him, what matter that the rose is red?*

He cannot love the sun, nor rue the rain.
Winds, unregarded, lave his heedless head.
Deaf, blind, and speechless, all perceptions fled,
Save one, the sense of loss, he gropes his way,
And will, until his final hours are sped;
An orphaned, witless wanderer, far astray,
His stolen soul estranged, mislaid in yesterday!

"Does not that exactly describe the child? 'Mislaid in yesterday,'" Cal repeated, with the writer's sense of satisfaction at his own successful phrase.

And then stopped short, aghast at the sight of Thomas, outraged, stiff with icy dislike, close beside him.

"*So! So, sir!*" All the suppressed dislike of two months' enforced propinquity came hissing out like concentrated poison in Thomas's exclamation. "So *that* is what you think of my son! Deaf and speechless! You—miserable—conceited—young *puppy!* How *dare* you? How dare you come here, you confounded—misbegotten interloper—eat my food—make use of my house—and insult me so?"

"Thomas, Thomas!" implored Fanny. "Remember that Cousin Cal is our guest!"

"I am not likely to forget it!"

"Cousin Juliana's guest, rather," said Cal, white about the nostrils. "Also I might remind you that my sister and I make a substantial contribution to the housekeeping! And I might further mention that we are *not* misbegotten—our parents were, I understand, married by a perfectly legal process known as chadar dalna—"

"Oh, hush, Cal! What does it matter? You are only exasperating him further," interpolated Scylla. "Do, for heaven's sake, apologize!"

"He certainly *will* apologize!" said Thomas, ominously flushed. "Or leave my house directly!"

"Apologize? What for? For pointing out what everybody else has observed long ago—that your wretched child is slow in his wits, if not actually feeble-minded?"

For all reply Thomas snatched up Cal's crutch, which was leaning against the sopha, and with it aimed a blow at Cal's head which must have knocked him senseless if he had not moved sharply aside; as it was, it struck his shoulder and sent him sprawling. He fell, striking his injured leg on the harp, which overbalanced. The twang of the strings mingled with Cal's shout of pain. He was up the next instant, however, perfectly white, his lips compressed and his eyes blazing.

"You cowardly scoundrel! I'll require satisfaction for that!"

"Cal, *Cal!*" his sister besought him. "This is folly! Remember yourself, think where we are. Think of Fanny!"

"Thomas!" begged Fanny likewise. "Stop, stop! This must go no further—you should *not* have struck your cousin!"

"Oh, why not?" said Cal coldly. "Knocking down an injured man with his own crutch is only such behavior as might be expected from Cousin Thomas."

Thomas, who did seem almost mad with fury, appeared quite capable of repeating the act, but fortunately, at that moment, a loud peal at the front doorbell brought all the protagonists to a sense of their surroundings; Thomas took himself off with an angry exclamation, bawling for one of the servants to answer the door; Scylla managed to drag her brother away to his chamber, where he paced up and down, fulminating against Thomas, until obliged to lie down through a sudden sickness and weakness brought on by the pain of his fall.

The ring at the door, which had interrupted the cousins' quarrel so fortunately, was equally fortunate in its purport, for it proved to have been an express messenger from Cal's friend Lieutenant, now Captain, Howard, who, at Portsmouth, having achieved his promotion and been posted into an 18-gun sloop, the *Asp,* was sending to inform Cal of his good fortune and beg his friend to join him as senior lieutenant and second in command without delay.

At any other time Scylla would have cried out against the notion of his putting out to sea in his present state, so very soon after his injured leg had healed; but now even she could see that there was no possibility of Cal remaining at the Hermitage any longer; he and Thomas would be continually at loggerheads. Miserably she helped him pack up his belongings and sent Jem to the White Hart to order a post chaise for six o'clock the following morning.

"That way I shan't be under the necessity of seeing that skulking fellow again; which is as well, for if I got my hands on him I'd never let go till I wrung his neck. Poor Fanny! I do sincerely pity her! My consolation is that it can't be too long before he has his deserts. There must be twenty people within five miles who would be glad to murder Thomas Paget.—But what will *you* do now, love? Shall you stay here? Or"—with a faint smile Cal recalled Miss Musson's letter—"do you want to go up to London and try your luck at Almack's?"

"Oh, Cal, how can I tell? I think I must stay here for a while. I do not feel in the mood for London."

"I am glad to hear it." Cal's rage was ebbing fast, with the prospect of interest and action ahead; he said ruefully, "I fear it will be upon Fanny that the brunt of this confounded quarrel will fall. Thomas will be as sore as a bear for days. She will be glad of your company."

"And I shall be glad of hers. But if"—Scylla did not wish to say, *If Thomas's attentions to me become too marked or too intolerable;* she did not want to wake Cal's ire again—"if I decide to go to London, I shall stay with our cousins the Lambournes, who have a house in Berkeley Square. They came to call when I was in Egremont House, and though I did not greatly care for Caroline Lambourne, she was perfectly civil, and indeed pressing in her invitation to me to make their house my own."

"Humph!" remarked Cal, stuffing neckcloths into his portmanteau. "Just like our cousin Juliana and our cousin Thomas!"

"Or there is an old great-uncle living in Hampshire," said Scylla despondently.

"Well, if I write to you, I shall direct my letters here."

"Oh, *pray* write, Cal—I shall miss you so unspeakably—indeed I do not know how I will be able to bear it."

"Now, goose—do not be shedding tears all over my clean linen! You know we should have had to part sometime."

"I wish we might have a house together and live in it."

"Well, so we will, when I am an admiral. Come, cheer up; go to Mrs. Strudwick for me and coax out of her a pasty or something, so that I need not see Thomas at the dinner table."

But Mrs. Strudwick, who had taken a strong fancy to Cal, insisted on putting up for him a whole box of eatables, including a spare Christmas pudding and half a ham. "For," she said, "I know that on those ships they gets nothing but nasty salt beef and biscuits all a-squirming with weevils."

Scylla too, avoiding the family dinner table, retired early to her couch and got up in the black, icy dawn to walk down to the White Hart and say good-by to her brother there, as he did not wish to rouse the rest of the household by having the chaise come to the door. A new fall of snow, from the previous evening, muffled their footsteps, but it was not above half an inch and had already melted from the cobblestones in the street.

Goble obligingly carried Cal's bag for him, refused a shilling for his pains, and seemed genuinely sorry to say good-by.

"Watch out, then, Mus Cal! Don't 'ee goo camsteary on that leg, now. I'm in behopes you'll be back, when old Boney's been put to bed with a shovel."

"Ah, I'll be back then, Mr. Goble, and we'll make a grand sossel of it!" Cal said, clapping him on the shoulder affectionately. "And don't you worry any further about what you told me. Done is done, and telling over won't help it."

"Ah, you're just about right there, sir," said Goble, and hobbled off.

"What had he been worrying about?" Scylla inquired.

"Never mind! Something he'd done that can't be mended now. He's a strange old fellow—we got talking—I couldn't sleep last night, my mind was whirling about like a windmill. I rose at three and spent the rest of the night outside, wandering about in the snow and listening to the owls." Scylla could believe that, for Cal was pale and hollow-eyed. "I couldn't get Fanny out of my mind, Scylla; you'll keep an eye on her, won't you? She is so frail—like those windflowers we saw growing on the banks of the Kunar River—do you remember? Say"—for a moment his voice cracked—"say good-by to her for me, will you? And give her this"—he dropped a light kiss on her mouth. "I can't give her anything more tangible, or Thomas would infalliby discover it! Anyway—as I was about to say—at four o'clock or thereabouts, what should I see but old Goble standing in the garden like a ghost. I said to him, 'What in the world are you doing here at this time of night, Goble?' and he said, 'I've summat on my mind, Mus Cal, what puts me all in a cold clam. I dreamed I saw a shim out here by the well-head, an' I got so fidgety I came down from my bed to see if 'twas so."

"What is a *shim?*"

"A ghost, I fancy."

Scylla shivered. "Poor old man! Perhaps he has not enough bed-clothes up there in that loft. I'll mention it to Fanny."

"By all means do so—but he had more than blankets on his mind. Ah, here is my chaise. Good-by, love—don't forget me"—and he gave her a quick hug and swung himself up, awkwardly, with the driver's help. The horses clattered off on the icy cobbles, and Scylla found herself suddenly alone, her throat full of tears, hungry, hollow in the heart, and freezing cold.

She returned home, wrapped herself in shawls, and climbed into her cold bed. I shall never sleep, she thought, but she, like Cal, had spent the early part of the night in wide-eyed restless wakefulness, looking ahead into what seemed a black and hopeless future; she did in fact fall quite quickly into a heavy slumber and slept long and late.

When she woke next it was full day, and there was a feeling of uneasiness and urgency so strong about the house that, even before she was washed and dressed, Scylla felt certain that something was badly amiss. Indeed, while she was combing out her curls, a tap came at the door.

"Who is it?" she called.

"It's Tess, miss. Oh, miss! Have you little Master Thomas in there with you?"

"Master Thomas?" Scylla flung open the door. "Good gracious, no! Why should I have him in here? Is he not in his cot or with his mother?"

"No, ma'am, he's not nowhere! He've gone missing, and, oh, I'm afeered the gipsies must have taken him!"

"Oh, what nonsense! I dare say he is in Miss Bet's room."

"No, we have looked all over, miss, and now Master is calling the constables," Tess said tearfully.

Scylla was appalled and hurried to the parlor, where she found Fanny, shivering and pale, but composed.

"Fanny! Can this be true?"

Fanny turned and speechlessly grasped both Scylla's hands. In the dining room the nursemaid Jemima could be heard sobbing hysterically and being scolded by Mrs. Strudwick. Bet and Patty, aghast and wide-eyed, huddled in a corner; Thomas, somewhere outside the house, was shouting orders.

"Yes, it is true," Fanny said at last. "Who could have done such a thing I cannot—" She gulped, and fell silent. Outside, the constables had now apparently arrived. Thomas was instructing them to interrogate the turnpike tollkeepers on the Midhurst and London roads, as to any strangers who might have passed by during the night. Scylla suddenly realized that the reason she could hear all this so clearly was because one of the windows was open six inches, although there was no fire in the hearth and the morning was bitterly cold. She moved to shut the window, but Fanny put out a hand to stop her.

"Thomas says we must leave it so. It was like that when I came down."

"How very strange! Was it not fastened last night?"

Scylla knew that it was Thomas's habit to make a circuit of all the downstairs windows and doors before going to bed, checking bars and bolts. But perhaps last night he had forgotten. Perhaps he had been as distracted, as thrown off balance, as Cal—

Cal!

Hoarsely, finding that her voice came out two tones deeper than she expected, Scylla said:

"Fanny, Cal has gone back to sea. He went off by post chaise this morning. He—he thought it best not to say good-by to you. He asked me to say it for him—"

Fanny stared at her in silence. It seemed to take a moment for the impact of the news to sink in. Then she said, almost inaudibly:

"Cal has *gone?*"

"Yes; gone to Portsmouth, to join a ship, the *Asp.* . . ."

Thomas came into the room with two burly men in top hats, the town constables, who gravely inspected the open window.

"Arr," said one of them. "Anybody could-a clumb in there."

" 'Countable easy, they could," said the other.

Then they followed Thomas upstairs to inspect the baby's empty cradle and, finally, to interrogate Jemima, who, heavy-eyed and husky from crying, could only declare that she had fallen into a deep sleep on the previous evening—"Dunnamany hours I slept, I never had sich a slumber before, never!"—and had awoken in the morning to find the baby gone.

"Were it not best to send for Lord Egremont?" whispered Scylla to Fanny while this was going on. "Is he not lord lieutenant of the county? I dare say these men are doing their duty as best they can—but they do not seem very sharp-witted."

Slowly Fanny nodded.

"Yes, that would be best. I wonder Thomas has not already done so." She spoke slowly and dazedly.

● Thomas was rushing about in a kind of wild, frenetic activity—now urging the maids to make yet another search of the attics and cellar; now ordering Goble and Jem to search the garden and outhouses. The well, with memories of the previous incident, was opened and inspected but found to contain nothing; nor did the stables, nor Thomas's garden room, nor the cellar beneath it.

Quietly, Scylla went out to Goble.

"Goble, will you please go to Petworth House and—and have Lord Egremont informed as to what has happened here?"

Dull-eyed, the old man looked up at her.

"Ah, that'd be best, missy; I'll go an' fet'n drackly."

"Goble," said Scylla—she could hardly trust her voice, her breath was coming in irregular gulps—"Goble, you don't *know* anything about this, do you? About—about little Master Thomas being lost?"

His expression was that of a desolate dog, beaten for some fault it does not understand.

"God's my witness I don't, missy; I only wish I did; by the pize, I do."

She let him go on that; she could not bear to ask the question that trembled in her mind: whether he thought that Cal had anything to do with it. *Cal?* No, it was just not possible. Not as a prank; no, he would never do anything so horrible. Not when it involved Fanny. . . .

Wearily Scylla returned to her chamber—which bore evidence of having been roughly searched—and sat on the bed, staring straight in front of her.

Presently she pulled out Miss Musson's letter and looked at it.

"I think you should know of the depth, the strength, and disinterested attachment of his feeling for you—"

After she had looked at them for a while the lines swam before her eyes.

XIX

Lord Egremont arrived at noon. Thomas, by that time, having learned that Cal had left Petworth, was insisting that his cousin must have stolen little Thomas and demanding that he be fetched back.

"Skulking off like that at nighttime! It's as plain as day that that's what he must have done. The man is mad—epileptic—spiteful and raving!"

"Oh, tush, my dear fellow. Lieutenant Paget? Absurd! Why should he commit such an act? He is a *gentleman!* Stealing babies? Good God, man, you must have a maggot in your idea box. No, no, depend upon it, you will find that some local ruffians are responsible for this. Bad business, shocking business, but I hope we'll very soon get to the bottom of it."

Egremont, as Scylla had expected, initiated a far more intelligent and speedy inquiry than the constables had done, sending out members of his own staff to question half the town, dispatching a message to London for Bow Street runners, and organizing an intensive search of the Hermitage and its environs.

At about four in the afternoon, when early winter dusk was already beginning to close in, a kind of shocked hush succeeded the uneasy bustle that had surrounded the house all day. Scylla, Fanny, Bet, and Patty were huddled in the parlor, over a dismal fire which nobody had the heart to blow brighter.

All of a sudden—"I believe they have found something," said Scylla.

They all listened, straining their ears. The sounds had been coming from outside and seemed to have centered around the ash tree. Scylla, moving to the window and parting the curtains, could see nothing; all beyond appeared already black as midnight. But in a few minutes the hall door opened and they heard low voices.

"Who's to tell her?"

"Not I, for sure."

"*I* will tell her," said Lord Egremont's voice, firm and clear; and he came into the room. He was still wearing his greatcoat and had mud daubed on his hessian boots; for once he was not smiling; his face was grave and stern.

He glanced about the room, observed Scylla, made her an infinitesimal signal with his head, as if to gesture her toward Fanny, then, moving up to the latter, took her hand, saying, gently but firmly:

"My child, I have some very bad news for you. I see no means of softening the blow but by telling you directly."

Fanny looked up into his face.

"The child is dead?"

"Yes," he said.

"Wh-where did you find him?"

"He was buried under the tree outside. The ash tree. Had it not snowed in the night he must have been found sooner, but the snowfall disguised the broken earth."

"The ash?" Fanny said. Her lips scarcely moved. "He was buried under the ash tree?"

"I am afraid so. Yes."

Scylla moved to take Fanny's arm but the latter seemed almost unconscious of her surroundings.

"What had—how had he been killed? He had not—he had not been buried *alive?*"

"No." Lord Egremont's face was set as if he hated to speak, but there was no help for it. "His throat was cut."

"Oh, dear God," Fanny whispered to herself, and then, puzzled, blindly looking up. "Who would *do* such a thing? To a *child?*"

"My dear, I do not know. But we will find out, depend upon it.— Now I want you to come with me up to Petworth House, where Liz will look after you." His eyes met those of Scylla; she nodded, agreeing with the plan. "You should not be staying here just now. This is too sad a place for you." Fanny, however—shocked, appalled as she was— would not budge. "I must remain here. Thomas will need me. Where is Thomas?" For the first time a gust of emotion shook her. Tears started from her eyes. "Oh, Thomas—*poor* Thomas! What will this *do* to him? I must go to him directly."

Again Egremont's eyes met those of Scylla, and he slightly shook his head.

"No, ma'am, I do not think you should do that just now. Your husband is—not himself."

"Where—where is the baby? Can I see him?"

Egremont shook his head decisively.

"The constables have—have taken charge of the body, ma'am. There must be an inquest, you see."

"An inquest. Yes." Fanny nodded. "Like poor Miss Fox." A kind of shudder went through her. After a moment she said:

"I think I should like to lie down on my bed for a little."

"Very sensible, my dear—though I wish you will come back with me. But if you remain here—somebody must be with you."

Scylla said, "Bet—why do you not take your stepmother upstairs? I will come in a moment."

Patty followed her sister and stepmother. Directly she was alone with Lord Egremont, Scylla went on:

"Sir, I have to tell you something. I—I feel it is my duty. My brother, as you know, returned to sea today. Yesterday evening he had a violent quarrel with Captain Paget."

"Yes, my dear, so I have heard." Lord Egremont smiled faintly. "After such a quarrel, witnesses are not backward in coming forward! Half the servants seem to have overheard it. And indeed Thomas told me himself."

"Of course." Scylla swallowed; then went on to relate the story of Cal's vigil in the garden. "I do not—do not know if this has anything to do with the crime, but I thought it right to inform you." Should she mention that Goble had something on his conscience? No—that was between him and Cal.

"Has—has Captain Paget accused my brother?"

"Indeed he has," said Egremont calmly. "And in no uncertain terms! But we have made due allowance for his distressed state of mind. I do not doubt but that he will have had second thoughts by to-morrow. We shall have to send for your brother, however." He took Scylla's hand and added, "Ma'am, it is with reluctance that I leave you in charge of this stricken household. Do not hesitate to send for me, though, if anything occurs to trouble or distress you.—Now I will bid you good night."

Scylla went slowly upstairs to Fanny, whom she found lying perfectly motionless on her bed, wrapped in a shawl, staring at the ceiling.

Scylla sat down on the bed by her and took her hand. After a moment Fanny said:

"Is Thomas accusing Cal?"

"Yes."

By next day, however, Thomas had changed his tune and was accusing Fanny. And with more apparent justification. For early next day two Bow Street runners arrived and proceeded to conduct an exceedingly intensive and thorough search of the house and garden, sifting through ashes of fires, prodding patches of loose earth, raising loose floor boards. One of the first things they discovered, in the vault of an outside privy at some distance from the house, was a blood-soaked garment which proved to be one of Fanny's cambric nightdresses. And wrapped up in it was a discarded razor of Thomas's, which Fanny had been in the habit of keeping in one of her bedroom drawers. She said vaguely, when questioned about it, that she had made use of it for undoing seams "when taking out tucks, so as to enlarge garments."

Meanwhile an express messenger, sent posting after Cal, had arrived too late; the sloop *Asp*, under command of its new captain, had sailed last night with the evening tide, under sealed orders from the Admiralty. Where was its destination? Nobody knew.

During this period gossip ran rife in the town. Who could have done the horrid deed? Most townspeople suggested that for the criminal the runners need look no further than one of the inmates of the Hermitage itself. "Very likely one o' the daughters—the eldern's a plain, spiteful mawk, an' 'tis well known the liddle maid were tarnal jealous o' the babby, allus tormenting and tarrifying of it."

Since it hardly seemed possible, however, that little Patty was capable of lifting a large baby from its cradle and cutting its throat, let alone digging a two-foot hole and burying it in frozen ground, suspicion rested more heavily upon Bet.

Indeed the Bow Street runners questioned her intensively for several hours, and at the inquest she was subjected to a formidable interrogation by Captain Dallyn, the chief constable.

Dr. Chilgrove gave evidence as to the state of the body: "The child's throat had been cut to the bone by a sharp instrument; there had also been several stab wounds in the corpse, which was quite drained of blood. At least three pints must have been lost. The body was cold and stiff when I examined it at 4:30 P.M. I am of the opinion that death had taken place at least twelve hours previously, probably more."

Parsons, one of the constables, gave evidence as to the open window. This produced a considerable sensation in the town hall (where the inquest was held) and public opinion veered back to the theory that some piker, mumper, or waygoer had broken into the house, possibly with the intention of burglary, had accidentally roused the child, and murdered him to stifle his noise.—But then, what about the nurse Jemima's unnaturally heavy slumber? What about Mrs. Paget's nightdress soaked in blood? And the razor, which had been kept in her drawer? The inquest jury demanded that Mrs. Paget be questioned; but this Dr. Chilgrove flatly refused to allow, informing Captain Dallyn that she was in a state of collapse. Scylla, Bet, and the maids all gave evidence, but none of them had anything useful to contribute. Thomas, again by Dr. Chilgrove's order, was not questioned; his grief and distress were too profound to make him capable of answering rationally.

The inquest jury returned a verdict of murder by person or persons unknown.

Later on that day, quietly, without stir or commotion, Fanny was arrested and taken away; not to Petworth jail, where she might become the target of local hostile and angry feeling, but to Chichester, fifteen miles distant, over the Downs. She was treated with civility and consideration; allowed to take a small bag of her own toilet things and nightwear; and assured that, owing to Lord Egremont's good offices, she was to be incarcerated in a cell by herself, and even be allowed a cot bed instead of a straw pallet. She received this news unemotionally, with the distrait, absent calm which had characterized her behavior since she first received the account of the child's death. It was Scylla who, outraged and furious, demanded by what right they took her off, how dared they accuse her? Surely Lord Egremont could not countenance such a miscarriage of justice?

"Lord Egremont be lord lieutenant o' the county, miss," one of the arresting constables pointed out phlegmatically. "Nothing can't be done without he knows about it."

"Do not trouble about me, pray, Scylla," Fanny said wearily. And she added in a low tone, "I never loved either of them. I have only my own self to blame."

"*Fanny!* Do not talk so!" Scylla was horrified. "I shall go to see Lord Egremont directly—I—I shall be coming to visit you in pr—over there—as soon as possible. I am *certain* that, very shortly, this injustice will be set right."

Thomas was not present when his wife was taken away. Indignantly, Scylla went in search of him and found him in his bedroom, methodically instructing Mrs. Strudwick and the weeping Tess to pack up all of Fanny's clothes and belongings.

"Thomas! What are you doing?"

"She is a murderess," he said coldly. "She killed my son. I do not want any relic of her to remain in this house."

"Have you gone mad? You know Fanny could not do such a thing! To her own child!"

"I know nothing of the sort. She had always neglected the child. She would not take it about with her. She disliked it, she was ashamed of it; she would not show it to people. For a long time she had been wishing it dead. *I know her nature!*" He lifted his eyes—angry, bloodshot, full of dreadful suffering—to those of Scylla. "Pray do not refer to this again, cousin; it is inexpressibly painful to me." Scylla left him and took herself up to Petworth House, where she found Liz Wyndham, alone and deeply troubled.

"George has gone over to Chichester; he is doing what he can to ensure that Fanny will be used with civility and given comfortable quarters."

"He is very good," Scylla mechanically said. Then she burst out, "Liz! For God's sake! How *could* he permit her arrest? He cannot believe she did it?"

"I do not think he does." Liz looked even more distressed. "But George cannot flout the processes of law. And the evidence against her is very strong, Scylla."

"But *Fanny*—so good, so gentle, who would not hurt a fly—her own *baby?* The *hours* I have seen her trying to teach that poor little thing to crawl, to take food, to talk—"

"Yes, that is true. But, Scylla, I don't believe she loved the baby—in fact I know she did not, she once said as much to me. . . . And she may well have come to hate her husband—"

"She had cause." Scylla's tone was bitter.

"Very likely. But that is why—don't you see, I am so afraid that, in the end, the baby may have come to *represent* Thomas in Fanny's eyes."

"I do not believe it." But, in spite of herself, Scylla was shaken again. She exclaimed, "Oh, God! Why did Cal and I ever come to Petworth? If we had not come here, Fanny and Thomas might never—might never—Oh, how I wish Cal were here now."

"Well, George is doing his best to get him back," Liz said. "He has applied to the Admiralty for an urgent message to be dispatched after the *Asp*—wherever it has gone. We can only wait." She added doubtfully, "Let us hope that whatever your brother has to say will clear Fanny entirely."

Scylla shivered. "In fact, I do not see how it can. He did not see Fanny again after—after his quarrel with Thomas. His last words to me were a request to say good-by to Fanny—"

Her voice faltered.

Liz gave her a very piercing glance.

"Did they love one another?"

"It is possible," Scylla had to admit. "I have sometimes thought . . . They dealt so happily together, with his poetry and her music."

"Possible? Say rather, inevitable. Your brother such a contrast to—How could she help it? And Thomas intensely jealous, no doubt?" Liz added dryly, "How does he behave himself to you?"

"Oh—he has been friendly enough." Scylla was not going to mention that look in Thomas's eye. She went on, "But now—after this—as Cal's sister—I am not sure how he will feel—I believe he thinks that Cal and Fanny somehow connived together to do the deed."

Liz said, "Would it not be best if you were to come and stay here with us? You must necessarily feel uncomfortable, alone in the house with Thomas, and only those two dismal girls as chaperones."

"Well—indeed I must say that I should be only too thankful—that house is horrible to me now. But perhaps it is my duty to stay there and comfort the girls—" Scylla began doubtfully.

"Fudge! Let their father do that. Do you go home and pack your things—I will send down a carriage for you in an hour's time. Indeed we shall be glad of your company!"

Acknowledging to herself her own relief at being thus firmly taken in hand, Scylla returned to the Hermitage. The house which, only three days before, had been so cheerfully brimming with life and activity was like a stricken place, mournfully silent, except when a gust of January wind elicited in some quarter the wild keening wail which made the servants shiver and exchange looks pregnant with ominous meaning.

"It were a-waiting—all the time—for summat to happen," commented Tess, helping Scylla pack her clothes. "I'll be out o' this place so fast—when me time's up—you 'on't see me for dust!"

"Tess," said Mrs. Strudwick, putting her head around the door, "have you seen Master's old pea jacket? Missus was on at me t'other day to sew on a couple of buttons that were coming loose, and I can't seem to lay me hands on it anywhere."

Tess disclaimed any knowledge of it. "But there's Master a-coming down the stairs this minute, ask him himself, why don't you?"

"I'm half afeered to speak to him, he looks so mazed and dreesome."

Indeed Thomas, when applied to, glowered at the housekeeper and told her not to pester him with trifles at such a time; and then, apparently recollecting, he said that he had given the jacket to a beggar several weeks ago.

"Well, I never!" muttered Tess to Mrs. Strudwick out of hearing. "I never knew Master give anything away afore—leastways, not something that still had some wear in it!"

"Saves me a job," said Mrs. Strudwick, and returned to the kitchen.

Thomas followed Scylla to her room, where she was packing a few books into a box.

"Why, what is this!" he exclaimed in great displeasure, looking at the stripped, tidy chamber. "I do not understand. What is going on here?"

"I am removing myself to Petworth House," Scylla told him composedly. "Mrs. Wyndham has invited me."

"*Removing to Petworth House?* But why should you do such a thing?" He seemed really shocked and disturbed; much more so, Scylla thought angrily, than at the news of Fanny's arrest.

"I do not wish to remain here, cousin."

Now he became angry. "You cannot leave me like this! What about my poor girls—with no one to comfort or advise them?"

"They have you, Thomas," Scylla coldly pointed out. "For the rest, they must manage as I presume they did before you married Fanny."

"It will look very bad if you leave me! People will say that it looks as if we have quarreled—as if you do not trust me!"

"To tell you the truth," Scylla replied, vigorously knotting a cord around her box, "I do not care a groat what people say. You and my brother *had* quarreled—I think it best that I leave your house."

Glancing about her, she stepped toward the door.

"No! I shall not let you slip away as easily as that!" cried Thomas.

He moved swiftly to intercept her and grasped her by the wrist. Even with only three fingers, his grip was unnervingly strong.

"Thomas! Will you please let me go!"

"No, I will not!" Now he had both wrists. "Can you not see—do you not realize—what your presence means to me? You *cannot* leave me now! You are my one comfort, my one hope for the future—the only star in the blackness that surrounds me!"

She exclaimed in horror, "You should *not* be saying these things to me! You are not yourself! I wish to hear no more—*pray* be silent and do not give me pain by talking in this manner. Have you no thought for Fanny—for your wife?"

As only answer, he encircled her with his arms and kissed her violently, repeatedly, bruising her mouth, while she struggled in vain to free herself. Indeed, she was amazed at his strength; short, thin, sallow, unassuming Thomas seemed to have the vigor, the tenacity and power, of a man twice his size.

"I love you, I love you!" he panted. "You and only you! I do not care any more what you may have been to other men—which, I must confess, did trouble me at first. But now my love for you has grown so great that I can overlook such considerations—" kissing her furiously and beginning to thrust her toward the tidy bed. "I must have you! I must and will make you mine."

Sobbing with rage, Scylla managed to tear herself loose from him and ran to the door. Snatching the key from the lock, she slammed the door as he started after her, and locked it on the outside. Then she ran to the front hall. Her luggage could be fetched later—she would return to Petworth House on foot. But outside the door she found Lord Egremont's chaise waiting for her, and her larger bags already bestowed in the boot. She had only to put on her pelisse and go. She had left the Hermitage only just in time, she told herself. Her lip was beginning to swell up—she would have to tell Liz that she had knocked it against the bedpost. Describe the scene that had just passed she *could* not—it was too horrible, too disgusting.

Scylla remained at Petworth House for a number of weeks. Her life there settled into a quiet routine. Other visitors came and went, but she saw little of them, Lord Egremont and Liz fully comprehending that she preferred dinner on a tray in her room or in the library.

Almost every day she went to visit Fanny in the jail at Chichester; one of the Egremont carriages was placed unreservedly at her disposal. Fanny's demeanor on those visits was always the same: quiet, uncomplaining, withdrawn. She expressed thanks for whatever was brought her in the way of fruit, reading matter, and clean linen. She would not accept pity or sympathy, reiterating that the calamity had been her own fault. She never asked why her stepdaughters did not come to see her.

The family at the Hermitage were far from happy. Permission had been given, after the inquest, for the funeral of the murdered child. This took place privately at night, little Thomas being interred next to his grandmother. In spite of the precautions taken to keep the ceremony secret, however, word leaked out, and a number of townspeople made their way to the spot and watched in silent hostility while the tiny coffin was lowered into the ground. As Thomas and his daughters hastily climbed into the carriage afterward, a voice cried: "Murderers! Who killed your own child?" and the crowd shook their fists and booed. Handfuls of snow and stones from the roadside were thrown after them. Later that night several ground-floor windows were broken, and the word MURDERER was written on the door in red paint. Thomas was obliged to keep the downstairs windows shuttered, even in the daytime, to protect his daughters from the hostility of his neighbors, who walked down the lane and stared at the house as if they expected to see somebody emerge from it red-handed.

Scylla heard this news from the Petworth House servants, who were perfectly well informed as to local feeling. Rumors about the illness and death of Thomas's first wife had now percolated through the town, and suspicion had swung back from Bet to her father; it was generally agreed that a man who had murdered his first wife would think nothing of doing away with his child; any question as to *motive* was easily dismissed.—" 'E be a broody, niggly sort o' fellow—likely the child grizzled and riled 'im. Or maybe he were where he didn't oughter be, making up to the nursegirl—an' the child woke, an' seed 'im there!" Poor Jemima came in for some suspicion, and so did Scylla —she had to give up walking in the town after one or two shouts of "Paget's whore!" had disconcerted her in the street.

After four weeks the case was due to come up before the Petworth magistrates. Lord Egremont had instructed his own solicitor, a man called Burrows, to act for Fanny, since Thomas, both in public and private, continued to accuse Fanny of having committed the crime, so that Throgmorton, the Paget family lawyer, could hardly act for her. No word had come yet from the *Asp* or from Cal. But one evening, a couple of days before the court was due to sit, Lord Egremont came into the library where Scylla was sitting. He looked harassed and perplexed, as he so often did these days.

"I have the man Goble here," he told her.

"Oh? What does he say?" Scylla inquired eagerly. She was much inclined to think that in Goble there lay some clue to the whole affair.

"Oh, I do not know! He is a strange fellow, a little touched in his wits, I fear. He spun a long rigmarole about the ghost of Paget's dead brother—I think he would have me believe that *he* came back from the next world and committed the murder. A most unlikely notion! He did say one thing that struck me, though," pursued Egremont. "It seems that when he can't sleep he rambles about the Hermitage garden, which he did on that particular night; though, from his account, somewhat *after* the time when the crime must have been committed; and he says that first he saw a ghost, or Token, flitting about—

the ghost of poor Ned Wilshire, he asserts; and then, later, he saw Thomas Paget himself come through the gate from the Glebe Path and enter the Hermitage by the garden door."

Scylla's interest quickened. She asked, "Was Cal with Goble at this time?"

"Yes. The two of them were sitting quietly in the little shelter at the end of the yew-tree walk. Cal said to Goble, 'Hush, there goes Paget. Don't let him know we are here, I've no wish to be further embrangled with him.' I asked Goble was he sure, and he said he could not mistake; Paget was wearing a waistcoat and an open-necked shirt."

"An open-necked shirt? On a snowy night? Goble must have been dreaming!"

"Well, so I began to think; especially as, at that point in the tale, he ran off into a long Bible quotation about the children of the unrighteous. I fear that his evidence would be laughed down in any court."

"He said nothing more? He did not mention anything that was on his mind, that had been troubling him?"

Egremont gave her a quick look.

"No, he did not. But I felt that he *was* troubled. What makes you ask?"

"I think he divulged something to my brother—perhaps confessed something he had done. But I have no right to speak of it—my brother did not tell me what it was. It was a confidence." Uncontrollably she burst out, "Lord Egremont! Suppose they find Fanny guilty—what then?"

"My dear, there is no need to be looking so far ahead. This is only a preliminary hearing, you know, at the Magistrates' Court. Next will come the Assizes—by which time, more evidence may have come to light."

"But suppose they do find her guilty?"

He said reluctantly, "It is very unlikely that she would hang. She might serve a life sentence in prison—perhaps thirty years."

"Thirty years!"

"Very likely she might be transported to one of the penal settlements in the colonies."

This information was of small comfort to Scylla.

Meanwhile the Admiralty had divulged that the *Asp* had been ordered to the Mediterranean, with dispatches for Lieutenant General Charles Stuart, now campaigning against the French in Minorca. Lord Egremont had sent messengers posthaste to intercept the ship at Plymouth, where she would be likely to put in to take water; but, as ill luck would have it, she put in at Falmouth instead and set sail before they could catch up with her. The *Asp* was a particularly swift vessel, and, though messages were sent after her by other ships, it was plain that Cal could not be expected back within a couple of months.

The Magistrates' Court session was brief and businesslike. Fanny, brought back to Petworth for the occasion, appeared pale, quiet, and collected, dressed in a plain black gown with a veil over her head. Thomas was in court, but he did not approach her, and she never looked in his direction. Formal evidence was taken. Fanny's solicitor announced her intention of pleading not guilty, and the session was adjourned "pending the return of further witnesses, at present unavailable." Public curiosity was aroused by the plural case of "witnesses"; whom else, besides Lieutenant Paget, could this denote? From mouth to mouth passed the information that the gardener at the Hermitage, Henry Goble, was to have been called, but he was missing; had not been seen for several days. Where could he be?

An unpleasant feature of the proceedings was the behavior of the accused's husband, Captain Paget. Dr. Chilgrove had endeavored to prevent his being called, on the grounds that he was suffering from "mental incoherence" and was so shaken by what he had undergone that no reliance could be placed on his testimony. The objection was set aside, however, and he was called, but immediately burst into a loud, screaming denunciation of his wife, "who had turned his son into a half wit," and became so hysterical that he had to be led from the courtroom. This outburst increased the public prejudice against him, and he was booed, while a murmur of "Shame" went up as Fanny was led away back into custody. Indeed, her solicitor demanded that she be released on bail, but this the magistrates refused to allow, giving the reason that her incarceration was for her own protection.

Scylla had hoped to speak to Fanny after the hearing, but the behavior of the crowd outside the town hall became so ungovernable that the constables had to smuggle the prisoner away by a side entrance and into a closed carriage, before her enthusiastic sympathizers could mob and trample her.

Thomas, gloomily returning home, was startled by the sight of his daughter Martha, blooming and pretty, with an unusual air of matronly decision about her.

"Where the devil have *you* come from?" he growled at her. "Wherever it is, you may just go back there! You have no place in my house any more!"

"I have not the least wish to stay in your house," sharply retorted Martha. "I came to hear the court session, and what I heard decided me to take Patty back with me to my house. This is no place for a child her age. You may come too, Bet, if you like."

Bet, though affronted at this casual invitation from her younger sister, nevertheless decided that almost any place would be more cheerful than the Hermitage and went off to pack up some clothes for herself and Patty. Thomas raged at them all, but somehow without conviction; he did not really care if his daughters remained or departed. Without waiting to bid them farewell, he strode away to his garden room.

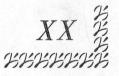

XX

The body of Henry Goble was discovered beside a tombstone in the new graveyard. Public shock and horror at this second death, following so rapidly after that of poor little Thomas Paget, was mitigated by Dr. Chilgrove's assurance that no foul play need be suspected. Inspection of the body had satisfied him that Goble had been carried off by the dangerous disorder of peripneumony, evidently brought on by chill and exposure acting on an already strained and enlarged heart which the doctor had been treating for some time with foxglove essence. It seemed plain that the poor man had been taken ill while tending the grave of Edward Wilshire, for he still clasped in his hand a bunch of crocuses that he must have been intending to place in a crock that stood nearby.

"Wretched man!" exclaimed Scylla when Lord Egremont brought her this news. "Cal will be excessively sad to hear of his death. I think he had grown truly attached to the old man, even in the short space of time that they had known one another. And now what is to be done? His testimony in court, however distracted, might have been worth *something;* now it is lost. All circumstances seem to favor my cousin Thomas! I believe he has sold his soul to the devil."

"Not *quite* all circumstances," Lord Egremont said. "I have here a letter from my friend James Henriques—"

"That good-for-nothing," muttered Liz Wyndham, who was sitting with them in the Petworth House library. "What use in the world can he be?"

"Not quite good for nothing, love, for he writes:

> *"Relative to your recent disturbances in Petworth, I am indeed shocked to read in* The Times *that your charming little neighbor has been charged with the murder of her child. It may have some bearing on this matter & be worth your knowing that Mrs. Liliane Baggot (who is at present living under my protection) affirms with certainty the following: viz., that Capt. Paget during an unguarded and expansive moment once swore to her that* he had succeeded in doing away with the first Mrs. P. & *wd not hesitate to get rid of the second should she prove as intransigeant as she bid fair to do. Mrs. B. wd be prepared to repeat this statement in Court but asks that, if possible, she may be spared this Horrid ordeal."*

"She might as well," remarked Liz, shrugging. "What is it, after all, but a spiteful piece of tittle-tattle?"

"Yes, very true, but investigations as to the death of the first Mrs. Paget might bring something to light. If only we had one piece of evidence of a more substantial nature!"

Unknown to Lord Egremont, such a piece of evidence was preparing, but it was not to come to light until some weeks later in that cold, bleak spring.

Meanwhile in Calcutta the new Governor General, the Earl of Mornington, resolved to strike at Tippoo Sahib's French-trained army and instructed his younger brother, Arthur Wellesley, with General Harris, to begin moving troops toward Seringapatam, the capital of Mysore. In the Mediterranean a combined Russian and Turkish fleet had captured Corfu. Marshal Suvorov, at the head of his Russian troops, had entered Milan. Buonaparte, having written urging Tippoo Sahib to overthrow the British in India, had set out on an overland march across the eastern desert toward Syria. Only the port and fortified town of Acre barred his passage eastward. And toward Acre the sloop *Asp* was making all speed with urgent dispatches.

In England the snow melted, fell again, melted again. And on the far side of the Shimmings Valley, Farmer Fewkes's cows, having scavenged in vain over the sodden hillside for a few mouthfuls of nourishing grass, raised their voices in complaint, lowing and bellowing their hunger and dissatisfaction.

"Drat 'em," said Farmer Fewkes to his man Tom. "They be growing as thin as clothes props. Ye'll have to give 'em a few more prongfuls o' Rector's hay, Tom."

Some weeks later, in Chichester jail, Fanny received an unexpected visitor. She had endeared herself to the wardresses by her gentle, diffident politeness; although accorded special privileges, she never presumed upon these, and performed any tasks set her with diligence and docility. Several of her kindly jailers were prepared to swear that she "could never have done that wicked deed" and would have been glad to shut their eyes to any small infringements of prison discipline. But Fanny never asked for any. Now, however—

"Here's a Lieutenant Paget to see you, love," said the day wardress, putting her head around the cell door. "By rights you're only allowed to be visited by husband, lawyer, or closest female relative—but we'll just say this one's your husband, eh? It's the same name, so what's the difference? And *he* never comes, anyway," she muttered disapprovingly, retreating and shutting the door.

Fanny almost fainted from surprise.

"Cal! I had thought you were in the Mediterranean Sea!"

"So I was. Oh, Fanny! My dearest dear! How can you *bear* it here? My poor love—what you have been through!"

It was very natural to find herself in Cal's arms, and the comfort of being there was so great that she was tempted to embrace him back, but withdrew herself, saying shakily:

"Indeed, we must not! Besides, what would they think—" glancing toward the grille in the door. "But, Cal, how in the world do you come to be here? I was never so astonished!"

She gazed at him, still hardly believing in his appearance, absently taking in the fact that he was very thin and looked pale under his sea tan.

"How do I come to be here? I posted direct from Portsmouth—and am on my way now to Petworth to make a deposition to the magistrates there. I shall tell them—what, I am sure, Goble already has but my testimony will add strength to his—that we saw Thomas in the garden on the night of—of your baby's death; that he wore shirt and trowsers only, and looked wild and haggard. At the time I thought his strange appearance to be a result of our quarrel, but now I believe it was due to guilt and horror over the deed he had just committed. Do you not think so too?"

Fanny shivered. "I do not know! He is very pertinacious in accusing me; and I know that *I* did not do it—but still—I find it so hard to believe that he could—that even *Thomas* could do such a thing—"

She raised pain-filled eyes to Cal, who exclaimed in horror, "You did not think that *I* had done it, Fanny?"

"No—oh, how could I tell? I did not know what to think."

"Have you no one to comfort you? Where is my sister?"

"Oh, she has come almost every day. She has been very kind. Everyone has indeed."

Now Cal glanced about the cell and saw that it was filled with tokens of people's good will—newspapers and books lay piled on the floor, jam pots of flowers, baskets of fruit stood ranged against the wall.

"Many Petworth people—whom I do not even know—so often send little things—eggs, cheeses—and the children send posies—somebody comes every single day with these—" Fanny indicated a very beautifully arranged bouquet of woodland flowers and evergreens—old-man's-beard, feathery broom, brilliant rose hips, pine fronds and cones, a few snowdrops and early wild daffodils. "Every day I receive a new one, but I do not know who brings them. Is it not beautiful?"

"Yes—very—but, Fanny, it is so dreadful to see you in this place. —To set you free I would gladly admit to the murder myself—"

"Cal, no! You are not to think of such a thing!"

"Well, I dare say it will not be necessary," he agreed. "I will go to see old Goble, and, between us, I dare say we may be able to piece together enough evidence to point the finger of justice at your abominable husband."

Fanny had not been told of Goble's death. Lord Egremont and Scylla had agreed that there was no point in additionally burdening her with this painful news.

She murmured, "I wish you need not! Oh—I do not want to die—and yet I feel that it may be better this way. Poor Thomas—I never loved him—indeed it was hard not to hate him—which was very wrong. I feel I am being punished deservedly."

"Arrant nonsense!" said Cal.

"No, it is not. I have a foreboding that, if I do not accept this as my just desert for not being a good wife to Thomas, something worse will happen. Oh, Cal—pray do not do anything rash or wild!"

"Not being a good wife to him? You were the best wife a man could hope for—far, far better than he deserved. Fanny, I dare say I should not be saying this to you now, but if—but when—when you are free of all this horror, free from Thomas—as you will, you *must* be—for he has quite disowned you—will you marry me? Will you be my wife? Indeed, I love you with my whole heart! Loving you has changed me from a boy to a man." He smiled at her ingenuously, and her heart was pierced by a curious pang—belying his words, he looked so much a boy, still, a lock of soft dark hair hanging, as usual, over his eyes, which gazed pleadingly into hers. "Fanny? Will you? Please say yes!"

She felt too much at ease with him to pretend shock, or surprise, or disapproval. But she shook her head.

"No. Dearest, dearest Cal—no! I love you as much as anybody in the world—but it cannot be. It can never be."

"Why not? You can divorce him, or—"

"Hush! It would be wrong. I know, I feel, it would be very wrong."

"No! It would not! It would be right—right for both of us!"

She said quietly, "Please do not go on."

"No, of course not." He was humbled. "Forgive me! I am always—importuning you when I should not—when you have too many troubles already. I just wanted you to know.—But you are right! I will leave you now. I will see you again as soon as may be. In the meantime—perhaps these may speak for me—" and he pulled a bundle of manuscript pages out of his pocket and handed them to her, saying with a slight smile, "Is it not strange? All the time I was under your roof, I could write nothing—not a single line—though I was feeling it in my heart. But the moment I was back at sea again, out it all came pouring, and the burden of it was Fanny—Fanny—Fanny! These are for you. Let them plead my case. Now I will bid you good-by."

And, first gently touching her forehead with his lips, he limped to the door and knocked to be let out.

During the hour's drive to Petworth he lay back against the cushions and sank into a profound sleep of exhaustion. Since receiving the news of Fanny's arrest he had hardly known a full night's repose—he had been riven by remorse over his quarrel with Thomas, which must have begun this whole train of events, harrowed by anxiety for Fanny, and consumed with a longing to affirm his love. The relief of having done this was so great that he slept like a child until awoken by his coach wheels clattering over the cobbled streets of Petworth.

He had told the driver to go straight to Petworth House, Fanny having informed him that Scylla was there. His need to see her almost equaled his need to see Fanny, and he was bitterly disappointed to be told by the major-domo that Miss Paget was not in the house just then.

"She'll be back here in two–three hours, though, sir; she and Mis' Wyndham have driven over to Chichester. They'll be back come dinnertime."

"How vexatious! We must have passed on the road."

However, Cal found the master of the house at home and unfeignedly delighted to see him.

"My dear Paget! You are welcome indeed. Where did my message finally catch up with you?"

"At Acre, sir."

"Acre? By heaven, you have made good time back, then!"

"We were bringing dispatches from Captain Sydney Smith, you see, sir. Boney is marching in his direction—hoping to go on to India—I believe he is at Jaffa now—so it was urgent to bring the news back to England. In that way, fortune favored me—otherwise I might not have got back so fast."

"You look worn to a bone, my poor boy. Will you eat a nuncheon?"

"No, I thank you, sir. I could not eat. I wish to make a deposition as soon as may be, regarding this horrible business."

"Of course you do! Let us go into the library, and I will ask Frank Goodyear to write it all down as you tell me. Frank! Frank!" he called to his secretary. "Come along, I wish you to write down Lieutenant Paget's statement."

In the library they found a young man studying a large number of elaborate plans which he had spread out on the great table. He rose politely at Lord Egremont's entrance and made to leave the room.

"Shan't disturb you long, Talgarth, my dear fellow," Lord Egremont said. "You go out and take some air, now, prune a tree or something, you look pale as a plateful of tripe! I wish you would obey my orders and go off to study the gardens at Corsham Court, instead of fagging yourself to death over those plans—all work and no play, you know!"

He shook his head at Talgarth as the latter, bowing, left the room, and added to Cal, "Capital young fellow that—capital. Obstinate as a bear, of course, never listens to my orders—but I believe he will be outstripping Capability Brown, by and by, he has a remarkable natural genius. He don't look well at present, though. Silly fellow! He spends too long over those confounded plans—schemes for my new pleasure grounds, you know. However that ain't to the purpose. Well, Frank—are you ready to write?"

"I believe, sir," said Cal, who had been thinking, "that it may be better if old Goble is brought here to confirm my testimony—that is, if it is possible to fetch him without arousing Captain Paget's suspicions?"

"Goble? What, hadn't you heard—No, but of course, how could you have? Why, he is dead, my dear fellow, dead and gone these six weeks."

"What?" exclaimed Cal, horribly startled. "Goble *dead?* How can this be? He was not murdered also?"

"No—no, poor old fellow, natural causes took him off—" and Lord Egremont described the circumstances. "Chilgrove said he was not surprised; Goble had been ailing for some time, never took much care of himself; probably never ate a proper meal. I doubt if he was given much in that cheeseparing Paget's establishment."

This news distressed Cal deeply. "I dare say the trouble he confided to me may have hastened his end; he told me that guilt and remorse had kept him from sleeping for many weeks."

"Guilt and remorse for what, my dear boy?"

"He told me that he was the person who threw Thomas's child down the well."

"Goble was?" exclaimed Egremont, very much astonished. "Good God! Bless my soul! Why in the world did he do that?"

"He told me that he had seen the ghost of Paget's brother, twenty years ago, in the Petworth jail, crying out for vengeance. Ever since, it had preyed on his mind, and one day when he was in the garden, he told me, 'something come over him and he took and heaved the babby down the well.' Then he was sorry for what he had done, but it was too late. So it was a relief to him when the baby was rescued. But he began to worry more and more, in case fate still intended him to punish Thomas in some other way."

"God bless my soul," Egremont muttered again. "And he told you all this?"

"Yes, it came out, bit by bit, on snowy days in the stable. I think," Cal said seriously, "that he began to confuse me in his own mind with this younger brother of Thomas who died in jail."

"Looked up Wilshire's case," Lord Egremont muttered. "Lost all his money at Goodwood races—drunk and disorderly—clapped into Petworth jail till his friends could pay his debts—contracted the jail fever and died. Before we built our new prison that was, of course. Poor stupid young fellow. Not a bad sort, I dare say.—But come, now, let us have your deposition, let us get that over with."

The deposition, however, as Lord Egremont soberly said, did little more than bear out Goble's previous testimony.

"We know the snow stopped falling at three. We have the night watchman's word for that. We know the child's burial place was covered with snow; therefore the murder must have been committed at least a half hour to an hour previously. You found Goble in the garden at half past three, you say—you do not think that he had committed the murder? Repeating his previous act?"

"No," said Cal, very positively. "His remorse over the previous act was too real. Also—as far as I know—Goble had but the one suit of clothes. I never saw him wearing anything else. And there was no blood on him—not a speck."

"I am afraid we are not advanced much further," Lord Egremont was saying disappointedly, "after fetching you all the way back from Acre, too!"—when the Rev. Martin Socket was announced.

"Mr. Socket informed me that it was a matter of some urgency, my lord," said the footman.

"In that case, show him in.—Well, Martin, my friend—what can I do for you?"

Mr. Socket did indeed appear quite agitated. He had another man with him, who carried a canvas parcel.

"Giles Fewkes, eh?" said Lord Egremont, recognizing one of his tenants. "What's all this about, then, eh?"

"Lord Egremont, Farmer Fewkes, here, has made a discovery which we think may be of considerable importance in the case of the Paget baby. We thought it best to lay the matter before you without delay."

"The Paget case?" Lord Egremont suddenly looked very alert. "Now *there's* a coincidence for you. But what is this discovery, then?"

The Rev. Mr. Socket, glancing at Mr. Fewkes, who appeared tongue-tied, continued with the story.

"Six weeks ago, you see, sir, as—owing to the splendid hay harvest last year, I had more than enough provender for my three horses and two milch cows—I sold the contents of my smaller barn, the one in the valley, to Mr. Fewkes, here; and he sent a couple of men with a wagon to cart it all over to one of his empty Dutch barns, in two big loads, rather than waste time going back and forth every time they wanted a truss of hay to feed his heifers."

"Yes? But what has this to say to anything?" demanded Egremont, somewhat puzzled.

"Patience, sir; I am just coming to the point. The hay was removed in two wagonloads and the barn—which, as you know, is halfway down the slope below the Hermitage—was left empty. This, as it happened, was on the day following the Paget baby's death."

"Oh-ho? Indeed?"

"Mr. Fewkes has been feeding the hay to his cattle, sir, truss by truss, and today discovered in the middle of a bundle this jacket, which we have brought to you."

Here Farmer Fewkes, undoing the canvas parcel, revealed a stiff, dusty, dirty-looking garment, with tarnished brass buttons, which could just be recognized as a pea jacket. It was stained dark brown, and flecked with stalks and seeds of hay. Rolled up in it was a short sword, which at first glance looked to be rusty, but on closer inspection appeared stained with the same dark substance as the jacket.

"Good God!" said Lord Egremont, staring at these exhibits. "That looks like one of the Petworth Troop issue swords. And that jacket—"

"I have seen that jacket—or one very like it," said Cal quietly. "It resembles one worn about the house by my cousin Thomas."

Lord Egremont stood up and, without touching it, carefully inspected the handle of the sword, which was made of plain metal, bound with wire to give it a better grip. "Look there, what do you see?" he said to Cal.

Cal scrutinized it likewise.

"I see the print of a three-fingered hand," he said.

Egremont began to mutter to himself. "He *knew* the house and grounds would be searched. He wore his wife's nightdress over his jacket to catch the blood. That was why Goble thought he was a ghost. But even so the jacket was soaked. He had to get rid of it. He left the nightdress and a razor in the privy to incriminate his wife—he made a mistake there. The child was stabbed as well as slashed. You cannot inflict a stab wound with a razor. He buried the child—that was before the snow had stopped falling. By the time you came into the garden the loose earth had been screened by snow, and he was in the valley, hiding his jacket and the weapon. An hour earlier, and you would have caught him digging."

Cal shuddered. "I must confess, sir, I am just as glad we did not. What a sight!"

"He hid the jacket in the barn, probably intending to return at a later time and burn it, after the Bow Street runners had completed their search. But, when he did go back to the barn, the hay had all been removed. He must have wondered where it had gone. He must have been horrified—"

"Why!" exclaimed the rector. "Paget did come to me—three or four days later! He told me his hay supply was running low and asked if I had any to spare. I told him that I had none left, save for my own use."

"He must have been on tenterhooks to know where your hay had gone," Lord Egremont said grimly. "Did he not ask you?"

"No—I suppose he was afraid his interest might seem too particular."

Egremont rang vigorously for a footman.

"Pringle: see that the constables are brought here directly. And—wait; as a magistrate and lord lieutenant, I can order the release of Mrs. Paget from jail; Frank, write this order from me to the governor of the prison at Chichester—Talgarth can take it over. Don't go, Socket, my dear fellow, or you, Fewkes, we shall want your depositions for the constables—Where is Paget gone off to, now? I suppose he is weary from traveling and needs to rest. Now then, Frank, take this down: 'I hereby authorize the immediate release of Mrs. Frances Paget—' "

Cal had not, in fact, gone to rest but was making his way across the Bartons graveyard to the Hermitage. By now, after his weeks at sea, he was quite nimble on his wooden leg, assisted by a heavy cane which he carried with him everywhere.

Entering the Hermitage garden, he noticed, first, the difference that the changing season had made since he was last there: the snow was all gone, the daffodil stalks were sprouting, slim and green, the cherry and apple trees were in bud.

Cal glanced through the garden-room window. The place was empty, so he swung his way across the lawn to the house.

The door was opened by Mrs. Strudwick, who gasped in astonishment.

"*Master Cal!* We never looked to see you back!"

"Is your master—is Captain Paget in?" he asked quickly.

"Yes, sir—he's in the dining room—shall I say you're here?" she added doubtfully, evidently recalling the quarrel. "He's in a very strange, twitty mood these days, sir."

"Don't trouble, Mrs. Strudwick, I will announce myself.—Where are the young ladies?" he added, for the house seemed strangely silent.

"They've gone, sir; their sister, Miss Martha, come and took them away. Master's all on his own now."

Cal entered the dining room where Thomas, having evidently finished an early and solitary meal, was sitting in the half-light as if he had not the energy to get up and move to another place. A gruel bowl and a plate with a half-eaten piece of bread stood before him.

Cal was startled at the difference that the intervening weeks had made in his cousin. Thomas looked as if he had aged by ten years. His brow was wrinkled, there were deep furrows in his sallow cheeks, the hair above his eyes had turned completely white, and the patches by his ears were grizzled with gray. He looked gaunt and dry, like some half-starved old bird of prey, huddled on its perch, with rusty feathers, its head hunched between its shoulders.

When Cal walked in Thomas, who was staring unseeingly at the shuttered window, did not turn his head, but said harshly:

"Get out, woman, and do not come troubling me. I said that I wanted nothing more."

"It is I, Thomas," Cal said.

Even then Thomas did not move at once, but Cal caught the white gleam as his eyes slid sideways. After a moment he slowly turned his head—again reminding Cal of a bird tilting its poll—and, looking up sidelong, muttered:

"You? What the devil are *you* doing here?" And, after a pause, irritably, "Leave my house!"

"No," Cal said. "It's all up, Thomas. Your run of luck is over."

"What are you talking about? Get out, I say!"

"Your jacket has been found. The one that you hid in the hay. And the sword—the sword that you used. Lord Egremont has them."

Thomas remained silent for so long after these words that Cal almost began to wonder whether he had grasped their import. But then he suddenly stood up. In the dusk he looked taller than his real height.

"What have you come here for?" he demanded.

"I have come—because I left with our business half-finished! Because, at that time, I dared not tell you what I thought of you, as I knew it would only rebound on *her*. I have to tell you what a detestably base, cruel, miserly wicked *brute* I think you are! You treated Fanny abominably—she was a thousand times too good for you! Only a monster like you could conceive the notion of killing your own child and attempting to pin the blame on her. But your plan has misfired, I am happy to say. The constables will be here soon to arrest you. But before that I have come to demand satisfaction for that cowardly blow you gave me—I will fight you in any way you choose!"

"The constables," Thomas muttered, more to himself than Cal.

"Will you fight?" demanded Cal. "Come on, you cur, *fight!* I am not afraid of you—even though I have only one leg!"

"Why, you stupid puppy!" growled Thomas. "What do I care for you? With your poetry and all your talk? *I* saw that you were in love with Frances, but you didn't even have the guts to *do* anything about it! I hate you for that! All you were fit for was to write verses—"

"Wait till I get my hands on your throat!" cried Cal in a passion, and he swung himself around the corner of the table.

Thomas stepped swiftly back.

"Oh no, you don't! I am my own master—I do not choose to engage in fisticuffs with *you*."

Calmly, without haste, he picked up a pistol which had been lying on a chair beside him, out of Cal's line of vision, and discharged it, at practically point-blank range. Cal staggered, and fell headlong on the floor.

Mrs. Strudwick came running and screaming. As she entered at one door, Thomas, still without haste, made his way out of the other. Mrs. Strudwick took one look at Cal and flew out of the front door, shrieking for Jem to fetch the doctor.

When Lord Egremont and the constables arrived, they met her in the lane.

"Oh, sirs," she cried distractedly, "mind what you're about with the master, he's dangerous. He've killed Master Cal, and now he's outside somewhere!"

The party of men stared cautiously around the dusk-filled garden.

"How'll we ever find the fellow in this light?" grunted one of them. "He might be lurking in any bush."

"More likely gone over the meadows and escaped," said another.

But they did not have very far to search for Thomas. He had pushed a wheelbarrow under the weeping ash, thrown a rope over one of its boughs, and, with a skill probably remembered from his naval days, made a couple of slip knots. Then he had thrust the barrow away.

By the time they found him he had stopped kicking and was hanging motionless, almost directly over the spot where he had buried his son. His cousin Cal, who had succeeded in crawling out of the house before dying, lay beneath him, against the trunk of the tree.

"I *still* do not understand," said Lady Mountague. "Why should he kill the child? And why bury it under the ash tree?"

She focused her keen, nearsighted gray eyes on those of Fanny and repeated, "Now why should he do a thing like that?"

In fact, Lady Mountague had a perfectly clear notion as to the motives behind Thomas's actions, but she was not going to allow Fanny to brood in silence; let the child cry her heart out at night if she must, but in the daytime the history of the past few months was going to be thoroughly dealt with and disposed of, until it was completely aired, disinfected, and made harmless.

"Well—you see, he was jealous. He was so jealous of us, we were all so happy together. And he was especially jealous of Cal—because Cal had succeeded in all the ways that Thomas had failed. Cal was young, too—he could have a son in course of time—a proper son, not a poor b-backward baby—"

"Now, child. *Child!* You have been told a hundred times over that if there was anything the matter with little Thomas it was not your fault. And that, in any case, most likely he would have grown up perfectly normal."

"That makes it all the worse!" wept Fanny. "Thomas just *gave up*—as if little Thomas were some undertaking that had turned out badly—not as if he were a person."

"Well, do not *you* be accusing yourself of giving up too soon, my dear, for your cousin has told me how patient you were, and how you endeavored to teach the child."

"But I didn't love him."

"Very well!" said Lady Mountague. "Let that be a lesson to you! Take pains to love everything else that you come across! And now, put it behind you. That is enough of crying and moping for one day; I want you to put on your bonnet and come for a drive with me. We are going over to Petworth; I dare say you will like to see your cousin and Liz Wyndham."

"You are very good to bear with me, ma'am, the way you do."

"I am fond of you, child. It is a pleasure to have you staying with me."

During the drive from Midhurst to Petworth, Fanny, gazing at the daffodils and tulips blazing in the cottage gardens, said wistfully:

"Should you object, ma'am, if I were to go and look at the Hermitage garden? I—I promise not to mope or brood."

"Very well, my child. Do you wish me to accompany you?"

Fanny said that must be as Lady Mountague pleased, and the latter, giving her a shrewd glance, observed that the place had rather disagreeable associations for her and she had as lief drop Fanny there and go on to Petworth House for a coze with that shatterbrained creature, Liz Wyndham, provided that Fanny would undertake not to fall into a melancholy, and not to spend more than twenty minutes there on her own. And she trusted Fanny not to do anything foolish.

"Yes, you may trust me, ma'am," Fanny said.

Left alone in the garden, she stared about her rather hesitantly, as if waiting for ghosts to come out and beckon. The wellhead, the stable, the orchard . . . But no ghosts moved, the sun shone warm on her back, birds scattered their songs like cascades of diamonds through the young-leaved trees.

Fanny walked around to look at the weeping ash and found that somebody had been there before her. The wire and leather thongs which had tied down its branches were all cut away, and the branches hung free, vibrating gently in the mild spring wind.

"Oh, I am glad for you!" breathed Fanny. "You poor thing!" And she laid a hand gently on the trunk. The tree would never be the same again; but at least it was free, now, to grow as best it could. Who had done that? she wondered.

Emboldened, she went around the house and opened the front door. Nobody was living there at present; Mrs. Strudwick and Tess had left, the place was empty. Would it feel very drear, very deserted? She walked inside and stopped, amazed at the warmth of welcome the house seemed to be sending out to her. It was not just the lozenges of sunlight on the parlor floor, or the scent of lavender from the pot-pourri on the hall table—there was a strong positive emanation of love and friendliness, an unheard but most emphatically felt message of joy at her return.

She did not go far inside; she stood in the hallway, feeling and re-ciprocating the waves of welcome; then, silently promising: I will come back! Don't grieve—wait for me! I will come back very soon! she walked outside again and turned the key in the lock.

Lingering in front of the house, she saw to her astonishment that there was a total stranger striding along the yew-tree walk: a tall, auburn-haired man wearing some kind of uniform. Who could he pos-sibly be, and what was he doing here? Unafraid, for her heart was filled now with grateful peace, Fanny crossed the grass toward the in-terloper.

Could it be Count van Welcker? Juliana Paget's husband?

"Good day, sir," she said politely when she was within speaking range. "Can I be of assistance to you?"

"Good day, ma'am! I must ask your pardon for this intrusion. I did ring at the bell first, but nobody answered. I am looking for Miss Scylla Paget—"

"*Oh!*" Fanny exclaimed in lively astonishment. "Is it possible—can you be—?"

She studied him, liking what she saw. Those absurd, luxuriant russet mustaches and beard—*nobody* in England wore hair like that any more—yet they suited him, he had a decidedly buccaneering look. The red hair, equally thick, under his turban-cap, the tartan uniform, the blue eyes that met hers in keen, friendly appraisal—

"Are you Colonel Cameron?"

"That I am!"

"Oh, she will be so *happy* to see you!" Fanny cried out. "I cannot tell you how she has longed for you. Since her brother died—"

"Yes, that was a bad business—a shocking business." His face clouded. "I heard about it in London—and your husband too, ma'am —am I right in thinking that you are Mrs. Paget?" He glanced at her black dress.

"Yes, I am," she said absently. "You have just come from London, Colonel Cameron? Not from the East?"

"I returned from Acre in the same sloop as Lieutenant Paget," he explained. "He had sent me a letter from Minorca, and by good fortune it found me in Baghdad, about to leave for Acre. So I was able to meet him there, and we returned to England together. I had concluded some business in Afghanistan. Since America went to war with France," he explained with a slight smile, "I have been acting as a kind of courier, both for this country and my own, and I had some intelligence for the British government regarding the movements of Tippoo Sahib's forces and the campaign being conducted against him by General Arthur Wellesley. My affairs in London being completed, I heard this dreadful news just as I was about to post down here—for Lieutenant Paget had told me on the voyage back that his sister might —might be prepared to reconsider an answer she had once given me—"

"Reconsider!" cried Fanny. "Oh, what are you waiting *here* for? Go up to Petworth House directly. Do you know where it is?"

"Yes, I observed the entrance while making my way here."

"Then go!" She almost pushed him.

"Will you not come with me, ma'am?"

"No—no. I will follow you—very soon. But do you go now!"

"You are a woman of decision, Mrs. Paget. I can see we shall be friends," he said, and walked off up the lane.

A footman at Petworth House told Colonel Cameron that Miss Paget was walked out in the park, as she mostly did at this time of day; the gentleman would very likely find her by the lake. Did he wish to see Mrs. Wyndham or Lady Mountague first? No, he wished only to see Miss Paget.

He was directed out into the pleasure garden, where an ornamental iron gate gave entrance into the park proper. Crossing the ha-ha by a wooden bridge, he looked across the great sweep of grass.

Far away by the lake he saw a tiny figure in black, slowly strolling. He recognized the silvery dot of Scylla's hair; and a splash of blue over the shoulder must be a parasol. The figure's slow, dejected gait went to his heart—when had he ever seen her walk at such a dawdling pace, as if she hardly cared whether she moved or stood still?

He began walking briskly in her direction, taking large strides. She had not noticed him; she was watching the waterfowl on the lake. But when he had covered about three quarters of the distance she heard his step and turned her head.

By now he could distinguish her features—her pale, startled face. She looked completely incredulous—frozen in disbelief. As he came closer he took off his cap and waved it. Then a kind of tremor went through her; she became galvanized. Dropping her parasol, she started to run toward him, fast—faster. Two more gigantic strides and he came up with her and caught her in his arms.

"Scylla! My love, my dear love!"

"Oh, Rob! Is it you? Is it really you? How did you find me? How did you know I was here? Where in the world have you come from?"

"All that is a long story. It can wait." He held her tightly and buried his face in her hair. "The main thing is that I have found you."

"Rob—you have heard about Cal?"

"Yes, I have heard," he said gravely. "And I am inexpressibly sorry —for the dreadful waste—and for you. We will talk later about Cal— we will be talking many times."

"—But he was right about his poetry!" she said with pride. "He has left a name behind him."

"Yes, he was right. He will not be forgotten.—And now, my love," said Cameron firmly, "we are going to talk about *us*." He glanced about him. "I feel there ought to be a tiger lurking in those rhododendrons."

"And Therbah—dear Therbah—waiting to shoot it!"

"Therbah sends his salaams to the sahiba and hopes to see her again in Baghdad. We shall have to travel by way of Turkey," he added thoughtfully. "Acre is going to be too hot for comfort during the next few months. Fortunately I am on excellent terms with the Porte."

"*Turkey—?*"

"We shall have to be married first, of course," he mentioned as an afterthought. "Therbah would not approve of our traveling together in the single state.—And this time I am not taking no for an answer. Oh, how monstrous you were to me! A repugnant alliance! Not if I were the last man on earth! Good God, what a setdown you gave me! I crept away feeling as if I had been blasted by one of my own cannon at point-blank range. It took me days—weeks—to recover."

"But you *did* recover in the end?" suavely suggested his love, from the security of an almost throttling embrace.

"Not at all. I am still in a shattered condition. Why do you think I had to take the trouble to travel all the way to England but to seek you out, you—you infernal baggage?"

"But how was *I* supposed to guess that you—that you really entertained such feelings? When you were such a martinet? When you shouted at me and ordered me about and snapped my head off at the least word of disagreement? Why were you always so severe? How could I help but assume that you thought me the greatest bore in the world?"

"My darling simpleton." He held her at arms' length a moment, then snatched her close again. "What do you take me for? I am only human! I was dying of love for you from—from about the second time I saw you—"

"Oh? Not the first? I think I am ahead of you there, Colonel Cameron!"

"Quiet, you! If I had relaxed my guard for a moment—"

"Oh, you men, with your notions of honor and propriety! We should then have been saved a great, great deal of trouble. However I dare say I had better give you this—" She was struggling with a wool-wrapped ring on her finger.

"Have you been to Almack's yet, my love?" inquired the colonel.

"No, I have not, but what is that to the purpose?"

"Then I fear," said Colonel Cameron, possessing himself of her hand in order to kiss the two small cross-shaped scars on her palm and wrist, "I fear that you have lost your chance of going there during this present visit to England. But I assure you, it is a dismally dull place!"

Fanny glanced across the Hermitage garden at the church clock. She still had five minutes left of the twenty allotted her by Lady Mountague. Smiling at the thought of Colonel Cameron—what a forthright, unexpected man, how different from what she had imagined, but she could see that he was just what Scylla needed—she moved slowly along the yew-tree walk, then paused to lean on the wall looking out over the valley.

She carried with her—as always, just now—Cal's last batch of poems; and presently she took them out and read them. They were so beautiful and mysterious! They created a whole scene, in words on the paper—the valley, the house—and herself, part of it all yet a spectator, sharing, yet observing. How curious it is to be a human, she thought— born of the natural world, growing from it, yet containing something more; a spirit that endures, that transcends. Could some part of Cal be here, now, still? Or did he exist only in the lines that he had left? " 'Odin, transfixed, above the whispering sea,' " she murmured, looking down at the brook among the alder trees. " 'Mimir's dark waters, flowing to eternity.' " And, with her chin propped on her hands, she sank into a kind of waking dream. How strange it had been—Cal, Scylla, the weeping ash, the feeling that it had all been predestined. Even poor Thomas—poor, poor Thomas!—in course of time the pain she felt when she thought of him would abate, or she would somehow turn it to account; pain was a harvest like any other, it must be used, not allowed to go to waste.

How long Fanny had remained there, leaning on the wall, she could not have said. It seemed like an immensity of time. She came back slowly to a full waking state with the feeling that all this had happened before. . . . Only, on the former occasion, she had been in London, had found herself in the thoroughfare called the Strand, with gulls calling and carriages passing; and the water on the other side of the wall had been the river Thames.

But now, as then, she had a feeling of guardianship, of loving company; as if somebody to whom she was inexpressibly dear, somebody she had always known, and always would know, waited close at hand.

The church clock said three o'clock; time to be going. Yet still she lingered. And now she saw somebody climbing up the steep side of the valley toward her; approaching the rector's empty hay barn, out of sight where the path bent around the building, then reappearing, coming closer: a young man, black-haired. He looked up, saw her, and raised a hand in serious greeting, walking on steadily in her direction.

It was the gardener, Andrew Talgarth.